Dead as a Doornail

"Are you going to tell me what's going on?" I felt like I had fallen into a bad dream.

"You got anyone who'll say where you were between six-thirty and now?"

"I already told you. I've been right here at the hotel, mostly asleep."

The first cop rolled his eyes. "Isn't that what they all say, Willy? I was asleep the whole time."

"Now wait a minute. You'd better tell me what's happening."

"Well, sir," Willy said, savoring the words. "It's about this lady we found along the road a little while ago. She had your card in her pocket with a room number on the back."

"Is she all right?"

"Didja hear that!" Joe exclaimed. "She's dead as a doornail, and he wants to know if she's all right. You'd better move on over to the wall, Beaumont . . . "

Other Detective J. P. Beaumont Mysteries by
J. A. Jance
From Avon Books

UNTIL PROVEN GUILTY
TRIAL BY FURY
TAKING THE FIFTH
IMPROBABLE CAUSE
A MORE PERFECT UNION
DISMISSED WITH PREJUDICE
MINOR IN POSSESSION
PAYMENT IN KIND

J·A·JANCE

INJUSTICE FOR ALL

AVON BOOKS ◆ NEW YORK

INJUSTICE FOR ALL is an original publication of Avon Books. This work has never before appeared in book form. This work is a novel. Any similarity to actual persons or events is purely coincidental.

AVON BOOKS
A division of
The Hearst Corporation
105 Madison Avenue
New York, New York 10016

First Avon Books Printing: May 1986

AVON TRADEMARK REG. U.S. PAT. OFF. AND IN OTHER COUNTRIES, MARCA REGISTRADA, HECHO EN CANADA.

Printed in Canada.

UNV   10   9   8   7

To Norman and Evie,
from their "only" child

Chapter 1

THERE's nothing like a woman's scream to bring a man bolt upright in bed. I had been taking a late-afternoon nap in my room when the sound cut through the stormy autumn twilight like a knife.

I threw open the door of my cabin. The woman screamed again, the sound keening up from the narrow patch of beach below the terrace at Rosario Resort. A steep path dropped from my cabin to the beach. I scrambled down it to the water's edge. There I spotted a woman struggling to drag a man's inert form out of the lapping sea.

She wasn't screaming now. Her face was grimly set as she wrestled the dead weight of the man's body. I hurried to help her, grasping him under the arms and pulling him ashore. Dropping to his side, I felt for a pulse. There was none.

He was a man in his mid to late fifties wearing expensive cowboy boots and a checkered cowboy shirt. His belt buckle bore the initials LSL. A deep gash split his forehead.

The woman knelt beside me anxiously, hopefully. When I looked at her and shook my head, her face contorted with grief. She sank to the wet sand beside me. "Can't you do something?" she sobbed.

Again I shook my head. I've worked homicide too many years not to know when it's too late. Footsteps pounded down the steps behind us as people in the bar and dining room hurried to see what had happened. Barney, the bartender, was the first person to reach us.

"Dead?" he asked.

I nodded. "Get those people out of here, every last one of them. And call the sheriff."

With unquestioning obedience Barney bounded up the steps and herded the onlookers back to the terrace some twenty-five feet above us. Beside me the woman's sobs continued unabated. It was a chilly autumn evening to begin with, and we were both soaked to the skin. Gently I took her arm, lifting her away from the lifeless body.

"Come on," I said. "You've got to get out of those wet clothes." She allowed me to pull her to her feet. "Is this your husband?"

She shook her head. "No, a friend."

"Are you staying here at the hotel?" She nodded. "Where's your room?"

"Up by the tennis courts."

She was shaking violently. The tennis courts and her room were a good quarter of a mile away. My cabin was just at the top of the path. "You can dry off and warm up in my room. The sheriff will need to talk to you when he gets here."

Like a dazed but pliant child, she followed me as I half led, half carried her up the path. By the time we reached my room, her teeth chattered convulsively. It could have been cold or shock or a little of both. I pulled her into the bathroom and turned on the water in the shower. "Get out of those wet things," I ordered. "I'll send someone to get you some clothes."

Kneeling in front of her, I fumbled with the sodden laces of her tennis shoes with my own numbed fingers. "What's your name?" I asked.

"Gi . . . Ginger," she stammered through chattering teeth.

"Ginger what?"

"Wa . . . Watkins."

I stood up. Her arms hung limply at her sides. "Can you undress, or do you need help?"

Clumsily she battled a button on her blouse, finally unfastening it. Leaving her on her own, I let myself out of the bathroom. "I'll be outside if you need anything."

Alone in the room, I stripped off my own soaked clothing and tossed the soggy bundle on a chair near the bed. I pulled on a shirt, a sweater, and two pair of socks before I picked up the phone and dialed the desk clerk. "This is Beaumont in Room Thirteen," I said. "Did someone call the sheriff?"

"Yes we did, Mr. Beaumont. The deputy's on his way."

"Have someone stay down on the beach with the body until

he gets here. Make sure nothing is moved or disturbed. The woman who found him is here in my room. She was freezing. She's taking a hot shower. Her name is Watkins. Can you send someone to her room for dry clothes? Does she have a husband?"

"There's no Mr. Watkins registered, Mr. Beaumont, but I'll send someone after the clothes right away."

"She'll need the works, underwear and all."

"I'll take care of it as soon as I can."

"Good," I replied. "And when the deputy comes, be sure he knows she's here with me. Since she's the one who found the body, he'll want to talk to her."

The desk clerk himself brought the clothes, handing them to me apologetically. His nametag labeled him Fred. "I hope I have everything," he said.

I opened the bathroom door wide enough to slip them inside onto the floor before turning back to Fred. "The deputy isn't here yet?"

"There's an accident down by the ferry dock. He can't come until he finishes with that."

"Did the dispatcher call for a detective from Friday Harbor?" I asked.

He shrugged. "I guess, but I don't know for sure. You seem to know about this kind of thing, Mr. Beaumont."

I ought to. I've worked homicide in Seattle for the better part of twenty years.

Fred moved uncertainly toward the door. "I'd better be getting back."

"Who was he?" I asked. Fred looked blank. "The dead man," I persisted.

"Oh," he replied. "His name was Sig Larson. He was here with the parole board."

"The parole board!" Cops don't like parole boards. Cops and parole boards work opposite sides of the street. Parole boards let creeps go faster than cops can lock them up. "What's the parole board doing here?"

Fred shrugged. "They came for a three-day workshop. They'll probably cancel now."

I glanced toward the bathroom door where the rush of the shower had ceased. "And her?" I asked.

"She's a member too, as far as I know. Her reservation was made along with all the rest."

"But her husband isn't here?"

"No, she's by herself."

"What about Larson?" Asking questions is a conditioned response in a detective. I asked the question, ignoring that I was more than a hundred miles outside my Seattle jurisdiction. Someone was dead. Who, How, and Why were questions someone needed to ask. It might as well be me.

"His wife is due in on one of tonight's ferries. I don't know which one. She isn't here yet."

I went to the bathroom door and tapped lightly. "I'm going to order a couple of drinks from Room Service. Would you like something?"

"Coffee," was the reply. "Black."

I turned back to Fred. "Did you hear that?"

He nodded.

"Send up a pot of coffee for her and two McNaughton's and water for me. Barney knows how I like them."

"Will do," the clerk replied, slipping from the room into the deepening darkness.

The door reopened. "I almost forgot. She's supposed to call Homer in Seattle. It's urgent. He said she knew the number."

Fred shut the door again, disappearing for good this time. Still cold, I turned up the thermostat in the room, mulling the turn of events. The lady showering in my bathroom was a married member of the Washington State Parole Board. The dead man on the beach was married too, but not to her, although it was evident there was some connection.

Room Service was on the ball. Coffee and drinks arrived before the bathroom door opened. Ginger Watkins, wearing a pale green dress, stepped barefoot into my room, a huge bath-towel turban wound around her head. She was fairly tall, five-eight or five-nine, with a slender figure, fine bones, and a flawlessly fair complexion. Her eyes were vivid uncut emeralds.

Coming up from the beach, I hadn't noticed she was beautiful. Standing across the room from me, swathed in the gentle light of the dressing room behind her, she took my breath away.

She returned my unabashed stare, and I looked away, embarrassed. "Better?" I managed.

"Yes, but I'm still cold."

I rummaged through the closet and brought out a tweed jacket which I put over her shoulders. I handed her a cup and saucer. "Here's your coffee."

She slipped into one of the two chairs at the table. "I left my wet clothes on the floor," she said.

I pointed to the chair. "There mine are." I poured more coffee. Her hands trembled as she raised the cup to her lips.

"What did you say your name was?"

"Beaumont," I answered. "J. P. Beaumont. My friends call me Beau."

"And I'm Ginger Watkins."

"You told me. The desk clerk said the man's name was Larson. You knew him?"

She nodded somberly, her eyes filling with tears. "Sig," she murmured, her throat working to stifle a sob.

"A friend of yours?"

She nodded again.

"How did you happen to find him? It wasn't much of a day for a walk on the beach."

"We planned to meet down there to talk, after the meeting. I was late. Darrell called. I didn't get there until forty-five minutes after I was supposed to."

"Who's Darrell?" I asked.

She gave me a funny look, as though I had asked a stupid question. "My husband," she answered.

The name sounded familiar, but I didn't put it together right then. I let it go. "Why meet him there? Why not in the lobby or the bar?"

"I told you, we needed to talk."

She set her coffee cup down, got up, and walked away from the table, her arms crossed, her body language closed.

"What about?"

"It was personal," she replied.

That's not a good answer at the beginning of an inquiry into death under unusual circumstances. Accidental drownings in October are unusual. My gut said murder, and murder is very personal. The ties between killer and victim are often of the most intimate kind. "How personal?"

She turned on me suddenly. "You don't have any right to ask me a question like that."

"Someone's going to ask it, sooner or later."

She met my gaze for a long moment before she wavered. "Sig

had some business dealings with my family. That's why I needed to talk to him."

"Privately?" I asked. She nodded. "Do you know his wife?"

Her mouth tightened. Her fingers closed tightly on her upper arms. "Yes. I know her."

"What's she like?"

"Mona's a calculating bitch." It was a simple statement spoken with a singular amount of venom.

"I take it you're not friends."

"Hardly." She walked back over to the table and sat down opposite me. "Mona thought Sig and I were having an affair."

"Were you?"

She looked at me, her eyes clear and steady in the glow of the light. "No," she said.

Irate husbands and wives don't always verify their spouses' indiscretions before they rub out a presumed lover. "Is Mona the jealous type? Or Darrell?"

She laughed. "Darrell? Are you kidding? He could care less. Mona called him with the story, and he was afraid it would hit the papers and screw up his campaign."

Suddenly the names shifted into focus. Darrell Watkins, candidate for lieutenant governor. Boy Wonder tackling the longtime incumbent. I whistled. "You mean *the* Darrell Watkins?"

Ginger Watkins peered at me across a cup of coffee. "One and the same," she said softly. "The sonofabitch."

It was no wonder I forgot to give her the message that someone had called.

Chapter 2

DEPUTY Jake Pomeroy arrived about seven. He made a very poor first impression. He was a fat-faced, pimpled kid who looked like he had stepped out of his high school graduation picture into a rumpled deputy sheriff's uniform. Until the detective arrived from Friday Harbor, Deputy Pomeroy was in charge. The deputy considered Sig Larson's death to be the crime of the century on Orcas Island.

He was trolling for suspects. He tossed his first hook in my direction. "Your name's Beaumont, is that correct?" I nodded. "What do you do?"

"Homicide detective. Seattle P.D." I handed him my ID.

He gave me a shrewd, appraising look. "I understand you moved the body. Is that also correct?"

"Yes."

His look became a contemptuous sneer. "Surely you know better than that."

I wanted to slug the officious bastard, but I answered evenly. "We thought he might still be alive."

"When you say 'we,' you mean you and Mrs. Watkins?"

"She found him. I heard her scream."

"And what time was that?" he asked, addressing Ginger.

"A quarter to six," she replied. "I was late."

"Late for what?"

"I was supposed to meet Sig there. At five."

The deputy tapped his front teeth with the eraser of his pencil and eyed her speculatively. "Why?"

"To talk."

His look narrowed. "Wasn't it cold down by the water?"

"We wanted to talk privately."

Pomeroy said nothing as he made a note. "How would you describe your relationship with Mr. Larson?"

"Friends."

"That's all?"

"That's all."

"How long have you known Mr. Beaumont here?"

"We just met. Down on the beach."

She was in my room, wearing my robe, her hair wet from my shower, with my bath towel wrapped around her head. She was also barefoot, because the desk clerk had forgotten to bring her shoes. Jake Pomeroy didn't believe for one minute we were recent acquaintances.

I attempted what must have sounded like a lame explanation. "We were freezing. I was afraid she'd go into shock. Her own room is way up the hill."

Jake gave Ginger an overt leer. "You're sure the two of you never met before this afternoon?"

"I'm sure!" Ginger snapped, a tiny flush marking her delicate cheekbone.

"You did say 'Mrs. Watkins,' isn't that right?" She nodded. "But your husband isn't here with you?" He recast his hook.

"I'm here on parole board business. So was Sig." She was rapidly losing patience.

"Was your husband also a friend of Mr. Larson's?"

The emerald in her eyes gleamed hard and brittle. "They had some business dealings, that's all."

"We'll check this out, of course," he said.

His questions had gone far enough. I resented the insinuations in his clumsy quest for an infidelity motive. "Look, Pomeroy," I told him, "if you want to ask questions about the position of the body, or what time it was, or whether we saw anyone else on the beach, that's fine. But if you're making accusations, you'd better read us our rights and let us call an attorney. If not, I'll shove that gold star where the sun don't shine."

A stunned expression spread over his flabby countenance. He lumbered to his feet. "I'll go back and wait for Detective Huggins."

"You do that."

I banged the door shut behind him and returned to the table. Ginger had unwrapped her turban and was toweling her hair dry. She looked relieved.

I picked up the phone and dialed the desk. "You didn't bring shoes," I growled when Fred answered.

"I didn't? Sorry. I can't do anything about it right now. A whole bunch of people just got here. I have to get them settled."

"Never mind," I told Fred. "I'll get them myself."

Ginger gave me her key. I walked to her room through a lightly falling evening mist. Opening her door, I expected to find the room well ordered and neat. Instead, it was a shambles. The place had been ransacked. I picked up the telephone receiver. Holding it at the top in an effort to disturb as few prints as possible, I called the desk. "Was Mrs. Watkins' room torn apart when you came after her clothes?" I asked.

"Why no, Mr. Beaumont. It was fine."

"It isn't now," I said grimly. "When that detective gets here, send him up."

"He's right here. Want to speak to him?"

"Put him on."

"Hello," a voice mumbled. "This is Detective Huggins."

"I'm Beaumont.

"J. P. Beaumont? Are you shitting me? This is Hal, Hal Huggins. Haven't seen you since I left the force ten years ago. How the hell are you?"

It took me a minute to place the name and the face and the mumbling speech. Hal Huggins had opted for being a big fish in a very small pond when he left Seattle's homicide squad to go to work for the San Juan County Sheriff's Department in Friday Harbor, hiring on as their chief detective. Probably their only detective.

"I'm fine," I replied.

"What are you up to?"

"I was with the woman who discovered the body this afternoon."

"No shit. Pomeroy is lining me up to go talk to her."

"You'd better come to her room first. Have the desk clerk bring you up."

"Okay, we'll be right there. Hey, by the way. There's someone else here you know. I just ran into him in the lobby. Remember Maxwell Cole?"

Does Captain Ahab remember Moby Dick? Cole is a crime columnist for the *Post-Intelligencer*. He's been on my case ever since I beat him out of a college girl friend, packed her off, and married her. As a reporter, he has dogged my career for as long as I've been on the force. Karen and I have been divorced for years, but I'm still stuck with Max. It's like I threw out the baby and ended up having to keep the dirty bathwater.

"Don't tell him I'm here," I cautioned. "What's he doing here anyway? The Sig Larson story?"

"Probably, although he didn't say."

"Don't ask. And don't bring him along."

Fred led Huggins and Pomeroy into Ginger's room. The clerk's mouth gaped. "What happened here? It wasn't like this when I picked up her clothes."

"What time was that?" Huggins asked.

Fred walked around the room as if at a loss for words, examining the debris. "What time?" Huggins repeated.

"Forty-five minutes ago," Fred replied. "No more than that."

Huggins looked at me. "So what's this got to do with the stiff on the beach."

"I took Ginger Watkins to my room to warm up after we left

the beach. Fred here," I said, indicating the desk clerk, "came up to get her some dry clothes. Not quite an hour later, I discovered this when I came to pick up a pair of shoes."

"Maybe she trashed it herself."

"No. She's still in my room. It's too cold to be wandering around barefoot."

Huggins glared sorrowfully around the room before turning to Pomeroy. "Call the crime-lab folks, Jake. Have them come take a look. Coroner's got the body, and the beach is covered with water, but they'd better see this all the same." He turned stiffly to me. "Take me to the lady. She can answer questions barefoot. Nobody's taking any shoes out of this room until the lab's done with it."

Pomeroy lingered near the door. "I told you to get, Jake, and I mean it," Huggins growled. Jake got, with the desk clerk right behind him.

Hal and I strolled back toward my room. "You're a little out of your territory, aren't you, Beau?" It was a comment rather than a question, asked without rancor.

"I'm here on vacation, an innocent bystander."

"Pomeroy seems to think otherwise."

"Pomeroy's got a dirty mind."

He chuckled. "How'd you get dragged into this, anyway?"

"I heard a lady scream and went to check it out. I never saw her before six o'clock this evening."

"Pomeroy says if you only met her tonight, how come she's sitting in your room barefoot with a towel around her head, wearing your bathrobe? He told me she had just stepped out of your shower. He thinks you're a hell of a fast worker."

"She was cold, goddammit. I tried to tell him that."

"He's not buying. Envious, I think. Claims she's pretty good looking."

"She is that," I acknowledged.

"What did you say her name is?"

"Ginger Watkins. Her husband's Darrell Watkins."

He stopped short and whistled. "The guy who's running for lieutenant governor against old man Chambers?"

"That's right."

Huggins shook his head. "What did I ever do to deserve this?" he asked plaintively.

"I don't know," I said, "but whatever it was, it must have been pretty bad."

Ginger rose to let us in, a worried frown on her face. "What took so long?" she asked. "I was afraid something had happened to you."

"This is Detective Hal Huggins," I said as he stepped forward, hand extended. "He's from the sheriff's department in Friday Harbor. Hal needs to ask you some questions. Hal, Ginger Watkins."

She offered him a firm handshake, while Hal examined her with care.

"Glad to meet you, Mrs. Watkins, but I'm afraid I have some disturbing news."

Her face darkened. "What?"

"We've just come from your room. The place has been ransacked."

She paled. "Ransacked! When?"

"Between the time the desk clerk picked up your clothes and when I went to get your shoes," I told her.

"But who would do something like that?" she demanded.

"We were hoping you could tell us, Mrs. Watkins." Hal settled himself on the edge of the bed. "Any ideas?"

Ginger shook her head. "None," she said.

"No one else had a key to your room?"

"Sig did. We always kept keys to each other's rooms on trips, as a precaution in case one of us was sick or hurt. I was sick once and he had to break in. It was just a safety precaution."

Huggins looked at her closely. "We'd better go over the whole thing," he said, leaning stiffly against the headboard. "Tell me everything. From the beginning."

Chapter 3

Huggins had barely asked his first question when the phone rang. I answered it—the phone, not the question. The voice on the other end of the line was one degree under rude. "I'm told Ginger Watkins is there. Let me speak to her."

"May I say who's calling?"

"No you may not! If she's there, put her on."

I don't like imperious *schmucks*. I fought fire with fire. "Mrs. Watkins is busy at the moment. Can I take a message?"

He fired off a verbal volley. I held the phone away from my ear long enough for the shouting to stop. "Give me your name and number," I told him. "She'll call back."

"I already left one message, damn it. Put her on. Tell her it's Homer."

When I heard his name, I remembered the forgotten message. I hung up the phone, cutting short his tirade. "It was Homer," I told Ginger. "He wants you to call."

Something flickered across her face, but I couldn't tell what. Anger? Fear? She turned her attention back to Huggins. "What were you saying?"

He regarded her with a sad-eyed glower. "I understand you discovered Mr. Larson's body. Now someone has ransacked your room. These incidents may or may not be related. We can't afford to assume they're not." He shifted on the bed, trying to find a more comfortable position. "Isn't it unusual for coworkers to have keys to each other's rooms?"

"Sig and I were close." Huggins waited as though expecting her to say something further. She didn't.

He sighed. "Did you have any valuables in your room? Items of jewelry, something like that?"

She shook her head. "No."

"Anything else of value—cameras, prescription medications?" Again she shook her head. He continued doggedly. "Any paperwork concerning parole board business that might be considered damaging or in some way usable? Maybe something you and Mr. Larson were working on together?"

There was a slight hesitation. "I brought some papers from home. They have nothing to do with work."

"May I ask what they are?"

"I'm filing for divorce on Monday," she said levelly. "I brought the paperwork with me. Sig and I planned to discuss it this evening." Her answer was calm, but her eyes betrayed a turmoil of warring emotions. I noticed it. So did Huggins. "That's why I was late to see Sig,'' she went on. ''Darrell called. Someone told him.''

Hal sat up. ''You didn't tell him before you left?''

''No.'' Ginger gave him a wan smile. ''It was a surprise.''

''Someone told him. Who?''

Ginger shrugged. ''I don't know, not for sure.''

''Did he mention what time?''

''Sometime today, I know that much.''

''Can you guess who it was?''

''Probably Mona.''

''Mona?''

''Sig's wife, Mona Larson.'' The antagonism in Ginger's voice set little alarm bells ringing. Had Sig Larson died in a matrimonial crossfire between his wife and Ginger's husband?

''But how did Mrs. Larson know?''

''I wrote Sig a letter last week, the day I made up my mind. He suggested I not file until after we had a chance to discuss it.''

''Why talk it over with him? What did he have to do with it?''

''I told you before, he was my friend. . . . My best friend,'' she added defiantly. ''Why wouldn't I discuss it with him? We weren't having an affair, if that's what you mean.'' Her denial of an unspoken accusation gave credence to Huggins' line of questioning. Sig's having her room key made it even more plausible.

Hal's disbelief must have showed. She continued. ''Our families were involved in a joint venture, a condominium project in Seattle. I didn't want to jeopardize Sig's position.''

''Would you have?''

Her smile was caustic. ''Evidently not. Homer and Darrell seem to have covered all possible contingencies.''

I had sat quietly as long as I could. ''Who the hell is Homer?'' I demanded.

''Homer Watkins,'' she replied, her answer permeated with sarcasm. ''My illustrious father-in-law.''

''I don't know him.''

''You haven't missed a thing.''

Huggins pulled himself to a sitting position and studied his notes. ''How will a divorce go over with the voters?'' he asked, approaching from another direction.

Ginger bit her lip. ''It won't make much difference. No one

will pay any attention. It certainly won't cost him the election."
She looked at Huggins closely. "Does Mona know about Sig?"
she asked.

"Not yet. We still haven't located her." Huggins sighed.
"Let's talk about today, from the beginning."

"I came over on the ferry early this morning," Ginger said.

"Alone?"

She nodded.

"Did you bring your car?"

"No. It's in Anacortes. I didn't think I'd need it."

"What time did you check in?"

"Our meeting started at one. I checked in sometime before
that."

"What time did Mr. Larson get here?"

"I don't know. I didn't see him before the meeting. During
our afternoon break we arranged to meet on the beach. That's
when I gave him my key."

"Do you have a key to his room?"

"No. Mona was coming." Her answer spoke volumes.

"Oh, I see," Huggins said. "Was anyone else aware you
planned to meet on the beach?"

Ginger shook her head. "Not as far as I know."

Hal Huggins was meticulous. "You got out of the meeting at
four. What did you do then?"

"I went back to my room. I took a nap. Then Darrell called."

"What time?"

"I was almost ready to go meet Sig. It must have been right
at five."

"What did he say?"

"He asked me to reconsider."

"And you said?"

"No."

Huggins reminded me of a doctor, probing and poking to find
out where it hurts. "Was he upset?"

"He seemed to be. That surprised me. If I didn't know him
better, I would have said he was jealous." Her tone was re-
signed. Ginger Watkins had long since come to terms with her
losses, whatever those might be.

"Why wouldn't he be jealous?"

"He's not the type." She gave a half-assed grin, the kind
people use to cover their real feelings, to hide something that

hurts more than they're willing to admit. Huggins skirted the issue, leaving me wondering what kind of husband wouldn't be jealous of Ginger Watkins.

I had never met the man, but I decided I didn't like Darrell Watkins, candidate for lieutenant governor. As a matter of fact, I was sure I wouldn't vote for him.

"Where did he call from?"

"He didn't say. It could have been anywhere in the state. He's out campaigning."

"You don't keep a copy of his schedule?"

"No."

"Supposing he were jealous. Would he have done something to Sig Larson or maybe hired someone to do it?"

"You mean put out a contract? No, for two reasons. Number one, he wouldn't have the money. Number two, I don't believe he's that much of a hypocrite."

"I see," Huggins said sagely. "You mean he fools around himself?" Ginger's lips trembled. She dropped her gaze and nodded.

Hal's questions had led circuitously to the heart of the matter. I had to give him credit. He made another note. "Watkins is an old, respected name in Seattle. Long on reputation and money both. Supposing Darrell did want to get rid of Sig Larson, why wouldn't he have the money? It only costs a few grand to put out a contract."

"Appearances can be deceiving," she said. "I'm not working gratis, you know."

"Which means?" Hal prompted.

"It means we need the money. Some of Homer's investments haven't turned out so well. The parole board job was designed to help out. Connections are nice. How else do you think someone without a degree could walk into a forty-thousand-dollar-a-year job?" Her voice carried a defensive edge.

The phone rang, and I answered, recognizing Deputy Pomeroy's officious voice. "Detective Huggins," he demanded.

I handed the phone to Hal. He listened for a few seconds before he said, "Keep her at the desk until I get there. And, Jake, if one of those goddamned reporters gets near her before I do, I'll have your badge, understand?"

Hal bolted for the door, then stopped, turning slowly back into the room. "It would be best if you stayed here," he told Ginger. "I'll let you know when you can return to your room."

She nodded. "All right."

"The lab guys'll call when they finish." He strode into the darkness to the sound of steady rain. I closed the door behind him, feeling uncomfortable, not knowing what to say. Ginger Watkins was a stranger I knew far too much about. "Warm enough?" I asked awkwardly.

"I am now." She paused. "I might as well call Homer and get it over with."

"Why call him at all? You can afford to ignore your soon-to-be ex-father-in-law."

She picked up the phone. "Ignoring him is the worst thing you can do to Homer." She dialed the desk to charge the call to her room number, but the desk didn't answer.

"Dial it direct," I told her, and she did.

"You called?" she asked. From across the room I could hear a renewal of his verbal barrage. "What do you want?" She interrupted him bluntly, dealing with rudeness in kind.

There was a long pause while she listened. I watched her. Her hair had dried. Honey-blond waves framed her face. She paced back and forth, tugging on a phone cord that didn't give her quite enough leash.

"I'm not going to change my mind, Homer," she said at last. "I've finally seen through the fog well enough to know what's going on."

Again there was a pause. "When I wanted to do something about it, he couldn't be bothered. Now it's too late. I don't care if he's upset. I'm getting out."

She waited. "That's not true, and you know it. What I do won't make a bit of difference, one way or the other. Besides, why should I care who wins?"

His answer to that question was brief, and she stiffened. "I've found jobs before. I'll find one again." She slammed the phone down, eyes blazing. "That bastard," she muttered.

The phone rang again, and she angrily snatched it off the hook. "Hello!" Sheepishly, she handed me the receiver. "It's for you," she said.

The desk had a message for me from Maxwell Cole. He would be in Room 143. He wanted to talk to me. I put the phone down and turned to Ginger. "Are you all right?" The phone call had genuinely disturbed her.

"I'm fine," she answered without conviction. She walked across the room and stared blindly out the darkened window like a lost, lonely child in need of comforting.

"He threatened to pull your job?"

"It's no idle threat," she returned. "He can do it."

I stood near her, wanting to put an arm around her shoulder and tell her everything would be all right, to give her some of my world-famous Beaumont Bromides. Determinedly she wiped away a tear.

"I'm sorry," she apologized. "I didn't mean to cry."

"You have plenty of reason," I offered.

She looked up at me with a faint smile. "I guess I do. I was thinking about Sig."

"What about him?"

"He gave me back my self-respect," she answered. "Nothing's going to change that. I'll resign if I have to, work as a waitress or a salesclerk, but nobody can take away what Sig Larson gave me." She paused tremulously. "I can't believe he's dead."

Abandoning her attempt to stave off tears, she fell helplessly into my arms, sobbing uncontrollably against my chest. I held her and let her cry, hoping no one was outside my window. Ginger Watkins was, after all, still very much a married lady with a husband who was a well-known statewide political candidate. This would provoke a terrific scandal if it ever hit the press.

I wondered briefly how I had fallen into such a mess. As her sobs subsided, I decided what the hell. Lie back and enjoy it.

Chapter 4

ONCE Ginger regained her composure, I suggested we order dinner from Room Service. It was close to nine. My three-meal-a-day system was going into withdrawal. I ordered two steaks, medium-rare. "Some wine?"

She shook her head. "I don't drink."

I ordered two bottles of Perrier. When in Rome, and all that. With her emotional outburst quelled, we waded toward dinner through a mire of meaningless chitchat. "Where are you from?" I asked.

"Centralia. My dad runs the Union 76 station down there."

It was a long way from small-town girl to big-time politics. She readily followed my thoughts. "Good looks help," she said with a smile. "Add some stupidity, and this is what you get."

"What do you mean?"

"I was pregnant when we got married. Homer offered to buy me off, send me to Sweden for an abortion. Darrell only married me because his father was dead set against it. I was a first and last gesture of independence." Her directness was unsettling. I was relieved when Room Service knocked on the door.

Our waiter was a young, local kid with a mouthful of braces and a winning smile. He wore a cutaway coat with a white towel draped casually over one arm. He spread the small round table with a linen cloth and served us with the arch panache of a British butler.

"That kid will go places," I said to Ginger after he bowed his way out of the room.

"At least he seems to enjoy what he's doing," she responded.

I poured two glasses of Perrier and handed her one. "You don't?" I asked.

"I was ready to," she began, "but then after Sig—" She broke off, unable to continue.

"What about Sig?"

"He saved my life," she said. "It's that simple."

"What did he do? Pull you out of a burning car?"

Ginger studied me in silence for a long time. "Something like that," she said quietly. "He got me to quit drinking."

"Drinking?" I'm sure I sounded incredulous.

She picked up the empty Perrier bottle and examined it. "I used to drink vodka, Wolfschmidts, on the rocks."

I grimaced. "We're not talking one drink before dinner."

"I almost died, Mr. Beaumont."

"Beau," I corrected. "My friends call me Beau."

"Beau," she added. "As long as I drank myself into oblivion

every night, it didn't matter if Darrell had a steady girl friend down in Olympia when the legislature was in session, or that he was screwing around with some secretary after work. If I drank hard enough and long enough, I could almost forget. Not forgive, just forget.

"Sig was like a father to me. Never laid a glove on me, as far as sex is concerned. He just kept telling me I deserved better."

"He was right," I interjected.

She smiled at me then, green eyes flashing momentarily. "Are you going to take up where Sig left off?"

"At your service." I waved my Perrier glass in a gallant flourish.

Her smile disappeared. "I can't understand why both Homer and Darrell are trying to talk me out of the divorce. Homer never liked me, and Darrell hasn't shown any interest in me for longer than I care to remember."

"Come on, you have to be kidding!"

"Do I?" Her face was devoid of humor.

I groped for a thread of non-threatening conversation. She had said she was pregnant when they married. "You have a child?"

"Had," she corrected. "A girl. Her name was Katy, after my mother. She was almost six months old when I found her dead in her crib. They call it Sudden Infant Death Syndrome, now. Back then it didn't have a name. I blamed myself. The kooks came out of the woodwork, told me God was punishing me for my sins. It was awful!" She closed her eyes, reliving the pain.

I wanted to say something, but it was a little late to offer condolences.

"That's when I started to drink," she continued as naturally as if she were discussing the weather. "I never got pregnant again. I couldn't sleep. I started having a drink or two in the evening to put me under, to blot out the pain. Eventually I had to drink to live. It's only been since I dried out that I've come to terms with Katy's death, accepted it, allowed myself to grieve. Booze is like that, you know. It buries feelings, keeps you from dealing with them."

The last sentence hit close to home. It was what Peters had told me I was doing, and Ralph Ames, and the chaplain. They told me to stop hiding out in McNaughton's and come to grips with grief. They said I should cry for Anne Corley and let her go. I wasn't ready.

I veered the conversation away from me and back to Ginger. "Sig helped you do that?"

She nodded. "We were in Shelton doing a series of hearings. Board members travel in pairs, like nuns. One morning I couldn't get out of bed. I had the shakes too bad. That was when Sig broke into my room. He dragged me to my first Alcoholics Anonymous meeting that night. We were scheduled to go home the next morning, but we stayed over. Sig got us rooms in a different motel. It took three days for him to walk me through the DTs. That's when Mona started thinking Sig and I were having an affair."

I looked at Ginger's trim figure and flawless grace. She didn't fit any of the standard stereotypes of a recovering alcoholic. Had she not told me, I never would have suspected.

"I won't go through that again, ever," she continued. "Nothing can be worse than DTs. Sig kept me in the program, talked to me when I got discouraged, kept telling me I was a worthwhile person long before I could see it for myself. I'd be dead by now if it weren't for him."

"He sounds like a hell of a nice guy," I commented.

"He was." She lapsed into silence.

"Do you love Darrell?" It was none of my business, yet I asked anyway. I already knew a great deal about Ginger Watkins, far more than our few hours together warranted, but I wanted to know more. It had nothing to do with Detective J. P. Beaumont. It was Beau, the man, who needed to know.

"I used to," she said softly. "Not anymore."

She met my gaze, then looked down at her plate. "I didn't mean to bore you."

"I'm not bored. What will you do?"

"Live one day at a time. I'll file on Monday, resign from the board if I have to, and go looking for a job."

"What kind of job?"

"Maybe I'll go back to school and get a degree in alcoholism counseling. I'd like to repay Sig Larson."

"Somehow I don't think Sig expected to be repaid."

"No," she agreed, "he didn't. That's why I want to do it." Suddenly she put the brakes on my questioning. "What about you? Who is J. P. Beaumont?"

I gave her an evasive grin. "A homicide cop in the middle of a mid-life crisis, trying to decide what I want to be when I grow up."

"Married?"

"Not anymore."

"Involved?"

I sighed. It was six months later, but the hurt was still there. Not bleeding, but raw nonetheless. "No, I'm footloose and fancy-free."

"You don't sound very footloose," she observed.

"That's very perceptive of you," I said. "You're right." I couldn't match her candor. The kind of open self-revelation that came easily to her eluded me. The telephone jangled a welcome interruption.

"Detective Beaumont?"

"Yes."

"This is Smitty with the crime lab. Could you bring Mrs. Watkins up to take a look around the room?"

"Sure. Find anything?"

"Can't tell." It was a standard answer. "Maybe she can tell us if anything's missing."

"Okay, we'll be right there."

I put down the phone and turned to Ginger. "Traveling time."

She peered in dismay at her stockinged feet. "What about shoes?"

Scrounging the bottom of the closet, I turned up my ancient bedroom slippers. "Put these on. They'll fit like a pair of snowshoes, but it's better than going barefoot."

Ginger stumbled across the room in a trial run. "Not much better," she commented.

The walk to Ginger's room was cold and windy. The rain had stopped. Wispy clouds scudded before a half-moon. Ginger scuffed along, gripping my arm in case she tripped over the out-sized slippers.

"Have you ever been the victim of a break-in before?"

She shook her head. I wanted to warn her, to ease the shock of seeing her things strewn and disheveled by unknown hands. She knew of the break-in from Huggins, but hearing it and seeing it are two different things.

We made it to her room without incident. If Rosario was crawling with reporters, they weren't in evidence. Thank God Huggins had managed to keep Ginger's room out of the limelight. By now members of the Fourth Estate would have filed their stories. They'd be settled in the Vista Lounge, drowning their sorrows or entertaining one another. The Seattle Press Corps Traveling Dog and Pony Show.

Pomeroy opened the door, grunting with displeasure when he saw me.

I ignored him, pushing my way past without any kind of acknowledgment. His face flushed angrily, but he said nothing.

Ginger followed me into the room. She stopped short inside the door, her face blanching, her hands involuntarily covering her mouth.

A man came forward and introduced himself. "I'm Dayton Smith," he said. "Smitty for short. This your room?"

Ginger nodded.

"We've dusted for prints. We'll want your prints and those of any other people known to have been in the room—the desk clerk, maids, Room Service. That's the only way to discover unidentified prints. We'll go down to the lobby after we finish here."

Again Ginger nodded, incapable of speech.

"Look around. Can you see if anything is missing?"

Walking trancelike through the room, Ginger fingered the heap of clothing piled on the floor, sifted through the contents of her makeup case strewn on the counter while those of us in the room watched in silence.

All the officers, with the possible exception of Pomeroy, understood the deep sense of violation a break-in victim feels. Fear, anger, and outrage passed over her face in rapid succession. She knelt beside a scatter of papers dumped near an overturned Gucci briefcase, awkwardly attempting to straighten them. When she finished, I pulled her to her feet.

"Is anything gone?"

She shook her head. "I don't think so."

I looked at Smitty. "No sign of forced entry?"

"No. Whoever came in evidently had a key."

I looked down at Ginger. She was pale and shaking. "Gather what you need," I said. "You can't stay here. We'll have the desk send someone to clean up this mess."

She approached the task purposefully, moving through the room, scooping up nightgown, robe, and shoes from the tangled heap on the floor. She sorted through the things on the counter, placing makeup, hairbrush, and toothbrush in a small case along with her clothing. Pomeroy watched her leeringly from the door. I wanted to kick him.

At last, still wearing my slippers, she turned to me. "I'm ready. Can we go?"

I led her from the room. She sank against me. I supported her willingly, J. P. Beaumont, Good Samaritan in an hour of need.

"Thank you," she whispered.

"You're welcome," I replied, guiltily conscious of savoring the slight pressure of her slender body against mine.

Chapter 5

SMITTY's partner from the Washington State Crime Lab took Ginger into the hotel kitchen for fingerprinting. I went to the desk where I tackled Fred, demanding another room. "I'm sorry Mr. Beaumont. We're full. We were almost booked before the reporters showed up, and now—"

"Look," I said. "The crime lab's still not done with her room. Besides, she can't go back there. The lock wasn't broken. Whoever got in had a key."

"As I said, we don't have any other rooms."

I turned away from the desk in disgust, only to run headlong into the mustached human walrus who calls himself Maxwell Cole. "Hello, J. P. Why didn't you return my call?"

"Didn't want to, Max. Get out of my way."

"You're being rude," he chided. "I only need to talk to you for a minute."

"What about?" I was pretty sure I knew what Max was after. For once in his life, he surprised me.

"Don Wilson."

"Who the hell is Don Wilson?"

"You remember, Denise Wilson's husband. DeAnn's father. The Lathrop case."

There isn't a cop in Washington State who isn't sickened by the very name. Philip Lathrop sits over on Death Row in Walla Walla, a slime thumbing his nose at the system. Seven years ago, he followed Denise Wilson home from the laundromat and raped her in front of her two-year-old daughter. Denise testified against him, and Lathrop got sent up. He went to prison vowing revenge.

Six years later he was placed in a work/release program. Nobody remembered that the Wilsons lived less than three miles away. He came back to their house one hot July day and finished the job, killing both Denise and DeAnn in a bloody carnage that left hardened detectives puking at the scene. It'll be years before he exhausts the appeals process. It's called a miscarriage of justice!

"What about Don Wilson?" I asked.

"I was to meet him here at four. He never showed."

"So? What does that have to do with me?"

"I wondered if you had seen him. He turns up at parole board hearings, demonstrating, protesting—that kind of thing. He's lobbying for a statewide victim/witness protection program."

"Look, Max, I wouldn't recognize him if I saw him. There hasn't been a protester in sight."

Max blinked at me nearsightedly through thick glasses. "You're sure?"

"Yes, I'm sure, goddammit," I snapped. "Now leave me alone." I was still worrying about Ginger, wondering if there might be a room available somewhere in Eastsound.

Max backed away from me warily. The last time he and I had a confrontation, I loosened a couple of teeth for him.

Just then Ginger returned from the kitchen. She walked past Cole. "I'm done, Beau," she said. "Did you get a room?" It was an innocent question, but I wondered how it would read in the morning edition. As recognition and wonder washed across Max's fat face, I wanted to crawl into a hole.

"Why, Mrs. Watkins, how nice to see you again."

Ginger turned on him coolly. "I don't believe I know you."

"Cole," he said with an affable grin. "Maxwell Cole of the *Post-Intelligencer*. Would you care to comment on Sig Larson's death?"

Her manner changed from cool to frigid. "I would not."

He shrugged and looked at me. "Doesn't hurt to ask."

"Get out of here, Max." I was in no mood to put up with any of his crap.

"Just one more question, Mrs. Watkins. Have you seen Don Wilson today?"

Ginger's reaction was totally out of proportion to the question.

"Is . . . he . . . here?" she stammered. Color drained from her face. She groped blindly for my arm.

The change wasn't lost on Max. He stepped toward her, and she shrank against me. "He was supposed to be," Max continued lightly. "We had an interview scheduled at four. He called late this morning. Said something was about to break. I barely had time to get here."

I stepped between Max and Ginger. "Why did he call you? Why not someone else?"

"I've been working on a special piece—"

I took Ginger's arm, cutting him off. "Come on. Let's get out of here."

"But—" Max protested.

"Stay away from her and stay away from me, Max. If you don't, I'll give your dentist and your eye doctor a little more business."

His walrus mouth opened and closed convulsively. They weren't empty words, and he knew it. When Ginger and I left the building, he made no effort to follow.

I led Ginger back to my room and helped her into the chair before I went back to shut and lock the door. "What is it, Ginger?" I asked gently. "Tell me."

"He did it," she said decisively. "It has to be him."

"Who did what?"

"Don Wilson. He killed Sig, I'm sure of it. I had no idea he was here. I never thought—"

"What are you talking about?"

"Don Wilson. He threatened us, both Sig and me. Sig just laughed it off. So did Darrell. No one took it seriously."

"Why did he threaten you? I don't understand."

"We—" She swallowed hard. "Sig and I conducted the hearing that sent Lathrop to that work/release program."

My gut gave a wrench. I remembered the public outcry. There had been talk that the parole board should resign *en masse*. I had been standing next to her. Turning, I moved away, distancing myself. I couldn't help it.

"Please, Beau, it wasn't our fault. We were given incomplete records. We made the decision as best we could with the information at hand." Her voice pleaded for understanding, for me not to abandon her.

"What did Wilson say?" My tone was flat and empty.

"That we'd pay for his wife and daughter. We didn't know, Beau. Can you understand that? There was an administrative foul-up. The rest of Lathrop's records weren't found until much later. We didn't know he had sworn to get even with Denise Wilson. We had no idea where she lived. Washington doesn't keep track of witnesses or victims, not even to protect them."

"When did Wilson threaten you?" I could tell from her voice it was important that I believe her.

"I don't know. Several times. He's always hanging around. In fact, Sig and I were surprised Wilson wasn't here today. He stands outside every meeting, carrying signs, passing out petitions, but I never thought he'd really do it."

"Petitions for what?"

"For a victim/witness protection program."

"But he wasn't here today?"

"No. Sig even mentioned it." I got up and went to the phone. "What are you doing?" she asked.

"I'm calling Huggins. He needs this information." Fred answered. "Is Detective Huggins still around?"

"No," came the reply. "He left in the police boat right after the crime-lab guys took off. He's probably in Friday Harbor by now."

"Call him and tell him to come back," I ordered. "It's urgent."

Fred's response wasn't hopeful. "I doubt he'll want to come back tonight."

"Tell him we've got a suspect. That'll bring him back." I hung up.

Ginger followed me to the door. "Where are you going?" she asked.

"I've got to find Maxwell Cole. You stay here, understand?" She nodded. "Lock the door behind me. Don't let anyone in."

I dashed outside and headed up the path to Room 143. No one answered my knock. I glanced at my watch. It was after eleven. The Vista Lounge was still open. I hurried back toward the main building, a converted mansion that serves as lobby, dining room, and bar. The lounge is a long, narrow room facing Rosario Strait. In its previous life it had been a sun porch. Now it was a posh watering hole.

Maxwell Cole's ample figure slouched on a stool at the end of the bar. He was downing handfuls of salted cracker goldfish and regaling the poor guy next to him with one-sided conversation. I tapped his shoulder.

"Hey, Max. I need to talk to you."

He heaved himself around on the bar stool to face me. "What's this? A change of heart? Decided you can afford to spend some time with your old fraternity buddy after all? Fuck off, J. P. Who needs it?"

He turned away and picked up his beer. I tapped his shoulder again. "I want to talk to you."

Barney is a good bartender. He has a sixth sense for trouble and can spot it before it starts. He ambled down the bar to where Cole was sitting.

"What seems to be the problem?"

"This guy's bothering me," Max whined. "I was sitting here minding my own business."

Barney glanced up at me. "I need to talk to him," I said tersely over Max's head. "About what happened this afternoon."

Max set down his half-empty glass. Barney swept it away and poured the contents into the sink. "After you talk to this gentleman," he said, "I'll buy you another beer."

"Why you—" Max objected.

"You'd better go, fella, before I get upset."

Barney is a beefy former Green Beret who looks as though he could inflict a considerable amount of bodily harm with his bare hands. Max finally scrambled down from the bar stool and reluctantly followed me into the next room, muttering under his breath. Once we were out of earshot of the bar, I turned on him. "You have any pictures of Wilson on you?"

"Hell no. Why should I?"

"Because you just might."

"Maybe one, but it'll cost you."

"How much?"

"An exclusive interview with Ginger Watkins."

"Ginger Watkins is not for sale."

"You say that in a rather proprietary manner, J. P. You got something going with her? I heard what she said about getting a room. She's a married lady, you know. Her husband is big. Very big."

"I want the picture, Max."

"No way."

He was wearing an ugly striped tie, still knotted, but hanging loose around his neck. I grasped it in my fist and lifted him to the tops of his toes. "I'm not on duty, Maxey, so don't tempt me."

"Okay, okay," he sputtered. "It's in my room."

"Go get it and bring it to me. I'll wait in the lobby."

He shambled off. I hurried to the pay phone near the front desk and dialed Peters, my partner, at home, long-distance, collect. I figured that would get his attention. He sounded half-asleep when he answered the phone. "What's up?" he asked when he recognized my voice. "Where are you? And why the hell are you calling me collect?"

"Rosario," I growled. "Send me the bill. Now listen. Remember the Lathrop case? Get down to the department and gather everything you can find on it. A detective from Friday Harbor will be calling for it. I want it ready when he does."

"Just a fucking minute, Beau. Do you know what time it is? It's a long way from Kirkland to the department."

"So move to town. It's not rush hour. It won't take more than twenty minutes to get to Seattle."

"Beau, you're supposed to be on vacation, for chrissake. What's gotten into you?"

"I'm asking a favor, Peters. Please."

"Oh, all right, but I'm gonna remember this. The Lathrop case, you said?"

"Yes, and everything you can find out about the victims' family, particularly Don Wilson, the father."

"Anything else? I'm already awake. Don't you want me to pick up some groceries or a newspaper while I'm at it?"

Maxwell Cole was lumbering toward the building. "Cut the comedy, Peters. This is serious."

"Okay, Beau, okay. I'm on my way."

"Thanks. I owe you one."

"This better count for more than one."

"It does."

Chapter 6

I KNOCKED. "Who is it?" Ginger called.

"Me, Beau." I opened the door with my key. Ginger stood near the bed, her face drawn and wary. She glanced at the manila envelope in my hand. "What's that?"

I came inside, shutting and locking the door behind me. I opened the envelope and handed her the picture Maxwell Cole had given me. She looked at Don Wilson's likeness.

"Where'd you get that?"

"Good ol' Max saves the day for a change."

Ginger retreated to a chair in the corner of the room, where she curled up with her legs folded under her and began brushing her hair with a vengeance.

"Huggins is on his way," I told her. "He'll want to go to work on this picture tonight. He'll show it to everyone he can find on or near the ferries, passengers and workers alike. He'll try to get to them while someone still remembers seeing Wilson, either coming over or going back."

Ginger put the brush in her lap. Her voice when she spoke was very small. "Do you think he's still here?"

"I don't know. My gut instinct says yes."

"What can we do?"

"First we talk to Huggins. After that, I don't know."

"Can I stay here, Beau? With you?" Anxious green eyes held mine.

I felt a catch in my throat, remembering the feel of her body against mine as she wept for Sig Larson. "I don't know why not. I'd as soon have you here where I can keep an eye on you. I was going to see if there were any rooms available in Eastsound, but this makes more sense."

She picked up her brush and silently resumed brushing her hair. I called the desk. Fred and I had gone round and round over the room problem one more time after Max gave me the picture.

I had pulled rank on him, hoping Detective Beaumont would elicit more action than Mr. Beaumont. No such luck. His tone was somewhat guarded. "Yes, Detective Beaumont. What can I do for you?"

"You have a roll-away bed down there?"

"Yes."

"I want one up here, on the double. Mrs. Watkins will stay here with me. We have reason to believe Larson's killer is still in the area. He may try to reach her next. Don't leak a word of this, is that clear?"

"Yes, sir. I'll deliver it myself. Not even the maids will know. I can pick it up in the morning before I leave."

"And if she has any calls," I continued, "put them on hold and check with me before you put them through."

"I understand."

"When's your shift over?"

"I'm pulling an extra one tonight. I won't get off until eight tomorrow morning."

"All right. Have the roll-away back out of here before you go. I guess that's all."

"Detective Beaumont?"

"Yes."

"Someone said Detective Huggins is just pulling up at the dock."

"Good. See if you can locate any coffee, would you?"

"Sure thing."

When Huggins knocked on the door, he was carrying a tray with a pot of coffee and three cups and saucers. "Somebody handed me this tray. Whatever you've got, Beaumont, it better be good."

"It is, Hal," I assured him. "Believe me."

Ginger poured coffee while I brought Hal up to date and showed him the photograph of Wilson. When I finished, he shook his head sadly. "It's a pisser. The wrong goddamned people get killed. Wilson'll end up on Death Row with Lathrop, and probably beat him to the gallows."

I interrupted Huggins' grim soliloquy. "Look, Hal, I called my partner in Seattle. He's gathering everything Seattle P.D. has on Lathrop and Wilson. It'll be ready when you call. He'll bring it out himself if you ask for him."

"Is he one of the old-timers?" Hal asked. "Somebody I'd remember?"

"No. He's brand-new, but a hell of a nice guy."

"What's his name?"

"Peters. Ron Peters."

He made a note of the name before turning to Ginger. "Can you remember exactly what Wilson said when he threatened you and Mr. Larson?"

Ginger shook her head. "Not the exact words. Just that he'd make us pay, that it wasn't fair for his wife and child to be dead while we were still alive."

"But you didn't think of him this afternoon when you discovered Mr. Larson's body. Why not?"

"I didn't think Wilson was here. If he's around, he's usually out front picketing with all his signs and paraphernalia. I forgot about him completely until that reporter said Wilson didn't show for a meeting."

"Which reporter?"

I answered him. "Max, Maxwell Cole. Wilson called him this morning and set up an interview here at Rosario at four o'clock. Max waited. Wilson never came."

Huggins focused once more on Ginger. "You said you mentioned the threats to your husband. He advised you to disregard them?"

Ginger nodded. "He said the world is full of harmless crazies."

"This one is far from harmless." Huggins sighed, glancing in my direction. "Any ideas, Beaumont?"

There was a quiet tap on the door. When I answered it, Fred stood outside with a roll-away bed. "This is the first I could get away," he said. "It's all right if Detective Huggins knows, isn't it?"

Since the bed was already there, it was too late to debate secrecy. I stepped aside and helped pull the bed over the threshold. He pushed the bed just inside the door, then ducked back into the night. Fearless Fred.

"This is my brainstorm," I said, turning to Huggins. "She stays with me tonight. Without knowing whether Wilson is still on the island, I'm not willing to risk leaving her alone."

He nodded in agreement. "Good thinking. I was going to suggest flying her to Seattle, but I'd prefer having her here in case

there are more questions in the morning. The county budget
doesn't handle a whole lot of commuting back and forth to the
big city."

Huggins stood up. "I'm going, then." He held Wilson's picture up to the light, examining it minutely. "I'll copy this sucker
tonight and plaster the island with it tomorrow—the island and
every single ferry that stops here. I'll send someone by Wilson's
house. It's late. I'd better hit the trail."

I followed him to the door. He turned to me and said in an
undertone, "You got a piece on you?"

"It's locked up in a suitcase, but—"

"I'm deputizing you as of right now, Beaumont. I don't want
there to be any jurisdictional fuss. Besides, I need you. Get it
out, and keep it handy." He poked his head back inside the door.
"You're in good hands, Mrs. Watkins. J. P. Beaumont is the
best there is."

"You'll give me a swelled head, Hal," I said.

I came back into the room, once more carefully locking the
door behind me. I went around the room, double-checking the
locks on the windows. Ginger watched me, her eyes gravely following my every move. I took my suitcase from its place in the
closet and removed my .38. I put the gun on the bed beside me.
Women usually retreat from firearms. Ginger held her ground.

"Are you?" she asked.

"Am I what?"

"The best there is?"

"I don't know about that." I sat looking at my revolver. A
gun is a tool, an instrument, until it kills something you love.
Then it takes on a life of its own, alien, evil.

"What are you thinking?"

"Nothing," I answered quickly. "Just wool-gathering."

"What happened to your wife?"

"Karen?" I shrugged. "She ran off with a chicken magnate
from Cucamonga, California."

"Chicken?"

"Yeah. He was an accountant scouting for a new plant site for
an egg conglomerate. Karen was supposed to be selling him real
estate."

"He married her?"

"Eventually."

"Kids?"

"Two. A boy and a girl, Scotty and Kelly. They're mostly grown, thriving in California. I see them during the summers." I didn't mention Anne Corley. It was a deliberate oversight.

"Girl friend?"

"None at the moment. Why all the questions?"

"Everyone's been asking me questions all evening. Turnabout is fair play. You said earlier you were having a mid-life crisis. How come?"

"Mid-life crises are very trendy these days." I responded with a congenial grin I hoped would derail the question. I didn't want to go into that, to examine motives and lost illusions.

"Will you still be a cop?"

I shrugged. I couldn't imagine being anything else. "Unless you have some other bright idea."

She looked at me seriously, squarely. "You've been hurt too."

"Does it show that much?"

"It shows."

I winced at her direct hit and changed the subject. "You said something earlier that's been bothering me: that you were working because you and Darrell needed the money. How come?"

"We're part of a syndicate that put together a downtown luxury high-rise project, just before the bottom dropped out of the real estate market. Most of our capital—ours, Homer's, and Sig's—has been tied up keeping the project afloat, waiting for the market to turn. Meantime, ready cash is in short supply."

"That's why you and Sig ended up on the parole board?"

She nodded. "Sig was actually well qualified. He knew it from the inside out without ever being either a prisoner or a guard. He did volunteer work at Walla Walla for years. He used to live near there, even started an A.A. group inside. He had every right to be on the board. I was the hanger-on."

Ginger looked at me earnestly. "I tried, though, Beau. Especially after Sig got me dried out. I read everything I could lay my hands on. I did a good job. The Lathrop case was an administrative nightmare." She willed me to believe her. It was important to her that I not lay blame.

"Those things happen," I conceded.

She accepted my remark as a form of absolution. "Thank you," she murmured.

"What will you do if you resign from the board?"

She shrugged. "Something," she replied. "Homer told me tonight he'll see to it that I don't get a penny."

"That's just a threat. He can't get away with it. You have an attorney. He'll see that you get a fair shake."

She laughed. "You don't understand. Homer Watkins' name isn't up in lights. He doesn't make headlines, but he's a mover and shaker in this state. Stone-cold broke, he can still pull enough strings to get anything he wants, including electing his son lieutenant governor. I'll be lucky to get out of the house with the clothes on my back."

"I have an attorney," I offered. "Maybe he could help." I was thinking about Ralph Ames, who even then was preparing for a custody hearing to wrest my partner's two kids out of a religious cult in Broken Springs, Oregon.

Ginger smiled, condescendingly. "How far do you think I'd get paying for an attorney on my own? It takes money to fight the system. I won't have any."

"Ames would do it if I asked him. He's from Arizona. Phoenix. He handles all my personal affairs. Let him take a look at your situation. It wouldn't cost you anything."

A smile flickered around the corner of her mouth. "Beau, listen to me. These are big-time lawyers with big-time staffs. They'd chew up your little guy and spit him out. But thanks. It's kind of you to offer."

"Promise me you'll let Ames look it over first. Talk about the best there is, Ames is it."

Ginger laughed aloud. "All right, all right. If you insist, but he'd better not show up wearing cowboy boots and riding a horse."

Chapter 7

I SPENT some time looking for a delicate way to suggest we get ready for bed. There was no easy way. I finally said it straight out. Ginger retreated into the bathroom to change while I grappled with the Chinese-puzzle roll-away bed. Partial assembly required.

The bed was unfolded and sitting in front of the outside door when Ginger emerged from the bathroom. She wore a jade-colored silk robe with a hint of filmy nightgown underneath. Seeing her, I realized I didn't have a pair of pajamas to my name. I'd been a bachelor so long, my last pair of Christmas pajamas had bitten the dust.

"What are you staring at?" she demanded, one hand on her hip. "Haven't you ever seen a woman in a robe before?"

"Sorry. I was thinking about something else."

I retired to the bathroom to contemplate my dilemma, finally opting for skivvies and no lights. That, of course, presented another problem. No light in a familiar room is one thing, and no light in a city apartment is another. But no light in a strange room where they've never heard of streetlights can be murder on shins, toes, and other unprotected parts of the anatomy. I blundered my way into bed after a bruising game of blindman's buff.

Settling into the roll-away, I discovered the bed frame formed a rigid hump directly under the small of my back. It was a long way from the king-sized comfort I had grown accustomed to. At last I concluded the bed wasn't any worse than some of the rocks I had slept on just for the hell of it during my hunting and camping phase. This at least had a somewhat higher purpose.

I tossed around a few minutes before dozing off. I had just entered that deep, initial alpha sleep when I heard her say, "Beau?"

Adrenaline pumping, I made a dive for the .38 on the floor beside me. The roll-away tipped up on one corner, pitching me headlong onto the floor in a tangle of sheets, pillow, and blankets. Ginger switched on the bedside lamp.

"What happened?"

"I fell out of bed, goddammit! What's wrong? Did you hear something?"

"No, I was wondering if you were awake."

"I am now," I grumbled. I didn't want to get up. The light still blazed while I sat on the floor clad in a discreet loincloth of sheet. I glared at her, and she started to giggle.

"It's not funny," I muttered.

She nodded, covering her mouth with her hand to contain increasing ripples of laughter. "Yes it is," she gasped at last. "You ought to see yourself."

I looked down. I had to admit that what I could see was pretty funny. The gun had skidded under the bed. No way was I going to crawl around on hands and knees searching for it. With as much dignity as I could muster, I unraveled my legs. At last, wearing the sheet as a toga, I stood on my feet, surveying the debris that had once been a tidy roll-away bed.

"This is a very large bed," Ginger said seriously, stifling her mirth. "It's probably more comfortable than that thing, too." That much was inarguable. I said nothing. "Care to join me?"

"Come on, Ginger. Get serious."

"I am serious." All laughter was gone from her mouth and eyes. "There's plenty of room," she added. "We're consenting adults. We haven't crossed any state lines."

"But you're the wife of the soon-to-be-elected lieutenant governor."

"The soon-to-be-former wife of the soon-to-be-elected lieutenant governor," she corrected with a hint of a smile.

I moved to the far side of the bed and alighted cautiously on the edge of it. I waited for lightning to strike. It didn't.

"Would you like me to call the desk and see if they have any bundling boards?"

I turned on her. "You're making fun of me."

"I can't help it."

Tentatively I slid first one leg, then the other under the covers, clutching the sheet firmly in one hand as a security blanket. I settled warily on my pillow before I turned to look at her. She sat propped up in bed observing me with undisguised interest.

The deep neckline of her gown fell away revealing a firm swell of breast.

"Do you think I'm beautiful?" she asked gravely.

I looked up guiltily, convinced she had caught me peeking. "Of course you're beautiful. Very beautiful."

"Sig used to tell me that. I never knew if I should believe him."

"My God, Ginger! How could you not believe him?"

"I still see a drunk when I look in the mirror." It was a comment made without guile. She wasn't fishing for a compliment: she was attempting to understand, to sort out what was real and what wasn't.

Obviously we weren't going right to sleep. I propped my pillow next to hers, examining her carefully, critically in the golden glow of the bedside lamp behind her. I studied the curve of her forehead, the clear green eyes under delicately arched brows, the fine, straight nose, the gentle pout of her lower lip. "You're not the same person now. I think that's what Sig wanted you to realize."

She drew her knees up and rested her chin on them, musing aloud. "I thought if I once quit drinking, that I'd be good enough, that Darrell would finally pay some attention to me. There are a lot of stories like that in A.A., you know, marriages that bounce back from the brink of disaster. But this is a thirty-six-year-old body. I can't compete with tender blossoms from the secretarial pool."

Silence lengthened between us. Never glib, I could think of nothing to say. But then, I had never before found myself in quite this situation.

"What's the scar on your chest?"

"Huh?" Her question startled me. I looked down as though I had forgotten it was my chest and my scar, the stark white of an incision highlighted against the rest of my skin. "It's from a bullet," I said.

"When did it happen?"

"Last spring sometime," I said carefully. The time, the date, the place are as indelibly inked on my soul as the scar is on my flesh.

"Did you catch him?"

"Who?"

"The man who shot you."

"It was a woman. She's dead."

"Oh."

"Do you mind turning out the lights?" I asked. I didn't want to talk anymore. The conversation was circling too close to my own hurt. It was one thing to help Ginger with hers. Dealing with my own was something else.

The light snapped off. I could feel Ginger settling on her side of the bed. I groped under the bed and located my .38. Once it was within easy reach, I lowered my pillow, resting on it as if it were full of thumbtacks or nails.

"Beau?"

"Yes."

"Could I just lie next to you? I need an arm around me. Some-one to hold me."

Tentatively, I held up the covers. She slid across the bed and nestled into the crook of my arm. I inhaled the fragrant perfume of her freshly washed hair. I felt the curve of her hip next to mine, the gentle swell of her breast under a layer of covers. For a long time we were quiet. I think I was holding my breath.

"Beau?"

"Yes."

"What are you thinking?"

"I'm trying to remember which of the Ten Commandments says 'Thou shalt not covet thy neighbor's wife.' "

"Do you?"

"Do I what?"

"Covet me?"

Right then I realized the Garden of Eden was a put-up job. "Yes."

Her hand flitted across my chest, her touch inflaming every strained nerve in my body. She pulled herself up until she lay on my chest, her lips grazing mine.

I was conscious of the tantalizing feel of silk against my skin, the musky odor of a woman's awakening body. She kissed me, cautiously, as though unsure of my response. I wasn't sure either. I waited long enough to be sure lightning still didn't strike, then I pulled her to me, my mouth seeking hers, finding her hungry, willing, eager.

She guided my hand through the cleft in her gown. Her breast was taut and expectant beneath my cupped fingers. I sampled her ear and traced the slender curve of her neck with my teeth and tongue. She gasped, and her body arched as gooseflesh swept across her skin beneath my fingertips.

She slipped from my grasp. I heard her impatiently cast off the silken barrier of gown. My Fruit of the Loom hit the floor as well. Ginger came back to me naked, sleek, and ready. Beyond pleasure, she sought only release.

She slid her body onto mine, moisture finding moisture, need finding need, plunging me deep within her. I grasped her slim waist, raising her, lowering her, hearing her sharp intake of breath each time I probed closer to home, each time I led her to the brink then drew her back, offering and withholding the final gift.

"Now," she whispered. "Please."

When the flood came, it engulfed us both. We surfaced in a quiet pool, spent and out of breath. "That was wonderful," she whispered.

"I'll bet you say that to all the guys," I teased.

She was suddenly subdued. "There's only been one other," she said. "He's never been this good. Ever."

"Flattery will get you everywhere." I drew her into my arms, cradling her head on my shoulder. "Are you going to shut up and go to sleep? It's late. The desk clerk is coming for the goddamn roll-away at eight in the morning."

"I'll be quiet," she said. "I promise."

She snuggled against me. We lay like that for a long time. Her breathing steadied and slowed. I listened as her heart beat next to mine, a thud followed by a smaller echo. Deliberately I tried to slow my breathing, hoping to God I wouldn't snore. Time passed slowly. I stared, sleepless, at the empty space above the ed, wondering how long it takes to learn to sleep double in a double bed, to misquote a familiar song. Probably a long time.

"Beau?"

"What now?"

"I can't do it."

"Do what?"

"Sleep like this. I don't know how to sleep with anyone but Darrell."

I pulled her to me, holding her for a moment in a crushing bear hug. I kissed the top of her forehead, then shoved her playfully toward the other side of the bed. "Go sleep over there, then, spoilsport."

"I'm sorry."

"Don't be. I understand."

And I did understand. Ginger Watkins had been caught up in the need to know she was still alive—a normal phenomenon in the aftermath of death, an instinctive affirmation of survival. If I hadn't been there, she would have found someone else. I just got lucky.

Chapter 8

THE telephone jarred me awake at seven. "Detective Beaumont? Darrell Watkins is on the phone. He wants to speak to Mrs. Watkins. Should I put him through?"

I felt the unaccustomed warmth of a body snuggled close to mine. It took time to clear my head. I turned, and Ginger stirred, nestling comfortably against me. She had evidently moved there in the middle of the night, our sleeping bodies overcoming our conscious objections. "Sure, that's fine," I said into the phone.

With a noisy clatter I fumbled the phone back into place. "Ginger. Wake up. You've got a call."

Her eyes opened and focused on mine with a look of startled dismay. The phone rang again before she could say anything. I handed it to her.

"Hello?" Ginger said, her voice still thick with sleep. "Oh, hello Darrell." There was a long silence as she listened to what he had to say. Meanwhile, I lay naked under the covers, considering the best way to get to the bathroom while maintaining some degree of modesty.

"No. I haven't changed my mind," she said firmly. That galvanized me to action. I had no intention of eavesdropping on her domestic conversation. I groped on the floor, found the discarded roll-away sheet, and wrapped it around me. With clean clothes from the closet, I withdrew into the bathroom and took a bracing hot shower.

The water pounded me. Despite lack of sleep, I was invigorated, stimulated. Exhaustion, my constant companion for months, dissolved. I was incredibly happy, except for one small cloud on my horizon. Ginger might be remorseful.

I didn't want guilt or regret to tarnish what had happened between us, even if it was nothing more than the survivor's time-honored, near-death screwing syndrome. Maybe that's all it had been for Ginger, but not for me. It had reawakened J. P. Beaumont's lost libido. I was glad to have the old boy back.

Humming under my breath, I emerged from the bathroom. Ginger sat on her side of the bed with her legs tucked under her. She was wearing the lush silk robe.

"Good morning," I said.

"Do you always sing in the shower?"

"Only when I'm happy," I told her.

"I see."

I looked at her, trying to assess the effect of her husband's phone call, hoping for some sign to indicate if she was glad to see me or if she wanted me to drop into a hole someplace. Her face remained inscrutable.

"Is Darrell coming up?" I asked, for want of something better to say.

"He wanted to, but I told him no. He thinks he can talk me into changing my mind. It won't work. I told him I'm staying here the rest of the weekend. I had planned to, anyway. There's no sense in going home just to fight."

"Will they cancel the workshop?"

She smiled mirthlessly. "Not even Trixie Bowdeen has nerve enough to go through with it after what happened to Sig."

"Who's she?"

"Chairman of the parole board."

"You don't like her much, do you."

"No," she responded.

With my hair combed and a splash of after-shave on my face, I surveyed the roll-away with an eye to making it look more like someone had slept in it and less as though a heavyweight wrestling match had occurred. I gathered up the sheets and blankets and started to put it to rights.

"Beau?"

Busy with the bed, I didn't look up when she spoke. "What?"

"Do you think badly of me?"

I abandoned the roll-away. "Think badly of you! Are you kidding? Why should I?"

"Because of last night. I didn't mean to . . . I—"

In two steps I stood beside her. "Look, lady," I said gruffly, placing my hand on her shoulder and giving her a gentle shake. "It's the blind leading the blind. I was worried about how you'd feel this morning, afraid you'd be embarrassed, think I'd taken advantage.''

She reached out and took my hand. She kissed the back of it, then turned it over and moved it from her hairline to her chin, guiding my fingers in a slow caress along the curve of her cheek.

"I'm not embarrassed," she said softly. "Greedy, but not embarrassed." She allowed my hand to stray down her neck and invade the soft folds of her robe. She was wearing nothing underneath.

Her robe fell open before me. Our coupling the night before had been in pitch-blackness. Now my eyes feasted hungrily on her body. She was no lithe virgin. Hers was the gentle voluptuousness of a grown woman, with a hint of fullness of breast and hip that follows childbearing. A pale web of stretch marks lingered in mute testimony.

My hand cupped her breast. It changed subtly but perceptibly. The nipple drew erect, the soft flesh taut and warm beneath my fingers. She caught my chin in her hand and turned my face to hers until our lips met. "Please, Beau," she whispered, her mouth against mine.

I shed my clothes on the spot while she lay naked before me, tempting as a pagan sacrifice offered to me alone. My fingers and tongue searched her body, exploring her, demanding admittance. She gave herself freely, opening before me, denying me nothing. She took all I had to give and more, her body arching to meet my every move. A final frenzy left her trembling against my shoulder, my face buried in her hair.

"It wasn't an accident, was it?" she said, when she could talk.

"What wasn't an accident?"

"Last night."

"I don't understand." I was mystified.

"While you showered, I was wondering if last night was an accident or if it could have been that way all along."

I raised up on one elbow to look at her. Her face was serious, contemplative.

Understanding dawned slowly. No one had ever before made love to her like that. Darrell Watkins had never tapped the wellspring of woman in her—not in eighteen years of marriage. I kissed her tenderly. "That's the way it's supposed to be."

"The bastard!" she said fiercely. "The first-class bastard! I'll take him to the cleaners."

I had unwittingly unleashed Hurricane Ginger into the world. "Maybe he doesn't know any better." I inadvertently defended him, and she gave me a shove that sent me sprawling from the bed onto the floor.

"He's been giving it away to everyone else. By God, it's going to cost him." Angry tears appeared on her cheeks.

The phone rang on the other side of the bed. I scrambled to reach it. "This is the desk. Can I come get that roll-away now? I'm almost ready to leave."

I cleared my throat. "Sure. Anytime. The bed's all ready to go." I spoke casually, all the while motioning frantically to Ginger. She hopped out of bed and made a beeline for the bathroom.

"By the way," I continued, stalling for time, "before you come, would you ask the dining room to have my usual table set for two? We'll be down for breakfast in a few minutes. I don't want to wait in a crush of reporters."

"No problem," Fred replied.

I rushed back into my clothes and made the room as presentable as possible. I went so far as to beat an indentation in the pillow on the roll-away. I also did my best to straighten one side of the king-size bed.

Ginger's transformation was speedy. Dressed, brushed, and wearing a subtle cologne, she emerged from the bathroom well before the clerk arrived. She may have worn some makeup other than a dash of pale lipstick, but I couldn't tell for sure. She looked refreshed and beautiful. Smiling, she surveyed my clumsy efforts to conceal our activities. Walking to the far side of the bed, she expertly straightened the bedding.

"Whose reputation are you trying to protect?" she asked.

"All of the above," I told her.

"I see."

The desk clerk knocked. We managed to fold up the roll-away contraption and move it out of the room.

"Hungry?" I asked after Fred was gone.

"Famished," she replied.

"Let's go do it, then," I told her. We walked through a quiet Rosario morning. The only noise was an occasional squawking gull. No one else from her group seemed to be up, although several of the dining room tables were occupied. The hostess led us directly to my preferred table, one by the window overlooking Rosario Strait.

"Morning, folks," said the same cheery waiter who had served us the night before. "What can I get you?"

"The works," I told him. "Eggs over easy, hash browns, toast, juice, coffee."

He looked questioningly at Ginger. "I'll have the same," she said with a smile.

My water glass had a narrow sliver of lemon in it. I speared the lemon with my fork, then offered it to Ginger across the table. Puzzled, she sat holding it.

"What's this for?" she asked.

"To wipe that silly grin off your face," I replied. "People might get suspicious."

She laughed outright, but soon a cloud passed over her face. "I believe," she said thoughtfully, "I'm beginning to understand what Sig meant."

Outside our window the sky directly overhead was blue. As we watched, a thick bank of fog marched toward us, rolling across the water, obscuring the strait beyond the resort's sheltered bay.

We were well into breakfast when, over Ginger's shoulder, I saw an obese but well-groomed woman pause at the dining room entrance, survey the room, then make her way toward us like a frigate under full sail. She wore a heavy layer of makeup. Her fingers were laden with a full contingent of ornate rings. A thick cloud of perfume preceded her.

"Ginger." Her voice had a sharp, schoolmarmish tone. Ginger started instinctively, then composed herself.

"Good morning, Trixie."

The woman stopped next to our table and appraised me disapprovingly. "I went by your room several times last night and this morning, but you weren't there." She paused as if waiting for Ginger to offer some kind of explanation. None was forthcoming.

"Trixie, I'd like you to meet a friend of mine, J. P. Beaumont. Beau, this is Trixie Bowdeen, chairman of the parole board."

"Glad to meet you," I said.

Trixie ignored me. "Have you gotten word that the meeting's canceled?" she asked coldly.

Ginger countered with some ice of her own. "I think that's only appropriate."

Trixie forged on. "We're all leaving this morning. Do you need a ride back to Seattle?"

"No, thanks. I can manage."

"All right." Trixie turned her ponderous bulk and started away. Then she stopped and returned to our table. "Under the circumstances, it's probably best if you don't go to Sig's funeral."

All color seeped from Ginger's cheeks, but she allowed herself no other visible reaction to Trixie's words. "Why not?" Ginger asked.

Her question seemed to take Trixie aback. "Well, considering . . ." Trixie retreated under Ginger's withering gaze, turned, and in a rustle of skirt and nylons, left the room.

Ginger carefully placed her fork on her plate and pushed it away. "Can we go?"

I took one look at her face and knew I'd better get her out of there fast. Trixie Bowdeen had just layered on the straw that broke the camel's back.

Chapter 9

THE fastest way out of the building was down the back stairs and out past the long, narrow, bowling-alley-shaped indoor pool. By the time we reached the terrace outside, Ginger's sob burst to the surface. She rushed to the guardrail and stood leaning over it, her shoulders heaving, while I stood helplessly to one side with my hands jammed deep in my pockets so I wouldn't reach out to hold her.

I've never seen fog anywhere that quite compares to Orcas Island fog. One moment we stood in the open; the next we were alone in a private world. As the fog swept in, Ginger faded to a shadow. I moved toward her, grasping her hand as the building disappeared behind us. She was still crying, the sound strangely muffled in the uncanny silence.

Pulling her to me, I rocked her against my chest until she quieted. I continued to hold her, but I also glanced over my shoulder to verify we were still invisible to the dining room windows. She drew a ragged breath.

"Are you all right now?"

She nodded. "I am. Really."

"That was an ugly thing for her to do."

"Trixie enjoyed passing along Mona's message." There was a shift in Ginger's voice, a strengthening of resolve. "I've got to resign. Without Sig, I can't stand up to those people. They're all cut from the same cloth."

Ginger broke away from me and moved along the terrace, running her hand disconsolately along the guardrail. I trailed behind her, at a loss for words, wondering what made her think Trixie had served as Mona's emissary.

"The fog feels like velvet," Ginger commented. "I wish I could hide in it forever and never come out."

"That's not the answer."

"Isn't it? When you're drunk you don't feel the hurt."

"What are you going to do?" Her remark had sounded like a threat to start drinking. If she was truly a recovering alcoholic, a drink was the last thing she needed.

"It's okay. Don't worry. I'll go to a meeting. There's one in Eastsound tonight."

"What meeting?"

"An A.A. meeting. Whenever Sig and I were on the road, we went to meetings together. We planned to go to this one tonight. I don't remember where it is."

"Can I come?"

Ginger stopped and faced me, looking deep into my eyes before she shook her head. "It's a closed meeting, Beau, not an open one where everyone is welcome. I'll go by myself. If I'm not going to Sig's funeral, it'll be my private remembrance for him."

She made the statement with absolute conviction. I couldn't help but respect her desire to have a private farewell for the man who had pulled her from the mire. We didn't discuss it again. The subject was closed.

The fog lifted as quickly as it had come. I moved discreetly away from her. "You're one hell of a woman, Ginger Watkins, I'll say that for you." She gave me a halfhearted smile and started toward the building.

"Are you sure you want to go in there? There's probably a

whole armload of reporters having breakfast by now. The murder
of a public official is big news.''

She stopped, considering my words. ''Reporters? In there?''
She nodded toward the dining room overhead.

''The desk clerk told me last night that some of them stayed
over. I know for a fact Maxwell Cole did.''

''He was that funny-looking fat man you were talking to in the
lobby when I came back from being fingerprinted? The one who
was supposed to meet Don Wilson?''

''One and the same.''

''Who does he work for?''

''The *P.I.* He writes a crime column.''

She paused thoughtfully. ''Is that all he's interested in?
Crime?''

I couldn't see where the discussion was going. ''Why are you
asking?''

She grinned impishly. ''I told you I'd get Darrell, starting
now. I'll file on Monday, but it'll hit the papers Sunday morning.
The only reason they want me to reconsider is to keep it quiet
until after election day. Believe me, Darrell doesn't want me
back. Now, where do I find what's-his-name?''

''Max? Probably under a rock somewhere.''

''I mean it, Beau. I want to talk to him.''

Hell hath no fury, and all that jazz. I figured Darrell Watkins
deserved just about anything Ginger could dish out. ''Go on into
the Moran Room and wait by the fireplace. I'll see if I can find
him and send him there. I'm also going to have your things moved
to another room for tonight, if you're going to stay over.''

''Why? Can't I stay with you?''

I shook my head. ''Discretion is the better part of valor, my
dear. You can sleep wherever you damn well please, but you'd
better have a separate room with your clothes in it or you'll get
us both in a hell of a lot of trouble.''

''Oh,'' she said. ''I guess I should've thought of that.''

Maxwell Cole was eating breakfast. Talking to him was tough
because all I could see was the blob of egg yolk that dangled
from one curl of his handlebar mustache. ''Ginger Watkins wants
to talk to you,'' I said.

His eyes bulged. ''No shit? Where is she?''

''In the Moran Room, just off the lobby, waiting.''

Cole lurched to his feet, signaling for the waiter to bring his check. "Hey thanks, J. P. I can't thank you enough."

Max persists in calling me by my initials. My real name is Jonas Piedmont Beaumont. Mother named me after her father and grandfather as a conciliatory gesture after my father died in a motorcycle crash before he and Mother had a chance to tie the knot. It didn't work. Her family never lifted a finger to help us. She raised me totally on her own. They never forgave her, and I've never forgiven them. It's a two-way street.

I shortened my name to initials in high school. In college people started calling me Beau. Except for Max. He picked my initials off a registration form, and he's used them ever since, mostly because he knows it bugs me.

"How about if you drop the 'J. P.' crap, Maxey? That would be one way of thanking me."

With a hangdog expression on his face, Max followed me out of the dining room to the crackling fireplace in the Moran Room. Afterwards I stopped at the desk to reserve a new room for Ginger. Just as I finished, someone walked up behind me and clapped me on the shoulder. It was Peters.

I shook his hand. "Huggins got ahold of you, then?"

"No. I came because a little bird told me." Peters grinned. Then in a lower voice, "What the hell are you doing packing hardware? You're supposed to be on vacation."

"It's a long story," I said.

"I'm sure it is. The ferry was crawling with deputies. They're handing out copies of Wilson's picture to everyone who gets on or off the boat. What's up?"

Peeking around the corner, I could see Ginger and Max in deep conversation. I had noticed a small, glass-walled conference room just off the dining room. I asked to use it. Once inside, with the doors safely closed against unwanted listeners, I told Peters all I knew. Maybe not quite all. I left out a few details. He didn't have any business messing around in my personal life.

Peters shook his head when I finished. "I wouldn't be in Huggins' shoes for all the tea in China. If this thing gets blown out of proportion, lots of political heads could roll. Homer Watkins isn't a lightweight."

"How come you know so much about him?"

"There's enough in the papers that you can piece it together.

Your problem is, you only read the crossword puzzles. Crosswords do not informed citizens make."

"Leave me alone. They're nothing but propaganda."

"Let's don't go into that, Beau. I like current events. You like history. I like sprout sandwiches. You like hamburgers. Neither of us is going to change."

I reached for the file folder Peters held in his hand. "Wait a minute. I'm supposed to give this to a Detective Huggins. You're not the investigating officer."

"For God's sake, Peters," I protested. "Don't be an ass. I'm the one who called and asked for it, remember?"

"Captain Powell gave me specific orders that the report goes to Huggins. You're on vacation. Powell doesn't want you screwing around in somebody else's case."

"I'll be a sonofabitch," I said.

Peters ignored my outburst. He had joined forces with the captain and the chaplain to corner me into a "vacation." He, more than the rest, understood my loss. "How're you doing, Beau?" he asked solicitously, changing topics. "You're looking better, like you're getting some rest."

I smiled to myself, considering my total sleep from the night before. I decided against depriving Peters of his illusions. "Sleeping like a baby," I said, grinning.

Huggins showed up about then. He saw us through the plate-glass windows and knocked to be let in. I introduced him to Peters. Within minutes the table was strewn with the grisly contents of the envelope. Maybe Peters couldn't give them to me, but nobody told Huggins not to.

The pictures were there—the senseless slaughter, the bloodied house. Denise Wilson had fought Lathrop. She hadn't died easily. She had battled him through every room before it was over. The pictures sickened me, as did Lathrop's smirking mug shot. There was no picture of Donald Wilson in the file. Without Maxwell Cole's contribution, we would have been up a creek.

"We're screening all the people on the ferries. We'll be talking to employees and guests here today," Huggins told us. "Someone will have seen him. You don't just appear and disappear like that unless you're a goddamned Houdini."

"He's not at his house?" I asked. Huggins shook his head. "Is there any other way to get here besides a ferry?" I continued. "There are float planes and charter boats. We're checking all of them, but it doesn't look to me as though he has that kind of money. He came over on the ferries, I'm sure of it, and we've got those babies covered.''

Peters smiled. ''You've heard that old joke going around Seattle, haven't you?''

''What's that?''

''What does a San Juan County police officer use for a squad car? A Washington State Ferry with blinking blue lights.''

Huggins glared at him. ''Very funny,'' he said, ''but we do a hell of a good job around here.''

Every once in a while Peters pulls a stunt that convinces me he's not nearly so old as his years. Then there are times when he's as wise as the old man of the sea.

This wasn't one of those times.

Chapter 10

I CALLED Ralph Ames, my attorney in Phoenix. Along with the car, I inherited Ames from Anne Corley. In six months' time, he had become an invaluable friend over and above being my attorney. I called him at home.

''What're you doing?'' I asked.

''Cleaning the pool,'' he replied.

I have little patience with people who own pools or boats. They're both holes you pour money into. Not only that, it's a point of honor to do all the work yourself, from swabbing decks to cleaning filters.

''Did you ever consider hiring someone to do it?''

''No, Beau. I don't jog. Cleaning the pool makes me feel self-righteous.''

''To each his own. What are you doing tomorrow?''

''Flying to Portland. Didn't Peters tell you?''

''Tell me what?''

''We have a custody hearing in The Dalles on Tuesday. Keep your fingers crossed.''

Peters was at war with his ex-wife. She got religion in a big way and went to live with a cult in Broken Springs, Oregon, taking their two little girls with her. Peters wanted them back. Ames took the case, joining the fray at my request and on my nickel. What's the point in having money if you can't squander it?

"That closemouthed asshole. That's good news."

"So what do you want, Beau? This is my day off. It is Saturday, you know."

"How about flying into Sea-Tac today instead of Portland tomorrow? I'm up on Orcas Island. There's someone here I'd like you to meet. I told her you'd take a look at her situation."

"Which is?"

"Divorce. Messy. With political ramifications. Looks like collusion between her husband and her father-in-law to toss her out without a pot to piss in."

"Are you giving my services away again, Beau?"

"I care enough to send the very best."

He laughed. "All right. I'll see what I can do. Let me call you back."

I gave him the number. As I hung up, Ginger appeared at my elbow. "Who was that?"

"Ames, my attorney from Phoenix, remember? I told you about him. I asked him to come talk to you."

"Here? On Orcas?"

"Sure."

"But you said he was in Phoenix."

"He is. He was coming up tomorrow, anyway. He's trying to get a reservation for this afternoon."

"From Phoenix?"

"If you're going to file on Monday, you need to talk to him tonight or tomorrow."

"How much is it going to cost?"

"Nothing. He'll put it on my bill."

I correctly read the consternation on Ginger's face. "How do you rate?" she asked. "I thought you were just a plain old, ordinary homicide detective. How come you have a high-powered attorney at your beck and call?"

"It's a long story," I said. "I came into a little money."

"A little?" she echoed.

"Some," I conceded.

"I see," Ginger said.

"You done with Cole?" I asked, changing the subject.

"He's one happy reporter." She grinned. "That story will make Darrell's socks roll up and down. It should hit the paper tomorrow."

"What did you say?"

"Enough. I named names. At least a few of them. A private detective had already checked those out. Darrell will come across as an active philanderer. Hot stuff."

We left the lobby and walked toward the new room where housekeepers had moved Ginger's things. "What do you think Darrell will do?" I asked.

She gave a mirthless laugh. "He'll huddle with Homer and the PR man. The three of them will decide how to play it. Name familiarity is name familiarity. They may get more press if they do an active denial. They'll take a poll and decide."

"That's pretty cold-blooded."

"Um-hum."

"But how are you going to feel with your personal life splashed all over the front page?"

We reached the building where her new room was. Ginger stepped to one side, waiting for me to open the door. The eyes she turned on me were luminously green and deep.

"I just found out about personal," she said softly. "None of that is going in the paper."

There was a tightening in my chest and a catch in my throat. Mr. Macho handles the compliment. I tripped over my own feet and stumbled into the hallway. I found her room, unlocked the door, and handed her the key.

"Are you coming in?"

The invitation was there, written on her face, but I shook my head. "Ames is supposed to call my room. I'd better not."

"Does that mean I can't see you? Have I been a bad girl and you're sending me to my room?" she teased.

"No. Let me see what's happening as far as Ames and Peters are concerned. Maybe you and I can go on a picnic."

"Terrific. I'll change into jeans."

"Wait a minute. I said maybe."

She looked both ways, up and down the hall, then gave me a quick kiss on the cheek. "Please."

"Well, all right, now that you put it that way."

Smiling, she disappeared into her room. I returned to mine. I had gotten a second key for Peters, and he was there waiting when I arrived. "Who's your roommate?" he asked casually as I flopped onto the bed. "Her makeup case is still in the bathroom."

I wasn't any better at sneaking around than Ginger was. I made a stab at semi-full disclosure. "Ginger Watkins stayed here last night. Didn't I tell you?"

Peters' eyes narrowed. "I don't think so."

"There weren't any more rooms, and she couldn't go back to hers. Whoever got in had a key."

"Right." Peters nodded complacently, humoring me.

"We got a roll-away. She's married, for chrissake!"

"Okay, okay," he said. "Have it your way. What's the program?"

"You didn't tell me Ames has a court date in The Dalles."

"Small oversight." Peters grinned. "So we're even. What's going on?"

"I asked Ames to come up here tonight. I'm hoping he can help Ginger with her divorce."

"And you still expect me to fall for that crap about a roll-away bed?" He laughed.

As I threw a pillow at him, the phone rang. It was Ames. "I get into Sea-Tac at five-fifty. Can someone meet me?"

"We'll flip a coin," I told him. "One of us will be there. What airline?"

"United."

"Okay. I'll book rooms here."

"Rooms?"

I glared at Peters. "Peters snores," I growled into the phone. "I sure as hell don't want him in my room, and you won't want him in yours, either. Besides, they've just had a bunch of cancellations. I know rooms are available."

"Rooms," Ames agreed.

Peters and I flipped a coin. He called heads, and it was tails. I figured it was my lucky day. Considering the ferry schedule, he didn't have much time to hang around. I called the desk and reserved two more rooms. Up at the far end of the complex. By the tennis courts. Adjoining.

I was still on the phone when someone knocked. Peters went to the door.

"My name is Ginger Watkins. Is Beau here?"

Peters stepped to one side and rolled his eyes at me once he was behind her. She wore a full-sleeved apricot blouse and a pair of tight-fitting Levi's that did justice to her figure. With a jacket slung nonchalantly over one shoulder, Ginger was a class act all the way.

"This is Detective Ron Peters," I said, "my partner on the force in Seattle."

"I'm pleased to meet you." Her smile of genuine goodwill had its desired effect.

Peters' appraising glance was filled with admiration. "Pleasure's all mine," he murmured.

Ginger turned to me. "Did I leave my calendar here?" she asked. "It isn't in the room, and I checked with the maids. They said they moved everything."

"I haven't seen it. When did you have it last?"

"I don't remember. I may have taken it with me when I went to meet Sig. It's got the address for the meeting tonight. I'm sure someone else can tell me where the meeting is, but I keep all kinds of phone numbers in the calendar. It would be hard to replace."

"Could you have left it in the car in Anacortes?"

She considered that possibility. "No," she said. "I don't think so."

I picked up the phone and called the desk to ask if anyone had turned in the missing calendar. No one had.

"Come on," I said when I got off the phone. "We'll walk Peters to his car. He's just leaving for the airport."

"You are?" she asked. "You barely got here."

"I did," Peters agreed sullenly, "but shore leave just got canceled."

Peters took off in his beat-up blue Datsun. Ginger and I diligently searched the meeting rooms, the dining room, the bar, and the lobby to no avail. The calendar wasn't there.

Rosario is nothing if not a full-service resort. While we were busy, the kitchen packed us a picnic lunch, complete with basket and tablecloth. Ginger's enthusiasm was unrestrained. She practically skipped on her way to the parking lot. A genuine Ford Pinto, white with splotches of rust, was parked next to my bright red Porsche 928. As I went to unlock the rider's side, Ginger assumed I was going to the junker. She started for the rider's side of that one, stopping in dismay when I opened the Porsche.

She came around the Pinto grinning sheepishly. "Isn't this a little high-toned for a homicide cop?"

I placed the picnic basket in the back and helped her inside. "Conspicuous consumption never hurt anybody," I said.

With a switch of the key, the powerful engine turned over. When she was alive, Anne Corley drove the car with casual assurance. I always feel just a little out of my league, as though the car is driving me.

"Have you seen Moran State Park?" I asked. Ginger shook her head. "Why don't we try that? This late in October it isn't crowded."

"You're changing the subject, Beau," she accused.

I feigned innocence. "What do you mean?"

"Tell me about the car," she insisted.

And so I told her about the car. About finding Anne Corley and losing Anne Corley. One by one I pulled the memories out and held them up in the diffused autumn light so Ginger and I could look at them together. We drove and walked and talked. We climbed the stairs in the musty obelisk without really noticing our surroundings. It was my turn to talk and Ginger's to listen.

By the time I finished, we were seated at a picnic table in a patch of dappled sunlight with the food laid out before us. There was a long pause. "You loved her very much, didn't you?" Ginger said at last.

"I didn't think I'd ever get over her."

"But you have?"

"I'm starting to, a little."

"Meaning me?" From someone else, that question might have sounded cynical, but not from Ginger.

I nodded. "Today is the first I've felt like my old self. Peters attributed it to my getting enough sleep."

"That shows how much he knows."

"He's young. What can I tell you?"

"And I'm the first, since Anne Corley?"

"Yes."

"And I was good?" It was a pathetic question. She was looking for the kind of reassurance most women don't need after age eighteen or so.

We were alone in the park. I came around the table and sat

behind her, my hands massaging her tight shoulders, rubbing the rigid muscles of her neck. Her body moved under the pressure of my kneading fingers, relaxing as stiffness succumbed to the balm of human touch.

"You were terrific," I whispered in her ear.

She turned to me, two huge teardrops welling in her eyes. "That was stupid. I shouldn't have asked."

She leaned against me, and I continued to rub her neck, feeling her tension soften and disappear.

"No one's ever done that to me before," she said.

"Done what?"

"Rubbed my neck like that."

I kissed her forehead. "All I can say, sweetheart, is you've been married to a first-class bastard."

Unexpectedly, she burst out laughing. I don't think anyone had ever referred to Darrell Watkins in quite those terms in her presence. She turned her neck languidly from side to side like a cat stretching in the sun. "That felt good," she murmured.

We repacked the picnic basket. "Could I stop by your room for a little while before I go? The meeting doesn't start until eight."

"Sure," I said. "By the way, how do you plan to get to that meeting?"

She clapped her hand over her mouth. "I forgot. I don't have my car. I can probably catch a ride with the van that goes to the ferry."

"Don't be silly. Take the Porsche," I said.

"I couldn't do that."

"Oh yes you can."

It was almost our first quarrel, but finally she knuckled under to my superior intellect and judgment. Besides, I had the clinching argument: by taking my car, she wouldn't have to leave nearly so early. She capitulated. Who says women can't be swayed by logic?

And hormones. And expensive toys.

Chapter 11

WE took a meandering route back to Rosario. At one point we paused, laughing, at a large hand-painted sign on a ninety-degree curve that said, "Slow Duck Crossing."

"Does that mean the ducks are dumb, or are you supposed to slow down?" Ginger asked.

"Possibly a little of both," I observed, braking to negotiate the narrow corner.

A flurry of yellow slips of paper awaited us at the desk. The first, a message from Huggins, was jubilant. A ticket-seller at the Anacortes ferry terminal remembered Don Wilson as a mid-afternoon walk-on passenger. The evidence was speculative and purely circumstantial, but that gave Wilson opportunity. He already had motive.

Huggins' second note was more ominous. Results of the autopsy were in. Larson's cause of death was a blow to the base of the skull with a blunt object. He was dead before he hit the water. The cut on his forehead had occurred after he was dead. The news hit Ginger pretty hard. In addition, her room key had not been found among Sig Larson's personal effects.

A message from Peters said he and Ames were skipping dinner in order to make it back to Orcas. Since the food on the ferries wasn't fit to eat, he advised me to make dinner reservations for after their arrival.

Ginger passed me her own fan-fold of messages, enough to form a formidable canasta hand. Darrell Watkins had called every half-hour. Homer Watkins had called several times. All of the messages, with increasing urgency, said for Ginger to call back.

She returned the calls from my room. I think she wanted the moral support of my presence. She spoke with Darrell first. He had learned of the impending column in the *P.I.* and wanted her to retract it. She was adamant. She would stand by every word of the story as written. He threatened to come up. She told him not to bother, that nothing he could say would make her change her mind.

The call to Homer was much the same. His attempts at browbeating also came to nothing. I wondered if either of them recognized a subtle shift in her from the day before, an undercurrent of gritty determination. J. P. Beaumont, posing as Professor Henry Higgins, heard the difference and gave himself a little credit.

Nonetheless, the phone calls had a subduing effect on our high spirits. I think we had intended to take advantage of each other's bodies before Ginger left, to recapture the magic of commingled enjoyment to last us until she returned from her meeting. Instead, we sat in my room without even holding hands, talking quietly as the sun went down.

I can't remember now what we talked about. We ranged over a wide variety of topics, finding surprising areas of common interest and knowledge. For someone with little formal education, Ginger was a widely read, challenging conversationalist.

I invited her to join Peters, Ames, and me for dinner after the meeting. She waited until the very last minute to leave for Eastsound, delaying her departure so long that she finally decided to change clothes after the meeting. She was clearly torn between wanting to go to the meeting and wanting to stay with me. I could probably have talked her out of going had I half tried. Out of respect to Sig Larson, I didn't make the attempt.

I walked her to my car. "Be careful," I said. "That's a hot little number."

She smiled. "I've driven one before."

"What time will you be back?"

"Ten. At the latest."

"I'll make reservations for then," I told her.

"Kiss me good-bye?" she asked.

I looked around. The parking lot was deserted. As near as I could tell, all the media types, including Maxwell Cole, had abandoned Rosario on the heels of the rest of the parole board, but years of being a cop have made me paranoid about reporters. I gave her a quick, surreptitious kiss. "Give old Sig a hail and farewell for me too," I said huskily. I had a lot to thank him for.

"I will," she whispered and was gone.

I went into the bar. Barney smiled when he saw me. "Find that calendar yet?" he asked, bringing me a McNaughton's and water.

"Not yet."

"You get what you needed from that fat slob last night?"

"Yeah," I answered. "Thanks."

"All those yahoos went home this morning," he continued. "They were a bunch of animals, especially that creep, what's-his-name . . . Dole?"

"Cole," I corrected. "And yes, he is a creep."

I drank my drink, aware of how much better I felt. Unburdening myself to Ginger had somehow lifted the pall that had paralyzed me since Anne Corley's death. I set down my empty glass and pushed back the stool.

"Only one?" Barney asked, surprised.

"Later," I told him. "I've got places to go, people to meet."

In actual fact, I went back to my room for the second shower and shave of the day. I dressed carefully. I wanted Ginger to see me at my best, wearing one of the hand-tailored suits Ames had insisted I purchase.

At nine forty-five I went back to the lobby. "Oh there you are," the desk clerk said. "I just this minute had a call for you." He handed me a slip of paper with Homer Watkins' name and number on it.

"He called for me, not Mrs. Watkins?" I asked.

"He was very specific," the clerk assured me. I walked to the pay phone and dialed the number. He answered on the second ring.

"This is Detective Beaumont," I said curtly into the phone.

"It's good of you to call," he said. His voice was smooth as glass, with the resonance of an old-fashioned radio announcer. It was a long way from our first telephone conversation. "I talked to a friend of yours today, a Maxwell Cole. He's under the impression that you have some influence with my daughter-in-law."

"That's correct," I replied. It was also something of an understatement.

"I thought you should be advised that Ginger has been somewhat unstable of late."

"Ginger Watkins' mental health is none of my business," I said.

"I couldn't be happier to hear you say that. She's been under a great deal of stress and can't be held responsible for her actions."

"What are you driving at?" I demanded.

"That's all I wanted to discuss," he said. "I have another call." Having another call on a second or third line constitutes a high-tech version of the brush-off. I put down the phone.

I went into the Moran Room to wait for Ames and Peters. The ferry was due in at nine-thirty, so I expected them at Rosario right around ten. I waited in front of the massive marble fireplace with its cheerful fire.

Ralph Ames was laughing as he came into the lobby. He and Peters were having a good time. I met them at the door. We left word for Ginger, and the three of us went on into the dining room. It was late, and the room was almost empty. We sat at a candlelit table and had a drink.

"You breaking training?" I asked as the waiter handed Peters a gin and tonic.

He raised his glass. "Just this once." He grinned.

We were so busy talking and catching up that I didn't notice the time. At ten-thirty the waiter suggested that if we wanted to eat before the kitchen closed, we'd better place our order. Suddenly I wasn't hungry. I told Peters and Ames to go ahead and order, that I'd wait for Ginger. I excused myself and went to the lobby, where I had the desk clerk call Ginger's room. No answer.

When Fred shook his head, I felt a sickening crunch in my stomach. "Something may have happened to her," I said. "Would you let me check her room?"

After the roll-away bed escapade, he could hardly say I had no business doing so. He put a Back in a Minute sign on the desk, and we hurried to Ginger's room. It was empty, undisturbed.

Back in the Mansion, I checked the dining room. Ames and Peters were happily working their way through salads, but Ginger was nowhere in sight. I went to the pay phone and dialed the sheriff's substation at Eastsound.

The dispatcher answered eventually, her response to my question short and to the point. There had been no reports of any traffic accidents. I tried to fend off rising panic. "Do you know any of the people who go to the Saturday-night A.A. meeting in Eastsound?" I asked.

"Yes, but I can't give out those names. It's confidential."

"Get one of them to call me back, then. It's urgent."

"I'll see what I can do."

I paced the floor in tight circles, trying to hold panic in check. When the phone rang, I pounced on it like a cat attacking a paralyzed mouse.

"My name is James," the voice on the phone drawled. "You wanted to talk to someone from A.A.?"

"Yes, I did. Did you go the meeting tonight?"

" 'Course I did. I was one of the speakers."

"Was there a woman there, a woman in a pale orange blouse and Levi's?"

"Sorry, mister, I can't give out that information. Whoever joins our fellowship is strictly confidential. That's why people feel safe in coming."

"You don't understand," I said desperately. "She left here at twenty to eight, going to the meeting. She hasn't come back. All I want to know is whether she made it that far."

There was a long pause. "No," he said.

"No *what*? No, you won't tell me?" I wanted to reach through the phone line and throttle him.

"No, she wasn't there. I woulda remembered someone like that. It was only locals tonight. No visitors."

Cold fear rose in my stomach, my throat. "Thank you," I managed, depressing the switch on the phone. I released it and redialed the substation. The dispatcher was annoyed.

"You'd better get ahold of Huggins over in Friday Harbor. Tell him to call Detective Beaumont. We've got trouble."

Hal called me back within minutes. "What's up?"

"It's Ginger. She's disappeared. She went to a meeting tonight and never got there. I've checked. The meeting was over at nine. She's still not back."

"It's almost eleven!"

"I know," I responded bleakly.

"What kind of car?" he asked.

"A Porsche 928. Red."

He whistled. "No shit? A Porsche? What's the license number?'' I gave it to him. ''Okay,'' he added, ''I'll be there in half an hour,'' he said. ''Where are you—Rosario?''

''Yes.''

''I'll come straight to the docks. I'll call the dispatcher and have her send Pomeroy. I think he's on duty tonight.'' He paused. ''Why'd you let her go by herself, Beau?''

I winced at his implied accusation. I had already asked myself the same question. ''She wanted to.''

''Oh,'' he said.

It wasn't a very convincing reason, not then, not now.

With leaden steps I walked back to the dining room to let Ames and Peters know that Ginger Watkins wouldn't be joining us for dinner. Not then. Not ever.

Chapter 12

THEY found the Porsche at seven Sunday morning in the pond by the Slow Duck Crossing sign. I stood to one side, watching the tow truck drag my 928 from the muck. Ginger, still wearing her apricot blouse, lay dead inside.

Huggins opened the door, and water cascaded out, leaving her body slumped over the steering wheel. Pomeroy gave me a half-smirk as I walked over to look inside and make positive identification. I nodded to Hal and walked away as the lab crew surrounded the car.

Peters was down the road, pacing the blacktop. ''From the looks of it, she ploughed into the water full throttle and never tried to stop.''

He was voicing my own thoughts. I said nothing.

''Is there a chance she passed out?''

''No,'' I said quickly. ''Absolutely not.''

Peters eyed me questioningly. ''Why not?''

''She didn't drink.''

Huggins left the car and came over to where we were standing.

"Watkins is on his way," he said. "It'll be a madhouse when he gets here. I understand he's got a whole press entourage."

"Great," I muttered.

"Did you see anything along the road?" Huggins' question was addressed to both Peters and me. Peters pointed. "There's a place back there where she laid down a layer of rubber. Looks like she floorboarded it from a dead stop." The three of us walked back to the place Peters had indicated. Huggins examined the mark, then nodded in agreement. He looked at me.

"Suicide, you think?"

"No way!" I declared vehemently. Huggins and Peters exchanged glances.

"We were going to have dinner," I continued. "She was looking forward to it." My rationale landed with a resounding thud, convincing no one, not even me.

As soon as I saw Darrell Watkins, I recognized him. I had indeed seen pictures of him. Politicians are never as tall or as good-looking as their publicity shots make them seem. Darrell Watkins was no exception. He was three or four inches shorter than I am, maybe five-ten or so. His face boasted classically handsome features topped by dark brown wavy hair, but a hint of potbelly protruded over his belt. A little too much of the good life showed around the edges.

Beside Darrell walked a taller, distinguished-looking man with a shock of white hair. There was a definite family resemblance. Homer Watkins, although pushing seventy, carried himself with the easy grace of an aging athlete. His son might have gone to seed, but not Homer. I looked at them with the kind of curiosity one reserves for snakes in a zoo. They didn't look like evil incarnate, but they had made Ginger Watkins' life hell on earth.

Huggins walked forward to greet them, waving back the crush of newsmen, photographers, and cameras that swirled around them. Ginger would have been offended that the aftermath of her death created a media event that would give her candidate/widower hours of free broadcasting coverage and hundreds of newspaper column-inches all over the state. I thought I was going to be sick.

"Hey, Beau, are you all right?" I had turned my back on the mêlée and was walking away. Peters followed.

"I've got to get out of here," I groaned. "I can't stand this bullshit."

I continued walking. Peters worked his way back through the crowd to redeem his car. I was several hundred yards down the road by the time he caught up with me. He pulled alongside. "Get in, Beau. Don't be a hard-ass." I was too sick at heart to argue.

"The press was handling Watkins with kid gloves," Peters said apropos of nothing.

I glowered at him. "What did you expect?"

Peters shrugged and broke off any further attempt at conversation. In the silence that followed, I tried to come to terms with what had happened. How could Ginger Watkins be the lifeless form slouched in my car? And what could I have done to prevent it? And where the hell was Don Wilson?

Ralph Ames waited for us in the driveway outside the Mansion. "I heard," he said as I dragged myself out of the car. "Is there anything I can do?"

"Not unless you can figure out a way to bring her back." I choked out the words and beat it for my cabin, leaving Peters and Ames standing there together. I didn't want to talk to anybody or hear any mumbled words of sympathy. I didn't have any right to sympathy. That was Darrell Watkins' exclusive territory.

I threw myself across the bed, aware of a faint trace of Ginger Watkins lingering in the bedclothes. I wanted to lock it out of my consciousness, but at the same time I wanted to hold onto it.

There was a gentle tap on the door. Ames came into the room, alone. He sat down on one of the chairs beside the table. For a long time he sat there without speaking. "You can't blame yourself," he said at last.

"Why not? I never should have let her go alone."

"It's not your fault."

I wanted to bellow at him, to rant and rave and vent my anger and frustration. "It is! Don't you see that it is?"

Ames remained unperturbed. "It was an A.A. meeting, is that right?"

"Yes," I said wearily.

"How long had it been since she quit drinking?"

My anger boiled back to the surface. "She wasn't drunk, and she didn't commit suicide. Doesn't anybody understand that, for God's sake?"

He ignored me. "It's possible, Beau. She had lost a good friend the day before—"

"Goddammit, Ames, I'm trying to tell you. Something happened between us. She didn't want to die."

Ames studied me carefully. "I see," he said slowly. He rose to his feet. "I'm sorry, Beau. I didn't know." His quiet understanding rocked me. Hot tears rose in my eyes. I didn't bother to brush them away. Ames paused in the doorway. "It's still not your fault," he added.

The hell it's not, I thought savagely as the door closed behind him. Wilson was here all the time, and I let her walk right into his trap.

I don't know how long I lay on the bed. Long enough to get a grip on myself. Long enough to know that if I walked outside I wouldn't embarrass myself and everyone around me.

I had been awake all night. Exhaustion claimed me, and I slept. In a dream Don Wilson and Philip Lathrop were together, both locked in the same cell. Armed with a gun, I tried to shoot them through iron bars. Each time I pulled the trigger, nothing happened. They laughed and pointed, both of them, together.

I woke in a sweat. Peters was sitting in the chair by the window. Ginger's chair.

"Bad dream?" he asked.

Not answering, I heaved my feet over the edge of the bed and sat there with my face buried in my hands, hoping the whole thing was a nightmare. It wasn't. Ginger Watkins was dead.

"They've released your car," Peters said.

I felt as if I'd been shot. "They've what?"

"Released the Porsche," Peters repeated. "Had it towed into Ernie's Garage in Eastsound."

"That's impossible! Murder was committed in that car. No one should go near it until the crime lab has gone over it with a fine-toothed comb."

"They've gone over it, all right. Not with a fine-toothed comb. The consensus is that she went drinking instead of to her meeting. They're treating it as a DWI, calling it an accident, pending the outcome of the autopsy. They found an empty vodka bottle in the car. The San Juan County Sheriff's Department says it can't afford to be responsible for a car like that. Too valuable."

I got up and went into the bathroom, where I splashed my face with cold water. My square-jawed reflection in the mirror was haggard, drained. When I came out of the bathroom, Peters hadn't moved.

"It wasn't an accident," I said.

"How are we going to prove it?"

It took a few seconds for the meaning of his words to sink in, to understand that I wasn't in it alone, that Peters would help—and so would Ames, for that matter. But even though his "we" eased my burden, the question remained: How would we prove it?

"Drive me to Eastsound," I said. "I want to talk to the mechanic."

"Huggins says he's tops."

"Sure he is. In a backwater like this, you can just bet they've got a top-drawer mechanic. He's probably one step under highway robbery."

We got into Peters' Datsun. He managed to drive us to Eastsound without having to pass the duck pond. "Are you going to tell me what happened?" Peters asked.

"No." My answer was abrupt. "Not now."

Peters deserved better than that. We had been partners for almost a year. He, more than anyone, had seen me through the Anne Corley crisis. I had learned to respect his quiet reserve and to tolerate his health fetishes. In the world of partners, alfalfa sprouts are a small price to pay for someone you can count on.

He didn't take offense. He brought our discussion back to the Porsche. "Huggins says Ernie can dry it out. If he gets to work on it fast enough, he might be able to prevent it from mildewing."

"So by releasing the car, Hal thinks he's doing me a favor?" Peters nodded. "God damn him," I said.

Ernie's Garage wasn't tough to find. It's the only one in town. I walked into the clapboard building, wondering for a moment if anyone was there. "Just a sec," an invisible voice called.

A mechanic's dolly wheeled out from under an upraised pickup. On it sat a man with his left leg missing below the knee and his left arm missing below the elbow. Where his hand should have been, a complicated metal gripper was strapped to his arm with a leather gauntlet. The gripper held a small wrench. Ernie Rogers had bright blue eyes, a curly red mustache, and a shiny bald spot on the back of his head. "How'do, mister," he drawled. "What can I do for you?"

"That's my car over there," I said, pointing. The Porsche huddled in a darkened corner of the garage.

"She's a pretty little thing." He clucked sympathetically. "Too bad about what happened."

"Huggins says you can dry it out and get it working. That true?"

He nodded, removing the wrench from its gripper and wiping his metal hand on greasy pants in the typical mechanic's gesture. "It'll cost you," he said. "How long you had 'er?"

"About six months."

"Ever done any major repairs on a Porsche?" Ernie asked. He was still sitting on the dolly, squinting up at me.

"No," I said. "Never have."

"I gotta take the whole damn thing apart, clean it with solvent, dry it, and put it back together."

"How much?"

"Six or seven grand."

In the old days, that's how much I would have spent on a brand-new car. Luckily, these weren't the old days. "How long will it take?"

"Depends on how soon you want me to start. Should do it as soon as possible if you want to save the interior. It'll take time— a couple weeks, maybe. I gotta get the money up front, though. Know what I mean?"

In the old days I never would have had a checking account with ten thousand dollars in it, but Ames had made me open a market-rate account. I pulled the checkbook out of my jacket pocket and wrote out a check for seven thousand dollars, payable to Ernie's Garage. I handed it to him. He looked at it, folded it deftly with one hand, and stuck it in his overall pocket.

"Thanks, Mr. Beaumont. That your phone number on the check in case I need to get ahold of you?"

"Yes. Keep track of your expenses. The insurance company will reimburse me."

Peters and I started toward the door. "I'm sorry about the lady in the car," Ernie said. "She wasn't your wife or anything, was she?"

"No," I said. "We were just friends."

The lie came easily. Ginger had said the same thing about Sig Larson. I wondered if she had told the truth.

Chapter 13

PETERS stopped at the front desk and bought a paper. He showed me Sig Larson's picture on the front page. "Max's interview with Ginger should be there," I told him.

He flipped through the pages and double-checked the index in the bottom corner of the front page, looking for Cole's City Beat column. "It's not here, Beau," he said. "I looked."

"But he said it would be in today's paper."

"So he lied," Peters said. "What else is new?" Peters sorted through the paper and removed the crossword puzzles, setting them aside for me to work later. "I'm going up to my room to get some rest," he said. "Ames wants to go back to Seattle on the seven-forty ferry tonight. You're welcome to ride along."

"Let me think it over, Peters. I can't quite see the three of us crammed in that Datsun, but—"

"Don't look a gift horse in the mouth," he told me. "It's a hell of a long walk from Anacortes to Seattle."

I accompanied Peters as far as his room. When he went inside, I knocked on Ames' door. Ralph was sprawled on his bed with the contents of a briefcase strewn around him. "Working on Peters' case?" I asked. He nodded. "Are we going to win?"

He looked at me squarely. "Maybe. Maybe not. Our best bet is to work out a negotiated settlement instead of going to court."

"Will they settle?"

He shrugged. "Justice is blind. Money talks. They'll settle if the price is right."

"It pisses me off to think of donating money to that ranting, chanting asshole." It was my money. Although I was willing to do whatever was necessary to buy Peters' kids a chance at a normal childhood, it still made me mad.

Ames regarded me mildly. "You want to bail out?"

"Hell, no. I just don't like that guru making money hand over fist."

Shaking his head, Ames gathered up his papers and shuffled them into a neat stack. "What do you want, Beau?"

I eased myself into the chair by his window, aware that my back hurt. Despite the nap, fatigue railed at me from every muscle in my body. "I want to offer a reward."

"For what?"

"For information leading to the arrest and conviction of the person or persons who murdered Sig Larson."

He picked up a yellow pad and a pen and made several notes in his small, cramped handwriting. "I can do that," he said. "From an anonymous donor, I presume?"

I nodded.

"How much?"

"Five."

"Thousand?"

I nodded again.

"Anything else?"

My mind started to click, like a car that has to be jump-started but runs fine after that. "What are you going to do, once you finish up in Oregon?"

"Go back to Phoenix. Why?"

"You told me I ought to do some investing, remember?"

He nodded. "What do you have in mind?"

"I understand there are a couple of condo projects in trouble in Seattle. Maybe now would be a good time to look into one of those. Would you mind sticking around and researching them?"

"Not as long as you're footing the bill." I got up to leave. "Are you coming back to town tonight?" he asked.

Pausing at the door, I considered my options. Riding with Ames and Peters would be physically uncomfortable but convenient. "No," I said, making up my mind, "I have some thinking to do. I'm better off here, away from everybody."

"And because you think Don Wilson is still on Orcas?"

He caught me red-handed. "So what?" I flared. "I'm on vacation. I can do as I damn well please."

"You don't have any objectivity in this case, Beau."

"Don't lecture me, Ralph. I'm your client, not some half-grown kid." I stormed from the room, slamming the door behind me, knowing he was more than half right.

I headed for the Mansion and the Vista Lounge. I wanted the taste of McNaughton's in my mouth, the feel of an icy glass in my hand. I almost ran over Maxwell Cole, who was about to climb into the hotel room in front of the building. I was surprised to see him. I thought he was already gone.

"What happened to your column?" I asked sarcastically. "Miss your deadline?"

"Deadline!" he echoed. "If you're talking about the piece I wrote yesterday, the one on Ginger Watkins, I didn't miss the deadline."

"So where is it?" I was looking for someone to bait, and Cole was a likely candidate. His handlebar mustache drooped lopsidedly, making him look more dreary than usual.

"They spiked the son of a bitch. The scoop of the year, and they spiked it!"

"Who did?"

"Beats the shit out of me. One minute it was in, the next minute it was out. My editor isn't talking."

The driver of the van honked. "Hey come on, man. Them ferries don't wait for nothing."

Cole scrambled into the van and settled in an aisle seat. The van pulled out of the gravel drive, leaving me lost in thought. It takes clout to spike a story, a hell of a lot of clout. I wondered who was flexing his muscle, Homer or Darrell, father or son, or father and son. It didn't matter. Whoever it was had robbed Ginger of her meager revenge, her sole token of defiance.

I charged into the lounge. It was deserted except for two slightly tipsy elderly ladies drinking sloe gin fizzes at a table by the arched windows. Barney folded a newspaper and shoved it under the bar as I sat down.

"McNaughton's?"

I nodded.

"It's too bad about Mrs. Watkins," he commented, placing the drink in front of me. "She seemed like a real nice lady, from what little I saw of her."

"She was." I agreed. I downed the drink and ordered another.

"Too bad about your car, too."

"Cars can be fixed," I said.

He grinned. "I guess old Ernie's in seventh heaven. Heard he's got himself a real-live Porsche to work on."

"You know him?"

"Hell, yes. Went to school together, kindergarten on. Ended up in Vietnam at the same time. Different outfits, though."

"That's where he lost his arm and leg?"

Barney nodded. "He doesn't let it bother him. Goes hunting every year, usually gets an elk. He's got a wife and two kids; another on the way."

"Is he any good?"

Barney grinned. "You'll have to ask his wife about that. He's not my type."

"As a mechanic, asshole. Is he a good mechanic?"

"He's good," Barney said seriously. "He'll put that car of yours back together better than it was before."

"Oh," I said.

A couple came in and sat at the other end of the bar. Barney left me to serve them. I sat there alone, nursing my drink, wondering where to start on a case that was not my case, on a murder that might be suicide or an accident, depending on your point of view.

In Seattle I knew what I'd do—sit down and try to pull together all the details on pieces of paper, set as many pieces of the puzzle on the table as possible, then move them around, trying to find a framework where they would fit.

Barney came back to me. "You want another?" he asked.

I looked at my glass. "Sure. Is that your paper under the bar?"

"It is, but you can have it. I'm done with it."

He pulled it out and laid it in front of me. I recognized Sig Larson's face looking up at me from under a screaming headline. I picked up the paper warily. I don't trust newspapers, don't like them, usually wouldn't be caught dead reading them; but this was different.

This time I was outside the official circle of information, and I needed a starting point. I was going to do something about Ginger Watkins' death, jurisdictions be damned. Sig Larson's death and Ginger's were inextricably linked. I intended to find out how.

I read every word of the laudatory obituary. A retired Eastern Washington wheat farmer, Lars Sigfried Larson had been widely respected. The article mentioned his volunteer work at Walla Walla and his involvement with Babe Ruth Baseball east of the mountains. It mentioned his widow, Mona, as well as his three grown children, married and scattered throughout the West. The funeral would be held in Welton on the banks of the Touchet River on Tuesday at two o'clock. The governor himself was expected to attend.

And so would J. P. Beaumont, I decided. I read on. The family requested that remembrances be sent to A.A. Even in death, Sig Larson didn't duck the issue of sobriety.

I had finished the article and was folding the paper when Peters came in and caught me. "What are you doing?"

"What the hell does it look like I'm doing? I'm trying to fold this goddamned newspaper."

"You haven't been reading it, have you?" Peters' eyes flashed with sly amusement. "You feeling all right, Beau? Maybe a little feverish?"

I stood up and struggled to return the newspaper to its place under the counter. When I flopped back down, Peters' grin faded. "Ames and I are getting ready to take off. Want to have a bite with us before we go?"

I signaled Barney for a new drink. When he set it in front of me, I raised the glass in Peters' direction in a sloppy salute. "Who needs food?"

"You're drinking too much . . ."

I cut him off. "Butt out, Peters."

Without arguing the point, he stalked from the bar. Misery does not necessarily love company. I made short work of that drink and the next one. Detective J. P. Beaumont disappeared with a subsequent dose of McNaughton's. All that remained was me, the man, or whatever bits and pieces were left of him.

"You're hitting it pretty hard, aren't you?" Barney asked, as he delivered my next drink.

"So what?" I returned. He handed me the glass, and I stared morosely into it. I swirled the amber liquid, listening to the crushed ice rustle against the glass.

Gradually, my carefully constructed defenses gave way. Pain leaked from every pore. Ginger's touch had reawakened that part of me that had died with Anne. Now Ginger's death released the grief I had kept so carefully bottled up inside me. It washed across me like a gigantic wave, choking me, drowning me.

The next thing I remember is Barney taking my last drink away and leading me, sobbing, from the bar. He got me as far as the door to my room before I was sick in a bordering flower bed.

It was still light when I staggered out of the bathroom and crawled into bed. I have a dim memory of Barney closing the curtains before he went outside and shut the door behind him.

Chapter 14

WHEN I woke up, cold sober, at two o'clock in the morning, I felt painfully alive again. I still hurt, but I had somehow bridged the chasm between the past and the present and was ready to go on. I had Ginger Watkins to thank for that, and there was only one way to repay her.

Ignoring my hangover, I rummaged around for paper, finally locating a fistful of Rosario stationery. I assigned each person a separate sheet of paper—Ginger, Sig, Wilson, Darrell, Homer, Mona. Under each name I noted everything I knew about them: things Ginger had told me, things I had heard from other sources. Maybe there's a better way of sorting out the players than by using paper and pencil, but I've never found one.

If I were keeping score, I'd have to say that Sig Larson dropped a few points in the process. I have an innate suspicion of perfection. Both Ginger's comments and the newspaper's undiluted praise made me wonder if the paragon had feet of clay. Being dead is only part of the qualifications for sainthood. Over and over, I recalled my offhand denial to Ernie, "Just friends," and so was Sig to Ginger. Just friends, right? Like hell.

A twinge of tardy jealousy caused me to turn to Mona Larson's sheet. What about her? Ginger had dismissed her as a calculating bitch. What suspicious wife isn't a calculating bitch, especially if she has some reason, especially from the other woman's point of view?

I could see Mona Larson in my mind's eye, a woman from sturdy farm stock, someone well beyond her middle years who had stood by her man through thick and thin only to see herself losing him to an attractive younger woman. It would give the fruits of her labors a bitter aftertaste.

So, how jealous was Mona Larson? Enough to make her anger public by sending Trixie Bowdeen with the message for Ginger not to attend Sig's funeral. Where had Mona been when she was supposedly en route to Orcas? Huggins had been unable to locate her to notify her of Sig's death. It was an item that merited exploration, but it wasn't top priority. Not that many jealous spouses actually murder their spouses and their spouses' friends.

Friends. There was that word again. Even in private thoughts I tended to gloss over it. *Lover*, then. Ginger and I had been lovers, briefly. And maybe Sig and Ginger had been, too. But if so, Sig was just as bad as Darrell. Ginger hadn't faked her surprise or enjoyment, had she?

No. My ego wouldn't accept that, and no woman could be so unlucky as to have two men as insensitive and unfeeling as Darrell. No. My thoughts chased themselves full-circle. Ginger and Sig could not have been lovers.

What about Homer and Darrell? What did I know of them? Homer and Jethro, I thought. Between them they wielded a large amount of power. With it they had imprisoned Ginger. Neither had wanted to let her go; both had tried to get her to delay the divorce. I recalled Homer's resonant voice on the phone, explaining how erratic Ginger had been, trivializing her motives, warning me to disregard whatever she might say. And all the while Ginger had been dying, or was already dead.

Darrell. What about Darrell, the boozing, whoring scion of an old, established family? A scion who had fallen on hard times, whose wife had to go to work to keep the wolf from the door. I recalled Ginger's response to Hal's question about a contract on Sig's life. No money, she had said. Not no reason, but no money. And no justification, either, since Darrell himself had been screwing around for years. Darrell Watkins, one-man stud service, who never rubbed his wife's neck, who never . . .

I couldn't believe Darrell would have had the nerve to confront Ginger on infidelity. That caliber of double standard is fast approaching extinction. But where had Darrell Watkins been on Saturday night? It would be interesting to know, just for the record.

Ginger. Ginger laughing, crying, stretching her neck as my thumbs massaged the muscles of her shoulders. Ginger's face transformed by a pleasure she had never known or suspected. Remembering that hurt too much, so I stopped.

She had seemed totally carefree as she drove away, waving to me through the window of the Porsche. Respect for Sig had dictated that she go to the meeting and say good-bye, but she would have come back to me, to what I alone had given her. Of that I was sure. Who or what had stopped her? Not suicide. Not booze.

That brought me to the last sheet of paper. Don Wilson. Bereaved husband and father, plunged into the world of political activist, parading his grief on placards and sandwich boards, trying to get someone to listen, attempting to change the system that had robbed him of his wife and child. He had a point, but he had gone after the wrong people.

Why had he agreed to meet Max? Max said something was about to break. What, other than Sig Larson's head? Had the phony interview been a ploy, a device to guarantee press coverage? Maybe Wilson had believed that killing Sig and Ginger would give his cause the public airing necessary to bring it to the top of the silent majority's consciousness. As if they gave a damn.

But it's a long way from political activism to cold-blooded murder, and there was nothing to prove Wilson's conversion—nothing but motive and opportunity.

Wilson had come to Orcas Island. That much we knew—not beyond a shadow of a doubt, but with relative certainty. And, as near as we could tell, he had not left it, at least not by any of the regular routes. He could have hired a boat or a plane, but that was unlikely. It would be too obvious. Besides, Huggins said he had checked all charters and tracked down all private parties who had booked moorage.

Assuming Wilson was still on Orcas, where was he hiding? Did he have an accomplice? Was this the end of it, since Sig and Ginger's decision had placed Lathrop in the work/release program, or was the entire Washington State Parole Board in jeopardy?

Questions. Homicide detectives always have far more questions than they do answers. I analyzed the pieces of paper, pondering each word, poring over each scrap of information until I could have quoted it back verbatim. Hours later, eyes swimming with fatigue, I stumbled to the bed and fell across it, not bothering to undress or pull the covers over me.

Questions continued to buzz in my head. Who had known of the A.A. meeting besides Sig, Ginger, and me? And how would the killer have known she would be in my Porsche?

The human brain is the oldest and best random-access memory. I had almost dozed off when a single word roused me. Calendar. I sat up in bed. The meeting had been noted in her calendar, and the calendar was missing. In fact, it was the only item still unaccounted for in the aftermath of the break-in.

I groped through the darkness for the phone, knocking it to the floor. "What happens to your garbage?" I asked a startled Fred, who answered sleepily on the fourth ring.

It took him a couple of seconds to get his brain in gear. "It goes to the landfill," he mumbled.

"Do you have garbage cans? Dumpsters?"

"Dumpsters, one by each wing, and two here at the Mansion." Fred sounded more awake now. He was gradually becoming accustomed to my middle-of-the-night requests.

"When were they emptied last?"

"Friday afternoon, late. We're on a Monday/Wednesday/Friday schedule."

I banged down the phone and rummaged through my clothes for my most disreputable Levi's and the dung-colored sweater Karen's mother knitted for me the Christmas before we were divorced. I had sworn to wear that sucker out. This would finish the job.

I stopped by the desk and begged a flashlight from Fred. It was cold, and rain was falling as I started my five A.M. assault on Rosario's garbage dumpsters.

Those who think being a detective is romantic ought to try rummaging through three-day-old garbage with a raging hangover, flashlight in hand, in a driving rainstorm. Things happen to apple cores and orange peels and banana skins that can't be described in polite company. If I had known about garbage cans, maybe I would have taken my mother's advice and become a schoolteacher.

I started with the wing where Ginger's original room had been, searching through each carefully fastened black plastic bag. I did the same to the second-wing dumpster, and again found nothing. In terms of garbage, this was lightweight stuff—tissues and soda cans, discarded hairspray cans, and a couple of pornographic magazines. Clean garbage. No calendar.

The last two dumpsters were by the Mansion itself. They contained GARBAGE, foul-smelling foodstuffs that had sat around for several days and gotten surly. I took one whiff and almost gave up, but some of my mother's stubborn determination must have stuck. I dug in and got lucky. At the bottom of the first dumpster, I found it—a leather-bound, gold-embossed executive planner with Ginger Watkins' name imprinted on the front.

Carefully I laid the book to one side and refilled the rancid container. After carrying the calendar back to my room, I stripped to the skin on the rainy porch, leaving my wrecked clothes by the door. I set the calendar on the floor just inside the doorway while I attempted to shower the odor off my body and out of my nose.

I came out of the shower wrapped in a towel and picked up the phone. I dialed Hal's number. On the third ring I realized it was only six o'clock. Homicide is always much more urgent when someone near and dear is dead.

"Guess what?" I asked when he finally answered.

"I give up," Hal mumbled groggily.

"I found Ginger's calendar, the one that was lifted from her room the other night."

"So big fucking deal. Do you know what time it is?"

"It was in the trash, down near the Mansion. You want to come out and pick it up, or should I bring it over to Friday Harbor myself?"

"Beau, give me a break, I didn't get to bed until three."

"Sorry, Hal, but I just found it. I thought you'd want to know."

"I'll pick it up later," he said grudgingly. "But it won't make any difference."

"What do you mean?"

He yawned, fully awake now. "Got the coroner's report just before I went to bed. Said her blood-alcohol reading was point-fifteen. She was dead drunk. Probably passed out cold when she hit the water."

"That's preposterous! It doesn't make sense."

"Of course it makes sense. Blood-alcohol counts don't lie. I'm telling you what they told me. It was an accident, and that's official."

I wanted to argue, but he wasn't having any. "The crime lab dusted for prints, enough to confirm that she was driving."

"You mean you're going to drop it just like that?"

"Look, Beau, we've already got one homicide. We don't need to change a DWI into homicide just for drill."

"But she wasn't drinking. She had nothing before she left here."

"You don't get a point-fifteen reading by osmosis. It was too much for her. The divorce, Sig Larson's death. She was despondent and slipped. It's the classic recovering-alcoholic story. She didn't live long enough to dry out a second time."

Ginger's words rang in my ears. "I won't go through that again. Ever." But I was the only one who had heard her make that categorical statement, the only one who knew that in twenty-four hours she had taken several giant steps beyond grief and found a reason for living.

"What was the time of death? Did they say?"

"Between eight-thirty and nine-thirty, give or take."

"I tell you, Hal, she had nothing to drink before she left here at twenty minutes to eight. How could she get that drunk in such a short time?"

He sighed. "You've been around boozers. With some of them, falling off the wagon is like stepping off a thirty-story building." Hal Huggins didn't budge. Neither did I.

"Do you want this calendar or not?" I demanded.

"I already said I'd come by later this morning and pick it up, but I'm not making any promises."

"Don't patronize me, Hal, goddammit. Will you have it analyzed or not? Don't pick it up just to humor me."

"For cripe's sake. I'll have it analyzed. Good-bye!" The receiver banged in my ear.

I looked at the calendar skulking by the door, its pungent odor invading the room. It made me wonder if I still wanted to be a cop when I grew up. I kept it in the room, odor and all. Considering the phone call, it didn't make much sense to keep it. I might just as well have pitched it outside into the drizzle, but I didn't.

I went to bed and tried to nap, without much luck.

Chapter 15

HAL Huggins was in a foul mood when he showed up an hour later. He called me from the lobby. "Bring that goddamned calendar down here and buy me breakfast, Beaumont."

Huggins was seated at a table before a steaming coffee cup

when I ventured into the dining room. Grudgingly, he pushed out a chair for me. "I'm not very good company when I don't get my beauty sleep," he growled. "Where the hell is that calendar?"

I handed it to him, wrapped in a Rosario pillowcase.

"What do you expect to find in there?" he asked, nodding toward it.

"Prints, I hope. Especially on last week's pages."

He leaned back in his chair and glowered at me. "Let me ask you this, Beau. Do you think this calendar has anything to do with Sig Larson's death? The break-in occurred after he was already dead."

"No, but—"

"But what?"

"The meeting was listed in there, the one Sig and Ginger planned to attend together."

"Were you awake when you called me this morning?"

"Sure I was awake."

"I told you then and I'll tell you now, Ginger Watkins' death has been ruled accidental. We are not treating it as a possible homicide. Do I make myself clear?"

"Very. So you won't have the calendar analyzed?"

"I'll take it, just for old time's sake, but that's the only reason." Huggins glared at me, his face implacable.

"What are you so pissed about, Hal?"

"I'm pissed because I've got a homicide to work, and I'm shorthanded, and I didn't get enough sleep, and my neck hurts. Any other questions?"

"None that I can think of."

The waiter brought Huggins his food and took my order. Halfway through breakfast, Hal's savage beast seemed somewhat soothed. "You going back today?"

"Probably." Rosario had lost its charm. I wanted to go home and lick my wounds.

"You need a ride?"

"Naw. I can take the shuttle bus."

The waiter brought my coffee and freshly squeezed orange juice. "Find any trace of Wilson?"

Huggins shook his head. "Not yet. Looks like he stepped off the face of the earth once he got on the ferry."

"Maybe he did," I said. "Still no sign of him at his house?"

"Not a trace. King County has round-the-clock surveillance on the place. It doesn't make sense."

"Unless he's dead, too," I suggested.

Huggins' flint-eyed scrutiny honed in on my face. "He might be, at that," he said.

I didn't like the tone, the inflection. "Is that an accusation?" I asked.

"Could be," he allowed, "if I thought vigilante mentality had caught you by the short hairs."

"Look, Hal, I was only trying to help."

He nodded. "I'd hate to think otherwise, Beau."

It sounded like the end of a beautiful friendship. I tried to put the conversation on a less volatile track. "How'd she get the booze, then? It had to come from somewhere. It wasn't in the Porsche when she left here."

"When she left *you*," he corrected. "She might have gone back to her room and gotten it. She might have bought it on the way."

I was shaking my head before he finished speaking. Huggins' face clouded. "You're sure you never met Ginger Watkins before last Friday?"

"I'm sure," I answered, trying to keep anger out of my voice. From one moment to the next, Huggins and I shifted back and forth to opposite sides, like two kids who can't decide if they're best friends or hate each other's guts.

"Why's it so goddamned important to you that she wasn't drunk?" he demanded.

How does a man answer a question like that without his ego getting in the way? If she was drunk, then I'm not the man I thought I was. A psychiatrist would have a ball with that one. I know she was coming back. She and I had a date to screw our brains out after dinner. That one had a good macho ring to it. I had given her a reason for living. She wouldn't have thrown it all away. That dripped with true missionary fervor.

I said, "It's important to me, that's all."

"My mind's made up; don't confuse me with the facts, right?"

"Something like that."

"Beau—"

"Will you have the calendar analyzed?"

"I told you I will, but—"

"And you'll let me know what you find?"

There was a momentary pause. "I guess." He stirred his coffee uneasily, looking at me over the cup. "It's probably a good thing you're going home today. We might end up stepping on each other's toes."

"I take it that means you're firing me as a San Juan County deputy?"

He nodded. "Yup." He gave me a lopsided grin. "If it's possible to fire someone who's working for free." The tension between us evaporated. Huggins rose, taking his check and the calendar. I snagged the check away from him.

"It's on me, Hal, remember? Your beauty sleep?"

We shook hands. "No hard feelings?" he asked.

"None."

"All right then. I'll be in touch. If I were a betting man, I'd say there won't be a goddamned thing in this sonofabitch." He strode out of the dining room.

It's too bad I didn't take that bet, but hindsight is always twenty/twenty.

I went into the bar because I didn't want to go back to my room. Without Ginger, my room seemed empty. Barney was industriously polishing the mirror.

"Morning," he said to my reflection. "Want a drink?"

"Just coffee," I replied. "I need to think."

He brought a mug and set it in front of me. "On the house," he said, refusing my money. Barney had a sense of when to leave people alone. He said nothing about my making an ass of myself. Instead he returned to his mirror and his Windex.

The question I had asked Hal was far more than rhetorical. He was right, of course. Blood-alcohol readings don't lie. No matter how much I wanted to deny it, Ginger Watkins had been drunk when she ploughed into the water. So where had she gotten the booze? From her room? A liquor store? Where?

"Hey, Barney," I said, "does Orcas Island have a liquor store?"

He grinned. "Hell, no. We're too small. We've got Old Man Baxter, though. He's the official agent. Lives up above Eastsound, about a half-mile beyond Ernie's."

"Did Huggins leave one of Don Wilson's pictures with you?"

"Are you kidding?" He reached under the bar and pulled out a whole handful. "Why, you want some?"

"One," I said. "I only need one." He handed me a picture.

I pulled out a pen to write on the back. "Tell me again how to get there."

"Where?"

"Mr. Baxter's."

"Now wait a minute. You come in here, and I give you free coffee. Next thing I know, you want to go see our agent so you can mix your own drinks? No way! I'd lose one of my best customers."

"I promise I won't buy anything," I protested. "I just want to show him this picture."

"Well, in that case. . . . Go past Ernie's. It's the fourth mailbox on the left."

"Thanks, have the desk call me a cab, would you?"

"Why?"

"So I don't have to walk."

"No, I mean why do you want to see Baxter?"

"I want to know if either Ginger Watkins or this man bought something from him Friday or Saturday. Make the call, would you?"

Instead, Barney reached into his pants pocket and extracted a ring of keys. He tossed them across the bar, and I caught them in midair. "What's this?"

"It's the key to an old Chevy pickup parked over by the moorage. You're welcome to use it if you like."

It was a small-town gesture, one that caught me by surprise. When I thought about it, though, there's no such thing as auto theft on Orcas Island. I pocketed the keys. "Thanks, Barney. Appreciate it."

The pickup looked old and decrepit; but ugliness, like beauty, is only skin-deep. The engine ran like a top beneath a rusty hood. I drove into Eastsound, past Ernie's and stopped at the fourth mailbox on the left. The house was a picturesque gray-and-white bungalow that might have been lifted straight off Cape Cod. I knocked on the door.

Mr. Baxter himself opened it. He was a small man with a belly much too large for the rest of him. The living room of the house had been converted into a mini–display room, with a stack of hand-held shopping baskets sitting beside the door. The house had the smell and look of an aging bachelor pad—not much cooking and not enough cleaning.

"Help yourself," he said, motioning me inside.

I pulled Don Wilson's picture out of my pocket. "I didn't come to buy anything," I said. "I was wondering if you'd ever seen this man before."

He peered at the picture, then looked up at me. "You a cop?" he asked. His face was truculent, arms crossed, chin jutting. Mr. Baxter was a short man embattled by a tall world.

Huggins had pulled the plug on my unofficial deputy status. "No," I said. "The woman who died the other night was a friend of mine. I'm trying to find out what happened to her."

"Not from me you won't."

"I'm only asking if you recognize him."

"You ever hear of the confidentiality statute of nineteen and thirty-three?"

"Not that I remember."

"It says no liquor-store clerk tells nobody nothing, excepting of course federal agents checking revenue stamps. We can talk to them."

"All I'm asking is, Did you see him?"

"And if I give out information, they stick me with a high misdemeanor. Nosiree. I'm not talking to nobody."

I could see right off I wasn't going to change his mind. I left. Something made me stop at Ernie's. The doors of the Porsche were wide open, and the insides of the car were scattered all over the garage in a seemingly hopeless jumble. Ernie glanced up as I walked in. He was bent over the engine, a grimy crutch propped under his good arm.

"How'do, Mr. Beaumont. I was just gonna call you."

I figured it was time to jack up the price, now that the car was in pieces and I was a captive audience.

"Why?" I asked.

"You ever have any work done on the linkage?"

I shrugged. "No. Not that I know of."

He hopped away from the car to a nearby tool bench, picked up something in his gripper, and handed it to me. I looked down at two pieces of metal, slightly smaller in diameter than a pencil.

"What's this?"

"That's the throttle linkage cable. Looks to me like it's been cut."

"What does that mean?"

"With that thing cut, Mr. Beaumont, all you have to do is put that baby in motion and you've got a one-way ride."

I looked down at the shiny crimped ends of metal. "It couldn't have broken in the accident?"

He shook his head. "No way."

"Mind if I use your phone?" I asked, keeping my voice calm. It was time for Hal Huggins to eat a little crow.

Chapter 16

HAL marched into Ernie's Garage looking thunderous. "What do you mean the linkage was cut?" he stormed.

Ernie pointed him in the direction of the tool bench where the two pieces of cable were once more lying in state. Silently Hal examined them, then he straightened. "How the hell could those crime-lab jokers miss something like this?"

"They were investigating an accident, remember?" I reminded him. "A DWI. Maybe even a suicide."

He glared at me. "That's no excuse."

"So where do we go from here?"

"Damned if I know." Hal settled on a bench near the door. "Not a chance of getting fingerprints now, either," he lamented.

Ernie, back under the hood, peered over his shoulder at Hal, grinning. "Only half as many as there could have been," he said.

Hal didn't bother to acknowledge Ernie's black humor. "Two homicides," he muttered. "Two goddamned homicides in as many days. Do you know how long we usually go up here without a homicide?"

"Did you tell anybody on the way over?"

"Hell, no. I tried to raise Pomeroy to come down to the dock and pick me up. I couldn't find that lard-ass anywhere. Luckily, somebody gave me a ride."

My mind was working. "Then the only people who know are you, Ernie, me, and the murderer."

"That's right. So what?"

"Let's keep it that way."

"What good will that do?" Hal asked.

"It'll give us a chance to investigate without the media breathing down our necks."

Hal nodded, slowly. "That does have some appeal." For a time we sat in silence. "How far could it have been driven like that, Ernie?" Hal asked finally.

Ernie answered without looking up from his work. "A couple hundred feet if the front end was aligned and it was on a straight stretch."

"What gear was it in?"

"Neutral when I got it, but I'm sure the tow-truck driver shifted it so he wouldn't tear up the transmission."

"Can you check with him?"

"Sure."

"And not a word of this to anyone," Hal admonished. "It's important."

Ernie straightened and favored Hal with a sly grin. "Had a feeling it was, or you wouldn't have been here in twenty-five minutes flat. Last time I seen you move that fast was at the Fireman's Picnic when a wasp was after you."

Hal laughed. "I set all-time world records with that sucker on my butt." The camaraderie was small-town stuff, foreign in a nice way.

"Don't worry. I'll keep it quiet." Ernie resumed working on the car, as though we were no longer there.

"What about Wilson?" I asked. "Any sign of him?"

Huggins shook his head. "We're looking, still keeping his house under surveillance, but so far nothing."

We rose and started toward the door; Ernie called after me, "By the way, Mr. Beaumont, maybe it won't cost you the whole seven grand after all."

Hal's eyes widened. "Seven grand?"

"Maybe six and a half." Ernie's head disappeared, dismissing us. Hal looked at me, stunned.

"Six and a half thousand? To fix the car?"

"It's a Porsche," I said. It seemed to me that no further explanation was necessary.

"How much they paying you these days? When I worked Seattle P.D., I was lucky to afford a lube and oil. Matter of fact, I still am. You into graft and corruption?"

"I happened into some money, Hal, that's all."

Hal glowered at me. "Some people have all the luck," he sniffed, walking outside. I followed.

"Where you going?" I asked.

"I'm looking for Pomeroy. He was supposed to come pick me up. I can't drive the goddamned police launch all over the goddamned island."

"Where do you want to go?"

"The duck pond, you asshole. Where else?"

That's how two homicide detectives, one legal and one not, returned to the scene of the crime in a bartender's borrowed pickup. It wasn't much, but it was a whole lot better than walking.

The place where the Porsche had laid down the layer of rubber made better sense now. The car had leaped forward from a dead stop. Even piecing that together didn't give us everything we needed to know. We gave up about mid-afternoon. I took Hal back to his boat.

"What are you going to do now?" he asked.

"Go home, I guess. Hanging around here won't do any good."

He sat in Barney's idling pickup, one hand on the door handle. "We'll get him, Beau. I promise." It was as close as Hal Huggins ever came to making an apology.

"Are you going to warn the rest of the parole board? What if he goes after the whole board, one by one."

Hal looked stricken. "I'll check it out," he agreed. "He could go through them like a dose of salts." He climbed from the pickup and headed for the dock.

Back at Rosario, I packed and checked out of my room. I had the desk clerk call for a float plane. I could have taken the ferry to Anacortes, but without a car, I'd still be a long way from Seattle. A charter pilot could drop me on Lake Union a mile or so from my apartment.

I dragged a newspaper along in the noisy little plane. I suffer from a fear of flying. There's nothing like reading a newspaper to make me forget that I'm scared. Newspapers always piss me off.

The editor opined that the tragic deaths of two members of the Washington State Parole Board over the weekend—one an apparent homicide and the other in a motor vehicle accident—pointed out the high cost of public service. He went on to say that Darrell

Watkins was showing great personal courage in continuing to campaign in the face of the loss of his beloved wife.

Bullshit! There was no hint that the beloved wife, now deceased, would have filed for a divorce had she lived to Monday morning. In the editorial, Ginger's and Darrell's life had been a Cinderella story, poor girl marries rich boy and lives happily ever after. As far as Ginger was concerned, the fairy tale had suffered in translation. Somehow I had an idea that Maxwell Cole's interview would never see the light of the day. It wasn't just spiked, it was buried. For good.

The article on Ginger made no mention of drinking. The accident was described as a one-car accident on a narrow road. Darrell Watkins was quoted at some length. "I am going on with the race because I believe Ginger would want me to."

The unmitigated ass! Ginger had been wrong. Darrell Watkins had developed hypocrisy into an art form.

The float plane dropped me at a dock on Lake Union. Without luggage, I could have walked. With luggage, I called a cab. It was early evening when I got home—the city boy glad to be back in familiar territory, with the comforting wail of sirens and the noise of traffic.

My apartment is in the Royal Crest, a condo at Third and Lenora. *Condo* conjures images of swinging singles. There are singles here, all right, mostly retired, who do very little swinging. It's a vertical neighborhood where people bring soup when you're sick and know who comes and goes at all hours. I moved in five years ago on a temporary basis, hoping Karen and I would get back together. We didn't. Five years later, my escape hatch has become home.

In the elevator two people welcomed me back, and on the mat in front of my door I found a stack of crossword puzzles culled from various newspapers and left for me by my next-door neighbor and crony, Ida Newell. Yes, it was very good to be home.

I put my suitcases in the bedroom and looked around the tiny apartment with satisfaction. One of my first concessions to having money was to hire a housekeeper who comes in once every two weeks whether I need it or not. The house smelled of furniture polish and toilet-bowl cleaner. It was a big improvement over the old days when it smelled like a billygoat pen and I needed two hours' notice before I could invite someone up to visit.

The mail was mostly of the bill/occupant variety, although I noticed that some of the occupant stuff was a lot more upscale than occupant mail I used to receive. Somewhere there's a mass-mailing company that knows when you move from one income bracket to another. The whole idea makes me paranoid.

I thumped into my favorite leather chair, a brown monstrosity that gives people with "taste" indigestion. I examined the bill from Rosario with its detail of all calls made from my room. I recognized most of them. Two of the numbers were unfamiliar. One had to be Homer's and the other Darrell's. I chose one at random.

Homer answered on the second ring. I didn't identify myself. "I'm a friend of Ginger's. I was calling to find out about her services."

"In keeping with Darrell's wishes, the services will be private."

"But I wanted—"

"I'm sorry. This is a very difficult time. Darrell wants to maintain a sense of dignity by keeping Ginger's funeral simple. Only family members and close personal friends. I'm sure you understand." He hung up without giving me an opportunity to explain why I thought I qualified as a close personal friend.

Remembering Ginger's description of how Darrell's campaign would handle news of the divorce, I understood all too well. A steering committee had decreed that Ginger's funeral should be handled with classic understatement and simplicity. Not too splashy. That would attract the sympathy vote.

I wanted to gag. Ginger had known news of the divorce wouldn't cost Darrell the election, but she had hoped to sting him with it. Instead, her death would provide the impetus for a come-from-behind victory. I wanted to protest to someone, but I didn't know who.

Restless, I walked two blocks to Avis and rented a car for the next morning. If I was going to make it to a funeral in Welton by two o'clock in the afternoon, I'd have to get an early start. My garage door opener was still with the Porsche on Orcas— probably wrecked, now that it had been wet. I parked the rented Rabbit on the street and went upstairs to get some sleep.

In a dream, Anne Corley and Ginger Watkins were together someplace. It seemed to be some kind of spa. They were both wrapped in thick white towels, with their hair hanging loose and wet. I came into the room. They waved at me and motioned for me to join them, but they were across a large room and between us lay a huge swimming pool. They motioned to me again, and I dove in, clothes and all. I tried to swim toward them, but the current was too swift. It caught me and carried me away, changing from a pool to a river. The dream ended with the sound of both of them laughing.

I awoke drenched with sweat. It was almost four o'clock in the morning. For a while I tried going back to sleep, but it didn't work. Remembering them both together haunted me. At last I got up and made coffee. The city was silent around me—not as silent as Orcas, but silent for the city. As I drank my coffee, I made up my mind that nothing would keep me from showing up at Ginger's funeral to offer my respects.

I consulted the map. I would go east on Interstate 90; but after Sig Larson's funeral, when I came back to Seattle, I would detour south to Centralia and find myself a Union 76 station. Ginger's father lived in Centralia. I was sure he would give me an invitation to the funeral if I explained to him that I was one of Ginger's old friends.

I filled a Thermos with the last of the coffee and headed out. I figured I'd have breakfast somewhere along the way.

Chapter 17

THE State of Washington is divided into two parts, east of the mountains and west of the mountains. They could just as well be separate countries.

West of the mountains is a fast-track megalopolis that is gradually encroaching on every inch of open space. East of the mountains seems like a chunk of the Midwest that has been transported and reassembled between the Cascades and the Rockies. It contains small towns, large farms, and the kind of vast horizons that brings to mind Robert Goulet's old song, "On a Clear Day You Can See Forever."

Welton is definitely east of the mountains. It's a tiny burg nestled in a hilly curve of the Touchet River, where two Walla Walla County roads meet in a casual Y that doesn't merit so much as a Yield sign, to say nothing of a blinking amber light.

Welton boasts a general store, a Grange Hall, a deserted schoolhouse, five or six dilapidated frame houses, and a double-wide mobile home perched on cement blocks behind the store. The Lutheran church burned down six years ago and has not been replaced. A sign on the light post next to the gas pump announced the schedule for the Walla Walla County Bookmobile. Next to it, another handbill posted notice of Sig Larson's funeral.

The gas jockey at the Texaco Station/General Store, a toothless old geezer named Gus, informed me that Lewis and Clark's party had once camped overnight on the river, supposedly somewhere near where the Grange Hall now stood. As far as he knew, Sig Larson's funeral was the biggest event to hit town since then.

"It isn't ever' day we have this kinda excitement around here," he commented as he scrubbed the rented Rabbit's windshield and checked the oil. "We're gonna shut 'er down and go over to the Hall for the funeral. Least we can so for old Sig, that's for sure."

"He lived around here?"

"Not anymore. Sold out a couple years back when that there wife of his decided Welton warn't good enough. Talked him into one of them highfalutin condanubians over to Lake Chelan. T'was a shame, a dad-gummed shame, if you ask me."

"But he'll be buried here?"

"First wife's buried here, you know. Think the kids had something to do with bringing him back. Son John's a bigwig lawyer down to California. He's the one took it on hisself to see things got done right."

"So Mona's Sig Larson's second wife?"

Gus snorted and spat a brown stream of tobacco juice over his shoulder. "She was already hanging round while Elke—that was Sig's first wife—was dyin' in the hospital over to Spokane."

"I take it you don't like Mona much."

He nodded sagely. "That's for sure," he said. "You can say that again."

Gus wore the logger trademark of mid-calf Levi's held up by a pair of bright red suspenders. Finished with my car, he stood with both thumbs stuck through his suspenders and surveyed the scatter of cars parked haphazardly around the Grange Hall. "Heard the governor hisself is coming. Wonder if ol' Mona'll get herself all gussied up or if she'll show up on that there motorcycle of hern.''

Motorcycle! That hardly tallied with the white-haired, displaced-homemaker farm wife I had imagined Sig Larson's widow to be—someone wearing an apron who baked her own bread and canned her own tomatoes.

A mobile television unit bearing a Spokane station's call letters and logo lumbered past us and parked under a tree near the Grange Hall. ''Don't that just beat all?'' Gus asked. ''All them television cameras and ever'thin', just for Old Sig's funeral.'' He spat again in disbelief.

As we watched, a helicopter dropped noisily from the sky and landed on the weedy playfield of the abandoned schoolhouse next door. Governor Reynolds stepped out, ducking under the blades, accompanied by none other than Homer Watkins himself.

Seeing Homer there was something of a shock. Ginger had implied that highly placed family connections had resulted in her appointment to the parole board, but seeing Homer with the governor brought the reality home.

''I'd better get going,'' I told Gus. I hurried to the Grange Hall and took an unobtrusive seat in the next-to-last row of ancient folding chairs. From there I could see who came and went without being observed.

I had stopped in Kenniwick and bought a huge bouquet of flowers, which now sat prominently displayed near the foot of Sig Larson's coffin. I had signed the card from ''A Friend'' and let it go at that. The flowers were a remembrance from Ginger to Sig through me. If Ginger and Sig were flapping around upstairs somewhere, then they both knew what I meant. If they weren't, it didn't matter anyway.

Unlike Lewis and Clark's historic visit, Sig Larson's funeral was immortalized by the press, the same teeming mob that had invaded Orcas Island. They were joined by troops from Spokane and Tri Cities as well. A full contingent of the Fourth Estate was there, jockeying for position and camera angle, elbowing one another out of the way.

It was simple to divide the guests into two parts: the plainly dressed quiet folk who had probably been lifelong friends and neighbors of Sig and Elke Larson, and the public officials and anxious candidates whose attendance was calculated to pick up a little free publicity over and above the paid political announcements.

The entire front row, on both sides of the aisle, was marked Reserved. As the pianist attempted a frail, halting prelude on an old upright píano, a group of six handsome young people, three couples in their late twenties to early thirties, was ushered to the front row. I surmised they were Sig's children and their spouses. Gus had told me there were two Larson boys and one girl, all married. They sat together on one side of the front row, leaving two places open next to the aisle.

The surviving members of the parole board, five of them, straggled down the aisle behind Trixie Bowdeen like a bunch of dazed sheep. Next came Governor Reynolds and Homer Watkins.

There was some confusion about seating arrangements as they reached the front row. Homer and Governor Reynolds held a hurried, private consultation before both men crossed the aisle to speak solemnly with the young couples. Then they rejoined the parole board.

Darrell Watkins was notable only in his absence.

The room filled quickly, until every chair was taken and people stood two-deep in the back of the room. It was then Mona Larson staged her grand entrance. She wore a black dress with a bold V neckline and a flared skirt over a pair of high-heeled black boots. Her hair, black and glossy, hung straight to her shoulders, with a fringe of bangs that made her look far younger than I had expected. Her tiny waist was encircled by a wide turquoise and silver belt. A weighty squash-blossom necklace with matching earrings completed the ensemble. It wasn't exactly mourning, but it made the point. It was also very striking.

A murmur rustled through the room. Mona strode down the aisle, well aware of the sensation she caused. At the front of the room she paused momentarily to get her bearings, then she turned her back on Sig Larson's children and took the empty seat next to Governor Reynolds. Another flurry of comment whispered through the hall.

From the back of the room it looked more like a shotgun wedding between feuding clans than the funeral of a highly regarded public official. Mona Larson was behaving badly by Welton standards, and it was clear she didn't give a damn.

A minister took his place behind the podium. "Dearly beloved," he intoned, "we are here this afternoon to say good-bye to our dear friend Lars Sigfried Larson . . .'' The cameras whirred and the circus got under way.

I don't remember much about the service. As far as I was concerned, I was there on official/unofficial business. I kept my eyes open in case Wilson thought Welton far enough away from Orcas that he could afford to turn up and savor his handiwork. Murderers do that in a kind of cutthroat one-upmanship, but Don Wilson was nowhere to be seen.

At the end of the service, the reverend announced that the Ladies Aid would be serving a potluck lunch, and all were welcome to come back to the hall after interment in the cemetery beyond the school.

The pallbearers hoisted the coffin. Mona Larson, followed by the governor and Sig's children, led a slow procession out of the hall, across the road, and into the cemetery. A man sat smoking on an idled backhoe near the fence, waiting to perform his essential role in the process. Once Sig's coffin was lowered into the grave, Mona turned and left the cemetery alone. Without speaking to or acknowledging anyone, she climbed into one of three waiting limousines and left Welton with an air of regal contempt.

Gus hobbled up next to me. "Ain't she somethin'?" he demanded, with just a hint of awe. "Actin' like she's the dad-gummed Queen of Sheba."

The press corps descended on the food like an army of ravenous ants. I spied Maxwell Cole packing around a paper plate piled high with ham and scalloped potatoes, but I managed to avoid him. The local folks clustered around the Larson children, expressing condolences, relieved now that Mona's abrupt departure had reduced the tension.

Homer Watkins materialized at my elbow. "I understand you're J. P. Beaumont. Aren't you the one I talked to on the phone the night Ginger died?"

I wondered who had squealed on me, but with Max in the room, it wasn't hard to figure it out. "Yes," I said.

"Tragic, tragic," he murmured.

"It is, isn't it," I agreed. "I was a little surprised there was no mention of the impending divorce in the paper."

His eyes hardened. "She told you about that?"

"We talked," I replied noncommittally.

"She wouldn't have gone through with it. She had been under

a great deal of stress. I'm sure once things settled down, she would have been fine."

"Fine or quiet?" I asked.

One eyebrow arched. He stepped back half a pace.

"Darrell didn't come?" I asked. The question was more to irk him than to have an answer.

Homer replied nonetheless. "He didn't feel up to it. Good day, Mr. Beaumont. I won't trouble you further."

As people lined up for second and third helpings, Governor Reynolds raised his hand for attention. "I'd like to make an announcement," he said. The media folks abandoned their plates and hustled off in search of equipment. Reynolds moved to the front of the room.

He put on his glasses and read from a prepared text. "This has been a sad occasion for the State of Washington. Sig Larson was a public servant, and he was murdered in the course of that service. He paid with his life. We have reason to believe that his death was related to his being on the parole board. Consequently, as of today, I am placing all members of the parole board under the protection of the Washington State Patrol. That is all."

There was a momentary lull after he finished speaking, then a rush of comment. Reporters attempted to call questions to him from the floor, but he turned away. Reynolds and Homer hurried out of the building. People followed them upstairs and outside, but they dashed to the waiting helicopter without speaking to anyone. With the governor gone, people moved back into the basement, where Trixie Bowdeen assumed the role of spokesman.

"Were you aware the governor was taking this action, Mrs. Bowdeen?"

"Yes," she said. "Each of us has been assigned round-the-clock protection, starting today."

"Is there any idea who the killer or killers might be?"

"No comment."

"How does your husband feel about your having a round-the-clock bodyguard?"

"Fortunately, he's not the jealous type." Trixie Bowdeen flashed what was supposed to be a charming smile. Her quip was greeted by general laughter. I didn't laugh. Governor Reynolds had not specifically mentioned Ginger's death, but I was sure Huggins had notified him regarding the changed status of the investigation. In any event, the protection was probably a good idea.

I left the hall and was halfway across the road when Maxwell Cole called my name. "Hey, J. P."

I turned to find him huffing behind me, carrying a plate of half-consumed pumpkin pie. "What do you want?"

"Any line on Wilson?"

I kept my expression blank. "No," I said. "Nobody's seen him."

"How come Ginger Watkins was driving your car?"

"None of your business," I snarled, walking away. He trotted after me. "I heard her blood-alcohol count was point-fifteen, but she was supposed to be on the wagon."

"Shut up," I said savagely.

He shut up, but only momentarily. "Do you know anything about the governor's victim/witness protection program? Is Reynolds going to drop that idea? That's what Wilson was after."

I stopped in my tracks. "What do you mean?"

Cole looked a little reluctant, as though he had said more than he intended. "Wilson expected an announcement that day at Rosario."

"From the governor's office?"

"That's what he told me on the phone."

"This is the first I've heard anything about an announcement," I said, turning to walk away.

"But, J. P.—"

Ignoring him, I walked back to the gas station where I had left the Rabbit. I climbed in and drove to where two uniformed limo drivers stood smoking under a tree. I rolled down the window. "Did that other driver say where he was taking Mrs. Larson?" I asked.

One looked at the other, who shrugged. "The Red Lion in Pasco, I think," he said. "You know where that is?"

"No," I replied, rolling up the window and putting the Rabbit in gear, "but I'll bet I can find it."

Chapter 18

I drove the forty miles into Pasco thinking about Ray Johnson. Ray and I were partners on the homicide squad for eleven years before he took off to become Chief of Police in Pasco. That's what happens to longtime Seattle P.D. folks. They get tired of the rat race and go looking for some one- or two-horse town where they can settle down and not have to look at the slice of life that turns up dead or drunk or both in Seattle's parks and alleys.

Ray had abandoned ship almost ten months earlier, and I had started working with Peters. It takes time to adjust to a new partner, but in the course of that ten months so much had happened that now it seemed Peters and I had been together for years, and Ray Johnson was ancient history.

Ten months is a long time to go without seeing an old friend, and I decided I'd eat a chili-burger and down a whole pot of thick coffee with Ray Johnson before I left town. For old time's sake. Without having Peters lecture me on the evils of the caffeine or red meat.

The sign at the Red Lion in Pasco said, "Welcome Mary Kay." I mistakenly thought Mary Kay was a waitress or barmaid who had returned for a visit.

That shows how wrong you can be.

The Red Lion in Pasco, like Red Lions everywhere, is built on the kind of grand scale that says, "Conventions welcome; all others enter at your own risk." As I drove up, a car pulled out of a parking place directly in front of the lobby. I grabbed the spot, feeling smug. Getting out of the Rabbit, I noticed that the car next to me, and two on the other side of that, were all recent-model pink Cadillacs. They had matching bumper stickers which read, "Ask me about Mary Kay."

Still musing about that, I entered the lobby. A huge banner solved the mystery. Stretched across the lobby, it proclaimed,

"Welcome Mary Kay Cosmetics." A regional sales convention was in full swing, and the hotel was thronged with troops of motivated, energetic ladies, all dressed in pink, who periodically burst into disturbingly impromptu choruses of company songs. I should have recognized it as an omen and realized I was headed for trouble.

A harried desk clerk managed to find me a room. Once safely shut away, I picked up the phone and asked for Mona Larson. "I'll ring," the operator told me.

"Hello." The voice was low and husky. For a second I thought I was talking to a man.

"Mona Larson, please," I stammered.

"This is she."

"My name is Beaumont. I'm here investigating a homicide. I need to talk to you."

"How the hell did you find me? That's why I didn't go home. I'm sick of being hounded."

"I'm a detective; that's how I found you. But it's only me. I've ditched the press."

Her tone mellowed a little. "That's a relief. Those bastards have been driving me crazy."

"Would you care to have a drink . . . coffee?"

"I could use a drink. Where are you?"

"In my room. I can meet you in the coffee shop or the bar." Sig Larson didn't drink. Maybe Mona didn't either. It was best to offer the lady a choice.

"All right. It'll take me a few minutes. I'll meet you in the bar. How will I know you?"

"From the looks of the lobby as I came in, I'll probably be the only man in the place."

She laughed. "You'll be the onion in the Mary Kay petunia patch."

She was right. Walking into the Starlight Lounge unnerved me. It was cocktail hour. All the old jokes about salesmen on convention came to mind and did a flip-flop. Saleswomen were just as bad. They sat in groups of twos and threes, giving me a clothes-stripping once-over. Other than the bartender, I was the only man in the room.

I had barely sat down when a woman in her mid-forties sidled up to my table. "Care for a drink?"

I looked around in consternation, hoping she wasn't talking to me. She was. Her face was a paper-smooth mask, eyes shadowed with a disconcerting blend of several different colors. Her lips, darker on the outside than on the inside, made me wonder what a two-toned tube of lipstick looked like.

"Sorry," I answered. "I'm meeting someone."

"Too bad," she said with a wink. She returned to her table while the bartender appeared at my elbow. "Drink, fella?"

"A McNaughton's and water," I said. He paused to wipe the table. "This is a little weird," I commented under my breath.

He laughed. "You think it's bad now, wait until nine o'clock when they're all on their lips."

The bartender returned to the bar. I sat there, conspicuously alone, waiting for Mona Larson. At Welton she had looked quite bizarre, but now I was anxious to see her. Mona's dramatic clothing would be a welcome contrast to the unrelenting pink, her disdain an antidote to the uncomfortable attention I was receiving at the moment.

Mona rescued me, all right. She had changed her black dress for a black, zippered jumpsuit. Her hair had been pulled up to the top of her head and stuck there with an unlikely comb. A few loose tendrils of hair trailed softly down her neck. Still wearing several pounds of silver and turquoise, she sauntered into the bar with a feline grace that disposed of the pink ladies once and for all.

"Mr. Beaumont?" she asked, extending her hand.

I half rose in greeting. Her handshake was firm, her dark brown eyes straightforward. "Don't bother getting up," she said, sinking gratefully into a low-backed chair opposite me.

"Thanks for saving my bacon," I said.

She glanced around the room disdainfully. "From what? These horny broads?" She turned to me and grinned. "You look like you can take care of yourself."

From what Ginger had said about Mona Larson and from what I had seen at the funeral, I was prepared not to like her, but her manner had a disarming forthrightness about it, and very little of the grieving widow.

"Sorry it took so long," she apologized. "I had a phone call. Are you from Orcas?"

The bartender brought my drink and took her order for Chivas on the rocks while I contemplated my situation. I was in no way from Orcas, and as a Seattle homicide detective, I had no business asking her anything at all.

I took a sip of my drink. "No. I'm from Seattle."

"I didn't know Seattle was involved in the case."

"We are now," I said.

"Do you have a card?"

There are times when I think I'll just stick my little toe in some water. Before I know it, I'm in over my head. I reached into my pocket and pulled out my leather cardholder. I handed her one of my business cards, which she examined without comment and put into a zippered pocket on the leg of her pants. Her fingers were long and slender, but the nails were close-cropped.

"So what do you want to know?"

"How well did you know Ginger Watkins?"

"Well enough."

"What do you mean?"

"We were shirttail relatives. Homer and Sig's first wife were brother and sister. Our families had some business dealings together."

So that was the connection. I had wondered about it.

"Were you and Ginger friends?"

"No."

I waited, hoping she'd expand on the subject. She didn't. "You and Darrell, then?"

"Darrell Watkins is an asshole," Mona said. "He's why I was late. He called from Seattle while I was at the funeral, wanted to explain why he wasn't there. As if I give a rat's ass." She extracted a pack of cigarettes from another zippered pocket. I hurried to offer her a light. She leaned back inhaling.

"Did you know Ginger was going to get a divorce?"

"You bet. I called Darrell to tell him."

"Why?"

She regarded me coolly. "Look, Mr. Beaumont, I played that side of the fence once. You're married to a jerk. Some nice guy sympathizes, listens to you, tells you what a bad deal you've got. First thing you know, you ditch the jerk and marry the nice guy. That's the name of the game, survival of the fittest."

"You think Ginger was trying to pack Sig off?"

She blew a languid cloud of smoke. "Not on purpose. She was so fucked up, she probably didn't know she was doing it. They were nice people, both of them."

I tried reconciling Mona's words with the person who had
forbidden Ginger to attend Sig's funeral. It didn't add up. "Why
didn't you want Ginger to come to the funeral?"

"Who said?"

"That's what I understood," I replied. "It came from someone, maybe Trixie Bowdeen."

"That cow? All she does is make trouble. She minds everybody else's business. Ginger could have come if she wanted to.
It wouldn't have bothered me."

She glanced away from me, angrily swiping a tear. Pain lurked
behind Mona Larson's tough exterior, under the brittle wit.

"You loved him very much, didn't you."

She looked at me, her eyes bright with tears. "That's not how
they see it in Welton," she said. "I'm the gold digger who married Sig Larson for his money. What a laugh!"

"Did you?" Mona's manner encouraged a direct approach.

She didn't deny it. "There's not much left," she countered.

"The money from the farm?"

"Gone. He left me a mortgaged condo on Lake Chelan, plus
my share of the Seattle project, whatever that's worth. I own my
Harley free and clear, and that's it, except for my jewelry." She
fell silent. I felt sorry for her. Ginger Watkins' calculating bitch
wasn't nearly as ruthless, close at hand.

"You work on the Harley yourself?"

She cocked her head. "What made you ask that?"

"Your nails are a whole lot more serviceable than the rest of
the nails in this room, like maybe they get a little grease under
them on occasion."

"Good guess," she said.

"What do you know about Don Wilson?" I asked, switching
topics.

She looked me straight in the eye. "I told him if he called
again I'd file a complaint."

"For what?"

"Telephone harassment. I knew all about his wife and kid, but
he'd call in the middle of the night, making wild threats. He
finally stopped."

"When?"

She thought. "A month or so ago, maybe longer."

"He threatened Sig?"

"Constantly."

"What did he say?"

"That he'd make Sig pay."

"Did Sig do anything about it?"

"Mostly he laughed it off. Initially he tried reasoning with the guy, but you can't talk to someone like that. They won't listen." She paused. "Do you think he did it?" The question was quiet. The noise of the room ebbed and flowed around us.

"It looks like it, at least for now."

She signaled the bartender for a drink. When he brought it, she lit another cigarette. "It's funny. Sig was so glad to get the appointment to the board. He thought, with his experience at Walla Walla, he could help; that he'd make a real contribution." She stopped, words giving way to reflection. It was an awkward silence.

"I understand Sig didn't drink."

She took a sip from her Chivas. "He wanted me to quit, too. There's nothing like a reformed drunk." She gave me a forlorn smile. "I would have, eventually." There was another long pause. She needed comforting and I was at a loss.

"Would you like to have dinner?" I asked at last.

She shook her head. "Not now, maybe later. I have some things I need to do first."

"How long will it take?"

"An hour or so. I'll give you a call when I finish."

She jotted my room number on the back of my card, and returned it to her pocket. We talked a while longer before she got up to leave. She held out her hand. "It was nice meeting you, Detective Beaumont. I'll see you later."

I watched her walk away, striding purposefully out of the room, a lady with places to go and people to see. It was only after she was out of sight that a wave of concern washed over me. I left money on the table and hurried after her, but she was nowhere in sight. I found a house phone and dialed her room. It rang and rang, but there was no answer.

Stopping by the desk, I asked what kind of car Mona Larson had registered. The clerk didn't bother to look at her card. "She's the one with the Harley, mister." He grinned. "Doesn't seem possible someone her size could handle one of those suckers."

I roamed through acres of parking lot to no avail. Finally I went back to my room and tried calling Ray in Pasco. No answer. I tried Mona's room several times as well, but there was still no answer. Giving up, I turned on the movie channel. I don't know when I fell asleep.

Chapter 19

A SHARP rap on the door jarred me awake. Flipping off the droning television set, I opened the door to find two uniformed police officers standing in the hallway.

"Are you J. P. Beaumont?" the first one asked, stepping uninvited through my open door. He wore gold-rimmed glasses and chewed a cud of gum with unbridled enthusiasm.

"Yes. What do you want?"

The second officer was heavyset: not fat, but with a definite paunch. "You know a lady named Mona Larson?"

"Yes, I do. What's up?"

"When's the last time you saw her?"

"I don't know. What time is it?"

The one in glasses looked at his watch. "Eight-thirty," he said, wrapping the gum around the tip of his tongue and giving it a small, interior pop.

"I saw her about six-thirty. She said she had some things to do."

"Did she say what?"

I shook my head. "No. What's going on?" I kept asking the question, but they disregarded it.

The heavyset one pulled a business card out of his inside jacket pocket and turned it over, examining both sides. I recognized it as one of my own. "Says here you're Detective Beaumont. You here in Pasco on official business?"

A twinge of uneasiness warned me something wasn't right. "No," I said after a pause. "I was at a funeral in Welton this afternoon and decided to spend the night."

"Sig Larson's funeral?" There was an unpleasant undertone to his question.

"Yes. As a matter of fact, it was."

The gum-chewer wandered over to the window. "Mind if we have a look around?"

"No. Yes. What's this all about?" I demanded, getting my back up.

"He asked you nice like," the heavyset one warned. "Now, can we look around or not?"

I retreated to the bed and sat down, more than half angry. Obviously there was some mistake. They had no business pushing me around like a common criminal. I wanted to get to the bottom of whatever it was. "Go ahead," I said, managing to control myself.

Glasses searched the whole room—under the bed, in the closet, in all the drawers, in the bathroom—while Fatso kept an eye on me, all the while fingering his nightstick. "No luggage?" Glasses asked when he finished.

"I didn't plan to spend the night."

"No, I suppose not."

"Are you going to tell me what's going on?" I felt as though I had fallen into a bad dream where things happen and no one tells you why. There wasn't much I could do about it. It was two against one. They were calling the shots.

"You got anyone who'll say where you were between six-thirty and now?"

"I already told you. I've been right here at the hotel, mostly asleep. Now tell me what the fuck is going on!"

Glasses rolled his eyes. "Isn't that what they all say, Willy? I was asleep the whole time. All by myself."

Willy grinned. "That's what they say."

"Now wait just a goddamned minute. You'd better tell me what's happening."

"You want to tell him, Joe?" Willy asked.

"Naw, you go ahead. Since he's so anxious to hear."

"Well sir," Willy said, savoring the words, "it's about this lady we found along the road a little while ago. Victim of a hit-and-run. She had your card in her pocket with a room number written on the back."

"Mona?" I asked. "Is she all right?"

"Didja hear that!" Joe exclaimed. "She's dead as a doornail, and he wants to know if she's all right. You'd better move on over to the wall. Put your hands above your head."

For a second I sat there, too stunned to move. Mona too? I

had just had a drink with her, talked to her. We were going to have dinner. Willy took a menacing step toward me. "He said move."

I was in no position to argue. I did as I was told. Willy patted me down. Removing my jacket from a chair, he discovered my shoulder holster underneath. "Why, looky here, Joe." Willy tossed my .38 to Glasses. "Read him his rights." Willy pulled a pair of handcuffs out of his pocket and held them in front of me. "Turn around, buster," he ordered. "You're under arrest."

"What the hell do you clowns think you're doing?"

"Clowns, Joe. You hear that? This renegade big-time cop from Seattle thinks we're a couple of clowns."

"You have the right to remain silent—" Joe began.

"You guys have to be shitting me. Ray Johnson used to be my partner—"

"You have the right to an attorney—"

"And your uncle George sits on the Supreme Court. Right, funnyman?" Willy sneered.

"Anything you say may be held—"

"I said turn around," Willy repeated, his words taking on an ominous edge. I turned. The handcuffs snapped shut behind me. "Did you hear your rights now, Mr. Beaumont?" He gave the cuffs a sharp yank, making sure they were fastened securely.

"I heard them."

"Did you understand them?"

"Yes."

He spun me around so I faced him. "We wouldn't want any question of abrogating your rights, now would we?"

"You asshole—" I began.

He grabbed me by the shoulder and shoved me toward the door. "Where are your car keys?"

"Find them yourself," I snapped.

"Here they are, Willy," Glasses called from the dresser.

"Bring 'em. We'll check out the car on the way." They led me handcuffed through the front lobby of the Red Lion, where several dozen women watched in openmouthed wonder.

I've arrested plenty of people in my time, but being arrested was an entirely new and painful experience. Handcuffed wrists in the small of the back make you feel humiliated and trapped and scared and guilty, even if you're not. I wanted to hide my face in my hands, to shield myself from gaping, prying eyes. I couldn't, not with my hands cuffed behind me.

I had parked the Rabbit near the front door. Now it was nowhere to be seen.

"Where is it?" Willy demanded.

"I don't know. It's gone. Somebody moved it."

Glasses and Fatso nodded at each other knowingly. "Sure they did," Willy said. "What kind of car is it?"

"A Rabbit, a red, rented Rabbit."

"Sounds about right," Willy said. "Bring the car, Joe. We'll drive around through the parking lot and see if Mr. Beaumont here can remember where he left it. Musta been driving in his sleep."

Maybe the reason cops hate reporters and vice versa is that we're so much alike. The same kind of questioning minds end up in both professions. The difference lies in what we do with the answers.

It came as no surprise that the same thought process that had brought me to the Red Lion in search of Mona Larson would do the same for a reporter. Fate alone dictated that the reporter should be Maxwell Cole. He arrived just as Willy shoved me into the backseat of a patrol car, blue lights flashing. Cole almost walked past us, but then he spied me. "J. P." he yelped. "Hey, what's going on?"

I prayed we'd leave right then, but we didn't. Joe meandered through the well-lit parking lot, searching for my car. By the time we located the Rabbit in the back row of the lot, a noisy cortege of people had formed behind us. "That's it," I said, nodding toward the Rabbit.

Joe left the patrol car idling and sauntered over to it. Through the open door, I could hear a chorus of questions. Glasses ignored them. He knelt in front of the car and examined the front bumper, then he stopped long enough to peer into all the windows. He hurried back to the patrol car. "Hand me the pliers, Willy."

With my key, Glasses unlocked the door on the rider's side. He used the pliers to lift the latch and open the door. I was grateful for that. At least he wasn't disturbing my evidence. He leaned into the Rabbit, then straightened and came back to the patrol car. "Call for a backup, Willy. Tell them to get someone to impound the car while we drag our friend here off to jail."

"Why? What have you got?"

"Remember the desk clerk told us she was wearing a bunch of Indian jewelry?"

"Yeah."

"Looks like it's all there, and the front end is smashed all to shit."

"That's impossible! I tell you, I've been asleep in my room since seven o'clock."

"We've got you dead to rights, mister," Glasses said.

"I swear I didn't do it."

"Save it for the judge," he said.

We waited in the car interminable minutes until a second patrol car with flashing blue lights and a wailing siren worked its way through the onlookers.

By the time we got to the station, there was a crowd of reporters milling outside, with Maxwell Cole leading the pack. Many of the out-of-town newsies had decided to stay over, thus gaining admittance to the third media event of the day. When Willy opened the door, I didn't want to get out. My mouth was dry; my knees shook, not with fear so much as helpless rage and indignation.

"Get out," Willy commanded.

I didn't, couldn't. Willy grabbed me by the shoulder and bodily pulled me from the car. Again I wanted a shield, a sack, a cloak of invisibility—anything to lock out the eyes and the cameras and the voices and the nightmare. Willy and Joe herded me into the station and handed me over to a woebegone detective named Barnes.

Barnes struck me as a detective's detective, an old-time cop who used common sense as opposed to some computerized procedural manual. He brought me a Styrofoam cup of bitter coffee. "They read you your rights?" I nodded. Over his voice, in the background, I could hear the demanding questions of the reporters who were laying siege to the Pasco City Police Department.

Barnes cocked his ear as if listening to the uproar outside. "You want to tell me what happened?"

How could I tell him what happened when I didn't know? Mona Larson was dead, but I didn't know how or why or where. "Where do you want me to start?"

"How long did you know Mrs. Larson?"

"I just met her this afternoon."

"At her husband's funeral?"

"No, later, when she came back to the hotel, after the funeral."

"You followed her?" It was a leading question.

"Yes."

"You went to her room?"

"No. I called her, from my room. We met for a drink."

"Why?"

"To talk."

"About?"

"Sig, her husband."

"You knew him, then?"

The questions were getting worse. So were the answers. "No. Not until after he was murdered."

Barnes' eyes glittered with that now-we're-getting-somewhere look. I recognized it. I've used it myself during interrogations. "After?"

"I heard a woman screaming from my room at the Rosario Resort on Orcas Island. I checked it out and found Ginger Watkins with Sig Larson's body. I've been working unofficially with Hal Huggins, the detective from Friday Harbor. Call and ask him. It's the San Juan County Sheriff's Department."

"I probably will give him a call," Barnes said reasonably. "After we finish here. So you met Mrs. Larson for a drink, in the bar?"

"Yes. I think it's called the Star Light Lounge."

"And you talked about?"

"I don't remember exactly . . . her marriage, Welton, her stepchildren. Lots of things. Then she had to leave."

"Did you go with her?"

"No."

"Follow her?"

"No. I told you, I went back to my room for a nap."

"Come on, Detective Beaumont. Let's get to the bottom of this. Did you and Mrs. Larson quarrel about something?" His position solidified. Up till then, I had answered his questions in a warily cooperative fashion, but something in his manner shifted, warning me. Before, I had believed we were on the same side. It was now clear that we weren't.

"Where's Ray Johnson?" I asked.

"The Chief? What business is that of yours?"

"Call him," I said flatly. "Ray and I used to be partners on the force in Seattle."

I could tell my words made some impact. Barnes got up and walked across the room, hands deep in his pockets. "Mrs. Larson was deliberately run down by a man driving a red car. Witnesses saw a Rabbit leaving the scene. Aren't you driving a red Rabbit?"

I didn't answer. He walked back across the room and looked down at me accusingly. "So what have you got against the parole board, Detective Beaumont? Did they let out a crook you thought should have stayed locked up?"

"I'm trying to tell you—"

"You've been on the scene of two recent homicides before this one." He picked up a newspaper that had been lying face-down on his desk. "Not only that, Mrs. Watkins died in your car, a red Porsche. How come you like red so much?"

"Call Ray Johnson, for chrissake! He'll vouch for me."

"The chief is unavailable. He and his wife are celebrating their twenty-fifth wedding anniversary with a second honeymoon in Spokane. I'm not calling him for anybody."

"What about Hal Huggins, the detective over in Friday Harbor?" I struggled to restrain my temper.

Barnes smiled indulgently, as if I were a not-too-bright kid who had screwed up some simple directions. "If you want to call somebody, I'd suggest you call your attorney, not a character witness. You want to use the phone?"

"No, I don't want to use the phone. I want out."

His smile disappeared. "I don't believe you understand, Mr. Beaumont. You're being booked on an open charge of murder."

The words filled the room, sucking out the atmosphere. It was suddenly difficult to breathe. "You're right," I said, caving in, "I want to use the phone." I tried Peters first. No dice. He was in The Dalles, with Ames, for the custody hearing. I didn't know where they were staying.

It's easy to panic in a situation like that, to decide that you're totally isolated and there's no way to get help. I finally dialed Ida Newell's number, collect. Ida, my next-door neighbor, is a retired schoolteacher, the proverbial little old lady in tennis shoes. She collects crossword puzzles for me and mothers me as much as I'll tolerate. It was ten-thirty, but she stays up late to watch the news.

"Why, Beau," she said pleasantly, once the operator connected us. "Where are you?"

I didn't entirely answer that question. "I need your help, Ida. I've got to get in touch with my partner and my attorney. I won't be able to call out after this. Could you please find them and give them a message?"

"Certainly." Thankfully, she didn't ask any questions.

"Their names are Ron Peters and Ralph Ames. They're staying somewhere in The Dalles."

"Where?"

"I don't know."

"Look here, Beau, if you don't know where they're staying, how do you expect me to find them?"

I wanted to bully her to action, but I fought to keep impatience out of my voice. "They'll be at the best hotel or motel in town. Try the phone book, the Yellow Pages."

Ida sounded dubious. "If I find them, what do I say?"

"Have Ames call me." I glanced at Barnes, who nodded reluctantly. I read her the number off the phone.

"That's all?"

"Tell him it's urgent."

"Well, all right."

"Thanks, Ida. You've no idea how much I appreciate this."

I put down the phone. Twenty minutes later, after fingerprints and a mug shot, I was locked up in a cell. Out of deference to my being a police officer, they gave me a private cell.

It was small consolation.

Chapter 20

I SLEPT. I don't know how, but I did. Maybe when you're up against something you can do absolutely nothing about, sleep is Mother Nature's balm for the insoluble problem. I slept, blissfully ignorant of what went on around me. Everyone told me about it. Later.

Through the wonders of modern telecommunications, old J. P. Beaumont hit the eleven o'clock news on every major television station in the Pacific Northwest—Spokane, Seattle, Portland, and Boise. The lead story was all about Seattle's rogue cop being booked into Pasco City Jail on an open charge of murder. It made for very splashy journalism and pushed Sig Larson's funeral back to just before Sports.

As far as the press was concerned, my guilt was a foregone conclusion. Not everyone had access to the kind of material Maxwell Cole did. They had to content themselves with only the immediate story. Max sat down and composed an in-depth piece that he transferred by modem to the *P.I.* in downtown Seattle. He dredged it all out of his fertile memory—the kid in the alley when I was a rookie, Anne Corley, Ginger dead in my Porsche. His column would have done the *National Enquirer* proud.

I slept.

Peters saw the story on a Portland station in The Dalles. He dialed Ames' number and found it busy. Ida Newell had just reached Ames at the Papadera Inn, The Dalles' only Best Western motel. Peters came to Ames' room while Ralph was still talking to Ida. Before the news was over, Ames and Peters were checked out of their rooms and driving hell-bent-for-leather to Tri Cities.

I sawed logs. It's called the sleep of the just.

In the bridal suite of Spokane's Ridpath Hotel, Evie Johnson fell asleep while Ray congratulated himself on his performance, not bad for twenty-five years of marriage. He could still hold his own in the bedroom department.

With Evie drowsing contentedly beside him, he switched the TV on low. He'd watch the news for a couple of minutes. He woke Evie scrambling out of bed. She sat up as he pulled on his clothes.

"Where are you going?" she demanded.

"I've gotta go, hon," he said. "You stay here. I'll leave the car so you can come home tomorrow."

"Why? What's wrong?"

"Someone back home lost his marbles and arrested Beau for first-degree murder."

"Can't you call?"

"I can't knock heads over the phone."

By the time Ray was ready, Evie had called the airport and

discovered that the last plane for Tri Cities left at ten fifty-five. She dressed quickly, throwing things into the suitcase. "I'll go with you," she told him. "There's no sense in staying here alone."

And still I slept.

San Juan County Sheriff Bill Yates woke Hal Huggins out of a sound sleep. "What the hell is going on?"

"How should I know?"

"I rented a float plane. He'll put you down on the Columbia. Get over to Pasco and find out."

So Hal Huggins, too, began a midnight trek to Tri Cities while I slept on, dreaming I was slicing off one of Maxwell Cole's gaudy ties with a huge pinking shears. No wonder I didn't want to wake up.

Ray hit town first. He came roaring into the jail, waking everybody, including a couple of drunks in the next cell who complained bitterly about being disturbed. "Why the hell didn't someone call me? I could have told you . . ." he shouted over his shoulder as he came down the hall. I could see Barnes hovering at a discreet distance.

"Come on, come on," he growled as the jailer fumbled with the key. "Open up, you nitwit!"

I swung off my cot and slipped into the plastic slippers that had replaced my shoes. I was wearing a bright orange jail jumpsuit that was more than slightly too short in the crotch and, as a consequence, more than moderately uncomfortable.

"Where the hell are his clothes?" Ray rumbled at Barnes. "Go get 'em."

Barnes disappeared down the hall. Ray hurried into the cell as the door opened. "Are you all right, Beau?"

"Sure, Ray. I'm fine. It was a mistake, that's all."

"Why the hell didn't you call me?"

"They said you were celebrating your twenty-fifth anniversary and couldn't be disturbed."

"I'm disturbed, all right! You can bet your ass I'm disturbed!"

Ray hustled me down the hall and into a restroom where Barnes brought me my clothes. "How did you hear about it?" I asked.

"It was on the news. At eleven."

"Where, in Spokane?"

"That's where I saw it, but I'll bet it was all over. You should see the mob of reporters outside right now. The place is crawling.''

''Great,'' I muttered. ''That's just great.''

He led me into his office, a place not much bigger than the cubbyhole the two of us had shared in the Public Safety Building in Seattle. This one boasted a polished wooden desk, not the institutional gray/green metal of Seattle P.D.

''Where is Evie?'' I asked. ''I'll bet she's pissed.''

Ray grinned. ''She was until she found out it was you. She drove back with me. Evangeline always had a soft spot in her heart for you, Beau. There's no accounting for taste. You hungry?'' he asked.

Once he reminded me, I was actually far beyond hunger. ''Starved,'' I told him.

He picked up the phone and dialed a number. I heard a phone ringing somewhere outside. ''Go pick up a couple of chili-burgers from Marie's,'' he barked into the phone. ''Tell her they're for me, with extra cheese and onions. And make a new pot of coffee. We're going to be a while.''

He leaned back in his chair and folded his hands across his gradually widening girth. ''What the hell is going on?''

Partway into my story, there was a knock on the door. A pretty young woman entered, carrying two steaming platters of chiliburgers. She left us with them and went out, returning with two freshly brewed cups of coffee. ''Thanks, LeAnn,'' Ray murmured as she set a mug in front of him. LeAnn flashed him a shy smile.

''See there?'' He grinned once the door closed behind her. ''Around here I get some respect.''

The two platters contained burgers smothered with thick chili, melted cheese, and chunks of chopped onions. Ray took a bite, followed by a sip of coffee. ''Reminds me of the Doghouse,'' he said. ''Sometimes I really miss that old place.''

The Doghouse is a restaurant a few blocks from my condo in Seattle. Ray and I frequented it the whole time we were partners. I go there less often now that Peters and I work together.

I was ravenous. We had barely made a dent in the two platters when we heard a commotion outside. Ray's phone rang. ''What is it?'' He listened, then held the phone away from his ear and covered the mouthpiece.

''Somebody named Ames. Says he's your attorney.''

"Ames! Ida must have found him."

"You want to see him?"

"Sure."

"And a guy named Peters?"

"Him too."

LeAnn opened the door. Ames strode purposefully into the room, talking as he came. "Look here, Chief Johnson, I demand to see my client at once!" Ames stopped abruptly when he spotted me sitting with a plate on top of Ray's desk scarfing down chili-burger as fast as I could shovel. Peters, directly behind Ames, almost rear-ended him.

"What the hell!" Peters exclaimed. The looks on their faces would have been comical if they hadn't been so serious. They had broken speed laws in two states, driving through the night to rescue me from jail, only to find me happily chowing down with the Chief of Police.

I stood up, wiping my mouth with a napkin. "Ralph, I'd like you to meet my former partner, Chief Ray Johnson. Ray, this is Ralph Ames, my attorney, and my new partner, Detective Ron Peters."

"You guys hungry?" Ray asked, indicating the half-consumed chili-burgers. "We could order a couple more. It would only take a minute."

Peters stifled a shudder of disgust and shook his head. Ames said a polite "no thank you" and got straight to the point. "What's going on?"

So I started the story again, from the beginning. I had reached almost the same point where Ames and Peters had made their entrance when the phone rang again. "No lie? He's here?" Ray said. "Send him in."

Hal Huggins came in. Ray showered him with the effusive cordiality one reserves for a late arrival at a class reunion. Once pleasantries were exchanged, the story reverted to square one. I was beginning to wish I had taped it on the first go down so I could turn on a machine and listen to it, rather than repeating it again and again. When I finally finished, there was a long silence.

Huggins spoke first. "I didn't figure him to be that smart," he said.

"Who?" I demanded. Obviously, Huggins knew something the rest of us didn't.

"Wilson. Don Wilson."

"Why him?" Peters asked.

"The calendar," Hal answered. "Ginger Watkins' calendar. Beau found it in a garbage can up at Rosario Sunday night. Wilson's prints are all over it."

"Where'd you get a copy of his prints?" I asked.

"From the F.B.I. Wilson served in the army."

Ray looked dubious. "How'd you get an F.B.I. report back so fast? Those things take months."

"You forget. Parole board members are political appointees. Governor Reynolds placed a call to the White House, and the F.B.I. found his prints in short order."

"So it is Wilson after all," I mused.

"Looks that way," Huggins agreed. "I'm getting a search warrant today." He turned on me. "You're sure he wasn't at the funeral?"

"I'm sure. Believe me, I looked."

Huggins was thinking aloud. "I wonder if we could request any of the television videotape and have someone go over it looking for him."

"Could be," Ray agreed. "Some of them are pretty good about it."

Hal continued. "He had to be there, must have followed you to the Red Lion. He saw you meet Mona Larson and decided to add one more notch to his scorecard. And frame you in the process."

I thought back on my drive into Pasco. I could remember no cars on the road behind me, but I hadn't been looking. I shook my head. "I didn't see any," I said. "But why frame me? It doesn't make sense."

"Muddy the water a little," Huggins suggested. Peters nodded in agreement.

"Had you told anyone that you planned to stay overnight in Pasco?" Ray's homicide instincts were still good, even though he had kicked himself upstairs.

"No. How could I have told someone? I didn't make up my mind until I was almost here and decided to see you."

"Either he followed you or knew where Mona was staying," Peters put in. "How did you find out?"

"I asked one of the limo drivers over in Welton."

"And they told you?"

"They didn't act as if it was any big secret."

The phone rang again. Ray answered. "Put it through," he said. He switched on the speakerphone on his desk.

"Is this Chief Johnson?" a voice asked.

"Yes."

"This is Lee Hawkins. I'm an aide to Governor Reynolds. We're just confirming that you have a suspect in custody in the deaths of Mona and Sig Larson."

"We do not have a suspect."

"But we were told—" There was a pause. "What about Ginger Watkins? We understand her death has been reclassified as a homicide."

"I repeat. We do not have a suspect in custody. In fact, I'll be calling a press conference at seven." Ray paused, turning his chair to consult an old pendulum clock that hung on the wall behind him. In Roman numerals the clock said the time was six-eighteen. "I'll be issuing the Pasco Police Department's official apology to Detective J. P. Beaumont."

"But the paper said—" Hawkins began.

"The paper's wrong," Ray interjected. "They often are, you know. Detective Beaumont is not a suspect in any of the cases, and we have no one else in custody."

"But the governor is ready to announce that he is withdrawing protection from the parole board."

"He's better retract that withdrawal," Ray said into the phone. "In fact, if I were him, I think I'd extend protection to all parole board family members as well."

I waved a hand to get Ray's attention. "Ask him about the victim/witness protection program."

Ray shot me a questioning look, then shrugged. "Someone here is asking about the victim/witness protection program." I mouthed my question to Ray, and he repeated it into the phone. "Someone wants to know when it will be ready."

Hawkins knew exactly what we were talking about. "Tell him not until the next legislative session convenes in January."

"Is that all you need to know?" Ray asked me.

I nodded. Ray put down the phone. "What's that all about?"

"Maxwell Cole said Wilson thought an announcement on that program was imminent."

"Doesn't sound like it to me," Ray replied, getting up and opening the door. "LeAnn, let the members of the press know that I'll be holding a press conference at seven A.M. In the city council chamber.''

He turned back inside the room, grinning. "You know," he said, "I think I'm actually going to enjoy this one."

Chapter 21

WE did enjoy the press conference. For once we caught the media absolutely flat-footed. When I walked to the podium with Ray, you could have heard a pin drop.

Ray Johnson went straight to the microphones as naturally as if he had been doing it all his life. In ten months he had indeed become a police chief rather than a homicide detective. He was totally at ease.

"Before I issue my statement, I want to introduce you to some guests. On my right is Detective J. P. Beaumont of Seattle P.D. Next to him is Ralph Ames, Mr. Beaumont's personal attorney. Next to him is Detective Hal Huggins of the San Juan County Sheriff's Department.

"What I have to say is short and sweet. The City of Pasco and its Police Department deeply regret that Detective Beaumont here was mistakenly arrested as a suspect in the murder of Mona Larson. We wish to express our sincere apology for any inconvenience this may have caused.

"We are pursuing several leads in the Larson case and are, in fact, working on a major suspect. I repeat, Detective Beaumont is not that suspect. My understanding is that, after consulting his attorney, Detective Beaumont has agreed not to press false-arrest charges against this jurisdiction. However, some legal action may be contemplated. I believe Mr. Ames will be speaking to that issue. Mr. Ames?" He yielded the platform to Ralph.

Ralph Ames looks unassuming. He dresses conservatively and well, but he's a real tiger in negotiations or in court. He stepped to the bank of microphones.

"Thank you, Chief Johnson. Yes, I have advised my client

that false-arrest proceedings would be ill-advised. However, in the next few days we will be reviewing all media coverage of my client's arrest to determine whether we have grounds for defamation of character or libel suits in conjunction with media treatment of the incident. It's possible some of the reports were in fact libelous.''

Ames sat down, leaving the hall in utter silence. I happened to be looking directly at Maxwell Cole when Ames made his pronouncement. Max blanched visibly, his complexion turning a pukey shade of green.

Ray resumed the microphone. ''Any questions?''

There were none immediately. No one was eager to leap into the breach. Eventually, one brave soul near the back tentatively raised his hand. ''Do you believe there's a connection between Mona Larson's death and that of her husband?''

I could see Ray's smile coming a mile away. ''No comment,'' he said.

''I understand the governor has now extended State Patrol protection to all family members of the parole board as well as to board members themselves. Is that true?''

''''You'll have to ask Governor Reynolds about that.''

''Can you tell us why Detective Huggins is here?''

Ray turned to Hal. ''Hal,'' he said, ''would you care to answer that?''

We were having a good time. I could see Peters in the back of the room with a broad grin plastered across his face.

''No comment,'' Hal said.

That got the message across. The reporters could see we were having fun at their expense. There were no more questions.

''Well then,'' Ray announced, ''I guess we're finished.''

We left the council chambers together. Back in Ray's office, we couldn't help chortling. We milled around for a few minutes, deciding on the next move. Ames and Peters had been up all night; they were worn out. They wanted to use my room at the Red Lion for a nap. My rented car had been impounded, pending investigation. The crime lab agreed to release it to Avis when they were done with it.

Peters left Ames and me in the station lobby and walked two blocks to get his Datsun. For the first time I noticed how haggard and drawn Ames looked. He was weary beyond words. ''You look like hell,'' I said.

"You wouldn't win any prizes yourself," he returned, his voice cracking with exhaustion, "now that his press conference adrenaline had worn off." He flopped down in one of the brown leather waiting-room chairs, resting his head on the wall behind him.

"We lost." His voice was low. I almost didn't hear him. It took a minute for me to realize what he was saying. At last I tumbled. "The custody hearing?"

He nodded. "We got an old-fashioned, dyed-in-the-wool conservative judge who figures only mothers are fit to raise children. No matter what."

I dropped into the chair beside him, chagrined that I hadn't given the custody hearing a moment's thought. I had never seen Ames so down. He's usually the steady one, the eye of the hurricane.

"I'm sorry," I murmured. "How's Peters taking it?" I felt responsible. Peters had pretty much given up the idea of ever getting his kids back until I butted in, encouraged him to fight for them, and told him we'd turn the problem over to Ames. I had watched Peters' hopes rise as the custody hearing neared. Now all that hope had come to nothing.

"Not well," Ames said. He looked at me closely. "Have you ever seen those two girls of his?"

I shook my head. "He was divorced long before we started working together."

"They're cute as buttons, both of them, and they were ecstatic to see him."

"What happens now?"

"I don't know. I need to think about it. The New Dawn attorney made a couple of broad hints, but I'm not sure he's on the level."

Peters pulled up outside and honked. We went out. Ames crawled into the backseat while I slipped into the front with Peters. While we had been involved with the reporters, his face had been animated, alive. Now a morose mask covered his handsome features.

"I'm sorry about the hearing," I said.

He put the car in gear. "Win some, lose some," he said, feigning nonchalance. It didn't work.

"But the girls are all right?" I insisted.

"Sure," he flared. "They can't have shots because shots show a lack of faith. They live on a diet or brown rice and fruit. Milk is a luxury. They have it once a week. On Sundays." Peters' anger played itself out. He fell silent.

"So what do we do now, coach?" I asked, turning to Ames in the backseat.

He shook his head. "I don't know. We took our best shot. I'll have to see what other avenues are open." Ames didn't elaborate, and silence lengthened in the little car.

"Thanks for coming to get me, you guys," I said. "Both of you."

"It's okay," Peters responded. "My turn will come."

Peters and Ames went up to my room to get some sleep. I was wide-awake. I went down to the lobby. On one of the lobby chairs I found an abandoned *P.I.* Curiosity got the better of me, overcoming my natural aversion to newspapers. I wanted to see what had made Maxwell Cole turn green when Ames mentioned libel suits. By picking up a discarded paper, I could read the column without giving them the satisfaction of paying for it.

Max used the words "rogue cop" over and over. He might have coined the expression himself. The story didn't contain much that was different from the other garbage he's written about me over the years, except for the Mona Larson allegations.

I had a feeling this was one instance where Max's retraction would receive prominent coverage. If I were in his shoes and thought Ralph Ames was coming after me with a libel suit, I'd be looking for cover.

I did pick up one other piece of useful information from reading the newspaper. Ginger Watkins' funeral would be held on Thursday afternoon. No time or place was given, but included in the brief announcement was Ginger Watkins' father's name. He was listed as a resident of Centralia. Tucking that tidbit away in the memory bank, I worked the crossword puzzle in ten minutes flat. For me, that was something of a record.

My presence in the lobby created a continuing stir. Mary Kay ladies sporting May Kay nametags and Mary Kay faces wandered by, staring openly. When I finished the puzzle, I approached the desk and asked if I could use a house phone to bill some calls to my room. The clerk, a sweet young thing with long blond hair, dropped her pen when I announced who I was.

"I'll have to check," she stammered, retreating into a back office. She returned a few minutes later. "Mr. Dixon says that will be fine," she gulped.

I smiled. "If anyone asks, tell them I was framed."

She nodded, wide-eyed, and said, "Thank you." She was so flustered she forgot to tell me to have a nice day.

I gave the hotel operator my room information, and asked Centralia Information for Tom Lander's number.

"The number is 763-4427."

I hung up and dialed. There was no answer. I dialed Information again. I'm a longtime believer in the old phone-factory adage, "Let your fingers do the walking," except mine walk straight to directory assistance. This time I asked for a Union 76 station. Again I dialed.

A man answered, an older man whose voice was deep and whose speech was slow. "Tom's Seventy-six. Tom speaking."

"My name is J. P. Beaumont. I'm a friend of Ginger's. I wanted to let you know how sorry I am."

"Thanks." There was a pause. I could hear him struggling to gain control. "It was your car she was driving, wasn't it?" he asked.

I was surprised that he recognized my name. "That's right," I told him. "I understand the funeral is tomorrow afternoon."

"Yes," he said. "Two o'clock."

"I tried calling Darrell but was told the services will be private. I was sorry to hear that. I'd very much like to attend. Do you think that's possible?"

"Far as I'm concerned. I don't know where those characters get off making it private. Funerals should have lots of people. It shows folks care."

"Where is it? The paper didn't say."

"Two o'clock in the Congregational Church downtown. In the chapel."

"Could I come as your guest?"

"Sure."

"I'll meet you at the church. About one forty-five."

"How will I know you?"

"I'll be able to find you," I told him.

"If anybody tries to stop you, tell 'em Tom Lander said you could come."

The next call was to a florist in the Denny Regrade near my apartment. I ordered a bouquet of flowers for Ginger Watkins from Sig Larson. While I was at it, I called a Pasco florist and ordered flowers for Mona Larson, too. I told the clerk to check with the Pasco Police Department to see where and when they should be sent.

She took my credit-card number and wanted to know what to put on the card.

"Sign the card 'A friend,' " I told her, and let it go at that.

I hoped like hell it would be the last batch of flowers I'd be ordering for a while.

Chapter 22

IT was pouring rain the morning of Ginger Watkins' funeral, the kind of hard, driving rain that demands umbrellas and confirms for unfortunate tourists that everything they say about Seattle's weather is true.

I rummaged through a closet searching for my one battered umbrella, a fold-up relic with two broken ribs and a bent handle. I hardly ever use it. Seattle's rain is usually no more than a misty drip, a dry drizzle that seldom merits use of what Seattlites fondly refer to as "bumbershoots," otherwise known as umbrellas.

Ames settled into the Westin Hotel. He had work to do and didn't want to be disturbed. Peters went back to the department where one of our Battered Wife/Dead Husband cases was about to come to trial. He spent the day locked up in a series of depositions.

J. P. Beaumont, still on vacation, was left to his own devices. I stopped by to thank Ida Newell for tracking down Ames and Peters.

"I was glad to," she assured me. "Why, the way they wrote you up in the paper was criminal. Are you going to sue them? They deserve it, especially that columnist fellow."

"Ames is looking into it," I told her. "I will if he tells me."

Later, I went to get a haircut. Virgil has been my barber ever since I moved to the city. I've followed him from his first little hole-in-the-wall shop to gradually more prosperous surroundings.

Now he's located in an attractive brick rehab on the corner of Third and Vine.

Busy, Virgil waved me into a chair to wait. "It's about time you came in here," he griped. "Saw you on TV, and I says to Betty, I says, wouldn't cha know he'd go and get himself on TV when he needs a haircut? Pray God he doesn't tell who cuts his hair, know what I mean?"

I knew exactly what he meant. I was long overdue. Getting haircuts was one of the things I had neglected in the previous months of malaise.

Virgil finished with a retiree from the Grosvenor House and beckoned me into the chair. "Saved all those articles from the paper for you," he said. "Figured if you was out of town, you might not get 'em, you know?"

"Thanks, Virgil."

"Understand your car got wrecked, too."

"They're working on it up at Orcas. I guess it'll be all right, eventually."

He clipped away, humming a country-western tune under his breath. I know enough about music to know he hummed very badly. When he finished, it was only eleven. I walked over to Seventh and stopped at the Doghouse, more for the company than the coffee. Doghouse regulars greeted me as a celebrity. After all, the idea of a cop gone bad is a real attention-grabber. I sat in a back corner booth and did some serious thinking.

About Sig and Ginger and Mona. I had never met Sig while he was alive, but his death had profoundly affected me. Ginger and Mona I knew briefly, only a matter of hours, before they too were dead. The three deaths plagued me, weighed me down. I kept going back to Mona and Ginger. Different, yes, but both young and vital, and both cut down. Something about the two of them nagged at the back of my mind, but I couldn't put my finger on it. The harder I tried to capture it, the more elusive it became.

The fingerprints accused Don Wilson, but where was he? How was he outmaneuvering all efforts to find him? Was he operating alone or with help? These were questions without answers; or if the answers were there, I couldn't see them.

I ambled back to my apartment and made myself a peanut butter sandwich. Sometimes, out of respect for Peters, I occasionally add sprouts to the peanut butter, but the plastic bag of sprouts in the vegetable drawer of my refrigerator had deteriorated to a vile greenish goo. With the sandwich and a glass of milk, I settled in my recliner and dialed the San Juan County Sheriff's Department.

I more than half expected to be told that Huggins was in Seattle attending a funeral. Instead, he answered.

"Hal? Beau here. You coming to Seattle for Ginger Watkins' funeral?"

"I was going to ask you to go, Beau. I'm up to my neck around here. Think you can swing it?"

"Sure. Homer tried to keep me away, saying Senator Watkins wanted a small, private ceremony, but I got my name on the guest list anyway."

"How'd you manage that?"

"Her father invited me. As his guest."

Hal clicked his tongue. "Homer won't like that." I was sure that was true.

"I take it you've had a couple run-ins with the old man?"

"Like running into a brick wall. I've tried to talk to the husband, and he's stonewalled me at every turn."

"Homer has?"

"Yes, goddammit. Homer."

"Any word on Wilson?"

"Hell no."

"Keep me posted if you hear anything, Hal."

"Sure thing. The search warrant didn't come through yesterday. I'm hoping for this afternoon. And Beau?"

"What?"

"You do the same. If anything turns up at the funeral, give me a call."

I dressed and walked down Fifth to University. The Congregational Church is located at the corner of Sixth and University. The tiny chapel at the south end of the building pinch-hits as a downtown Catholic chapel for weekday noontime business Masses. Ecumenism is alive and well and living in Seattle.

Taking up a position in the lobby of the Park Place building across the street, I watched as people arrived or were dropped off at the church. The first black limo accompanied by two state patrolmen deposited Homer and his illustrious son, Senator Darrell Watkins. The second limo, also with an armed guard, brought Governor Reynolds.

When the third, unattended by official motorcycles dropped off an older, nondescript man who paused uncertainly on the sidewalk, I left my vantage across the street and approached him.

"Are you Tom Lander?" I asked.

"Mr. Beaumont?" he returned, his tone doubtful.

"Yes." Relief passed over his face. We shook hands. He looked down at his old-fashioned suit and dusted an imaginary fleck of lint from his arm.

"Big cities make me nervous," he said uncomfortably.

Homer materialized out of nowhere. "Hello, Tom," he said, elbowing me aside. "They're ready for us now." He scowled at me, trying to place me. "This is a private service, Mr.—"

"Beaumont," I supplied.

"It's all right, Homer," Tom said. "He's with me."

Homer Watkins gave Tom a constrained nod. "Very well," he said, walking stiffly toward the church. Tom Lander and I followed. The chapel couldn't have held more than forty people. An usher showed Tom to a front-row seat, while I took one near the door.

As people came in, I realized Peters would have recognized the political personalities from their pictures. I was an outsider, with no program or scorecard. My only hope of identifying the various guests was to lay hands on the guest book in the vestibule.

I did recognize the parole board, however. Led by Madame Bowdeen, they appeared far more nervous than they had been in Welton. Pressure was taking its toll. Had I been in their shoes, I would have been nervous, too. Looking around, however, I could have assured them with reasonable accuracy that Don Wilson was nowhere to be seen.

A young, bearded minister conducted the service in a smooth, professional way, telling us that Ginger Watkins was a person who had found herself in service to others. His comments made me hope that maybe he had at least a passing acquaintance with the lady.

As the eulogy began, my eyes were drawn to Darrell Watkins' heaving shoulders. He sat in the front row head bowed, silent sobs wracking his body. Next to him Tom Lander reached over and laid a consoling hand across his grieving son-in-law's shoulder.

I can stand anything but hypocrisy. Darrell was making an obvious play for sympathy, and Tom Lander fell for it—comforting the asshole who had screwed around on his daughter the whole time they were married, who had never bothered to give her the smallest satisfaction in lovemaking, who had kept her locked in a confining, stifling marriage, trotting her out on command when his rising political star demanded the display of a pretty wife.

It put a lump in my throat to realize I had given Ginger more pleasure by accident than that whining bastard had in eighteen years of marriage. I didn't hear the rest of the service. I seethed, watching Darrell's bitter, remorseful, crocodile tears. Too little too late. When the pallbearers carried the white coffin out the door, Darrell followed, his face contorted with anguish, supported on one side by Homer and on the other by Tom.

"That son of a bitch," I muttered to myself. I don't think anyone heard me.

Outside, people milled on the sidewalk, waiting for the funeral cortege to form and lead us to Woodlawn Cemetery. I paused as long as I could over the guest book, mentally noting as many names as possible. Then I waited by Tom's limo, expecting to tell him good-bye. Instead, he asked me to come along, to ride to the cemetery with him.

I didn't particularly want to go, but it was hard to refuse the old man. He was so isolated and alone that, in the end, I went.

We rode in silence. I was still seething over the funeral, and Tom seemed lost in thought. I stayed in the car during the graveside ceremony, refusing to be an audience to any more theatrics on Darrell's part. I used the time to jot down as many names as I could remember from the guest book. Once we started downtown, I had myself fairly well in hand.

"What now?" I asked, initiating conversation.

Tom shrugged. "Darrell said I was welcome to come over to the house, but I don't know. I don't feel comfortable with all those mucky-mucks."

"Do you know most of those people?" I asked.

"No."

"How about a cup of coffee before you decide?"

He seemed to welcome the delay. He nodded. "That would be real nice."

The limo driver raised a disapproving eyebrow when I dismissed him, telling him to drop us at the Doghouse. I knew Tom would be far more at home there than in the rarefied atmosphere of the Four Seasons-Olympic or the Westin. He settled gratefully into a booth and smiled when the waitress, calling me by name, brought a coffee pot with the menus.

"I guess even big-city folks can be friendly," he said.

"This is my neighborhood, Tom. I live just a few blocks from here."

We both ordered coffee. I watched Tom shovel three teaspoons of sugar into his cup. "How did you know Ginger?" he asked, stirring absently.

"I only met her the day before she died," I said quietly, "but she helped me, more than I can say. She talked me through a problem I had been avoiding for months. I had to go today. I owed her."

"Ginger was like that," he said. He smiled sadly. "Always ready to help the other guy, always a friend in need. She was the kind of kid who dragged home broken-winged birds and expected me to fix them." He paused. "They mostly died," he added. He stared disconsolately into his cup. "Did you know about the drinking?" he asked.

His question jarred me. "Yes."

"I thought she had beaten it. Sig Larson helped her. What made her start again?"

"I don't know." I didn't have a clue. I ached for him as he pondered Ginger's death. His child's death. Why had she died drunk? Someone had neglected to tell him that her death had been reclassified as a homicide, and I figured it wasn't my place to tell him. That was up to Hal Huggins.

"There was some gossip about them, you know," Tom continued, "Sig and Ginger. But I never put any store in it. Ginger wasn't like that."

"No," I agreed. "I'm sure she wasn't." The topic made me very uneasy. "Did you know she intended to file for a divorce?"

"She wouldn't have," he answered with firm conviction. "She might have threatened, to get Darrell to shape up, but she wouldn't have left him. We Landers hang in there. It's a family tradition."

I wanted to say that Ginger had hung in there more than long enough but I didn't. That would have been kicking him while he was down. Besides, it would have given away too much about Ginger and J. P. Beaumont. Better to let sleeping dogs lie. As far as Tom Lander was concerned, Ginger Watkins and I had been just friends. Nothing more.

"Do you want to go to the house?" I asked.

"Would you come along?" he countered.

He needed an ally, and I was it. "Why not?" I said, rising. "Between the two of us, we should be able to handle that bunch."

We took a cab to the motel where Tom was staying, then we drove to Darrell Watkins' Capitol Hill mansion in a GMC pickup with "Tom's Union 76" emblazoned on the door.

Chapter 23

THE Watkins mansion sits atop Capitol Hill with a spectacular view of downtown Seattle and Puget Sound. At the base of the hill, Interstate 5 bisects the city. As we rounded the circular driveway and drove past a gurgling fountain, I could imagine Homer and Darrell sipping cocktails and watching the freeway turn to a parking lot each evening as commuters tried to go home.

"Who lives here?" I asked.

"Homer used to," Tom said, "but now he's moved into a condominium."

"This is where Ginger lived, then?"

"For about a year," Tom answered.

The mansion itself was a spacious white colonial, set in a manicured, parklike setting. By the time we arrived, the drive was already teeming with a variety of trendy late-model vehicles. Ginger had described the last few years as a struggle for financial survival. That was why she had gone to work for the parole board. These surroundings gave no hint of encroaching poverty.

"They bought this from Homer?"

Tom shrugged. "Ginger never talked to me about their private affairs. They used to live over there someplace." He gestured down the back of Capitol Hill. "Nice enough place, if you didn't need to find it in the dark."

We rang the bell, setting off a multinote chime. A uniformed maid opened the door. "Yes," she said in a truculent manner designed to frighten off gate-crashers.

"Tom Lander."

"Oh, yes, Mr. Lander." She stepped back, opening the door in welcome. "You're expected."

We entered a foyer with an intricate parquet floor and a magnificent chandelier that hung from a vaulted ceiling far above us. Polished mahogany handrails lined a circular staircase. From behind a closed door to our left came a murmur of voices. "This way, please," the maid told us.

As the door opened, we heard a small burst of laughter from a group of people gathered near a fireplace at the opposite end of an enormous room. To one side an arched doorway led into the dining room where a lavish buffet supper lay spread across a gleaming tabletop.

A scatter of twenty-five or thirty fashionably attired people chatted amiably over drinks and hors d'oeuvres. It would have made a wonderful cocktail party. Any relation to a funeral was purely coincidental.

Our host was nowhere in sight, but Homer broke away from the congenial group and came to meet us, a careful smile displayed on his face. "I'm glad you decided to come, Tom. You too, Mr. Beaumont. Care for a drink?"

"I'll have a beer," Tom said.

"McNaughton's and water," I answered. Homer nodded to the maid, and she disappeared.

Gravely solicitous, Homer guided Tom toward the fireplace. I trailed behind. "Let me introduce you to some of the folks, Tom. There wasn't enough time at the church."

Several of the names were preceded by "Representative" or "Senator." Clearly this was more a gathering of Darrell's peers than it was one of Ginger's friends. I tried keeping track of names, attempting to remember only those I hadn't already gleaned from the guest book.

Senator George Berry and Representative Dean Rhodes. Ray Johnson always told me that the secret to remembering names was creating colorful word pictures using the names. I had seen him do it for years. I made a stab at it.

Rhodes and Berry. I imagined several roads and saw them intersecting at one giant strawberry. Representative Doris Winters. I covered the strawberry with a giant load of winter snow.

Berry, Rhodes, Winters. So far, so good. Representative Larry Vukevich. Shit. Vukevich! Race car driver. Okay. Vukevich racing past the berry. Senator Toshiro Kobayashi. I gave up.

The maid handed me my McNaughton's. I wandered away from the introductions to a chair beside a leaded-glass window. I needed Peters. He'd know all those people. The room was stifling. I belted that drink and ordered another when the maid walked past again.

The door at the end of the room opened, letting in a welcome rush of cool air. Darrell Watkins—accompanied by a handsome, smiling young brunette—entered the room. Tom's back was to the door. Homer, facing both Darrell and Tom, gave an almost imperceptible shake of his head over Tom's shoulder. Darrell caught the warning and spoke quietly to the woman, who melted smoothly into the crowd.

So this was the tender blossom, the competition Ginger had talked about, already marking her territory and claiming her prize. I downed my second McNaughton's and sauntered over to where the brunette had settled on a green velvet love seat. She crossed her legs, revealing a rather lengthy stretch of shapely thigh.

"Would you like a drink?" I asked.

She smiled up at me. "Sure. Vodka tonic."

I found the maid and placed the order. "It's for the young woman over there, I forget her name."

"Miss Lacy," the maid supplied helpfully.

"I'll have another McNaughton's," I said, returning my glass. Casually I meandered back to the sweet young thing on the love seat. "My name's Beau," I said. "You're Miss Lacy?"

"Darlene," she replied, smiling.

"Glad to meet you, Darlene. Mind if I sit down?"

"No." She moved to make room, demurely covering some of the visible thigh. "Are you a lobbyist?" she asked.

"No, I'm a friend of Ginger's"

"Oh," she said, a trifle too quickly.

I don't believe any of Ginger's friends had been expected.

"It's too bad about Ginger," Darlene continued. "I didn't know her personally, but everyone says she was a very nice person."

"She was," I replied.

The maid brought the drinks. Darlene sipped hers, eyes holding mine over the top of her glass.

"What do you do?" I asked.

"I'll go to Olympia in January. I'll be on staff, either with the lieutenant governor's office or the senate. It doesn't matter to me." She laughed. "A job's a job."

Homer caught sight of us sitting together and hastened toward the love seat. "Mr. Beaumont, I didn't mean to ignore you. Would you care for a sandwich, deviled eggs, salad?"

"No, thanks. I was just chatting with Miss Lacy here. She was telling me about her new job. Sounds like a good deal to me." I managed a hollow grin, hoping it adequately expressed my feelings on the subject.

"Have you met Darrell?" Homer asked.

"No," I replied. "Haven't had the pleasure." I took another belt of McNaughton's—for luck, maybe. Or maybe because the room was uncommonly hot and I was very thirsty. I set my empty glass on a polished table and followed Homer to where Darrell was waxing eloquent with the lady from my memory word picture. Snow, I decided fuzzily. That was her name.

Homer caught Darrell's attention. "Darrell, this is Mr. Beaumont. It was his—"

Darrell turned toward me, his smile turning sallow. "Oh yes, Mr. Beaumont. I hope your Porsche isn't ruined."

"No. It'll be fine. It takes time. I wanted to express my condolences," I said.

"Thanks," he said, his face assuming the grieved air that had offended me at the funeral. "So nice of you to stop by." I resisted the temptation to smack that phony look right off his face. Homer steered Representative Snow away from us, leaving Darrell and me together. Darrell signaled the maid for two more drinks. "It's scary," he said, turning back to me. "First Sig, then Ginger, now Mona."

I was sure he knew all about Don Wilson. Considering the family's close ties to the governor's office, that was hardly surprising.

"I hope to God they catch that guy before he gets anyone else," Watkins continued.

"Me too," I said. "We usually do, sooner or later."

He gave me an appraising look. "We? Is Seattle P.D. involved too?" he asked.

"No, not officially. I'm here because Ginger and I were friends." The maid broke in to deliver drinks. My series of

McNaughton's had come in rapid enough succession that I was getting a little buzz.

"I don't recall her mentioning your name." It did my heart good to note the subtle shift in Darrell's manner, a wariness. I was something he didn't expect. How about that! Maybe Ginger had some secrets too, asshole. How d'you like them apples? The thoughts bubbled unspoken through my new glass of McNaughton's.

"You can't tell about women," I said jokingly. "Ginger and I go back a long way. We ran into each other up at Orcas by accident; but then, life is full of little surprises, right?"

"Right," he replied lamely.

The door opened, and a new trio of people entered. Darrell excused himself to greet them. The room had grown more crowded. There were far more people sipping drinks than had been at the chapel earlier.

The coffee, the McNaughton's, and the water asserted themselves. Searching for a restroom, I wandered into the kitchen, slipping through the swinging door when a maid carried a new tray of deviled eggs into the dining room.

The kitchen, massive and polished, was a combination of old and new. An ancient walk-in refrigerator covered one wall while, on the other side of the room, a long commercial dishwasher steamed under the hand of a heavyset woman rinsing a tray of plates. On a third wall sat a huge eight-burner range, while the middle of the room held a sleek stainless steel worktable laden with food. The woman looked up from the dishwasher and saw me at the doorway. "Can I help you?" she demanded.

"I'm looking for a restroom."

"No restrooms here," she stated flatly. "Upstairs. On the right."

Chastised, I retreated the way I had come, threading my way through the chatting guests to the foyer and up the stairs. A dizzying trip up the circular stairway convinced me I had had too much to drink. The first likely-looking door I found was locked. I tried the next floor. Bingo.

I had already flushed and was splashing my face with cool water in an effort to sober up when I heard voices in the hall outside. I'm sure it never occurred to anyone that a guest might have ventured all the way upstairs in search of a restroom. I opened the door and stepped into the hall. "It looks great, Dar-

rell," a voice was saying from a room farther up the corridor.
"The fact that it was private makes it that much better."

"That's what we pay you for, Sam." I recognized Darrell
Watkins' voice. "That's what a campaign manager is supposed
to do."

"Name familiarity's way up, up five points over last week.
That's a tremendous change this late in the campaign. I'd say
you have it in the bag."

"I'd better get back downstairs. Leave that paper up here when
you go," Darrell said. "We wouldn't want Tom to stumble across
it before he leaves."

I was standing outside the door when Darrell Watkins stepped
into the hall. He almost ran over me.

"You son of a bitch!" I muttered.

"What are you doing up here?"

"Taking a leak," I said.

"I think maybe you'd better go, Mr. Beaumont."

"I'll go when I'm good and ready, asshole."

Another man appeared behind Darrell, a young blond man in
casual clothes who looked as if he had just stepped out of a
racquet club advertisement. Behind both of them stood the newly
hired Darlene Lacy.

"Who's this, Darrell?" the other man asked.

I answered. "The name's Beaumont, Detective J. P. Beaumont, Seattle P.D." I was riding a boozy wave of moral indignation. "So you ran a poll, did you?" I sneered. "Figured the
voters would like it better if you made it look quiet and dignified.
That's how Ginger said you'd handle the divorce, too."

"I don't know what you're talking about."

"Oh yes you do. You got the newspapers to bury the story,
but Ginger was filing on Monday morning."

"Shut up," Darrell said.

"I won't shut up. How much does it cost to buy the press?"

"You're drunk, Mr. Beaumont. You'd better leave."

"I'm more pissed than I am drunk."

"Get out," he snarled. He moved toward me, reaching out to
put a hand on my shoulder.

"Get your hands off me!" I flung him away. What happened
next was in slow motion. I reached for him, wanting to grab him
by the shoulders and shake his teeth out. Instead, I lost my balance and slipped, shoving him backward toward the stairs. He

fell, catching his face on the heavy mahogany ball at the top of the handrail. When he straightened, blood spurted from his nose.

"I said get out!"

"I'm going."

"What's happening up there?" Homer called from below.

Darrell held a hanky to his nose. "Nothing," he replied. "Mr. Beaumont here has had one too many."

I charged down the stairs, shoving my way past Homer in the foyer. The air outside the house was sharp and cold, with a stiff breeze blowing off the water. It cleared the smoke-laden air from my lungs and cut through the haze of McNaughton's in my head, enough so I was shocked by what I had done. Taking a drunken swing at Darrell Watkins would add credence to the J. P. Beaumont legend—the hotheaded, killer-cop myth promoted by Maxwell Cole and his cohorts.

I took a deep breath of the biting, cold air. "You're not doing a whole hell of a lot to live it down," I told myself aloud.

A horn honked beside me, startling me out of my reverie. Tom Lander's GMC pulled up beside me. Tom leaned over and rolled down the window. "Get in," he ordered.

I did.

"What happened back there?" he asked, putting the pickup in gear.

"I had to get the hell out of there. They were driving me crazy."

"Me too," he said, accepting what I said at face value. "Where to?"

I directed him to my building at Third and Lenora. I didn't invite him up. I was sure he'd be reading all about it in the morning edition, and I didn't feel like doing any explanations beforehand.

"Thanks for coming along," Tom said as I opened the door to get out. "I'm glad at least one of Ginger's friends was there."

Nodding in agreement, I climbed out onto the sidewalk, then I reached back into the truck to shake his hand. "Your daughter was a very special lady, Tom. I'm sorry she's gone."

"Thanks," he said. He drove away without further comment.

Words are never enough in a situation like that. Actions were what was needed. I turned and walked into the lobby of the Royal Crest.

By then I was stone-cold sober.

Chapter 24

FRIDAY morning. My last day of vacation, and I was hung over as hell. It seemed like all I had done was drink and go to funerals, a regular busman's holiday. I called Ames to invite him to breakfast. Reluctantly, he agreed.

"I'm very busy, you know," he said crossly as we picked up our menus. "I'm working on the condominium thing, and I'm still negotiating with New Dawn. What do you want?"

"Well," I parried, "as my attorney I thought you ought to know I was in a mild altercation with a Washington State senator last night. Bloodied his nose, probably blacked his eyes. . . . Accidentally," I added.

Ames put down his menu. "This is a joke, right?"

"Wrong. No joke."

"Maybe you'd better tell me about it."

For an answer, I handed him a copy of a newspaper. Ames read silently:

"In a private funeral ceremony attended only by family and close friends, State Senator Darrell Watkins said a tearful farewell to his wife Ginger yesterday afternoon.

"Mrs. Watkins, a member of the Washington State Parole Board, died in a one-vehicle accident on Orcas Island, Saturday, October 25. Her funeral services were delayed to allow fellow board members to travel to Welton for the funeral of another board member, Sig Larson, who was the victim of a homicide the previous day.

"Initially thought to be the underdog against longtime incumbent, Lieutenant Governor Rod Chambers, Sen. Watkins has seen his political base increase even as he has faced personal tragedy. Public-opinion polls now show him running neck and neck with Lt. Governor Chambers.

"A Watkins family spokesman said services for Mrs. Watkins

were kept private to avoid a 'sensationalizing press from taking advantage of an unfortunate situation.'

"Senator Watkins, in a terse statement issued late last night, said that he is canceling all campaign appearances for the remainder of the week."

Ames looked up from the paper. "Don't I remember reading that it was his wife's wish that he continue with the campaign? When did you break his nose?"

"Last night. After the funeral. I'll bet he's not a pretty sight this morning."

"No wonder he canceled his public appearances."

"That sorry son of a bitch deliberately staged a 'private ceremony' in order to gain the sympathy vote." I relayed to Ames the conversation I had overheard.

"This the first you've been around politics?" Ames inquired dryly. "That's how it works. Will he bring charges?"

"I don't know. That's why I called you."

"Were there any reporters there at the time?"

"You mean when he fell? Not that I know of."

"I'm surprised they're downplaying it like this. By all rights, you should be plastered all over the front page for the second time this week."

"Maybe I just got lucky," I suggested.

Ames shook his head. "I doubt it. They probably won't go for criminal charges, but my guess is we'll be hearing from their attorneys. They'll sue for damages."

"Wonderful," I mumbled.

"Considering their financial situation, they'd be crazy not to."

"What do you mean?"

Just then the waitress brought our food and put it in front of Ames. He had taken a file folder out of his briefcase. He sighed, put the folder down, and picked up his fork. "You know which of the condominium projects are in trouble, don't you?"

"I wasn't asking about that. You said it wouldn't make sense for them not to sue me."

"Beau, listen to me. I'm trying to explain. The two that are in trouble are Belltown Terrace and Waterview Place. Belltown Terrace is theirs. Scuttlebutt says the project will go on the auction block by the end of the year unless they pick up some new capital. They might go for a fat out-of-court settlement in order to pick up some quick cash.''

"Slow down. You're talking about two different things.''

"I'm talking money.''

"Look, Ralph, if they're going bankrupt, then I'd better not get involved. I didn't realize they were almost to sheriff's-sale time.''

Ames looked at me sadly and shook his head. "You haven't been listening.''

"Yes, I have. Why would I want to buy a unit from someone who's about to go belly-up? More specifically, why would I want to buy in a building owned by someone who's about to sue me?'' Waiting for Ames' answer, I chased a slippery chunk of egg across my plate with a piece of whole-wheat toast. Peters had convinced me to give up white bread, not cholesterol.

"A unit!'' Ames exploded. "Who's talking about a unit? I'm talking about the building. You said you wanted to invest. It would be a great write-off. You rent the units for five to seven years; then go in, do some remodeling, and sell them. It's a heck of a good deal.''

I put down my toast. I put down my fork. "You were supposed to be looking for a condominium for me to buy.''

"The penthouses in Belltown aren't sold. You could live there, but in order to keep our noses clean with the IRS, you'd have to pay rent back to the corporation.''

"Ames, I can't buy a whole building.''

"Well, not by yourself. I can get you in with a syndicate. I know of one in the market for just this kind of deal, five of you altogether. What do you think?''

I didn't know what to think. I knew my inheritance was considerable, but I still hadn't gotten a handle on the magnitude of it. I kept trying to get my arms around it.

"You do what you think is best,'' I said to Ames. "You know a hell of a lot more about this stuff than I do, but I can't see myself doing business with Homer and Darrell Watkins, especially after last night.''

"Forget last night. We'll be dealing with the bank, not Homer and Darrell. The FDIC is ready to eat the bank alive if they don't get out from under this loan. Want to go over the financial papers?''

I shook my head. "That's your job.''

Ames patted his mouth with his napkin and returned the file folder to his briefcase. "Very well," he said, rising. "I've got to run. I'm expecting a call from The Dalles."

"How's that going?" I asked.

He shrugged. "I'm not talking. I don't want to get Peters' hopes up, but it's not a dead issue."

He left me in the restaurant. After I paid the bill, I walked down Second to Belltown Terrace. It was a twenty-story building with a small grassy courtyard setting it back from the street. The sign said "Model Open," so I went inside. A real estate lady came down to meet me. She showed me through the entire project, from the indoor pool and exercise room to the outdoor racquetball court and running track. A gas barbecue grill sat on a small patio near the party room.

I lost the barbecue and also my only form of cooking expertise when Karen and I split up. The number of decent barbecued ribs I'd had since then could be counted on one hand. I decided that if Ames could negotiate my way into the building, it might not be such a bad idea.

Taking the woman's card, I promised to call her once I made up my mind. Back on the street, I dealt with the problem of my last day of vacation. The bug was on me. Jurisdictions notwithstanding, I had to do something.

I didn't bother going back to Avis. Considering my track record, they wouldn't be eager to rent me another car. I tried Hertz instead. I drove north on I-5 and took the Lynnwood exit. Using the phone book, I located Don Wilson's address. When I got there, I found that both the front and back doors were secured with police padlocks. Huggins had made the place off-limits. A quick check of the neighborhood showed no surveillance vehicles.

Wilson's house was set back by itself on a wooded lot. The nearest neighbor was a good half-block away in a tiny clapboard cottage. I walked to it and knocked. After a time the door inched open the length of a security chain.

"Yes?" a woman's voice demanded.

I held one of my cards up to the door so she could see it. "I need to ask a couple questions about Mr. Wilson."

"You and everybody else," the woman grumbled, but the door closed long enough for her to unfasten the chain. "What do you want to know?"

The woman was more than middle-aged, with a white apron

spread across an ample figure. With an exasperated glare, she pointed her index finger at her ear and made several quick circular gestures.

"What else do you want to know?"

"Crazy enough to kill someone?"

"Wouldn't you be if you was him? You know what happened to his wife and kid."

"When did you last see him?"

"Look," she said, "I'm trying to cook dinner. I don't have all day. I already said this once. Do I have to say it again?"

"It would help," I said.

She sighed. "Well, follow me into the kitchen, then—before I burn it up." Opening the door wide, she motioned me inside. I followed her into a small kitchen where she was peeling vegetables for what looked like a stew. "Last I saw him was Friday morning. He was unloading signs from his car."

"Unloading?"

"That's what I said. Unloading. Packing them into the house."

It struck me as odd. If he was on his way to Orcas to demonstrate, he should have had his signs along. "Why?" I said, more to myself than to the woman.

"How should I know?"

I spent a while longer in the steamy kitchen, but other than stoutly defending Don Wilson's right to go off the deep end, the woman told me nothing more of consequence. I drove back into Seattle with the unsettling feeling that I knew both more and less than I had known before.

By the time I got home, late-afternoon sun had broken through the clouds. I called Peters at the Department.

"How's it going?" I asked.

"I hate depositions," he answered.

"What are you doing tonight?"

"Oh, I don't know. I thought I'd hang around here long enough to wait out the traffic." Friday afternoon rush-hour traffic is worse on Seattle's two floating bridges than it is during the rest of the week, as weekend travelers join regular commuters trying to cross Lake Washington to get to the suburbs and beyond.

"Why don't you stop by and have dinner? Maybe Ames could join us."

"What kind of food?" Peters asked.

I hadn't planned that far in advance. "I don't know."

"Tell you what," Peters offered. "I'll stop by the market and pick up something."

He didn't fool me for a minute. That way he could control the menu. "Sure," I said. "That'll be fine."

Hal Huggins called right after I talked to Peters. "Where've you been? I've been calling all afternoon."

"Out," I said without explanation. "What do you want?"

"We searched Wilson's house," Huggins said. "All his picketing stuff was there—the signs, the brochures, the petitions. Nothing out of the ordinary except one thing."

"What's that?"

"He left a half-chicken thawing on the counter, like he planned to be home in time for dinner. And he didn't leave food out for his cat. By the time we got there, the cat had helped himself to the chicken."

"Smart cat," I said.

"Get serious, Beau. What does that say to you?"

"He didn't expect to be gone long."

"Yeah," Huggins agreed.

We talked a few more minutes before my Call Waiting signal buzzed me to say Peters was downstairs. He carried a box of marinated vegetables, a pound of cooked spinach tortellini, and some fresh sole that he proceeded to bake in my oven. Ames turned us down cold, so it was only Peters and I who sat down to a gourmet dinner overlooking Seattle's nighttime skyline. Peters glanced at his watch as we finished eating.

"I'd be lucky to be home now, even if I left right at five. It takes an hour on Fridays. Longer if there's an accident on the bridge."

"Why don't you move downtown?" I asked.

A shadow crossed his face. "I keep thinking I'll get the girls back. You can't raise kids in the city."

I told him then about what I had seen at Belltown Terrace—the running track, the pool, the facilities. "You could raise kids there," I told him, "and not have to spend half your life commuting in a car."

"I don't have the kids. . . . Probably never will," he replied bitterly. "Besides," he added, "I don't have that kind of money."

Respecting Ames' wishes, I said nothing about continuing negotiations in The Dalles.

Our evening was pleasant. I told Peters about the reception at the Watkins mansion, including my taking a swing at Darrell Watkins. I tried unsuccessfully to recall the names of some of the people there. Vukevich was the only one I could remember for certain. "There was a Representative Snow, I think, and maybe somebody named Lane."

Peters shook his head. The names didn't sound familiar. So much for using word pictures to enhance my memory. You can't teach an old dog new tricks.

Chapter 25

ERNIE Rogers called at six forty-five Saturday morning. The car was ready; would I like him to bring it to Seattle?

"Sure, but—" I thought about the Porsche and wondered how he'd handle it. Ernie heard the pause and understood it.

"My wife will drive," he said.

"Well, sure. Do you know your way around Seattle?"

"Some."

I gave him directions, describing the electronic gate into the garage on Lenora at the base of the building. "The Genie may not work now that it's been wet."

"It should," Ernie said. "I fixed it. We'll be there early afternoon."

"How will you get back to Orcas?"

"We're going to make a weekend of it. My mother-in-law is keeping the kids. We won't catch the bus back to Anacortes until Monday afternoon. Jenny wants to do some shopping. We thought we'd turn this into a mini-vacation."

"Do you have reservations somewhere?" I asked.

"No, we'll check into a motel after we get to town."

"Do I owe you any more money?" I asked, wondering if I should be prepared to write another check.

"As a matter of fact," he answered, "you'll be getting back some change."

"I'll look for you when you get here," I said. "My parking space is number forty-eight. After you park, come on up to 1106. We'll go to lunch."

"Sounds great."

Peters called from home while I was drinking my second cup of coffee. He was reading his morning paper. "Somebody blabbed about the search warrant. I'll bet Huggins is pissed. The paper names Wilson as the major suspect in both Larson murders. Who's the leak?"

Peter and I had hammered away on Don Wilson's thawing chicken over drinks after dinner. "Does the article mention Ginger Watkins?" I asked.

"Not so far."

"I've gotta go, Peters." I hung up and dialed Hal Huggins' number in Friday Harbor. It was busy and stayed that way. I tried the Sheriff's Department. "I'm sorry. Detective Huggins is unavailable."

"This is Detective Beaumont from Seattle. I'll hold. He'll talk to me."

I was right. Hal came on the line a minute later. "Sorry to keep you waiting, Beau. This place is a zoo. We've got reporters hanging from the ceiling fans. Somebody told them about the search warrant."

"Who?"

"How the hell should I know?"

"Pomeroy, maybe?" I asked. He was my first choice.

"I don't think so. I asked him. He denied it six ways to Sunday. I think he's telling the truth. Musta been somebody else."

A voice spoke to Hal in the background, and I heard his muffled reply. "Hey," he said into the phone. "I've gotta run. The press is eating me alive. I'll let you know if anything breaks."

I put down the phone and sat for a while. Eventually I called Ray in Pasco. He was at home. He sounded glad to hear from me.

"What did they find in the Rabbit?" I asked him after the niceties.

"Not in the Rabbit, on it. Mona's hair, and fibers from her jacket on the front bumper."

"No fingerprints?"

"Yours, smudged. Must have worn gloves."

"Great. Terrific. When's Mona's funeral?"

"It's over. Her brother brought in a bunch of Hell's Angels types from Idaho, cowboys on motorcycles. I went to the service. Except for the brother and his friends, no one was there."

At least I had sent flowers.

I made a late lunch reservation for the Space Needle. It's one of Seattle's best-known tourist attractions. The combination of food and view are unbeatable.

As I hung up the phone after making the reservation, I congratulated myself. It would be the first time I had visited the Space Needle since that night months ago when I went with Anne Corley. Maybe I was finally getting better.

I said a small thank-you to Ginger Watkins wherever she was.

Downtown is deserted on weekends. All the business people are home in the suburbs, mowing lawns and raking leaves. Farther downtown where the stores are, there are still crowds of shoppers, but not up in the Denny Regrade where I live. The flat stretches of the Regrade form a quiet village.

Actually, the Regrade used to be as hilly as the rest of Seattle, but sometime during the early nineteen-hundreds, a city engineer named R. H. Thompson got carried away with his work and decided to sluice Denny Hill into Puget Sound. He wanted flat, and he got it; only the Depression stopped him before he got started on Queen Anne Hill. That kind of nonsense wouldn't get past environmentalists today, but it did then. Now the Denny Regrade is flat as a pancake.

Expansion from downtown, also stopped by the Depression, left the Regrade as it is today, a neighborhood of condominiums and apartment buildings interspersed with offices and small businesses. New luxury high-rises and flea-bitten hotels coexist in relative harmony.

I opened the door to my solitary lanai and went out to soak up some quiet morning sun. I needed to think.

A couple of things were right at the top of my list. For one, why would the killer have carefully worn gloves to drive my car when he had blatantly left prints all over Ginger's calendar? Of course, he didn't expect the calendar to be found, but still, it was taking a hell of a chance.

And the half-chicken bothered me. My mother was a firm believer in "Waste not, want not." The idea of thawing meat when you had no intention of coming home didn't make sense. And how had he disappeared into thin air? And why had he unpacked all his protest materials before he left for Orcas?

Questions. Always questions with no answers. And reporters buzzing around with their own sets of questions, never having brains enough not to print everything they knew, or thought they knew.

Stymied, I went back inside to shower, shave, and dress. I was ready and waiting when Ernie and Jenny showed up at one-thirty. Jenny Rogers was a smiling woman, several years younger than Ernie. They were a matched set. Her flaming red hair and blue eyes made them look more like brother and sister than husband and wife. She had a pregnant shelf of tummy that could easily have held a coffee cup and saucer.

"Any trouble with the car?" I asked.

Jenny giggled. "Some," she replied.

I looked anxiously at Ernie, afraid something was wrong with the Porsche that he hadn't been able to fix. He grinned. "She had a hard time steering," he explained. "The baby kept getting in the way."

Sports cars are not necessarily built for pregnant drivers.

We decided to walk from my place to Seattle Center. I guess I had never noticed all the curb cuts in the sidewalks. Ernie wheeled along, easily keeping pace with Jenny and me.

They found the Space Needle enchanting. Jenny had never been there, not even on the observation deck. She was delighted with the revolving restaurant, exuberant about the food. Her enjoyment was contagious. We had a great time. Eventually, however, conversation turned to business. Ernie reached in a pocket and pulled out an envelope which he handed to me. In it was a check for five hundred dollars, made out in my name. "What's this?" I asked.

"The job didn't take nearly as long as I thought," he answered. "That's your change."

I remembered Barney at Rosario telling me that Ernie was the best. I had doubted it then, but now I believed it. I'd checked, and couldn't have gotten the work done nearly that fast or cheap anywhere else. Taking a pen, I endorsed the check back to Jenny Rogers and handed it to her.

She was stunned. "Why?" she asked.

"For driving the car back, saving me a day of traveling. And for the baby. Ernie said you wanted to go shopping."

She looked at him quickly, questioning whether she should accept it. He shrugged, and she put the check in her purse.

"Thank you," she said.

Ernie looked uncomfortable. He changed the subject. "Did you see the paper this morning?"

"I didn't see it, but I heard."

"The paper said it's because the parole board let that Lathrop guy out and he killed Wilson's wife."

I shrugged. "Could be," I said.

"Well, they still shouldn't have fired Blia," Jenny said. Ernie shot a quick silencing glance in Jenny's direction. "Well, they shouldn't have," she insisted, with a defiant shake of her head. "It's not fair."

"What's not fair?"

"Blia Vang was a maid working at Rosario who got fired because she lost her keys. They said someone found them and used them to break into Mrs. Watkins' room."

I felt as if I had wandered into a conversation twenty minutes late. "Who's this again?"

"Blia Vang. A friend of ours." Jenny's blue eyes smoldered with indignation. "Somebody stole her keys, so they fired her."

"When?"

Ernie broke in with an explanation. "Blia worked the day that man was murdered. She left her keys on a cart, and someone took them. The hotel claimed she was careless and fired her."

My mind raced. Sig's key to Ginger's room had never been found, but the fact that the maid's keys had been stolen the same day was too much of a coincidence. My gut told me the missing keys were somehow related to the murder.

"Does Hal Huggins know?"

Ernie shrugged. "I don't know. She was too scared to say anything. The manager didn't find out until yesterday. When he did, he fired her on the spot."

"But has Hal talked to her?"

"I doubt it. She took off on the next ferry," Jenny interjected. "She would have been long gone before he knew."

I felt a mounting surge of excitement. Maybe she had seen someone in the hall, someone she could identify. "A material witness can't just walk away. She'll have to tell the authorities what she knows."

"She won't," Jenny said.

"She has to. She could be charged with obstruction of justice."

Jenny gave a sharp laugh. "Try explaining obstruction of justice to a H mong refugee. That's why she ran away. She's scared. She almost died when they took her fingerprints. She won't talk to a cop."

"Does anyone know where she went?"

Jenny and Ernie exchanged glances. "Maybe," Jenny said reluctantly. "But I tell you, she won't talk to you or Hal either. She's scared."

It occurred to me suddenly that Jenny and Ernie Rogers seemed to be far more than casually involved. "Wait a minute. How do you know so much about her?"

Jenny looked shyly at Ernie. He answered with a mildly reproving glare. "We work with the refugees," he explained. "An H mong saved my life while I was in 'Nam. I'm the one who got her the job at Rosario in the first place. I feel pretty bad about it. We both do."

I was like an old, flop-eared hound stumbling across a fresh scent. "Would you help me find her?" I asked, attempting to contain my elation. Their heads shook in silent unison.

"I'll get an interpreter," I argued. "I'd be off duty, no uniform, no badge. This could be important. She may have seen someone or something nobody else saw."

Jenny's manner softened when she understood I believed Blia innocent of any wrongdoing. Ernie remained adamant.

"There might be a reward," I added as a last resort.

"She won't talk to you," Ernie said. "Even if you find her, she won't talk."

"She would if you went along to translate," Jenny suggested. Ernie gave Jenny a black look, but his resistance was weakening. He sat for a long time, looking at me, weighing the pros and cons.

"You're sure she wouldn't get into any trouble?" he asked.

"I guarantee it."

"In that case," Ernie Rogers said gruffly, "I guess it couldn't hurt to talk to her."

Chapter 26

I COULD hardly wait to get home. Jenny had told me there was a possibility Blia Vang was staying with relatives in Seattle. I wanted to start looking for her.

While Ernie waited in the cab, Jenny and I retrieved luggage from the Porsche. In the elevator, Jenny thanked me again for both the money and lunch. It made me uneasy. Being an anonymous benefactor is a hell of a lot easier than looking gratitude in the face.

"Buy something nice for the baby," I said, patting her tummy.

She smiled and stood on tiptoe, leaning over her pregnant belly to give me a peck on the cheek as the elevator door opened to let her off. She gave me the name of a motel near Green Lake in case I needed to get in touch with them.

Back in my apartment I called Detective Henry Wu, a third-generation Seattleite of Chinese extraction. Hank came to homicide from the University of Washington with a major in police science and a minor in Far Eastern studies.

"Hey, Beau," he said, when I told him who was calling. "When you coming back?"

"Monday," I said. "But I need your help today. What do you know about H mong refugees here in town?"

"A very tightly knit group," he replied. "They don't trust outsiders. With good reason, mostly."

"Do you have any friends there?"

"I've got an ear there," he allowed. "Not a friend. Why? What do you need?"

"There's a young woman, used to be a maid up at Rosario. Her name is Blia Vang. They fired her for losing a set of keys. I need to talk to her."

"What about? Is this official police business?"

"More like unofficial police business. Remember old Hal Huggins?"

"Sure."

"He's working a homicide on Orcas. This woman may have a lead for him. She took off before he could talk to her. Rumor has it she's in Seattle, staying with relatives. I've got an interpreter, someone she knows, a fellow named Ernie Rogers. I need to ask her a couple questions. Off the record. No badge, no uniform, nothing. There's even a reward, if that helps."

"Money isn't going to make a hell of a lot of difference if she has to talk to a cop."

"Don't tell her I'm a cop. Say a friend of Ernie Rogers needs to talk to her."

"I'll try," Hank agreed, "but don't hold your breath. Is that all?"

"Well, actually, there's one more thing."

"Shoot."

"My interpreter is in town until four-thirty Monday afternoon. That's when the bus leaves for Anacortes."

"Jesus Christ, Beau! This is Saturday."

"Call somebody. Leave a message. It's important."

"Right," he said sarcastically. "The H mong all have phones and folks to take messages. I'll see what I can do."

"Thanks, Hank. I appreciate it."

I hung up. One of the hardest things about this business is waiting. You put an idea out into the ether, then you wait to see if anything happens. Television detectives notwithstanding, a lot of times nothing does.

On Saturday, nothing happened. I finally got around to unpacking the suitcases I had brought home and stashed in the bedroom without opening. On the table beside my recliner, I discovered the bill from Rosario. Ames had impressed on me the value of saving copies of all bills as potential weapons in future battles with the IRS. I stowed the bill away in a shoe box reserved for that purpose, your basic low-tech-filing system.

I tried Ames. Since it was cocktail hour on Saturday evening, I thought he might be persuaded into coming over. No dice. Claimed he was in the middle of something vital and couldn't take a break. More than a little put out, I walked across the street to the Cinerama and watched the original uncut version of *Oklahoma* for the seventh time.

Afterward, I went home, to bed but not to sleep. Thoughts of

Ginger Watkins and Mona Larson haunted me. There was a common denominator, but I couldn't put my finger on it.

It was after three when I fell asleep. The phone rang at six. It was Ames—bright, cheerful, energetic Ames—calling on the security phone from the lobby. "Let me in, Beau. I'm downstairs."

I staggered into the kitchen and started coffee. When I opened the door, Ames bounced into the apartment, brimming over with excitement. "I have the deal put together. The other syndicate members want to know if you're going to buy the penthouse before the purchase of the building, or if you want to rent it back." Words tumbled out in a torrent.

"In that case, you wouldn't be able to buy it outright for five years, but considering the tax write-offs on the building, you needn't worry."

"Wait a goddamned minute here, Ames! Do you mean to tell me you woke me up at six o'clock on Sunday morning because you put a real estate package together?"

Chastised, Ames accepted a proffered cup of coffee. "I had to wait for one guy's plane to land in Japan."

"Which building?" I asked. "The one with the barbecue?"

"Belltown Terrace," he said.

"Okay, that's the one with the grill. What's next?"

"Tomorrow I make them an offer."

I sat down opposite Ames with my own coffee cup. "I have a hard time seeing myself as a real estate magnate."

"It'll grow on you," he assured me, smiling.

"What do I do with this?" I asked, indicating the small apartment that had been my first and only haven after the painful split from Karen and the kids.

"Sell it, or keep it and rent it out. It's up to you."

I remembered when the mortgage on the unit plus the child-support I sent Karen had been an almost insurmountable problem every month. Things had changed. For the better.

I scrambled a couple of eggs while Ames fixed toast. I could summon no enthusiasm for this real-life game of Monopoly. Even though it was theoretically my money, I didn't feel any sense of its belonging to me—or of my belonging to it, for that matter.

"What's wrong, Beau?" he asked, finally noticing my genuine disinterest.

"Mona Larson and Ginger Watkins," I told him.

"What about them, other than the obvious?"

"Something bothers me, and I can't get a handle on it: some common denominator, besides Sig."

"They were both broke," Ames said.

"I beg your pardon?"

"They were both broke," he repeated. "Mortgaged up the yingyang. Belltown didn't work out the way they expected. First the cement strike caught them. When the units finally hit the market, they got clobbered by high interest rates.

"For a long time nothing sold. They all lost a bundle. The whole group mortgaged everything to pay the first segment of the construction loan last year, thinking they could hold out and make the money back through sales. The next segment is due the end of December. There's no way they'll meet it. If they could even pay the interest, they might forestall a sheriff's sale, but after looking at the PDCs, I don't think they can."

"PDCs. What are they?"

"Public Disclosure Commission statements. Elected and appointed state officials fill out financial disclosure forms showing their earnings and holdings . . . that sort of thing. They're a matter of public record. After looking them over, it's clear that the parole board income was keeping both the Larson and Watkins households afloat."

"What about Homer?"

Ames laughed. "He's exempt. He holds no public office. He's always a bridesmaid but never a bride. He's involved in campaigns all over the map, but he's never a candidate himself. I'd guess he's as bad off as everybody else, but he doesn't have to fill out a form saying so."

"Both broke," I mused.

"You have to have pretty deep pockets to be able to weather the kind of financial storm there's been in Seattle's real estate market the last couple of years. My indicators say it's starting to turn around."

"Are mine?"

"Are your what?"

"Are my pockets deep enough?"

Ames laughed again. "They are, Beau. Believe me, you'll do fine. Now, we should take a look at that penthouse. If you're going to buy it separately, I can draw up an earnest-money agreement today."

I rummaged through my wallet and found the business card of

the real estate lady at Belltown Terrace. "Call her," I said. "I liked the water view best. Two bedrooms with a den."

Ames seemed startled as he took the card. He had asked for a decision. I don't think he expected one quite that fast. "Just like that?" he asked.

"I looked at it Friday. It has a grill. I'm a sucker for barbecues."

Ames left a short time later, setting off happily on his various missions. At least one Seattle real estate agent was in for a pleasant surprise that Sunday.

Alone, I mulled Ames' information. Broke. Both Ginger and Mona had been dead broke, battling for survival, trying to stay afloat. I found it hard to imagine Ginger living in that palatial estate, running like hell to keep up appearances. In Chelan, Mona and Sig must have been caught on the same kind of treadmill.

Ginger and Mona—both of them married above their station, both young and attractive, and both dead within days of one another, probably at the hands of the same killer. Mona Larson and Ginger Watkins indeed had a lot in common.

Peters' phone call interrupted my reverie. We see each other so little during the week that we have to check in on weekends. Indulging in his favorite vice, current events, he was determined to keep me well informed, whether or not I wanted to be.

"I don't suppose you've read the paper."

"Good hunch."

"Your friend Max has hit an all-time-record low for bad taste, a Death Row telephone interview with Philip Lathrop from Walla Walla. Asked Lathrop what he thought about Wilson knocking off Sig and Mona Larson."

"I don't think I want to hear this," I said.

"Lathrop's comment was, 'It serves 'em right.' "

"That's why I don't read papers," I told Peters.

"Maybe you've got a point," Peters muttered.

Ida Newell dropped off my Sunday collection of crossword puzzles. I was working the second one when the phone rang. It was Hal Huggins. "They found him, Beau."

"Who?"

"Wilson."

"Where? When can I question him?"

"In Prosser. I'm on my way over there right now." Hal hardly sounded jubilant. "But St. Peter's the only one who'll be asking him any questions."

"He's dead? You're kidding! Who found him?"

"A troop of Boy Scouts out cleaning the bank along the Yakima River."

"How long's he been dead?" My mind did a quick geographic review. Prosser was in Benton county, the county next to Pasco where Mona Larson died.

"I don't know, but I'm going over to find out."

"What's the cause of death?"

"Initial report says drowning."

"Drowning?" I repeated.

"I'll find out when I get there."

I heard weariness and frustration in Hal's voice. He had followed a trail of questions, only to be robbed of both his suspect and his answers. To a homicide detective, answers are life's blood.

"Tough break, Hal," I said.

"I know." He paused. "I'd better go." With that, he hung up.

I sat for a long time afterward holding the phone. When a recorded voice threatened me with bodily harm, I returned the receiver to its cradle.

Don Wilson was dead. That finished it, right? Supposedly.

Maybe it did for Hal Huggins. It sounded as if he was buying the whole program.

But I wasn't. Several things demanded consideration: Don Wilson's thawing chicken, his hungry cat, his unpacked protest gear, and an extraneous set of missing keys. All were perplexing loose ends that wouldn't go away, that refused to be tied up in neat little packages.

Loose ends bug me. If they didn't, I guess I'd be in another line of work.

Chapter 27

ANYONE who's ever been on vacation knows how hard it is to return to work that first day. In my case, the vacation had been the culmination of months of being miserable and disconnected. It felt like I was going back to work after six months rather than a mere two weeks.

Peters spent the day at the courthouse on the dead wife-beater case. Both Peters and I were rooting for the woman, Delphina Sage. Delphina's husband, Rocky, came home drunk one Friday night and beat the crap out of her, same as he did every payday. The only difference was that, the day before, Delphina had bought herself a .22 pistol.

If she had shot him while he was beating her up, it wouldn't have been so bad. We would have called it self-defense and let it go at that. Instead, Delphina waited until Rocky was sound asleep, then plugged him full of holes. From talking to the kids and the neighbors, Peters and I figured Rocky was a bully badly in need of plugging, but Barbara Guffy, King County's chief prosecutor, has a thing about premeditation. She was after a murder conviction.

Peters and I had been working another case just prior to my leaving for Rosario. In two separate but—we believed—related incidents, some jackass had set fire to sleeping transients downtown. Detectives Lindstrom and Davis had one case, while Peters and I had the other. Our victim had died almost immediately, but the other transient still clung stubbornly to life in the burn unit at Harborview Hospital. Both victims remained unidentified.

I was reviewing what little we had to go on when Hank Wu stopped by my desk. "Any luck?" I asked.

He shook his head. "This stuff takes time, Beau. The H mong don't come out of the woodwork and spill their guts just because Henry Wu snaps his finger. What time did you say your interpreter leaves?"

"Today on the four-thirty Greyhound for Anacortes."

"I'd say chances aren't very good."

"Keep after it anyway."

"Sure, glad to." Hank sauntered away from my desk.

Ames had promised to call as soon as he heard anything on the real estate transactions. The penthouse earnest-money agreement called for a March closing date. "That way," Ames had told me with a sly grin, "we'll keep the money in the family."

He called just before lunch, sounding perplexed. "What's the matter, Ames? You sound upset."

"I don't understand. They jumped on the penthouse deal, but they refused to consider the syndicate offer."

"Why?"

"I don't know. Must have come up with another investor who's willing to buy in. That's all I can figure."

"What happened?"

"That's what's so strange. When I talked to the project manager this morning, he was hot on the idea. Said he had to talk to one of the principals. Five minutes later, the deal was off. Just like that. One minute they needed the money; the next minute they didn't. The way they grabbed at that penthouse deal, even with a delayed closing, they don't expect to lose Belltown between now and March."

At Ames' insistence I had studied the project's financial sheet. We were talking big money, several million dollars.

"How can someone come up with that kind of cash in five minutes' time?" I wondered aloud.

"I don't know," Ames told me, "but I intend to find out."

Ames was in no mood to go to lunch. Craving companionship, I tracked down Peters at the courthouse. The two of us walked to a salad bar at Fourth and Madison. He dismissed my questions about Delphina Sage with an impatient shake of his head. "I don't want to talk about it. You do any good this morning?" he asked.

"I went over everything we have on our charbroiled John Doe. This afternoon I thought I'd check to see if Manny and Al's guy up in the burn unit can talk."

"Don't hold your breath," Peters said. "He couldn't last week."

It sounded hopeless to me, and I said as much. "We'll never

crack this one. There's nothing to go on. Besides, if bums kill bums, who gives a shit?"

Peters gave me a long, critical look. "We sure as hell won't crack it with that kind of attitude," he responded. "You were supposed to come back from vacation with your enthusiasm back, all pumped up and rarin' to go, remember?"

"Go to hell," I retorted. "What do you think about them finding Wilson?"

"We're talking burning transients, remember?" he reminded me.

"I'm not interested in burning transients. I want to talk about Don Wilson."

"What about him? According to the papers, Hal Huggins has him dead to rights. Left a note and everything. What's there to talk about?"

"A note!" I exclaimed. "Are you serious?"

"Damn it, Beau. When are you going to stop being stubborn and start reading the papers? Yes, a note."

For the first time I felt the smallest prick of annoyance toward Hal Huggins. My phone had worked well enough when he needed my help. So why hadn't he called me with the news of the note? "God damn that Huggins," I grumbled. "What did the paper say?"

"That they found Wilson's body on the banks of the Yakima River just outside Prosser. Said he died of exposure, but that somebody found a suicide note."

"Exposure? Initially they said drowning. Since when is exposure suicide?"

"I'm just telling you what it said in the paper."

"And where did they find the note?"

"The article didn't say."

I left Peters at the table and prowled the restaurant for a pay phone. Locating one in a hallway between the men's and ladies' restrooms, I placed a call to Friday Harbor. Hal Huggins was not in. The woman who answered had no idea when he was expected. I left word for him to call me and went back to Peters.

"Did they say how long he'd been dead?"

Peters shrugged and shook his head. "A couple of days, I guess. At least that's what they implied."

"What about the note?"

"Just that there was one."

I stared morosely into my cup. Peters was fast losing patience. "Look. This Wilson character isn't our case. When are you going to the hospital?"

"Right after lunch, I guess."

He watched me drain my cup. "Know what your problem is, Beau?"

"What?"

"You just don't give a shit about burned-up bums."

"We've been partners too long," I told him.

I drove up to First Hill, Pill Hill as it's called because of all the hospitals. The burn victim in Harborview was in no condition to talk, at least not according to the dogfaced intensive-care nurse who barred my way. She said he had been hit by an infection and wasn't expected to make it.

I went down to Pioneer Square. I walked around talking to people, asking questions. It was tough. All of the drunks were too fuzzy to know who was sitting next to them right then, to say nothing of remembering someone who had been missing from the park bench almost three weeks. In their world, three weeks ago was ancient history.

By four o'clock I was parked outside the Greyhound terminal at Seventh and Stewart as Jenny and Ernie arrived by taxi. Ernie held two suitcases on his lap; Jenny struggled with a collection of shopping bags.

"Want some help?" I asked, coming up behind them.

They both turned. Jenny's face was radiant with that peculiar glow common to pregnant women. Ernie seemed relieved to find someone to help her with the luggage.

"She didn't spend it all," he said, grinning. "But she came real close." He wheeled along beside me as I carried bags and packages into the terminal and checked them onto the proper bus. "You never found Blia?" Ernie asked.

"No, and we've been looking."

"If you find her, I'd still be willing to talk to her, but I hate to miss a full day's work."

"What about a telephone conference call?" I asked. "We could get you, Blia, and me all on the phone together."

Ernie shook his head doubtfully. "You gotta remember that for the H mong, coming to this country is like stepping into a time machine. She was raised one step out of the Stone Age. A telephone conference call is asking too much."

"It was just an idea," I said dismally.

Promptly at four-thirty the bus left for Anacortes. I dropped my company car off at the department and rode a free bus as far as the Westin. I needed to talk. Ames was stuck with me whether he liked it or not.

As it turned out, Ames was glad to see me. "I've been hitting one brick wall after another on the Belltown thing," he complained. "I have some sources here in town, one in particular over at the *Daily Journal of Commerce*. He's mystified, too. Says nobody's acting like there's an outside investor. The real estate community is watching Belltown Terrace because of the sheriff's sale. He doesn't know who bailed them out."

"Well, somebody did," I said, settling onto Ames' bed. "Am I buying the penthouse?"

"If you still want it, considering you'd be buying it from them rather than the syndicate."

I thought about it, but I had been fantasizing about barbecued ribs for three days. My mind was made up. "I want it," I declared.

Ames nodded. "All right." He changed the subject. "Tomorrow I have to go back to The Dalles. They left word this afternoon. I catch an early plane to Portland."

"Want a ride to the airport? My car's back."

He shook his head. "I'll take the hustle bus."

We were ready to discuss our dinner when Peters called. "I figured I'd find you there. I just got out of court. What are you up to?"

"Ames and I are plotting dinner. Care to join us?"

He did. Afterwards, Ames returned to the Westin and Peters dropped by my apartment to chat. Around ten, just as Peters was ready to head home, the phone rang. It was the department. Another transient had been set afire in an alley encampment between First and Western off Cedar. Officers were on the scene. We took Peter's Datsun.

The building at First and Cedar is an office building with a penthouse restaurant on the fifth floor. The narrow alley behind it separates the building from two pay-parking lots. Between them sits a no-man's-land of blackberry bramble eight feet high. A small clearing had been carved beneath the thorny, dense branches with pieces of cardboard for flooring and walls.

Al Lindstrom and Manny Davis were at the scene. We didn't

need to ask what was under the blanket in the blackberry clump. Once you've smelled the sweetish odor of charred human flesh, you never forget it.

"Same MO as before," Al told us grimly. "Only it's a woman this time, one of the Regrade regulars. We've got a positive ID. Teresa Smith's her name. Looks like she was sleeping it off here in the brush when someone doused her with gasoline and lit a match." The very fact that someone knew her name gave us a big leg up over the other two cases.

"Who reported it?" I asked.

He gestured toward the building above us. "A guy up there in the bar looked down and saw the fire just as it started. The bartender called 911, but it was too late by the time they got here."

"Did he see anyone?"

"Saw a car drive off. Only headlights and taillights. No make or model."

"So we're not dealing with another transient," Peters commented. It was true. Downtown bums don't drive. They wander, foot-patrol style, throughout the downtown area, hanging out in loosely organized, ever-changing packs.

"How come she was by herself?"

One of the uniformed officers came up as I asked the question. "We found her boyfriend. The food bank up the street was open, and she passed out. The group left her to sleep it off while they went to get food."

A tall, weaving Indian with shoulder-length greasy hair broke free from a scraggly group at the end of the alley. He pushed his way toward us. "Where is she?" he mumbled.

Manny moved to head him off, but the drunk brushed him aside. "Where is she?" he repeated. He stopped in front of me and stood glaring balefully, swaying from side to side.

I brought out my ID and opened it in front of him. I motioned wordlessly toward the heap of blanket. He swung blearily to look where I pointed. When his eyes focused on the blanket, his knees crumpled under him. He sank to the ground, his face contorted with grief, shoulders heaving.

This was an empty hulk of humanity with nothing left to lose, yet I watched as he sustained still another loss. He stank. His hair and clothes were filthy. Blackened toes poked through his duct-taped shoes. But his anguish at the woman's death was real and affecting.

Grief is grief on any scale.

One of the patrolmen knelt beside him. "We've sent for Reverend Laura," he said.

In the old days, Reverend Laura would have gone searching for heathens in Africa or South America. Today, the tall, raw-boned woman is a newly ordained Lutheran minister with a pint-sized church in a former Pike Place tavern. She ministers to downtown's homeless. Wearing her hair in a severe bun and with no makeup adorning her ruddy cheeks, she is both plain and plainspoken, but her every action brims with the milk of human kindness. She appeared within minutes and knelt beside the weeping man, taking his elbow and raising him to his feet.

"Come on, Roger," she said kindly, "let's go to the mission."

"Will you keep him there so we can reach him tomorrow?" I asked.

She nodded. An officer helped her load him into a car. We fanned out, asking questions of all bystanders, interviewing the patrons in Girvan's, including the man who had first reported the incident.

We found nothing. It took us until two A.M. to ascertain we had found nothing. Peters dropped me off at my place. "Why don't you stay here?" I offered. "You can have the bed. I'll sleep on the couch."

"No, thanks," he replied. "I'd better get home."

I'm sure I was sound asleep before he reached the floating bridge.

Chapter 28

I WOKE up Tuesday morning, tired but with a renewed sense of purpose. Roger Bear Claw's grief had catapulted burning transients out of the realm of the inconsequential. Years of discipline took over, bringing focus and motivation. Ginger, Mona, and

Wilson were Hal's bailiwick. Teresa Smith and a dead John Doe were mine.

By seven-thirty I was at my desk. Peters stopped by on his way to the courthouse. He dropped a newspaper onto my desk. "Thought you'd want to read Max's column," he said.

It was there in lurid black and white, all about Ginger Watkins' murder. He told the whole story, including the blood-alcohol count, speculating what conversation she and Wilson might have shared over those last few drinks. Columnists speculate with impunity. They also rationalize. Cole's conclusion was that Wilson had taken his own life after destroying those responsible for the deaths of his wife and child. With typical tunnel vision, he ignored the fact that Mona Larson had never served on the parole board.

The moral of the story—and with Max there is always a moral—was couched in snide asides about inept law-enforcement officers. No one was exempt—from the Washington State Patrol and the San Juan County Sheriff's Department to the Pasco City Police. There was, however, one notable omission. J. P. Beaumont's name wasn't mentioned, not once. Evidently Ralph Ames' threat of libel had struck terror in Max's black little heart.

Peters was still there when I finished reading the article. I tossed the paper back to him. "Where the hell does he get his information? Huggins swears there's no leak in his department, but the stuff about the throttle linkage was known only by Huggins, Rogers, me and the killer."

Peters shrugged. "It doesn't really matter, does it? Wilson's dead; the case is closed. Maybe now you can get your mind back on the job. I should be done with the Sage case by noon."

After Peters left, Al, Manny, and I did a quick huddle. "So who's got a grudge against bums?" Manny asked.

"Every taxpaying, law-abiding citizen," Al Lindstrom grumped. Al is a typical hardworking Scandinavian squarehead with a natural aversion to any able-bodied person who beats the system by not holding down a real job.

Al and Manny went to the Pike Place Mission for another talk with Roger Bear Claw, while I was dispatched to Harborview Hospital to check on the surviving John Doe. Before I had a chance to leave my desk, the phone rang. It was Hal Huggins. I tried to check the annoyance in my voice. "It's about time you got around to calling me."

"Lay off, Beau. I'm up to my neck. It's just as well Wilson's dead. The county couldn't afford two first-degree murder trials."

"You're sure Wilson did it? All three of them?"

"Absolutely. Didn't you hear about the note?"

"Vaguely. But exposure? People don't just go out in the woods and wait to die. Besides, it hasn't been cold."

"Who knows? Maybe he fell in some water. That'll do it. Look, Beau, I'm not calling the shots, the coroner is. . . . By the way," he added, "we found his car parked on a side street in Prosser. The note was there."

"How long had it been there?"

"I can't tell you that. We're trying to reconstruct Wilson's movements from the time he left Orcas. So far we're not having much luck, but there's no doubt the note is his. The prints check. Handwriting checks. What more do you want?"

"What about the chicken?"

"Oh, for God's sake, Beau, lay off that chicken. Maybe he didn't plan to kill them when he left home; but after he did, he couldn't very well go back without getting caught, not even to eat his chicken or feed his goddamned cat."

"So you're closing the case?" I asked.

"Not completely. As I said, we're still retracing his movements from the time he left Orcas until he showed up in the river."

"How long has he been dead?"

"Old man Scott says two to three days at the most."

"Not 'Calls It Like I Sees 'Em' Scott!"

"That's right. One and the same. He's still Benton County Coroner. He's up for reelection next week."

Only three counties in Washington—King, Pierce, and Whatcom—have medical examiners. All the rest rely on an antiquated county coroner system. Whoever runs for office is elected without any consideration of qualifications. Garfield Scott had earned both his nickname and a permanent place in the Bungler's Hall of Fame when he declared a man dead of a heart attack, only to turn him over and discover a knife still buried in the victim's chest.

"Can't you get another opinion? What if Wilson's been dead longer than that, like since before Mona died?"

"Dammit, Beau. I already told you, I'm not calling the shots.

There's an election next week, remember? Scott would never hold still for a second opinion."

I changed the subject. "Who went to Maxwell Cole with Ginger's murder?" I asked.

There was a moment's pause. "I don't have any idea."

"Somebody did," I told him grimly. "It's front-page stuff in this morning's *P.I.*"

"Not anybody from my department, I can tell you that!" Huggins' hackles were up, and so were mine. He attempted to smooth things over. "Thanks for all your help, Beau."

"Think nothing of it," I said. Obviously he didn't.

On my way up to Harborview, I tried to shift gears from one case to another. The same intensive-care nurse stopped me. "He can't talk to you," she snapped. "He's dying."

"Look," I said wearily. "Can he communicate at all?"

"He can nod and shake his head. That's it."

"Even that may tell me something. Someone else died last night, a woman. She never made it as far as the hospital. Without his help, the toll could go higher."

She relented a little. I could see it in the set of her mouth.

"Please," I wheedled, taking advantage of her hesitation. She glared at me, then marched briskly down the hall, her rubber-soled shoes squeaking on the highly polished tile floor. I stood there waiting, uncertain if she was throwing me out or taking it under advisement. She came back a few minutes later carrying a sterilized uniform, booties, and a face mask. Wordlessly, she helped me don compulsory ICU costume.

"You can see him for five minutes. No more."

One look convinced me that Teresa Smith was a hell of a lot better off for dying on the spot. What little was visible of the man's puffy face was fused in a featureless mass of flesh that bore little resemblance to a human being. Tubes went in and out his arms and throat. His breathing was labored.

"He's awake," the nurse said, although I don't know how she knew that. "We call him Mr. Smith."

I stood by the bed, astonished by my revulsion. I'm a homicide cop. I'm supposed to be used to the worst life can dish out. Five minutes left no time for niceties. He was dying. I think he knew it.

"I'm a cop, Mr. Smith. A detective. They'll only let me talk for five minutes. Somebody else got burned last night, up on First Avenue. We think it's the same guy who burned you. Can you help us?"

There was no response. I couldn't tell if he heard me.

"Did you see anyone?"

He nodded, so slightly, that I wasn't sure he had moved.

"Someone you knew?"

This time there was no mistaking it. The mass of flesh moved slightly from side to side. The answer was no.

"One person?"

A minute nod. We were playing hardball Twenty Questions. Every question had to count. There wouldn't be any second chances, not with this Mr. Smith.

"Male?" Another nod. He groaned with the effort.

"Young?"

He nodded again, barely, but his breathing changed. The nurse took me by the arm. "Enough," she said firmly. "He's fallen asleep. You've worn him out."

She led me outside the intensive care unit, where I shed the sterile clothes. "Thank you," I said. She bustled away without acknowledgment. She was a tough old bat, but nobody with the least tendency to a soft heart could work there.

Back in the office I had a despondent Peters on my hands. "They convicted her," he said. "Not Murder One, but a minimum of twenty years for killing that worthless bastard. What the hell ever happened to justice?"

"Sometimes there's no such thing," I told him. "So get to work."

We did. We spent the afternoon with Manny and Al. The information that it was somebody young, probably a kid, constituted the first tiny break in the case. One kid, one young punk, who liked to burn people up. Who was he? Where was he from? Was he black, white, Asian?

Back to questions, always questions. The consensus was that, whoever he was, he wasn't a regular inhabitant of the downtown area. This wasn't your usual drunken brawl over a half-consumed bottle of Big Red. Fights over booze are generally harmless—a little gratuitous bloodshed among friends. This was deliberately malicious. And deadly.

We hit the streets, talking to known gang leaders and toughs. The patrolmen in what the department calls the David Sector of downtown Seattle know most of the street kids by name. They guided us to the various groups, pointing out kids who would talk and kids who liked to throw their weight around. All of them could have gotten gasoline; none of them had cars.

To quote one, a scrawny-looking kid named Spike who wore a black leather vest over a hairless bare chest, "Nobody knew nothin'," although he hinted darkly that there might be a club down at Franklin High with some allegedly vicious initiation rites.

Peters and I drove to Franklin High School in Rainier Valley. The principal, a tall black former Marine, sounded more like a drill sergeant than an educator. He admitted he had some tough kids in his school, but none who would go around setting fire to sleeping drunks, he'd stake his reputation on it. I was inclined to believe him.

Driving back to the department, Peters asked me what I thought. "He seems to know what's going on with those kids," I told him.

"Bullshit," Peters replied. "Nobody ever knows what's going on with a bunch of kids."

We agreed to disagree. It wasn't the first time, and it wouldn't be the last.

I found a note from Henry Wu on my desk. "See me."

Hank sat with his feet propped on his desk reading a copy of the *International News.* "What have you got?"

He put down the paper, a wide smile spreading under his impeccable mustache. "I think I've found her, Beau, in the Stadium Apartments out in Rainier Valley. You know where that is, out on Martin Luther King Way?"

"I think so."

"My source says she lives with her aunt and uncle and some cousins out there. Your interpreter's gone?"

"Yesterday," I said.

I must have sounded ungrateful. Hank bristled. "Look, I moved heaven and earth to get this far. Nobody rushes a grapevine."

"I know. Sorry. It's just that Ernie had to go home." Hank appeared somewhat mollified. "So what do you suggest?" I asked. "Is there anybody on the force who speaks H mong?"

"Even if there was, I wouldn't advise your taking them along, not if you want her to talk."

"What should I do then, go by myself?"

"That guy who left on the bus—Ernie. . . . My source recognized the name, knew who he was. He's evidently widely respected in the Seattle H mong community. It wasn't until I mentioned him that I started getting to first base. My suggestion is that you do whatever it takes to get him back down here.''

If you call in an expert, you have to be prepared to take his advice. Henry Wu was the expert. ''Thanks, Hank. I'll see what I can do.''

I went back to my desk. Peters looked up as I sat down. ''What gives?''

''Hank's got a line on the hotel maid from Orcas,'' I answered. I picked up the phone, ready to call Ernie.

Peters scowled. ''Look, Beau, we're already on a case. Two and a half by actual count, if that guy at Harborview is still alive.''

I felt like he'd stepped on my toes. ''Don't tell me what to do,'' I snapped. I couldn't very well call Ernie right then, not with Peters peering over my shoulder. We spent the rest of the afternoon circling each other like a squabbling old married couple. By five, we still weren't ready to bury the hatchet.

''You having dinner with Ames?'' Peters asked as we waited uneasily for the Public Safety Building's snaillike elevator. I hadn't told him Ames had returned to The Dalles. I didn't tell him then.

''Naw, he's busy,'' I replied noncommittally.

If Peters was fishing for an invitation to dinner, I didn't bite. We parted company in the lobby, and I walked home to the Royal Crest. I called Ernie right away.

''I think we've found Blia,'' I said, once he answered the phone. ''Could you come down tomorrow if I had a float plane pick you up and take you back?''

''It won't work,'' he said. ''I've got a motor home to overhaul. The Hansens are leaving for Arizona Saturday. I've got that job to do and another due by Friday.''

''Nobody else can do it?'' I insisted.

''I'm a one-man shop. Without me, nothing happens.''

I couldn't very well argue the point. ''Call me as soon as you see your way clear,'' I told him.

''Sure thing,'' he replied. ''Glad to.''

Disappointed, I hung up. Outside it was raining a steady fall drizzle. I put on a waterproof jacket and walked to the golden arches at Sixth and Westlake. I picked up a Big Mac and an order of fries to go. Peters would have pitched a fit if he'd glimpsed my evening menu.

Back at the house, I set the table with my good dishes and dined in solitary splendor. Bachelors are allowed their small eccentricities. After dinner I settled into my old-fashioned recliner and let my mind wander.

Maybe the guy who sent us to Franklin had been playing some game of his own, creating a wild-goose chase among the predominantly minority kids there. I was smart enough to recognize that the suggestion played on our own prejudices. Maybe our bum-killing fanatic was to be found at the other end of the spectrum, concealed among the well-heeled kids of Bellevue or the North End.

It was a thought that merited further consideration. Meantime, all we could do was keep looking for that rarest of all birds, the eyewitness.

The discipline of focusing on one issue at a time pushed Ginger and Sig and Mona and Wilson further and further into the background. I had to leave them alone until Ernie could return to Seattle.

For the time being, inconsequential as they might seem, three dead transients took precedence. Harborview Hospital had called the department to say that Mr. Smith was no more. My interview with him had been his very last opportunity to give us any help.

I fell asleep in the chair and didn't wake up until morning. That's something else bachelors can get away with. I'm not sure the good outweighs the bad.

Chapter 29

My back was broken when I woke up. In my youth I could sleep all night in a recliner and not have it bother me the next day. Maybe I'm getting old.

I was in the bathroom, my face slathered with shaving cream, when the phone rang. I hurried to answer it, Colgate Instant Shave smearing into the holes of the mouthpiece.

"Did you know?" an unfamiliar voice asked.

"Know what?"

"That Ginger was—" Tom Lander's voice cracked.

I waited while he got hold of himself. "I knew," I said grimly, silently cursing Homer and Darrell Watkins and Hal Huggins and J. P. Beaumont for not having broken the news to Tom earlier.

"Why didn't you tell me? Why did I have to read it in the paper?"

I didn't have an answer. I had known he wasn't told, but I had shut the knowledge out of my mind.

"Was it Wilson?" he continued doggedly.

"That's what Hal Huggins thinks," I countered.

"What do you think?" he demanded.

"I don't know." It was an honest answer.

"You could have told me."

"I expected Homer or Darrell would do that."

"They didn't."

I felt like I owed him something, but not enough to lapse into idle speculation about thawing chickens and hungry cats and extra keys. "Look, Tom, I'm following up on some leads. I'll be in touch if I find anything out, okay?"

"Why should I believe you?"

"No reason," I answered. "Because I asked."

"All right," he agreed reluctantly. "But was she really drunk, or was that just part of the story?"

"Her blood-alcohol count showed she had been drinking, enough to be drunk."

"Oh," he said, disappointment thick in his voice.

"Why, Tom? What does it matter?"

"It's personal," he replied and hung up.

I went to the bathroom and finished shaving, thinking about Maxwell Cole. I couldn't help wondering how he had gotten his information, particularly since Huggins was so sure it hadn't come through his department. I decided to pay a call on Max, for old time's sake. I called the *P.I.* He wasn't in and wasn't expected before ten.

I checked the phone book. Bingo. Maxwell Cole. It gave a Queen Anne phone number but no address. I dialed. He sounded groggy.

"Hello, Max. This is Beaumont. I want to talk to you."

"To me? How come?"

"Just a couple of questions. Can I come over?"

"I guess."

"Good. What's the address?"

He gave me a number on Bigelow North, an old-fashioned street strewn with fallen chestnuts and mounds of moldering leaves. The house was an eighteen-nineties gingerbread type set among aging trees and crowned with leaded glass gable windows. It surprised me. I had always figured Max for the swinging hot tub and cocktails type. This hardly fit that image.

I pulled up and parked. Before I could get out of the car, Max blustered out the front door and down the walk. He heaved himself into the Porsche.

"What are you doing here?" he demanded.

"You invited me, remember?"

"I was asleep. Let's go someplace for coffee." We drove to an upstairs coffee-and-croissant place on top of Queen Anne Hill. "So what do you want?" Max asked, once we settled at a table.

"I want to know where you got your information on Ginger Watkins."

Wariness crept over his flabby face. "Why do you want to know?"

"I do, that's all."

"My sources are confidential."

"You'd be forced to tell, under oath."

"There won't be a trial. Wilson's dead."

"Did Wilson tell you about Ginger? Were you in touch with him after that day on Orcas?"

Max shook his head. "Don't try to trick me, J. P. Why do you want to know? Huggins says the case is closed. He's satisfied Wilson did it."

"Who set up the meeting on Orcas? Was it Wilson?"

Max nodded.

"What did he say?"

"That something big was going to break, that it would be announced during the parole board retreat. He thought it should go in the special feature I was doing on him."

"Did he say what this 'something big' was?"

"He didn't. I thought it would be about the Victim/Witness

Protection Program. That's what he was working on, but nobody's mentioned it since. He must have had his wires crossed.''

"Did you ever publish it? The feature, I mean?''

Max looked stunned to think that I had missed a word of his deathless prose. ''I used some of it in the column after Wilson died, but not much. I was still pissed at him for dragging me all the way to Orcas and then missing the interview.''

"Was it Pomeroy?'' I asked in a feint-and-thrust maneuver designed to throw him off guard. It didn't work.

"I'm not talking,'' Max returned stubbornly. ''I already told you that.'' I wasn't able to get any more out of him. We finished coffee, and I took him home.

I turned up at the department around ten. Peters, glancing up from a stack of papers, glared at me. ''What'd you do? Forget to set your alarm?''

I didn't answer. I sat down at my desk, hoping to reshuffle my priorities and get the two John Does and Teresa Smith back on top of the desk. Don Wilson, the wild card, refused to go away.

"I talked to Hal,'' I said to Peters as I passed his desk. ''Old Man Scott swears up and down Wilson was dead two to three days at most. If that's true, how come he floated to the surface? That usually takes five days to a week.''

"Current,'' Peters offered helpfully. ''The current could have washed him up on shore without him necessarily floating to the surface.''

"I wish Baker could take a look at him.'' Dr. Howard Baker is King County's crackerjack medical examiner. Nothing gets by him. Dr. Baker is no coroner, but then King County isn't Benton County, either. ''Why the hell couldn't Wilson have died inside King County? It would simplify my life.''

"Wish in one hand, shit in the other, and see which hand gets full first.'' Peters' comment was philosophical. I love it when he lectures me in parables.

Just then Peters' phone rang. He listened briefly, then slammed down the receiver and jumped to his feet. ''Come on,'' he said. ''We've gotta go.''

"Where?''

"Manny and Al are down in Pioneer Square. They may have a lead in the transient case.''

That effectively put the cap on Ginger and Sig and Mona and Wilson. I followed Peters through the fifth-floor maze and out of the building. Pioneer Square is only a few blocks from the department, down the hill, off James.

As the name implies it's an old neighborhood made up of stately old buildings whose insides have been gutted and brought up to code. Gentrification has brought new tenants—law firms, trendy shoppes, and tiny espresso bars. The only glitch is that the new tenants haven't quite convinced the old ones, the bums, that they don't live there anymore. The merchants and the bums are constantly at war to see who controls the turf.

Peters and I walked down the hill. Manny and Al were in the Elliott Bay Bookstore, downstairs in the book-lined espresso bar. With them was a young woman in tennis shoes and a ponytail. She might have been any well-built teenager poured into a tank top and tightly fitting jeans, nipples protruding under the knit material. She looked like a teenager until you saw her close up. Her face was still attractive, but it showed signs of excessive wear.

Periodically she popped a bubble with a wad of gum, but she kept a nervous watch on a flashily dressed black man two tables away. He sat with both arms folded across his chest, silently observing the proceedings.

"So nothing happened," she was saying as Peters and I approached the table. "It washed off. He never lit the match, but I told Lawrence I'll bet it's the same guy. When I heard it on the news, I told him." She nodded toward the man I assumed to be Lawrence. "He said I could tell."

Al motioned us into two empty chairs while Manny spoke earnestly to the girl. "These are Detectives Peters and Beaumont," he explained. "They're working the case with us. Would you be willing to do a composite drawing, Sandra?"

She glanced questioningly toward Lawrence. He nodded. Evidently, anything that damaged the merchandise was bad for business. It didn't make sense to let someone set fire to the stable.

"Yes," she answered.

"This was three nights ago?"

I think she forgot she was talking to a cop. She gave Manny a bat of her long lashes as she answered. "Yes."

"And there were two of them?"

"Yes."

"Black or white?"

"White."

"Blond? Brunet?"

"One of each."

"How tall?

"I don't pay much attention. I mean, it's not important, you know? Maybe six feet or so."

"How old?"

"Twenty. Maybe younger."

"And they both paid?"

"I charge extra for two." Lawrence shifted uneasily in his chair, but I don't think Sandra noticed. At least he didn't tell her to shut up.

"Where did you go?"

"To a room at The Gaslight up on Aurora."

"So what happened?"

"Nothing. . . . Nothing kinky," she added. "Not even both together. But while the second one was getting it up, the first one pulled a bottle out of his coat pocket and poured something on me. It smelled terrible. It burned my eyes.

"The second one started yelling, 'What are you crazy?' and the first one said 'Just having a little fun.' I jumped up to call Lawrence, but one of them knocked me down, and they took off. The second guy didn't even get his shirt and shoes on. I followed them to the door, screaming like mad. They drove off before Lawrence could catch them."

"You're sure it was gasoline he poured on you?"

"Yeah. From one of those screw-top Coke bottles. Lawrence said if they'da lit a match I'da died."

Manny nodded. "It's true," he said. Sandra swallowed hard. I wondered how old she was. Probably no more than seventeen, although she looked half again that old.

"After that woman died, Lawrence said I could tell. He said this was one time we'd better cooperate."

Manny nodded again, encouragingly. "Lawrence is absolutely right," he agreed. "What kind of car was it?"

"White. One of those little foreign cars like maybe a Toyota or a Datsun. I don't know which."

"What year?"

She shrugged. "But it had some of those university parking stickers in the window. We watch for those. They're usually bad news."

Lawrence stood and motioned toward the door. Sandra caught the signal and rose obediently. "I gotta go."

"Can we call you for the composite?" Manny asked.

She nodded. "Lawrence knows how to get ahold of me."

Lawrence made a quick exit with the girl trailing behind him on an invisible leash.

"I'll just bet he does, the son of a bitch," Al Lindstrom muttered under his breath. "That makes me sick."

Manny glared at his partner. "Don't look a gift horse in the mouth, Al. We get paid for solving murders, not for busting hookers and pimps. She's the best thing that's happened to us all week."

Chapter 30

I FELT like a goddamned rubber band. Teresa and friends bubbled to the surface while Ginger and friends receded. The four of us went to lunch—Manny, Al, Peters, and I. Manny was high as a kite, while Al was still pissed, speculating that Lawrence made more than all four of us put together. Well, three of us, anyway. I wasn't talking.

Other than comparing notes on what Sandra had said, there wasn't much to do until she completed the composite. We agreed that since Manny had done most of the talking with Sandra, he should make the next contact and set up the appointment. There was no sense in causing Lawrence to be any more squirrelly than he already was.

The idea that the car was a white Datsun or Toyota with a university sticker was some help, but not much. There are literally thousands of cars registered at the U Dub, as locals refer to the University of Washington. We figured somebody should contact the campus police and ask for a preliminary list.

Seattle P.D. and the campus police get along fairly well. As law-enforcement officers, campus cops suffer from a severely restricted sphere of influence. They do a lot of PR work within the confines of their narrow jurisdiction, keeping a lid on anything that might offend the tender sensibilities of well-heeled alumni. Peters and I were to brief them on the current situation. We figured they'd be overjoyed to be involved in a real crime that didn't involve property theft.

As soon as lunch was over, we split up the act. Manny and Al headed for the medical examiner's office to pick up the preliminary report on the Harborview John Doe. Dental charts were our only possible means of identification. There sure as hell wouldn't be any fingerprints. Peters and I were supposed to go to the university. About ten to one, we stopped by the department to pick up a car, but Margie Robles, our clerk, caught us before we got away.

"There you are!" she exclaimed. "I've been looking all over for you."

"Why? What's up?"

"Somebody named Ames. He's called three times so far. For you or Detective Peters."

"Why would he call me?" Peters wondered.

"Did he leave a number?" I asked.

"Not the last time. Said you should meet him at the airport at one forty-five. Both of you. Here's the flight number." She handed me a yellow slip of paper.

Once she was out of earshot, Peters turned on me.

"What's this about? More footwork for Hal Huggins?"

"I guess," I said.

He glowered at me. "We'd better not take a company car, then. We can just barely make it." He angrily strode toward the door with me right on his tail. I had an idea Ames wasn't calling about Ginger and friends. He had been in The Dalles, negotiating with New Dawn. If he had sprung the kids, it would be a kindness to give Peters some advance warning, but if he hadn't . . . I wasn't about to make that kind of mistake. I let Peters stay pissed.

The Datsun was parked in a cheapo monthly garage at the bottom of James. Peters ground it into gear and angrily fishtailed us out of the parking stall. "You've got more nerve than a bad tooth. We shouldn't work an unauthorized case during regular hours. You'll get us both in trouble."

I said nothing. It was pure luck that got us to Sea-Tac without a speeding citation. The parking garage was crammed to the gills.

We searched through three levels before we finally spotted a little old lady vacating a spot. Peters beat two other cars to it. We were inside the terminal by one thirty-five. Naturally we had to hassle with the security guards over our weapons.

By the time we reached the gate, Northwest Orient Flight 106 from Portland was already parked in place at the jet bridge. Passengers were disembarking. I saw Ames first. He was packing one kid on his hip and dragging the other along by the hand. The girl Ames was carrying spotted Peters. "Daddy, Daddy," she squalled.

Peters whirled toward her, a look of stunned amazement on his face. As he stood glued to the floor, unable to move, the girl who was walking broke loose from Ames' grip and raced for Peters' knees. She hit him with a full flying tackle that almost toppled him. Meantime, the kid Ames was carrying set up such a howl, he had no choice but to set her on the floor and let her run too.

Peters sank to the floor, buried under a flurry of bawling kids. I moved to where Ames, looking inordinately proud, was attempting to smooth the wrinkles from his usually immaculate jacket. What appeared to be the better part of a Tootsie Roll was stuck to his silk tie.

I grabbed his hand and pumped it. "How the hell did you pull it off?"

"You've just funded their mother on a five-year mission to Nicaragua. No children allowed, of course."

"Of course," I said.

"Fully deductible," he added.

"Of course." With Ames in charge I should have known the solution would be fully deductible. Peters gradually emerged from the mêlée and came over to Ames and me, one child in each arm. They were cute little imps, five and six years old with baby teeth, long dark hair, thick lashes, and brown eyes.

Peters was more than a little choked up. "I don't know what to say," he blurted.

"How about introducing me?"

"This is Heather," he said, indicating the smaller one, "and this is Tracie. My friend, Detective Beaumont."

"Beau," I corrected.

The smaller of the two regarded me seriously. "Hello. Mommy says my name is Joy and she's Truth." She pointed at her sister.

They had evidently lived under different names in Broken Springs, Oregon.

"I like Heather better," I said.

We stood there awkwardly, bottling up the hallway, not knowing what to say or do. It was a moment that could have become maudlin, given half a chance, but Ames took charge. He herded us down the hallway like a bunch of errant sheep, leaving us long enough to pick up luggage. When he rejoined us, he carried only his own suitcase and a briefcase.

"What about them?" I asked, indicating the girls.

"New Dawn's attorney told me I could have them this morning, as is, take it or leave it. I took it. I decided we could get them clothes once they got here."

One glance at Peters told me Ames had made the right choice. You can always buy new clothes. I doubted he would have gotten a second crack at the kids.

We crowded into the Datsun for the trip back to Seattle. Peters sat in the backseat with the girls. I drove while Ames attempted to clean the chocolate off his tie.

"I guess you're taking the rest of the afternoon off?" I asked.

Peters grinned. "Looks that way. I can't believe you did it!" he said to Ames.

I could believe it, all right. I counted on Ames to smooth it over so Peters would never know exactly how it happened. It would be better for him to believe that his ex-wife had experienced a sudden change of heart. There was no need to tell him certain amounts of money had changed hands.

I got out at the department, and Ames assumed the driver's seat. I tracked down Captain Larry Powell and told him that Peters was gone for the day, explaining that his kids had come home unexpectedly. Powell was glad to hear it, but he didn't press for details. I didn't volunteer any, either.

Once Peters dropped me at the department, I checked out a car and drove to the university. Driving there, I suddenly recalled an old undergraduate pastime that had been called Bum Bashing in my day. It involved dragging home a bum on one pretext or another and then beating the crap out of him once he was there. Of course, back in the old days, I couldn't remember anyone's ever dying of it. Obviously the current generation had elevated the sport from intramural to semipro. By actual count we had three victims dead. My hope was that Sandra's encounter had been with the same bunch and that we could somehow nail them.

As I expected, the officer of the day, Joseph Randolph, was more than happy to help me. He listened carefully as I explained the problem, then left me in a waiting room while he went to work on it. Forty minutes later, he called me back into his office. With a triumphant grin, he handed me a huge computer printout that must have weighed ten pounds.

"Here it is," he said. "Every single car that's registered on campus this quarter—make and license number."

I could tell he was proud of getting it for us so fast. I hated to burst his bubble. "Can you break it down by make and model?" I asked.

His face fell. "I don't know when we could schedule that much computer time."

I took the whole list back to the department. Manny, Al, and I divided it three ways and began weeding through it. By quitting time, we had found 73 Datsuns and 51 Toyotas. No colors. We called it a job and went home. That's one thing about this kind of work. When you're looking for a needle in the haystack, you don't have to do it all at once. Both the needle and the haystack will stay right there and wait until the next day.

I called Peters at home to find out how things were going. They had just come in from buying bedroom furniture. He said he'd decided to take the rest of the week off. It would take that long to get the girls registered for school and locate a baby-sitter. I told him not to worry, since sorting through the vehicle list would probably take the better part of a week.

Ames turned up, wearing a clean tie and jacket. The two of us went out for a celebratory dinner, co-conspirators congratulating each other behind Peters' back. With the kids in Peters' custody and the major real estate deal canceled, Ames planned to return to Arizona on Saturday. I was sorry to hear it. It cost me money, but I enjoyed having Ames around. I supposed, however, that he did have other clients.

"You making any progress on the Watkins case?" he asked as we left Rosselini's Four Ten Restaurant to walk home.

I shook my head. "Huggins is sure Wilson did it. Since it isn't my case, I don't have much to say about it."

Ames looked thoughtful. "I can't help but think that the murders and the project might be related."

"How's that?"

"I'm not sure. It's just a thought."

We walked together as far as Fourth and Lenora, then split up. I went up to my apartment, mulling Ames' words along with thawing chickens, hungry cats, and extra keys.

Chapter 31

ONCE more I had a face full of shaving cream when the phone rang. It was Peters looking for a good pediatrician. In order to register the girls for school, they had to have a complete set of vaccinations. New Dawn believed in prayer, not science. As I tried to keep shaving cream out of the receiver, I considered growing a full beard.

I returned to the bathroom and had barely put razor to chin when the phone rang again. I jumped and left a good-sized nick. I'm sure I sounded exasperated when I answered. "Is this Detective Beaumont?" The voice was female, sultry, and dripping with the honeyed accents of the Deep South.

"Yes," I answered tentatively.

"My name's Colleen Borden with Armour Life Insurance." I steeled myself for the inevitable pitch. Various estate planners and financial advisors had crawled out of the woodwork ever since my windfall. "Ah'd like to make an appointment with you."

"I'm not interested in any life insurance. I'm going to live forever." It was the line that had given me the most luck in getting rid of pushy bastards.

"Ah'm not tryin' to sell you somethin,' Mr. Beaumont." She sounded clearly affronted. "Ah'm not a salesman. Ah'm a claims inspector."

That caught my attention. "A claims inspector?"

"Yes. Ah investigate death claims."

"Whose claim are you investigating?"

"That's why Ah want to see you. Ah'll be comin' to town

tomorrow and wondered if maybe we could get together for dinner, say at the Westin, the Palm Court, at six.''

"How will I know you?"

"The reservation will be in my name."

She hung up. I spent the next few minutes taking the phone apart and prying Colgate Instant Shave out of the holes with a toothpick. A death-claim inspector. I wondered which one. There were any number of deaths in need of inspecting.

I finished my shave on the third try. I was almost late by then. I hit the elevator with a tiny piece of tissue stemming the flow of blood on my chin.

Manny and Al were hard at work on the list when I got to my desk. I settled down with my portion of it, wishing Peters were there to lighten the load. Manny took off about eleven to oversee Sandra's composite drawing, while Al and I grappled with the list until our eyes burned.

Manny came back about two, practically walking on air. He had two drawings. Each pictured a clean-cut, ordinary-looking kid. It gets me when a cold-blooded killer looks like the kid next door or maybe even *is* the kid next door.

But it wasn't the drawings that had Manny excited. Sandra had come up with one other tiny scrap of information. The white car had carried a bumper sticker. She couldn't remember the whole thing, just that some of the letters had been funny, maybe backwards or upside down. The only one she remembered for sure was a K, and maybe a backwards E.

A frat rat! From a house with *kappa* in it and maybe a *sigma*. Sandra, bless her little heart of gold, had saved our eyesight. Instead of having to go through the computer printout listing every car on campus, she had narrowed our investigation to the much smaller world of sororities and fraternities. A quick consultation with Ma Bell's Yellow Pages told us the university boasted only ten Greek houses with *kappa* in their names.

Manny, Al, and I drove to what we call Never Never Land in two separate cars. If Seattle is a liberal egg, then the University of Washington is the yolk, although the kids there now are far more conservative than the students of, say, the sixties or seventies. They still do drugs, and they still live in an aura of permissiveness where some students literally get away with murder, but it's a hell of a lot better than it used to be.

We didn't notify the campus police. It wasn't necessary. Greek Row isn't on campus proper.

Parking places are at a premium. We finally parked in front of two separate fire hydrants on Seventeenth NE. Manny and Al took one side of the street, and I took the other, wishing the whole time that Peters were there to back me up instead of sitting in a doctor's office somewhere waiting to have his kids vaccinated for polio, tetanus, typhoid, and God knows what else.

I was the one who got lucky, if you can call it that. Kappa Sigma Epsilon at 4747 Seventeenth NE was a white, New England-style building. I remembered it as an old-line, socially prominent Eastern fraternity. Like fraternities in general, it had fallen on hard times. The paint was chipped and peeling, and a couple of broken windows were patched with plywood.

I knocked and waited. Finally a wide-eyed kid answered the door. I pulled out the two sketches. "I wondered if you could help me. Do you recognize either of these guys?"

He looked at the pictures, then back at me. "You a cop?" he asked.

I pulled out my ID. Five years ago, a kid at the university wouldn't have given me the time of day. That's what I expected now. I was wrong.

He nodded, pointing. "That's Howard Rayburn. The other's Vince Farley. Howie's upstairs. Want me to get him?"

Sometimes you make a decision that you spend the rest of your life regretting, playing it back over and over; wondering, if you had done something differently, would disaster have been averted. At that moment in the vestibule of Kappa Sigma Epsilon I made one of those bad decisions.

I didn't know what I was up against, and I didn't want to go in without a backup. "No, thanks," I said. "I'll be right back." I hurried to the grass median and waited until I saw Manny coming back down a sidewalk. I motioned for him to come. He in turn called Al.

"What have you got?" Manny demanded.

"Looks like they both live there. Only one is home."

"Want me to radio for more units?" Al asked. I nodded. He loped off toward their car. I motioned Manny to cover the back door, while I returned to the front porch. This time I didn't bother to knock. I met the same kid, coming down the stairs.

"I told Howie you were here," he said helpfully.

It was the worst thing he could have done, but I hadn't told him not to. "What room?" I said, taking the stairs three at a time.

"Turn left. Third door on the left."

I drew my .38 as I dashed down the hall. The third door on the left was ajar. I tapped on it, but there was no answer. I pushed the door open, but nothing happened. Cautiously I looked inside. No one was there. A dresser drawer sat open with half its contents spilled onto the floor. Someone had left the room in a hell of a hurry.

I flew back down the hall to the vestibule at the bottom of the stairs. The same kid was still standing there. When he saw my Smith and Wesson, his jaw dropped.

"Did he come this way?" I demanded.

Incapable of speech, he shook his head.

"Is there another way down from up there?"

He nodded dumbly.

"For chrissake talk to me! Where is it?"

"The fire escape comes out down by the kitchen."

I raced in the direction he pointed. I came to the backdoor and looked outside long enough to see Manny crouched behind a dumpster. I turned around and almost ran over the kid who had trailed behind me down the hall.

"If he didn't get out here, where else could he be? Is there a basement?"

This time he pointed to a darkened stairway leading down from the kitchen. I heard wailing sirens as backup units charged through traffic. Sprinting to the bottom of the stairs, I paused on a musty landing before dashing down a narrow hall. I checked rooms as I went—laundry room, boiler room, bicycle room, poolroom. All of them were empty.

If Howie hadn't made a run for it before Manny got to the dumpster, he was still hiding somewhere in the building. The question was Where.

I had started up the stairs to begin a systematic, room-to-room search when I remembered chapter rooms. Every fraternity had one—at least they used to—a secret room hidden somewhere in the house, where the whole fraternity gathered for formal meetings and initiations. I went back to the poolroom. One wall curved in a semicircle.

"Where's the chapter room?" I snapped. "There?"

The boy nodded.

"Where's the entrance?"

He opened the door to a seemingly small closet which became a black-walled stucco room, an Aeolian cave for initiation rites. He pointed toward a small door. I motioned him away from it and knocked. No answer. I tried the doorknob. It turned in my hand. I pushed the door open, but stayed outside.

"Howie?" I asked into the blackened room.

There was no answer, but I could sense another person's presence. Maybe I could smell his terror, hear his heart thumping. I knew he was there.

"Police, Howie. We know you're in there. Give yourself up." Still there was no answer.

"Come on out, Howie. We know all about you and Vince. It's no use."

I heard a half-sob. "I didn't do it." His voice was a choked whisper. "I made him leave, but he said I was an accessory after the fact."

"Come on out, Howie. We can talk about it later."

I stood with one eye closed, hoping to adjust my vision to the deeper darkness of the other room. It didn't help.

There is no silence quite as stark as that between hunter and hunted. The two of us were alone in a frozen universe. The small click of a released safety catch shattered the silence.

"Throw it down," I commanded. "Come out with your hands up."

Instead, Howard Rayburn, age nineteen, put the gun to his head and blew his brains out.

Chapter 32

I WAS sick as I walked through the process. Howie Rayburn was almost the same age as my own son, Scott. The media showed up outside, including the ubiquitous Maxwell Cole. I stumbled across him when I went outside with the medical examiner's team.

He waved to me, but I ignored him. It's a double standard. No one had been particularly interested when Teresa Smith burned to death. She wasn't as newsworthy as someone who might have lit the match. I returned to the building without acknowledging him.

Nobody could tell us where Vince Farley was. We sealed off both Rayburn's and Farley's rooms until Al came back with search warrants. By late afternoon we knew more about Vince Farley than we wanted. His father owned a string of racetracks all over the Southwest. Vince was flunking out of school. He kept a little scrapbook. We found clippings, not only of the three incidents in Seattle, but also one from Iowa City, Iowa. Same MO. Vince Farley himself was nowhere to be found.

Howard Rayburn's mother, a widow, showed up. She appeared to be a nice lady—shocked, disbelieving, grieving, hurt. Al talked to her; I didn't. Couldn't.

The afternoon turned sunny, the blue clarity of the sky mocking what was going on below. We worked the rest of the afternoon. It was dark before we got back downtown and started writing reports; midnight before I came home and took a long shower, trying to wash away the day's filth. I fell into bed but couldn't sleep. I finally got up and administered a bottle of medicinal McNaughton's. It worked; I slept.

I stumbled to my desk at eight the next morning—sick, hungover, exhausted. Peters called to touch bases. "You guys got a line on Farley?" he asked.

"Not yet." I sighed wearily. "We've got a dragnet out, but it hasn't turned up anything. We heard rumors late last night that he might have crossed into Canada. His mother is divorced and lives in Toronto."

"That means extradition?"

"Fat chance, right?"

"Right," Peters echoed. "So what are you doing today?"

"We'll be back at the U, interviewing fraternity brothers. We didn't get to all of them last night."

And that's what we did. All day long. Back downtown late in the afternoon, we tried to put some international tracers on Vince Farley. Still no luck. We heard through the grapevine that his father's attorney was raising hell with the Chief about his son's name being plastered all over the media. It was the age-old story.

Poor little rich kid fucks up, and Daddy's attorneys ride to the rescue.

I got back to my apartment about five-thirty. I sat down in the chair long enough to take off my shoes. I made the mistake of leaning back, intending to rest my eyes a minute. The next thing I knew, it was six-thirty and the phone jangled me awake.

"Hello," I mumbled into the phone.

"Detective Beaumont, am Ah to understand you're standin' me up?" An angry Southern belle is anything but sultry.

"I'm sorry," I stammered. "I'll be right there."

"Ah've already been waitin' a whole half-hour."

"No, really, I'm only a couple of minutes away."

The Palm Court maître d' greeted me with a knowing smile. "You must be Mr. Beaumont. Right this way, please."

I had been far too preoccupied during the preceding thrity-six hours to give Ms. Colleen Borden from Armour Life Insurance Company any thought. Had I done so, I'm sure I wouldn't have pictured a platinum blonde in her late forties with an hourglass figure and a crimson smile. Her hair was pulled back ballerina-style and covered with a broad, brimmed fedora. A well-cut lavender dress, softly draped, showed her figure to good advantage. At the base of her throat lay a gleaming diamond pendant. Her eyes were a startling shade of violet, set in a timeless face.

The waiter held my chair. I slipped into it while she gave me a shrewdly appraising once-over. "Well now," she drawled, "Ah don't believe anybody told me you were quite this cute, Detective Beaumont. Seein' you in the flesh maybe Ah'm not so mad at you for fallin' asleep."

It wasn't how I had expected our conversation to start. I mumbled an apology. She held up her hand. "No, now Ah don't want to hear another word about it. We'll just have ourselves a little drink and a little dinner. Then, if you still feel like apologizin', maybe we can work somethin' out." She gave me a sly grin. I would have had to be blind, deaf, and dumb not to have known what she meant.

I put a bland smile on my face and ordered a hair-of-the-dog McNaughton's. "What can I do for you?"

She took a long sip of Southern Comfort. "Mah daddy owns Armour Life Insurance Company," she drawled. "And his daddy owned it before that. We're not very big, but we're solid."

She paused and gave me a dazzling smile. "Years ago, Daddy

called me into his office. He doesn't have any sons, you see, and he says, 'Cody.' That's what he calls me. 'Cody, Ah want you to come into the business so you'll know how to run it when the time comes, but Ah don't want you out sellin' none o' this stuff. That's too hard a life for a little lady. What Ah'd like you to do is make sure that when we pay a claim it's on the up and up.' And that's what Ah've been doin' ever since."

"What does this have to do with me?"

Instead of answering my question, she motioned to a waiter who hovered in the background. "You decided what you want?" she asked. "Ah do believe Ah'll have the pheasant. Ah just love pheasant." Without looking, I nodded, and she ordered two of them. She turned back to me, the smile once more in place.

"Why do you suppose Homer and Darrell Watkins turned you down when you made them such a right tolerable offer?"

With that, any notion that Colleen Borden was a lightweight went right out the window.

"Ames says they found another investor."

"Ralph Ames is your attorney, the one who was handlin' your deal?"

"Yes."

"Do you have any idea where that man is?"

"Ames? Why, no. He said he'd head back to Phoenix tomorrow, but I don't know where he's been today."

"Ah've hung around here all day long, hopin' to run into him, left him messages. He hasn't returned a single call, not one."

"That's not like him," I said contritely, as though both Ames and I had been remiss. "Have you tried in the last few minutes?"

"Ah left word that he should join us." As if on cue, the maître d' hurried to our table. "Excuse me, Miss Borden. There's a gentleman outside who says his name is Mr. Ames. Should I show him in?"

"Oh, by all means. Do have him come in."

There was a flurry of activity around our table as a third place was set. Ames followed the maître d' uncertainly, as though not sure what to expect. I stood to introduce them. It was comical to see. Ames fell into those violet eyes and never knew what hit him.

"Ah'm very pleased to make your acquaintance, Mr. Ames," Cody drawled. "Ah've been doin' my very best to find you all day long."

"I'm sorry to be so difficult," Ames apologized. "I've been out in Kirkland helping a friend of ours. I was actually . . ." Ames paused and cleared his throat. "Interviewing baby-sitters. He has to have one by Monday, you know."

Colleen nodded seriously, as though she understood perfectly.

"And then," Ames continued, Colleen's undivided attention making him babble, "once we got the girls registered for school, we had to take them shopping for clothes, shoes, lunch pails, bedding, everything."

I burst out laughing. The very idea of Ralph Ames, attorney extraordinaire, interviewing nannies and dragging tykes through Nordstroms and The Bon on a full-scale shopping marathon struck my funnybone, especially since he was so dead serious about it. Colleen took offense at my laughter. That moment sealed Ralph Ames' fate.

"Mr. Beaumont, Ah think it's perfectly wonderful that Mr. Ames has been helpin' his friend, and Ah don't see any reason for you to be laughin' at him."

Ames turned an interesting shade of red and took a long sip of the Southern Comfort that Colleen had ordered for him. By the time we were into the main course—three pheasants instead of two—Colleen Borden knew as much about Peters' custody fight as confidentiality would allow.

Then, just when I thought we were never going back to Armour Life Insurance Company, Colleen delicately laid down her fork, turned her violet-eyed charm full on Ames, and said softly, "Supposin' we get down to business."

Cody Borden was the consummate iron fist in a velvet glove. "To begin with, Ah've talked to Hal Huggins. He's a nice man, but Ah don't believe he's ever been involved in an insurance case of this magnitude." She blinked a long blink with her very long eyelashes. "You see," she drawled, "we're talkin' about three million dollars altogether."

"Insurance fraud!" Ames exclaimed. "A buy/sell agreement funded with life insurance. Why didn't I think of that?" Ames came on-line without missing a beat.

Colleen smiled at him. "That's right, sweetie. Five hundred thousand apiece, with a five hundred thousand accidental-death benefit."

Ames' accountant mentality took over. He whistled. "That

would be plenty to get them out of the woods. When would the claim be paid?"

"Well, now," Colleen murmured, "that all depends, doesn't it? Two to three weeks if everythin's in order. Much longer than that if there's a problem."

"Three weeks would be in time to ward off the sheriff's sale."

Colleen nodded. "These policies are all well beyond the contestable period. We'll be payin' the claims, regardless. Ah just want to be sure in my own mind that we're not payin' good money to a murderer."

She removed a sheaf of papers from a slender briefcase, handing them to Ames rather than me. Swiftly he skimmed through them. "It's essentially a buy/sell arrangement," he explained to me a few minutes later, "with all proceeds going to the surviving partners."

"And the surviving partners are?" I asked.

"Why, Darrell Watkins and his daddy, of course," Colleen answered sweetly.

"Have you talked to Hal Huggins about this?" I demanded.

"He's got it stuck in his craw that somebody named Wilson did it. But in talkin' to him, Ah kept comin' up with your name, Mr. Beaumont. And then, when Ah started looking into the Belltown Terrace situation, Ah saw your name again." She smiled. "Seemed like too much of a coincidence to me, wouldn't you say?"

Ames had been studying the papers throughout this exchange. He looked around as though waking from a long sleep. "If both surviving beneficiaries were implicated in the deaths of the other partners, what would happen?"

Colleen smiled again. "Why, sweetie, if someone proves that, the proceeds go to the insured's next of kin."

Dinner wasn't over. I believe we had dessert and coffee, but I bowed out of the conversation. I sat there thinking about Mona Larson's brother from Idaho and Sig Larson's three kids and Ginger Watkins' father, Tom Lander.

Maybe Hal Huggins was buying the Don Wilson story, but I wasn't. Cody's idea made perfect sense. Darrell and Homer could knock off the others, frame Wilson, and use the three million to bail themselves out of the hole. Greed for motive rather than revenge.

I made up my mind on the spot that, if Hal Huggins wouldn't do something about it officially, then I would unofficially.

I left the table with Ames and Colleen still huddled over a sheaf of papers. I had the distinct impression, however, that they wouldn't stick to business forever.

Chapter 33

HAL Huggins didn't answer either at home or at the office when I got back from the Westin. Why should he? After all, it was Friday night. As far as Hal was concerned, he had solved three murders that week. He was probably out celebrating.

I tried again the next morning, as soon as I woke up. Woke him, too. "What's going on?" he muttered, half asleep.

"Did you talk to Colleen Borden?"

"That dingey broad? Yes, I talked to her. Goddamned insurance companies are all alike—do anything to avoid paying a claim. All they want to do is take your money; then, as soon as somebody dies—"

"Hal," I interrupted, "did you listen to her? I think she's onto something."

"Look here, Beau," Huggins bristled. "I'm telling you once and for all. Wilson did it. We've got motive, opportunity, witnesses that place him near the scene, fingerprints on a confession. What the hell do you want?"

"I want to nail the guilty party."

"You know, Beau, I keep wondering why you're so involved. I heard you were up nosing around Wilson's house the other day. This isn't your case, remember?"

"Are you going to investigate Colleen Borden's allegations or not?"

"The case is closed as far as my office is concerned."

"My mind's made up, don't confuse me with the facts. Didn't you tell me that once? Does it have anything to do with the fact that Tuesday is election day and Darrell Watkins is a major political candidate? Did the sheriff tell you to stifle?''

"Go fuck yourself," Huggins replied, hanging up.

I got Ernie Rogers' home number from the Directory Assistance. "It's Saturday. What time are you coming over?" I asked, once I got him on the phone.

Ernie sounded surprised. "I didn't think you still needed me. I thought the case was closed. That's what the paper said."

"It may be closed there," I returned grimly. "It isn't here. How long will it take you to get to Seattle?"

"I'll check the ferry schedule and call you back."

"Screw the ferry schedule. Charter a float plane. I'll pay for it. Get here as soon as you can. Have him land at the Lake Union dock. I'll pick you up."

He called back a little while later to say that the soonest he could arrive would be one o'clock. It was almost ten. I had three hours to do what I needed to do.

I had kept one of Don Wilson's pictures. I needed to assemble a few others for a rogue's gallery. While I was at it, I decided to kill two birds with one stone.

Directory Assistance gave me Darrell Watkins' campaign headquarters. A quavery-voiced old lady answered the phone. "Do you have access to Mr. Watkins' calendar?" I asked.

"Certainly," she responded. "It's right here on the wall above my head. That way we all know what's going on at all times. Of course, he's canceled everything now that his wife . . ." Her voice trailed off.

"I know. I was wondering about some appearances during the last couple of weeks." I was playing liar's poker and doing my best to sound casual, unhurried. "I'm writing an article about Mr. Watkins. My records show he was in Vancouver and Longview on the eighteenth, and Chehalis, Centralia, and Olympia on the nineteenth. Is that correct?"

"I don't know where you got that," she snorted. "He was scheduled to be in Bellingham and Everett on the eighteenth and nineteenth."

There was a catch of excitement in my throat. Everett is a short hop from Anacortes and the ferry to Orcas.

"Is that all you wanted?" she demanded impatiently.

"Do you have any brochures with his picture?"

"Certainly. We could send you a whole packet. Are you interested in doorbelling?"

"No. All I need is one brochure. Can I pick it up?"

"Our campaign headquarters is at the corner of Denny and First North."

"Good," I said. "I'll be right over."

Getting a picture of Homer Watkins proved somewhat more difficult. Not impossible. I finally managed to dredge one out of a newspaper file. It was several years old and dated from Homer's tenure as president of the Washington Athletic Club. It was good enough for my purposes.

I stopped by the department and sifted through the collection of pictures we keep on hand to build montages for witnesses to use when they're trying to identify a suspect. You can't just hand them a picture and say, "Is this the one?" You have to give them a batch of pictures and say, "Do you see anyone you recognize?"

Ernie was true to his word. The float plane pulled up to the dock on Lake Union right at one. The pilot said he'd have lunch and then come back to the plane. Ernie had left his wheel chair at home. Assisted by a steel crutch, he hopped from the plane to the Porsche. Once inside, Ernie and I took off for Rainier Valley.

The Porsche created quite a stir among some kids playing a spirited game of soccer in the parking lot of the Stadium Apartments, a low-income housing complex on Martin Luther King Way. From the way he had put the Porsche back together, it was clear Ernie Rogers was a top-drawer mechanic, but his skill with language dumbfounded me. The kids broke up their game and admiringly surrounded the car, giving us a thumbs-up greeting. Within moments Ernie was speaking to them in a language I had never heard before. They responded by enthusiastically directing us to a building near the back of the complex.

People with two good legs never notice stairways. We were directed to a set of dingy stairs thick with the stale odor of boiled rice, rancid cooking oil, and old fish. Ernie turned around, sat down, handed me his crutch, then made his way up the steps on his butt without a word of complaint. We located the correct apartment number and knocked on a flimsy, hollow door.

It opened slowly, revealing an old woman, gray-haired and tiny, who peered cautiously up at us. Ernie spoke to her rapidly but softly in the same musical language he had used on the chil-

dren outside. Her face brightened, and she favored him with a
benign smile. A slight inclination of her head motioned us into
the room.

It was empty except for one derelict chair and a floor covering
of woven mats. I had the feeling that, moments before we entered, the room had teemed with people. Now it contained only
two, the old woman and a venerable old man with white hair and
a twisted driftwood walking stick. He sat regally on the only
chair—a cane-backed wooden one that leaned slightly to one side.
He nodded to Ernie, and spoke to the old woman who disappeared and returned with a folding chair for Ernie. The old man
spoke again, addressing Ernie, who turned to me.

"He wants to know if Blia is in trouble."

"No," I answered. "We're looking for the man who stole her
keys."

The old man studied me closely as Ernie translated. "The
hotel didn't believe her when she said someone stole them."

"I do," I told him. When Ernie translated, the old man nodded
sagely.

"He wants to know what you want with Blia."

I reached into my coat pocket and removed the packet of pictures. I handed them directly to the old man. "I want to show
her these. One of those men may have been the one who stole
her keys. Maybe she'll recognize him."

The old man examined the pictures minutely in the dim light
of the curtained window, then he spoke quickly to the old woman
who shuffled from the room. Moments later she returned, leading
a shy young woman with waist-length jet-black hair. The younger
woman seemed reluctant, but the old woman prodded her forward. When Blia saw Ernie, her face brightened. She moved
forward more willingly.

The woman led Blia to the old man, who handed her the pictures. "Ask her if she saw any of those men at Rosario the day
she lost her keys."

Ernie translated. The girl walked to the curtained window and
studied the pictures. I held my breath as she leafed through them
one by one. It was possible she had seen nothing, would recognize no one. Suddenly she stopped. She handed one of them back
to Ernie, who passed it to me.

The face in the picture was that of Homer Watkins.

I'm sure my face betrayed the impact the picture had on me.

I had expected it to be Darrell Watkins, wanted it to be him so badly I could taste it. There are very good reasons why neither doctors nor detectives should work on cases too close to home. It warps perspective.

I looked up. Everyone in the room was staring at me. "Ask her when she saw him," I said to Ernie.

He translated for her, then turned to me with Blia's long response. "She was cleaning her last room. Someone had checked in and then changed his mind. The desk wanted the room re-cleaned because they thought they could rent it again. When she came out of the room, he was standing by her cart. A few minutes later she realized her keys were missing."

"Can she remember exactly what time it was?"

"Late. After dark. Around seven o'clock." Blia hadn't moved from her place near the window. She watched me warily, gauging my reactions to each translation.

"Tell her thank you," I said. "And tell her there's a reward. Someone will be in touch with her next week to arrange it. He will be authorized to pay her five thousand dollars, but she may have to testify in court."

Ernie looked at me quickly before he translated. He spoke for a long time. Blia's face changed several times, mirroring surprise, joy, doubt, and, finally, after the old man spoke sternly, agreement.

"She'll testify," Ernie said. "If you need it."

The old woman showed us out of the apartment. "Five thousand dollars is a lot of money," Ernie said as he bumped his way down the stairs. "Where'd it come from?"

"Beats me," I replied. We were both quiet after that until we were in the car and halfway back downtown. "Whose picture?" Ernie asked.

"Not the guy I expected," I said.

"You can't tell me who, though?"

"No, I'd better not." He accepted my refusal good-naturedly. I felt obliged to explain. "If word leaks out before we're ready on this one—"

"Forget it," he said. "It's no big deal."

We stopped at the Doghouse for coffee before I took him back to the plane. Once the float plane was airborne above Lake Union, I went home.

There was no sense in calling Huggins. His mind was made

up. And there was no sense in calling Peters. His hands were full. I called the Westin and was told Mr. Ames had changed his mind. He hadn't checked out, after all. I left a message saying that I would need him in Seattle during the week and that he shouldn't leave without checking with me first. I had a feeling Ames' virtue was no longer intact.

I settled into my recliner. I'm not one of the trendy types who sits in a half-lotus position to do his thinking. My legs would stick permanently. A recliner and a steaming cup of strong coffee are all I need to get the creative juices flowing.

The ball was definitely back in my court. What I had to do more than anything was think it through. There was far too much at stake to go off half-cocked.

Homer. Blia Vang had fingered Homer. He had been at Rosario that Friday afternoon, and no one had known it. So he had gotten the keys and then let Wilson into Ginger's room to get the calendar? That didn't make sense, but that was the way it looked.

I tried to put myself back in that Friday afternoon, to remember all the events in the exact order in which they had occurred. It can be done. It's a process very much like a self-induced hypnotic trance. Or a time machine.

The parole board meeting got out at four. Ginger and Sig were supposed to meet at five, but Darrell called and held Ginger up, made her late. By the time she reached the rendezvous, Sig Larson was dead.

Homer Watkins and Don Wilson, an unholy alliance. Unless . . . Something Blia Vang had said jumped out at me.

Someone had rented a room at Rosario and then changed his mind. Who? And what about Darrell Watkins' campaign appearances in Everett and Bellingham?

The thought had no more than crossed my mind when I was out of my chair, emptying my cup in the sink and shrugging my way into the shoulder holster.

Either Homer and Darrell were in it together, or Darrell was next on the list.

Chapter 34

THE Porsche loves to get on the freeway and go. I headed north to Everett, driving directly to the offices of the *Everett Herald*. It's a small-town paper. The receptionist, a bored teenager, was happy to have some company.

I flashed my badge at her, and she bustled around, finding me what I needed—all papers from the two-week period prior to October eighteenth. I located the information I wanted, eventually. Buried among wedding announcements, Pop Warner football scores, and pre-holiday church bazaars was an article detailing Darrell Watkins' campaign swing through Bellingham and Everett. He was to address the Bellingham Rotary and Jaycees on Friday afternoon and a League of Women Voters convention at the Everett Holiday Inn Friday evening. Saturday morning he was scheduled to be the keynote speaker at a Merchant's Fair breakfast.

Thanking the receptionist for her help, I drove to the Holiday Inn. I didn't mess around with the desk clerk. I asked to speak directly to the manager. He was an eager Young Turk, fresh out of school with a degree in hotel management. His nametag pegged him as Mr. Young, which seemed entirely appropriate.

"What can I do for you?" he asked, after minutely examining my identification.

"I'd like to see your guest register for the night of October eighteenth."

"This is, of course, highly irregular."

"Mr. Young," I said firmly, "I'm attempting to prevent another homicide. There's not much time."

"Can't this wait until Monday when I could check with my superiors in Seattle?"

"No. Someone else could be dead by then." Youth can often be intimidated by a steady, middle-aged stare. It worked like a charm.

"Oh, all right. I don't see how it could hurt."

There were lots of registration slips. Many of the women had registered separately, even though they were staying in the same room—a variation on the female penchant for separate checks. I thumbed through them carefully. I was close to the bottom before I found the one I wanted, a slip that read Darrell Watkins. I jotted down the license number of the car, an '81 Audi.

Mr. Young had stood peering over my shoulder the whole time. "Did you find what you needed?" he asked.

"Yes. Can you make me a copy of this?" I showed him the slip.

"This is nuts. I shouldn't have shown it to you in the first place without a court order. Now you want me to make you a copy?"

"By the time I can get a court order," I said, "the killer may strike again. The score is four to nothing right now. The killer's winning."

He made me a copy. "One more question," I said as he handed me the paper. "Who on your catering staff handled the League of Women Voters convention?"

"That would have been Sue Carleton."

"Is she here?"

He sighed, exasperated. "She's upstairs."

Sue Carleton turned out to be a heavyset dame in her middle years. I had a feeling she had come up through the ranks—without a degree in hotel management but with a healthy regard for and an easy ability to work with other people. She had a pleasant manner and a sparkling sense of humor.

"What can I do for you, Detective Beaumont?" she asked.

"I wanted to talk to you about the League of Women Voters."

"They were awful." She smiled. "Too many chiefs and not enough Indians. I almost lost my mind."

"I wanted to ask you about one of the speakers, Darrell Watkins."

"That jerk. He was late. I had to pay my people overtime because they didn't finish on time."

"What happened?"

"He was supposed to speak at the beginning of the program. He didn't show up until nine when they were almost finished. They let him give his whole speech anyway. I was livid."

I stood. "That's all I needed to know. Did he offer any explanation?"

"Car trouble, I think. Does this help?"

"You'd better believe it. Thanks."

Galloping out of the Holiday Inn, I sped north to Anacortes, hoping I'd hit the ferry schedule right. No such luck. A ferry was just pulling away from the dock as I drove up to the ticket booth. There was nothing to do but cool my heels and wait for the next one.

It was possible Darrell could have been on Orcas with Homer at the time Ginger's room was broken into and still have made it back to Everett by nine. If, that is, he had better luck with the ferries than I did.

Once on Orcas, I drove straight to Rosario without notifying Huggins. I wanted to get in, verify the information, and get back out—without arousing attention.

It was Saturday evening. A laughing crowd was grouped around the massive fireplace in the Moran Room, and a clutch of people stood in front of the desk, waiting to register. The overtaxed desk clerk was far too busy to help me right then.

I went into the Vista Lounge. Barney was at his station. He glanced up and waved as I walked past. I had no more than taken a seat on a stool at the end of the bar when he brought me a McNaughton's and water.

"That's pretty good," I said as he set the drink in front of me.

He grinned. "I don't do much, but I'm good at what I do."

Someone signaled for a beer. Barney drew one from the tap, delivered it, then came back to me. "So what's up? You get your car back all right?"

I nodded. "Ernie did a great job. I'm up here looking for some answers," I told him.

"What kind?"

"I need to see the guest register for the eighteenth. . . . Quietly," I added.

"Unofficially?" I nodded, and he grinned. "I might be able to help. Did you see the lady at the desk?"

"Just a glimpse. She was busy."

"We're engaged," he said proudly. "Tell me what you want. She'll get it for you."

Another customer summoned him. When he returned, he stood

in front of me, vigorously polishing the bar. "What are you looking for?" he asked.

"At least one room was rented twice that day. Someone checked in, changed his mind, and checked back out. I need a copy of any registration slips on rooms that were rented twice that day."

He gave me a sly wink. "Looking for somebody sneaking around, eh?" He glanced at my glass. "You want another?"

"No. I'd better switch to coffee. It's a long drive."

"You're not staying over? We've got rooms."

I shook my head. I drank a couple of cups of coffee and ate a hamburger while I waited. It was almost an hour before Barney's fiancée delivered the goods. There were three rooms that had been rented twice on the eighteenth. Using a lighted hurricane lamp from one of the tables, I studied the copies Barney gave me. Five of the six names didn't ring any bells. Three of them had actually spent the night. The other two were probably respectably married people sneaking an illicit afternoon without their lawfully wedded husbands and wives.

The last name stopped me cold. Don Lacy. The address was in Burien. I wrote it down, 12823 S. 124th. The clincher was that the car was a 1981 Audi, the same make and model listed on Darrell Watkins' guest registration at the Holiday Inn. Naturally the license numbers didn't match. What a surprise! Don Lacy and Darrell Watkins had to be one and the same.

I left the lounge and walked to the last wing of the hotel where Ginger's original room had been. The room registered to Lacy was right next door to Ginger's. When Darrell had been talking to her, pleading with her not to divorce him, he had been directly on the the other side of a narrow wallboard partition, not calling long-distance from somewhere on the mainland.

Hurrying back to my car, I barely had time to catch the last ferry to Anacortes. I sat by one of the huge windows, staring at glass that reflected the bright lights inside the boat rather than the midnight water outside.

My mind jumped to a dozen different conclusions. Wilson, Homer, and Darrell all had to be involved together. Somehow. All three of them had been at Orcas that afternoon. Funny how both Darrell and Homer had neglected to mention it. The question remained, Were they in it together, or was one covering for the other?

I wanted to be the one to find the answers. I owed Ginger that much, but I wasn't working with a full contingent of soldiers. I didn't have all the resources of Seattle P.D. standing behind me, backing me up. I suppose I could have called Huggins and insisted he reopen the case, but I didn't. Pride, I guess. I wanted to nail the case down with a fistful of incontrovertible evidence before I called for reinforcements.

My mother used to say, "Pride goeth before a fall." It's true.

By the time I reached Anacortes, I had a game plan mapped out in my mind.

It was almost two in the morning when I hit Seattle. I drove straight through town and took the Sea-Tac exit to Burien. The address on S. 124th street wasn't hard to find. A silver Audi was parked in the driveway. I drove home.

Once in the house, I went searching for the phone book. I looked under Lacy, Darlene, 12823 S. 124th Street. That answered a lot of questions. I put the phone book away and went to bed.

Ames woke me Sunday morning. According to my count, that was two Sundays in a row. He wondered if I would care to join Cody and him for brunch at the Westin. Ames sounded smug. He couldn't quite conceal his lack of disappointment when I said no. Ames had never struck me as much of a ladies man. He was proud of what he regarded as a personal conquest.

I wasn't the kind of guy to tell him that he had been duck soup for someone like Colleen Borden, and she was far too much of a lady to tell him herself. I left his delusions of adequacy intact.

"Too much to do, Ames, sorry. But I'll want to talk to you later today or tomorrow about some of the reward money."

"Okay," he said. "But if you don't reach me in my room, you might try Cody's."

"Right," I said.

I waited until ten o'clock before I called Janice Morraine at home. She's a criminalist in Seattle's Washington State Patrol Crime Lab. Over the months, she and I had become friends. I couldn't call the crime lab directly to ask for help. I didn't have an official case number.

"How are you at handwriting analysis?"

"So-so," she answered.

"How about trading breakfast for an off-the-record opinion."

She laughed. "Smooth talker," she said.

We went to an omelet house at the bottom of East Madison, right on Lake Washington. There, amid the early-afternoon Sunday brunch crowd, she smoked one cigarette after another and compared the two signatures from copies of the guest-registration forms. She studied them in silence for several long minutes, leaving me to sip my coffee and stare at the top of her head bent over the papers in total concentration. At last she looked up at me.

"You know I'm not the final word," she said. I nodded. "But in my opinion, they were signed by the same person."

"That's what I thought."

"Is this *the* Darrell Watkins?" she asked, pointing at his signature. I nodded again. "If this is something bad, you'd better not just take my word for it," she warned.

"I won't."

"And we haven't had this conversation?"

"How did you guess? Now, what do you want to eat?"

We each had huge omelets with crisp hash browns and thick, jam-covered toast. As far as I was concerned, it was a celebration. I was getting closer and closer to nailing those bastards. Nothing definite. Strictly circumstantial, but closer nonetheless.

Darrell Watkins, Homer Watkins, and the deceased Don Wilson. Gradually I was closing in on the truth.

Hurrying back to my apartment, I pawed through the receipt shoebox until I found my bill from Rosario. The long-distance phone calls were there—time, duration, phone numbers, and charges. Thank God for computer printouts.

I saw the problem immediately. How could Homer have been seen by Blia Vang at seven o'clock Friday night, less than an hour after he had phoned my room and left word for Ginger to call? Her answering call to Seattle was right there on my bill, dialed direct from my room. The time on the printout said seven-forty. The call from Orcas to Seattle had lasted six minutes.

Settling into my recliner, I studied the list of phone calls with minute care. Again on Saturday, there were calls to Seattle numbers, one to Homer in the early evening and one to Peters much later.

I didn't bother to work the crossword puzzles Ida Newell had dropped outside my door. I sat there and wondered why Blia Vang had lied to me, or if she hadn't, how had Homer Watkins managed to be in two places at once.

Chapter 35

MONDAY morning I woke up early and waited until six before I called Ray Johnson in Pasco. Evie answered the phone. "Just a minute, Beau. Ray's in the shower." Evie and I chatted amiably until Ray came on the phone.

"How the hell are you?" he boomed.

"I need your help, Ray."

"Sure thing. What's up?"

"Remember that morning when we were all there in your office and the governor's office called?"

"I remember. Just before the press conference. They wanted to make sure we had you safely under lock and key."

"Do you happen to remember the man's name? The governor's aide?"

Ray Johnson is an encyclopedia of names. Once he hears one, he doesn't forget it. When he left Seattle for Pasco, I felt as though I had lost my right arm. I had come to depend on him to remember names for both of us.

"Just a minute now," he said. "Hold on and it'll come to me. Something to do with a bird. Hawk . . . Hawkins. That's it, I'm almost sure. What do you need him for? I thought the case was all sewed up."

"Except for a couple of loose ends," I said.

By ten to eight I was suffering from a serious case of twenty-four-minute flu. I called the Department at eight. Peters wasn't in yet. Margie took the call.

"I'm not feeling well, Marge," I said, doing my best to sound feeble.

"I hope it's not stomach flu," Margie sympathized. "That's going around. My kids were both down with it last week and missed two whole days of school."

By five after eight, I was in the Porsche heading south on the freeway, feeling much better. It was a miracle. As I drove toward

Olympia, my mother's words came back to me. "One thing about Jonas, he doesn't let good sense stand in the way of what he wants."

My mother's twenty-five-year-old words still held the ring of prophecy. What I was doing didn't make good sense. J. P. Beaumont, good sense to the contrary, was turning up the heat under Homer and Darrell Watkins, attempting to smoke them into the open. It was best not to use a direct attack.

I parked as close as I could to the governor's office on the governmental campus and walked in as big as life. I asked the doe-eyed young receptionist for Mr. Hawkins.

"Do you have an appointment?" she asked.

"No," I said, flashing my ID in her direction. "But I'm sure he'll see me just the same."

I was right. Within five minutes I was shown into Lee Hawkins' office. I handed him my City of Seattle business card which he examined with some care.

"Weren't you the one—"

"Who was mistakenly arrested in Pasco?" I supplied helpfully. "Yes, I am."

He nodded. "I thought so. The name looked familiar. What can I do for you?" He dropped my card onto his desk.

"I'm actually here about the Washington State Victim/Witness Protection Program."

"I see."

"What's going on with that?"

"Well, we've been involved in negotiations with the Senate and House Judiciary Committees. There's no question that the program will cost money, although the governor's office supports the idea wholeheartedly." He paused and looked at me. "Is this on or off the record?"

"Off."

"We've about ironed out all resistance. We're hoping it'll be presented as a joint bill early next session."

"No announcement will be made prior to that?"

"That would be premature, Mr. Beaumont."

"And no announcement was planned for the parole board retreat on Orcas?"

"Absolutely not."

Just in case my message hadn't gotten through, I added one

final hook. "That's funny. Don Wilson was sure there would be an announcement at Orcas."

Lee Hawkins smiled. "He must have been mistaken."

"Of course," I replied. "Thanks." I left and drove straight back to Seattle. If somebody called to check on my health, the invalid should be at home, in bed. And if somebody took the bait, the fisherman should be hanging onto the other end of the pole for dear life.

Predictably, the phone was ringing as I got off the elevator. It was Peters. "Where the hell have you been? You're supposed to be sick."

"I needed some medicine," I lied. "How're the girls?"

"They're in school. The baby-sitter Ames hired will pick Heather up after kindergarten. Tracie can walk home by herself. Mrs. Keen—that's the baby-sitter's name—will stay until I get home tonight. Do you have everything you need? Yogurt, or maybe some Pepto-Bismol?"

"Everything, thanks. I'm much better. What are you doing?"

"Manny and Al are trying to negotiate a peace treaty with the feds to extradite Farley from Canada."

"Good luck." I was glad I wouldn't be there to fight and lose the opening rounds of the paperwork war. I've seen more than one crook hole up across the border, hiding out in plain sight behind a mountain of red tape.

"Get well," Peters said. "See you tomorrow."

I fixed a pot of coffee, sat down, and put my feet up. The next caller was Ames, totally focused on business. "What about the reward money?"

"Never mind. The witness may have lied to me. We'll have to see."

"Okay," Ames said agreeably. "Whatever you say."

"How's Cody?" I couldn't resist catching him off base. Ames was trying with some difficulty to concentrate on work. His obvious confusion was laughable.

He hesitated, half switching gears, attempting to maintain his dignity. "She's working today. I don't know doing what." He paused again, scrambling for what to say next. "I guess, as long as I'm here, I'll go ahead and mother-hen the penthouse deal. Are you going to do any customizing?"

I hadn't thought about it. "What do you suggest?"

Ames sighed. "I'll get a couple of decorators to take a look and see what they say."

"Just one thing, Ames."

"What's that?"

"Wherever I go, my recliner goes."

"Right," he said.

He hung up. I poured myself a cup of coffee. And waited. It was the calm before the storm. I was convinced the storm was coming. Who would call, Darrell or Homer? I figured it was a toss-up.

When the phone finally rang at four that afternoon, it was a delivery boy bringing flowers. I buzzed him into the building and opened the door without even bothering to check the peekhole. The crime prevention unit would have drummed me off the force.

"Hello, Detective Beaumont," Darrell Watkins said easily. "I've got a gun. You're coming with me." He raised a snub-nosed .38 from behind the box of flowers.

He lifted my Smith and Wesson out of its holster and dropped it into a jacket pocket, all the while keeping me covered.

"I understand you were making inquiries about the Victim/Witness Protection Program."

"That's right."

"Was your interest personal or professional?"

"Both."

"Since that's a program I'm interested in, too, I thought maybe we should get together and talk. Where's your car?"

"In the garage."

"Let's go."

He directed me to the Watkins mansion on Capitol Hill. I walked ahead of him to the house and pushed the door open, half expecting to find Homer waiting inside, but the entryway was empty, the house itself quiet.

I stepped over the threshold, tensing as I realized we were alone, hoping I could catch him off guard, take him by surprise.

Instead, something hit me behind my right ear. I went down like a sack of potatoes.

The cold woke me. I opened my eyes, thinking I'd gone blind. I could see nothing. I struggled to move, and ran my nose into my knee. It startled me to find my knee jammed directly in front of my face. It shouldn't have been there. I tried moving my fingers and felt my feet. Slowly it started making sense. I was tied, trussed in a fetal position, with my hands and feet fastened together at my ankles.

I was also stark naked.

It's tough getting your bearings in pitch darkness. Under me were what seemed to be wooden slats. A humming motor clicked off, followed by ominous silence.

I was trapped in a refrigerator waiting to die.

Rocking painfully on the small of my back, I tried rolling as far as I could in one direction, hoping to find a door and figure out a way to open it. I rolled until I encountered a smooth, hard surface. Before I could ascertain whether it was door or wall, a door at the other end of the compartment jerked open. A single light bulb next to the door snapped on, momentarily blinding me.

When I could see, Darrell Watkins was standing over me. "My, my. Aren't we clever. I didn't think you'd wake up before I got back. I had to take your car downtown and park it on Third Avenue. In the bus zone. By now it's being towed at owner's expense. It'll take days to find it."

"You're crazy."

"Maybe," he said agreeably. "But smart."

"Is this how Wilson died of exposure?"

He nodded. "I let him hang around long enough for the drug to get out of his system, then I sprayed him with cold water. Worked like a charm. I never had to tie him up. I'm afraid your rope burns will show."

I wanted to keep him talking. I gauged the distance between us, wondering if I could roll against his legs with enough strength to knock him down.

"You met him on the ferry?"

"He met me on the car deck so I could give him a copy of the governor's proclamation."

"But there was no proclamation."

Watkins shrugged. "Don Wilson didn't know that. He got in the car, I gave him one little prick with this, and he went night-night."

He held up a hypo, the needle glinting in the light from the bulb near the door. I made a tentative roll toward him. He laughed and stepped away. "None of that," he said.

"Wilson went off the ferry in your car?"

"That's right. Out cold on the floor of the backseat. I put him in the trunk later. He slept like a baby until Sunday when I finally got him back to Seattle. I had plenty of time to see Sig Larson."

"And kill him?"

He grinned. "That too." He sobered suddenly. "You puzzle me, Detective Beaumont. As far as I can tell, you're the only one who doesn't believe Wilson did it. How come?"

"Gut instinct. Wilson left a chicken thawing at home, and he didn't feed his cat. Looked like he planned to come back."

"He did. You think you're pretty smart, don't you! Guess that's why you're there and I'm here, right?" He laughed—the maniacal laughter of someone losing his grip. "Except for that, I was good, though, wasn't I? Framed Wilson every step of the way, that poor, stupid bastard. He wanted to make headlines."

"You're the one who called him to Orcas?"

He nodded, grinning. "You bet. I even arranged for that reporter to do a series on him. That was brilliant."

His words reeked of ugly truth. "You've been planning this for a long time."

"Months. This was my last chance before the sheriff's sale. After that it would have been too late."

"Mona too?"

"Mona too."

"How did you know she was at the Red Lion?"

"My father. I told him I wanted to explain why I couldn't go to Sig's funeral. I was waiting. When you drove up, I decided to use your car. That was masterful, don't you think?"

"You did it for the money?"

"Money isn't everything, but it helps. I'll need every penny to get back on even ground."

"You think you'll get away with it?"

"Absolutely!"

"How did you get Ginger drunk?"

He laughed. "You should have seen her face. She was real surprised to see me. I was waiting just outside the gate. I almost missed her because she was driving a different car. Your car. How come?"

I ignored his question and repeated my own. "How'd you get her drunk?"

"A hose, a soft plastic hose. That was for Tom's benefit. She promised him she'd never drink again. Little Miss Perfect. Shoved it down her throat and poured the booze through it. She was already unconscious. It worked, too. Did you see old Tom at the funeral?''

''What about the calendar. Did you take it?'' If I was going to die, it would at least be *with* some answers.

''Sure. I had to put Wilson's fingerprints on something while he was passed out in the back of the car.''

Far away, through the chill, I heard the chime of the doorbell. Darrell jumped as though shot. I tried to call for help. He covered the distance between us in one long step. A hand clamped over my mouth, and a needle pricked my arm.

The lights went out, literally and figuratively.

Chapter 36

WHEN I awakened again, my fingers and toes were numb. Trying not to succumb to panic, I moved them as much as possible, hoping to force circulation back into them. There was a gag in my mouth with sticky tape holding it in place.

The humming motor clicked off. In the subsequent silence, I could hear another person's breathing.

I strained to listen. The roaring beat of my own heart threatened to drown out the shallow sound. The person was sleeping a sleep very close to the big one. Panting with effort, I rocked toward the sound. Four painful rocks away, I encountered another naked body, bound and trussed as I was, with legs as hairy as my own. Another man. For some unaccountable reason, that made me feel better.

Positioning my back against his, I tried to jar him awake. He stirred a little, but immediately resumed his shallow breathing. Again I attempted to shake him. Exertion caused beads of sweat to pop out on my body. I was aware of further heat loss as cold, dry air met perspiration.

Painfully I scooted around until my feet were in his face. I kicked him, and his breathing changed. He was awake now, whoever he was. Some circulation had returned to my fingers and toes. I felt for the tape that covered his mouth. Grasping a corner of it between my thumbs and forefingers, I rolled away from him, taking the tape with me.

It took long, precious minutes to roll back again and reposition myself to remove the cloth material that had been stuffed into his mouth behind the tape. "Thank you," he choked once the gag was out. I recognized the voice.

Homer Watkins lay on the wooden slats beside me.

He had not yet mastered the fundamentals of movement in our condition. I rolled around until my face was against his fingers. His first numbed attempts at grasping the tape on my gag didn't work. It took numerous tries before he was at last able to hold the tape while I rolled away. Then I manuevered my way back so he could remove the gag.

"Who are you?" he asked as soon as I could speak.

"Beaumont," I answered. "What time is it?"

"I don't know. It was morning when he put me in here. He kept me up all night, raving. He's crazy."

"We'll discuss that later. Let's get out of here first before we die of cold or suffocation. Can you untie me?"

We struggled in the dark, our fingers too numb and clumsy to know what they were about. Time passed, I don't know how much. Finally I gave up in defeat. "Stay here," I ordered. "I'm going to find a bottle to break."

I remembered seeing a wine rack, but in the struggle to free us, I had become disoriented. I rocked back and forth across the confines of our prison, searching for the rack, my muscles screaming at the unaccustomed position. After what seemed like hours, I finally bumped up against the stack of corked bottles.

Deliberately breaking a bottle seems easy, but not if your hands and feet are tied together. The adult male body has long since lost the newborn limberness which allows a baby to suck its toes. Each movement was an agony, each failure unbearable. I wanted desperately to break the bottle in the farthest corner of our cage. There's an atavistic fear of bleeding to death in the dark. I didn't want to roll blindly and helplessly on broken glass.

At last I managed to return to Homer with a jagged shard from a bottle. "You do me," I said. "If anybody gets cut, it'll be me."

Fortunately, the insides of our wrists were tied together. The cuts and slices in my flesh, though painful and bloody, were also superficial. As Homer sawed at my restraints I asked him questions. The exercise served two purposes. It gave me some answers, and it took both our minds off the sticky blood that accompanied his work.

"Why did you go to Rosario that Friday?"

"Darlene said she thought that's where Darrell went. I was worried about him. He was upset."

"Why?"

"God knows he had no right to be jealous, but he couldn't believe she'd go ahead and divorce him."

"You took the maid's keys and broke into Ginger's room?"

"Someone had already been there. The room was a mess. I panicked."

"But I talked to you. Ginger called you back."

"When she didn't return my call at first, I was afraid he might have killed her too."

"Ginger called you in Seattle. I have the phone number on my bill."

"I have a phone in the car. I forwarded calls there."

A long silence ensued between us, with only the scraping of glass on the fibrous rope filling the emptiness left by the stilled motor. "Why didn't you turn him in?"

He waited a long time to answer me. "When they said it was Wilson, I believed it, wanted to believe it."

"It wasn't."

"I know," he said hollowly.

Eventually, after what seemed an eternity, the rope parted. My hands and feet were freed.

To my complete frustration, I wasn't instantly able to straighten up and walk to the light switch. My muscles were too cramped and stiff. I lurched across the wooden slats, crawling awkwardly on my knees, dreading the broken glass, groping blindly for the elusive switch I knew was there. Eventually I found it.

The sudden light from the single 40-watt light was dazzling. I found the thermostat and turned the refrigeration unit off, then I cut through Homer's bonds. Movement returned slowly. Even then, it didn't do us a hell of a lot of good: there was no latch inside the refrigerator door, only a smooth, seemingly impenetrable metal surface.

I turned from the door to Homer. "How long have you known for sure?"

"Since last night. I wouldn't let myself believe it. I never saw him in a jealous rage before."

"Jealous rage hell!" I said harshly, stripping away Homer's last vestige of justification. "He's after money, the insurance. He set it up to frame Wilson for the first three. You can bet he has some plan so it will look like J. P. Beaumont did away with you."

Homer swayed dangerously. I caught him and broke his fall. "He would, wouldn't he! He'd kill me too." Homer Watkins sank the rest of the way to the floor. You don't fake the kind of shock that spread across his face. Seeing it told me once and for all that Homer was innocent. Darrell Watkins had acted alone.

The naked old man, diminished, squatted brokenly on his haunches, a picture of abject defeat. I looked down, thinking to help him to his feet. In looking down, I saw our way out.

Our cell's wooden slats were actually the tops of pallets, wooden lathing on frames of sturdy two-by-fours. "Get up, Homer, quick," I urged, grasping him by the wrist and pulling him to his feet.

The pallets were about three and a half feet square. I picked one up, hefted it, stood it on edge. With both of us swinging in concert, we could use it as a battering ram. The latches on the outside of the door couldn't hold forever under that kind of treatment.

I explained the plan. "If the door opens and he's outside, chances are he'll have a weapon. Keep swinging, and hope we can hit him."

We took a first tentative swing at the door. The noise of the blow seemed deafening. We waited, breathless, expecting Darrell to charge through the door. Nothing happened. We swung again. Again nothing happened.

"All right," I said, "here goes. Swing together in rhythm. Back and forth. Eventually we'll build momentum."

I didn't tell Homer my other worry, that our air would run out and we'd suffocate before we ever broke through to the outside. At least we'd die warm.

Swing, blam. Swing, blam. Swing, blam. Obviously the house was empty, or the noise would have aroused a response. Swing, blam. Swing, blam. Swing, blam. The metal dented as the inside of the door crushed against an outer shell. Swing, blam. Swing, blam. Swing, blam. The door shuddered each time we hit it, giving way under every blow. Swing, blam. Swing, blam. Swing, blam. As the hinges crumbled, momentum carried us into the kitchen. We were out. We were free. We weren't going to die.

At least not then, and not in a refrigerator.

The kitchen was dark. It was night. Homer crossed the floor and switched on a light. A clock over the sink said nine o'clock. "What night?" I asked.

"Tuesday," he said. "Election night." The strength that had sustained him as we battered the door ebbed away. He leaned heavily against the stainless steel table in the center of the room. "What are you going to do?" he asked.

I gave the first answer that came to mind. It had no bearing on the question he was really asking. "I'm going to find some clothes."

There is something implacably sane about insanity. I found all our clothes, both Homer's and mine, in a dirty-clothes hamper in the laundry room. Where else? It was as though Darrell expected a maid to appear and wash them for him, maybe even dispose of the corpses in his refrigerator—a kind of macabre *noblesse oblige*. Darrell Watkins was no more accustomed to living without money than I was used to living with it.

Homer was still leaning against the table when I returned to the kitchen. He hadn't moved. "What are you going to do?" he asked again, his voice a plaintive monotone.

I countered with another question. "Where is he?"

"The victory party."

"Where?"

Homer took the clothes I handed him. "I won't tell," he said stubbornly. "I'll show you. Will you arrest him?"

"If I can."

"Don't," he said.

I was bent over, tying my shoe, convinced I had misunderstood him. "What did you say?"

"Don't arrest him. Put him out of his misery. He's a mad dog."

I knew what he was asking and why. I shook my head. "I'm an officer of the law, Homer. I can't do that."

My .38 had been in its holster at the bottom of the clothes hamper. I checked it now, making sure it was loaded, that it wasn't jammed. "Will he be armed?"

"No." Homer stopped speaking abruptly and stood examining

his shoes as though unsure which shoe went on what foot. "I can't say," he resumed at last. "He's killed four people so far. What do I know?"

A phone hung on the kitchen wall. I had seen it the moment the light came on, but I waited to use it until we were both dressed. Homer's dignity had suffered enough.

While I waited, I washed the dried blood from my hands and wrists. When Homer finally finished tying his shoelaces, I picked up the phone and dialed the department. It was late, after nine, but I knew Peters would be there. We were partners. He would be working, trying to find me.

"Beau!" he exclaimed, relief evident in his voice. "Where the hell are you?"

Quickly I gave him the address. "Come as fast as you can. Bring a couple squad cars with you, but no sirens, understand?"

"Right," he replied without question.

Homer had disappeared from the kitchen while I talked on the phone. He returned now, wearing a heavy jacket over his suit. He still looked cold and pale. "Are you warming up?" I asked.

He nodded. "I'm coming with you." He was determined.

"You can't," I said. "It's too dangerous. It would be better if you stayed here."

"No. I know where he'll be. Maybe I can talk him into giving up."

It was remotely possible. "Where's the party?" I asked.

"Will you take me along?"

I relented. "Oh, all right. Now where are we going?"

"The Trade Center," Homer replied.

"Shit!" I remembered seeing live election-night coverage from the Muni-League party in previous years. It was usually held in the Seattle Trade Center. The candidates and their campaign workers would gather there, winners and losers alike, to watch the returns. There would be throngs of people, drunk and sober, television cameras, bands, lights, reporters. It would be chaos—the last place any cop in his right mind wants to go after a crazed killer.

Peters and four uniformed patrolmen arrived within minutes. The three of us—Peters, Homer, and I—rode in a squad car to the Trade Center at Elliott and Clay.

"Let me talk to him," Homer insisted as we made our way through traffic. "Maybe I can get him to surrender."

My initial reaction was to say no out of hand. We're not in this business to risk civilian lives. Peters, however, assumed the role of devil's advocate. "It's going to be a madhouse in there. If Homer can get him to come quietly, it could prevent wholesale bloodshed."

Spending well over twenty-four hours in cold storage had put me in a mood to listen to sweet reason. "All right," I agreed. "So how do we handle it?"

Homer let out his breath as though he had been holding it. "I'll lead the way to our spot. We're usually on the first floor, near the escalator. Give me a minute or so to find him."

It was better than no plan at all.

We approached the Trade Center with lights flashing but no sirens. Not wanting to broadcast a warning, we maintained radio silence. Surprising him was our only chance. Alerting the world could create a riot.

Once there, Peters designated an officer to assume command outside the center. He deployed men to cover all building and parking-garage entrances. It was an empty gesture. We all knew that if panic ensued, no one would be able to tell Darrell Watkins from hundreds of other terrified partygoers crushing through the doors, racing to get outside.

Peters and I paused for a moment outside the door, giving Homer a head start in crossing the crowded room. "Are you sure you're okay?" Peters asked.

"Yeah. I'm all right."

"I'll go first," he said. "You follow."

"No deal, asshole," I told him. "You've got a couple little kids to raise. No fucking way you're sticking me with that job."

Before Peters had a chance to object, I pushed my way in front of him, following Homer Watkins into a wall-to-wall throng of people.

Chapter 37

AFTERWARDS, there were conflicting stories. A woman said she saw Homer Watkins walk up to Darrell, pull a gun out of his jacket, and try to shoot him. Others said there was a struggle, the gun went off, and Homer fell mortally wounded.

I heard the report of a pistol and a woman's scream. Time froze. The sea of people turned as one man, moving toward the disturbance and away from it at the same time, surging forward and back, closing ranks. I fought my way through, moving in slow motion, flinging people aside, only to have others blunder into my path.

"Out of the way. Police!" Peters roared behind me, but the crowd became denser, more compact. Absolutely silent, and compact. To this day, I don't know if that silence existed anywhere but in my mind. It ceased when I reached the escalators.

People coming down screamed and swirled back up the moving stairs, attempting to escape the carnage below. They encountered a wall of people above them who stood unable to move, transfixed by fear.

I saw Darrell Watkins as he broke and ran. Gun in hand, he dashed up the escalator three and four steps at a time, plunging over people, pushing them aside.

Delayed pandemonium erupted through the crowd as I touched the rail of the down escalator. Maybe the noise was there the whole time and I only just then heard it. Clearing the way with my drawn .38, I charged up the downward treadmill, desperate to reach the top. My only hope was to drive him farther up into the building. Away from the crowds. Away from doors that would lead him outside.

Peters must have been only one or two steps behind me at the outset, but the crowd caught him in a crushing wave of panic and carried him back toward the door with them. I paused and turned briefly at the top of the stairs, hoping he was with me. He wasn't.

It would be Darrell Watkins and J. P. Beaumont. Alone.

The Trade Center is made up of a soaring atrium, with a ground floor and two layers of shops arranged around circling balconies under a huge skylight. Watkins charged up the second escalator. On the second level the crowd had thinned. I raced across the landing to the up escalator and followed, watching in dismay as he disappeared around a corner and down a hall before I reached the next level.

He was halfway down the long corridor when I turned the corner in hot pursuit. "Stop or I'll shoot," I shouted.

I paused to fire, but he was out of range. My slug ponged harmlessly off the wall behind him. I ducked my chin into my chest and sprinted down the corridor after him as he vanished into a stairwell. Gasping for breath, I flung open the fire door. I stood on a concrete landing, listening to the echo of retreating footsteps. For one heart-stopping moment, I thought they were going down. Then a gust of fresh air rushed down the stairwell into my face, followed by the warning shriek of an alarm on an opened emergency exit.

He had gone to the roof.

I crept up the stairs. It could be a trap. He might have opened and shut the outside door to trick me. Maybe he was lying in wait around the blind corner of the stairs, ready to blast me into oblivion. I held my breath as I rounded the turn. He wasn't there. The stairs leading to the emergency exit were empty.

Below I heard the wail of sirens as ambulances and emergency vehicles raced to the scene. They would set up a command post and summon the Emergency Response Team, trying to position them to negotiate a surrender or, as a last resort, to fire off a clean shot. Peters would direct officers through the building, evacuating the crowd, securing first one area and then another.

But all that was happening in another world, far below us. Out on the roof, Darrell Watkins was waiting. For me.

I pushed open the heavy door. Over the wail of the alarm, I heard a bullet whine past the door's metal frame above my head. That was his second shot. I counted, wondering subconsciously what kind of a gun Homer had smuggled into his jacket. How many bullets? Did Darrell have four more shots, or seven? And did he have another gun of his own?

Standing in what amounted to a metal bunker at the top of the stairwell, I was better off trying to draw his fire and exhaust his ammunition while I could use the heavy door as armor between us. Each bullet he expended was one less available to slaughter innocent bystanders. Or me.

I yanked the alarm wire off the wall, silencing its bloodcurdling screech. In the sudden quiet that followed, a surprising calm settled over me. He was trapped. His only way out was past me. If I could drive him to a frenzy, force him to attack me in the open, maybe I could end it.

The irony struck me with the force of a physical blow. Darrell Watkins and J. P. Beaumont, men who had possessed the same woman, were locked in mortal combat.

I remembered Homer's hopeless pronouncement in the kitchen. "Put him out of his misery." I was tempted! God, was I tempted! But shooting was too easy, too good for him. I wanted him to live to know his loss, to pay a price, to suffer humiliation and defeat, to live out his days with Philip Lathrop as his lifelong companion. They deserved each other.

I would take him alive. I steeled myself to use every weapon at my disposal.

Somehow Ginger Watkins would forgive me. I opened the door a crack so he could hear me.

"She was a hell of a lay," I called into the night.

"What?"

"Ginger. She was one hell of a lay," I taunted. "Too bad you didn't know how good she was."

Another bullet whined off the metal door. That was three.

"You lying son of a bitch!"

"What's the matter. Can't take a dose of your own medicine? She was hot stuff, Darrell," I continued, soft enough so he had to strain to hear me. "She was so hungry. You never gave her what she wanted. She needed a man to take her, to make her know she was a woman."

I waited, silence brittle between us, hoping another bullet would crash into the wall near my head. Nothing happened. He was across the roof from me, crouched out of range behind a small fenced terrace outlined in a sudden splash of moonlight. Needing to draw his fire, I opened the door and spun around toward the back of the rooftop box that formed the top of the stairwell.

It worked. Too well. A slug ripped into my upper left arm, spinning me against the wall. Searing pain came quickly, making it hard to talk, to concentrate. How many bullets was that now, four or five?

"You couldn't handle that, could you?" I rasped through gritted teeth. "You had to have young ones like Darlene, girls you could impress with money if not performance. Ginger had been empty so long I couldn't fill her up."

"Liar," he said.

"Just because you couldn't get it up for her didn't mean nobody could."

"No," he croaked, his voice a hoarse, broken whisper. "It's not true."

"It is, too. Ask me. Ask Sig. Didn't he tell you? He could have."

"Maybe with him, not you." His voice rose dangerously. A tongue of flame spewed from his pistol in the darkness. The shot whistled harmlessly away into the night sky. Five or six? Let there be only six bullets, I prayed, not nine.

"I can prove it. How about the stretch marks from Katy? Remember those, or had it been so long since you looked at her that you forgot?"

I waited to see if he would reply. There was nothing. No response. "She'd have been stupid to divorce you," I continued. "She should have just screwed around behind your back. That would have been fair."

Several separate shots peppered the wall of the stairwell, followed by silence. For a long time we remained motionless, frozen in place, him across the fenced balcony and me behind the stairwell, a sticky stream of blood oozing through my jacket sleeve. I couldn't tell for sure if he had emptied the bullet chamber. Or if he had another gun.

It was time to play Russian roulette.

I stepped into the open. If he had only one shot left, he could squander it on me. Whether or not he got me, Darrell Watkins was finished.

"I always knew she was fucking around. She had to be."

"Is that why you killed her, Darrell, or was it the money?"

He raised up, his form outlined on the other side of the terrace. "Both," he said simply. "She was going to divorce me." He spoke with the wonder of a philosopher contemplating life's fundamental mysteries. He seemed quiet, subdued.

"Drop the gun, Darrell."

"I won the election. Did you know that?"

"Put your hands on your head. You're under arrest."

My words were a catalyst, spurring him to action. With an enraged roar, he vaulted over the fence, charging at me like a wounded bull. He landed on the terrace.

Except it wasn't a terrace at all.

It was the skylight.

The glass shattered. With an agonizing screech, he plunged out of sight, crashing into the mêlée of television cameras and milling people three stories below.

I walked over to the jagged hole and looked down. Far below, Darrell's crumpled body lay in a broken heap, seeping blood on the red brick floor. Around him television cameras hummed, fighting for focus and position, recording live footage for the people staying up late to watch election-night returns. Viewers would have their full recommended daily dose of blood and guts before they fell asleep. In living color.

The door behind me flew open. Peters burst onto the rooftop, his .38 glinting in the moonlight. "Are you all right?" he demanded.

"I am now."

Chapter 38

WE went to Peters' house in Kirkland the following Sunday for dinner. My left arm was in a sling. Cody Borden insisted she knew just what I needed. She would cook Southern for us— Southern Fried Chicken, black-eyed peas, and cornbread. She bustled around Peters' kitchen with Peters serving as cook's helper. She wore stiletto heels. One of Peters' oversized aprons was cinched tightly around her tiny waist. She looked better than any middle-aged woman has a right to look.

Peters was catering to the invalid. I had been off work the rest of the week, recuperating. In the interim, Peters, Cody, and Ames had joined forces to spoil me rotten.

Ames, content for once to let Cody out of his sight, sat on a couch with Heather and Tracie cuddled on either side of him. He was teaching them the Pledge of Allegiance. They had never learned it while they lived with New Dawn in Broken Springs, Oregon. At Greenwood School in Kirkland, they were required to memorize it.

I listened on the sidelines. Uncle Ralph, as they called Ames, showed infinite patience. It was funny that the man who inspired stark terror in the heart of Maxwell Cole was meek as a lamb with those two little ankle-biters. They had him wrapped around their fingers.

It was a quiet family setting, as American as apple pie. I sat in an easy chair across from them, my arm safe from squirming little bodies, sipping a McNaughton's. Physically, I remained in the room, but my thoughts roamed far afield.

Had Homer Watkins lived, things would have been different. Since there were no surviving partners, however, Armour Life would pay the insurance proceeds to each person's next of kin.

Tom Lander had put his 76 Station on the market. He planned to buy a motor home and hit the road. Sig's children had been notified and were in the process of filing a claim. No one had yet been able to locate Mona's brother, but Cody said she was working on it. Cody said it would be only a matter of days before death benefits owing them were paid.

As far as we could tell, Homer had no surviving kin, and his attorney said that his will left everything he owned to Children's Orthopedic Hospital.

I understood Blia Vang had used her reward money to make a down payment on a small house with room for a large garden. Ames was handling those details, including getting Blia hired on in the Westin laundry. Blia's whole family—aunt, uncle, and cousins—would be moving out of the low-income housing development and into a place of their own.

I didn't go to Homer and Darrell's double funeral. I sent flowers to Homer, not Darrell. The funeral was widely attended. And televised.

Thinking about Ginger still hurt, but Anne Corley's pain was a little more remote. I had Ginger to thank for that. She had helped me say good-bye to Anne, to move beyond that chapter in my life. Without her, I don't know how long it would have taken to get back on track.

I returned to Peters' living room in time to hear the girls repeating in singsong unison: "One nation, under God, invisible, with liverty injustice for all."

"And justice for all," Ames corrected gently.

I took a long sip of McNaughtons. Thinking about Ginger and Mona and Sig and Homer, I wondered if the girls hadn't gotten it right the first time.

— THE —
MATLOCK
PAPER

The name on the computer screen is James Barbour
Matlock. Vietnam veteran. College professor. He's Washington's choice to stop a far-reaching conspiracy, an
undercover assignment destined to put Matlock's neck
against the razor's edge of danger. And the faceless men
in Washington don't care if it means savaging the woman
Matlock loves, or trapping Matlock in a maze of unrelenting terror. They care about just one thing: that
Matlock is the perfect man for the job . . . for a reason
that is disturbing, violent, and very, very deadly.

—THE—
MATLOCK
PAPER

Robert Ludlum

A DELL BOOK

Published by
Dell Publishing Co., Inc.
1 Dag Hammarskjold Plaza
New York, New York 10017

For Pat and Bill—
As the ancient Bagdhivi proverb says:
When giants cast shadows, hope for the shade.
The "Due Macellis" are giants!

Dell ® TM 681510, Dell Publishing Co., Inc.

ISBN: 0-440-15538-X

Reprinted by arrangement with Doubleday & Company, Inc.
Printed in the United States of America
One Previous Dell Edition
New Dell Edition
March 1986

10 9 8 7 6 5 4 3 2 1

WFH

1

Loring walked out the side entrance of the Justice Department and looked for a taxi. It was nearly five thirty, a spring Friday, and the congestion in the Washington streets was awful. Loring stood by the curb and held up his left hand, hoping for the best. He was about to abandon the effort when a cab that had picked up a fare thirty feet down the block stopped in front of him.

"Going east, mister? It's O.K. This gentleman said he wouldn't mind."

Loring was always embarrassed when these incidents occurred. He unconsciously drew back his right forearm, allowing his sleeve to cover as much of his hand as possible—to conceal the thin black chain looped around his wrist, locked to the briefcase handle.

"Thanks, anyway. I'm heading south at the next corner."

He waited until the taxi reentered the flow of traffic and then resumed his futile signaling.

Usually, under such conditions, his mind was alert, his feelings competitive. He would normally dart his eyes in both directions, ferreting out cabs about to disgorge passengers, watching the corners for those dimly lit roof signs that meant this particular vehicle was for hire if you ran fast enough.

Today, however, Ralph Loring did not feel like running. On this particular Friday, his mind was obsessed with a terrible reality. He had just borne witness to a man's being sentenced to death. A man he'd never met but knew a great deal about. An unknowing man of thirty-three who lived and worked in a small New England town four hundred miles away and who had no idea of Loring's existence, much less of the Justice Department's interest in him.

Loring's memory kept returning to the large conference room with the huge rectangular table around which sat the men who'd pronounced the sentence.

He had objected strenuously. It was the least he could do for the man he'd never met, the man who was being maneuvered with such precision into such an untenable position.

"May I remind you, Mr. Loring," said an assistant attorney general who'd once been a judge advocate in the navy, "that in any combat situation basic risks are assumed. A percentage of casualties is anticipated."

"The circumstances are different. This man isn't trained. He won't know who or where the enemy is. How could he? We don't know ourselves."

"Just the point." The speaker then had been another assistant AG, this one a recruit from some corporation law office, fond of committee meetings, and, Loring suspected, incapable of decisions without them. "Our subject is highly mobile. Look at the psychological profile, 'flawed but mobile in the extreme.' That's exactly what it says. He's a logical choice."

" 'Flawed but mobile'! What in heaven's name does that mean? May *I* remind this committee that I've worked in the field for fifteen years. Psychological profiles are only screening guidelines, hit-and-miss judgments. I would no more send a man into an infiltration problem without knowing him thoroughly than I would assume the responsibility for NASA mathematics."

The chairman of the committee, a career professional, had answered Loring.

"I understand your reservations; normally, I'd agree. However, these aren't normal conditions. We have barely three weeks. The time factor overrides the usual precautions."

"It's the risk we have to assume," said the former judge advocate pontifically.

"*You're* not assuming it," Loring replied.

"Do you wish to be relieved of the contact?" The chairman made the offer in complete sincerity.

"No, sir. I'll make it. Reluctantly. I want that on the record."

"One thing before we adjourn." The corporation lawyer leaned forward on the table. "And this comes right from the top. We've all agreed that our subject is motivated. The profile makes that clear. What must also be made clear is that any assistance given this committee by the subject is given freely and on a voluntary basis. We're vulnerable here. We cannot, repeat *cannot*, be responsible. If it's possible, we'd like the record to indicate that the subject came to *us*."

Ralph Loring had turned away from the man in disgust.

If anything, the traffic was heavier now. Loring had about made up his mind to start walking the twenty-odd blocks to his apartment when a white Volvo pulled up in front of him.

"Get in! You look silly with your hand up like that."

"Oh, it's you. Thanks very much." Loring opened the door and slid into the small front seat, holding his briefcase on his lap. There was no need to hide the

thin black chain around his wrist. Cranston was a
field man, too; an overseas route specialist. Cranston
had done most of the background work on the assignment which was now Loring's responsibility.

"That was a long meeting. Accomplish anything?"

"The green light."

"It's about time."

"Two assistant ACs and a concerned message from
the White House were responsible."

"Good. Geo division got the latest reports from
Force-Mediterranean this morning. It's a regular mass
conversion of source routes. It's confirmed. The fields
in Ankara and Konya in the north, the projects in Sidi
Barrani and Rashid, even the Algerian contingents are
systematically cutting production. It's going to make
things very difficult."

"What the hell do you want? I thought the objective was to rip them out. You people are never satisfied."

"Neither would you be. We can exert controls over
routes we know about; what in God's name do we
know about places like . . . Porto Belocruz, Pilcomayo,
a half dozen unpronounceable names in Paraguay,
Brazil, Guiana? It's a whole goddamn new ballgame,
Ralph."

"Bring in the SA specialists. CIA's crawling with
them."

"No way. We're not even allowed to ask for maps."

"That's asinine."

"That's espionage. We stay clean. We're strictly according to Interpol-Hoyle; no funny business. I
thought you knew that."

"I do," replied Loring wearily. "It's still asinine."

"You worry about New England, USA. We'll handle
the pampas, or whatever they are—it is."

"New England, USA, is a goddamn microcosm. That's what's frightening. What happened to all those poetic descriptions of rustic fences and Yankee spirit and ivied brick walls?"

"New poetry. Get with it."

"Your sympathy is overwhelming. Thanks."

"You sound discouraged."

"There isn't enough time. . . ."

"There never is." Cranston steered the small car into a faster lane only to find it bottlenecked at Nebraska and Eighteenth. With a sigh, he shoved the gearshift into neutral and shrugged his shoulders. He looked at Loring, who was staring blankly at the windshield. "At least you got the green light. That's something."

"Sure. With the wrong personnel."

"Oh . . . I see. Is that him?" Cranston gestured his head toward Loring's briefcase.

"That's him. From the day he was born."

"What's his name?"

"Matlock. James B. Matlock II. The B is for Barbour, very old family—two very old families. James Matlock, B.A., M.A., Ph.D. A leading authority in the field of social and political influences on Elizabethan literature. How about that?"

"Jesus! Are those his qualifications? Where does he start asking questions? At faculty teas for retired professors?"

"No. That part of it's all right; he's young enough. His qualifications are included in what Security calls 'flawed but mobile in the extreme.' Isn't that a lovely phrase?"

"Inspiring. What does it mean?"

"It's supposed to describe a man who isn't very nice. Probably because of a loused-up army record, or a divorce—I'm sure it's the army thing—but in spite of that insurmountable handicap, is very well liked."

"I like him already."

"That's my problem. I do, too."

The two men fell into silence. It was clear that Cranston had been in the field long enough to realize when a fellow professional had to think by himself. Reach certain conclusions—or rationalizations—by himself. Most of the time, it was easy.

Ralph Loring thought about the man whose life was detailed so completely in his briefcase, culled from a score of data-bank sources. James Barbour Matlock was the name, but the person behind the name refused to come into focus. And that bothered Loring; Matlock's life had been shaped by disturbing, even violent, inconsistencies.

He was the surviving son of two elderly, immensely wealthy parents who lived in handsome retirement in Scarsdale, New York. His education had been properly Eastern Establishment: Andover and Amherst, with the proper expectations of a Manhattan-based profession—banking, brokerage, advertising. There was nothing in his precollege or undergraduate record to indicate a deviation from this pattern. Indeed, marriage to a socially prominent girl from Greenwich seemed to confirm it.

And then things happened to James Barbour Matlock, and Loring wished he understood. First came the army.

It was the early sixties, and by the simple expedient of agreeing to a six-month extension of service, Matlock could have sat comfortably behind a desk as a supply officer somewhere—most likely, with his family's connections, in Washington or New York. Instead, his service file read like a hoodlum's: a series of infractions and insubordinations that guaranteed him the least desirable of assignments—Vietnam and its escalating hostilities. While in the Mekong Delta, his military behavior also guaranteed him two summary courts-martial.

Yet there appeared to be no ideological motivation behind his actions, merely poor, if any, adjustment.

His return to civilian life was marked by continuing difficulties, first with his parents and then with his wife. Inexplicably, James Barbour Matlock, whose academic record had been gentlemanly but hardly superior, took a small apartment in Morningside Heights and attended Columbia University's graduate school.

The wife lasted three and a half months, opting for a quiet divorce and a rapid exit from Matlock's life.

The following several years were monotonous intelligence material. Matlock, the incorrigible, was in the process of becoming Matlock, the scholar. He worked around the calendar, receiving his master's degree in fourteen months, his doctorate two years later. There was a reconciliation of sorts with his parents, and a position with the English department at Carlyle University in Connecticut. Since then Matlock had published a number of books and articles and acquired an enviable reputation in the academic community. He was obviously popular—"mobile in the extreme" (silly goddamn expression); he was moderately well off and apparently possessed none of the antagonistic traits he'd displayed during the hostile years. Of course, there was damn little reason for him to be discontented, thought Loring. James Barbour Matlock II had his life nicely routined; he was covered on all flanks, thank you, including a girl. He was currently, with discretion, involved with a graduate student named Patricia Ballantyne. They kept separate residences, but according to the data, were lovers. As near as could be determined, however, there was no marriage in sight. The girl was completing her doctoral studies in archeology, and a dozen foundation grants awaited her. Grants that led to distant lands and unfamiliar facts. Patricia Ballantyne was not for marriage; not according to the data banks.

But what of Matlock? wondered Ralph Loring. What did the facts tell him? How could they possibly justify the choice?

They didn't. They couldn't. Only a trained professional could carry out the demands of the current situation. The problems were far too complex, too filled with traps for an amateur.

The terrible irony was that if this Matlock made errors, fell into traps, he might accomplish far more far quicker than any professional.

And lose his life doing so.

"What makes you all think he'll accept?" Cranston was nearing Loring's apartment and his curiosity was piqued.

"What? I'm sorry, what did you say?"

"What's the motive for the subject's acceptance? Why would he agree?"

"A younger brother. Ten years younger, as a matter of fact. The parents are quite old. Very rich, very detached. This Matlock holds himself responsible."

"For what?"

"The brother. He killed himself three years ago with an overdose of heroin."

Ralph Loring drove his rented car slowly down the wide, tree-lined street past the large old houses set back beyond manicured lawns. Some were fraternity houses, but there were far fewer than had existed a decade ago. The social exclusivity of the fifties and early sixties was being replaced. A few of the huge structures had other identifications now. *The House, Aquarius* (naturally), *Afro-Commons, Warwick, Lumumba Hall.*

Connecticut's Carlyle University was one of those medium-sized "prestige" campuses that dot the New England landscape. An administration, under the guidance of its brilliant president, Dr. Adrian Sealfont, was restructuring the college, trying to bring it into the second half of the twentieth century. There were inevitable protests, proliferation of beards, and African studies balanced against the quiet wealth, club blazers, and alumni-sponsored regattas. Hard rock and faculty tea dances were groping for ways to coexist.

Loring reflected, as he looked at the peaceful campus in the bright spring sunlight, that it seemed inconceivable that such a community harbored any real problems.

Certainly not the problem that had brought him there.

Yet it did.

Carlyle was a time bomb which, when detonated, would claim extraordinary victims in its fallout. That it *would* explode, Loring knew, was inevitable. What happened before then was unpredictable. It was up to him to engineer the best possible probabilities. The key was James Barbour Matlock, B.A., M.A., Ph.D.

Loring drove past the attractive two-story faculty residence that held four apartments, each with a separate entrance. It was considered one of the better faculty houses and was usually occupied by bright young families before they'd reached the tenure necessary for outlying homes of their own. Matlock's quarters were on the first floor, west section.

Loring drove around the block and parked diagonally across the street from Matlock's door. He couldn't stay long; he kept turning in the seat, scanning the cars and Sunday morning pedestrians, satisfied that he himself wasn't being observed. That was vital. On Sunday, according to Matlock's surveillance file, the young professor usually read the papers till around noon and then drove to the north end of Carlyle where Patricia Ballantyne lived in one of the efficiency apartments reserved for graduate students. That is, he drove over if she hadn't spent the night with him. Then the two generally went out into the country for lunch and returned to Matlock's apartment or went south into Hartford or New Haven. There were variations, of course. Often the Ballantyne girl and Matlock took weekends together, registering as man and wife. Not this weekend, however. Surveillance had confirmed that.

Loring looked at his watch. It was twelve forty, but Matlock was still in his apartment. Time was running short. In a few minutes, Loring was expected to be at Crescent Street. 217 Crescent. It was where he would make cover-contact for his second vehicle transfer.

He knew it wasn't necessary for him to physically watch Matlock. After all, he'd read the file thoroughly, looked at scores of photographs, and even talked briefly with Dr. Sealfont, Carlyle's president. Nevertheless, each agent had his own working methods, and his included watching subjects for a period of hours before making contact. Several colleagues at Justice claimed it gave him a sense of power. Loring knew only that it gave him a sense of confidence.

Matlock's front door opened and a tall man walked out into the sunlight. He was dressed in khaki trousers, loafers, and a tan turtleneck sweater. Loring saw that he was modestly good looking with sharp features and fairly long blond hair. He checked the lock on his door, put on a pair of sunglasses, and walked around the sidewalk to what Loring presumed was a small parking area. Several minutes later, James Matlock drove out of the driveway in a Triumph sportscar.

The government man reflected that his subject seemed to have the best of a pleasant life. Sufficient income, no responsibilities, work he enjoyed, even a convenient relationship with an attractive girl.

Loring wondered if it would all be the same for James Barbour Matlock three weeks from then. For Matlock's world was about to be plunged into an abyss.

2

Matlock pressed the Triumph's accelerator to the floor and the low-slung automobile vibrated as the speedometer reached sixty-two miles per hour. It wasn't that he was in a hurry—Pat Ballantyne wasn't going anywhere—just that he was angry. Well, not angry, really; just irritated. He was usually irritated after a phone call from home. Time would never eliminate that. Nor money, if ever he made any to speak of—amounts his father considered respectable. What caused his irritation was the infuriating condescension. It grew worse as his mother and father advanced in years. Instead of making peace with the situation, they dwelled on it. They insisted that he spend the spring midterm vacation in Scarsdale so that he and his father could make daily trips into the city. To the banks, to the attorneys. To make ready for the inevitable, when and if it ever happened.

". . . There's a lot you'll have to digest, son," his father had said sepulchrally. "You're not exactly prepared, you know. . . ."

". . . You're all that's left, darling," his mother had said with obvious pain.

Matlock knew they enjoyed their anticipated, martyred leave-taking of this world. They'd made their mark—or at least his father had. The amusing part was that his parents were as strong as pack mules, as healthy as wild horses. They'd no doubt outlast him by decades.

The truth was that they wanted him with them far more than he wished to be there. It had been that way for the past three years, since David's death at the Cape. Perhaps, thought Matlock, as he drew up in front of Pat's apartment, the roots of his irritation were in his own guilt. He'd never quite made peace with himself about David. He never would.

And he didn't want to be in Scarsdale during the midterm holidays. He didn't want the memories. He had someone now who was helping him forget the awful years—of death, no love, and indecision. He'd promised to take Pat to St. Thomas.

The name of the country inn was the Cheshire Cat, and, as its title implied, it was Englishy and pubbish. The food was decent, the drinks generous, and those factors made it a favorite spot of Connecticut's exurbia. They'd finished their second Bloody Mary and had ordered roast beef and Yorkshire pudding. There were perhaps a dozen couples and several families in the spacious dining area. In the corner sat a single man reading *The New York Times* with the pages folded vertically, commuter fashion.

"He's probably an irate father waiting for a son who's about to splash out. I know the type. They take the Scarsdale train every morning."

"He's too relaxed."

"They learn to hide tension. Only their druggists know. All that Gelusil."

"There are always signs, and he hasn't any. He looks positively self-satisfied. You're wrong."

"You just don't know Scarsdale. Self-satisfaction is a

registered trademark. You can't buy a house without it."

"Speaking of such things, what are you going to do? I really think we should cancel St. Thomas."

"I don't. It's been a rough winter; we deserve a little sun. Anyway, they're being unreasonable. There's nothing I want to learn about the Matlock manipulations; it's a waste of time. In the unlikely event that they ever *do* go, others'll be in charge."

"I thought we agreed that was only an excuse. They want you around for a while. I think it's touching they do it this way."

"It's not touching, it's my father's transparent attempt at bribery. . . . Look. Our commuter's given up." The single man with the newspaper finished his drink and was explaining to the waitress that he wasn't ordering lunch. "Five'll get you ten he pictured his son's hair and leather jacket—maybe bare feet—and just panicked."

"I think you're wishing it on the poor man."

"No, I'm not. I'm too sympathetic. I can't stand the aggravation that goes with rebellion. Makes me self-conscious."

"You're a very funny man, Private Matlock," said Pat, alluding to Matlock's inglorious army career. "When we finish, let's go down to Hartford. There's a good movie."

"Oh, I'm sorry, I forgot to tell you. We can't today. . . . Sealfont called me this morning for an early evening conference. Said it was important."

"About what?"

"I'm not sure. The African studies may be in trouble. That 'Tom' I recruited from Howard turned out to be a beaut. I think he's a little to the right of Louis XIV."

She smiled. "Really, you're terrible."

Matlock took her hand.

The residence of Dr. Adrian Sealfont was imposingly appropriate. It was a large white colonial mansion with wide marble steps leading up to thick double doors carved in relief. Along the front were Ionic pillars spanning the width of the building. Floodlights from the lawn were turned on at sundown.

Matlock walked up the stairs to the door and rang the bell. Thirty seconds later he was admitted by a maid, who ushered him through the hallway toward the rear of the house, into Dr. Sealfont's huge library.

Adrian Sealfont stood in the center of the room with two other men. Matlock, as always, was struck by the presence of the man. A shade over six feet, thin, with aquiline features, he radiated a warmth that touched all who were near him. There was about him a genuine humility which concealed his brilliance from those who did not know him. Matlock liked him immensely.

"Hello, James." Sealfont extended his hand to Matlock. "Mr. Loring, may I present Dr. Matlock?"

"How do you do? Hi, Sam." Matlock addressed this last to the third man, Samuel Kressel, dean of colleges at Carlyle.

"Hello, Jim."

"We've met before, haven't we?" asked Matlock, looking at Loring. "I'm trying to remember."

"I'm going to be very embarrassed if you do."

"I'll bet you will!" laughed Kressel with his sardonic, slightly offensive humor. Matlock also liked Sam Kressel, more because he knew the pain of Kressel's job—what he had to contend with—than for the man himself.

"What do you mean, Sam?"

"I'll answer you," interrupted Adrian Sealfont. "Mr. Loring is with the federal government, the Justice Department. I agreed to arrange a meeting between the three of you, but I did not agree to what Sam and Mr. Loring have just referred to. Apparently Mr. Loring has seen fit to have you—what is the term—under surveillance. I've registered my strong objections." Sealfont looked directly at Loring.

"You've had me *what?*" asked Matlock quietly.

"I apologize," said Loring persuasively. "It's a personal idiosyncrasy and has nothing to do with our business."

"You're the commuter in the Cheshire Cat."

"The what?" asked Sam Kressel.

"The man with the newspaper."

"That's right. I knew you'd noticed me this afternoon. I thought you'd recognize me the minute you saw me again. I didn't know I looked like a commuter."

"It was the newspaper. We called you an irate father."

"Sometimes I am. Not often, though. My daughter's only seven."

"I think we should begin," Sealfont said. "Incidentally, James, I'm relieved your reaction is so understanding."

"My only reaction is curiosity. And a healthy degree of fear. To tell you the truth, I'm scared to death." Matlock smiled haltingly. "What's it all about?"

"Let's have a drink while we talk." Adrian Sealfont smiled back and walked to his copper-topped dry bar in the corner of the room. "You're a bourbon and water man, aren't you, James? And Sam, a double Scotch over ice, correct? What's yours, Mr. Loring?"

"Scotch'll be fine. Just water."

"Here, James, give me a hand." Matlock crossed to Sealfont and helped him.

"You amaze me, Adrian," said Kressel, sitting down in a leather armchair. "What in heaven's name prompts you to remember your subordinates' choice of liquor?"

Sealfont laughed. "The most logical reason of all. And it certainly isn't confined to my . . . colleagues. I've raised more money for this institution with alcohol than with hundreds of reports prepared by the best analytic minds in fund-raising circles." Here Adrian Sealfont paused and chuckled—as much to himself as to those in the room. "I once gave a speech to the Organization of University Presidents. In the question and answer period, I was asked to what I attributed Carlyle's endowment. . . . I'm afraid I replied, 'To those ancient peoples who developed the art of fermenting the vineyards.' . . . My late wife roared but told me later I'd set the fund back a decade."

The three men laughed; Matlock distributed the drinks.

"Your health," said the president of Carlyle, raising his glass modestly. The toast, however, was brief. "This is a bit awkward, James . . . Sam. Several weeks ago I was contacted by Mr. Loring's superior. He asked me to come to Washington on a matter of utmost importance, relative to Carlyle. I did so and was briefed on a situation I still refuse to accept. Certain information which Mr. Loring will impart to you seems incontrovertible on the surface. But that is the surface: rumor; out-of-context statements, written and verbal; constructed evidence which may be meaningless. On the other hand, there might well be a degree of substance. It is on that possibility that I've agreed to this meeting. I must make it clear, however, that I cannot be a party to it. Carlyle *will not* be a party to it. Whatever may take place in this room has my un-acknowledged approval but not my official sanction. You act as individuals, not as members of the faculty or staff of Carlyle. If, indeed, you decide to act at all. . . . Now, James, if that doesn't 'scare you,' I don't know what will." Sealfont smiled again, but his message was clear.

"It scares me," said Matlock without emphasis.

Kressel put down his glass and leaned forward on the chair. "Are we to assume from what you've said that you don't endorse Loring's presence here? Or whatever it is he wants?"

"It's a gray area. If there's substance to his charges, I certainly cannot turn my back. On the other hand, no university president these days will openly collab-orate with a government agency on speculation. You'll forgive me, Mr. Loring, but too many people in Wash-ington have taken advantage of the academic com-munities. I refer specifically to Michigan, Columbia, Berkeley . . . among others. Simple police matters are one thing, infiltration . . . well, that's something else again."

"Infiltration? That's a pretty strong word," said Matlock.

"Perhaps too strong. I'll leave the terms to Mr. Lor-ing."

Kressel picked up his glass. "May I ask why we— Matlock and I—have been chosen?"

"That, again, will be covered in Mr. Loring's dis-cussion. However, since I'm responsible for *your* being here, Sam, I'll tell you *my* reasons. As dean, you're more closely attuned to campus affairs than anyone else. . . . You will also be aware of it if Mr. Loring or his associates overstep their bounds. . . . I think that's all I have to say. I'm going over to the assembly. That filmmaker, Strauss, is speaking tonight and I've got to put in an appearance." Sealfont walked back to the bar and put his glass on the tray. The three other men rose.

"One thing before you go," said Kressel, his brow wrinkled. "Suppose one or both of us decide we want no part of Mr. Loring's . . . business?"

"Then refuse." Adrian Sealfont crossed to the library door. "You are under no obligation whatsoever; I want that perfectly clear. Mr. Loring understands. Good evening, gentlemen." Sealfont walked out into the hallway, closing the door behind him.

3

The three men remained silent, standing motionless. They could hear the front entrance open and close. Kressel turned and looked at Loring.

"It seems to me you've been put on the spot."

"I usually am in these situations. Let me clarify my position; it will partly explain this meeting. The first thing you should know is that I'm with the Justice Department, *Narcotics* Bureau."

Kressel sat down and sipped at his drink. "You haven't traveled up here to tell us forty percent of the student body is on pot and a few other items, have you? Because if so, it's nothing we don't know."

"No, I haven't. I assume you *do* know about such things. Everyone does. I'm not sure about the percentage, though. It could be a low estimate."

Matlock finished his bourbon and decided to have another. He spoke as he crossed to the copper bar table. "It may be low or high, but comparatively speaking—in relation to other campuses—we're not in a panic."

"There's no reason for you to be. Not about that."

"There's something else?"

"Very much so." Loring walked to Sealfont's desk and bent down to pick up his briefcase from the floor. It was apparent that the government man and Carlyle's president had talked before Matlock and Kressel arrived. Loring put the briefcase on the desk and opened it. Matlock walked back to his chair and sat down.

"I'd like to show you something." Loring reached into the briefcase and withdrew a thick page of silver-colored stationery, cut diagonally as if with pinking shears. The silver coating was now filthy with repeated handling and blotches of grease or dirt. He approached Matlock's chair and handed it to him. Kressel got up and came over.

"It's some kind of letter. Or announcement. With numbers," said Matlock. "It's in French; no, Italian, I think. I can't make it out."

"Very good, professor," said Loring. "A lot of both and not a predominance of either. Actually, it's a Corsican dialect, written out. It's called the Oltremontan strain, used in the southern hill country. Like Etruscan, it's not entirely translatable. But what codes are used are simple to the point of not being codes at all. I don't think they were meant to be; there aren't too many of these. So there's enough here to tell us what we need to know."

"Which is?" asked Kressel, taking the strange-looking paper from Matlock.

"First I'd like to explain how we got it. Without that explanation, the information is meaningless."

"Go ahead." Kressel handed the filthy silver paper back to the government agent, who carried it to the desk and carefully returned it to his briefcase.

"A narcotics courier—that is, a man who goes into a specific source territory carrying instructions, money, messages—left the country six weeks ago. He was more than a courier, actually; he was quite powerful in the distribution hierarchy; you might say he was on a busman's holiday, Mediterranean style. Or perhaps he was checking investments. . . . At any rate, he was killed by some mountain people in the Toros Daglari—that's Turkey, a growing district. The story is, he canceled operations there and the violence followed. We accept that; the Mediterranean fields are closing down right and left, moving into South America. . . . The paper was found on his body, in a skin belt. As you saw, it's been handed around a bit. It brought a succession of prices from Ankara to Marrakesh. An Interpol undercover man finally made the purchase and it was turned over to us."

"From Toros Dag-whatever-it-is to Washington. That paper's had quite a journey," said Matlock.

"And an expensive one," added Loring. "Only it's not in Washington now, it's here. From Toros Daglari to Carlyle, Connecticut."

"I assume that means something." Sam Kressel sat down, apprehensively watching the government man.

"It means the information in that paper concerns Carlyle." Loring leaned back against the desk and spoke calmly, with no sense of urgency at all. He could have been an instructor in front of a class explaining a dry but necessary mathematics theorem. "The paper says there'll be a conference on the tenth of May, three weeks from tomorrow. The numbers are the map coordinates of the Carlyle area—precision decimals of longitude and latitude in Greenwich units. The paper itself identifies the holder to be one of those summoned. Each paper has either a matching half or is cut from a pattern that can be matched—simple additional security. What's missing is the precise location."

"Wait a minute." Kressel's voice was controlled but sharp; he was upset. "Aren't you ahead of yourself,

Loring? You're giving us information—obviously restricted—before you state your request. This university administration isn't interested in being an investigative arm of the government. Before you go into facts, you'd better say what you want."

"I'm sorry, Mr. Kressel. You said I was on the spot and I am. I'm handling it badly."

"Like hell. You're an expert."

"Hold it, Sam." Matlock raised his hand off the arm of the chair. Kressel's sudden antagonism seemed uncalled for. "Sealfont said we had the option to refuse whatever he wants. If we exercise that option—and we probably will—I'd like to think we did so out of judgment, not blind reaction."

"Don't be naïve, Jim. You receive restricted or classified information and instantly, *post facto*, you're involved. You can't deny receiving it; you can't say it didn't happen."

Matlock looked up at Loring. "Is that true?"

"To a degree, yes. I won't lie about it."

"Then why should we listen to you?"

"Because Carlyle University *is* involved; has been for years. And the situation is critical. So critical that there are only three weeks left to act on the information we have."

Kressel got out of his chair, took a deep breath, and exhaled slowly. "Create the crisis—without proof—and force the involvement. The crisis fades but the records show the university was a silent participant in a federal investigation. That was the pattern at the University of Wisconsin." Kressel turned to Matlock. "Do you remember that one, Jim? Six days of riots on campus. Half a semester lost on teach-ins."

"That was Pentagon oriented," said Loring. "The circumstances were entirely different."

"You think the Justice Department makes it more palatable? Read a few campus newspapers."

"For Christ's sake, Sam, let the man talk. If you don't want to listen, go home. I want to hear what he has to say."

Kressel looked down at Matlock. "All right. I think I understand. Go ahead, Loring. Just remember, no obligations. And we're not bound to respect any conditions of confidence."

"I'll gamble on your common sense."

"That may be a mistake." Kressel walked to the bar and replenished his drink.

Loring sat on the edge of the desk. "I'll start by asking both of you if you've ever heard of the word *nimrod.*"

"Nimrod is a Hebrew name," Matlock answered. "Old Testament. A descendant of Noah, ruler of Babylon and Nineveh. Legendary prowess as a hunter, which obscures the more important fact that he founded, or built, the great cities in Assyria and Mesopotamia."

Loring smiled. "Very good again, professor. A *hunter* and a *builder.* I'm speaking in more contemporary terms, however."

"Then, no, I haven't. Have you, Sam?"

Kressel walked back to his chair, carrying his glass. "I didn't even know what you just said. I thought a nimrod was a casting fly. Very good for trout."

"Then I'll fill in some background. . . . I don't mean to bore you with narcotics statistics; I'm sure you're bombarded with them constantly."

"Constantly," said Kressel.

"But there's an isolated geographical statistic you may not be aware of. The concentration of drug traffic in the New England states is growing at a rate exceeding that of any other section of the country. It's a startling pattern. Since 1968, there's been a systematic erosion of enforcement procedures. . . . Let me put it into perspective, geographically. In California, Illinois, Louisiana, narcotics controls have improved to the point of at least curtailing the growth curves. It's really the best we can hope for until the international agreements have teeth. But not in the New England area. Throughout this section, the expansion has gone wild. It's hit the colleges hard."

"How do you know that?" asked Matlock.

"Dozens of ways and always too late to prevent distribution. Informers, marked inventories from Mediterranean, Asian, and Latin American sources, traceable Swiss deposits; that *is* restricted data." Loring looked at Kressel and smiled.

"Now I know you people are crazy." Kressel spoke disagreeably. "It seems to me that if you can substantiate those charges, you should do so publicly. And loud."

"We have our reasons."

"Also restricted, I assume," said Kressel with faint disgust.

"There's a side issue," continued the government man, disregarding him. "The eastern prestige campuses—large and small, Princeton, Amherst, Harvard, Vassar, Williams, Carlyle—a good percentage of their enrollments include VIP kids. Sons and daughters of very important people, especially in government and industry. There's a blackmail potential, and we think it's been used. Such people are painfully sensitive to drug scandals."

Kressel interrupted. "Granting what you say is true, and I don't, we've had less trouble here than most other colleges in the northeast area."

"We're aware of that. We even think we know why."

"That's esoteric, Mr. Loring. Say what you want to say." Matlock didn't like the games some people played.

"Any distribution network which is capable of systematically servicing, expanding, and controlling an entire section of the country has got to have a base of operations. A clearing house—you might say, a command post. Believe me when I tell you that this base of operations, the command post for the narcotics traffic throughout the New England states, is Carlyle University."

Samuel Kressel, dean of the colleges, dropped his glass on Adrian Sealfont's parquet floor.

Ralph Loring continued his incredible story. Matlock and Kressel remained in their chairs. Several times during his calm, methodical explanation, Kressel began to interrupt, to object, but Loring's persuasive narrative cut him short. There was nothing to argue.

The investigation of Carlyle University had begun eighteen months ago. It had been triggered by an accounts ledger uncovered by the French Sureté during one of its frequent narcotics investigations in the port of Marseilles. Once the ledger's American origins were established, it was sent to Washington under Interpol agreement. Throughout the ledger's entries were references to "C-22°-59°" consistently followed by the name *Nimrod*. The numbered degree marks were found to be map coordinates of northern Connecticut, but not decimally definitive. After tracing hundreds of possible trucking routes from Atlantic seaboard piers and airports relative to the Marseilles operation, the vicinity of Carlyle was placed under maximum surveillance.

As part of the surveillance, telephone taps were ordered on persons known to be involved with narcotics distribution from such points as New York, Hartford, Boston, and New Haven. Tapes were made of conversations of underworld figures. All calls regarding narcotics to and from the Carlyle area were placed to and from public telephone booths. It made the intercepts difficult, but not impossible. Again, restricted methods.

As the information files grew, a startling fact became apparent. The Carlyle group was independent. It had no formal ties with structured organized crime; it was beholden to no one. It *used* known criminal elements, was not used *by* them. It was a tightly knit unit, reaching into the majority of New England universities. And it did not—apparently—stop at drugs.

There was evidence of the Carlyle unit's infiltration into gambling, prostitution, even postgraduate employment placement. Too, there seemed to be a purpose, an objective beyond the inherent profits of the illegal activities. The Carlyle unit could have made far greater profit with less complications by dealing outright with known criminals, acknowledged suppliers in all areas. Instead, it spent its own money to set up its organization. It was its own master, controlling its own sources, its own distribution. But what its ultimate objectives were was unclear.

It had become so powerful that it threatened the leadership of organized crime in the Northeast. For this reason, leading figures of the underworld had demanded a conference with those in charge of the Carlyle operation. The key here was a group, or an individual, referred to as *Nimrod*.

The purpose of the conference, as far as could be determined, was for an accommodation to be reached between Nimrod and the overlords of crime who felt threatened by Nimrod's extraordinary growth. The conference would be attended by dozens of known and unknown criminals throughout the New England states.

"Mr. Kressel." Loring turned to Carlyle's dean and seemed to hesitate. "I suppose you have lists—students, faculty, staff—people you know or have reason to suspect are into the drug scene. I can't assume it because I don't know, but most colleges do have."

"I won't answer that question."

"Which, of course, gives me my answer," said Loring quietly, even sympathetically.

"Not for a minute! You people have a habit of assuming exactly what you want to assume."

"All right, I stand rebuked. But even if you'd said yes, it wasn't my purpose to ask for them. It was merely by way of telling you that we *do* have such a list. I wanted you to know that."

Sam Kressel realized he'd been trapped; Loring's ingenuousness only annoyed him further. "I'm sure you do."

"Needless to say, we'd have no objection to giving you a copy."

"That won't be necessary."

"You're pretty obstinate, Sam," said Matlock. "You burying your head?"

Before Kressel could reply, Loring spoke. "The dean knows he can change his mind. And we've agreed, there's no crisis here. You'd be surprised how many people wait for the roof to cave in before asking for help. Or accepting it."

"But there aren't many surprises in your organization's proclivity for turning difficult situations into

disasters, are there?" countered Sam Kressel antago-
nistically.

"We've made mistakes."

"Since you have names," continued Sam, "why
don't you go after them? Leave us out of it; do your
own dirty work. Make arrests, press charges. Don't try
to deputize *us*."

"We don't want to do that. . . . Besides, most of our
evidence is inadmissible."

"That occurred to me," interjected Kressel.

"And what do we gain? What do *you* gain?" Loring
leaned forward, returning Sam's stare. "We pick up a
couple of hundred potheads, a few dozen speedfreaks;
users and low-level pushers. Don't you understand,
that doesn't *solve* anything."

"Which brings us to what you really want, doesn't
it?" Matlock sank back into the chair; he watched the
persuasive agent closely.

"Yes," answered Loring softly. "We want Nimrod.
We want to know the location of that conference on
May 10. It could be anywhere within a radius of fifty
to a hundred miles. We want to be prepared for it. We
want to break the back of the Nimrod operation, for
reasons that go way beyond Carlyle University. As
well as narcotics."

"How?" asked James Matlock.

"Dr. Sealfont said it. Infiltration. . . . Professor Matlock, you are what's known in intelligence circles as a
highly mobile person within your environment. You're
widely accepted by diverse, even conflicting factions
—within both the faculty and the student body. We
have the names, you have the mobility." Loring
reached into his briefcase and withdrew the scissored
page of filthy stationery. "Somewhere out there is the

information we need. Somewhere there's someone who has a paper like this; someone who knows what we have to know."

James Barbour Matlock remained motionless in his chair, staring at the government man. Neither Loring nor Kressel could be sure what he was thinking but both had an idea. If thoughts were audible, there would have been full agreement in that room at that moment. James Matlock's mind had wandered back three, almost four years ago. He was remembering a blond-haired boy of nineteen. Immature for his age, perhaps, but good, kind. A boy with problems.

They'd found him as they'd found thousands like him in thousands of cities and towns across the country. Other times, other Nimrods.

James Matlock's brother, David, had inserted a needle in his right arm and had shot up thirty mg. of white fluid. He had performed the act in a catboat in the calm waters of a Cape Cod inlet. The small sailboat had drifted into the reeds near shore. When they found it, James Matlock's brother was dead.

Matlock made his decision.

"Can you get me the names?"

"I have them with me."

"Just hold it." Kressel stood up, and when he spoke, it wasn't in the tone of an angry man—it was with fear. "Do you realize what you're asking him to do? He has no experience in this kind of work. He's not trained. Use one of your *own* men."

"There isn't time. There's no time for one of our men. He'll be protected; you can help."

"I can *stop* you!"

"No, you can't, Sam," said Matlock from the chair.

"Jim, for Christ's sake, do you know what he's asking? If there's *any* truth to what he's said, he's placing you in the worst position a man can be in. An informer."

"You don't have to stay. My decision doesn't have to be your decision. Why don't you go home?" Matlock rose and walked slowly to the bar, carrying his glass.

"That's impossible now," said Kressel, turning toward the government agent. "And *he knows it.*"

Loring felt a touch of sadness. This Matlock was a good man; he was doing what he was doing because he felt he owed a debt. And it was coldly, professionally projected that by accepting the assignment, James Matlock was very possibly going to his death. It was a terrible price, that possibility. But the objective was worth it. The conference was worth it.

Nimrod was worth it.

That was Loring's conclusion.

It made his assignment bearable.

4

Nothing could be written down; the briefing was slow, repetition constant. But Loring was a professional and knew the value of taking breaks from the pressures of trying to absorb too much too rapidly. During these periods, he attempted to draw Matlock out, learn more about this man whose life was so easily expendable. It was nearly midnight; Sam Kressel had left before eight o'clock. It was neither necessary nor advisable that the dean be present during the detailing of the specifics. He was a liaison, not an activist. Kressel was not averse to the decision.

Ralph Loring learned quickly that Matlock was a private man. His answers to innocuously phrased questions were brief, thrown-away replies constituting no more than self-denigrating explanations. After a while, Loring gave up. Matlock had agreed to do a job, not make public his thoughts or his motives. It wasn't necessary; Loring understood the latter. That was all that mattered. He was just as happy not to know the man too well.

Matlock, in turn—while memorizing the complicated information—was, on another level, reflecting on his own life, wondering in his own way why he'd been selected. He was intrigued by an evaluation that could describe him as being *mobile;* what an awful word to have applied!

Yet he knew he was precisely what the term signified. He *was* mobile. The professional researchers, or psychologists, or whatever they were, were accurate. But he doubted they understood the reasons behind his . . . "mobility."

The academic world had been a refuge, a sanctuary. Not an objective of long-standing ambition. He had fled into it in order to buy time, to organize a life that was falling apart, to understand. To get his *head straight,* as the kids said these days.

He had tried to explain it to his wife, his lovely, quick, bright, ultimately hollow wife, who thought he'd lost his senses. What was there to understand but an *awfully* good job, an *awfully* nice house, an *awfully* pleasant club, and a *good* life within an *awfully* rewarding social and financial world? For her, there *was* nothing more to understand. And he understood that.

But for him that world had lost its meaning. He had begun to drift away from its core in his early twenties, during his last year at Amherst. The separation became complete with his army experience.

It was no one single thing that had triggered his rejection. And the rejection itself was not a violent act, although violence played its role in the early days of the Saigon mess. It had begun at home, where most life-styles are accepted or rejected, during a series of disagreeable confrontations with his father. The old gentleman—too old, too gentlemanly—felt justified in demanding a better performance from his first son. A direction, a sense of purpose not at all in evidence. The senior Matlock belonged to another era—if not another century—and believed the gap between father and son a desirable thing, the lower element being dismissible until it had proved itself in the marketplace. Dismissible but, of course, malleable. In ways, the father was like a benign ruler who, after generations of power, was loath to have the throne abandoned by his rightful issue. It was inconceivable to the elder Matlock that his son would not assume the leadership of the family business. Businesses.

But for the younger Matlock, it was all *too* conceivable. And preferable. He was not only uncomfortable thinking about a future in his father's *marketplace*, he was also afraid. For him there was no joy in the regimented pressures of the financial world; instead, there was an awesome fear of inadequacy, emphasized by his father's strong—overpowering—competence. The closer he came to entering that world, the more pronounced was his fear. And it occurred to him that along with the delights of extravagant shelter and unnecessary creature comforts had to come the justification for doing what was expected in order to possess these things. He could not find that justification. Better the shelter should be less extravagant, the creature comforts somewhat limited, than face the prospects of continuing fear and discomfort.

He had tried to explain *that* to his father. Whereas his wife had claimed he'd lost his senses, the old gentleman pronounced him a misfit.

Which didn't exactly refute the army's judgment of him.

The army.

A disaster. Made worse by the knowledge that it was of his own making. He found that blind physical discipline and unquestioned authority were abhorrent to him. And he was large enough and strong enough and had a sufficient vocabulary to make his unadjustable, immature objections known—to his own disadvantage.

Discreet manipulations by an uncle resulted in a discharge before his tour of service was officially completed; for that he *was* grateful to an influential family.

And at this juncture of his life, James Barbour Matlock II was a mess. Separated from the service less than gloriously, divorced by his wife, dispossessed—symbolically if not actually—by his family, he felt the panic of belonging nowhere, of being without motive or purpose.

So he'd fled into the secure confines of graduate school, hoping to find an answer. And as in a love affair begun on a sexual basis but growing into psychological dependence, he had married that world; he'd found what had eluded him for nearly five vital years. It was the first real commitment he'd ever experienced.

He was free.

Free to enjoy the excitement of a meaningful challenge; free to revel in the confidence that he was equal to it. He plunged into his new world with the enthusiasm of a convert but without the blindness. He chose a period of history and literature that teemed with energy and conflict and contradictory evaluations. The apprentice years passed swiftly; he was consumed and pleasantly surprised by his own talents. When he emerged on the professional plateau, he brought fresh air into the musty archives. He made startling innovations in long-unquestioned methods of research. His doctoral thesis on court interference with English Renaissance literature—news management—blew into the historical ashcan several holy theories about one benefactress named Elizabeth.

He was the new breed of scholar: restless, skeptical, unsatisfied, always searching while imparting what he'd learned to others. Two and a half years after receiving his doctorate, he was elevated to the tenured position of associate professor, the youngest instructor at Carlyle to be so contracted.

James Barbour Matlock II made up for the lost years, the awful years. Perhaps best of all was the knowledge that he could communicate his excitement to others. He was young enough to enjoy sharing his enthusiasm, old enough to direct the inquiries.

Yes, he was *mobile;* God, was he! He couldn't, *wouldn't* turn anyone off, shut anyone out because of disagreement—even dislike. The depth of his own gratitude, the profoundness of his relief was such that he unconsciously promised himself never to discount the concerns of another human being.

"Any surprises?" Loring had completed a section of the material that dealt with narcotics purchases as they'd been traced.

"More a clarification, I'd say," replied Matlock. "The old-line fraternities or clubs—mostly white, mostly rich—get their stuff from Hartford. The black units like Lumumba Hall go to New Haven. Different sources."

"Exactly; that's student orientation. The point being that none buy from the Carlyle suppliers. From Nimrod."

"You explained that. The Nimrod people don't want to be advertised."

"But they're here. They're used."

"By whom?"

"Faculty and staff," answered Loring calmly, flipping over a page. This *may* be a surprise. Mr. and Mrs. Archer Beeson . . ."

Matlock immediately pictured the young history instructor and his wife. They were Ivy League conformity itself—falsely arrogant, aesthetically precious. Archer Beeson was a young man in an academic hurry; his wife, the perfect faculty ingenue, carelessly sexy, always in awe.

"They're with LSD and the methedrines. Acid and speed."

"Good Lord! They fooled the hell out of me. How do you know?"

"It's too complicated to go into, also restricted. To oversimplify: they, he, used to purchase heavily from a distributor in Bridgeport. The contact was terminated and he didn't show up on any other lists. But he's not off. We think he made the Carlyle connection. No proof, though . . . Here's another."

It was the coach of varsity soccer, a jock who worked in physical education. His items were marijuana and amphetamines; his previous source, Hartford. He was considered a pusher on campus, not a user. Although the Hartford source was no longer employed, the man's varied and dummied bank accounts continued to grow. Assumption: Nimrod.

And another. This one frightening to Matlock. The assistant dean of admissions. An alumnus of Carlyle who returned to the campus after a brief career as a salesman. He was a flamboyant, open-handed man; a proselytizer for the cause of Carlyle. A popular enthusiast in these days of cynicism. He, too, was considered a distributor, not a user. He covered himself well through second- and third-level pushers.

"We think he came back here through the Nimrod organization. Good positioning on Nimrod's part."

"Goddamn scarey. That son of a bitch makes parents think he's a combination of astronaut and chaplain."

"Good positioning, as I said. Remember? I told you and Kressel: the Nimrod people have interests that go beyond drugs."

"But you don't know what they are."

"We'd better find out. . . . Here's the breakdown of the kids."

The names of the students seemed endless to Matlock. There were 563 out of a total enrollment of 1200 plus. The government man admitted that many were included not because of confirmation of individual use, but due to their campus affiliations. Clubs and fraternities were known to pool resources for the purchase of narcotics.

"We haven't the time to ascertain the validity of every name. We're looking for relationships; any, no matter how remote. You've got to have all kinds of avenues; we can't restrict them. . . . And there's one aspect to this list; I don't know whether you see it or not."

"I certainly do. At least, I think I do. Twenty or thirty names here ring loud bells in several high places. Some very influential parents. Industry, government. Here." Matlock pointed. "The president's cabinet, if I'm not mistaken. And I'm not."

"You see." Loring smiled.

"Has any of this had any effect?"

"We don't know. Could have, could be. The Nimrod tentacles are spreading out fast. That's why the alarms are sounding; louder than your bells. Speaking unofficially, there could be repercussions no one's dreamed of. . . . Defense overruns, union contracts, forced installations. You name it. It *could* be related."

"Jesus Christ," said Matlock softly.

"Exactly."

The two men heard the front door of Sealfont's mansion open and shut. As if by reflex, Loring calmly took the papers from Matlock's hand and quickly replaced them in his briefcase. He closed the case and then did an unexpected thing. He silently, almost unobtrusively, whipped back his jacket and curled his fingers around the handle of a revolver in a small holster strapped to his chest. The action startled Matlock. He stared at the hidden hand.

The library door opened and Adrian Sealfont walked in. Loring casually removed his hand from inside his coat. Sealfont spoke kindly.

"I *do try*. I honestly do. I understand the words and the pictures and take no offense whatsoever at the braided hair. What confuses me is the hostility. Anyone past thirty is the natural enemy of these fellows."

"That was Strauss, wasn't it?" asked Matlock.

"Yes. Someone inquired about the New Wave influence. He replied that the New Wave was ancient history. Prehistoric, was his word. . . . I won't interrupt you gentlemen. I would, however, like to know Kressel's status, Mr. Loring. Obviously, James has accepted."

"So has Mr. Kressel, sir. He'll act as liaison between us."

"I see." Sealfont looked at Matlock. There was a sense of relief in his eyes. "James, I can tell you now. I'm extremely grateful you've decided to help."

"I don't think there's an alternative."

"There isn't. What's frightening is the possibility of such total involvement. Mr. Loring, I'll want to be advised the minute you have anything concrete. At that point, I shall do whatever you wish, follow any instructions. All I ask is that you supply me with proof and you'll have my complete, my official cooperation."

"I understand, sir. You've been very helpful. More than we had a right to expect. We appreciate it."

"As James said, there is no alternative. But I must impose limits; my first obligation is to this institution. The campuses these days might appear dormant; I think that's a surface evaluation. . . . You have work to do and I have some reading to finish. Good night, Mr. Loring. James."

Matlock and the government man nodded their goodnights as Adrian Sealfont closed the library door.

By one o'clock, Matlock could absorb no more. The main elements—names, sources, conjectures—were locked in; he would never forget them. Not that he could recite everything by rote; that wasn't expected. But the sight of any particular individual on the lists would trigger a memory response. He knew Loring was right about that. It was why the agent insisted that he say the names out loud, repeating them several times each. It would be enough.

What he needed now was a night's sleep, if sleep would come. Let everything fall into some kind of perspective. Then in the morning he could begin to make initial decisions, determine which individuals should be approached, selecting those least likely to come in contact with one another. And this meant familiarizing himself with immediate friends, faculty or student body status—dozens of isolated fragments of information beyond the data supplied by Loring. Kressel's files—the ones he disclaimed having—would help.

Once in conversations he'd have to make his way carefully—thrusting, parrying, watching for signs, looks, betrayals.

Somewhere, with someone, it would happen.

"I'd like to go back to something," said Loring. "Background material."

"We've covered an awful lot. Maybe I should digest what I've got."

"This won't take a minute. It's important." The agent reached into his briefcase and withdrew the filthy, scissored paper. "Here, this is yours."

"Thanks for I-don't-know-what." Matlock took the once-shining silver paper and looked at the strange script.

"I told you it was written in Oltremontan-Corsican and, except for two words, that's correct. At the bottom, on a single line, you'll see the phrase *Venerare Omerta*. That's not Corsican, it's Sicilian. Or a Sicilian contraction, to be precise."

"I've seen it before."

"I'm sure you have. It's been given wide distribution in newspapers, movies, fiction. But that doesn't lessen its impact on those concerned by it. It's very real."

"What does it mean?"

"Roughly translated: Respect the law of Omerta. Omerta is an oath of allegiance *and* silence. To betray either is asking to be killed."

"Mafia?"

"It's involved. You might say it's the party of the second part. Bear in mind that this little announce-

ment was issued jointly by two factions trying to reach
an accommodation. 'Omerta' goes across the board;
it's understood by both."

"I'll bear it in mind, but I don't know what I'm
supposed to do with it."

"Just know about it."

"O.K."

"One last item. Everything we've covered here tonight is related to narcotics. But if our information is
correct, the Nimrod people are involved in other fields.
Sharking, prostitution, gambling . . . perhaps, and it's
only perhaps, municipal controls, state legislatures,
even the federal government. . . . Experience tells us
that narcotics is the weakest action, the highest rate
of collapse among these activities, and that's why
we've centered on it. In other words, concentrate on
the drug situation but be aware that other avenues
exist."

"It's no secret."

"Maybe not to you. Let's call it a night."

"Shouldn't you give me a number where I can reach
you?"

"Negative. Use Kressel. We'll check with him several
times a day. Once you start asking questions, you may
be put under a microscope. Don't call Washington.
And *don't* lose our Corsican invitation. It's your ultimate clout. Just find another one."

"I'll try."

Matlock watched as Loring closed his briefcase,
looped the thin black chain around his wrist, and
snapped the built-in lock.

"Looks very cloak-and-daggerish, doesn't it?" Loring laughed.

"I'm impressed."

"Don't be. The custom began with diplomatic couriers who'd take their pouches to hell with them, but today it's simply a protection against purse-snatching. ... So help me, that's what they think of us."

"I don't believe a word you say. That's one of those cases that make smoke screens, send out radio signals, and trigger bombs."

"You're right. It does all those things and more. It's got secret compartments for sandwiches, laundry, and God knows what else." Loring swung the briefcase off the desk. "I think it'd be a good idea if we left separately. Preferably one from the front, one from the rear. Ten minutes apart."

"You think that's necessary?"

"Frankly, no, but that's the way my superiors want it."

"O.K. I know the house. I'll leave ten minutes after you do, from the kitchen."

"Fine." Loring extended his right hand by steadying the bottom of his case with his left. "I don't have to tell you how much we appreciate what you're doing."

"I think you know why I'm doing it."

"Yes, we do. Frankly, we counted on it."

Loring let himself out of the library and Matlock waited until he heard the outer door open and close. He looked at his watch. He'd have one more drink before he left.

By one twenty Matlock was several blocks away from the house. He walked slowly west toward his apartment, debating whether to detour around the campus. It often helped him to walk out a problem; he knew sleep would come fitfully. He passed a number of students and several faculty members, exchanging low-keyed, end of the weekend greetings with those he recognized. He'd about made up his mind to turn north on High Street, away from the direction of his apartment, when he heard the footsteps behind him. First the footsteps, then the harshly whispered voice.

"Matlock! Don't turn around. It's Loring. Just keep walking and listen to me."

"What is it?"

"Someone knows I'm here. My car was searched. . . ."

"Christ! How do you know?"

"Field-threads, preset markings. All over the car. Front, back, trunk. A very thorough, very professional job."

"You're sure?"

"So goddamn sure I'm not going to start that engine!"

"Jesus!" Matlock nearly stopped.

"Keep walking! If anyone was watching me—and you can be damned sure someone was—I made it clear I'd lost my ignition key. Asked several people who passed by where a pay phone was and waited till I saw you far enough away."

"What do you want me to do? There's a phone booth on the next corner. . . ."

"I know. I don't think you'll have to do anything, and for both our sakes, I hope I'm right. I'm going to jostle you as I pass—pretty hard. Lose your balance, I'll shout my apologies. Pretend you twisted an ankle, a wrist, anything you like; *but buy time!* Keep me in sight until a car comes for me and *I nod that it's o.k.* Do you have all that? I'll get to the booth in a hurry."

"Suppose you're still phoning when I get there?"

"Keep walking but *keep checking.* The car's cruising."

"What's the point?"

"This briefcase. That's the point. There's only one thing Nimrod—if it *is* Nimrod—would like more than this briefcase. And that's the paper in your coat pocket. So be careful!"

Without warning, he rushed up beside Matlock and pushed him off the sidewalk.

"Sorry, fella! I'm in an awful hurry!"

Matlock looked up from the ground, reflecting that he'd had no reason to *pretend* to fall. The force of Loring's push eliminated that necessity. He swore and rose awkwardly. Once on his feet, he limped slowly toward the phone booth several hundred yards away. He wasted nearly a minute lighting a cigarette. Loring was inside the booth now, sitting on the plastic seat, hunched over the phone.

Any second, Matlock expected Loring's car to drive up the street.

Yet none came.

Instead, there was the tiniest break in the spring noises. A rush of air through the new leaves. Or was it the crush of a stone beneath a foot, or a small twig unable to take the weight of the new growth in the trees? Or was it Matlock's imagination? He couldn't be sure.

He approached the booth and remembered Loring's orders. *Walk by and pay no attention.* Loring was still huddled over the phone, his briefcase resting on the floor, its chain visible. But Matlock could hear no conversation, could see no movement from the man within. Instead, again, there was a sound: now, the sound of a dial tone.

Despite his instructions, Matlock approached the booth and opened the door. There was nothing else he could do. The government man had not even *begun* his call.

And in an instant, he understood why.

Loring had fallen into the gleaming gray metal of the telephone. He was dead. His eyes wide, blood trickling out of his forehead. A small circular hole no larger than a shirt button, surrounded by a spray of cracked glass, was ample evidence of what had happened.

Matlock stared at the man who had briefed him for hours and left him minutes ago. The dead man who had thanked him, joked with him, then finally warned him. He was petrified, unsure of what he should do, *could* do.

He backed away from the booth toward the steps of the nearest house. Instinct told him to stay away but not to run away. Someone was out there in the street. Someone with a rifle.

When the words came, he realized they were his, but he didn't know when he'd decided to shout them. They just emerged involuntarily.

"Help . . . *Help!* There's a man out here! He's been *shot!*"

Matlock raced up the steps of the corner house and began pounding on the door with all his strength. Several lights went on in several different homes. Matlock continued shouting.

"For God's *sake,* someone call the *police! There's a dead man out here!*"

Suddenly, from the shadows underneath the full trees in the middle of the block, Matlock heard the roar of an automobile engine, then the sound of swerving tires as the vehicle pulled out into the middle of the street and started forward. He rushed to the edge of the porch. The long black automobile plunged out of the darkness and sped to the corner. Matlock tried to see the license plates and, realizing that was impossible, took a step down to identify the make of the car. Suddenly he was blinded. The beam of a searchlight pierced the dimly lit spring night and focused itself on him. He pulled his hands up to shield his eyes and then heard the quiet slap, the instant rush of air he had heard minutes ago.

A rifle was being fired at him. A rifle with a silencer.

He dove off the porch into the shrubbery. The black car sped away.

5

He waited alone. The room was small, the window glass meshed with wire. The Carlyle Police Station was filled with officers and plainclothesmen called back on duty; no one could be sure what the killing signified. And none discounted the possibility that others might follow.

Alert. It was the particular syndrome of midcentury America, thought Matlock.

The gun.

He'd had the presence of mind after reaching the police to call Sam Kressel. Kressel, in shock, told him he would somehow contact the appropriate men in Washington and then drive down to the station house.

Until further instructions, they both agreed Matlock would restrict himself to a simple statement on finding the body and seeing the automobile. He had been out for a late night walk, that was all.

Nothing more.

His statement was typed out; questions as to time, his reasons for being in the vicinity, descriptions of the "alleged perpetrator's vehicle," direction, estimated speed—all were asked routinely and accepted without comment.

Matlock was bothered by his unequivocal negative to one question.

"Did you ever see the deceased before?"

"No."

That hurt. Loring deserved more than a considered, deliberate lie. Matlock recalled that the agent said he had a seven-year-old daughter. A wife and a child; the husband and father killed and he could not admit he knew his name.

He wasn't sure why it bothered him, but it did. Perhaps, he thought, because he knew it was the beginning of a great many lies.

He signed the short deposition and was about to be released when he heard a telephone ring inside an office beyond the desk. Not *on* the desk, beyond it. Seconds later, a uniformed policeman emerged and said his name in a loud voice, as if to make sure he had not left the building.

"Yes, officer?"

"We'll have to ask you to wait. If you'll follow me, please."

Matlock had been in the small room for nearly an hour; it was 2:45 A.M. and he had run out of cigarettes. It was no time to run out of cigarettes.

The door opened and a tall, thin man with large, serious eyes walked in. He was carrying Loring's briefcase. "Sorry to detain you, Dr. Matlock. It is 'Doctor,' isn't it?"

" 'Mister' is fine."

"My identification. Name's Greenberg, Jason Greenberg. Federal Bureau of Investigation. I had to confirm your situation. . . . It's a hell of a note, isn't it?"

" 'A hell of a note'? Is that all you can say?"

The agent looked at Matlock quizzically. "It's all I care to share," he said quietly. "If Ralph Loring had completed his call, he would have reached me."

"I'm sorry."

"Forget it. I'm out-briefed—that is, I know something but not much about the Nimrod situation; I'll get filled in before morning. Incidentally, this fellow Kressel is on his way over. He knows I'm here."

"Does this change anything? . . . That sounds stupid, doesn't it? A man is killed and I ask you if it changes anything. I apologize again."

"No need to; you've had a terrible experience. . . . Any change is up to you. We accept the fact that Ralph's death could alter tonight's decision. We ask only that you keep your own counsel in what was revealed to you."

"You're offering me a chance to renege?"

"Of course. You're under no obligation to us."

Matlock walked to the small, rectangular window with the wire-enclosed glass. The police station was at the south end of the town of Carlyle, about a half a mile from the campus, the section of town considered industrialized. Still, there were trees along the streets. Carlyle was a very clean town, a neat town. The trees by the station house were pruned and shaped.

And Carlyle was also something else.

"Let me ask you a question," he said. "Does the fact that I found Loring's body associate me with him? I mean, would I be considered a part of whatever he was doing?"

"We don't think so. The way you behaved tends to remove you from any association."

"What do you mean?" Matlock turned to face the agent.

"Frankly, you panicked. You didn't run, you didn't take yourself out of the area; you flipped out and started shouting your head off. Someone who's programmed for an assignment wouldn't react like that."

"I wasn't programmed for *this*."

"Same results. You just found him and lost your head. If this Nimrod even *suspects* we're involved . . ."

"Suspects!" interrupted Matlock. "They *killed* him!"

"*Someone* killed him. It's unlikely that it's any part of Nimrod. Other factions, maybe. No cover's absolutely foolproof, even Loring's. But his was the closest."

"I don't understand you."

Greenberg leaned against the wall and folded his arms, his large, sad eyes reflective. "Ralph's field cover was the best at Justice. For damn near fifteen years." The agent looked down at the floor. His voice was deep, with faint bitterness. "The kind of goddamn cover that works best when it doesn't matter to a man anymore. When it's finally used, it throws everyone off balance. And insults his family."

Greenberg looked up and tried to smile, but no smile would come.

"I still don't understand you."

"It's not necessary. The main point is that you simply stumbled on the scene, went into panic, and had the scare of your life. You're dismissible, Mr. Matlock. . . . So?"

Before Matlock could respond, the door swung open and Sam Kressel entered, his expression nervous and frightened.

"Oh, Christ! This is terrible! Simply terrible. You're Greenberg?"

"And you're Mr. Kressel."

"Yes. What's going to happen?" Kressel turned to Matlock, speaking in the same breath. "Are you all right, Jim?"

"Sure."

"Well, Greenberg, what's *happening!*? They told

me in Washington that you'd let us know."

"I've been talking to Mr. Matlock and . . ."

"Listen to me," interrupted Kressel suddenly. "I called Sealfont and we're of the same opinion. What happened was terrible . . . tragic. We express our sympathies to the man's family, but we're most anxious that any use of the Carlyle name be cleared with us. We assume this puts everything in a different light and, therefore, we insist we be kept out of it. I think that's understandable."

Greenberg's face betrayed his distaste. "You race in here, ask me what's happening, and before you give me a chance to answer, you tell me what *must* happen. Now, how do you want it? Do I call Washington and let them have *your* version or do you want to listen first? Doesn't make a particle of difference to me."

"There's no reason for antagonism. We never asked to be involved."

"Nobody does." Greenberg smiled. "Just please let me finish. I've offered Matlock his out. He hasn't given me his answer, so I can't give you mine. However, if he says what I think he's going to say, Loring's cover will be activated immediately. It'll be activated anyway, but if the professor's in, we'll blow it up a bit."

"What the hell are you talking about?" Kressel stared at the agent.

"For years Ralph was a partner in just about the most disreputable law firm in Washington. Its clients read like a cross section of a Mafia index. . . . Early this morning, there was the first of two vehicle transfers. It took place in a Hartford suburb, Elmwood. Loring's car with the D.C. plates was left near the home of a well-advertised capo. A rented automobile was waiting for him a couple of blocks away. He used that to drive to Carlyle and parked it in front of 217 Crescent Street, five blocks from Sealfont's place. 217 Crescent is the residence of a Dr. Ralston. . . ."

"I've met him," interjected Matlock. "I've heard he's . . ."

". . . an abortionist," completed Greenberg.

"He's in no way associated with this university!" said Kressel emphatically.

"You've had worse," countered Greenberg quietly. "And the doctor is still a Mafia referral. At any rate, Ralph positioned the car and walked into town for the second transfer. I covered him; this briefcase is prime material. He was picked up by a Bell Telephone truck which made routine stops—including one at a restaurant called the Cheshire Cat—and finally delivered him to Sealfont's. No one could have known he was there. If they had, they would have intercepted him outside; they were watching the car on Crescent."

"That's what he told me," said Matlock.

"He knew it was possible; the trace to Crescent was intentionally left open. When he confirmed it, to his satisfaction, he acted fast. I don't know what he did, but he probably used whatever stragglers he could find until he spotted you."

"That's what he did."

"He wasn't fast enough."

"What in God's name does this have to do with *us?* What *possible* bearing can it have?" Kressel was close to shouting.

"If Mr. Matlock wants to go on, Loring's death will be publicized as an underworld killing. Disreputable lawyer, maybe a bag man; undesirable clients. The capo and the doctor will be hauled in; they're expendable. The smoke screen's so thick everyone's off balance. Even the killers. Matlock's forgotten. It'll work; it's worked before."

Kressel seemed astonished at Greenberg's assured glibness, his confidence, his calm professionalism. "You talk awfully fast, don't you?"

"I'm very bright."

Matlock couldn't help but smile. He liked Greenberg; even in—perhaps because of—the sadly disagreeable circumstances. The agent used the language well; his mind was fast. He was, indeed, bright.

"And if Jim says he washes his hands of it?"

Greenberg shrugged. "I don't like to waste words. Let's hear him say it."

Both the men looked at Matlock.

"I'm afraid I'm not going to, Sam. I'm still in."

"You can't be serious! That man was killed!"

"I know. I found him."

Kressel put his hand on Matlock's arm. It was the gesture of a friend. "I'm not an hysterical shepherd watching over a flock. I'm concerned. I'm *frightened*. I see a man being manipulated into a situation he's not qualified to handle."

"That's subjective," broke in Greenberg quietly. "We're concerned, too. If we didn't think he was capable, we never would have approached him."

"I think you would," said Kressel. "I don't for a minute believe such a consideration would stop you. You use the word *expendable* too easily, Mr. Greenberg."

"I'm sorry you think so. Because I don't. We don't. . . . I haven't gotten the detailed briefing, Kressel, but aren't you supposed to act as liaison? Because if that's true, I suggest you remove yourself. We'll have someone else assigned to the job."

"And give you a clear field? Let you run roughshod over this campus? Not on your life."

"Then we work together. As disagreeable as that may be for both of us . . . You're hostile; perhaps that's good. You'll keep me on my toes. You protest too much."

Matlock was startled by Greenberg's statement. It was one thing to form an antagonistic coalition, quite another to make veiled accusations; insulting to use a literary cliché.

"That remark requires an explanation," said Kressel, his face flushed with anger.

When Greenberg replied, his voice was soft and reasonable, belying the words he spoke. "Pound sand, mister. I lost a very good friend tonight. Twenty minutes ago I spoke with his wife. I don't give explanations under those conditions. That's where my employers and me part company. Now, shut up and I'll write out the hours of contact and give you the emergency telephone numbers. If you don't want them, get the hell out of here."

Greenberg lifted the briefcase onto a small table and opened it. Sam Kressel, stunned, approached the agent silently.

Matlock stared at the worn leather briefcase, only hours ago chained to the wrist of a dead man. He knew the deadly pavanne had begun. The first steps of the dance had been taken violently.

There were decisions to make, people to confront.

6

The implausible name below the doorbell on the two-family faculty house read: Mr. and Mrs. Archer Beeson. Matlock had elicited the dinner invitation easily. History instructor Beeson had been flattered by his interest in coordinating a seminar between two of their courses. Beeson would have been flattered if a faculty member of Matlock's attainments had asked him how his wife was in bed (and most wondered). And since Matlock was very clearly male, Archer Beeson felt that "drinks and din" with his wife wriggling around in a short skirt might help cement a relationship with the highly regarded professor of English literature.

Matlock heard the breathless shout from the second-floor landing. "Just a sec!"

It was Beeson's wife, and her broad accent, over-cultivated at Miss Porter's and Finch, sounded caricatured. Matlock pictured the girl racing around checking the plates of cheese and dip—very unusual cheese and dip, conversation pieces, really—while her husband put the final touches on the visual aspects of his bookcases—perhaps several obscure tomes carelessly, carefully, placed on tables, impossible for a visitor to miss.

Matlock wondered if these two were also secreting small tablets of lysergic acid or capsules of methedrine.

The door opened and Beeson's petite wife, dressed in the expected short skirt and translucent silk blouse that loosely covered her large breasts, smiled ingenuously.

"Hi! I'm Ginny Beeson. We met at several *mad* cocktail parties. I'm *so* glad you could come. Archie's just finishing a paper. Come on up." She preceded Matlock up the stairs, hardly giving him a chance to acknowledge. "These stairs are *horrendous!* Oh, well, the price of starting at the bottom."

"I'm sure it won't be for long," said Matlock.

"That's what Archie keeps saying. He'd better be right or I'll have muscles all over my legs!"

"I'm sure he is," said Matlock, looking at the soft, unmuscular, large expanse of legs in front of him.

Inside the Beeson apartment, the cheese and dip were prominently displayed on an odd-shaped coffee table, and the anticipated showcase volume was one of Matlock's own. It was titled *Interpolations in Richard II* and it resided on a table underneath a fringed lamp. Impossible for a visitor to miss.

The minute Ginny closed the door, Archie burst into the small living room from what Matlock presumed was Beeson's study—also small. He carried a sheaf of papers in his left hand; his right was extended.

"Good-oh! Glad you could make it, old man! . . . Sit, sit. Drinks are due and overdue! God! I'm flaked out for one! . . . Just spent three hours reading twenty versions of the Thirty Years' War!"

"It happens. Yesterday I got a theme on *Volpone* with the strangest ending I ever heard of. Turned out the kid never read it but saw the film in Hartford."

"With a new ending?"

"Totally."

"God! That's marvy!" injected Ginny semihysterically. "What's your drink preference, Jim? I may call you Jim, mayn't I, Doctor?"

"Bourbon and a touch of water, and you certainly better, Ginny. I've never gotten used to the 'doctor.' My father calls it fraud. Doctors carry stethoscopes, not books." Matlock sat in an easy chair covered with an Indian serape.

"Speaking of doctors, I'm working on my dissertation now. That and two more hectic summers'll do the trick." Beeson took the ice bucket from his wife and walked to a long table underneath a window where bottles and glasses were carelessly arranged.

"It's worth it," said Ginny Beeson emphatically. "Isn't it worth it, Jim?"

"Almost essential. It'll pay off."

"That and *publishing*." Ginny Beeson picked up the cheese and crackers and carried them to Matlock. "This is an interesting little Irish *fromage*. Would you believe, it's called 'Blarney'? Found it in a little shop in New York two weeks ago."

"Looks great. Never heard of it."

"Speaking of publishing. I picked up your *Interpolations* book the other day. *Damned fascinating!* Really!"

"Lord, I've almost forgotten it. Wrote it four years ago."

"It should be a *required text!* That's what Archie said, isn't it, Archie?"

"Damned right! Here's the poison, old man," said Beeson, bringing Matlock his drink. "Do you work through an agent, Jim? Not that I'm nosy. I'm years from writing anything."

"That's not true, and you know it," Ginny pouted vocally.

"Yes, I do. Irving Block in Boston. If you're working on something, perhaps I could show it to him."

"Oh, no, I wouldn't . . . that'd be awfully presumptuous of me. . . ." Beeson retreated with feigned humility to the couch with his drink. He sat next to his wife and they—involuntarily, thought Matlock—exchanged satisfied looks.

"Come on, Archie. You're a bright fellow. A real comer on this campus. Why do you think I asked you about the seminar? *You* could be doing *me* the favor. I might be bringing Block a winner. That rubs off, you know."

Beeson's expression had the honesty of gratitude. It embarrassed Matlock to return the instructor's gaze until he saw something else in Beeson's eyes. He couldn't define it, but it was there. A slight wildness, a trace of panic.

The look of a man whose mind and body knew drugs.

"That's *damned* good-oh of you, Jim. I'm touched, *really.*"

The cheese, drinks, and dinner somehow passed. There were moments when Matlock had the feeling he was outside himself, watching three characters in a scene from some old movie. Perhaps on board ship or in a sloppily elegant New York apartment with the three of them wearing tightly fitted formal clothes. He wondered why he visualized the scene in such fashion—and then he knew. The Beesons had a thirties quality about them. The thirties that he had observed on the late night television films. They were somehow an anachronism, of this time but not of the time. It was either more than camp or less than put-on; he couldn't be sure. They were not artificial in themselves, but there was a falseness in their emphatic small talk, their dated expressions. Yet the truth was that they were the *now* of the present generation.

Lysergic acid and methedrine.

Acid heads. Pill poppers.

The Beesons were somehow forcing themselves to show themselves as part of a past and carefree era. Perhaps to deny the times and conditions in which they found themselves.

Archie Beeson and his wife were frightening.

By eleven, after considerable wine with the "interesting-little-veal-dish-from-a-recipe-in-an-old-Italian cookbook," the three of them sat down in the living room. The last of the proposed seminar problems was ironed out. Matlock knew it was time to begin; the awful, awkward moment. He wasn't sure how; the best he could do was to trust his amateur instincts.

"Look, you two. . . . I hope to hell this won't come as too great a shock, but I've been a long time without a stick." He withdrew a thin cigarette case from his pocket and opened it. He felt foolish, uncomfortably clumsy. But he knew he could not show those feelings. "Before you make any judgments, I should tell you I don't go along with the pot laws and I never have."

Matlock selected a cigarette from the dozen in the case and left the case open on the table. Was that the proper thing to do? He wasn't sure; he didn't know. Archie and his wife looked at each other. Through the flame in front of his face, Matlock watched their reaction. It was cautious yet positive. Perhaps it was the alcohol in Ginny, but she smiled hesitantly, as if she was relieved to find a friend. Her husband wasn't quite so responsive.

"Go right ahead, old man," said the young instructor with a trace of condescension. "We're hardly on the attorney general's payroll."

"Hardly!" giggled the wife.

"The laws are archaic," continued Matlock, inhaling deeply. "In all areas. Control and an abiding sense of discretion—self-discretion—are all that matter. To deny experience is the real crime. To prohibit any intelligent individual's right to fulfillment is . . . goddamn it, it's repressive."

"Well, I think the key word is *intelligent*, Jim. *In*discriminate use among the *un*intelligent leads to chaos."

"Socratically, you're only half right. The other half is 'control.' Effective control among the 'iron' and 'bronze' then frees the 'gold'—to borrow from *The Republic*. If the intellectually superior were continually kept from thinking, experimenting, because their thought processes were beyond the comprehension of their fellow citizens, there'd be no great works—artistically, technically, politically. We'd still be in the Dark Ages."

Matlock inhaled his cigarette and closed his eyes. Had he been too strong, too positive? Had he sounded too much the false proselytizer? He waited, and the wait was not long. Archie spoke quietly, but urgently nevertheless.

"Progress is being made every day, old man. Believe that. It's the truth."

Matlock half opened his eyes in relief and looked at Beeson through the cigarette smoke. He held his gaze steady without blinking and then shifted his stare to Beeson's wife. He spoke only two words.

"You're children."

"That's a relative supposition under the circumstances," answered Beeson, still keeping his voice low, his speech precise.

"And that's talk."

"Oh, don't be so sure about that!" Ginny Beeson had had enough alcohol in her to be careless. Her husband reached for her arm and held it. It was a warning. He spoke again, taking his eyes off Matlock, looking at nothing.

"I'm not at all sure we're on the same wavelength . . ."

"No, probably not. Forget it. . . . I'll finish this and shove off. Be in touch with you about the seminar." Matlock made sure his reference to the seminar was offhanded, almost disinterested.

Archie Beeson, the young man in an academic hurry, could not stand that disinterest.

"Would you mind if I had one of those?"

"If it's your first, yes, I would. . . . Don't try to impress me. It doesn't really matter."

"My first? . . . Of what?" Beeson rose from the couch and walked to the table where the cigarette case lay open. He reached down, picked it up, and held it to his nostrils. "That's passable grass. I might add, just passable. I'll try one . . . for openers."

"For openers?"

"You seem to be very sincere but, if you'll forgive me, you're a bit out of touch."

"From what?"

"From where it's at." Beeson withdrew two cigarettes and lit them in *Now, Voyager* fashion. He inhaled deeply, nodding and shrugging a reserved approval, and handed one to his wife. "Let's call this an hors d'oeuvre. An appetizer."

He went into his study and returned with a Chinese lacquered box, then showed Matlock the tiny peg which, when pushed, enabled the holder to flip up a thin layer of wood on the floor of the box, revealing a false bottom. Beneath were two dozen or so white tablets wrapped in transparent plastic.

"This is the main course . . . the entrée, if you're up to it."

Matlock was grateful for what knowledge he possessed and the intensive homework he'd undertaken during the past forty-eight hours. He smiled but his tone of voice was firm.

"I only take white trips under two conditions. The first is at *my* home with very good, very old friends. The second is with very good, very old friends at *their* homes. I don't know you well enough, Archie. Self-discretion. . . . I'm not averse to a small red journey, however. Only I didn't come prepared."

"Say no more. I just may be." Beeson took the Chinese box back into his study and returned with a small leather pouch, the sort pipe smokers use for tobacco, and approached Matlock's chair. Ginny Beeson's eyes grew wide; she undid a button on her half-unbuttoned blouse and stretched her legs.

"Dunhill's best." Beeson opened the top flap and held the pouch down for Matlock to see inside. Again there was the clear plastic wrapped around tablets. However, these were deep red and slightly larger than the white pills in the Chinese box. There were at least fifty to sixty doses of Seconal.

Ginny jumped out of the chair and squealed. "I *love* it! It's the pinky-groovy!"

"Beats the hell out of brandy," added Matlock.

"We'll trip. Not too much, old man. Limit's five. That's the house rules for new old friends."

The next two hours were blurred for James Matlock, but not as blurred as they were for the Beesons. The history instructor and his wife quickly reached their "highs" with the five pills—as would have Matlock had he not been able to pocket the final three while pretending to have swallowed them. Once on the first plateau, it wasn't too hard for Matlock to imitate his companions and then convince Beeson to go for another dosage.

"Where's the almighty discretion, Doctor?" chuckled Beeson, sitting on the floor in front of the couch, reaching occasionally for one of his wife's legs.

"You're better friends than I thought you were."

"Just the *beginning* of a beautiful, *beautiful* friendship." The young wife slowly reclined on the couch and giggled. She seemed to writhe and put her right hand on her husband's head, pushing his hair forward.

Beeson laughed with less control than he had shown earlier and rose from the floor. "I'll get the magic then."

When Beeson walked into his study, Matlock watched his wife. There was no mistaking her action. She looked at Matlock, opened her mouth slowly, and pushed her tongue out at him. Matlock realized that one of Seconal's side effects was showing. As was most of Virginia Beeson.

The second dosage was agreed to be three, and Matlock was now easily able to fake it. Beeson turned on his stereo and played a recording of "Carmina Burana." In fifteen minutes Ginny Beeson was sitting on Matlock's lap, intermittently rubbing herself against his groin. Her husband was spread out in front of the stereo speakers, which were on either side of the turntable. Matlock spoke as though exhaling, just loud enough to be heard over the music.

"These are some of the best I've had, Archie. . . . Where? Where's the supply from?"

"Probably the same as yours, old man." Beeson turned over and looked at Matlock and his wife. He laughed. "Now, I don't know what you mean. The magic or the girl on your lap. Watch her, Doctor. She's a minx."

"No kidding. Your pills are a better grade than mine and my grass barely passed inspection. Where? Be a good friend."

"You're funny, man. You keep asking. Do I ask you? No. . . . It's not polite. . . . Play with Ginny. Let me listen." Beeson rolled back over face down on the floor.

The girl on Matlock's lap suddenly put her arms around his neck and pressed her breasts against his chest. She put her head to the side of his face and began kissing his ears. Matlock wondered what would happen if he lifted her out of the chair and carried her into the bedroom. He wondered, but he didn't want to find out. Not then. Ralph Loring had not been murdered to increase his, Matlock's, sex life.

"Let me try one of your joints. Let me see just how advanced your taste is. You may be a phony, Archie."

Suddenly Beeson sat up and stared at Matlock. He wasn't concerned with his wife. Something in Matlock's voice seemed to trigger an instinctive doubt. Or was it the words? Or was it the too normal pattern of speech Matlock used? The English professor thought of all these things as he returned Beeson's look over the girl's shoulder. Archie Beeson was suddenly a

man warned, and Matlock wasn't sure why. Beeson
spoke haltingly.

"Certainly, old man. . . . Ginny, don't annoy Jim."
He began to rise.

"Pinky groovy . . ."

"I've got several in the kitchen. . . . I'm not sure
where but I'll look. Ginny, I told you not to tease Jim.
. . . Be nice to him, be good to him." Beeson kept
staring at Matlock, his eyes wide from the Seconal,
his lips parted, the muscles of his face beyond relaxa-
tion. He backed away toward the kitchen door,
which was open. Once inside, Archie Beeson did a
strange thing. Or so it appeared to James Matlock.

He slowly closed the swing-hinged door and held it
shut.

Matlock quickly eased the drugged girl off his lap
and she quietly stretched out on the floor. She smiled
angelically and reached her arms up for him. He
smiled down, stepping over her.

"Be right back," he whispered. "I want to ask
Archie something." The girl rolled over on her stomach as Matlock walked cautiously toward the kitch-
en door. He ruffled his hair and purposely, silently,
lurched, holding onto the dining room table as he
neared the entrance. If Beeson suddenly came out, he
wanted to appear irrational, drugged. The stereo
was a little louder now, but through it Matlock could
hear the sound of Archie's voice talking quietly, excitedly on the kitchen telephone.

He leaned against the wall next to the kitchen door
and tried to analyze the disjointed moments that
caused Archie Beeson to panic, to find it so imperative to reach someone on the telephone.

Why? What?

Had the grand impersonation been so obvious? Had he blown his first encounter?

If he had, the least he could do was try to find out who was on the other end of the line, who it was that Beeson ran to in his disjointed state of anxiety.

One fact seemed clear: whoever it was had to be more important than Archer Beeson. A man—even a drug addict—did not panic and contact a lesser figure on his own particular totem.

Perhaps the evening wasn't a failure; or his failure —conversely—a necessity. In Beeson's desperation, he might let slip information he never would have revealed if he *hadn't* been desperate. It wasn't preposterous to force it out of the frightened, drugged instructor. On the other hand, that was the least desirable method. If he failed in that, too, he was finished before he'd begun. Loring's meticulous briefing would have been for nothing; his death a rather macabre joke, his terrible cover—so painful to his family, so inhuman somehow—made fruitless by a bumbling amateur.

There was no other way, thought Matlock, but to try. Try to find out who Beeson had reached *and* try to put the pieces of the evening back where Beeson might accept him again. For some insane reason, he pictured Loring's briefcase and the thin black chain dangling from the handle. For an even crazier reason, it gave him confidence; not much, but some.

He assumed a stance as close to the appearance of collapse as he could imagine, then moved his head to the door frame and slowly, quarter inch by quarter inch, pushed it inward. He fully expected to be met by Beeson's staring eyes. Instead, the instructor's back was to him; he was hunched over like a small boy trying to control his bladder, the phone clutched to his thin scrunched neck, his head bent to the side. It was obvious that Beeson thought his voice was muffled, indistinguishable beneath the sporadic crescendos of the "Carmina Burana." But the Seconal had played one of its tricks. Beeson's ear and his speech were no longer synchronized. His words were not only clear. They were emphasized by being spaced out and repeated.

". . . You *do not* understand me. I want you to understand me. *Please,* understand. He keeps asking questions. He's not *with* it. He *is not with it.* I swear to Christ he's a plant. Get hold of Herron. Tell Herron to reach him for *God's* sake. Reach him, *please!* I could lose everything! . . . No. No, I can tell! I *see* what I *see, man!* When that bitch turns horny I have *problems.* I mean there are appearances, old man. . . . Get Lucas. . . . For Christ's sake *get* to him! I'm in *trouble* and I can't. . . ."

Matlock let the door swing slowly back into the frame. His shock was such that thought and feeling were suspended; he saw his hand still on the kitchen door, yet he felt no wood against his fingers. What he had just heard was no less horrible than the sight of Ralph Loring's lifeless body in the telephone booth.

Herron. *Lucas Herron!*

A seventy-year-old legend. A quiet scholar who was as much revered for his perceptions of the human condition as he was for his brilliance. A lovely man, an honored man. There had to be a mistake, an explanation.

There was no time to ponder the inexplicable.

Archer Beeson thought he was a "plant." And now, someone else thought so, too. He couldn't allow that. He had to think, force himself to *act.*

Suddenly he understood. Beeson himself had told him what to do.

No informer—no one not narcotized—would attempt it.

Matlock looked over at the girl lying face down on the living room floor. He crossed rapidly around the dining table and ran to her side, unbuckling his belt as he did so. In swift movements, he took off his trousers and reached down, rolling her over on her back. He lay down beside her and undid the remaining two buttons on her blouse, pulling her brassiere until the hasp broke. She moaned and giggled, and when he touched her exposed breasts, she moaned again and lifted one leg over Matlock's hip.

"Pinky groovy, pinky groovy . . ." She began breathing through her mouth, pushing her pelvis into Matlock's groin; her eyes half open, her hands reaching down, stroking his leg, her fingers clutching at his skin.

Matlock kept his eyes toward the kitchen door, praying it would open.

And then it did, and he shut his eyes.

Archie Beeson stood in the dining area looking down at his wife and guest. Matlock, at the sound of Beeson's footsteps, snapped his head back and feigned terrified confusion. He rose from the floor and immediately fell back down again. He grabbed his trousers and held them in front of his shorts, rising once more unsteadily and finally falling onto the couch.

"Oh, Jesus! Oh, sweet Jesus, Archie! Christ, young fella! I didn't think I was this freaked out! . . . I'm far out, Archie! What the hell, what do I *do?* I'm *gone*, man, I'm sorry! Christ, I'm sorry!"

Beeson approached the couch, his half-naked wife at his feet. From his expression it was impossible to tell what he was thinking. Or the extent of his anger.

Or was it anger?

His audible reaction was totally unexpected: he started to laugh. At first softly, and then with gathering momentum, until he became nearly hysterical.

"Oh, *God*, old man! I said it! I *said* she was a minx! . . . Don't worry. No tattle tales. No rapes, no dirty-old-man-on-the-faculty. But we'll have our *seminar*. Oh, Christ, yes! That'll be some *seminar!* And you'll tell them all you picked *me!* Won't you? Oh, yes! That's what you'll tell them, isn't it?"

Matlock looked into the wild eyes of the addict above him.

"Sure. Sure, Archie. Whatever you say."

"You better believe it, old man! And don't apologize. No apologies are necessary! The apologies are mine!" Archer Beeson collapsed on the floor in laughter. He reached over and cupped his wife's left breast; she moaned and giggled her maddening, high-pitched giggle.

And Matlock knew he had won.

He was exhausted, both by the hour and by the tensions of the night. It was ten minutes past three and the choral strains of the "Carmina Burana" were still hammering in his ears. The image of the barebreasted wife and the jackal-sounding husband—both writhing on the floor in front of him—added revulsion to the sickening taste in his mouth.

But what bothered him most was the knowledge that Lucas Herron's name was used within the context of such an evening.

It was inconceivable.

Lucas Herron. The "grand old bird," as he was called. A reticent but obvious fixture of the Carlyle campus. The chairman of the Romance languages department and the embodiment of the quiet scholar with a deep and abiding compassion. There was always a glint in his eyes, a look of bemusement mixed with tolerance.

To associate him—regardless of how remotely—with the narcotics world was unbelievable. To have heard him sought after by an hysterical addict—for essentially, Archer Beeson *was* an addict, psychologically if not chemically—as though Lucas were some sort of power under the circumstances was beyond rational comprehension.

The explanation had to lie somewhere in Lucas Herron's immense capacity for sympathy. He was a friend to many, a dependable refuge for the troubled, often the deeply troubled. And beneath his placid, aged, unruffled surface, Herron was a strong man, a leader. A quarter of a century ago, he had spent countless months of hell in the Solomon Islands as a middle-aged infantry officer. A lifetime ago, Lucas Herron had been an authentic hero in a vicious moment of time during a savage war in the Pacific. Now over seventy, Herron was an institution.

Matlock rounded the corner and saw his apartment half a block away. The campus was dark; aside from the street lamps, the only light came from one of his rooms. Had he left one on? He couldn't remember.

He walked up the path to his door and inserted his key. Simultaneously with the click of the lock, there was a loud crash from within. Although it startled him, his first reaction was amusement. His clumsy, long-haired house cat had knocked over a stray glass or one of those pottery creations Patricia Ballantyne had inflicted on him. Then he realized such a thought was ridiculous, the product of an exhausted mind. The crash was too loud for pottery, the shattering of glass too violent.

He rushed into the small foyer, and what he saw pushed fatigue out of his brain. He stood immobile in disbelief.

The entire room was in shambles. Tables were overturned; books pulled from the shelves, their pages torn from the bindings, scattered over the floor; his stereo turntable and speakers smashed. Cushions from his couch and armchairs were slashed, the stuffing and foam rubber strewn everywhere; the rugs upended, lumped in folds; the curtains ripped from their rods, thrown over the upturned furniture.

He saw the reason for the crash. His large casement window, on the far right wall bordering the street, was a mass of twisted lead and broken glass. The window consisted of two panels; he remembered clearly that he had opened both before leaving for the Beesons. He liked the spring breezes, and it was too early in the season for screens. So there was no reason for the window to be smashed; the ground was perhaps four or five feet below the casement, sufficient to dissuade an intruder, low enough for a panicked burglar to negotiate easily.

The smashing of the window, therefore, was not for escape. It was intended.

He had been watched, and a signal had been given.

It was a warning.

And Matlock knew he could not acknowledge that warning. To do so was to acknowledge more than a robbery; he was not prepared to do that.

He crossed rapidly to his bedroom door and looked inside. If possible, his bedroom was in more of a mess than the living room. The mattress was thrown against the wall, ripped to shreds. Every drawer of his bureau was dislodged, lying on the floor, the contents scattered all around the room. His closet was like the rest —suits and jackets pulled from the clothes rod, shoes yanked from their recesses.

Even before he looked he knew his kitchen would be no better off than the rest of his apartment. The foodstuffs in cans and boxes had not been thrown on the floor, simply moved around, but the soft items had been torn to pieces. Matlock understood again. One or two crashes from the other rooms were tolerable noise levels; a continuation of the racket from his kitchen might arouse one of the other families in the building. As it was, he could hear the faint sounds of footsteps above him. The final crash of the window had gotten someone up.

The warning was explicit, but the act itself was a search.

He thought he knew the object of that search, and again he realized he could not acknowledge it. Conclusions were being made as they had been made at Beeson's; he had to ride them out with the most convincing denials he could manufacture. That much he knew instinctively.

But before he began that pretense, he had to find out if the search was successful.

He shook the stammering lethargy out of his mind and body. He looked once again at his living room; he studied it. All the windows were bare, and the light was sufficient for someone with a pair of powerful binoculars stationed in a nearby building or standing on the inclining lawn of the campus beyond the street to observe every move he made. If he turned off the lights, would such an unnatural action lend credence to the conclusions he wanted denied?

Without question. A man didn't walk into a house in shambles and proceed to turn off lights.

Yet he had to reach his bathroom, at that moment the most important room in the apartment. He had to spend less than thirty seconds inside to determine the success or failure of the ransacking, and do so in such a way as to seem innocent of any abnormal concerns. If anyone *was* watching.

It was a question of appearance, of gesture, he thought. He saw that the stereo turntable was the nearest object to the bathroom door, no more than five feet away. He walked over and bent down, picking up several pieces, including the metal arm. He looked at it, then suddenly dropped the arm and brought his finger to his mouth, feigning an imagined puncture on his skin. He walked into the bathroom rapidly.

Once inside, he quickly opened the medicine cabinet and grabbed a tin of Band-Aids from the glass shelf. He then swiftly reached down to the left of the toilet bowl where the cat's yellow plastic box was placed and picked up a corner of the newspaper underneath the granules of litter. Beneath the newspaper he felt the coarse grain of the two layers of canvas he had inserted and lifted up an edge.

The scissored page was still intact. The silver Corsican paper that ended in the deadly phrase *Venerare Omerta* had not been found.

He replaced the newspaper, scattered the litter, and stood up. He saw that the frosted glass of the small window above the toilet was partially opened, and he swore.

There was no time to think of that.

He walked back into the living room, ripping the plastic off a Band-Aid.

The search had failed. Now the warning had to be ignored, the conclusions denied. He crossed to the telephone and called the police.

"Can you give me a list of what's missing?" A uniformed patrolman stood in the middle of the debris. A second policeman wandered about the apartment making notes.

"I'm not sure yet. I haven't really checked."

"That's understandable. It's a mess. You'd better

look, though. The quicker we get a list, the better."

"I don't think anything *is* missing, officer. What I mean is, I don't have anything particularly valuable to anyone else. Except perhaps the stereo . . . and that's smashed. There's a television set in the bedroom, that's okay. Some of the books could bring a price, but look at them."

"No cash, jewelry, watches?"

"I keep money in the bank and cash in my wallet. I wear my watch and haven't any jewelry."

"How about exam papers? We've been getting a lot of that."

"In my office. In the English department."

The patrolman wrote in a small black notebook and called to his partner, who had gone into the bedroom. "Hey, Lou, did the station confirm the print man?"

"They're getting him up. He'll be over in a few minutes."

"Have you touched anything, Mr. Matlock?"

"I don't know. I may have. It was a shock."

"Particularly any of the broken items, like that record player? It'd be good if we could show the fingerprint man specific things you haven't touched."

"I picked up the arm, not the casing."

"Good. It's a place to start."

The police stayed for an hour and a half. The fingerprints specialist arrived, did his work, and departed. Matlock thought of phoning Sam Kressel, but reasoned that there wasn't anything Kressel could do at that hour. And in the event someone outside *was* watching the building, Kressel shouldn't be seen. Various people from the other apartments had wakened and had come down offering sympathy, help, and coffee.

As the police were leaving, a large patrolman turned in the doorway. "Sorry to take so much time, Mr. Matlock. We don't usually lift prints in a break and entry unless there's injury or loss of property, but there's been a lot of this sort of thing recently. Personally, I think it's those weirdos with the hair and the beads. Or the niggers. We never had trouble like this before the weirdos and the niggers got here."

Matlock looked at the uniformed officer, who was so confident of his analysis. There was no point in objecting; it would be useless, and Matlock was too tired. "Thanks for helping me straighten up."

"Sure thing." The patrolman started down the cement path, then turned again. "Oh, Mr. Matlock."

"Yes?" Matlock pulled the door back.

"It struck us that maybe someone was looking for something. What with all the slashing and books and everything . . . you know what I mean?"

"Yes."

"You'd tell us if that was the case, wouldn't you?"

"Of course."

"Yeah. It'd be stupid to withhold information like that."

"I'm not stupid."

"No offense. Just that sometimes you guys get all involved and forget things."

"I'm not absentminded. Very few of us are."

"Yeah." The patrolman laughed somewhat derisively. "I just wanted to bring it up. I mean, we can't do our jobs unless we got all the facts, you know?"

"I understand."

"Yeah. Good."

"Good night."

"Good night, Doctor."

He closed the door and walked into his living

room. He wondered if his insurance would cover the disputable value of his rarer books and prints. He sat down on the ruined couch and surveyed the room. It was still a mess; the carnage had been thorough. It would take more than picking up debris and righting furniture. The warning had been clear, violent.

The startling fact was that the warning existed at all.

Why? From whom?

Archer Beeson's hysterical telephone call? That was possible, even preferable, perhaps. It might encompass a motive unrelated to Nimrod. It could mean that Beeson's circle of users and pushers wanted to frighten him enough to leave Archie alone. Leave them all alone; and Loring had specifically said there was no proof that the Beesons were involved with the Nimrod unit.

There was no proof that they weren't, either.

Nevertheless, if it *was* Beeson, the alarm would be called off in the morning. There was no mistaking the conclusion of the night's engagement. The "near-rape" by a dirty, drugged "old man." He was Beeson's academic ladder.

On the other hand, and far less preferable, there was the possibility that the warning *and* the search were centered on the Corsican paper. What had Loring whispered behind him on the sidewalk?

". . . There's only one thing they want more than this briefcase; that's the paper in your pocket."

It was then reasonable to assume that he'd been linked to Ralph Loring.

Washington's assessment that his panic at finding Loring dissociated him from the agent was in error, Jason Greenberg's confidence misplaced.

Still again, as Greenberg had suggested, they might

test him. Press him before issuing a clean bill of health.

Might, could, possible, still again.

Conjectures.

He had to keep his head; he couldn't allow himself to overreact. If he was to be of *any* value, he had to play the innocent.

Might have, could have, it was possible.

His body ached. His eyes were swollen and his mouth still had the terrible aftertaste of the combined dosages of Seconal, wine, and marijuana. He was exhausted; the pressures of trying to reach unreachable conclusions were overtaking him. His memory wandered back to the early days in 'Nam and he recalled the best advice he'd ever been given in those weeks of unexpected combat. That was to rest whenever he could, to sleep if it was at all possible. The advice had come from a line sergeant who, it had been rumored, had survived more assaults than any man in the Mekong Delta. Who, it was also rumored, had slept through an ambush which had taken most of his company.

Matlock stretched out on the barely recognizable couch. There was no point in going into the bedroom —his mattress was destroyed. He unbuckled his belt and kicked off his shoes. He could sleep for a few hours; then he'd talk to Kressel. Ask Kressel and Greenberg to work out a story for him to use about the invasion of his apartment. A story approved by Washington and, perhaps, the Carlyle police.

The police.

Suddenly he sat up. It hadn't struck him at the time, but now he considered it. The crass but imperiously polite patrolman whose primitive detection powers had centered on the "weirdos and niggers" had addressed him as "Mister" throughout the nearly two hours of police investigation. Yet when he was leaving, when he insultingly referred to the possibility of Matlock's withholding information, he had called him "Doctor." The "mister" was normal. The "doctor" was most unusual. No one outside the campus community—and rarely there—ever called him "Doctor," ever called *any* Ph.D. "Doctor." It struck most holders of such degrees as fatuous, and only the fatuous expected it.

Why had the patrolman used it? He didn't know him, he had never seen him to his knowledge. How would the patrolman know he was even entitled to the name "doctor"?

As he sat there, Matlock wondered if the combined efforts and pressures of the last hours were taking their toll. Was he now finding unreasonable meanings where no meanings existed? Was it not entirely plausible that the Carlyle police had a list of the Carlyle faculty and that a desk sergeant, or whoever took emergency calls, had checked his name against the list and casually stated his title? Was he not, perhaps, consigning the patrolman to a plateau of ignorance because he disliked the officer's prejudices?

A lot of things were possible.

And disturbing.

Matlock fell back onto the couch and closed his eyes.

At first the noise reached him as a faint echo might from the far end of a long, narrow tunnel. Then the noise became identifiable as rapid, incessant tapping. Tapping which would not stop, tapping which became louder and louder.

Matlock opened his eyes and saw the blurred light

coming from two table lamps across from the couch. His feet were drawn up under him, his neck perspiring against the rough surface of the sofa's corduroy cover. Yet there was a cool breeze coming through the smashed, lead-framed window.

The tapping continued, the sound of flesh against wood. It came from the foyer, from his front door. He flung his legs over the side onto the floor and found that they both were filled with pins and needles. He struggled to stand.

The tapping and the knocking became louder. Then the voice. "Jamie! Jamie!"

He walked awkwardly toward the door.

"Coming!" He reached the door and opened it swiftly. Patricia Ballantyne, dressed in a raincoat, silk pajamas evident underneath, walked rapidly inside.

"Jamie, for God's sake, I've been trying to call you."

"I've been here. The phone didn't ring."

"I know it didn't. I finally got an operator and she said it was out of order. I borrowed a car and drove over as fast as I could and . . ."

"It's not out of order, Pat. The police—the police were here and a quick look around will explain why —they used it a dozen times."

"Oh, good Lord!" The girl walked past him into the still-disheveled room. Matlock crossed to the telephone and picked it up from the table. He quickly held it away from his ear as the piercing tone of a disengaged instrument whistled out of the receiver.

"The bedroom," he said, replacing the telephone and going to his bedroom door.

On his bed, on top of the slashed remains of his mattress, was his bedside phone. The receiver was off the hook, *underneath* the pillow, muffling the harsh sound of the broken connection so it would not be heard. Someone had not wanted it to ring.

Matlock tried to remember everyone who'd been there. All told, more than a dozen people. Five or six policemen—in and out of uniform; husbands and wives from other apartments; several late-night passersby who had seen the police cars and wandered up to the front door. It had been cumulatively blurred. He couldn't remember all the faces.

He put the telephone back on the bedside table and was aware that Pat stood in the doorway. He gambled that she hadn't seen him remove the pillow.

"Someone must have knocked it over straightening out things," he said, pretending irritation. "That's rotten; I mean your having to borrow a car. . . . Why did you? What's the matter?"

She didn't reply. Instead, she turned and looked back into the living room. "What happened?"

Matlock remembered the patrolman's language. "They call it 'break and entry.' A police phrase covering human tornadoes, as I understand it. . . . Robbery. I got myself robbed for the first time in my life. It's quite an experience. I think the poor bastards were angry because there wasn't anything of any value so they ripped the place apart. . . . Why'd you come over?"

She spoke softly, but the intensity of her voice made Matlock realize that she was close to panic. As always, she imposed a control on herself when she became emotional. It was an essential part of the girl.

"A couple of hours ago—at quarter to four to be exact—my phone rang. The man, it was a man, asked for you. I was asleep, and I suppose I didn't make much sense, but I pretended to be upset that anyone would think you were there. . . . I didn't know what to do. I was confused. . . ."

"Okay, I understand that. So?"

"He said he didn't believe me. I was a liar. I . . . I was so surprised that anyone would phone then— at quarter to four—and call me a liar . . . I was confused. . . ."

"What did you say?"

"It's not what *I* said. It's what *he* said. He told me to tell you to . . . not to stay 'behind the globe' or 'light the lower world.' He said it *twice!* He said it was an awful joke but you'd understand. It was frightening! . . . Do you? Do you understand?"

Matlock walked past her into the living room. He looked for his cigarettes and tried to remain calm. She followed him. "What did he mean?"

"I'm not sure."

"Has it anything to do with . . . this?" She gestured her hand over the apartment.

"I don't think so." He lit his cigarette and wondered what he should tell her. The Nimrod people hadn't wasted any time finding associations. If it *was* Nimrod.

"What did he mean by . . . 'standing behind the globe'? It sounds like a riddle."

"It's a quote, I think." But Matlock did not have to think. He knew. He recalled Shakespeare's words precisely: *Knowest thou not that when the searching eye of heaven is hid behind the globe and lights the lower world . . . then thieves and robbers range abroad unseen . . . in murders and in outrage bloody here.*

"What does it mean?"

"I don't *know!* I can't remember it. . . . Somebody's confusing me with someone else. That's the only thing

I can imagine. . . . What did he sound like?"

"Normal. He was angry but he didn't shout or anything."

"No one you recognized? Not specifically, but did you ever hear the voice before?"

"I'm not sure. I don't think so. No one I could pick out, but . . ."

"But what?"

"Well, it was a . . . cultivated voice. A little actorish, I think."

"A man used to lecturing." Matlock made a statement, he did not ask a question. His cigarette tasted sour so he crushed it out.

"Yes, I guess that would describe it."

"And probably not in a science lab. . . . That reduces the possibilities to roughly eighty people on campus."

"You're making assumptions I don't understand! That phone call *did* have something to do with what happened here."

He knew he was talking too much. He didn't want to involve Pat; he *couldn't* involve her. Yet someone else had—and that fact was a profound complication. "It might have. According to the best sources—naturally I refer to television detectives—thieves make sure people aren't home before they rob a place. They were probably checking me out."

The girl held his wavering eyes with her gaze. "Weren't you home then? At quarter to four? . . . The question is not inquisitorial, my darling, simply a point of information."

He swore at himself silently. It was the exhaustion, the Beeson episode, the shock of the apartment. Of course the question wasn't inquisitorial. He was a free agent. And, of course, he was home at quarter to four.

"I'm not sure. I wasn't that concerned with the time. It was one hell of a long evening." He laughed feebly. "I was at Archie Beeson's. Proposed seminars with young instructors promote a lot of booze."

She smiled. "I don't think you understand me. I really don't mind what Poppa Bear was doing. . . . Well, of course, I do, but right now I don't understand why you're lying to me. . . . You were *here* two hours ago, and that phone call wasn't any thief checking your whereabouts and you *know* it."

"Momma Bear's reaching. That doesn't go with the territory." Matlock was rude. It, too, like the lying, was obviously false. Whatever his past rebellions, whatever his toughness, he was a kind person and she knew that.

"All right. I apologize. I'll ask one more question and then I'll leave. . . . What does *Omerta* mean?"

Matlock froze. "What did you say?"

"The man on the phone. He used the word *Omerta*."

"How?"

"Very casually. Just a reminder, he said."

8

Field Agent Jason Greenberg walked through the borderless door of the squash court. "You're working up quite a sweat there, Dr. Matlock."

"I'd hate to have it analyzed. . . . Anyway, it was your idea. I would have been just as happy at Kressel's office or even downtown somewhere."

"This is better. . . . We've got to talk quickly, though. The gym registry has me listed as an insurance surveyor. I'm checking the extinguishers in the corridors."

"They probably need checking." Matlock walked to a corner where a gray sweatshirt was wrapped in a towel. He unwound it and slipped it over his head. "What have you come up with? Last night was a little hairy."

"If you discount confusion, we haven't come up with a thing. At least nothing specific. A couple of theories, that's all. . . . We think you handled yourself very well."

"Thanks. I was confused. What are the theories? You sound academic, and I'm not sure I like that."

Greenberg's head suddenly shifted. From the right wall there could be heard a dull thumping. "Is that another court?"

"Yes. There are six of them on this side. They're

practice courts, no balconies. But you know that."

Greenberg picked up the ball and threw it hard against the front wall. Matlock understood and caught it on the bounce. He threw it back; Greenberg returned it. They maintained a slow rhythm, neither man moving more than a foot or two, each taking his turn to throw. Greenberg spoke softly, in a monotone.

"We think you're being tested. That's the most logical explanation. You *did* find Ralph. You made a statement about seeing the car. Your reasons for being in the area were weak; so weak we thought they were plausible. They want to make sure, that's why they brought in the girl. They're being thorough."

"Okay. Theory number one. What's number two?"

"I said that was the most logical. . . . It's the only one, really."

"What about Beeson?"

"What about him? You were there."

Matlock held the squash ball in his hand for a few seconds before lobbing it against the side wall. The wall away from Greenberg's stare.

"Could Beeson have been smarter than I thought and sent out an alarm?"

"He could have. We think it's doubtful. . . . The way you described the evening."

But Matlock had *not* described the *entire* evening. He had not told Greenberg or anyone of Beeson's telephone call. His reasons weren't rational, they were emotional. Lucas Herron was an old man, a gentle man. His sympathy for troubled students was legendary; his concern for young, untried, often arrogant new instructors was a welcomed sedative in faculty crises. Matlock had convinced himself that the "grand old bird" had befriended a desperate young man, helping him in a desperate situation. He had no right to surface Herron's name on the basis of a phone call made by a panicked drug user. There were too many possible explanations. Somehow he'd speak with Herron, perhaps over coffee at the Commons, or in the bleachers at a baseball game—Herron loved baseball —talk to him, tell him he should back away from Archer Beeson.

"—about Beeson?"

"What?" Matlock had not heard Greenberg.

"I asked you if you had second thoughts about Beeson."

"No. No, I haven't. He's not important. As a matter of fact, he'll probably throw away the grass and the pills—except for *my* benefit—if he thinks he can use me."

"I won't try to follow that."

"Don't. I just had momentary doubts. . . . I can't believe you arrived at only one theory. Come on. What else?"

"All right. Two others and they're not even plausible—both from the same egg. The first is that there might be a leak in Washington. The second—a leak here at Carlyle."

"Why not plausible?"

"Washington first. There are fewer than a dozen men who know about this operation, and that includes Justice, Treasury, and the White House. They're the caliber of men who exchange secret messages with the Kremlin. Impossible."

"And Carlyle?"

"You, Adrian Sealfont, and the obnoxious Samuel Kressel. . . . I'd like nothing better than pointing at Kressel—he's a prick—but, again, impossible. I'd also take a certain ethnic delight in knocking a venerated

WASP like Sealfont off his pedestal, but there, too—no sense. That leaves you. Are you the one?"

"Your wit is staggering." Matlock had to run to catch the ball which Greenberg threw into a corner. He held it in his hand and looked at the agent. "Don't misunderstand me—I like Sam, or at least I think I do—but why is he 'impossible'?"

"Same as Sealfont. . . . In an operation like this we start at the beginning. And I *mean* the *beginning*. We don't give a goddamn about positions, status, or reputation—good or bad. We use every trick in the books to prove someone guilty, not innocent. We try to find even the flimsiest reason *not* to clear him. Kressel's as clean as John the Baptist. Still a prick, but clean. Sealfont's worse. He's everything they say. A goddamn saint—Church of England, of course. So, again, that leaves you."

Matlock whipped the ball up in a spinning reverse shot into the rear left ceiling. Greenberg stepped back and slashed the ball in midair into the right wall. It bulleted back between Matlock's legs.

"I gather you've played the game," said Matlock with an embarrassed grin.

"The bandit of Brandeis. What about the girl? Where is she?"

"In my apartment. I made her promise not to leave till I got back. Outside of safety, it's one way to get the place cleaned up."

"I'm assigning a man to her. I don't think it's necessary, but it'll make *you* feel better." Greenberg looked at his watch.

"It will and thanks."

"We'd better hurry. . . . Now, listen. We're letting everything take its normal course. Police blotter, newspapers, everything. No covers, no counter stories, nothing to obstruct normal curiosity or your perfectly normal reactions. Someone broke into your apartment and smashed up the place. That's all you know. . . . And there's something else. You may not like it, but we think it's best—and safest."

"What?"

"We think Miss Ballantyne should report the phone call she received to the police."

"Hey, come on! The caller expected to find me there at four o'clock in the morning. You don't spell that kind of thing out. Not if you're on a fellowship and expect to work for museum foundations. They still revere McKinley."

"The eye of the beholder, Dr. Matlock. . . . She just received a phone call; some man asked for you, quoted Shakespeare, and made an unintelligible reference to some foreign word or city. She was goddamn mad. It wouldn't rate five lines in a newspaper, but since your apartment was broken into, it's logical she report it."

Matlock was silent. He walked over to the corner of the squash court where the ball had settled and picked it up. "We're a couple of ciphers who got pushed around. We don't know what happened; just that we don't like it."

"That's the idea. Nothing is so convincing as someone who's a bewildered injured party and lets everybody know it. Make an insurance issue about those old books of yours. . . . I've got to go. There aren't that many extinguishers in the building. Anything else? What are you doing next?"

Matlock bounced the ball on the floor. "A fortuitous invitation. Fortuitously received over a number of beers at the Afro-Commons. I'm invited to a staged version of the original puberty rites of the Mau Mau tribes. Tonight at ten o'clock in the cellars of Lumumba Hall. . . . It used to be the Alpha Delt fraternity house. I can tell you there are a lot of white Episcopalians spinning in hell over that one."

"Again, I'm not following, Doctor."

"You don't do your homework, either. . . . Lumumba Hall is very large on your list."

"Sorry. You'll phone me in the morning?"

"In the morning."

"I'll call you Jim if you'll call me Jason."

"No kiss, but agreed."

"O.K. Practice some more in here. I'll take you when this is over."

"You're on."

Greenberg let himself out. He looked up and down the narrow corridor, satisfied that no one was there; no one had seen him enter or leave the court. Continuous thumping could be heard within the walls. All the courts were in use. Greenberg wondered, as he was about to turn the corner into the main hallway, why the Carlyle gymnasium was so heavily attended at eleven o'clock in the morning. It was never the case at Brandeis; not fifteen years ago. Eleven o'clock in the morning was a time for class.

He heard a strange noise that was not the sound of a hard ball against thick wood and turned quickly.

No one.

He entered the main hall and turned once again. No one. He left quickly.

The sound he heard was that of a stubborn latch. It came from the door next to Matlock's court. Out of that door a man emerged. He, too, as Greenberg had done less than a minute before, looked up and down the narrow corridor. But instead of being satisfied that no one was there, he was annoyed. The obstinate latch had caused him to miss seeing the man who'd met with James Matlock.

Now the door of court four opened and Matlock himself stepped into the corridor. The man ten feet away was startled, pulled his towel up to his face, and walked away, coughing.

But the man wasn't quick enough. Matlock knew that face.

It was the patrolman from his apartment at four o'clock in the morning.

The patrolman who had called him "Doctor." The man in uniform who knew beyond a doubt that the campus troubles were caused by the "weirdos and the niggers."

Matlock stared at the retreating figure.

Over the large cathedral doors one could see—if one looked closely, or the sun was shining at a certain angle—the faded imprint of the Greek letters ΑΔΦ. They had been there in bas-relief for decades, and no amount of sand blasting or student damage could eradicate them completely. The fraternity house of Alpha Delta Phi had gone the way of other such buildings at Carlyle. Its holy order of directors could not find it within themselves to accept the inevitable. The house had been sold—lock, stock, leaking roof, and bad mortgage—to the blacks.

The blacks had done well, even extremely well, with what they had to work with. The decrepit old house had been totally refurbished inside and out. All past associations with its former owners were obliterated wherever possible. The scores of faded photographs of venerated alumni were replaced with wildly theatrical portraits of the new revolutionaries—African, Latin American, Black Panther. Throughout the ancient halls were the new commands, screeched in posters and psychedelic art: *Death to the Pigs! Up Whitey! Malcolm Lives! Lumumba the Black Christ!*

Between these screams for recognition were replicas of primitive African artifacts—fertility masks, spears, shields, animal skins dipped in red paint, shrunken heads suspended by hair with complexions unmistakably white.

Lumumba Hall wasn't trying to fool anyone. It reflected anger. It reflected fury.

Matlock didn't have to use the brass knocker set beside the grotesque iron mask at the edge of the doorframe. The large door opened as he approached it, and a student greeted him with a bright smile.

"I was hoping you'd make it! It's gonna be a groove!"

"Thanks, Johnny. Wouldn't miss it." Matlock walked in, struck by the proliferation of lighted candles throughout the hallway and adjoining rooms. "Looks like a wake. Where's the casket?"

"That's later. Wait'll you see!"

A black Matlock recognized as one of the campus extremists walked up to them. Adam Williams' hair was long—African style and clipped in a perfect semicircle above his head. His features were sharp; Matlock had the feeling that if they met in the veldt, Williams would be assumed to be a tribal chief.

"Good evening," Williams said with an infectious grin. "Welcome to the seat of revolution."

"Thanks very much." They shook hands. "You don't look so revolutionary as you do funereal. I was asking Johnny where the casket was."

Williams laughed. His eyes were intelligent, his smile genuine, without guile or arrogance. In close quarters, the black radical had little of the firebrand quality he displayed on the podium in front of cheering supporters. Matlock wasn't surprised. Those of the faculty who had Williams in their courses often remarked on his subdued, good-humored approach. So different from the image he projected in campus—

rapidly becoming national—politics.

"Oh, Lord! We're lousing up the picture then! This is a happy occasion. A little gruesome, I suppose, but essentially joyful."

"I'm not sure I understand," Matlock smiled.

"A youngster from the tribe reaches the age of manhood, the brink of an active, responsible life. A jungle Bar Mitzvah. It's a time for rejoicing. No caskets, no weeping shrouds."

"That's right! That's right, Adam!" said the boy named Johnny enthusiastically.

"Why don't you get Mr. Matlock a drink, brother." And then he turned to Matlock. "It's all the same drink until after the ceremony—it's called Swahili punch. Is that O.K.?"

"Of course."

"Right." Johnny disappeared into the crowd toward the dining room and the punch bowl. Adam smiled as he spoke.

"It's a light rum drink with lemonade and cranberry juice. Not bad, really. . . . Thank you for coming. I mean that."

"I was surprised to be invited. I thought this was a very 'in' thing. Restricted to the tribe. . . . That didn't come out the way I meant it."

Williams laughed. "No offense. I used the word. It's good to think in terms of tribes. Good for the brothers."

"Yes, I imagine it is. . . ."

"The collective, protective social group. Possessing an identity of its own."

"If that's the purpose—the constructive purpose—I endorse it."

"Oh, it is. Tribes in the bush don't always make war on each other, you know. It's not all stealing, looting, carrying away women. That's a Robert Ruark hang-up. They trade, share hunting and farming lands to-gether, coexist in the main probably better than na-tions or even political subdivisions."

It was Matlock's turn to laugh. "All right, professor. I'll make notes *after* the lecture."

"Sorry. Avocational hazard."

"Avocational or occupational?"

"Time will tell, won't it? . . . One thing I should make clear, however. We don't need your endorse-ment."

Johnny returned with Matlock's cup of Swahili punch. "Hey, you know what? Brother Davis, that's Bill Davis, says you told him you were going to flunk him, then at midterm you gave him a High Pass!"

"Brother Davis got off his fat ass and did a little work." Matlock looked at Adam Williams. "You don't object to that kind of endorsement, do you?"

Williams smiled broadly and placed his hand on Matlock's arm. "No, sir, bwana. . . . In that area you run King Solomon's Mines. Brother Davis is here to work as hard as he can and go as far as his potential will let him. No argument there. Bear down on the brother."

"You're positively frightening." Matlock spoke with a lightness he did not feel.

"Not at all. Just pragmatic. . . . I've got some last-minute preparations to look after. See you later." Wil-liams hailed a passing student and walked through the crowd toward the staircase.

"Come on, Mr. Matlock. I'll show you the new al-terations." Johnny led Matlock into what used to be Alpha Delt's common room.

In the sea of dark faces, Matlock saw a minimum of

guarded, hostile looks. There were, perhaps, less overt greetings than he might expect outside on the campus, but by and large, his presence was accepted. He thought for a moment that if the brothers knew why he had come, the inhabitants of Lumumba Hall might turn on him angrily. He was the only white person there.

The alterations in the common room were drastic. Gone were the wide moldings of dark wood, the thick oak window seats beneath the huge cathedral windows, the solid, heavy furniture with the dark red leather. Instead, the room was transformed into something else entirely. The arched windows were no longer. They were now squared at the top, bordered by jet-black dowels an inch or two in diameter, which looked like long, rectangular slits. Spreading out from the windows into the walls was a textured pattern of tiny wooden bamboo strips shellacked to a high polish. This same wall covering was duplicated on the ceiling, thousands of highly glossed reeds converging towards the center. In the middle of the ceiling was a large circle, perhaps three feet in width, in which there was placed a thick pane of rippled glass. Beyond the glass shone a bright yellowish white light, its flood diffused in ripples over the room. What furniture he could see through the mass of bodies was not really furniture at all. There were various low-cut slabs of thick wood in differing shapes on short legs—these Matlock assumed were tables. Instead of chairs, there were dozens of pillows in vibrant colors scattered about the edge of the walls.

It didn't take Matlock long to realize the effect.

Alpha Delta Phi's common room had been transformed brilliantly into the replica of a large thatched

African hut. Even to the point of the blazing equatorial sun streaming through the enclosure's vent to the skies.

"This is remarkable! Really remarkable. It must have taken months."

"Almost a year and a half," Johnny said. "It's very comfortable, very relaxing. Did you know that lots of top designers are going in for this sort of thing now? I mean the back-to-nature look. It's very functional and easy to maintain."

"That sounds dangerously like an apology. You don't have to apologize. It's terrific."

"Oh, I'm *not* apologizing." Johnny retreated from his explanation. "Adam says there's a certain majesty in the primitive. A very proud heritage."

"Adam's right. Only he's not the first person to make that observation."

"Please don't put us down, Mr. Matlock. . . ."

Matlock looked at Johnny over the rim of his cup of Swahili punch. Oh, Christ, he thought, the more things change, the more they remain the same.

The high-ceilinged chapter room of Alpha Delta Phi had been carved out of the cellars at the farthest end of the fraternity house. It had been built shortly after the turn of the century when impressive alumni had poured impressive sums into such hobbies as secret societies and debutante cotillions. Such activities promulgated and propagandized a way of life, yet assuredly kept it selective.

Thousands of starched young men had been initiated in this chapel-like enclosure, whispering the secret pledges, exchanging the unfamiliar handshakes explained to them by stern-faced older children, vowing till death to keep the selected faith. And afterward, getting drunk and vomiting in corners.

Matlock thought these thoughts as he watched the Mau Mau ritual unfold before him. It was no less childish, no less absurd than the preceding scenes in this room, he considered. Perhaps the physical aspects —the simulated physical aspects—were more brutal in what they conveyed, but then the roots of the ceremony were not based in the delicate steps of a cotillion's pavanne but, instead, in harsh, animal-like pleas to primitive gods. Pleas for strength and survival. Not supplications for continued exclusivity.

The tribal rite itself was a series of unintelligible chants, each one growing in intensity, over the body of a black student—obviously the youngest brother in Lumumba Hall—stretched out on the concrete floor, naked except for a red loincloth strapped around his waist and legs, covering his genitals. At the finish of each chant, signifying the end of one canto and the commencement of the succeeding song, the boy's body was raised above the crowd by four extremely tall students, themselves naked to the waist, wearing jet-black dance belts, their legs encased in spirals of rawhide strips. The room was lighted by dozens of thick candles mounted on stands, causing shadows to dance across the upper walls and the ceiling. Adding to this theatrical effect was the fact that the five active participants in the ritual had their skins covered with oil, their faces streaked in diabolical patterns. As the singing grew wilder, the young boy's rigid body was thrown higher and higher until it left the hands of its four supporters, returning split seconds later into the outstretched arms. Each time the black body with the red loincloth was flung into the air, the crowd responded with growing volumes of guttural shouts.

And then Matlock, who had been watching with a degree of detachment, suddenly found himself frightened. Frightened for the small Negro whose stiff, oiled body was being flung into air with such abandon. For two additional blacks, dressed like the others, had joined the four in the center of the floor. However, instead of helping toss the now soaring figure, the two blacks crouched between the rectangular foursome—beneath the body—and withdrew long-bladed knives, one in each hand. Once in their squatting positions, they stretched out their arms so that the blades were held upright, as rigid, as stiff as the body above them. Each time the small Negro descended, the four blades inched closer to the falling flesh. One slip, one oily miscalculation on the part of just one of the four blacks, and the ritual would end in death for the small student. In murder.

Matlock, feeling that the ritual had gone as far as he could allow, began scanning the crowd for Adam Williams. He saw him in front, on the edge of the circle, and started pushing his way toward him. He was stopped—quietly but firmly—by the blacks around him. He looked angrily at a Negro who held his arm. The black didn't acknowledge his stare; he was hypnotized by the action now taking place in the center of the room.

Matlock saw why instantly. For the body of the small boy was now being *spun*, alternately face up and face down with each elevation. The danger of error was increased tenfold. Matlock grabbed the hand on his arm, twisted it inward, and flung it off him. He looked once more in the direction of Adam Williams.

He wasn't there. He was nowhere in sight! Matlock stood still, undecided. If he raised his voice between the crowd's roaring crescendos, it was entirely possible that he might cause a break in the concentration of those handling the body. He couldn't risk that, and yet he couldn't allow the dangerous absurdity to continue.

Suddenly Matlock felt another hand, this one on his shoulder. He turned and saw the face of Adam Williams behind him. It startled him. Had some primitive tribal signal been transmitted to Williams? The black radical gestured with his head for Matlock to follow him through the shouting crowd to the outer edge of the circle. Williams spoke between the roars.

"You look worried. Don't be."

"Look! This crap's gone far enough! That kid could be killed!"

"No chance. The brothers have rehearsed for months. . . . It's really the most simplistic of the Mau Mau rites. The symbolism is fundamental. . . . See? The child's eyes remain open. First to the sky, then facing the blades. He is constantly aware—every second—that his life is in the hands of his brother warriors. He cannot, he *must* not show fear. To do so would betray his peers. Betray the confidence he must place in their hands—as they will someday place their lives in *his* hands."

"It's childish, *dangerous stupidity*, and you *know* it!" cut in Matlock. "Now, I'm telling you, Williams, you put a stop to it or *I* will!"

"Of course," continued the black radical, as if Matlock had not spoken, "there are anthropologists who insist that the ceremony is essentially one of fertility. The unsheathed knives representing erections, the four protectors guarding the child through its formative years. Frankly, I think that's reaching. Also, it strikes me as contradictory even for the primitive mind. . . ."

"Goddamn you!" Matlock grabbed Williams by the front of his shirt. Immediately other blacks closed in on him.

Suddenly there was total silence in the eerily lit room. The silence lasted only a moment. It was followed by a series of mind-shattering screams from the mouths of the four Negroes in the center of the crowd in whose hands the life of the young student depended. Matlock whipped around and saw the shining black body descending downward from an incredible height above the outstretched hands.

It couldn't be true! It wasn't happening! Yet it was!

The four blacks suddenly, in unison, crouched into kneeling positions *away* from the center, their arms slashed to their sides. The young student came crashing down, *face toward the blades.* Two further screams followed. In a fraction of a second, the students holding the huge knives swung their weapons across one another and in an unbelievable display of wrist strength, *caught* the body on the flat of the blades.

The crowd of blacks went wild.

The ceremony was over.

"Do you believe me now?" Williams asked, speaking in a corner with Matlock.

"Whether I do or not doesn't change what I said. You can't *do* this sort of thing! It's too goddamn dangerous!"

"You exaggerate. . . . Here, let me introduce another guest." Williams raised his hand and a tall thin black with close-cropped hair and glasses, dressed in an expensively cut tan suit, joined them. "This is Julian Dunois, Mr. Matlock. Brother Julian is our expert. Our choreographer, if you like."

"A pleasure." Dunois extended his hand, speaking with a slight accent.

"Brother Julian is from Haiti. . . . Harvard Law out of Haiti. A most unusual progression, I think you'll agree."

"It certainly is. . . ."

"Many Haitians, even the Ton Ton Macoute, still get upset when they hear his name."

"You exaggerate, Adam," said Julian Dunois with a smile.

"That's what I just said to Mr. Matlock. *He* exaggerates. About the danger of the ceremony."

"Oh, there's danger—as there's danger if one crosses the Boston Commons wearing a blindfold. The petcock of safety, Mr. Matlock, is that those holding the knives watch closely. In the training there is as much emphasis on being able to drop the knives instantly as there is in holding them up."

"That may be so," Matlock acknowledged. "But the margin for error terrifies me."

"It's not as narrow as you think." The lilt in the Haitian's voice was as reassuring as it was attractive. "Incidentally, I'm a fan of yours. I've enjoyed your works on the Elizabethans. May I add, you're not exactly what I expected. I mean, you're far, far younger."

"You flatter me. I didn't think I was known in law schools."

"My undergraduate major was English literature."

Adam interrupted politely. "You two enjoy yourselves. There'll be drinks upstairs in a few minutes; just follow the crowd. I've got things to do. . . . I'm glad you've met. You're both strangers, in a way. Strangers should meet in unfamiliar areas. It's comforting."

He gave Dunois an enigmatic look and walked rapidly away through the crowd.

"Why does Adam feel he has to talk in what I'm sure he considers are profound riddles?" Matlock asked.

"He's very young. He strives constantly to make emphasis. Very bright, but very young."

"You'll pardon me, but you're not exactly ancient. I doubt more than a year or two older than Adam."

The black in the expensively cut tan suit looked into Matlock's eyes and laughed gently.

"Now you flatter *me*," he said. "If the truth were known—and why shouldn't it be?—and if my tropic color did not disguise the years so well, you'd know that I was precisely one year, four months, and sixteen days *older* than *you*."

Matlock stared at the Negro, speechless. It took him nearly a full minute to assimilate the lawyer's words and the meaning behind those words. The black's eyes did not waver. He returned Matlock's stare in equal measure. Finally, Matlock found his voice.

"I'm not sure I like this game."

"Oh, come, we're both here for the same reason, are we not? You from your vantage point, I from mine . . . Let's go upstairs and have a drink. . . . Bourbon and soda, isn't it? Sour mash, if it's available, I understand."

Dunois preceded Matlock through the crowd, and Matlock had no other course but to follow.

Dunois leaned against the brick wall.

"All right," Matlock said, "the amenities are over.

Everyone's acknowledged your show downstairs, and there's no one left for me to impress my white skin on. I think it's time you started explaining."

They were alone now, outside on the porch. Both held drinks.

"My, aren't we professional? Would you care for a cigar? I can assure you it's Havana."

"No cigar. Just talk. I came here tonight because these are my friends. I felt privileged to be invited. . . . Now, you've attached something else and I don't like it."

"Bravo! Bravo!" said Dunois, raising his glass. "You do that very well. . . . Don't worry, they know nothing. Perhaps they suspect, but believe me, only in the vaguest terms."

"What the hell are you talking about?"

"Finish your drink and let's walk out on the lawn." Dunois drained his rum and, as if by reflex, Matlock drank the remainder of his bourbon. The two men walked down the steps of the Lumumba Hall, Matlock following the black to the base of a large elm tree. Dunois turned suddenly and grabbed Matlock by the shoulders.

"Take your goddamn hands off me!"

"Listen to me! I want that paper! I *must have* that paper! And you must tell me *where it is!*"

Matlock flung his hands up to break Dunois's grip. But his arms did not respond. They were suddenly heavy, terribly heavy. And there was a whistling. A growing, piercing whistling in his head.

"What? What? . . . What paper? I don't have any paper. . . ."

"Don't be difficult! We'll get it, you know! . . . Now, just tell me where it is!"

Matlock realized that he was being lowered to the

ground. The outline of the huge tree above him began to spin, and the whistling in his brain became louder and louder. It was unendurable. He fought to find his mind again.

"What are you doing? What are you doing to me!?"

"The paper, Matlock! Where is the Corsican *paper?*"

"Get *off* me!" Matlock tried to yell. But nothing came from his lips.

"*The silver paper, goddamn you to hell!*"

"No paper . . . no. Haven't paper! No!"

"Listen to me! You just had a drink, remember the drink? . . . You just finished that drink. Remember? . . . You can't be alone now! You don't *dare* be alone!"

"What? . . . What? Get off me! You're crushing me!"

"I'm not even *touching* you. The drink is! You just consumed three tabs of *lysergic acid!* You're in trouble, Doctor! . . . *Now! You tell me where that paper is!*"

From his inner recesses he found an instant of clarity. From the spinning, turning, whirling spirals of mind-blasting colors, he saw the form of the man above him and he lashed out. He grabbed at the white shirt between the dark borders of the jacket and pulled it down with all the strength he could summon. He brought his fist up and hit the descending face as hard as he could. Once the face was jarred, he began hammering at the throat beneath it mercilessly. He could feel the shattering of the glasses and he knew his fist had found the eyes and crushed the glass into the rolling head.

It was over in a period of time he could never ascertain. Dunois's body was beside him, unconscious.

And he knew he had to run. Run furiously away! What had Dunois said? . . . Don't dare be alone. Don't *dare!* He had to find Pat! Pat would know what to do. He had to find her! The chemical in his body was going to take full effect soon and he knew it! Run, for Christ's sake!

But where?! Which way?! He didn't know *the way!* The *goddamn fucking way!* The street was there, he raced along the street, but was it the *right way?!* Was it the *right street?!*

Then he heard a car. It *was* a car, and it was coming close to the curb and the driver was looking at him. Looking at him, so he ran faster, tripping once over the curb and falling into the pavement and rising again. Running, for Christ Almighty's sake, running till the breath in his lungs was gone and he could no longer control the movement of his feet. He felt himself swerve, unable to stop himself, toward the wide gulf of the street, which suddenly became a river, a black putrid river in which he would drown.

He vaguely heard the screech of the brakes. The lights blinded him, and the figure of a man reached down and poked at his eyes. He didn't care any longer. Instead, he laughed. Laughed through the blood which flowed into his mouth and over his face.

He laughed hysterically as Jason Greenberg carried him to the car.

And then the earth, the world, the planet, the galaxy, and the entire solar system went crazy.

The night was agony.

The morning brought a degree of reality, less so for Matlock than for the two people sitting beside him, one on either side of the bed. Jason Greenberg, his large, sad eyes drooping, his hands calmly crossed on his lap, leaned forward. Patricia Ballantyne, her arm stretched out, held a cool washcloth on Matlock's forehead.

"The schvugs gave you one hell of a party, friend."

"Shh!" whispered the girl. "Leave him alone."

Matlock's eyes wandered as best they could around the room. He was in Pat's apartment, in her bedroom, her bed.

"They gave me acid."

"You're telling *us* . . . We had a doctor—a real doctor—brought in from Litchfield. He's the nice fella you kept trying to take the eyeballs from. . . . Don't worry, he's federal. No names."

"Pat? How come . . ."

"You're a very sweet acid head, Jamie. You kept yelling my name."

"It also made the best sense," interrupted Greenberg. "No hospitals. No out-patient records. Nice and private; good thinking. Also, you're very persuasive when you're violent. You're a hell of a lot stronger than

I thought. Especially for such a lousy handball player."

"You shouldn't have brought me here. Goddamn it, Greenberg, you shouldn't have *brought* me here!"

"Forgetting for the moment that it was your idea . . ."

"I was drugged!"

"It was a *good* idea. What would you have preferred? The emergency clinic? . . . 'Who's that on the stretcher, Doctor? The one screaming.' . . . 'Oh, just Associate Professor Matlock, Nurse. He's on an acid trip.' "

"You know what I mean! You could have taken me home. Strapped me down."

"I'm relieved to see you don't know much about acid," said Greenberg.

"What he means, Jamie . . . ," Pat took his hand, ". . . if it's bad, you should be with someone you know awfully well. The reassurance is necessary."

Matlock looked at the girl. And then at Greenberg. "What have you told her?"

"That you volunteered to help us; that we're grateful. With your help we may be able to prevent a serious situation from getting worse." Greenberg spoke in a monotone; it was obvious that he didn't wish to expand.

"It was a very cryptic explanation," Pat said. "He wouldn't have given me that if I hadn't threatened him."

"She was going to call the police." Greenberg sighed, his sad eyes sadder. "She was going to have me locked up for dosing you. I had no choice."

Matlock smiled.

"Why are you doing this, Jamie?" Pat found nothing amusing.

"The man said it: the situation's serious."

"But why *you?*"

"Because I can."

"What? Turn in kids?"

"I told you," said Jason. "We're not interested in students. . . ."

"What's Lumumba Hall, then? A branch of General Motors?"

"It's one contact point; there are others. Frankly, we'd rather *not* have gotten involved with that crowd; it's ticklish. Unfortunately, we can't choose."

"That's offensive."

"I don't think there's much I could say that wouldn't be offensive to you, Miss Ballantyne."

"Perhaps not. Because I thought the FBI had more important work to do than harassing young blacks. Obviously, you don't."

"Hey, come on." Matlock squeezed the girl's hand. She took it from him.

"No, I mean that, Jamie! No games, no radical chic. There are drugs all over this place. Some of it's a bad scene, most of it's pretty standard. We *both* know that. Why all of a sudden are the kids at Lumumba singled out?"

"We wouldn't *touch* those kids. Except to help them." Greenberg was weary from the long night. His irritation showed.

"I don't like the way you people help people and I don't like what happened to Jamie! Why did you send him there?"

"He didn't *send* me. I maneuvered that myself."

"Why?"

"It's too complicated and I'm too washed out to explain it."

"Oh, Mr. Greenberg did that. He explained all right. They've given you a badge, haven't they? They can't do it themselves so they pick a nice, easygoing fellow to do it for them. You take all the risks; and when it's over, you'll never be trusted on this campus again. Jamie, for God's sake, this is your *home*, your *work!*"

Matlock held the girl's eyes with his own, doing his best to calm her. "I know that better than you do. My home needs to be helped—and that's no game either, Pat. I think the risks are worth it."

"I won't pretend to understand that."

"You can't understand it, Miss Ballantyne, because we can't tell you enough to make it reasonable. You'll have to accept that."

"Do I?"

"I'm asking you to," said Matlock. "He saved my life."

"I wouldn't go that far, Professor." Greenberg shrugged as he spoke.

Pat stood up. "I think he threw you overboard and tossed you a rope as an afterthought. . . . Are you all right?"

"Yes," answered Matlock.

"I have to go; I won't if you don't want me to."

"No, you go ahead. I'll call you later. Thanks for the ministrations."

The girl looked briefly at Greenberg—it was not a pleasant look—and crossed to her dresser. She picked up a brush and rapidly stroked her hair, slipping an orange headband into place. She watched Greenberg through the mirror. He returned the stare.

"The man who's been following me, Mr. Greenberg. Is he one of your men?"

"Yes."

"I don't like it."

"I'm sorry."

Pat turned. "Will you remove him, please?"

"I can't do that. I'll tell him to be less obvious."

"I see." She took her purse from the dresser top and reached down to the floor, picking up her accordion briefcase. Without speaking further, the girl walked out of the bedroom. Several seconds later, the two men could hear the apartment door open and shut firmly.

"That is one very strong-willed young lady," said Jason.

"There's a good reason."

"What do you mean?"

"I thought you fellows were so familiar with the people you had to deal with. . . ."

"I'm still getting briefed. I'm the back-up, remember?"

"Then I'll save you time. In the late fifties her father got McCarthyized out of the State Department. Of course, he was very dangerous. He was a language consultant. He was cleared for translating newspapers."

"Shit."

"That's the word, brother. He never made it back. She's had scholarships all her life; the cupboard's bare. She's a little sensitive to your type."

"Boy, do you pick 'em!"

"You picked *me*, remember?"

Matlock opened the door to his apartment and walked into the foyer. Pat had done a good job putting the rooms in order—as he knew she would. Even the curtains were rehung. It was a little after three—most of the day wasted. Greenberg had insisted that the two of them drive over to Litchfield for a reexamination by the doctor. Shaken but operable, was the verdict.

They stopped for lunch at the Cheshire Cat. During

the meal, Matlock kept looking over at the small table where four days ago Ralph Loring had sat with his folded newspaper. The lunch was quiet. Not strained —the two men were comfortable in each other's company—but quiet, as if each had too much to think about.

On the road back to Carlyle, Greenberg told him to stay in his apartment until he contacted him. Washington hadn't issued any new instructions. They were evaluating the new information, and until they confirmed any further involvement, Matlock was to remain "OOS"—a term the English professor found hard to equate with grownups: *out of strategy.*

It was just as well, he thought. He had his own strategy to think about—Lucas Herron. The "grand old bird," the campus elder statesman. It was time to reach him, to warn him. The old man was out of his element, and the quicker he retreated, the better for everyone—Carlyle included. Yet he didn't want to telephone him, he didn't want to arrange a formal meeting—he had to be subtler than that. He didn't want to alarm old Lucas, have him talking to the wrong people.

It occurred to Matlock that he was acting as some sort of protector for Herron. That presumed Lucas was innocent of any serious involvement. He wondered if he had the right to make that assumption. On the other hand, by civilized standards, he had no right to make any other.

The telephone rang. It couldn't be Greenberg, he thought. He'd just left him at the curb. He hoped it wasn't Pat; he wasn't ready to talk to her yet. Reluctantly he lifted the instrument to his ear. "Hello!"

"Jim! Where have you *been!?* I've been calling since eight this morning! I was so goddamn worried I

went over there twice. Got your key from mainte-
nance." It was Sam Kressel. He sounded as though
Carlyle had lost its accreditation.

"It's too involved to go into now, Sam. Let's get together later. I'll come over to your place after dinner."

"I don't know if it can wait that long. Jesus! What
the hell got *into* you?"

"I don't understand."

"At Lumumba last night!"

"What are you talking about? What have you
heard?"

"That black bastard, Adam Williams, handed in a
report to my office accusing you of just about everything short of advocating slavery! He claims the only
reason he's not filing police charges is that you were
blind drunk! Of course, the alcohol stripped you of
your pretenses and showed clearly what a racist you
are!"

"What?!"

"You broke up furniture, slapped around some kids,
smashed windows. . . ."

"You know damned well that's bullshit!"

"I figured as much." Kressel lowered his voice. He
was calming down. "But my knowing it doesn't help,
can't you see that? This is the kind of thing we've got
to *avoid*. Polarization! The government walks onto
a campus, polarization follows."

"Listen to me. Williams' statement is a decoy—if
that's the word. It's camouflage. They drugged me last
night. If it hadn't been for Greenberg, I don't know
where I'd be right now."

"Oh, God! . . . Lumumba's on your list, isn't it?
That's all we *need!* The blacks'll scream persecution.
Christ knows what'll happen."

Matlock tried to speak calmly. "I'll come over

around seven. Don't do anything, don't say anything. I've got to get off the phone. Greenberg's supposed to call."

"Wait a minute, Jim! One thing. This Greenberg ... I don't trust him. I don't trust any of them. Just remember. Your loyalty's to Carlyle. . . ." Kressel stopped, but he had not finished. Matlock realized he was at a loss for words.

"That's a strange thing to say."

"I think you know what I mean."

"I'm not sure I do. I thought the idea was to work together. . . ."

"Not at the expense of ripping this campus apart!" The dean of colleges sounded nearly hysterical.

"Don't worry," Matlock said. "It won't tear. I'll see you later." Matlock hung up the phone before Kressel could speak again. His mind needed a short rest, and Kressel never let anyone rest where his domain was concerned. Sam Kressel, in his own way, was as militant as any extremist, and, perhaps, quicker to cry "foul."

These thoughts led Matlock to another consideration—two considerations. Four days ago, he had told Pat that he didn't want to change their plans for St. Thomas. Carlyle's midterm holiday, a short ten days at the end of April, would start after classes on Saturday, in three days. Under the circumstances, St. Thomas was out—unless Washington decided to retire him, and he doubted that. He'd use his parents as the excuse. Pat would understand, even be sympathetic. The other thought was his own classes. He had fallen behind. His desk was piled with papers—mostly themes and essay exams. He had also missed his two classes earlier in the day. He was not so much concerned for his students—his method was to accelerate in the fall and winter and relax in the spring—but he didn't want to add any fuel to such fires as Williams' false complaint. An absentee associate professor was a target for gossip. His class load for the next three days was medium—three, two, and two. He'd organize the work later. Between now and seven o'clock, however, he had to find Lucas Herron. If Greenberg called while he was out, he'd blame it on a forgotten graduate conference.

He decided to shower, shave, and change clothes. Once in the bathroom, he checked the litter box. The Corsican paper was there—he knew it would be.

The shave and shower completed, Matlock walked into his bedroom, selecting clothes and a course of action. He didn't know Herron's daily schedule, although it would be a simple matter to find out if Lucas had any late afternoon classes or seminars. If he didn't, Matlock knew Herron's house; it would take about fifteen minutes to get there by car. Herron lived eight miles from the campus, on a rarely traveled back road in a section once a part of the old Carlyle family estate. Herron's home had been a carriage house. It was out of the way, but as Lucas kept saying, "Once there, it's worth it."

The rapid tapping of the door knocker broke his concentration. It also frightened him—he felt himself gasping for breath; that was disturbing.

"Be right there," he yelled, slipping a white sport shirt over his head. He walked barefoot to the front door and opened it. It was impossible for him to conceal his shock. In the doorframe stood Adam Williams —alone.

"Afternoon."

"Jesus! . . . I don't know whether to hit you in the

mouth right now or first call the police! What the hell do you want? Kressel's already called me, if that's what you're checking on."

"Please let me talk to you. I'll be quick." The black spoke with urgency, trying, thought Matlock, to conceal his fear.

"Come on in. And *make* it quick." Matlock slammed the door as Williams passed by him into the foyer. The black turned and tried to smile, but there was no humor in his eyes.

"I'm sorry about that report. Truly sorry. It was an unpleasant necessity."

"I don't buy that and you can't sell it! What did you want Kressel to do? Bring me up before the board and burn me out of here? Did you think I'd just sit down and play doormat? You're a goddamn maniac!"

"We didn't think *anything* would happen. That's precisely why we did it. . . . We couldn't be sure where you went. You disappeared, you know. You might say we had to take the offensive and then later agree that it was all a disagreeable misunderstanding. . . . It's not a new tactic. I'll send Kressel another report, backing off—but not entirely. In a couple of weeks, it'll be forgotten."

Matlock raged, as much against Williams' attitude as his conscienceless pragmatism. But when he spoke he did not raise his voice. "Get out. You disgust me."

"Oh, come off it, man! Haven't we *always disgusted* you?!" Matlock had hit a nerve and Williams responded in kind. But just as suddenly, he took hold of himself. "Let's not argue theoretical practicalities. Let me get to the point and leave."

"By all means."

"All right. Listen to me. Whatever Dunois wanted

from you, *give* it to him! . . . That is, give it to me and I'll send it on. No forked tongue; it's last-extremity language!"

"Too pat a phrase. No sale. Why would I have anything Brother Julian wanted? Did he say so? Why doesn't he come over himself?"

"Brother Julian doesn't stay long in any one place. His talents are in great demand."

"Staging Mau Mau puberty rituals?"

"He really does that, you know. It's a hobby."

"Send him to me." Matlock crossed in front of Williams and went to the coffee table. He reached down and picked up a half-empty pack of cigarettes. "We'll compare notes on associative body movements. I've a hell of a collection of sixteenth-century folk dances."

"Talk seriously. There's no *time!*"

Matlock lit a cigarette. "I've got all the time in the world. I just want to see Brother Julian again; I want to put him in jail."

"No chance! No chance. I'm here for *your* benefit! If I leave without it, I can't *control* it!"

"Two pronouns signifying the same or different objects?"

"Oh, you're too much! You're really too much! Do you know who Julian Dunois *is?*"

"Part of the Borgia family? Ethiopian branch?"

"*Stop it, Matlock!* Do what he says! People could be hurt. Nobody wants that."

"I *don't* know who Dunois is and I don't much give a damn. I just know he drugged me and assaulted me and is exercising a dangerous influence on a bunch of children. Beyond this, I suspect he had my apartment broken into and many of my personal belongings destroyed. I want him put away. From you *and* from me."

"Be reasonable, *please!*"

Matlock walked swiftly to the curtains in front of his casement window and with a flourish, yanked them down, displaying the shattered glass and twisted lead.

"Is this one of Brother Julian's calling cards?"

Adam Williams stared, obviously shocked, at the mass of destruction. "No, man. Absolutely, no. That's not Julian's style. . . . That's not even my style. That's someone else."

11

The road to Lucas Herron's house was dotted with the potholes of winter. Matlock doubted that the town of Carlyle would fill them in; there were too many other commercially traveled streets still showing the effects of the New England freeze. As he approached the old carriage house, he slowed his Triumph to barely ten miles an hour. The bumps were jarring, and he wanted to reach Herron's house with little noise.

Thinking that Jason Greenberg might have had him followed, Matlock took the long route to Herron's, driving four miles north on a parallel road and then doubling back on Herron's street. There was no one behind him. The nearest houses to Herron's were a hundred yards away on either side, none in front. There'd been talk of turning the area into a housing development just as there'd been talk of enlarging Carlyle University, but nothing came of either project. Actually, the first depended upon the second, and there was strong alumni opposition to any substantial physical change at Carlyle. The alumni were Adrian Sealfont's personal cross.

Matlock was struck by the serenity of Herron's home. He'd never really looked at the house before. A dozen times, more or less, he'd driven Lucas home after faculty meetings, but he'd always been in a hurry. He'd never accepted Lucas's invitations for a drink and, as a result, he had never been inside the house.

He got out of the car and approached the old brick structure. It was tall and narrow; the faded stone covered with thousands of strands of ivy heightened the feeling of isolation. In front, on the large expanse of lawn, were two Japanese willow trees in full spring bloom, their purple flowers cascading toward the earth in large arcs. The grass was cut, the shrubbery pruned, and the white gravel on the various paths was gleaming. It was a house and grounds which were loved and cared for, yet one had the feeling that they were not shared. It was the work of and for one person, not two or a family. And then Matlock remembered that Lucas Herron had never married. There were the inevitable stories of a lost love, a tragic death, even a runaway bride-to-be, but whenever Lucas Herron heard about such youthful romanticizing he countered with a chuckle and a statement about being "too damned selfish."

Matlock walked up the short steps to the door and rang the bell. He tried practicing an opening smile, but it was false; he wouldn't be able to carry it off. He was afraid.

The door swung back and the tall, white-haired Lucas Herron, dressed in wrinkled trousers and a half-unbuttoned, oxford-blue shirt, stared at him.

It was less than a second before Herron spoke, but in that brief instant, Matlock knew that he'd been wrong. Lucas Herron knew why he had come.

"Well, Jim! Come in, come in, my boy. A pleasant surprise."

"Thank you, Lucas. I hope I'm not interrupting anything."

"Not a thing. You're just in time, as a matter of fact. I'm dabbling in alchemy. A fresh fruit gin Collins. Now I won't have to dabble alone."

"Sounds good to me."

The inside of Herron's house was precisely as Matlock thought it would be—as his own might be in thirty-odd years, if he lived that long alone. It was a mixed bag, an accumulated total of nearly half a century of unrelated gatherings from a hundred unrelated sources. The only common theme was comfort; there was no concern for style or period or coordination. Several walls were lined with books, and those which were not were filled with enlarged photographs of places visited abroad—one suspected during sabbaticals. The armchairs were thick and soft, the tables within arm's reach—the sign of practiced bachelorhood, thought Matlock.

"I don't think you've ever been here—inside, I mean."

"No, I haven't. It's very attractive. Very comfortable."

"Yes, it's that. It's comfortable. Here, sit down, I'll finish the formula and bring us a drink." Herron started across the living room toward what Matlock presumed was the door to the kitchen and then stopped and turned. "I know perfectly well that you haven't come all the way out here to liven up an old man's cocktail hour. However, I have a house rule: at least one drink—religion and strong principles permitting—before any serious discussion." He smiled and the myriad lines around his eyes and temples became more pronounced. He was an *old*, old man. "Besides, you look terribly serious. The Collins'll lessen the degree, I promise you."

Before Matlock could answer, Herron walked rapidly through the door. Instead of sitting, Matlock walked to the wall nearest him, against which was a small writing desk, above it a half-dozen photographs that hung in no discernible pattern. Several were of Stonehenge taken from the same position, the setting sun at dramatically different angles. Another was of a rock-bound coast, mountains in the distance, fishing boats moored offshore. It looked Mediterranean, possibly Greece or the Thracian Islands. Then there was a surprise. On the lower right side of the wall, only inches above the desk, was a small photograph of a tall, slender army officer standing by the trunk of a tree. Behind him the foliage was profuse, junglelike; to the sides were the shadows of other figures. The officer was helmetless, his shirt drenched with sweat, his large right hand holding the stock of a submachine gun. In his left hand the officer held a folded piece of paper—it looked like a map—and the man had obviously just made a decision. He was looking upward, as though toward some high terrain. The face was taut but not excited. It was a good face, a strong face. It was a dark-haired, middle-aged Lucas Herron.

"I keep that old photograph to remind me that time was not always so devastating."

Matlock snapped up, startled. Lucas had reentered and had taken him off guard. "It's a good picture. Now I know who really won that war."

"No doubt about it. Unfortunately, I never heard of that particular island either before or since. Someone said it was one of the Solomons. I think they blew it up in the fifties. Wouldn't take much. Couple of fire crackers'd do it. Here." Herron crossed to Matlock, handing him his drink.

"Thanks. You're too modest. I've heard the stories."

"So have I. Impressed the hell out of me. They grow better as I grow older. . . . What do you say we sit in the back yard. Too nice to stay indoors." Without waiting for a reply, Herron started out and Matlock followed.

Like the front of the house, the back was precisely manicured. On a flagstone patio, there were comfortable-looking, rubber-stranded beach chairs, each with a small table by its side. A large wrought-iron table with a sun umbrella was centered in the middle of the flagstones. Beyond, the lawn was close cropped and full. Dogwood trees were dotted about, each spaded around its trunk, and two lines of flowers—mostly roses—stretched lengthwise to the end of the lawn, about a hundred feet away. At the end of the lawn, however, the pastoral effect abruptly stopped. Suddenly there were huge trees, the underbrush thick, mangled, growing within itself. The side borders were the same. Around the perimeters of the sculptured back lawn was an undisciplined, overgrown forest.

Lucas Herron was surrounded by a forbidding green wall.

"It *is* a good drink, you'll admit." The two men were seated.

"It certainly is. You'll convert me to gin."

"Only in spring and summer. Gin's not for the rest of the year. . . . All right, young fellow, the house rule's been observed. What brings you to Herron's Nest?"

"I think you have an idea."

"Do I?"

"Archie Beeson." Matlock watched the old man, but Herron's concentration was on his glass. He showed no reaction.

"The young history man?"

"Yes."

"He'll make a fine teacher one day. Nice little filly of a wife, too."

"Nice . . . and promiscuous, I think."

"*Appearances,* Jim." Herron chuckled. "Never thought of you as Victorian. . . . One grows infinitely more tolerant of the appetites as one gets older. And the innocent whetting of them. You'll see."

"Is that the key? The tolerance of appetites?"

"Key to what?"

"Come on. He wanted to reach you the other night."

"Yes, he did. And you were there. . . . I understand your behavior left something to be desired."

"My behavior was calculated to leave that impression." For the first time Herron betrayed a trace of concern. It was a small reaction, the blinking of his eyes in rapid succession.

"That was reprehensible." Herron spoke softly and looked up at his imposing green wall. The sun was going below the line of tall trees; long shadows were cast across the lawn and patio.

"It was necessary." Matlock saw the old man's face wince in pain. And then he recalled his own reaction to Adam Williams' description of the "unpleasant necessity" of sending Sam Kressel the false report of his actions at Lumumba Hall. The parallel hurt.

"The boy's in trouble. He's sick. It's a disease and he's trying to cure himself. That takes courage. . . . This is no time for campus Gestapo tactics." Herron took a long drink from his glass while his free hand gripped the arm of the chair.

"How did you know about it?"

"That might be privileged information. Let's say I heard from a respected co-worker of ours—in the medical line—who ran across the symptoms and became concerned. What difference does it make? I tried to help the boy and I'd do it again."

"I'd like to believe that. It's what I wanted to believe."

"Why is that difficult for you?"

"I don't know. . . . Something at the front door a few minutes ago. Perhaps this house. I can't put my finger on it. . . . I'm being completely honest with you."

Herron laughed but still avoided Matlock's eyes. "You're too wound up in the Elizabethans. The plots and counterplots of *The Spanish Tragedy*. . . . You young faculty crusaders should stop trying to be an amateur Scotland Yard. Not too long ago it was fashionable around here to have Red Dogs for breakfast. You're just magnifying the situation out of proportion."

"That's not true. I'm not a faculty crusader. I'm no part of that crowd, and I think you know it."

"What was it then? Personal interest? In the boy. Or his wife? . . . I'm sorry, I shouldn't have said that."

"I'm glad you did. I have no interest in Virginia Beeson—sexual or otherwise. Although I can't imagine what else there would be."

"Then you put on quite an act."

"I certainly did. I took extreme measures to keep Beeson from knowing why I was there. It was that important."

"To whom?" Herron slowly put his glass down with his right hand, his left still gripped the arm of the chair.

"To people beyond this campus. Washington people. The federal authorities . . ."

Lucas Herron took a sudden, sustained intake of breath through his nostrils. In front of Matlock's eyes,

Herron's face began to drain itself of color. When he spoke, he did so barely above a whisper.

"What are you saying?"

"That I was approached by a man from the Justice Department. The information he showed me was frightening. Nothing was trumped up, nothing over-dramatized. It was straight data. I was given a free choice whether to cooperate or not."

"And you accepted?" Herron's words were uttered softly in disbelief.

"I didn't feel there was an alternative. My younger brother . . ."

"You didn't feel there was an *alternative?*" Herron rose from his chair, his hands began to shake, his voice grew in intensity. "You didn't *feel* there was an *alternative?*"

"No, I didn't," Matlock remained calm. "That's why I came out here. To warn you, old friend. It's much deeper—far more dangerous . . ."

"*You* came out here to warn *me?!* What have you done? What in the name of everything sacred *have you done?* . . . Now, you listen to me! You listen to what I say!" Herron backed off, bumping into the small side table. In one whip of his left arm, he sent it crashing onto the flagstones. "You let it *go*, do you hear me! You go back and tell them *nothing! Nothing exists!* It's all . . . all in their imaginations! *Don't touch it! Let it go!*"

"I can't do that," said Matlock gently, suddenly afraid for the old man. "Even Sealfont will have to agree. He can't fight it any longer. It's there, Lucas. . . ."

"Adrian! Adrian's been told? . . . Oh, my God, do you know what you're doing? *You'll destroy so much.*

So many, many . . . Get out of here! *Get out!* I don't know you! Oh, *Jesus! Jesus!"*

"Lucas, what is it?" Matlock got up and took several steps toward the old man. Herron continued backing away, an old man in panic.

"Don't come near me! Don't you *touch me!"*

Herron turned and started running as well as his ancient legs could carry him across the lawn. He stumbled, falling to the ground, and picked himself up. He didn't look back. Instead he ran with all his might toward the rear of the yard, toward the overgrown woods. And then he disappeared through his huge green wall.

"Lucas! For Christ's sake!" Matlock raced after the old man, reaching the edge of the woods only seconds behind him. Yet he was nowhere in sight. Matlock whipped at the overgrowth in front of him and stepped into the tangled mass of foliage. Branches slashed back at him, and the intricate webbings of giant weeds ensnared his feet as he kicked his way into the dense woods.

Herron was gone.

"Lucas! Where are you?!"

There was no answer, only the rustling of the disturbed growth behind him. Matlock went farther into the forest, ducking, crouching, sidling by the green barriers in front of him. There was no sign of Lucas Herron, no sound.

"Lucas! For God's sake, Lucas, answer me!"

Still no reply, no hint of presence.

Matlock tried to look around him, tried to spot a break in the patterns of foliage, a route to follow. He could see none. It was as if Lucas were matter one moment, vapor the next.

And then he heard it. Indistinct, from all sides of him, echoing softly from some unknown place. It was a deep-throated moan, a wail. Near, yet far in the dense distance. And then the wail diminished and became a plaintive sob. A single sob, punctuated by a single word—clear, and spoken in hatred.

The word was—

"Nimrod..."

"Goddamn it, Matlock! I told you to stay put until I contacted you!"

"Goddamn it, Greenberg! How did you get into my apartment?!"

"You didn't get your window fixed."

"You haven't offered to pay for it."

"We're even. Where have you been?"

Matlock threw his car keys on the coffee table and looked at his broken stereo set in the corner. "It's an involved story and I suspect . . . pathetic. I'll tell you all about it after I've had a drink. My last one was interrupted."

"Get me one, too. I've also got a story and mine's *definitely* pathetic."

"What do you drink?"

"Very little, so whatever you're having is fine."

Matlock looked out his front window. The curtains were strewn on the floor where he had torn them in front of Adam Williams. The sun was almost down now. The spring day was over. "I'm going to squeeze some lemons and have a fresh fruit Tom Collins."

"Your file says you drink bourbon. Sour mash."

Matlock looked at the federal agent. "Does it?"

Greenberg followed Matlock into the kitchen and watched in silence as he fixed their drinks. Matlock handed the federal man his glass.

"Looks fancy."

"It's not . . . Whose pathetic story gets first telling?"

"I'll want to hear yours, of course, but under the circumstances, mine has priority."

"You sound ominous."

"No. Just pathetic. . . . I'll start by asking you if you'd care to know where I've been since I dropped you off." Greenberg leaned against the counter.

"Not particularly, but you'll tell me anyway."

"Yes, I will. It's part of the pathos. I was out at your local airport—Bradley Field—waiting for a jet dispatched by Justice a few hours ago from Dulles. There was a man on the plane who brought me two sealed envelopes which I had to sign for. Here they are." Greenberg reached into his jacket pocket and took out two long business envelopes. He put one on the counter and began to open the second.

"They look very official," said Matlock, edging himself up so that he sat next to the sink, his long legs dangling over the side in front of the cabinets.

"They couldn't be more official. . . . This envelope contains the summary of our conclusions based on information you gave us—gave me. It ends with a specific recommendation. I'm allowed to convey this information in my own words as long as I cover all the facts. . . ."

"Jason Greenberg gets two points."

"However," continued the federal man without acknowledging Matlock's interruption, "the contents of the second envelope must be delivered verbatim. You are to read it thoroughly—*should it be necessary*—and if it's acceptable, you've got to acknowledge that by your signature."

"This gets better and better. Am I running for the Senate?"

"No, you're just running. . . . I'll start as instructed." Greenberg glanced at the unfolded paper and then looked across at Matlock. "The man at Lumumba Hall named Julian Dunois—alias Jacques Devereaux, Jésus Dambert, and probably several others we don't know about—is a legal strategist for the Black Left militants. The term *legal strategist* covers everything from court manipulations to agent provocateur. When involved with the former, he uses the name of Dunois, the latter—any number of aliases. He operates out of unusual places geographically. Algiers, Marseilles, the Caribbean—including Cuba—and, we suspect, Hanoi and probably Moscow. Perhaps even Peking. In the States he has a regular, bona fide law office in upper Harlem and a West Coast affiliate in San Francisco. . . . He's generally in the background, but wherever he's in evidence, bad news usually follows. Needless to say, he's on the attorney general's list of undesirables, and these days that's not respectable any longer. . . ."

"These days," broke in Matlock, "that includes almost everyone to the left of AT&T."

"No comment. To continue. The surfacing of Dunois in this operation adds a dimension not anticipated—a new aspect not considered before. It goes beyond domestic lawbreakers and enters the area of international crime and/or subversion. *Or* a combination of *both*. In light of the fact that drugs were used on you, your apartment broken into and ripped apart, your friend, Miss Ballantyne, indirectly threatened —and don't kid yourself, that's what it was—in light of all this, the recommendation is as follows. You withdraw from any further participation in this investigation. Your involvement is beyond the realm of reasonable risk." Greenberg dropped the paper on the counter and took several swallows of his drink. Matlock swung his legs slowly back and forth in front of the cabinet beneath him. "What say you, in the docket?" asked Greenberg.

"I'm not sure. It seems to me you're not finished."

"I'd like to be. Right here. The summary's accurate, and I think you should agree with the recommendation. Pull out, Jim."

"Finish first. What's the other letter? The one I'm supposed to read verbatim?"

"It's only necessary if you reject the recommendation. Don't reject it. I'm not instructed to lean that way, so that's off the record."

"You know damned well I'm going to reject it, so why waste time?"

"I *don't* know that. I don't want to *believe* that."

"There's no way out."

"There are counter explanations I can activate in an hour. Get you off the hook, out of the picture."

"Not any longer."

"What? Why?"

"That's *my* pathetic story. So you'd better continue."

Greenberg searched Matlock's eyes for an explanation, found none, and so picked up the second envelope and opened it.

"In the unlikely and ill-advised event that you reject our recommendation to cease and desist, you must understand that you do so against the express wishes of the Justice Department. Although we will offer whatever protection we can—as we would any citizen —you act under your own responsibility. We cannot be held liable for any injuries or inconveniences of any nature."

"Is that what it says?"

"No, that's *not* what it says, but that's what it means," said Greenberg, unfolding the paper. "It's much simpler and even more inclusive. Here." The federal agent handed Matlock the letter.

It was a statement signed by an assistant attorney general with a separate line on the left for Matlock's signature.

An investigative office of the Department of Justice accepted the offer of James B. Matlock to make inquiries of a minor nature with regard to certain illegal acts alleged to have occurred within the vicinity of Carlyle University. However, the Department of Justice now considers the situation to be a professional matter, and any further participation on the part of Professor Matlock is deemed unwarranted and against the policies of the Department. Therefore, the Department of Justice hereby informs James B. Matlock that it appreciates his previous cooperation but requests him to remove himself from any further involvement in the interest of safety and investigatory progress. It is the opinion of the Department that further actions on the part of Professor Matlock might tend to interfere with the aims of the Investigation in the Carlyle area. Mr. Matlock has received the original of this letter and so signifies by his signature below.

"What the hell are you talking about? This says that I agree to pull out."

"You'd make a lousy lawyer. Don't buy a bicycle on time before talking to me."

"What?"

"Nowhere! *Nowhere* does your signing this little stinkpot say you *agree* to retire from the scene. Only that Justice *requested* you to."

"Then why in hell should I sign it?"

"Excellent question. You may buy a bicycle. . . . You sign it if, as you say, you reject the recommendation to pull out."

"Oh, for Christ's sake!" Matlock slipped down from the edge of the sink and threw the paper across the counter next to Greenberg. "I may not know law but I know language. You're talking in contradictions!"

"Only on the surface. . . . Let me ask you a question. Say you continue playing undercover agent. Is it conceivable that you may want to ask for help? An emergency, perhaps?"

"Of course. Inevitable."

"You get no help whatsoever without that letter going back signed. . . . Don't look at *me!* I'll be replaced in a matter of days. I've been in the area too long already."

"Kind of hypocritical, isn't it? The only way I can count on any assistance—any protection—is to sign a statement that says I won't need it."

"It's enough to send me into private practice. . . . There's a new term for this sort of thing these days. It's called 'hazardless progress.' Use whatever—*who*ever—you can. But don't take the blame if a *game plan* gets fucked up. Don't be responsible."

"And I jump without a parachute if I don't sign."

"I told you. Take some free advice—I'm a good lawyer. Quit. Forget it. But *forget it.*"

"And I told *you*—I can't."

Greenberg reached for his drink and spoke softly. "No matter what you do, it's not going to bring your brother out of his grave."

"I know that." Matlock was touched, but he answered firmly.

"You might prevent other younger brothers but you probably won't. In either case, someone else can be recruited from professional ranks. I hate like hell to admit it, but Kressel was right. And if we don't get this conference—this convocation of peddlers in a couple of weeks—there'll be others."

"I agree with everything you say."

"Then why hesitate? Pull out."

"Why? . . . I haven't told you *my* pathetic little story, that's why. Remember? You had priority, but I've still got my turn."

"So tell."

And Matlock told him. Everything he knew about Lucas Herron—legend, giant, the "grand old bird" of Carlyle. The terror-stricken skeleton who had run into his personal forest. The wail of the single word: "Nimrod." Greenberg listened, and the longer Matlock talked, the sadder Jason Greenberg's eyes became. When Matlock finished, the federal agent drank the last of his drink and morosely nodded his head in slow motion.

"You spelled out everything for him, didn't you? You couldn't come to *me*, you had to go to *him*. Your campus saint with a bucket of blood in his hands. . . . Loring was right. We had to reach a conscience-stricken amateur. . . . Amateurs in front of us and amateurs behind us. At least I'll say this for you. You got a conscience. That's more than I can say for the rear flank."

"What should I do?"

"Sign the stinkpot." Greenberg picked up the Justice Department letter from the counter and handed it to Matlock. "You're going to need help."

Patricia Ballantyne preceded Matlock to the small side table at the far end of the Cheshire Cat. The drive out had been strained. The girl had hammered away—quietly, acidly—at Matlock's cooperating with the government, in particular and specifically the Federal Bureau of Investigation. She claimed not to be reacting to a programmed liberal response; there was simply too much overwhelming evidence that such organizations had brought the country ten steps from its own particular police state.

She knew firsthand. She'd witnessed the anguished aftermath of one FBI exercise and knew it wasn't isolated.

Matlock held her chair as she sat down, touching her shoulders as she did so. Touching, reaffirming, lessening the imagined hurt. The table was small, next to a window, several feet from a terrace that soon—in late May—would be in use for outside dining. He sat across from her and took her hand.

"I'm not going to apologize for what I'm doing. I think it has to be done. I'm not a hero and I'm not a fink. I'm not asked to be heroic, and the information they want ultimately will help a lot of people. People who need help—desperately."

"Will those people *get* help? Or will they simply be prosecuted? Instead of hospitals and clinics . . . will they find themselves in jail?"

"They're not interested in sick kids. They want the ones who make them sick. So do I."

"But in the process, the kids get hurt." A statement.

"Some may be. As few as possible."

"That's contemptible." The girl took her hand away from Matlock's. "It's so condescending. Who makes *those* decisions? You?"

"You're beginning to sound like a one-track tape."

"I've *been* there. It's not pleasant."

"This is entirely different. I've met just two men; one . . . left. The other's Greenberg. They're not your nightmares from the fifties. Take my word for that."

"I'd like to."

The manager of the Cheshire Cat approached the table. "There's a telephone call for you, Mr. Matlock."

Matlock felt a twinge of pain in his stomach. It was the nerves of fear. Only one person knew where he was—Jason Greenberg.

"Thanks, Harry."

"You can take it by the reservations desk. The phone's off the hook."

Matlock got out of his chair and looked briefly at Pat. In the months and months of their going out together, from restaurants to parties to dinners, he had never received a telephone call, had never been interrupted that way. He saw that realization in her eyes. He walked rapidly away from the table to the reservations desk.

"Hello?"

"Jim?" It *was* Greenberg, of course.

"Jason?"

"Sorry to bother you. I wouldn't if I didn't have to."

"What is it, for heaven's sake?"

"Lucas Herron's dead. He committed suicide about an hour ago."

The pain in Matlock's stomach suddenly returned. It wasn't a twinge this time, but instead a sharp blow that left him unable to breathe. All he could see in front of his eyes was the picture of the staggering, panicked old man running across the manicured lawn and disappearing into the dense foliage bordering his property. And then the wailing sound of a sob and the name of Nimrod whispered in hatred.

"Are you all right?"

"Yes. Yes, I'm all right." For reasons he could not fathom, Matlock's memory focused on a small, black-framed photograph. It was an enlarged snapshot of a dark-haired, middle-aged infantry officer with a weapon in one hand, a map in the other, the face lean and strong, looking up toward the high ground.

A quarter of a century ago.

"You'd better get back to your apartment. . . ." Greenberg was issuing an order, but he had the sense to be gentle about it.

"Who found him?"

"My man. No one else knows yet."

"Your man?"

"After our talk, I put Herron under surveillance. You get to spot the signs. He broke in and found him."

"How?"

"Cut his wrists in the shower."

"Oh, Christ! What have I done?"

"Cut that out! Get back here. We've got people to reach. . . . Come on, Jim."

"What can I tell Pat?" Matlock tried to find his mind but it kept wandering back to a helpless, frightened old man.

"As little as possible. But hurry."

Matlock replaced the receiver and took several deep breaths. He searched his pockets for cigarettes and remembered that he'd left them at the table.

The table. Pat. He had to go back to the table and think of something to say.

The truth. Goddamn it, the *truth*.

He made his way around two antique pillars toward the far end of the room and the small side table by the window. In spite of his panic, he felt a degree of relief and knew it was because he had decided to be honest with Pat. God knew he had to have someone other than Greenberg and Kressel to talk to.

Kressel! He was supposed to have gone to Kressel's house at seven. He'd forgotten all about it!

But in an instant Sam Kressel went out of his thoughts. He saw the small side table by the window and there was no one there.

Pat was gone.

13

"No one saw her leave?" Greenberg followed a frustrated Matlock into the living room from the foyer. Sam Kressel's voice could be heard from the bedroom, shouting excitedly into a telephone. Matlock took notice of it, his attention split in too many areas.

"That's Sam in there, isn't it?" he asked. "Does he know about Herron?"

"Yes. I called him after I talked to you. . . . What about the waitresses? Did you ask them?"

"Of course, I did. None of them were sure. It was busy. One said she thought she might have gone to the ladies' room. Another hinted, s'help me, hinted, that she might have been the girl who left with a couple from another table."

"Wouldn't they have had to pass you on the way out? Wouldn't you have seen her?"

"Not necessarily. We were in the back. There are two or three doors which lead to a terrace. In summer, especially when it's crowded, they put tables on the terrace."

"You drove out in your car?"

"Naturally."

"And you didn't see her outside, walking on the road, on the grounds?"

"No."

"Did you recognize any of the other people there?"

"I didn't really look. I was . . . preoccupied." Matlock lit a cigarette. His hand shook as he held the match.

"If you want my opinion, I think she spotted someone she knew and asked for a lift home. A girl like that doesn't go anywhere she doesn't want to go without a fight."

"I know. That's occurred to me."

"Have a fight?"

"You might say it was diminishing but not over. The phone call probably set her off again. Old English teachers rarely get calls while out at restaurants."

"I'm sorry."

"It's not your fault. I told you, she's uptight. She keeps thinking about her father. I'll try her apartment when Sam gets off the phone."

"*He's* a funny man. I tell him about Herron—naturally he goes off the deep end. He says he's got to talk privately with Sealfont so he goes into the bedroom and shouts so loud they can hear him in Poughkeepsie."

Matlock's thoughts shifted quickly to Herron. "His death—his *suicide*—is going to be the biggest shock this campus has had in twenty years. Men like Lucas simply don't die. They certainly don't die like *this*. . . . Does Sam know I saw him?"

"He does. I couldn't withhold that. I told him pretty much what you told me—shorter version, of course. He refuses to believe it. The implications, I mean."

"I don't blame him. They're not easy to believe. What do we do now?"

"We wait. I've made a report. Two lab men from

the Hartford Bureau are out there now. The local police have been called in."

At the mention of the police, Matlock suddenly remembered the patrolman out of uniform in the squash court corridor, who had walked rapidly away at the moment of recognition. He'd told Greenberg and Greenberg had never given him an explanation—if there was one. He asked again.

"What about the cop in the gym?"

"The story's reasonable. At least so far. The Carlyle police are assigned three mornings a week for limited use of the facilities. Town-gown relations. Coincidence."

"You're settling for that?"

"I said, 'so far.' We're running a check on the man. Nothing's turned up but an excellent record."

"He's a bigot, a nasty bastard."

"This may surprise you, but that's no crime. It's guaranteed in the Bill of Rights."

Sam Kressel walked through the bedroom door quickly, emphatically. Matlock saw that he was as close to pure fear as he'd ever seen a man. There was an uncomfortable similarity between Sam's face and the bloodless expression of Lucas Herron before the old man had raced into the woods.

"I heard you come in," Kressel said. "What are we going to *do*? What in hell are we *going to do*? . . . Adrian doesn't believe that absurd story any more than I do! *Lucas Herron! It's insane!*"

"Maybe. But it's true."

"Because *you* say so? How can you be sure? You're no professional in these matters. As I understand it, Lucas admitted he was helping a student through a drug problem."

"He . . . they aren't students."

"I see." Kressel stopped briefly and looked back and forth between Matlock and Greenberg. "Under the circumstances, I demand to know the identities."

"You'll get them," said Greenberg quietly. "Go on. I want to hear why Matlock's so wrong, the story so absurd."

"Because Lucas Herron isn't . . . wasn't the only member of the faculty concerned with these problems. There are dozens of us giving aid, helping wherever we can!"

"I don't follow you." Greenberg stared at Kressel. "So you help. You don't go and kill yourself when a fellow member of the faculty finds out about it."

Sam Kressel removed his glasses and looked momentarily reflective, sad. "There's something else neither of you know about. I've been aware of it for some time but not so knowledgeably as Sealfont. . . . Lucas Herron was a very sick man. One kidney was removed last summer. The other was also cancerous and he knew it. The pain must have been unbearable for him. He hadn't long."

Greenberg watched closely as Kressel returned his glasses to his face. Matlock bent down and crushed out his cigarette in an ashtray on the coffee table. Finally, Greenberg spoke.

"Are you suggesting that there's no relationship between Herron's suicide and Matlock's seeing him this afternoon?"

"I'm not suggesting any such thing. I'm sure there's a relationship. . . . But you didn't know Lucas. His whole life for nearly half a century, except for the war years, was Carlyle University. It's been his total, complete existence. He loved this place more than any man could love a woman, more than any parent a child. I'm sure Jim's told you. If he thought for a moment that his world here was going to be defaced, torn apart—that would be a greater pain than the physical torture his body gave him. What better time to take his own life?"

"*Goddamn you!*" roared Matlock. "You're saying *I killed him!*"

"Perhaps I am," Kressel said quietly. "I hadn't thought of it in those terms. I'm sure Adrian didn't either."

"But that's what you're *saying!* You're saying I went off half-cocked and killed him as much as if I'd slashed his wrists! . . . Well, you weren't there. *I was!*"

Kressel spoke gently. "I didn't say you went off half-cocked. I said you were an amateur. A very well-intentioned amateur. I think Greenberg knows what I mean."

Jason Greenberg looked at Matlock. "There's an old Slovak proverb: 'When the old men kill themselves, the cities are dying.'"

The telephone bell suddenly pierced the air; its sound acted as a jolt to the three men. Matlock answered it, then turned to Greenberg. "It's for you."

"Thanks." The federal agent took the phone from Matlock. "Greenberg. . . . O.K. I understand. When will you know? . . . I'll probably be on the road by then. I'll call you back. Talk later." He replaced the telephone and stood by the desk, his back to Matlock and Kressel. The dean of colleges couldn't contain himself.

"What was it? What happened?"

Greenberg turned and faced them. Matlock thought his eyes seemed sadder than usual, which Matlock had learned was a sign of trouble in Greenberg.

"We're making a request of the police—the courts —for an autopsy."

"*Why?!*" Kressel shouted as he approached the agent. "For God's sake, *why?!* The man killed himself! He was in *pain!* . . . Jesus Christ, you can't *do* this! If news of it gets out . . ."

"We'll handle it quietly."

"That can't be done and you *know* it! It'll leak out and all hell'll break loose around here! I won't *permit* it!"

"You can't stop it. Even I couldn't stop it. There's sufficient evidence to indicate that Herron didn't take his own life. That he was killed." Greenberg smiled wryly at Matlock. "And not by words."

Kressel argued, threatened, made another call to Sealfont, and finally, when it was obvious that all were to no avail, he left Matlock's apartment in fury.

No sooner had Kressel slammed the door than the telephone rang again. Greenberg saw that the sound disturbed Matlock—not merely annoyed him, but disturbed him; perhaps frightened him.

"I'm sorry. . . . I'm afraid this place has to be a kind of patrol base for a while. Not long. . . . Maybe it's the girl."

Matlock picked up the phone, listened, but did not say anything into it. Instead, he turned to Greenberg. He said only one word.

"You."

Greenberg took the telephone, uttered his name softly, and then spent the next minute staring straight ahead. Matlock watched Greenberg for half the time and then wandered into his kitchen. He didn't wish to stand awkwardly to one side while the agent listened to a superior's instructions.

The voice at the other end of the line had initially identified itself by saying, "Washington calling."

On the counter lay the empty envelope in which the brutally hypocritical statement had come from the Department of Justice. It had been one more sign that his worst fantasies were gradually becoming real. From that infinitesimal portion of the mind which concerns itself with the unthinkable, Matlock had begun to perceive that the land he had grown up in was changing into something ugly and destructive. It was far more than a political manifestation, it was a slow, all-embracing sense of morality by strategy. A corruption of intentions. Strong feelings were being replaced with surface anger, convictions and compromise. The land was becoming something other than its promise, its commitment. The grails were empty vessels of flat wine, impressive solely because they were possessed.

"I'm off the phone now. Would you like to try reaching Miss Ballantyne?"

Matlock looked up at Greenberg, standing in the frame of the kitchen door. Greenberg, the walking contradiction, the proverb-quoting agent deeply suspicious of the system for which he worked.

"Yes. Yes, I'd like to." He started into the living room as Greenberg stepped aside to let him pass. Matlock reached the center of the room and stopped. "That's one hell of a quotation. What was it? 'When the old men kill themselves, the cities are dying.'" He turned and looked at the agent. "I think that's the saddest proverb I've ever heard."

"You're not Hassidic. Of course, neither am I, but the Hassidim wouldn't think it sad. . . . Come to think of it, no true philosopher would."

"Why not? It *is* sad."

"It's truth. Truth is neither joyful nor sad, neither good nor bad. It is simply truth."

"Someday let's debate that, Jason." Matlock picked up the telephone, dialed Pat's number, and let it ring a dozen times. There was no answer. Matlock thought of several of Pat's friends and wondered whether to call them or not. When angry or upset, Pat usually did one of two things. She either went off by herself for an hour or so, or, conversely, sought out one or two friends and drove off to a film in Hartford or an out-of-the-way bar. It was just over an hour. He'd give her another fifteen minutes before phoning around. It had, of course, occurred to him that she might have been taken involuntarily—that had been his first thought. But it wasn't logical. The Cheshire Cat had been filled with people, the tables close together. Greenberg was right. Wherever she went, she went because she wanted to go.

Greenberg stood by the kitchen door. He hadn't moved. He'd been watching Matlock.

"I'll try in a quarter of an hour. Then, if there's no answer, I'll call some friends of hers. As you said, she's one strong-willed young lady."

"I hope you're not from the same cloth."

"What does that mean?"

Greenberg took several steps into the living room. When he spoke, he looked directly into Matlock's eyes.

"You're out. Finished. Forget the letter, forget Loring, forget me. . . . That's the way it's got to be. We understand you have reservations for St. Thomas on Pan Am for Saturday. Enjoy it, because that's where you're going. Much better this way."

Matlock returned the government man's look. "Any decision like that will be made by me. I've got a gentle old man on my conscience; and you've got that stinkpot in your pocket. I signed it, remember?"

"The stinkpot doesn't count anymore. D.C. wants you out. You go."

"Why?"

"Because of the gentle old man. If he *was* killed, you could be, too. If that happened, certain records might be subpoenaed, certain men who had reservations about recruiting you might voice those reservations to the press. You were maneuvered. I don't have to tell you that."

"So?"

"The directors at Justice have no wish to be called executioners."

"I see." Matlock took his eyes off Greenberg and wandered toward the coffee table. "Suppose I refuse?"

"Then I remove you from the scene."

"How?"

"I have you arrested on suspicion of murder one."

"*What?*"

"You were the last person of record to see Lucas Herron alive. By your own admission, you went out to his house to threaten him."

"To *warn* him!"

"That's subject to interpretation, isn't it?"

When the thunderous crash came, it was so ear-shattering both men threw themselves to the floor. It was as if the whole side of the building had collapsed in rubble. Dust was everywhere, furniture toppled, glass shattered, splinters of wood and plaster flew through the air, and the terrible stench of burning sulfur settled over the room. Matlock knew the smell of that kind of bomb, and his reflexes knew how to operate. He clung to the base of his couch waiting, waiting for a second explosion—a delayed detonator which would kill any who rose in panic. Through the mist, he saw Greenberg start to get up, and he leaped forward, tackling the agent at his knees.

"Get down! Stay. . . ."

The second explosion came. Parts of the ceiling blackened. But Matlock knew it was not a killer explosive. It was something else, and he could not figure it out at the moment. It was an eyegrabber, a camouflage—not meant to kill, but to deflect all concentration. A huge firecracker.

Screams of panic could now be heard mounting from all parts of the building. The sounds of rushing feet pounded on the floor above his apartment.

And then a single screech of terror from outside Matlock's front door. It would not stop. The horror of it caused Matlock and Greenberg to struggle to their feet and race to the source. Matlock pulled the door open and looked down upon a sight no human being should ever see more than once in a lifetime, if his life must continue beyond that instant.

On his front step was Patricia Ballantyne wrapped in a bloodsoaked sheet. Holes were cut in the areas of her naked breasts, blood flowing from gashes beneath the nipples. The front of her head was shaved; blood poured out of lacerations where once had been the soft brown hair. Blood, too, came from the half-open mouth, her lips bruised and split. The eyes were blackened into deep crevasses of sore flesh—but they moved! The eyes moved!

Saliva began forming at the corners of her lips. The half-dead corpse was trying to speak.

"Jamie . . ." was the only word she managed and then her head slipped to one side.

Greenberg threw his whole weight against Matlock, sending him sprawling into the gathering crowd. He roared orders of "Police!" and "Ambulance!" until he saw enough people running to execute his commands. He put his mouth to the girl's mouth, to force air into the collapsing lungs, but he knew it wasn't really necessary. Patricia Ballantyne wasn't dead; she'd been tortured by experts, and the experts knew their business well. Every slash, every crack, every bruise meant utmost pain but did not mean death.

He started to pick the girl up but Matlock stopped him. The English professor's eyes were swollen with tears of hate. He gently removed Greenberg's hands and lifted Pat into his arms. He carried her inside and stretched her out on the half-destroyed sofa. Greenberg went into the bedroom and returned with a blanket. Then he brought a bowl of warm water from the kitchen and several towels. He lifted the blanket and held a towel beneath the bleeding breasts. Matlock, staring in horror at the brutally beaten face, then took the edge of another towel and began wiping away the blood around the shaven head and the mouth.

"She'll be all right, Jim. I've seen this before. She'll be all right."

And as Greenberg heard the sounds of the sirens in the near distance, he wondered, really, if this girl would ever be right again.

Matlock, helpless, continued to wipe the girl's face, his tears now streaming down his cheeks, his eyes unblinking. He spoke through his controlled sobs.

"You know what this means, don't you? No one

pulls me out now. They try, I'll kill them."

"I won't let them," said Greenberg simply.

The screeching of brakes could be heard outside and the flashing lights of the police cars and the ambulances whipped in circles through the windows.

Matlock's face fell into the cushion beside the unconscious girl and he wept.

Matlock awoke in the antiseptic whiteness of a hospital room. The shade was up, and the sun reflected harshly on the three walls he could see. At his feet a nurse was writing efficiently, emphatically, on top of a clipboard attached to the base of the bed by a thin keychain. He stretched his arms, then quickly brought his left back, aware of a sharp pain in his forearm.

"You feel those the next morning, Mr. Matlock," droned the nurse without looking up from the clipboard. "Heavy intravenous sedations are murder, I can tell you. Not that I've ever had one, but Lord knows, I've seen enough who have."

"Is Pat . . . Miss Ballantyne here?"

"Well, not in the same *room!* Lord, you campus types!"

"She's here?"

"Of course. Next room. Which I intend to keep *locked!* Lord, you people from the hill! . . . There! You're all accounted for." The nurse let the clipboard crash down and vibrate back and forth. "Now. *You've* got special privileges. *You're* allowed breakfast even though it's past breakfast time—*way* past! That's probably because they want you to pay your bill. . . . You can be discharged any time after twelve."

"What time is it? Someone took my watch."

"It's eight minutes to nine," said the nurse, glancing at her wrist. "And no one *took* your watch. It's with any other valuables you had when you were admitted."

"How *is* Miss Ballantyne?"

"We don't discuss other patients, Mr. Matlock."

"Where's her doctor?"

"He's the same as yours, I understand. Not one of *ours*." The nurse made sure the statement was hardly complimentary. "According to your chart, he'll be here at nine thirty unless we phone for an emergency."

"Call him. I want him here as soon as possible."

"Now, really. There's no emergency. . . ."

"Goddamn it, get him here!"

As Matlock raised his voice the door of his room opened. Jason Greenberg came in quickly. "I could hear you in the corridor. That's a good sign."

"How's Pat?"

"Just a minute, sir. We have regulations. . . ."

Greenberg took out his identification and showed it to the nurse. "This man is in my custody, Miss. Check the front desk, if you like, but leave us alone."

The nurse, ever professional, scrutinized the identification and walked rapidly out the door.

"How's Pat?"

"A mess, but with it. She had a bad night; she's going to have a worse morning when she asks for a mirror."

"The hell with that! Is she *all right?*"

"Twenty-seven stitches—body, head, mouth, and, for variety, one on her left foot. But she's going to be fine. X-rays show only bone bruises. No fractures, no ruptures, no internal bleeding. The bastards did their usual professional job."

"Was she able to talk?"

"Not really. And the doctor didn't advise it. She needs sleep more than anything else. . . . You need a little rest, too. That's why we put you here last night."

"Anyone hurt at the apartment?"

"Nope. It was a crazy bombing. We don't think it was intended to kill anyone. The first was a short two-inch stick taped below the window exterior; the second—activated by the first—wasn't much more than a July Fourth rocket. You expected the second blast, didn't you?"

"Yes. I guess I did. . . . Terror tactics, wasn't it?"

"That's what we figure."

"Can I see Pat?"

"Rather you waited. The doctor thinks she'll sleep into the afternoon. There's a nurse in there with ice packs and stuff if localized pain bothers her. Let her rest."

Matlock cautiously sat up on the edge of the bed. He began flexing his legs, arms, neck, and hands, and found that he wasn't much below par. "I feel sort of like a hangover without the headache."

"The doctor gave you a heavy dose. You were . . . understandably . . . very emotional."

"I remember everything. I'm calmer, but I don't retract one goddamned word. . . . I have two classes today. One at ten and the other at two. I want to make them."

"You don't have to. Sealfont wants to see you."

"I'll talk to him after my last class. . . . Then I'll see Pat." Matlock stood on his feet and walked slowly to the large hospital window. It was a bright, sunlit morning; Connecticut had had a string of beautiful days. As he stared outside, Matlock remembered that he'd looked out another window five days ago when he'd first met Jason Greenberg. He'd made a decision then as he was making one now. "Last night you said you wouldn't let them pull me out. I hope you haven't changed your mind. I'm *not* going to be on that Pan Am flight tomorrow."

"You won't be arrested. I promised you that."

"Can you prevent it? You also said you were going to be replaced."

"I can prevent it. . . . I can morally object, an enigmatic phrase which is translated to mean I can embarrass people. However, I don't want to mislead you. If you create problems, you could be taken into protective custody."

"They can if they can find me."

"That's a condition I don't like."

"Forget you heard it. Where are my clothes?" Matlock walked to the single closet door and opened it. His slacks, jacket, and shirt were hung on hangers; his loafers were on the floor with his socks carefully inserted. The lone bureau held his undershorts and a hospital-furnished toothbrush. "Will you go down and see whoever you've got to see to get me out of here? Also, I'll need my wallet, cash, and watch. Will you do that, please?"

"What do you mean—if they could find you? What are you going to do?" Greenberg made no move to leave.

"Nothing earth-shattering. Merely continue making those inquiries . . . of a minor nature. That's the way the statement from your employers phrased it, wasn't it? Loring said it. Somewhere out there is the other half of that paper. I'm going to find it."

"You listen to me first! I don't deny you have a right . . ."

"You don't *deny!*" Matlock turned on the federal

agent. His voice was controlled but vicious. "That's not good enough. That's *negative* approval! I've got several *big* rights! They include a kid brother in a sailboat, a black son of a bitch named Dunois or whatever you call him, a man by the name of Lucas Herron, and that girl in there! I suspect you and the doctor know the rest of what happened to her last night, and I can *guess!* Don't talk to me about *a right!*"

"In principle, we agree. I just don't want your 'rights' to land you next to your brother. This is a job for professionals. Not an amateur! If you work at all, I want you to work with whoever takes my place. That's important. I want your word on it."

Matlock took off the top of his pajamas and gave Greenberg a short, embarrassed smile. "You have it. I don't really see myself as a one-man ranger team. Do you know who's taking your place?"

"Not yet. Probably someone from D.C. They won't take a chance on using a Hartford or a New Haven man. . . . The truth is . . . they don't know who's been bought. He'll be in touch. I'll have to brief him myself. No one else can. I'll instruct him to identify himself with . . . what would you like?"

"Tell him to use your proverb. 'When the old men kill themselves, the cities are dying.'"

"You like that, don't you?"

"I don't like it or dislike it. It's simply the truth. Isn't that the way it should be?"

"And very applicable. I see what you mean."

"Very."

"Jim, before I go this afternoon, I'm going to write out a telephone number for you. It's a Bronx number —my parents. They won't know where I am, but I'll check with them every day. Use it if you have to."

"Thanks, I will."

"I want your word on it."

"You have it." Matlock laughed a short laugh of gratitude.

"Of course, under the circumstances, I may just be on the other end of the line if you do call."

"Back in private practice?"

"The possibility is less remote than you think."

15

Between his two classes, Matlock drove to the small brokerage office in the town of Carlyle and emerged with a check for $7,312. It represented his total investment in the market, mostly from royalties. The broker had tried to dissuade him; it was no time to sell, especially at current prices. But Matlock had made up his mind. The cashier reluctantly issued the check.

From there Matlock went to his bank and transferred his entire savings into his checking account. He added the $7,312 to the slip and looked at the sum total of his immediate cash value.

It came to $11,501.72.

Matlock stared at the figure for several minutes. He had mixed feelings about it. On the one hand, it proved solvency; on the other, it was a little frightening to think that after thirty-three years of living he was able to pinpoint so accurately his net financial worth. There was no house, no land, no hidden investments anywhere. Only an automobile, a few possessions of minor value, and some published words of such a specialized nature that there would be no significant commercial rewards.

Yet by many standards, it was a great deal of money.

Only nowhere *near* enough. He knew that. It was why Scarsdale, New York, was on the day's schedule.

The meeting with Sealfont had been unnerving, and Matlock wasn't sure how much more his shattered nerves could take. The cold fury of Carlyle's president was matched only by the depth of his anguish.

The bewildering shadow world of violence and corruption was a world he could never come to grips with because it was not within the realm of his comprehension. Matlock had been startled to hear Sealfont say, as he sat in his chair staring out the bay window overlooking the most beautiful lawn on the Carlyle campus, that he might well resign.

"If this whole sordid, unbelievable business is true —and who can doubt it—I have no right to sit in this chair."

"That's not so," Matlock had answered. "If it's true, this place is going to need you more than ever before."

"A blind man? No one needs a blind man. Not in this office."

"Not blind. Unexposed."

And then Sealfont had swung around in his chair and pounded on the top of his desk in an enormous display of strength.

"Why *here*?! Why *here*?!"

As he sat in front of Sealfont's desk, Matlock looked at the pained face of Carlyle's president. And for a second he thought the man might weep.

The trip down the Merritt Parkway was made at high speed. He had to race; it was necessary for him. It helped take his mind off the sight of Pat Ballantyne as he had seen her a few minutes before leaving. He had gone from Sealfont's to the hospital; still he hadn't been able to talk with her. No one had yet.

She had awakened at noon, he'd been told. She'd gone into severe hysterics. The doctor from Litchfield had administered further sedatives. The doctor was worried, and Matlock knew it was Pat's mind he was worried about. The nightmare of terror inflicted upon her body had to touch her brain.

The first minutes with his parents at the huge Scarsdale house were awkward. His father, Jonathan Munro Matlock, had spent decades in the highest spheres of his marketplace and knew instinctively when a man came to him without strength.

Without strength but with need.

Matlock told his father as simply and unemotionally as he could that he wanted to borrow a large sum of money; he could not guarantee its repayment. It would be used to help—ultimately help—young people like his dead brother.

The dead son.

"How?" asked Jonathan Matlock softly.

"I can't tell you that." He looked into his father's eyes and the irrevocable truth of the son's statement was accepted by the father.

"Very well. Are you qualified for this undertaking?"

"Yes. I am."

"Are there others involved?"

"By necessity, yes."

"Do you trust them?"

"I do."

"Have they asked for this money?"

"No. They don't know about it."

"Will it be at their disposal?"

"No. Not that I can foresee. . . . I'll go further than that. It would be wrong for them to learn of it."

"I'm not restricting you, I'm asking."

"That's my answer."

"And you believe that what you're doing will help, in some way, boys like David? Practical help, not theoretical, not dream stuff, not charity."

"Yes. It has to."

"How much do you want?"

Matlock took a deep breath silently. "Fifteen thousand dollars."

"Wait here."

Several minutes later, the father came out of his study and gave the son an envelope.

The son knew better than to open it.

Ten minutes after the exchange—and Matlock knew it *was* an exchange—he left, feeling the eyes of his parents as they stood on the enormous porch and watched him drive out through the gates.

Matlock pulled into the apartment driveway, shut off the lights and the engine, and wearily climbed out. As he approached the old Tudor house, he saw that every light he owned was turned on. Jason Greenberg wasn't taking chances, and Matlock assumed that some part of Greenberg's silent, unseen army was watching his place from varying distances—none too far away.

He unlocked the door and pushed it open. There was no one there. At least, not in sight. Not even his cat.

"Hello? Jason? . . . Anybody here? It's Matlock."

There was no answer and Matlock was relieved. He wanted only to crawl into bed and sleep. He'd stopped at the hospital to see Pat, and the request had been denied. At least he'd learned that ". . . she is resting and her condition is deemed satisfactory." That was a step up. That afternoon she'd still been on the critical list. He would see her at nine in the morning.

Now was the time for him to sleep—peaceably if possible. Sleep at all costs. There was a great deal to do in the morning.

He went into his bedroom, passing the still unrepaired sections of wall and window as he did so. Carpenter's and plasterer's tools were neatly stacked in corners. He removed his jacket and his shirt and then thought, with a degree of self-ridicule, that he was becoming far too confident. He walked rapidly out of the bedroom and into his bathroom. Once the door was shut, he reached down to the litter box and lifted up the newspaper to the layer of canvas. The Corsican paper was there, the tarnished silver coating reflecting the light.

Back in the bedroom, Matlock removed his wallet, cash, and car keys, placing them on top of his bureau. As he did so, he remembered the envelope.

He hadn't been fooled. He knew his father, perhaps better than his father realized. He presumed there was a short note with the check stating clearly that the money was a gift, not a loan, and that no repayment was anticipated.

The note was there, folded inside the envelope, but the written words were not what Matlock expected.

I believe in you. I always have.
Love,
Dad

On top of the note, clipped to the paper on the reverse side, was the check. Matlock slipped it off and read the figure.

It was for fifty thousand dollars.

Much of the swelling on her face and around her eyes had subsided. He took her hand and held it tightly, putting his face once more next to hers.

"You're going to be fine," were the innocuous words he summoned. He had to hold himself in check to stop himself from screaming out his anger and his guilt. That this could be done to a human being by other human beings was beyond his endurance. And he was responsible.

When she spoke, her voice was hardly audible, like a small child's, the words only partially formed through the immobile lips.

"Jamie . . . Jamie?"

"Shh . . . Don't talk if it hurts."

"*Why?*"

"I don't know. But we'll find out."

"No! . . . No, don't! They're . . . they're . . ." The girl had to swallow; it was nearly impossible for her. She pointed to a glass of water on the bedside table. Matlock quickly reached for it and held it to her lips, supporting her by the shoulders.

"How did it happen? Can you tell me?"

"Told . . . Greenberg. Man and woman . . . came to the table. Said you were . . . waiting . . . outside."

"Never mind, I'll talk to Jason."

"I . . . feel better. I hurt but . . . feel better, I . . . really do. . . . Am I going to be all right?"

"Of course you are. I spoke with the doctor. You're bruised, but nothing broken, nothing serious. He says you'll be out of bed in a few days, that's all."

Patricia Ballantyne's eyes brightened, and Matlock saw the terrible attempt of a smile on her sutured lips. "I fought. . . . I fought and I fought . . . until I . . . couldn't remember any more."

It took all of Matlock's strength not to burst into tears. "I know you did. Now, no more talking. You rest, take it easy. I'll just sit here and we'll talk with our eyes. Remember? You said we always communicate around other people with our eyes. . . . I'll tell you a dirty joke."

When the smile came, it *was* from her eyes.

He stayed until a nurse forbade him to stay longer. Then he kissed her softly on the lips and left the room. He was a relieved man; he was an angry man.

"Mr. Matlock?" The young doctor with the freshly scrubbed face of an intern approached him by the elevator.

"Yes?"

"There's a telephone call for you. You can take it at the second floor reception, if you'll follow me."

The caller's voice was unknown. "Mr. Matlock, my name's Houston. I'm a friend of Jason Greenberg's. I'm to get in touch with you."

"Oh? How's Jason?"

"Fine. I'd like to get together with you as soon as possible."

Matlock was about to name a place, any place, after his first class. And then he stopped. "Did Jason leave any message . . . where he is now, or anything?"

"No sir. Just that I was to make contact pronto."

"I see." Why didn't the man say it? Why didn't Houston identify himself? "Greenberg definitely told me he'd leave word . . . a message . . . where he'd be. I'm sure he said that."

"Against department regulations, Mr. Matlock. He wouldn't be allowed to."

"Oh? . . . Then he didn't leave any message at all?"

The voice on the other end of the line hesitated slightly, perceptively. "He may have forgotten. . . . As a matter of fact, I didn't speak to him myself. I received my orders directly from Washington. Where shall we meet?"

Matlock heard the anxiety in the man's voice. When he referred to Washington, his tone had risen in a small burst of nervous energy. "Let me call you later. What's your number?"

"Now listen, Matlock. I'm in a telephone booth and we have to meet. I've got my orders!"

"Yes, I'll bet you do. . . ."

"What?"

"Never mind. Are you downtown? In Carlyle?"

The man hesitated again. "I'm in the area."

"Tell me, Mr. Houston. . . . Is the city dying?"

"What? What are you talking about?"

"I'm going to be late for my class. Try me again. I'm sure you'll be able to reach me." Matlock hung up the phone. His left hand shook and perspiration had formed on his brow.

Mr. Houston was the enemy.

The enemy was closing in.

His first Saturday class was at eleven, which gave him just about an hour to make what he felt were the most logical arrangements for the money. He didn't want to think that he had to physically be in the town of Carlyle—at the Carlyle Bank—on Monday morning. He wasn't sure it would be possible. He wasn't sure where he would be on Monday.

Since, on the surface, Carlyle was a typical New England college town, it had a particular way of life common to such places. One knew, generally on a first-name basis, all the people whose jobs made day-to-day living the effortless, unhurried existence that it was. The garage mechanic was "Joe" or "Mac," the manager at J. Press was "Al," the dentist "John" or "Warren," the girl at the dry cleaners "Edith." In Matlock's case, the banker was "Alex." Alex Anderson, a Carlyle graduate of forty, a local boy who'd made the jump from town to gown and then coordinated both. Matlock called him at home and explained his problem. He was carrying around a large check from his father. He was making some private family investments in his own name, and they were confidential. Since the robbery at his apartment, he wanted to divest himself of the check immèdiately. Could Alex suggest anything? Should he put it in the mail? How best to get it into his account, since he wasn't sure he would be in Carlyle on Monday, and he needed it cleared, the money available. Alex Anderson suggested the obvious. Matlock should endorse the check, put it in an envelope marked for Anderson's attention, and drop it in the night deposit box at the bank. Alex would take care of the rest first thing Monday morning.

And then Alex Anderson asked him the denomination and Matlock told him.

The account problem solved, Matlock concentrated on what he began to think of as his point of departure. There was no other phrase he could find, and he needed a phrase—he needed the discipline of a

definition. He had to start precisely right, knowing
that what might follow could be totally *undisciplined*
—completely without plan or orthodoxy. For he had
made up his mind.

He was going to enter the world of Nimrod. The
builder of Babylon and Nineveh, the hunter of wild
animals, the killer of children and old men, the beater
of women.

He was going to find Nimrod.

As were most adults not wedded to the precept
that all things enjoyable were immoral, Matlock was
aware that the state of Connecticut, like its sister
states to the north, the south, and the west, was in-
habited by a network of men only too eager to supply those divertissements frowned upon by the pul-
pits and the courts. What Hartford insurance executive in the upper brackets never heard of that string
of "Antique Shoppes" on New Britain Avenue where
a lithe young girl's body could be had for a reasonable amount of petty cash? What commuter from Old
Greenwich was oblivious to the large estates north of
Green Farms where the gambling often rivaled the
Vegas stakes? How many tired businessmen's wives
from New Haven or Westport were really ignorant of
the various "escort" services operating out of Hamden and Fairfield? And over in the "old country," the
Norfolks? Where the rambling mansions were fading
apotheoses to the *real* money, the blooded first families who migrated just a little west to avoid the new
rich? The "old country" had the strangest diversions,
it was rumored. Houses in shadows, lighted by candles, where the bored could become aroused by observation. Voyeurs of the sickest scenes. Female, male,
animal—all types, all combinations.

Matlock knew that in this world Nimrod could be found. It had to be. For although narcotics were but one aspect of the services rendered within this network, they were available—as was everything else.

And of all these games of indulgence, none had the fire and ice, none had the magnetism, of the gambling houses. For those thousands who couldn't find time for the junkets to San Juan, London, or Paradise Island, there were the temporary excursions into the manic moments where daily boredom could be forgotten—a stone's throw from home. Reputations were made quickly over the green felt tables—with the roll of the dice or a turn of a card. It was here that Matlock would find his point of departure. It was in these places where a young man of thirty-three years was prepared to lose thousands—until someone asked who he was.

At twelve thirty Matlock walked across the quadrangle toward his apartment. The time had come to initiate his first move. The vague outline of a plan was coming into focus.

He should have heard the footsteps, but he didn't. He only heard the cough, a smoker's cough, the cough of a man who'd been running.

"Mr. Matlock?"

Matlock turned and saw a man in his middle thirties, like himself, perhaps a bit older and, indeed, out of breath.

"Yes?"

"Sorry, I keep missing you. I got to the hospital just as you'd left, then waited in the wrong damn building for you, after your class. There's a very confused biology teacher with a name similar to yours. Even looks a little like you. Same height, build, hair . . ."

"That's Murdock. Elliott Murdock. What's the matter?"

"He couldn't understand why I kept insisting that when 'old men kill themselves, the cities are dying'!"

"You're from Greenberg!"

"That's it. Morbid code, if you don't mind my saying so. Keep walking. We'll separate at the end of the path. Meet me in twenty minutes at Bill's Bar & Grill by the freight depot. It's six blocks south of the railroad station. O.K.?"

"Never heard of it."

"I was going to suggest you remove your necktie. I'll be in a leather jacket."

"You pick classy spots."

"Old habit. I cheat on the expense account."

"Greenberg said I was to work with you."

"You better believe it! He's up to his Kosher ass in boiling oil for you. I think they're shipping him out to a job in Cairo. . . . He's one hell of a guy. We field men like him. Don't louse him up."

"All I wanted to ask was your name. I didn't expect a sermon."

"It's Houston. Fred Houston. See you in twenty minutes. Get rid of the tie."

Bill's Bar & Grill was a part of Carlyle Matlock had never seen before. Railroad laborers and freight-yard drifters were its predominant clientele. He scanned the filthy room; Houston sat in a back booth.

"It's cocktail hour, Matlock. A little early by campus standards, but the effects aren't much different. Not even the clothes these days."

"It's quite a place."

"It serves the purpose. Go up to the bar and get yourself a drink. The bunnies don't come on till sundown."

Matlock did as Houston instructed and brought back the best bourbon he could find. It was a brand he had given up when he reached a living wage.

"I think I should tell you right away. Someone using your name telephoned me at the hospital."

It was as if Houston had been hit in the stomach. "My God," he said quietly. "What did he say? How did you handle it?"

"I waited for him to identify himself . . . with Greenberg's proverb. I gave him a couple of chances but he didn't. . . . So I told him to call me later and hung up."

"He used *my* name?! *Houston.* You're sure?"

"Absolutely."

"That doesn't make sense. He *couldn't!*"

"Believe me. He did."

"No one knew I was the replacement. . . . *I* didn't know it until three this morning."

"Someone found out."

Houston took several swallows of his beer. "If what you say is true, I'll be out of here within a couple of hours. Incidentally, that was good thinking. . . . Let me give you an extra hint, though. Never accept a contact made by telephone."

"Why not?"

"If that *had* been me calling—how would *I* know it was *you* I was talking to?"

"I see what you mean. . . ."

"Common sense. Most everything we do is common sense. . . . We'll keep the same code. The 'old men' and 'the cities.' Your next contact will be made to-night."

"You're sure you'll be leaving?"

"I've been *spotted.* I'm not *about* to stick around. Maybe you forgot Ralph Loring. . . . We gave big at the office."

"All right. Have you talked to Jason? Did he brief you?"

"For two hours. From four till six this morning. My wife said he drank thirteen cups of coffee."

"What can you tell me about Pat? Patricia Ballan-tyne. What happened?"

"You know the medical facts. . . ."

"Not all of them."

"I don't know *all* of them, either."

"You're lying."

Houston looked at Matlock without offense. When he replied, he did so compassionately. "All right.

There was evidence of rape. That's what you want to know, isn't it?"

Matlock gripped his glass. "Yes," he said softly.

"However, you should know this, too. The girl doesn't know it. Not at this stage of her recovery. I understand the mind plays tricks. It rejects things until it thinks—or something tells it—that the remembering can be handled."

"Thanks for the lesson in psychology. . . . Animals. Filthy animals . . ." Matlock pushed his glass away. The liquor was intolerable to him now. The thought of dulling his senses even slightly was abhorrent.

"I'm supposed to play this by ear, so if I read you wrong, all I can do is apologize. . . . Be around when the puzzle gets put together for her. She's going to need you."

Matlock looked up from the table, from the sight of his tensed hands. "It was that bad?" he asked almost inaudibly.

"Preliminary lab tests—fingernails, hair, what have you—indicate that the assault was carried out by more than one person."

Matlock's hatred could find only one expression. He closed his eyes and lashed out at the glass, sending it across the floor, where it smashed in front of the bar. The bartender dropped his soiled rag and started toward his latch, looking over at the man who threw the glass. Then he stopped. Houston held up a bill quickly, gesturing the man to stay away.

"Get hold of yourself!" Houston said. "You're not going to do anyone any good like that. You're just calling attention to us. . . . Now, listen. You're cleared to make further inquiries, but there are two stipulations. The first is to check with our man—it was supposed to be me—before approaching anyone. The second—keep your subjects to students and only students. No faculty, no staff, no one outside—just students. . . . Make your reports every night between ten and eleven. Your contact will reach you daily as to where. Have you got that?"

Matlock stared at the agent in disbelief. He understood what the man was saying—even why he said it —but he couldn't believe that anyone who'd been briefed by Jason Greenberg would think he could deliver such instructions. "Are you serious?"

"The orders are explicit. No deviations. That's holy writ."

It was there again for Matlock. Another sign, another compromise. Another plastic order from the unseen plastic leaders.

"I'm there but I'm *not* there, is that the idea? I'm consigned to the outer limits and that fulfills the bargain?"

"Frig that."

Matlock's eyes wandered upward, at nothing. He was trying to buy a few seconds of sweet reason. "Frigga is the Norse goddess of the sky. She shares the heavens with Odin. Don't insult the lady, Houston."

"You're a nut!" said the agent. "I'm not sorry I'm getting out of here. . . . Look, it's for the best, take my word for it. And one last thing. I've got to take back the paper Loring gave you. That's a *must do.*"

"Is it, really?" Matlock slid across the filthy leatherette seat and started to get up. "I don't see it that way. You go back to Washington and tell them I see it as a *must don't.* Take care of yourself, holy writ."

"You're playing around with preventive custody!"

"We'll see who's playing," said Matlock as he pushed himself away from the table, angling it to block the agent's exit, and started for the door. He could hear the screech of the table's legs as Houston moved it out of his way. He heard Houston call his name softly, intensely, as if he were confused, wanting to make Matlock come back, yet afraid of identifying him. Matlock reached the door, turned right on the sidewalk, and started running as fast as he could. He found a narrow alley and realized that it was, at least, in the right direction. He raced into it and stopped, pressing himself into a doorway. At the base of the alley, on the freight-yard thorough-fare, he saw Houston walking rapidly past the phleg-matic noonday laborers on their lunch breaks. Houston looked panicked; Matlock knew he couldn't return to his apartment.

It was a funny thing to do, he considered, as he sat in the booth of Bill's Bar & Grill. Returning to the place he couldn't wait to get out of twenty minutes ago. But it made vague sense to him—as much as anything made sense at the moment. He had to be by himself and think. He couldn't take the chance of wandering the streets where some part of the Green-berg-Houston unseen army might spot him. Ironical-ly, the bar seemed safest.

He'd made his apologies to a wary bartender, offer-ing to pay for the broken glass. He implied that the man he'd had words with before was a deadbeat—into him for a lot of money with no ability to pay. This explanation, given by the now-relaxed customer, was not only accepted by the bartender, it elevated him to a status not often seen in Bill's Bar & Grill.

He had to marshal his thoughts. There were check-points he'd mentally outlined which were to be passed before he began his journey to Nimrod. Now, there was another checkpoint. Houston had supplied it, although he'd never know. Pat had to be totally safe. He couldn't have that worry on his mind. All other items on his list were subservient to this. The clothes, the ready cash, the unfamiliar automobile, all would have to wait. He might have to alter his strategy now, Matlock thought. Nimrod's associates would be watched, his apartment would be watched, every name and location on the Justice list would be under surveillance.

But first, Pat. He'd have her guarded night and day, around the clock, every minute. Guarded openly, with no pretense of secrecy. Guarded in such a way as to be a signal to both the unseen armies, a warning that she was out of the game. Money was no problem now, none at all. And there were men in Hartford whose professions would fit his requirements. He knew that. The huge insurance companies used them incessantly. He remembered an ex-faculty member from the math department who'd left Carlyle for the lucrative field of insurance actuaries. He worked for Aetna. He looked for a telephone inside the dingy bar.

Eleven minutes later, Matlock returned to the booth. The business was concluded with Blackstone Security, Incorporated, Bond Street, Hartford. There would be three men daily on eight-hour shifts, three hundred dollars for each twenty-four-hour period the subject was covered by Blackstone, Inc. There would, of course, be the additional charges for any expenses incurred and a fee attached for the use of a "Tel-electronic" if it was required. The Tel-electronic was a small device which signaled the bearer with short beeps if the telephone number designated was called. Blackstone, of course, suggested a different telephone number from a resident phone—which, of course, they

would have activated within twelve hours and for
which, of course, there was an additional charge.

Matlock agreed to everything, was grateful *for* everything, and said he'd be in Hartford to sign the
papers later in the afternoon. He wanted to meet Mr.
Blackstone—for another reason now. Blackstone, however, made it clear that since the head of Aetna's
actuarial department had personally contacted him
regarding Mr. Matlock, the formalities were not pressing. He'd dispatch his team to the Carlyle Hospital
within the hour. And by any chance, was Mr. Matlock related to Jonathan Munro Matlock . . . ? The
head of Aetna's actuarial department had mentioned . . .

Matlock was relieved. Blackstone *could* be useful.
The ex-faculty member at Aetna had assured him that
there was none better than Blackstone. Expensive, but
the best. Blackstone's personnel for the most part
were former officers of the Special Forces and Marine
Intelligence team. It was more than a business gimmick. They were smart, resourceful, and tough. They
were also licensed and respected by the state and local police.

The next item on his list was clothes. He had
planned to go to his apartment and pack a suit, several pairs of slacks, and a jacket or two. Now that was
out. At least for the time being. He would buy clothes
—what he needed—as he went along. The ready cash
could prove more of a problem, considering the
amount he wanted. It was Saturday—he wasn't going
to waste a Saturday night. The banks were closed, the
large money sources unavailable.

Alex Anderson would have to solve the problem.
He'd lie to Alex Anderson, tell him Jonathan Munro
Matlock would look kindly—financially kindly—on

Anderson if the banker would made available a large sum of cash on a Saturday afternoon. It would be confidential on both sides, of course. There would be a gratuity rendered for a coveted favor on a Saturday afternoon. Nothing which could be construed remotely indelicate. And, of course, again, confidential.

Matlock rose from the ripped, stained, dirty leatherette seat and returned to the telephone.

Anderson had only fleeting doubts about accommodating Jonathan Munro Matlock's son, and they concerned not the act but the confidence of the act. Once that concern was allayed, the fact that he was giving aid in the best traditions of banking became clear. It was important for any bank to accommodate the better client. If a particular client wished to show gratitude . . . well, that was up to the client.

Alex Anderson would secure James Matlock five thousand dollars in cash on a Saturday afternoon. He would deliver it to him at three outside the Plaza Movie Theatre, which was showing a revival of *A Knife in the Water*—with subtitles.

An automobile would be the least of his problems. There were two rent-a-car offices in the town, a Budget-National and a Luxor-Elite. The first for students, the second for affluent parents. He would rent a Luxor Cadillac or Lincoln and drive into Hartford to another Luxor lot and change cars. From Hartford he'd go to a Luxor branch in New Haven and do the same. With money, there would be the minimum of questions; with decent tips, there might even be cooperation.

He'd moved to his point of departure.

"Hey, mister. Your name Matlock?" The hairy bartender leaned over the table, the soiled bar rag squeezed in his right hand.

"Yes," answered the startled Matlock with a short, violent intake of breath.

"Guy just came up t' me. Said for me to tell you you forgot something outside. On the curb, he said. You should hurry, he said."

Matlock stared at the man. The pain in his stomach was the fear again, the panic. He reached into his pocket and pulled out several bills. Separating a five, he held it up to the bartender. "Come to the door with me. Just to the window. Tell me if he's outside."

"Sure. . . . To the window." The hairy bartender switched the soiled rag to his left hand and took the bill. Matlock got out of the booth and walked beside the man to the half-curtained, filthy glass looking out on the street. "No, he's not there. There's no one there. . . . Just a dead . . ."

"I see," said Matlock, cutting the man off. He didn't have to go outside, it wasn't necessary.

Lying on the edge of the curb, its body draping down into the gutter, was Matlock's cat.

Its head was severed, held to the rest of its body by a small piece of flesh. The blood poured out, staining the sidewalk.

The killing preyed on Matlock's mind as he approached the West Hartford town line. Was it another warning or had they found the paper? If they *had* found the paper, it didn't vitiate the warning, only reinforced it. He wondered whether to have a member of the Blackstone team check his apartment, check the litter box. He wasn't even sure why he hesitated. Why not have a Blackstone man find out? For three hundred dollars a day, plus charges, such an errand was hardly too much to ask. He was going to ask far more of Blackstone, Incorporated, but they didn't know it. Yet he kept balking. If the paper *was* secure, sending a man to check it might reveal its location.

He'd almost made up his mind to take the chance when he noticed the tan sedan in his rear-view mirror. It was there again. It had been there, off and on, since he'd entered Highway 72 a half hour ago. Whereas other cars turned off, passed him, or fell behind, this tan sedan was never really out of sight. Weaving in and around the traffic, it always managed to stay three or four cars behind him. There was one way to find out if it was coincidence. Off the next exit into West Hartford was a narrow street which wasn't a street at all but a cobblestone alley used almost exclusively for deliveries. He and Pat thought it was a shortcut one hectic afternoon and had been hemmed in for five minutes.

He swung off the exit and down the main street toward the alley. He made a sharp left and entered the narrow cobblestone lane. Since it was Saturday afternoon, there were no delivery trucks, and the alley was clear. He raced through, emerging in a crowded A & P parking lot, which in turn led to a parallel main road. Matlock drove to an empty parking space, shut off his motor, and lowered himself on the seat. He angled his side-view mirror so that it reflected the entrance of the alley. In roughly thirty seconds, the tan sedan came into view.

The driver was obviously confused. He slowed down, looking at the dozens of automobiles. Suddenly, behind the tan sedan, another car began blowing its horn. The driver was impatient; the tan sedan was blocking his progress. Reluctantly, the driver of the tan sedan started up; but before he did, he turned his face, craning his neck over his right shoulder in such a way that Matlock, now looking directly at the automobile, recognized him.

It was the patrolman. The police officer who'd been in his demolished apartment after the Beeson episode, the man who had covered his face with a towel and raced down the corridor of squash alley two days ago.

Greenberg's "coincidence."

Matlock was perplexed. He was also frightened.

The patrolman in mufti drove the tan sedan haltingly toward a parking lot exit, still obviously searching. Matlock saw the car turn into the flow of traffic and drive away.

The offices of Blackstone Security, Incorporated, Bond Street, Hartford, looked more like a wealthy, sedate insurance company than an investigatory agency. The furniture was heavy colonial, the wallpaper a subdued, masculine stripe. Expensive hunting prints above the glow of brass table lamps. The effect was immediately one of strength, virility, and financial solidity. Why not? thought Matlock, as he sat in the Early American two-seater in the outer office. At three hundred dollars a day, Blackstone Security, Incorporated, probably rivaled Prudential in ratio of investment to profits.

When he was at last ushered into the office, Michael Blackstone rose from his chair and walked around the cherrywood desk to greet him. Blackstone was a short, compact man, neatly dressed. He was in his early fifties, obviously a physical person, very active, probably very tough.

"Good afternoon," he said. "I hope you didn't drive down here just for the papers. They could have waited. Just because *we* work seven days a week, doesn't mean we expect the rest of the world to do so."

"I had to be in Hartford, anyway. No problem."

"Sit down, sit down. Can I offer you anything? A drink? Coffee?"

"No thanks." Matlock sat in a huge black leather chair, the kind of chair usually found in the oldest, most venerated men's clubs. Blackstone returned to his desk. "Actually, I'm in somewhat of a hurry. I'd like to sign our agreement, pay you, and leave."

"Certainly. The file's right here." Blackstone picked up a folder on his desk and smiled. "As I mentioned on the phone, there are questions we'd like answered, of course. Beyond what you've instructed us to do. It would help us carry out your orders. Take just a few minutes."

Matlock expected the request. It was part of his plan, why he wanted to see Blackstone. His assumption—once Blackstone entered the picture—was that Blackstone might be able to offer him shortcuts. Perhaps not willingly, but if it was a question of "an additional charge." . . . It was for this reason that he had to meet Blackstone face to face. If Blackstone could be bought, a great deal of time could be saved.

"I'll answer what I can. As I'm sure you've checked out, the girl was beaten severely."

"We know that. What puzzles us is the reluctance of anyone to say why. No one's given that sort of beating for kicks. Oh, it's possible, but that kind of case is generally handled quickly and efficiently by the police. There's no need for us. . . . Obviously you have information the police don't have."

"That's true. I do."

"May I ask why you haven't given it to them? Why you hired us? . . . The local police will gladly furnish protection if there's sufficient cause, and far less expensively."

"You sound like you're turning away business."

"We often do." Blackstone smiled. "It's never done happily, I can tell you that."

"Then why . . ."

"You're a highly recommended client," interrupted Blackstone, "the son of a very prominent man. We want you to know your alternatives. That's our reasoning. What's yours?"

"You're plainspoken. I appreciate it. I assume what you're saying is that you don't want your reputation tarnished."

"That's good enough."

"Good. That's my reasoning, too. Only it's not *my* reputation. It's the girl's. Miss Ballantyne's. . . . The

simplest way to put it is that she showed bad judgment in her choice of friends. She's a brilliant girl
with an exciting future, but unfortunately that intelligence didn't carry over into other areas." Matlock
purposely stopped and took out a pack of cigarettes.
Unhurriedly, he removed one and lit it. The pause
had its effect. Blackstone spoke.

"Did she profit financially from these associations?"

"Not at all. As I see it, she was used. But I can understand why you asked. There's a lot of money to be
made on campuses these days, isn't there?"

"I wouldn't know. Campuses aren't our field."
Blackstone smiled again, and Matlock knew he was
lying. Professionally, of course.

"I guess not."

"All right, Mr. Matlock. Why was she beaten?
And what do you intend to do about it?"

"It's my opinion she was beaten to frighten her
from revealing information *she doesn't have.* I intend
to find the parties involved and tell them that. Tell
them to leave her alone."

"And if you go to the police, her associations—past
associations, I assume—become a matter of record
and jeopardize this brilliant future of hers."

"Exactly."

"That's a tight story. . . . Who are these parties involved?"

"I don't know them by name. . . . However, I
know their occupations. The main line of work seems
to be gambling. I thought you might be able to help
me here. Naturally, I would expect an additional
charge for the service."

"I see." Blackstone got up and walked around his
chair. For no particular reason, he fingered the dials

on his inoperative air conditioner. "I think you presume too much."

"I wouldn't expect names. I'd like them, of course, and I'd pay well for them. . . . But I'd settle for locations. I can find them myself, and you know I can. You'd be saving me time, though."

"I gather you're interested in . . . private clubs. *Private* social organizations where members may meet to pursue activities of their choice."

"Outside the eye of the law. Where private citizens can follow their perfectly natural inclinations to place bets. That's where I'd like to start."

"Could I dissuade you? Is it possible I could convince you to go to the police, instead?"

"No."

Blackstone walked to a file cabinet on the left wall, took out a key, and opened it. "As I said, a tight story. Very plausible. And I don't believe a word of it. . . . However, you seem determined; that concerns me." He took a thin metal case from the file cabinet and carried it back to the desk. Selecting another key from his chain, he unlocked it and withdrew a single sheet of paper. "There's a Xerox machine over there," he said, pointing to a large gray copier in the corner. "To use it one places a page face down under the metal flap and dials the required duplicates. Records are kept of the numbers automatically. There's rarely a reason for more than one. . . . If you'll excuse me for approximately two minutes, Mr. Matlock, I must make a phone call in another office."

Blackstone held up the single sheet of paper, then placed it face down on top of Matlock's file folder. He stood erect, and, with the fingers of both hands, tugged at the base of his jacket in the manner of a man used to displaying expensive suits. He smiled and walked around his desk toward the office door. He opened it and turned back.

"It may be what you're looking for, and then again, it may not. I wouldn't know. I've simply left a confidential memorandum on my desk. The charge will be listed on your billing as . . . additional surveillance."

He went out the door, closing it firmly behind him. Matlock rose from the black leather chair and crossed behind the desk. He turned the paper over and read the typed heading.

FOR SURVEILLANCE: HARTFORD—NEW HAVEN AXIS
PRIVATE CLUBS: LOCATIONS AND CONTACTS (MANAGERS)
AS OF 3—15. NOT TO BE REMOVED FROM OFFICE

Beneath the short, capitalized paragraph were twenty-odd addresses and names.

Nimrod was closer now.

The Luxor-Elite Rental Agency on Asylum Street, Hartford, had been cooperative. Matlock now drove a Cadillac convertible. The manager had accepted the explanation that the Lincoln was too funereal, and since the registration papers were in order, the switch was perfectly acceptable.

So was the twenty-dollar tip.

Matlock had analyzed Blackstone's list carefully. He decided to concentrate on the clubs northwest of Hartford for the simple reason that they were nearer the Carlyle area. They weren't the nearest, however. Two locations were within five and seven miles of Carlyle respectively—in opposite directions—but Matlock decided to hold them off for a day or so. By the time he reached them—if he did so—he wanted the managements to know he was a heavy plunger. Not a mark, just heavy. The network gossip would take care of that—if he handled himself properly.

He checked off his first location. It was a private swimming club west of Avon. The contact was a man named Jacopo Bartolozzi.

At nine thirty Matlock drove up the winding drive-way to a canopy extending from the entrance of the Avon Swim Club. A uniformed doorman signaled a parking attendant, who appeared out of nowhere and slid into the driver's seat the moment Matlock stepped onto the pavement. Obviously no parking ticket was to be given.

As he walked toward the entrance, he looked at the exterior of the club. The main building was a sprawling, one-story white brick structure with a tall stockade fence extending from both ends into the darkness. On the right, quite far behind the fence, was the iridescent glow of greenish blue light and the sound of water splashing. On the left was a huge tent-like canopy under which could be seen the shimmering light of dozens of patio torches. The former was obviously an enormous pool, the latter some kind of dining area. Soft music could be heard.

The Avon Swim Club appeared to be a very luxurious complex.

The interior did nothing to dispel this observation. The foyer was thickly carpeted and the various chairs and odd tables against the damask walls seemed genuine antiques. On the left was a large checkroom, and further down on the right was a white marble counter not unlike a hotel information desk. At the end of the narrow lobby was the only incongruous structure. It was a black, ornate wrought-iron gate, and it was closed, obviously locked. Beyond the grilled enclosure could be seen an open-air corridor, subtly lit, with an extended covering supported by a series of thin Ionic pillars. A large man in a tuxedo was standing at attention behind the iron gate.

Matlock approached him.

"Your membership card, sir?"

"I'm afraid I don't have one."

"Sorry, sir, this is a private swimming club. Members only."

"I was told to ask for Mr. Bartolozzi."

The man behind the grill stared at Matlock, frisking him with his eyes.

"You'd better check the front desk, sir. Right over there."

Matlock walked back to the counter, to be greeted by a middle-aged, slightly paunchy desk clerk who had not been there when he first came in.

"May I help you?"

"You may. I'm fairly new in the area. I'd like to become a member."

"We're sorry. Membership's full right now. However, if you'll fill out an application, we'll be glad to call you if there's an opening. . . . Would that be a family application or individual, sir?" The clerk, very professionally, reached below the counter and brought up two application forms.

"Individual. I'm not married. . . . I was told to ask for Mr. Bartolozzi. I was told specifically to ask for him. Jacopo Bartolozzi."

The clerk gave the name only the slightest indication of recognition. "Here, fill out an application and I'll put it on Mr. Bartolozzi's desk. He'll see it in the morning. Perhaps he'll call you, but I don't know what he can do. Membership's full and there's a waiting list."

"Isn't he here now? On such a busy night?" Matlock said the words with a degree of incredulity.

"I doubt it, sir."

"Why don't you find out? Tell him we have mutual friends in San Juan." Matlock withdrew his money clip and removed a fifty-dollar bill. He placed it in front of the clerk, who looked at him sharply and slowly picked up the money.

"San Juan?"

"San Juan."

Matlock leaned against the white marble counter and saw the man behind the wrought-iron gate watching him. If the San Juan story worked and he got through the gate, he realized that he would have to part with another large-sized bill. The San Juan story *should* work, thought Matlock. It was logical to the point of innocence. He had spent a winter vacation in Puerto Rico two years ago, and although no gambler, he'd traveled with a crowd—and a girl—who made the nightly rounds of the casinos. He'd met a number of people from the Hartford vicinity, although he couldn't for the life of him remember a single name.

A foursome emerged from inside the grilled entrance, the girls giggling, the men laughing resignedly. The women had probably won twenty or thirty dollars, thought Matlock, while the men had probably lost several hundred. Fair exchange for the evening. The gate closed behind them; Matlock could hear the electric click of the latch. It was a very well-locked iron gate.

"Excuse me, sir?" It was the paunchy desk clerk, and Matlock turned around.

"Yes?"

"If you'll step inside, Mr. Bartolozzi will see you."

"Where? How?" There was no door except the wrought-iron gate and the clerk had gestured with his left hand, away from the gate.

"Over here, sir."

Suddenly a knobless, frameless panel to the right of the counter swung open. The outline was barely discernible when the panel was flush against the damask wall; when shut, no border was in evidence. Matlock walked in and was taken by the clerk to the office of Jacopo Bartolozzi.

"We got mutual friends?" The obese Italian spoke hoarsely as he leaned back in his chair behind the desk. He made no attempt to rise, gave no gesture of welcome. Jacopo Bartolozzi was a short, squat caricature of himself. Matlock couldn't be sure, but he had the feeling that Bartolozzi's feet weren't touching the floor beneath his chair.

"It amounts to the same thing, Mr. Bartolozzi."

"What amounts? Who's in San Juan?"

"Several people. One fellow's a dentist in West Hartford. Another's got an accounting firm in Constitution Plaza."

"Yeah. . . . Yeah?" Bartolozzi was trying to associate people with the professions and locations Matlock described. "What's the names? They members here?"

"I guess they are. They gave me *your* name."

"This is a swim club. Private membership. . . . Who are they?"

"Look, Mr. Bartolozzi, it was a crazy night at the Condado casino. We all had a lot to drink and . . ."

"They don't drink in the Puerto Rican casinos. It's a law!" The Italian spoke sharply, proud of his incisive knowledge. He was pointing his fat finger at Matlock.

"More honored in the breach, believe me."

"What?"

"We drank. Take my word for it. I'm just telling you I don't remember their names. . . . Look, I can go downtown on Monday and stand all day outside the Plaza and I'll find the CPA. I could also go out to West Hartford and ring every dentist's doorbell. What difference does it make? I like to play and I've got the money."

Bartolozzi smiled. "This is a swim club. I don't know what the hell you're talking about."

"O.K.," said Matlock with a disgruntled edge to his voice. "This place happened to be convenient, but if you want to show three lemons, there are others. My San Juan friends also told me about Jimmy Lacata's down in Middletown, and Sammy Sharpe's in Windsor Shoals. . . . Keep your chips, fink." He turned to the door.

"Hold it! Wait a minute!"

Matlock watched the fat Italian get out of the chair and stand up. He'd been right. Bartolozzi's feet couldn't have been touching the floor.

"What for? Maybe your limit's too small here."

"You know Lacata? Sharpe?"

"Know *of* them, I told you. . . . Look, forget it. You've got to be careful. I'll find my CPA on Monday and we'll both come back some other time. . . . I just felt like playing tonight."

"O.K. O.K. Like you said, we gotta be careful." Bartolozzi opened his top drawer and pulled out some papers. "C'mere. Sign 'em. You got an itch. Maybe I'll take your money. Maybe you'll take mine."

Matlock approached the desk. "What am I signing?"

"Just a couple of forms. Initiation's five hundred. Cash. You got it? No checks, no credit."

"I've got it. What are the forms?"

"The first is a statement that you understand that this is a nonprofit corporation and that any games of chance are for charitable purposes. . . . What are you laughing at? I built the Church of the Blessed Virgin down in Hamden."

"What's this other? It's a long one."

"That's for our files. A certificate of general partnership. For the five hundred you get a classy title. You're a partner. Everybody's a partner. . . . Just in case."

"In case?"

"In case anything good happens to us, it happens just as good to you. Especially in the newspapers."

The Avon Swim Club was certainly a place for swimming, no doubt about it. The enormous pool curved back nearly two hundred feet, and scores of small, elegant cabanas bordered the far side. Beach chairs and tables were dotted about the grassy edges beyond the tiled deck of the pool, and the underwater floodlights made the setting inviting. All this was on the right of the open-air corridor. On the left, Matlock could see fully what was only hinted at from the outside. A huge green-and-white-striped tent rose above dozens of tables. Each table had a candled lantern in the center, and patio torches were safely placed about the whole enclosure. At the far end was a long table filled with roasts, salads, and buffet food. A bar was adjacent to the long table; scores of couples were milling about.

The Avon Swim Club was a lovely place to bring the family.

The corridor led to the rear of the complex, where there was another sprawling, white-bricked structure similar to the main building. Above the large, black-enameled double doors was a wooden sign, in old English scroll:

The Avon Spa

This part of the Avon Swim Club was not a lovely place to bring the family.

Matlock thought he was back in a San Juan casino —his only experience in gambling rooms. The wall-to-wall carpet was sufficiently thick to muffle sound almost completely. Only the click of the chips and the low-keyed but intense mutterings of the players and the board men were heard. The craps tables were lined along the walls, the blackjack counters in the center. In between, in staggered positions to allow for the flow of traffic, were the roulette wheels. In the middle of the large room, raised on a platform, was the cashier's nest. All of the Avon Spa's employees were in tuxedos, neatly groomed and subservient. The players were less formal.

The gate man, pleased with Matlock's crisp fifty-dollar bill, led him to the half-circle counter in front of the cashier's platform. He spoke to a man counting out slips of paper.

"This is Mr. Matlock. Treat him good, he's a personal friend."

"No other way," said the man with a smile.

"I'm sorry, Mr. Matlock," muttered the gate man quietly. "No markers the first time around."

"Naturally. . . . Look, I'm going to wander about. . . ."

"Sure. Get the feel of the action. . . . I tell you, it ain't Vegas. Between you and me, it's Mickey Mouse most of the time. I mean for a guy like you, you know what I mean?"

Matlock knew exactly what the gate man meant. A fifty-dollar bill was not the ordinary gratuity in Avon, Connecticut.

It took him three hours and twelve minutes to lose $4,175. The only time he felt panic was when he had a streak at the craps table and had built up his reserves to nearly $5,000. He had begun the evening properly—for his purposes. He went to the cashier often enough to realize that the average purchase of chips was $200 to $300. Hardly "Mickey Mouse" in his book. So his first purchase was $1,500. The second was $1,000; the third, $2,000.

By one in the morning, he was laughing with Jacopo Bartolozzi at the bar underneath the green-and-white-striped tent.

"You're a game one. Lots'a creeps would be screaming 'ice pick' if they went for a bundle like you did. Right now I'd be showing them a few papers in my office."

"Don't you worry, I'll get it back. I always do. . . . You said it before. My itch was too much. Maybe I'll come back tomorrow."

"Make it Monday. Tomorrow it's only swimming."

"How come?"

"Sunday. Holy day."

"Shit! I've got a friend coming in from London. He won't be here Monday. He's a big player."

"Tell you what. I'll call Sharpe over in Windsor Shoals. He's a Jew. Holy days don't mean a fucking thing to him."

"I'd appreciate that."

"I may even drop over myself. The wife's got a Mothers of Madonna meeting, anyway."

Matlock looked at his watch. The evening—his point of departure—had gone well. He wondered if he should press his luck. "Only real problem coming into a territory is the time it takes to find the sources."

"What's your problem?"

"I've got a girl over in the motel. She's sleeping, we

traveled most of the day. She ran out of grass—no hard stuff—just grass. I told her I'd pick some up for her."

"Can't help you, Matlock. I don't keep none here, what with the kids around during the day. It's not good for the image, see? A few pills, I got. No needle crap, though. You want some pills?"

"No, just grass. That's all I let her use."

"Very smart of you. . . . Which way you headed?"

"Back into Hartford."

Bartolozzi snapped his fingers. A large bartender sprang into position instantly. Matlock thought there was something grotesque about the squat little Italian commandeering in such fashion. Bartolozzi asked the man for paper and pencil.

"Here. Here's an address. I'll make a phone call. It's an afterhours place right off the main drag. Down the street from G. Fox. Second floor. Ask for Rocco. What you couldn't use, he's got."

"You're a prince." And as Matlock took the paper, he meant it.

"For four grand the first night, you got privileges. . . . Hey, y'know what? You never filled out an application! That's a gas, huh?"

"You don't need credit references. I play with cash."

"Where the hell do you keep it?"

"In thirty-seven banks from here to Los Angeles." Matlock put down his glass and held out his hand to Bartolozzi. "It's been fun. See you tomorrow?"

"Sure, sure. I'll walk you to the door. Don't forget now. Don't give Sammy all the action. Come on back here."

"My word on it."

The two men walked back to the open-air corridor,

the short Italian placing his fat hand in the middle of Matlock's back, the gesture of a new friend. What neither man realized as they stepped onto the narrow causeway was that one well-dressed gentleman at a nearby table who kept punching at a fluidless lighter was watching them. As the two men passed his table, he put his lighter back into his pocket while the woman across from him lit his cigarette with a match. The woman spoke quietly through a smile.

"Did you get them?"

The man laughed softly. "Karsh couldn't have done better. Even got close-ups."

If the Avon Swim Club was an advantageous point of departure, the Hartford Hunt Club—under the careful management of Rocco Aiello—was an enviable first lap. For Matlock now thought of his journey to Nimrod as a race, one which had to end within two weeks and one day. It would end with the convocation of the Nimrod forces and the Mafiosi somewhere in the Carlyle vicinity. It would be finished for him when someone, somewhere produced another silver Corsican paper.

Bartolozzi's telephone call was effective. Matlock entered the old red stone building—at first he thought he had the wrong address, for no light shone through the windows, and there was no sign of activity within —and found a freight elevator at the end of the hallway with a lone Negro operator sitting in a chair in front of the door. No sooner had he come in than the black rose to his feet and indicated the elevator to Matlock.

In an upstairs hallway a man greeted him. "Very nice to make your acquaintance. Name's Rocco. Rocco Aiello." The man held out his hand and Matlock took it.

"Thanks. . . . I was puzzled. I didn't hear anything. I thought maybe I was in the wrong place."

"If you had heard, the construction boys would have taken me. The walls are eighteen inches thick, sound-proofed both sides; the windows are blinds. Very secure."

"That's really something."

Rocco reached into his pocket and withdrew a small wooden cigarette case. "I got a box of joints for you. No charge. I'd like to show you around, but Jock-O said you might be in a hurry."

"Jock-O's wrong. I'd like to have a drink."

"Good! Come on in. . . . Only one thing, Mr. Matlock. I got a nice clientele, you know what I mean? Very rich, very cube. Some of them know about Jock-O's operation, most of them don't. You know what I mean?"

"I understand. I was never much for swimming anyway."

"Good, good. . . . Welcome to Hartford's finest." He opened the thick steel door. "I hear you went for a bundle tonight."

Matlock laughed as he walked into the complex of dimly lit rooms crowded with tables and customers. "Is that what it's called?"

"In Connecticut, that's what it's called. . . . See? I got two floors—a duplex, like. Each floor's got five big rooms, a bar in each room. Very private, no bad behavior. Nice place to bring the wife, or somebody else, you know what I mean?"

"I think I do. It's quite something."

"The waiters are mostly college boys. I like to help them make a few dollars for their education. I got niggers, spics, kikes—I got no discrimination. Just the hair, I don't go for the long hair, you know what I mean?"

"College kids! Isn't that dangerous? Kids talk."

"Hey, what d'you think?! This place was originally started by a Joe College. It's like a fraternity home. Everybody's a bona fide, dues-paying member of a private organization. They can't getcha for that."

"I see. What about the other part?"

"What other part?"

"What I came for."

"What? A little grass? Try the corner newsstand."

Matlock laughed. He didn't want to overdo it. "Two points, Rocco. . . . Still, if I knew you better, maybe I'd like to make a purchase. Bartolozzi said what I couldn't use, you've got. . . . Forget it, though. I'm bushed. I'll just get a drink and shove off. The girl's going to wonder where I've been."

"Sometimes Bartolozzi talks too much."

"I think you're right. By the way, he's joining me tomorrow night at Sharpe's over in Windsor Shoals. I've got a friend flying in from London. Care to join us?"

Aiello was obviously impressed. The players from London were beginning to take precedence over the Vegas and Caribbean boys. Sammy Sharpe's wasn't that well known, either.

"Maybe I'll do that. . . . Look, you need something, you feel free to ask, right?"

"I'll do that. Only I don't mind telling you, the kids make me nervous."

Aiello took Matlock's elbow with his left hand and walked him toward the bar. "You got it wrong. These kids—they're not kids, you know what I mean?"

"No, I don't. Kids are kids. I like my action a little more subdued. No sweat. I'm not curious." Matlock looked up at the bartender and withdrew what was left of his bankroll. He removed a twenty-dollar bill and placed it on the bar. "Old Fitz and water, please."

"Put your money away," Rocco said.

"Mr. Aiello?" A young man in a waiter's jacket approached them. He was perhaps twenty-two or twenty-three, Matlock thought.

"Yeah?"

"If you'll sign this tab. Table eleven. It's the Johnsons. From Canton. They're O.K."

Aiello took the waiter's pad and scribbled his initials. The young man walked back toward the tables.

"See that kid? That's what I mean. He's a Yalie. He got back from Nam six months ago."

"So?"

"He was a lieutenant. An officer. Now he's studying business administration. . . . He fills in here maybe twice a week. Mostly for contacts. By the time he gets out, he'll have a real nest egg. Start his own business."

"What?"

"He's a supplier. . . . These kids, that's what I mean. You should hear their stories. Saigon, Da Nang. Hong Kong, even. Real peddling. Hey, these kids today, they're great! They know what's up. Smart, too. No worries, believe me!"

"I believe you." Matlock took his drink and swallowed quickly. It wasn't that he was thirsty, he was trying to conceal his shock at Aiello's revelation. The graduates of Indochina were not the pink-cheeked, earnest, young-old veterans of Armentières, Anzio, or even Panmunjom. They were something else, something faster, sadder, infinitely more knowing. A hero in Indochina was the soldier who had contacts on the docks and in the warehouses. That man in Indochina was the giant among his peers. And such young-old men were almost all back.

Matlock drank the remainder of his bourbon and

let Rocco show him the other rooms on the third floor. He displayed the controlled appreciation Aiello expected and promised he'd return. He said no more about Sammy Sharpe's in Windsor Shoals. He knew it wasn't necessary. Aiello's appetite had been whetted.

As he drove away, two thoughts occupied his mind. Two objectives had to be accomplished before Sunday afternoon was over. The first was that he had to produce an Englishman; the second was that he had to produce another large sum of money. It was imperative that he have both. He had to be at Sharpe's in Windsor Shoals the next evening.

The Englishman he had in mind lived in Webster, an associate professor of mathematics at a small parochial campus, Madison University. He had been in the country less than two years; Matlock had met him—quite unprofessionally—at a boat show in Saybrook. The Britisher had lived on the Cornwall coast most of his life and was a sailing enthusiast. Matlock and Pat had liked him immediately. Now Matlock hoped to God that John Holden knew something about gambling.

The money was a more serious problem. Alex Anderson would have to be tapped again, and it was quite possible that he'd find enough excuses to put him off. Anderson was a cautious man, easily frightened. On the other hand, he had a nose for rewards. That instinct would have to be played upon.

Holden had seemed startled but not at all annoyed by Matlock's telephone call. If he was anything other than kind, it was curious. He repeated the directions to his apartment twice and Matlock thanked him, assuring him that he remembered the way.

"I'll be perfectly frank, Jim," said Holden, admitting Matlock into his neat three-room apartment. "I'm simply bursting. Is anything the matter? Is Patricia all right?"

"The answers are yes and no. I'll tell you everything I can, which won't be a hell of a lot. . . . I want to ask you a favor, though. Two favors, actually. The first, can I stay here tonight?"

"Of course—you needn't ask. You look peaked. Come, sit down. Can I get you a drink?"

"No, no thanks." Matlock sat on Holden's sofa. He remembered that it was one of those hide-a-beds and that it was comfortable. He and Pat had slept in it one happy, alcoholic night several months ago. It seemed ages ago.

"What's the second favor? The first is my pleasure. If it's cash, I've something over a thousand. You're entirely welcome to it."

"No, not money, thanks just the same. . . . I'd like you to impersonate an Englishman for me."

Holden laughed. He was a small-boned man of forty, but he laughed the way older, fatter men laughed.

"That shouldn't be too demanding, now should it? I suspect there's still a trace of Cornwall in my speech. Hardly noticeable, of course."

"Hardly. With a little practice you may even lose the Yankee twang. . . . There's something else, though, and it may not be so easy. Have you ever gambled?"

"Gambled? You mean horses, football matches?"

"Cards, dice, roulette?"

"Not substantially, no. Of course, as any reasonably imaginative mathematician, I went through a phase when I thought that by applying arithmetical principles—logarithmic averages—one could beat the gambling odds."

"Did they work?"

"I said I went through the phase, I didn't stay there. If there's a mathematical system, it eluded me. Still does."

"But you've played? You know the games."

"Rather well, when you come right down to it. Laboratory research, you might say. Why?"

Matlock repeated the story he had told Blackstone. However, he minimized Pat's injuries and lightened the motives of those who assaulted her. When he finished, the Englishman, who'd lit his pipe, knocked the ashes out of the bowl into a large glass ashtray.

"It's right out of the cinema, isn't it? . . . You say Patricia's not seriously hurt. Frightened but nothing much more than that?"

"Right. If I went to the police it might louse up her scholarship money."

"I see. . . . Well, I don't really, but we'll let it go. And you'd rather I lost tomorrow night."

"That doesn't matter. Just that you bet a great deal."

"But you're *prepared* for heavy losses."

"I am."

Holden stood up. "I'm perfectly willing to go through with this performance. It should prove rather a lark. However, there's a great deal you're not telling me and I wish you would. But I shan't insist upon it. I will tell you that your story is boggled with a large mathematical inconsistency."

"What's that?"

"As I understand it, the money you are prepared to lose tomorrow evening is far in excess of any amount Patricia might realize in scholarship aid. The logical assumption, therefore, is that you do not wish to go to the police. Or perhaps, you can't."

Matlock looked up at the Englishman and wondered at his own stupidity. He felt embarrassed and very inadequate. "I'm sorry. . . . I haven't consciously lied to you. You don't have to go through with it; maybe I shouldn't have asked."

"I never implied that you lied—not that it matters. Only that there was much you haven't told me. Of course, I'll do it. I just want you to know I'm a willing audience when and if you decide to tell me everything that's happened. . . . Now, it's late and you're tired. Why don't you take my room."

"No, thanks. I'll sack out here. It has pleasant memories. A blanket's all I need. Also I have to make a phone call."

"Anything you say. A blanket you'll get, and you know where the phone is."

When Holden left, Matlock went to the phone. The Tel-electronic device he'd agreed to lease would not be ready until Monday morning.

"Blackstone."

"This is James Matlock. I was told to call this number for any messages."

"Yes, Mr. Matlock. There is a message, if you'll hold on while I get the card. . . . Here it is. From the Carlyle team. Everything is secure. The subject is responding nicely to medical treatment. The subject had three visitors. A Mr. Samuel Kressel, a Mr. Adrian Sealfont, and a Miss Lois Meyers. The subject received two telephone calls, neither of which the physician allowed to be taken. They were from the same individual, a Mr. Jason Greenberg. The calls were from Wheeling, West Virginia. At no time was the subject separated from the Carlyle team. . . . You can relax."

"Thank you. I will. You're very thorough. Good night." Matlock breathed deeply in relief and exhaustion. Lois Meyers lived across the hall from Pat in the graduate apartment house. The fact that Greenberg had called was comforting. He missed Greenberg.

He reached up and turned off the table lamp by the sofa. The bright April moon shone through the windows. The man from Blackstone's service was right —he could relax.

What he couldn't allow to relax were his thoughts about tomorrow—and after tomorrow. Everything had to remain accelerated; one productive day had to lead into another. There could be no letup, no sense of momentary satisfaction which might slow his thrust.

And after tomorrow. After Sammy Sharpe's in Windsor Shoals. If all went according to his calculations, it would be the time to head into the Carlyle area. Matlock closed his eyes and saw Blackstone's printed page in front of his mind.

CARMOUNT COUNTRY CLUB—CONTACT: HOWARD
STOCKTON
WEST CARLYLE SAIL AND SKI RESORT—CONTACT: ALAN
CANTOR

Carmount was east of Carlyle near the border of Mount Holly. The Sail and Ski was west, on Lake Derron—a summer and winter resort area.

He'd find some reason to have Bartolozzi or Aiello, or, perhaps, Sammy Sharpe, make the proper introductions. And once in the Carlyle area, he would drop the hints. Perhaps more than hints—commands, requirements, necessities. This was the boldness he needed to use, this was the way of Nimrod.

His eyes remained closed, the muscles in his body sagged, and the pitch darkness of exhausted sleep came over him. But before sleeping he remembered the paper. The Corsican paper. He had to get the paper now. He would need the silver paper. He would need the invitation to Nimrod.

His invitation now. His paper.

The Matlock paper.

If the elders at the Windsor Shoals Congregational Church had ever realized that Samuel Sharpe, attorney at law, the very bright Jewish lawyer who handled the church's finances, was referred to as Sammy the Runner by most of North Hartford and South Springfield, Massachusetts, vespers would have been canceled for a month. Fortunately, such a revelation had never been made to them and the Congregational Church looked favorably on him. He had done remarkable things for the church's portfolio and gave handsomely himself during fund drives. The Congregational Church of Windsor Shoals, as indeed most of the town, was nicely disposed toward Samuel Sharpe.

Matlock learned all of this in Sharpe's office inside the Windsor Valley Inn. The framed citations on the wall told half the story, and Jacopo Bartolozzi good-naturedly supplied the rest. Jacopo was actually making sure that Matlock and his English friend were aware that Sharpe's operation, as well as Sharpe himself, lacked the fine traditions of the Avon Swim Club.

Holden surpassed Matlock's expectations. Several times he nearly laughed out loud as he watched Holden take hundred-dollar bills—rushed into Webster by a harassed, nervous Alex Anderson—and flick them nonchalantly at a croupier, never bothering to count the chips but somehow letting everyone at whatever table he was at realize that he knew—to the dollar—the amount given him. Holden played intelligently, cautiously, and at one point was ahead of the house by nine thousand dollars. By the end of the evening, he had cut his winnings to several hundred and the operators of the Windsor Valley breathed grateful sighs of relief.

James Matlock cursed his second night of terrible luck and took his twelve-hundred-dollar loss for what it meant to him—nothing.

At four in the morning Matlock and Holden, flanked by Aiello, Bartolozzi, Sharpe, and two of their cronies, sat at a large oak table in the colonial dining room. They were alone. A waiter and two busboys were cleaning up; the gambling rooms on the third floor of the inn had closed.

The husky Aiello and the short, fat Bartolozzi kept up a running commentary about their respective clientele, each trying to upstage the other with regard to their customers' status; each allowing that "it might be nice" for the other to become "acquainted" with a Mr. and Mrs. Johnson of Canton or a certain Dr. Wadsworth. Sharpe, on the other hand, seemed more interested in Holden and the action in England. He told several funny, self-effacing stories about his visits to London clubs and his insurmountable difficulty with British currency in the heat of betting.

Matlock thought, as he watched Sammy Sharpe, that he was a very charming man. It wasn't hard to believe that Sharpe was considered a respectable asset to Windsor Shoals, Connecticut. He couldn't help comparing Sharpe to Jason Greenberg. And in the comparison, he found an essential difference. It was told in the eyes. Greenberg's were soft and compassionate, even in anger. Sharpe's were cold, hard, incessantly darting—strangely in conflict with the rest of his relaxed face.

He heard Bartolozzi ask Holden where he was off to next. Holden's offhand reply gave him the opportunity he was looking for. He waited for the right moment.

"I'm afraid I'm not at liberty to discuss my itinerary."

"He means where he's going," injected Rocco Aiello.

Bartolozzi shot Aiello a withering glance. "I just thought you should drop over to Avon. I got a real nice place I think you'd enjoy."

"I'm sure I would. Perhaps another time."

"Johnny'll be in touch with me next week," Matlock said. "We'll get together." He reached for an ashtray and crushed out his cigarette. "I have to be in . . . Carlyle, that's the name of the place."

There was the slightest pause in the conversation. Sharpe, Aiello, and one of the other two men exchanged looks. Bartolozzi, however, seemed oblivious to any deep meaning.

"The college place?" asked the short Italian.

"That's right," answered Matlock. "I'll probably stay at Carmount or the Sail and Ski. I guess you fellows know where they are."

"I guess we do." Aiello laughed softly.

"What's your business in Carlyle?" The unidentified man—at least no one had bothered to introduce him by name—drew deeply on a cigar as he spoke.

"*My* business," said Matlock pleasantly.

"Just asking. No offense."

"No offense taken. . . . Hey, it's damned near four thirty! You fellows are too hospitable." Matlock pushed his chair back, prepared to stand.

The man with the cigar, however, had to ask another question.

"Is your friend going to Carlyle with you?"

Holden held up his hand playfully. "Sorry, no itineraries. I'm simply a visitor to your pleasant shores and filled with a tourist's plans. . . . We really must go."

Both men rose from the table. Sharpe stood, too. Before the others could move, Sharpe spoke.

"I'll see the boys to their car and show them the road out. You fellows wait here—we'll settle accounts. I owe you money, Rocco. Frank owes me. Maybe I'll come out even."

The man with the cigar, whose name was obviously Frank, laughed. Aiello looked momentarily perplexed but within seconds grasped the meaning of Sharpe's statement. The men at the table were to remain.

Matlock wasn't sure he'd handled the situation advantageously.

He had wanted to pursue the Carlyle discussion just enough to have someone offer to make the necessary calls to Carmount and the Sail and Ski. Holden's refusal to speak about his itinerary precluded it, and Matlock was afraid that it also implied that he and Holden were so important that further introductions were unnecessary. In addition, Matlock realized that as his journey progressed, he banked more and more on the dead Loring's guarantee that none of those invited to the Carlyle conference would discuss delegates among themselves. The meaning of "Omerta" was supposedly so powerful that silence was inviolate. Yet Sharpe had just commanded those at the table to remain.

He had the feeling that perhaps he had gone too far with too little experience. Perhaps it was time to reach Greenberg—although he'd wanted to wait until he had more concrete knowledge before doing so. If he made contact with Greenberg now, the agent might force him—what was the idiotic phrase?—out of strategy. He wasn't prepared to face that problem.

Sharpe escorted them to the near-deserted parking lot. The Windsor Vally Inn wasn't crowded with overnight guests.

"We don't encourage sleeping accommodations," Sharpe explained. "We're known primarily as a fine restaurant."

"I can understand that," said Matlock.

"Gentlemen," began Sharpe haltingly. "May I make a request that might be considered impolite?"

"Go right ahead."

"May I have a word with you, Mr. Matlock? Privately."

"Oh, don't concern yourself," said Holden, moving off. "I understand fully. I'll just walk around."

"He's a very nice fellow, your English friend," Sharpe said.

"The nicest. What is it, Sammy?"

"Several points of information, as we say in court."

"What are they?"

"I'm a cautious man, but I'm also very curious. I run a fine organization, as you can see."

"I can see."

"I'm growing nicely—cautiously, but nicely."

"I'll accept that."

"I don't make mistakes. I've a trained legal mind and I'm proud that I don't make mistakes."

"What are you driving at?"

"It strikes me—and I must be honest with you, it has also occurred to my partner Frank and to Rocco Aiello—that you may have been sent into the territory to make certain observations."

"Why do you think that?"

"Why? . . . From nowhere comes a player like you. You got powerful friends in San Juan. You know our places like the back of your hand. Then you have a very rich, very nice associate from the London scene. That all adds up. . . . But most important—and I think you know it—you mention this business in Carlyle. Let's be honest. That speaks a whole big book, doesn't it?"

"Does it?"

"I'm not foolhardy. I told you, I'm a cautious man. I understand the rules and I don't ask questions I'm not supposed to ask or talk about things I'm not privileged to know about. . . . Still, I want the generals to realize they have a few intelligent, even ambitious, lieutenants in the organization. Anyone can tell you. I don't skim, I don't hold back."

"Are you asking me to give you a good report?"

"That about sizes it up. I have value. I'm a respected attorney. My partner's a very successful insurance broker. We're naturals."

"What about Aiello? It seems to me you're friendly with him."

"Rocco's a good boy. Maybe not the quickest, but solid. He's a kind person, too. However, I don't believe he's in our league."

"And Bartolozzi?"

"I have nothing to say about Bartolozzi. You'll have to make up your own mind about him."

"By saying nothing, you're saying a lot, aren't you?"

"In my opinion, he talks too much. But that could be his personality. He rubs me the wrong way. Not Rocco, though."

Matlock watched the methodical Sharpe in the pre-dawn light of the parking lot and began to understand what had happened. It was logical; he, himself, had planned it, but now that it was taking place, he felt curiously objective. Observing himself; watching reacting puppets.

He had entered Nimrod's world a stranger; possibly suspect, certainly devious.

Yet suddenly, that suspicion, that deviousness, was not to be scorned but *honored*.

The suspect honored for his deviousness—because it *had* to come from a higher source. He was an emissary from the upper echelons now. He was feared.

What had Greenberg called it? The shadow world. Unseen armies positioning their troops in darkness, constantly on the alert for stray patrols, unfriendly scouts.

The thin line he had to tread was precarious. But it was his now.

"You're a good man, Sharpe. Goddamn smart, too. ... What do you know about Carlyle?"

"Nothing! Absolutely nothing."

"Now you're lying, and that's *not* smart."

"It's true. I don't *know anything*. Rumors I've heard. Knowledge and hearsay are two different kinds of testimony." Sharpe held up his right hand, his two forefingers separated.

"What rumors? Give it straight, for your own sake."

"Just rumors. A gathering of the clan, maybe. A meeting of very highly placed individuals. An agreement which has to be reached between certain people."

"Nimrod?"

Sammy Sharpe closed his eyes for precisely three seconds. During those moments he spoke.

"Now you talk language I don't want to hear."

"Then you didn't hear it, did you?"

"It's stricken from the record, I assure you."

"O.K. You're doing fine. And when you go back inside, I don't think it would be such a good idea to discuss the rumors you've heard. That would be acting like a stupid lieutenant, wouldn't it?"

"Not only stupid—insane."

"Why did you tell them to stay, then? It's late."

"For real. I wanted to know what everybody thought of you and your English friend. I'll tell you now, though—since you have mentioned a certain name, no such discussion will take place. As I said, I understand the rules."

"Good. I believe you. You've got possibilities. You'd better go back in. . . . Oh, one last thing. I want you . . . *we* want you to call Stockton at Carmount and Cantor at the Sail and Ski. Just say I'm a personal friend and I'll be showing up. Nothing else. We don't want any guards up. That's important, Sammy. Nothing else."

"It's my pleasure. And you won't forget to convey my regards to the others?"

"I won't forget. You're a good man."

"I do my best. It's all a person can do . . ."

Just then, the quiet of the predawn was shattered by five loud reports. Glass smashed. The sounds of people running and screaming and furniture crashing came from within the inn. Matlock threw himself to the ground.

"John! John!"

"Over here! By the car! Are you all right?!"

"Yes. Stay there!"

Sharpe had run into the darkness by the base of the building. He crouched into a corner, pressing himself against the brick. Matlock could barely see the outline of his form, but he could see enough to watch Sharpe withdraw a revolver from inside his jacket.

Again there was a volley of shots from the rear of the building, followed once more by screams of terror. A busboy crashed through the side door and crawled on his hands and knees toward the edge of the parking lot. He shouted hysterically in a language Matlock could not understand.

Several seconds later, another of the inn's employees in a white jacket ran through the door pulling a second man behind him, this one obviously wounded, blood pouring from his shoulder, his right arm dangling, immobile.

Another shot rang out of nowhere and the waiter who had been screaming fell over. The wounded man behind him went pummeling forward, crashing face down into the gravel. Within the building, men were shouting.

"Let's go! Get *out!* Get to the *car!*"

He fully expected to see men come scrambling out of the side door into the parking lot, but no one came. Instead, from another section of the property, he heard the gunning of an engine and, moments later, the screeching of tires as an automobile made a sharp turn. And then, to his left, about fifty yards away, a black sedan came racing out of the north driveway toward the main road. The car had to pass under a street light, and Matlock saw it clearly.

It was the same automobile that had plunged out of the darkness moments after Ralph Loring's murder.

Everything was still again. The grayish light of dawn was getting brighter.

"Jim! Jim, come here! I think they've gone!"

It was Holden. He had left the sanctuary of the automobile and was crouching over the man in the white jacket.

"Coming!" said Matlock, getting off the ground.

"This fellow's dead. He was shot between the shoulders. . . . This one's still breathing. Better get an ambulance." Holden had walked over to the unconscious busboy with the bloodied, immobile right arm.

"I don't hear anything. Where's Sharpe?"

"He just went inside. That door. He had a gun."

The two men walked carefully to the side entrance of the inn. Matlock slowly opened the door and preceded Holden into the foyer. Furniture was overturned, chairs and tables on their sides; blood was glistening on the wooden floor.

"Sharpe? Where are you?" Matlock raised his voice cautiously. It was several seconds before the reply came. When it did, Sharpe could hardly be heard.

"In here. In the dining room."

Matlock and Holden walked through the oak-framed arch. Nothing in either man's life had prepared him for what he saw.

The overpowering horror was the sight of the bodies literally covered with blood. What was left of Rocco Aiello was sprawled across the red-soaked tablecloth, most of his face blown off. Sharpe's partner, the unintroduced man named Frank, was on his knees, his torso twisted back over the seat of a chair, blood flowing out of his neck, his eyes wide open in death. Jacopo Bartolozzi was on the floor, his obese body arched around the leg of a table, the front of his shirt ripped up to the collar, revealing his bulging stomach, the flesh pierced with a score of bullet holes, blood still trickling out over the coarse black hair. Bartolozzi had tried to tear his shirt away from his battered chest, and a portion of cloth was clutched in his dead hand. The fourth man lay behind Bartolozzi, his head resting on Bartolozzi's right foot, his arms and legs extended in a spread-eagle pattern, his entire back covered with a thick layer of blood, portions of his intestines pushed through the skin.

"Oh, my God!" muttered Matlock, not fully believing what he saw. John Holden looked as though he might become sick. Sharpe spoke softly, rapidly, wearily.

"You'd better go. You and your English friend better leave quickly."

"You'll have to call the police," said Matlock, bewildered.

"There's a man outside, a boy. He's still alive." Holden stuttered as he spoke.

Sharpe looked over at the two men, the revolver at his side, his eyes betraying only the slightest degree of suspicion. "I have no doubt the lines have been cut. The nearest houses are farms at least half a mile from here. . . . I'll take care of everything. You'd better get out of here."

"Do you think we should?" asked Holden, looking at Matlock.

Sharpe replied. "Listen, Englishman, personally I couldn't care less what either of you do. I've got enough to think about, enough to figure out. . . . For your own good, get out of here. Less complications, less risk. Isn't that right?"

"Yes, you're right," Matlock said.

"In case you're picked up, you left here a half hour ago. You were friends of Bartolozzi, that's all I know."

"All right."

Sharpe had to turn away from the sight of the murdered men. Matlock thought for a moment that the Windsor Shoals attorney was going to weep. Instead, he took a deep breath and spoke again.

"A trained legal mind, Mr. Matlock. I'm valuable. You tell them that."

"I will."

"You also tell them I need protection, *deserve* protection. You tell them that, too."

"Of course."

"Now, get out." Suddenly Sharpe threw his revolver on the floor in disgust. And then he screamed, as the tears came to his eyes, "Get out for Christ's sake! *Get out!*"

Matlock and Holden agreed to separate immediately. The English professor dropped off the mathematician at his apartment and then headed south to Fairfield. He wanted to register at a highway motel far enough away from Windsor Shoals to feel less panicked, yet near enough to Hartford so he could get to Blackstone's by two in the afternoon.

He was too exhausted, too frightened to think. He found a third-rate motel just west of Stratford and surprised the early morning clerk by being alone.

During the registration, he mumbled unpleasant criticisms about a suspicious wife in Westport, and with a ten-dollar bill convinced the clerk to enter his arrival at 2:00 A.M., single. He fell into bed by seven and left a call for twelve thirty. If he slept for five hours, he thought, things had to become clearer.

Matlock slept for five hours and twenty minutes and nothing much had changed. Very little had cleared up for him. If anything, the massacre at Windsor Shoals now appeared more extraordinary than ever. Was it possible that he was meant to be a victim? Or were the killers waiting outside, waiting silently for him to leave before committing their executions?

Mistake or warning?

By one fifteen he was on the Merritt Parkway. By

one thirty he entered the Berlin Turnpike, taking the back roads into Hartford. By five minutes past two he walked into Blackstone's office.

"Look," said Michael Blackstone, leaning over his desk, staring at Matlock, "we ask a minimum of questions, but don't for one minute think that means we give our clients blank checks!"

"It seems to me you like that process reversed."

"Then take your money and go somewhere else. We'll survive!"

"Just hold it! You were hired to protect a girl, that's all! That's what I'm paying three hundred dollars a day for! Anything else is marginal, and I'm paying for that, too, I expect."

"There'll be no extra charges. I don't know what you're talking about." Suddenly Blackstone bent his elbows, crouching forward. He whispered hoarsely. "Christ, Matlock? Two *men!* Two men on that goddamn list were murdered last night! If you're a hopped-up maniac, I don't want anything to do with you! That's no part of any deal here! I don't care *who* your old man is or *how* much money you've got!"

"Now I don't know what *you're* talking about. Except what I read in the papers. I was at a motel in Fairfield last night. I was registered there at two this morning. According to the papers, those killings took place around five."

Blackstone pushed himself off the desk and stood up. He looked at Matlock suspiciously. "You can verify that?"

"Do you want the name and number of the motel? Give me a phone book, I'll get it for you."

"No! . . . No. I don't want to know a thing. You were in Fairfield?"

"Get the phone book."

"All right. All right, forget it. I think you're lying, but you've covered yourself. As you say, we're only hired to protect the girl."

"Any change from Sunday afternoon? Is everything all right?"

"Yes. . . . Yes." Blackstone seemed preoccupied. "I've got your Tel-electronic. It's operative. It's an additional twenty dollars a day."

"I see. Wholesale price."

"We never implied we were cheap."

"You couldn't."

"We don't." Blackstone remained standing, pushed a button on his office intercom, and spoke into it. "Bring in Mr. Matlock's Tel-electronic, please."

Seconds later an attractive girl came into the office carrying a metal device no larger than a pack of cigarettes. She put it on Blackstone's desk and placed an index card beside it. She left as rapidly as she had entered.

"Here you are," Blackstone said. "Your code is Charger Three-zero. Meaning—Carlyle area, three-man team. The telephone number you call is five, five, five, six, eight, six, eight. We keep a list of numbers on reserve which we feel are easy to commit. The Tel-electronic will signal you by short beeps. You can shut it off by pushing this button here. When the signal is emitted, you are to call the number. A recording machine on that telephone will give you the message from the team. Often it will be to phone another number to make direct contact. Do you understand everything? It's really very simple."

"I understand," said Matlock, taking the small metal box. "What confuses me is why you don't just have the men call this office and then you contact me.

Outside of whatever profit there is, wouldn't it be easier?"

"No. Too much room for error. We handle a great many clients. We want our clients to be in direct contact with the men they're paying for."

"I see."

"Also, we respect the privacy of our clients. We don't think it's such a good idea for information to be transmitted through third and fourth parties. Incidentally, you can reach the team by the same procedures. Each one has a machine. Just phone the number and record the message for them."

"Commendable."

"Professional." And then Blackstone, for the first time since Matlock had entered the office, sat in his chair and leaned back. "Now I'm going to tell you something, and if you want to take it as a threat, you'd be justified. Also, if you want to cancel our services on the strength of what I say, that's O.K., too. . . . We know that you're being actively sought by agents of the Justice Department. However, there are no charges leveled against you, no warrants for your arrest. You have certain rights which the federal men often overlook in their zealousness—it's one of the reasons we're in business. However, *again*, we want you to know that should your status change, should there *be* charges or a warrant for your arrest, our services are terminated immediately, and we won't hesitate to cooperate with the authorities regarding your whereabouts. Whatever information we possess will be held for your attorneys—it's privileged—but not your whereabouts. *Capiche?*"

"I do. That's fair."

"We're more than fair. That's why I'm going to demand ten days' advance payment from you—unused portion returnable. . . . In the event the situation changes and the federal men get a court order for you, you will receive—*only once*—the following message on the telephone recorder. Just *these words.*"

Blackstone paused for emphasis.

"What are they?"

" '*Charger Three-zero is canceled.*' "

Out on Bond Street Matlock felt a sensation he knew wouldn't leave him until his journey, his race was over. He thought people were staring at him. He began to think strangers were watching him. He found himself involuntarily turning around, trying to find the unseen, observing eyes. Yet there were none.

None that he could distinguish.

The Corsican paper now had to be gotten out of his apartment. And considering Blackstone's statements, there was no point in his attempting to get it himself. His apartment would be under surveillance—from both camps, the seekers and the quarry.

He would use the Blackstone team, one of them, putting to the test the sartorial Blackstone's guarantee of privileged information. He would reach them—him —as soon as he placed one prior telephone call. A call that would make it clear whether the silver Corsican invitation was really necessary or not. A call to Samuel Sharpe, attorney at law, Windsor Shoals, Connecticut.

Matlock decided to show Sharpe a temporary, more compassionate side of his acquired personality. Sharpe himself had displayed a momentary lapse of control. Matlock thought it was the moment to indicate that even such men as himself—men who had influential friends in San Juan and London—had feelings beyond personal survival.

He walked into the lobby of the Americana Hotel and called him. Sharpe's secretary answered.

"Are you in an office where Mr. Sharpe can return your call momentarily?"

"No, I'm in a telephone booth. I'm also in a hurry."

There was silence, preceded by the click of a hold button. The wait was less than ten seconds.

"May I have the number you're calling from, Mr. Matlock? Mr. Sharpe will get back to you within five minutes."

Matlock gave the girl the number and hung up.

As he sat in the plastic seat, his memory wandered back to another telephone booth and another plastic seat. And a black sedan which raced past the dead man slouched in that booth, on that seat, with a bullet hole in his forehead.

The bell sounded; Matlock lifted the receiver.

"Matlock?"

"Sharpe?"

"You shouldn't call me at the office. You should know better. I had to go down to the lobby here, to a pay phone."

"I didn't think a respected attorney's telephone would be any risk. I'm sorry."

There was a pause at the other end of the line. Sharpe obviously never expected an apology. "I'm a cautious man, I told you. What is it?"

"I just wanted to know how you were. How everything went. It was a terrible thing, last night."

"I haven't had time for a reaction. There's so much to do. Police, funeral arrangements, reporters."

"What are you saying? How are you handling it?"

"There won't be any major mistakes. In a nutshell— if it comes to that—I'm an innocent victim. Frank's a victim, too, only he's dead. . . . I'm going to miss

Frank. He was a very good fellow. I'll close down the upstairs, of course. The state police have been paid. By you people, I assume. It'll be what the papers say it was. A bunch of Italian hoodlums shot up in a nice country restaurant."

"You're a cool operator."

"I told you," replied Sharpe sadly, "I'm a cautious man. I'm prepared for contingencies."

"Who did it?"

Sharpe did not answer the question. He did not speak at all.

"I asked you, who do you think did it?"

"I expect you people will find out before I do. . . . Bartolozzi had enemies; he was an unpleasant person. Rocco, too, I suppose. . . . But why Frank? You tell me."

"I don't know. I haven't been in touch with anyone."

"Find out for me. Please. It wasn't right."

"I'll try. That's a promise. . . . And, Sammy, make those calls to Stockton and Cantor, don't forget."

"I won't. I've got them listed on my afternoon calendar. I told you. I'm a methodical man."

"Thanks. My sympathies about Frank. He seemed like a nice guy."

"He was a prince."

"I'm sure he was. . . . I'll be in touch, Sammy. I haven't forgotten what I said I'd do for you. You've really impressed me. I'll . . ."

The sound of coins dropping into the telephone receptacle at Windsor Shoals interrupted Matlock. The time limit was up, and there was no point in prolonging the conversation. He had found out what he needed to know. He had to have the Corsican paper now. The horror of the dawn massacre had not caused the methodical Sharpe to forget the telephone calls he'd promised to make. Why it hadn't was a miracle to Matlock, but there it was. The cautious man had not panicked. He was ice.

The telephone booth was stuffy, close, uncomfortable, filled with smoke. He opened the door and walked rapidly across the hotel lobby to the front exit.

He rounded the corner of Asylum Street looking for an appropriate restaurant. One in which he could have lunch while awaiting the return call from Charger Three-zero. Blackstone had said that he should leave a number; what better than a restaurant?

He saw the sign: The Lobster House. The kind of place frequented by business executives.

He was given a booth to himself, not a table. It was nearly three; the luncheon crowd had thinned. He sat down and ordered a bourbon on the rocks, asking the waitress the whereabouts of the nearest telephone. He was about to get out of the booth to make his call to 555-6868 when he heard the muted, sharp, terrifying sound of the Tel-electronic from within his jacket. At first it paralyzed him. It was as if some part of his person, an hysterical organ perhaps, had gone mad and was trying to signal its distress. His hand shook as he reached inside his coat and withdrew the small metal device. He found the shut-off button and pressed it as hard as he could. He looked around, wondering if the sound had attracted attention.

It had not. No one returned his looks. No one had heard a thing.

He got out of his seat and walked quickly toward the telephone. His only thought was Pat—something had happened, something serious enough for Charger Three-zero to activate the terrible, insidious machine which had panicked him.

Matlock pulled the door shut and dialed 555-6868.

"Charger Three-zero reporting." The voice had the once-removed quality of a taped recording. "Please telephone five, five, five; one, nine, five, one. There is no need for alarm, sir. There's no emergency. We'll be at this number for the next hour. The number again is five, five, five; one, nine, five, one. Out."

Matlock realized that Charger Three-zero took pains to allay his fears immediately, perhaps because it was his first experience with the Tel-electronic. He had the feeling that even if the town of Carlyle had gone up in thermonuclear smoke, Charger Three-zero's words would have a palliative quality about them. The other reasoning, perhaps, was that a man thought more clearly when unafraid. Whatever, Matlock knew that the method worked. He was calmer now. He reached into his pocket and took out some change, making a mental note as he did so to convert some dollar bills into coins for future use. The pay telephone had become an important part of his life.

"Is this five, five, five; nineteen fifty-one?"

"Yes," said the same voice he had heard on the recording. "Mr. Matlock?"

"Yes. Is Miss Ballantyne all right?"

"Doing very well, sir. That's a good doctor you've got. She sat up this morning. A lot of the swelling's gone down. The doctor's quite pleased. . . . She's asked for you a number of times."

"What are you telling her?"

"The truth. That we've been hired by you to make sure she's not bothered."

"I mean about where I am."

"We've simply said you had to be away for several days. It might be a good idea to telephone her. She can take calls starting this afternoon. We'll screen them, of course."

"Of course. Is that why you contacted me?"

"In part. The other reason is Greenberg. Jason Greenberg. He keeps calling for you. He insists that you get in touch with him."

"What did he say? Who talked to him?"

"I did. Incidentally, my name's Cliff."

"O.K., Cliff, what did he say?"

"That I should tell you to call him the minute I reached you. It was imperative, critical. I've got a number. It's in Wheeling, West Virginia."

"Give it to me." Matlock withdrew his ballpoint pen and wrote the number on the wooden shelf under the telephone.

"Mr. Matlock?"

"What?"

"Greenberg also said to tell you . . . that 'the cities weren't dying, they were dead.' Those were his words. 'The cities were dead.' "

Cliff agreed without comment to retrieve the Corsican paper from Matlock's apartment. A rendezvous would be arranged later by telephone. In the event the paper was missing, Charger Three-zero would alert him immediately.

Matlock restricted himself to one drink. He picked at his lunch and left the Lobster House by three thirty. It was time to regroup his forces, resupply his ammunition. He had parked the Cadillac in a lot several blocks south of Blackstone's office on Bond Street. It was one of those municipal parking areas, each slot with its own meter. It occurred to Matlock as he approached it that he hadn't returned to insert additional coins since going to Blackstone's. The meters were only good for an hour; he'd been there for nearly two. He wondered what rental-car businesses did with the slew of traffic violations which had to mount up with transients. He entered the lot and momentarily wondered if he was in the right aisle. Then he realized he was not. The Cadillac was two lanes over, in the fourth aisle. He started to sidle past the closely parked vehicles toward his own and then he stopped.

In between the automobiles, he saw the blue and white stripes of a Hartford patrol car. It was parked directly behind his Cadillac. One police officer was trying the Cadillac's door handle, a second patrolman was leaning against the police vehicle talking into a radio phone.

They'd found the car. It frightened him, but somehow it didn't surprise him.

He backed away cautiously, prepared to run if he was spotted. His thoughts raced ahead to the problems to which this newest complication gave rise. First and most immediate was an automobile. Second was the fact that they knew he was in the Hartford vicinity. That ruled out other means of transportation. The railroad stations, the bus terminals, even the hack bureaus would be alerted. It came back to finding another car.

And yet he wondered. Blackstone made it clear there were no charges against him, no warrants. If there were, he would have received the message from 555-6868. He would have heard the words: "Charger Three-zero is canceled."

He hadn't. There'd been no hint of it. For a moment he considered going back to the patrol car, accepting a ticket for overtime.

He dismissed the thought. These police were not meter maids. There had been a previous parking lot beyond an alley, at the rear of an A&P. And another policeman—in civilian clothes—following him. A pattern was there, though it eluded definition.

Matlock walked swiftly up Bond Street away from the municipal lot. He turned into the first side street and found himself beginning to break into a run. Instantly he slowed down. There is nothing in a crowded street more noticeable than a man running—unless it is a woman. He resumed a pace equal to the afternoon shoppers, doing his best to melt into the flow of human traffic. He even paused now and then to stare blankly into store-front windows, not really seeing the displays of merchandise. And then he began to reflect on what was happening to him. The primitive instincts of the hunted were suddenly working inside his brain. The protective antennae of the would-be trapped animal were thrusting, parrying with their surroundings and, chameleonlike, the body did its best to conform to the environment.

Yet he wasn't the hunted! He was the hunter! Goddamn it, he was the *hunter!*

"Hello, Jim! How the hell are you? What are you doing in the big city?"

The shock of the greeting caused Matlock to lose his balance. To actually *lose his balance* and trip. He fell to the sidewalk and the man who had spoken to him reached down and helped him up.

"Oh! Oh, hello, Jeff! Christ, you startled me. Thanks." Matlock got up and brushed himself off. He looked around wondering who else besides Jeff Kramer was watching him.

"A long lunch, buddy?" Kramer laughed. He was a Carlyle alumnus with a graduate degree in psychology that had been impressive enough for an expensive public relations firm.

"Lord, no! Just have something on my mind. My bumbling old professor bag." And then Matlock looked at Jeff Kramer. Jeff Kramer was not only with an expensive firm, but he also had an expensive wife and two very expensive kids in extremely expensive prep schools. Matlock felt he should reemphasize his previous point. "For a fact, I had one unfinished bourbon."

"Why don't we rectify that," said Kramer, pointing

at the Hogshead Tavern across the street. "I haven't seen you in months. I read in *The Courant* you got yourself robbed."

"Goddamn, *did* I! The robbery I could take, but what they did to the apartment! And the *car!*" Matlock headed toward the Hogshead Tavern with Jeff Kramer. "That's why I'm in town. Got the Triumph in a garage here. That's my problem, as a matter of fact."

The hunted not only had antennae which served to warn the host of its enemies, but also the uncanny —if temporary—ability to turn disadvantage into advantage. Conceivable liabilities into positive assets.

Matlock sipped his bourbon and water while Kramer went through half his Scotch in several swallows. "The idea of a bus down to Scarsdale, with changes at New Haven and Bridgeport, defeats me."

"*Rent* a car, for Christ's sake."

"Just tried two places. The first can't let me have one until tonight, the second not until tomorrow. Some kind of convention, I guess."

"So wait until tonight."

"Can't do it. Family business. My father called his council of economic advisers. For dinner—and if you think I'm going to Scarsdale without my own wheels, you're out of it!" Matlock laughed and ordered another round of drinks. He reached into his pocket and put a fifty-dollar bill on the bar. The bill had to attract the attention of Jeff Kramer, who had such an expensive wife.

"Never thought you could balance a checkbook, say nothing of being an economic adviser."

"Ah, but I'm the prince royal. Can't forget that, can we?"

"Lucky bastard, that's what I can't forget. Lucky bastard."

"Hey! I've got one hell of an idea. Your car in town?"

"Hey, wait a minute, good buddy. . . ."

"No, listen." Matlock took out his bills. "The old man'll pay for it. . . . Rent me *your* car. Four or five days. . . . Here. I'll give you two, three hundred."

"You're nuts!"

"No, I'm not He wants me down. He'll pay!"

Matlock could sense Kramer's mind working. He was estimating the cost of a low-priced rent-a-car for a week. Seventy-nine fifty and ten cents a mile with an average daily mileage of, perhaps, fifteen or twenty. Tops, $105, and maybe $110, for the week.

Kramer had that expensive wife and those two very expensive kids in extremely expensive prep schools.

"I wouldn't want to take you like that."

"Not *me!* Christ, no. *Him!*"

"Well . . ."

"Here, let me write out a bill. I'll give it to him the minute I get there." Matlock grabbed a cocktail napkin and turned it over to the unprinted side. He took out his ballpoint pen and began writing. "Simple contract. . . . 'I, James B. Matlock, agree to pay Jeffrey Kramer three hundred' . . . what the hell, it's his money . . . 'four hundred dollars for the rental of his . . .' —what's the make?"

"Ford wagon. A white Squire. Last year's." Kramer's eyes alternately looked at the napkin and the roll of bills Matlock carelessly left next to Kramer's elbow on the bar.

" 'Ford Wagon, for a period of' . . . let's say one week, O.K.?"

"Fine." Kramer drank the remainder of his second Scotch.

" 'One week. . . . Signed, James B. Matlock!' There you are, friend. Countersign. And here's four hundred. Courtesy of Jonathan Munro. Where's the car?"

The hunted's instincts were infallible, thought Matlock, as Kramer pocketed the bills and wiped his chin, which had begun to perspire. Kramer removed the two car keys and the parking lot ticket from his pocket. True to Matlock's anticipation. Jeff Kramer wanted to part company. With his four hundred dollars.

Matlock said he would phone Kramer in less than a week and return the automobile. Kramer insisted on paying for the drinks and rapidly left the Hogshead Tavern. Matlock, alone, finished his drink and thought out his next move.

The hunted and the hunter were now one.

He sped out Route 72 toward Mount Holly in Kramer's white station wagon. He knew that within the hour he would find another pay telephone and insert another coin and make another call. This time to one Howard Stockton, owner of the Carmount Country Club. He looked at his watch; it was nearly eight thirty. Samuel Sharpe, attorney at law, should have reached Stockton several hours ago.

He wondered how Stockton had reacted. He wondered about Howard Stockton.

The station wagon's headlights caught the reflection of the road sign.

MOUNT HOLLY. INCORPORATED 1896

And just beyond it, a second reflection.

MOUNT HOLLY ROTARY
HARPER'S REST
TUESDAY NOON
ONE MILE

Why not? thought Matlock. There was nothing to lose. And possibly something to gain, even learn.

The hunter.

The white stucco front and the red Narragansett neons in the windows said all there was to say about Harper's cuisine. Matlock parked next to a pickup truck, got out, and locked the car. His newly acquired suitcase with the newly acquired clothes lay on the back seat. He had spent several hundred dollars in Hartford; he wasn't about to take a chance.

He walked across the cheap, large gravel and entered the bar area of Harper's Restaurant.

"I'm on my way to Carmount," said Matlock, paying for his drink with a twenty-dollar bill. "Would you mind telling me where the hell it is?"

"About two and a half miles west. Take the right fork down the road. You got anything smaller than a twenty? I only got two fives and singles. I need my singles."

"Give me the fives and we'll flip for the rest. Heads you keep it, tails I have one more and you still keep it." Matlock took a coin from his pocket and threw it on the formica bar, covering it with his hand. He lifted his palm and picked up the coin without showing it to the bartender. "It's your unlucky night. You owe me a drink—the ten's yours."

His conversation did not go unheeded by the other customers—three men drinking draft beer. That was fine, thought Matlock, as he looked around for a telephone.

"Men's room's in the rear around the corner," said a rustic-looking drinker in a chino jacket, wearing a baseball cap.

"Thanks. Telephone around?"

"Next to the men's room."

"Thanks again." Matlock took out a piece of paper

on which he had written: Howard Stockton, Carmount C.C., #203-421-1100. He gestured for the bartender, who came toward him like a shot. "I'm supposed to phone this guy," said Matlock quietly. "I think I got the name wrong. I'm not sure whether it's Stackton or Stockton. Do you know him?"

The bartender looked at the paper and Matlock saw the instant reflex of recognition. "Sure. You got it right. It's Stockton. Mr. Stockton. He's vice-president of the Rotary. Last term he was president. Right, boys?" The bartender addressed this last to his other customers.

"Sure."

"That's it. Stockton."

"Nice fella."

The man in the chino jacket and baseball cap felt the necessity of elaborating. "He runs the country club. That's a real nice place. Real nice."

"Country club?" Matlock implied the question with a trace of humor.

"That's right. Swimming pool, golf course, dancing on the weekends. Very nice." It was the bartender who elaborated now.

"I'll say this, he's highly recommended. This Stockton, I mean." Matlock drained his glass and looked toward the rear of the bar. "Telephone back there, you say?"

"That's right, Mister. Around the corner."

Matlock reached into his pocket for some change and walked to the narrow corridor where the rest rooms and telephone were located. The instant he rounded the corner, he stopped and pressed himself against the wall. He listened for the conversation he knew would be forthcoming.

"Big spender, huh?" The bartender spoke.

"They all are. Did I tell you? My kid caddied there a couple of weeks ago—some guy got a birdie and give the kid a fifty-dollar bill. Che-ryst! Fifty dollars!"

"My old woman says all them fancy dames there are *whoores*. Real whoores. She works a few parties there, my old woman does. Real whoores. . . ."

"I'd like to get my hands on some of them. Jee-*sus!* I swear to Christ most of 'em got no brazzieres!"

"Real whoores. . . ."

"Who gives a shit? That Stockton's O.K. He's O.K. in my book. Know what he did? The Kings. You know, Artie King who had a heart attack—dropped dead doin' the lawns up there. Old Stockton not only give the family a lotta dough—he set up a regular charge account for 'em at the A&P. No shit. He's O.K."

"Real whoores. They lay for money. . . ."

"Stockton put most of the cash up for the grammar school extension, don't forget that. You're fuckin' right, he's O.K. I got two kids in that school!"

"Not only—y'know what? He give a pocketful to the Memorial Day picnic."

"Real, honest-to-Christ whoores. . . ."

Matlock silently sidestepped his way against the wall to the telephone booth. He closed the door slowly with a minimum of noise. The men at the bar were getting louder in their appreciation of Howard Stockton, proprietor of the Carmount Country Club. He was not concerned that they might hear his delayed entrance into the booth.

What concerned him in an odd way was himself. If the *hunted* had instincts—protective in nature—the *hunter* had them also—aggressive by involvement. He understood now the necessity of tracking the scent, following the spoor, building a fabric of comprehensive habit. It meant that the hunter had abstract tools to complement his weapons. Tools which could build a base of entrapment, a pit in which the hunted might fall.

He ticked them off in his mind.

Howard Stockton: former president, current vice-president of the Mount Holly Rotary; a charitable man, a compassionate man. A man who took care of the family of a deceased employee named Artie King; who financed the extension of a grammar school. The proprietor of a luxurious country club in which men gave fifty-dollar tips to caddies and girls were available for members in good standing. Also a good American who made it possible for the town of Mount Holly to have a fine Memorial Day picnic.

It was enough to start with. Enough to shake up Howard Stockton if—as Sammy Sharpe had put it— "it came to that." Howard Stockton was not the formless man he was fifteen minutes ago. Matlock still didn't know the man's features, but other aspects, other factors were defined for him. Howard Stockton had become a *thing* in Mount Holly, Connecticut.

Matlock inserted the dime and dialed the number of the Carmount Country Club.

"It *suh*tainly is a pleasure, Mr. Matlock!" exclaimed Howard Stockton, greeting Matlock on the marble steps of the Carmount Country Club. "The boy'll take your car. Heah! Boy! Don't wrap it up, now!"

A Negro parking attendant laughed at his southern gentleman's command. Stockton flipped a half-dollar in the air and the black caught it with a grin.

"Thank you, suh!"

"Treat 'em good, they'll treat you good. That right, boy? Do I treat you good?!"

"Real good, Mister Howard!"

Matlock thought for a moment that he was part of an odious television commercial until he saw that Howard Stockton was the real item. Right up to his grayish blond hair, which topped a sun-tanned face, which, in turn, set off his white moustache and deep blue eyes surrounded by crow's nests of wrinkles belonging to a man who lived well.

"Welcome to Carmount, Mr. Matlock. It's not Richmond, but on the other hand, it ain't the Okefenokee."

"Thank you. And the name is Jim."

"Jim? Like that name. It's got a good, honest ring to it! My friends call me Howard. You call me Howard."

The Carmount Country Club, what he could see of it, reminded Matlock of all those pictures of antebellum architecture. And why not, considering the owner? It was rife with potted palms and delicate chandeliers and light blue toile wallpaper depicting rococo scenes in which cavorted prettified figures in powdered wigs. Howard Stockton was a proselytizer of a way of life which had collapsed in 1865, but he wasn't going to admit it. Even the servants, mostly black, were in liveries—honest-to-god liveries, knickers and all. Soft, live music came from a large dining room, at the end of which was a string orchestra of perhaps eight instruments gracefully playing in a fashion long since abandoned. There was a slowly winding staircase in the center of the main hall which would have done honor to Jefferson Davis—or David O. Selznick. Attractive women were wandering around, linked with not-so-attractive men.

The effect was incredible, thought Matlock, as he walked by his host's side toward what his host modestly claimed was his private library.

The southerner closed the thick paneled door and strode to a well-stocked mahogany bar. He poured without asking a preference.

"Sam Sharpe says you drink sour mash. You're a man of taste, I tell you that. That's *my* drink." He carried two glasses to Matlock. "Take your pick. A Virginian has to disarm a northerner with his complete lack of bias these days."

"Thank you," said Matlock, taking a glass and sitting in the armchair indicated by Stockton.

"This Virginian," continued Howard Stockton, sitting opposite Matlock, "also has an unsouthern habit of getting to the point. . . . I don't even know if it's wise for you to be in my place. I'll be honest. That's why I ushered you right in here."

"I don't understand. You could have told me on the phone not to come. Why the game?"

"Maybe you can answer that better than I can. Sammy says you're a real big man. You're what they call . . . *international*. That's just dandy by me. I like a bright young fella who goes up the ladder of success. Very commendable, that's a fact. . . . But I pay my bills. I pay every month on the line. I got the best combined operation north of Atlanta. I don't want trouble."

"You won't get it from *me*. I'm a tired businessman making the rounds, that's all I am."

"What happened at Sharpe's? The papers are full of it! I don't want *nothin'* like that!"

Matlock watched the southerner. The capillaries in the suntanned face were bloodred, which was probably why the man courted a year-round sunburn. It covered a multitude of blemishes.

"I don't think you understand." Matlock measured his words as he lifted the glass to his lips. "I've come a long way because I *have* to be here. I don't *want* to be here. Personal reasons got me into the area early, so I'm doing some sightseeing. But it's only that. I'm just looking around. . . . Until my appointment."

"What appointment?"

"An appointment in Carlyle, Connecticut."

Stockton squinted his eyes and pulled at his perfectly groomed white moustache. "You've got to be in Carlyle?"

"Yes. It's confidential, but I don't have to tell you that, do I?"

"You haven't told me anything." Stockton kept watching Matlock's face, and Matlock knew the southerner was looking for a false note, a wrong word, a hesitant glance which might contradict his information.

"Good. . . . By any chance, do you have an appointment in Carlyle, too? In about a week and a half?"

Stockton sipped his drink, smacking his lips and putting the glass on a side table as though it were some precious *objet d'art*. "I'm just a southern cracker tryin' to make a dollar. Livin' the good life and makin' a dollar. That's all. I don't know about any appointments in Carlyle."

"Sorry I brought it up. It's a . . . major mistake on my part. For both our sakes, I hope you won't mention it. Or *me*."

"That's the *last* thing I'd do. Far as I'm concerned, you're a friend of Sammy's lookin' for a little action . . . and a little hospitality." Suddenly Stockton leaned forward in his chair, his elbows on his knees, his hands folded. He looked like an earnest minister questioning a parishioner's sins. "What in tarnation happened at Windsor Shoals? What in hell was it?"

"As far as I can see, it was a local vendetta. Barto-lozzi had enemies. Some said he talked too goddamn much. Aiello, too, I suppose. They were show-offs. . . . Frank was just there, I think."

"Goddamn *Eye*talians! Mess up everything! *That* level, of course, you know what I mean?"

There it was again. The dangling interrogative—but in this southerner's version, it wasn't really a question. It was a statement.

"I know what you mean," said Matlock wearily.

"I'm afraid I got a little bad news for you, Jim. I closed the tables for a few days. Just plum scared as a jackrabbit after what happened at the Shoals."

"That's not bad news for me. Not the way my streak's been going."

"I heard. Sammy told me. But we got a couple of other diversions. You won't find Carmount lacking in hospitality, I promise you that."

The two men finished their drinks, and Stockton, relieved, escorted his guest into the crowded, elegant Carmount dining room. The food was extraordinary, served in a manner befitting the finest and wealthiest plantation of the antebellum South.

Although pleasant—even relaxing, in a way—the dinner was pointless to Matlock. Howard Stockton would not discuss his "operation" except in the vaguest terms and with the constant reminder that he catered to the "best class of Yankee." His speech was peppered with descriptive anachronisms, he was a walking contradiction in time. Halfway through the meal, Stockton excused himself to say good-bye to an important member.

It was the first opportunity Matlock had to look at Stockton's "best class of Yankee" clientele.

The term applied, thought Matlock, if the word *class* was interchangeable with *money*, which he wasn't willing to concede. Money screamed from every table. The first sign was the proliferation of suntans in the beginning of a Connecticut May. These were people who jetted to the sun-drenched islands at will. Another was the easy, deep-throated laughter echoing throughout the room; also the glittering reflection of jewelry. And the clothes—softly elegant suits, raw silk jackets, Dior ties. And the bottles of sparkling vintage wines, standing majestically in sterling silver stands upheld by cherrywood tripods.

But something was wrong, thought Matlock. Something was missing or out of place, and for several minutes he couldn't put his finger on what it was. And then he did.

The suntans, the laughter, the wrist jewelry, the jackets, the Dior ties—the money, the elegance, the aura was predominantly *male*.

The contradiction was the women—the girls. Not that there weren't some who matched their partners, but in the main, they didn't. They were younger. Much, much younger. And different.

He wasn't sure what the difference was at first. Then, abstractly, it came to him. For the most part, the girls—and they *were* girls—had a look about them he knew very well. He'd referred to it often in the past. It was the campus look—as differentiated from the office look, the secretary look. A slightly more careless attitude in conversation. The look of girls not settling into routines, not welded to file cabinets or typewriters. It was definable because it was real. Matlock had been exposed to that look for over a decade—it was unmistakable.

Then he realized that within this contradiction there was another—minor—discrepancy. The clothes the girls wore. They weren't the clothes he expected to find on girls with the campus look. They were too precisely cut, too designed, if that was the word. In this day of unisex, simply too feminine.

They wore costumes!

Suddenly, in a single, hysterically spoken sentence from several tables away, he knew he was right.

"Honest, I mean it—it's too groovy!"

That voice! *Christ, he knew that voice!*

He wondered if he was meant to hear it.

He had his hand up to his face and slowly turned toward the direction of the giggling speaker. The girl was laughing and drinking champagne, while her escort—a much older man—stared with satisfaction at her enormous breasts.

The girl was Virginia Beeson. The "pinky groovy" perennial undergraduate wife of Archer Beeson, Carlyle University's history instructor.

The man in an academic hurry.

Matlock tipped the black who carried his suitcase up the winding staircase to the large, ornate room Stockton had offered him. The floor was covered with a thick wine-colored carpet, the bed canopied, the walls white with fluted moldings. He saw that on the bureau was an ice bucket, two bottles of Jack Daniels, and several glasses. He opened the suitcase, picked out his toilet articles, and put them on the bedside table. He then removed a suit, a lightweight jacket, and two pairs of slacks, and carried them to the closet. He returned to the suitcase, lifted it from the bed, and laid it across the two wooden arms of a chair.

There was a soft tapping on his door. His first thought was that the caller was Howard Stockton, but he was wrong.

A girl, dressed in a provocative deep-red sheath, stood in the frame and smiled. She was in her late teens or very early twenties and terribly attractive.

And her smile was false.

"Yes?"

"Compliments of Mr. Stockton." She spoke the words and walked into the room past Matlock.

Matlock closed the door and stared at the girl, not so much bewildered as surprised.

"That's very thoughtful of Mr. Stockton, isn't it?"

"I'm glad you approve. There's whisky, ice, and glasses on your bureau. I'd like a short drink. Unless you're in a hurry."

Matlock walked slowly to the bureau. "I'm in no hurry. What would you like?"

"It doesn't matter. Whatever's there. Just ice, please."

"I see." Matlock poured the girl a drink and carried it over to her. "Won't you sit down?"

"On the bed?"

The only other chair, besides the one on which the suitcase was placed, was across the room by a French window.

"I'm sorry." He removed the suitcase and the girl sat down. Howard Stockton, he thought, had good taste. The girl was adorable. "What's your name?"

"Jeannie." She drank a great deal of her drink in several swallows. The girl may not have perfected a selection in liquor, but she knew how to drink. And then, as the girl took the glass from her mouth, Matlock noticed the ring on her third right finger.

He knew that ring very well. It was sold in a campus bookstore several blocks from John Holden's apartment in Webster, Connecticut. It was the ring of Madison University.

"What would you say if I told you I wasn't interested?" asked Matlock, leaning against the thick pole of the bed's anachronistic canopy.

"I'd be surprised. You don't look like a fairy."

"I'm not."

The girl looked up at Matlock. Her pale blue eyes were warm—but professionally warm—meaning, yet not meaning at all. Her lips were young. And full; and taut.

"Maybe you just need a little encouragement."

"You can provide that?"

"I'm good." She made the statement with quiet arrogance.

She was so young, thought Matlock, yet there was age in her. And hate. The hate was camouflaged, but the cosmetic was inadequate. She was performing—the costume, the eyes, the lips. She may have detested the role, but she accepted it.

Professionally.

"Suppose I just want to talk?"

"Conversation's something else. There are no rules about that. I've equal rights in that department. Quid pro, Mister No-name."

"You're facile with words. Should that tell me something?"

"I don't know why."

" 'Quid pro quo' isn't the language of your eight to three hooker."

"This place—in case you missed it—isn't the Avenida de las Putas, either."

"Tennessee Williams?"

"Who knows?"

"I think you do."

"Fine. All right. We can discuss Proust in bed. I mean, that *is* where you want me, isn't it?"

"Perhaps I'd settle for the conversation."

The girl suddenly, in alarm, whispered hoarsely, "Are you a cop?"

"I'm the furthest thing from a cop," laughed Matlock. "You might say that some of the most important policemen in the area would like to find me. Although I'm no criminal. . . . Or a nut, by the way."

"Now *I'm* not interested. May I have another drink?"

"Surely." Matlock got it for her. Neither spoke until he returned with her glass.

"Do you mind if I stay here awhile? Just long enough for you to have balled me."

"You mean you don't want to lose the fee?"

"It's fifty dollars."

"You'll probably have to use part of it to bribe the dormitory head. Madison University's a little old-fashioned. Some coed houses still have weekday check-ins. You'll be late."

The shock on the girl's face was complete. "You *are* a cop! You're a lousy *cop!*" She started to get out of the chair, but Matlock quickly stood in front of her, holding her shoulders. He eased her back into the chair.

"I'm not a cop, I told you that. And you're not interested, remember? But *I'm* interested. I'm *very* interested, and you're going to tell me what I want to know."

The girl started to get up and Matlock grabbed her arms. She struggled; he pushed her back violently. "Do you always get 'balled' with your ring on? Is that to show whoever gets laid there's a little class to it?!"

"Oh, my God! Oh, Jesus!" She grabbed her ring and twisted her finger as if the pressure might make it disappear.

"Now, listen to me! You answer my questions or I'll be down in Webster tomorrow morning and I'll start asking them down there! Would you like that better?"

"Please! *Please!*" Tears came to the girl's eyes. Her hands shook and she gasped for breath.

"How did you get here?!"

"No! No . . ."

"*How?*"

"I was recruited. . . ."

"By whom?"

"Other . . . Others. We recruit each other."

"How many are there?"

"Not many. Not very many. . . . It's quiet. We have to keep it quiet. . . . Let me go, *please*. I want to *go*."

"Oh, no. Not yet. I want to know how many and *why!*"

"I told you! Only a few, maybe seven or eight girls."

"There must be thirty downstairs!"

"I don't *know* them. They're from other places. We don't ask each other's *names!*"

"But you know where they're from, don't you!"

"Some. . . . Yes."

"Other schools?"

"Yes. . . ."

"*Why*, Jeannie? For Christ's sake, *why?*"

"Why do you *think? Money!*"

The girl's dress had long sleeves. He grabbed her

right arm and ripped the fabric up past the elbow. She fought him back but he overpowered her.

There were no marks. No signs.

She kicked at him and he slapped her face, hard enough to shock her into momentary immobility. He took her left arm and tore the sleeve.

There they were. Faded. Not recent. But there.

The small purple dots of a needle.

"I'm not on it now! I haven't been in *months!*"

"But you need the money! You need fifty or a hundred dollars every time you come over here! . . . What is it *now?* Yellows? Reds? *Acid? Speed?* What the hell is it *now?* Grass isn't that expensive!"

The girl sobbed. Tears fell down her cheeks. She covered her face and spoke—moaned—through her sobs.

"There's so much trouble! So much . . . *trouble!* Let me go, *please!*"

Matlock knelt down and cradled the girl's head in his arms, against his chest.

"What trouble? tell me, please. What trouble?"

"They *make* you do it. . . . You *have* to. . . . So many need help. They won't help *anyone* if you don't do it. Please, whatever your name is, let me alone. Let me go. Don't say anything. Let me *go! . . . Please!*"

"I will, but you've got to clear something up for me. Then you can go and I won't say anything. . . . Are you down here because they threatened you? Threatened the other kids?"

The girl nodded her head, gasping quietly, breathing heavily. Matlock continued. "Threatened you with what? Turning you in? . . . Exposing a habit? That's not worth it. Not today. . . ."

"Oh, you're outta sight!" The girl spoke through her

tears. "They can ruin you. For life. Ruin your family, your school, maybe later. Maybe. . . . Some rotten prison. Somewhere! Habit, pushing, supplying . . . a boy you know's in trouble and *they* can get him off. . . . Some girl's in her third month, she needs a doctor . . . *they* can get one. No noise."

"You don't need *them!* Where've you *been?!* There are agencies, counseling!"

"Oh, Jesus Christ, mister! Where have *you* been?! . . . The drug courts, the doctors, the judges! They run them *all!* . . . There's nothing *you* can do about it. Nothing *I* can do about it. So leave me alone, leave *us* alone! Too many people'll get hurt!"

"And you're just going to keep doing what they say! Frightened, spoiled little bastards who keep on whining! Afraid to wash your hands, or your *mouths,* or your *arms!*" He pulled at her left elbow and yanked it viciously.

The girl looked up at him, half in fear, half in contempt.

"That's right," she said in a strangely calm voice. "I don't think you'd understand. You don't know what it's all about. . . . We're different from you. My friends are all I've got. All any of us have got. We help each other. . . . I'm not interested in being a hero. I'm only interested in my friends. I don't have a flag decal in my car window and I don't like John Wayne. I think he's a shit. I think you all are. All shits."

Matlock released the girl's arm. "Just how long do you think you can keep it up?"

"Oh, I'm one of the lucky ones. In a month I'll have that scroll my parents paid for and I'm out of it. They hardly ever try to make contact with you later. They say they will, but they rarely do. . . . You're just supposed to live with the possibility."

He understood the implications of her muted testimony and turned away. "I'm sorry. I'm very, very sorry."

"Don't be. I'm one of the lucky ones. Two weeks after I pick up that piece of engraved crap my parents want so badly, I'll be on a plane. I'm leaving this goddamn country. And I'll never come back!"

He had not been able to sleep, nor had he expected to. He had sent the girl away with money, for he had nothing else he could give her, neither hope nor courage. What he advocated was rejected, for it involved the risk of danger and pain to untold children committed to the well-being of each other. He could not demand; there was no trust, no threat equal to the burdens they carried. Ultimately, it was the children's own struggle. They wanted no help.

He remembered the Bagdhivi admonition: *Look ye to the children; look and behold. They grow tall and strong and hunt the tiger with greater cunning and stronger sinews than you. They shall save the flocks better than you. Ye are old and infirm. Look to the children. Beware of the children.*

Were the children hunting the tiger better? And even if they were, whose flocks would they save? And who was the tiger?

Was it the "goddamn country"?

Had it come to that?

The questions burned into his mind. How many Jeannies were there? How extensive was Nimrod's recruiting?

He had to find out.

The girl admitted that Carmount was only one port

of call; there were others, but she didn't know where. Friends of hers had been sent to New Haven, others to Boston, some north to the outskirts of Hanover.

Yale. Harvard. Dartmouth.

The most frightening aspect was Nimrod's threat of a thousand futures. What had she said?

"They hardly ever make contact. . . . They say they will. . . . You live with the possibility."

If such was the case, Bagdhivi was wrong. The children had far less cunning, possessed weaker sinews; there was no reason to beware. Only to pity.

Unless the children were subdivided, led by other, stronger children.

Matlock made up his mind to go down to New Haven. Maybe there were answers there. He had scores of friends at Yale University. It would be a side trip, an unconsidered excursion, but intrinsic to the journey itself. Part of the Nimrod odyssey.

Short, high-pitched sounds interrupted Matlock's concentration. He froze, his eyes swollen in shock, his body tense on top of the bed. It took him several seconds to focus his attention on the source of the frightening sound. It was the Tel-electronic, still in his jacket pocket. But where had he put his jacket? It wasn't near his bed.

He turned on the bedside lamp and looked around, the unrelenting, unceasing sounds causing his pulse to hammer, his forehead to perspire. Then he saw his coat. He had put it on top of the chair in front of the French window, halfway across the room. He looked at his watch: 4:35 A.M. He ran to the jacket, pulled out the terrible instrument, and shut it off.

The panic of the hunted returned. He picked up the telephone on the bedside table. It was a direct line, no switchboard.

The dial tone was like any other dial tone outside the major utility areas. A little fuzzy, but steady. And if there was a tap, he wouldn't be able to recognize it anyway. He dialed 555-6868 and waited for the call to be completed.

"Charger Three-zero reporting," said the mechanized voice. "Sorry to disturb you. There is no change with the subject, everything is satisfactory. However, your friend from Wheeling, West Virginia, is very insistent. He telephoned at four fifteen and said it was imperative you call him at once. We're concerned. Out."

Matlock hung up the telephone and forced his mind to go blank until he found a cigarette and lit it. He needed the precious moments to stop the hammering pulse.

He hated that goddamn machine! He hated what its terrifying little beeps did to him.

He drew heavily on the smoke and knew there was no alternative. He had to get out of the Carmount Country Club and reach a telephone booth. Greenberg wouldn't have phoned at four in the morning unless it was an emergency. He couldn't take the chance of calling Greenberg on the Carmount line.

He threw his clothes into the suitcase and dressed quickly.

He assumed there'd be a night watchman, or a parking attendant asleep in a booth, and he'd retrieve his, Kramer's, automobile. If not, he'd wake up someone, even if it was Stockton himself. Stockton was still frightened of trouble, Windsor Shoals trouble—he wouldn't try to detain him. Any story would do for the purveyor of young, adorable flesh. The sunburned southern flower of the Connecticut Valley. The stench of Nimrod.

Matlock closed the door quietly and walked down the silent corridor to the enormous staircase. Wall sconces were lighted, dimmed by rheostats to give a candlelight effect. Even in the dead of night, Howard Stockton couldn't forget his heritage. The interior of the Carmount Country Club looked more than ever like a sleeping great hall of a plantation house.

He started for the front entrance, and by the time he reached the storm carpet, he knew it was as far as he would go. At least for the moment.

Howard Stockton, clad in a flowing velour, nine-teenth-century dressing gown, emerged from a glass door next to the entrance. He was accompanied by a large, Italian-looking man whose jet black eyes silently spoke generations of the Black Hand. Stockton's companion was a killer.

"Why, Mr. Matlock! Are you leavin' us?"

He decided to be aggressive.

"Since you tapped my goddamn phone, I assume you gather I've got problems! They're *my business, not yours!* If you want to know, I resent your intrusion!"

The ploy worked. Stockton was startled by Matlock's hostility.

"There's no reason to be angry. . . . I'm a business-man, like you. Any invasion of your privacy is for your protection. Goddamn! That's *true, boy!*"

"I'll accept the lousy explanation. Are my keys in the car?"

"Well, not in your *car.* My friend Mario here's got 'em. He's a real high-class Eyetalian, let me tell you."

"I can see the family crest on his pocket. May I have my keys?"

Mario looked at Stockton, obviously confused.

"Now, just a minute," Stockton said. "Wait a bit,

Mario. Let's not be impulsive. . . . I'm a reasonable man. A very reasonable, rational person. I'm merely a Virginia . . ."

"*Cracker,* trying to make a dollar!" interrupted Matlock. "I'll buy that! Now get the hell out of my way and give me the keys!"

"Good Lord, *you all* are downright *mean!* I mean, *mean!* Put yourself in my place! . . . Some crazy code like 'Chargin' Three-zero' and an urgent call from Wheelin', West *Virginia!* And instead of usin' my perfectly good telephone, you gotta make space and get *outta* here! C'mon, Jim. What would *you* do?!"

Matlock kept his voice chillingly precise. "I'd try to understand *who* I was dealing with. . . . We've made a number of inquiries, Howard. My superiors are concerned about you."

"What-do-you-mean?" Stockton's question was asked so swiftly the words had no separation.

"They think . . . we think you've called too much attention to yourself. President and vice-president of a *Rotary Club!* Jesus! A one-man fund-raiser for new school buildings; the big provider for widows and orphans—charge accounts included; Memorial Day picnics! Then hiring locals to spread rumors about the girls! Half the time the kids walk around half naked. You think the local citizens don't talk? *Christ,* Howard!"

"Who the hell are you?"

"Just a tired businessman who gets annoyed when he sees another businessman make an ass of himself. What the hell do you think you're running for? Santa Claus? Have you any idea how prominent that costume is?"

"Goddamn it, you got it in for me! I've got the finest combined operation north of Atlanta! I don't

know who you people been talkin' to, but I tell you—
this l'il old Mount Holly'd go to hell in a basket
for me! Those things you people dug up—they're
good things! *Real* good! . . . You twist 'em, make
'em sound bad! That ain't *right!*"

Stockton took out a handkerchief and patted his
flushed, perspiring face. The southerner was so upset
his sentences spilled over into one another, his voice
strident. Matlock tried to think swiftly, cautiously.
Perhaps the time was now—with Stockton. It had to
be sometime. He had to send out his own particular
invitation. He had to start the last lap of his journey
to Nimrod.

"Calm down, Stockton. Relax. You may be right. . . .
I haven't time to think about it now. We've got a
crisis. All of us. That phone call was serious." Matlock paused, looking hard at the nervous Stockton,
and then put his suitcase on the marble floor. "Howard," he said slowly, choosing his words carefully, "I'm
going to trust you with something and I hope to hell
you're up to it. If you pull it off, no one'll bother your
operation—ever."

"What's that?"

"Tell *him* to take a walk. Just down the hall, if you
like."

"You heard the man. Go smoke a cigar."

Mario looked both hostile and confused as he
trudged slowly toward the staircase. Stockton spoke.

"What do you want me to do? I told you, I don't
want trouble."

"We're *all* going to have trouble unless I reach a
few delegates. That's what Wheeling was telling me."

"What do you mean . . . delegates?"

"The meeting over at Carlyle. The conference with
our people and the Nimrod organization."

"That's not my affair!" Stockton spat out the words. "I don't know a thing about that!"

"I'm sure you don't; you weren't meant to. But now it concerns all of us. . . . Sometimes rules have to be broken; this is one of those times. Nimrod's gone too far, that's all I can tell you."

"You tell *me?* I live with those *preachers!* I *parlay* with them, and when I complain, you know what our own people say? They say, 'That's the way it is, old Howie, we all do business'! What kind of talk is that? Why do *I* have to do business with them?"

"Perhaps you won't much longer. That's why I have to reach some of the others. The delegates."

"They don't include me in those meetings. I don't know anyone."

"Of course you don't. Again, you weren't meant to. The conference is heavy; very heavy and very quiet. So quiet we may have screwed ourselves: we don't know who's in the area. From what organization; from what family? But I have my orders. We've got to get through to one or two."

"I can't help you."

Matlock looked harshly at the southerner. "I think you can. Listen to me. In the morning, get on the phone and pass the word. *Carefully!* We don't want panic. Don't talk to anyone you don't know and don't use my name! Just say you've met someone who has the Corsican paper, the silver Corsican paper. He's *got* to meet quietly with someone else who has it, too. We'll start with one person if we have to. Have you got that?"

"I got it but I don't like it! It's none of *my business!*"

"Would you rather close down? Would you rather lose this magnificent relic of yours and stare out of a cell window for ten or twenty years? I understand prison funerals are very touching."

"All right! . . . All right. I'll call my bag boy. I'll say I don't know nothin'! I'm just passin' along a message."

"Good enough. If you make a contact, tell whoever it is that I'll be at the Sail and Ski tonight or tomorrow. Tell him to bring the paper. I won't talk to anyone without the paper!"

"Without the paper. . . ."

"Now let me have my keys."

Stockton called Mario back. Matlock got his keys.

He swung south on Route 72 out of Mount Holly. He didn't remember precisely where, but he knew he'd passed several highway telephone booths on his way up from Hartford. It was funny how he was beginning to notice public telephones, his only connecting link with solidity. Everything else was transient, hit or miss, unfamiliar and frightening. He'd phone Greenberg as Charger Three-zero requested, but before he did, he was going to reach one of Blackstone's men.

A rendezvous would have to be arranged immediately. He now had to have the Corsican paper. He'd put out the word; he'd have to keep his end of the bargain or he would learn nothing. *If* Stockton's message got through and *if* someone *did* make contact, that someone would kill or be killed before breaking the oath of "Omerta" unless Matlock produced the paper.

Or was it all for nothing? Was he the amateur Kressel and Greenberg said he was? He didn't know. He tried so hard to think things through, look at all sides of every action, use the tools of his trained, aca-

demic imagination. But was it enough? Or was it possible that his sense of commitment, his violent feelings
of vengeance and disgust were only turning him into a Quixote?

If that were so, he'd live with it. He'd do his god-
damnedest and live with it. He had good reasons—a
brother named David; a girl named Pat; a gentle old
man named Lucas; a nice fellow named Loring; a confused, terrified student from Madison named Jeannie.
The sickening whole *scene!*

Matlock found a booth on a deserted stretch of
Route 72 and called the inanimate receiver at the other
end of 555-6868. He gave the number of the telephone
booth and waited for Charger Three-zero to answer
his call.

A milk truck lumbered by. The driver was singing
and waved to Matlock. Several minutes later a huge
Allied Van Lines sped past, and shortly after a produce truck. It was nearing five thirty, and the day was
brightening. Brightening to a dull gray, for there were
rain clouds in the sky.

The telephone rang.

"Hello!"

"What's the problem, sir? Did you reach your friend
in West Virginia? He said he's not kidding anymore."

"I'll call him in a few minutes. Are you the fellow
named Cliff?" Matlock knew it was not; the voice was
different.

"No, sir. I'm Jim. Same name as yours."

"All right, Jim. Tell me, did the other fellow do
what I asked him to? Did he get the paper for me?"

"Yes, sir. If it's the one on silver paper, written in
Italian. I think it's Italian."

"That's the one. . . ."

Matlock arranged for the pickup in two hours. It

was agreed that the Blackstone man named Cliff
meet him at an all-night diner on Scofield Avenue near
the West Hartford town line. Charger Three-zero insisted that the delivery be made rapidly, in the parking lot. Matlock described the car he was driving and
hung up the phone.

The next call would have to be Jason Greenberg in
Wheeling. And Greenberg was furious.

"Schmuck! It isn't bad enough you break your
word, you've got to hire your own army! What the
hell do you think those clowns can do that the United
States Government can't?"

"Those clowns are costing me three hundred dollars
a day, Jason. They'd better be good."

"You ran out! Why did you do that? You gave me
your word you wouldn't. You said you'd work with
our man!"

"Your man gave me an ultimatum I couldn't live
with! And if it was your idea, I'll tell you the same
thing I told Houston."

"What does that mean? What ultimatum?"

"You know goddamn well! Don't play that game.
And you listen to me. . . ." Matlock took a break before plunging into the lie, giving it all the authority he
could summon. "There's a lwayer in Hartford who has
a very precise letter signed by me. Along the same
lines as the letter I signed for you. Only the information's a bit different: it's straight. It describes in detail
the story of my recruitment; how you bastards
sucked me in and then how you let me hang. How
you forced me to sign a lie. . . . You try anything,
he'll release it and there'll be a lot of embarrassed
manipulators at the Justice Department. . . . You
gave me the idea, Jason. It was a damn good idea.
It might even make a few militants decide to tear

up the Carlyle campus. Maybe launch a string of riots, with luck, right across the country. The academic scene's ready to be primed out of its dormancy; isn't that what Sealfont said? Only this time it won't be the war or the draft or drugs. They'll find a better label: government infiltration, police state . . . *Gestapo* tactics. Are you prepared for that?"

"For Christ's sake, cut it out! It won't do you any good. You're not that important. . . . Now, what the hell are you talking about? *I briefed him!* There weren't any conditions except that you keep him informed of what you were doing."

"Bullshit! I wasn't to leave the campus; I wasn't to talk to anyone on the faculty or the staff. I was restricted to student inquiries, and I gathered those were to be cleared *first!* Outside of those minor restrictions, I was free as a bird! Come on! You *saw* Pat! You saw what they did to her. You know what else they did—the word is *rape*, Greenberg! Did you people expect me to *thank* Houston for being so *understanding?*"

"Believe me," said Greenberg softly, in anger. "Those conditions were added after the briefing. They should have told me, that's true. But they were added for your own protection. You can see that, can't you?"

"They weren't part of our bargain!"

"No, they weren't. And they should have told me. . . ."

"Also, I wonder whose protection they were concerned with. Mine or theirs."

"A good question. They should have told me. They can't delegate responsibility and always take away the authority. It's not logical."

"It's not *moral.* Let me tell you something. This little odyssey of mine is bringing me closer and closer to the sublime question of morality."

"I'm glad for you, but I'm afraid your odyssey's coming to an end."

"Try it!"

"They're going to. Statements in lawyers' offices won't mean a damn. I told them I'd try first. . . . If you don't turn yourself over to protective custody within forty-eight hours, they'll issue a warrant."

"On what grounds?!"

"You're a menace. You're mentally unbalanced. You're a nut. They'll cite your army record—two courts-martial, brig time, continuous instability under combat conditions. Your use of drugs. And alcohol—they've got witnesses. You're also a racist—they've got that Lumumba affidavit from Kressel. And now I understand, although I haven't the facts, you're consorting with known criminals. They have photographs—from a place in Avon. . . . Turn yourself in, Jim. They'll ruin your life."

Forty-eight hours! Why forty-eight hours? Why not twenty-four or twelve or immediately? It didn't make sense! Then he understood and, alone in the booth, he started to laugh. He laughed out loud in a telephone booth at five thirty in the morning on a deserted stretch of highway in Mount Holly, Connecticut.

The practical men were giving him just enough time to accomplish something—if he *could* accomplish something. If he couldn't, and anything happened, they were clean. It was on record that they considered him a mentally unbalanced addict with racist tendencies who consorted with known criminals, and they had given him warning. In deference to the delicate balance of dealing with such madmen, they allocated *time* in the hopes of reducing the danger. Oh, Christ! The manipulators!

He reached the West Hartford diner at six forty-five and ate a large breakfast, somehow believing that the food would take the place of sleep and give him the energy he needed. He kept glancing at his watch, knowing that he'd have to be in the parking lot by seven thirty.

He wondered what his contact at Charger Three-zero would look like.

The man was enormous, and Matlock had never considered himself small. Cliff of Charger Three-zero reminded Matlock of those old pictures of Primo Carnera. Except the face. The face was lean and intelligent and smiled broadly.

"Don't get out, Mr. Matlock." He reached in and shook Matlock's hand. "Here's the paper; I put it in an envelope. By the way, we had Miss Ballantyne laughing last night. She's feeling better. Encephalograph's steady, metabolism's coming back up to par, pupil dilation's receding. Thought you'd like to know."

"I imagine that's good."

"It is. We've made friends with the doctor. He levels."

"How's the hospital taking your guard duty?"

"Mr. Blackstone solves those problems in advance. We have rooms on either side of the subject."

"For which, I'm sure, I'll be charged."

"You know Mr. Blackstone."

"I'm getting to. He goes first class."

"So do his clients. I'd better get back. Nice to meet you." The Blackstone man walked rapidly away and got into a nondescript automobile several years old.

It was time for Matlock to drive to New Haven.

He had no set plan, no specific individuals in mind; he wasn't leading, he was being led. His information was, at best, nebulous, sketchy, far too incomplete to deal in absolutes. Yet perhaps there was enough for someone to make a connection. But whoever made it, or was capable of making it, had to be someone with an overall view of the university. Someone who dealt, as did Sam Kressel, with the general tensions of the campus.

However, Yale was five times the size of Carlyle; it was infinitely more diffuse, a section of the New Haven city, not really isolated from its surroundings as was Carlyle. There *was* a focal point, the Office of Student Affairs; but he didn't know anyone there. And to arrive off the street with an improbable story of college girls forming—or being formed into—a prostitution ring reaching, as so far determined, the states of Connecticut, Massachusetts, and New Hampshire, would create havoc if he was taken seriously. And he wasn't sure he *would* be taken seriously, in which case he'd learn nothing.

There was one possibility; a poor substitute for Student Affairs, but with its own general view of the campus: the Department of Admissions. He knew a man, Peter Daniels, who worked in Yale's admissions office. He and Daniels had shared a number of lecterns during prep school recruitment programs. He knew Daniels well enough to spell out the facts as he understood them; Daniels wasn't the sort to doubt him or to panic. He'd restrict his story to the girl, however.

He parked on Chappel Street near the intersection of York. On one side of the thoroughfare was an arch leading to the quadrangle of Silliman College, on the other a large expanse of lawn threaded with cement paths to the Administration Building. Daniels's office was on the second floor. Matlock got out of the car, locked it, and walked toward the old brick structure with the American flag masted next to the Yale banner.

"That's preposterous! This is the age of Aquarius and then some. You don't pay for sex; it's exchanged freely."

"I know what I saw. I know what the girl told me; she wasn't lying."

"I repeat. You can't be sure."

"It's tied in with too many other things. I've seen them, too."

"May I ask the obvious question? Why don't you go to the police?"

"Obvious answer. Colleges have been in enough trouble. What facts I have are isolated. I need more information. I don't want to be responsible for indiscriminate name-calling, any widespread panic. There's been enough of that."

"All right, I'll buy it. But I can't help you."

"Give me several names. Students *or* faculty. People you know . . . you're certain are messed up, seriously messed up. Near the center. You've got those kinds of names, I know you do; we do. . . . I swear, they'll never know who gave them to me."

Daniels got out of his chair, lighting his pipe. "You're being awfully general. Messed up how? Academically, politically . . . narcotics, alcohol? You're covering a wide territory."

"Wait a minute." Daniels's words evoked a memory. Matlock recalled a dimly lit, smoke-filled room inside a seemingly deserted building in Hartford. Rocco Aiello's Hunt Club. And a tall young man in a waiter's jacket who had brought over a tab for Aiello to sign. The veteran of Nam and Da Nang. The Yalie who was *making contacts, building up his nest egg* . . . the *business administration* major. "I know who I want to see."

"What's his name?"

"I don't know. . . . But he's a veteran—Indochina, about twenty-two or three; he's pretty tall, light brown hair . . . majoring in business administration."

"A description which might fit five hundred students. Except for premed, law, and engineering, it's all lumped under liberal arts. We'd have to go through every file."

"Application photographs?"

"Not allowed anymore, you know that."

Matlock stared out the window, his eyebrows wrinkled in thought. He looked back at Daniels. "Pete, it's May. . . ."

"So? It could be November; that wouldn't change the Fair Practices law."

"Graduation's in a month. . . . Senior class photographs. Yearbook portraits."

Daniels understood instantly. He took his pipe from his mouth and started for the door.

"Come with me."

His name was Alan Pace. He was a senior and his curriculum was not centered on business administration; he was a government major. He lived off campus on Church Street near the Hamden town line. According to his records, Alan Pace was an excellent student, consistent honors in all subjects, a fellowship in the offing at the Maxwell School of Political Science at Syracuse. He had spent twenty-eight months in the army, four more than was required of him. As with most veterans, his university extracurricular activities were minimal.

While Pace was in service, he was an officer attached to inventory and supply. He had volunteered for a four-month extended tour of duty in the Saigon

Corps—a fact noted with emphasis on his reapplication form. Alan Pace had given four months of his life more than necessary to his country. Alan Pace was obviously an honorable man in these days of cynicism.

He was a winner, thought Matlock.

The drive out Church Street toward Hamden gave Matlock the chance to clear his mind. He had to take one thing at a time; one item crossed off—on to the next. He couldn't allow his imagination to interpret isolated facts beyond their meaning. He couldn't lump everything together and total a sum larger than the parts.

It was entirely possible that this Alan Pace played a solo game. Unattached, unencumbered.

But it wasn't logical.

Pace's apartment house was an undistinguished brown brick building, so common on the outskirts of cities. Once—forty or fifty years ago—it had been the proud symbol of a rising middle class extending themselves out beyond the cement confines toward the country, but not so courageous as to leave the city completely. It wasn't so much run down as it was . . . not spruced up. The most glaring aspect of the apartment house to Matlock, however, was that it seemed to be a most unlikely place for a student to reside.

But he was there now; Peter Daniels had ascertained that.

Pace had not wanted to unlatch the door. It was only Matlock's strong emphasis on two points that made the student relent. The first point was that he wasn't from the police; the second, the name of Rocco Aiello.

"What do you want? I've got a lot of work to do;

I don't have time to talk. I've got comprehensives to-morrow."

"May I sit down?"

"What for? I told you, I'm busy." The tall, brown-haired student crossed back to his desk, piled with books and papers. The apartment was neat—except for the desk—and quite large. There were doors and short corridors leading to other doors. It was the sort of apartment that usually was shared by four or five students. But Alan Pace had no roommates.

"I'll sit down anyway. You owe that much to Rocco."

"What does that mean?"

"Just that Rocco was my friend. I was the one with him the other night when you brought him a tab to sign. Remember? And he was good to you. . . . He's dead."

"I know. I read about it. I'm sorry. But I didn't owe him anything."

"But you bought from him."

"I don't know what you're talking about."

"Come on, Pace. You don't have the time and nei-ther do I. You're not connected to Aiello's death, I know that. But I've got to have information, and you're going to supply it."

"You're talking to the wrong person. I don't know you. I don't know *anything*."

"I know *you*. I've got a complete rundown on you. Aiello and I were considering going into business to-gether. Now, that's none of your concern, I realize that, but we exchanged . . . personnel information. I'm coming to you because, frankly, Rocco's gone and there are areas that need filling. I'm really asking a favor, and I'll pay for it."

"I told you, I'm not your man. I hardly knew Aiello. I picked up a few dollars waiting tables. Sure, I heard rumors, but that's *all*. I don't know what you want, but you'd better go to someone else."

Pace was sharp, thought Matlock. He was disengaging himself but not foolishly claiming complete innocence. On the other hand, perhaps he was telling the truth. There was only one way to find out.

"I'll try again. . . . Fifteen months in Vietnam. Saigon, Da Nang; excursions to Hong Kong, Japan. I&S officer; the dullest, most exasperating kind of work for a young man with the potential that earns him honors at a very tough university."

"I&S was good duty; no combat, no sweat. Everybody made the tourist hops. Check the R&R route sheets."

"Then," continued Matlock without acknowledging Pace's interruption, "the dedicated officer returns to civilian life. After a four-month voluntary extension in Saigon—I'm surprised you weren't caught up on *that* one—he comes back with enough money to make the proper investments, and certainly not from his army pay. He's one of the biggest suppliers in New Haven. Do you want me to go on?"

Pace stood by the desk and seemed to stop breathing. He stared at Matlock, his face white. When he spoke, it was the voice of a frightened young man.

"You can't prove anything. I haven't done anything. My army record, my record here—they're both good. They're very good."

"The best. Unblemished. They're records to be proud of; I mean that sincerely. And I wouldn't want to do anything to spoil them; I mean that, too."

"You couldn't. I'm clean!"

"No, you're not. You're up to your fellowship neck. Aiello made that *clear*. On *paper*."

"You're lying!"

"You're stupid. You think Aiello would do business with *anyone* he didn't run a check on? Do you think he'd be *allowed* to? He kept very extensive books, Pace, and I've got them. I told you; we were going into business together. You don't form a partnership without audit disclosures, you should know that."

Pace spoke barely above a whisper. "There are no books like that. There never are. Cities, towns, codes. No names. Never any names."

"Then why am I here?"

"You saw me in Hartford; you're reaching for a connection."

"You know better than that. Don't be foolish."

Matlock's quickly put implications were too much for the tall, shocked young man. "Why did you come to me? I'm not that important. You say you know about me; then you know I'm not important."

"I told you. I need information. I'm reluctant to go to the high priests, anyone with real authority. I don't want to be at a disadvantage. That's why I'm willing to pay; why I'm prepared to tear up everything I've got on you."

The prospect of being cut free of the stranger's grip was obviously all that was on Pace's mind. He replied quickly.

"Suppose I can't answer your questions? You'll think I'm lying."

"You can't be worse off. All you can do is try me."

"Go ahead."

"I met a girl . . . from a nearby college. I met her under circumstances that can only be described as professional prostitution. Professional in every sense of the word. Appointments, set fees, no prior knowledge of clients, the works. . . . What do you know about it?"

Pace took several steps toward Matlock. "What do you mean, what do I know? I know it's there. What else is there to know?"

"How extensive?"

"All over. It's not news."

"It is to me."

"You don't know the scene. Take a walk around a few college towns."

Matlock swallowed. Was he really that far out of touch? "Suppose I were to tell you I'm familiar with a lot of . . . college towns?"

"I'd say your circles were cubed. Also, I'm no part of that action. What else?"

"Let's stick to this for a minute. . . . Why?"

"Why what?"

"Why do the girls do it?"

"Bread, man. Why does anyone do anything?"

"You're too intelligent to believe that. . . . Is it organized?"

"I guess so. I told you, I'm no part of it."

"Watch it! I've got a lot of paper on you. . . ."

"All right. Yes, it's organized. Everything's organized. If it's going to work."

"Where *specifically* are the operations?"

"I *told* you! All *over*."

"Inside the colleges?"

"No, not inside. On the outskirts. A couple of miles usually, if the campuses are rural. Old houses, away from the suburbs. If they're in cities—downtown hotels, private clubs, apartment houses. But not *here*."

"Are we talking about . . . Columbia, Harvard, Radcliffe, Smith, Holyoke? And points south?"

"Everyone always forgets Princeton," replied Pace with a wry smile. "A lot of nice old estates in those back roads. . . . Yes, we're talking about those places."

"I never would have believed it. . . ." Matlock spoke as much to himself as to Pace. "But, *why?* Don't give me the 'bread' routine. . . ."

"Bread is *freedom,* man! For these kids it's freedom. They're not psyched-up freaks; they're not running around in black berets and field jackets. Very few of us are. We've *learned.* Get the money, fella, and the nice people will like you. . . . Also, whether you've noticed it or not, the straight money's not as easy to come by as it once was. Most of these kids need it."

"The girl I mentioned before; I gathered she was forced into it."

"Oh, Jesus, nobody's *forced!* That's crap."

"She was. She mentioned a few things. . . . Controls is as good a word as any. Courts, doctors, even jobs. . . ."

"I wouldn't know anything about that."

"And afterward. Making contact later—perhaps a few years later. Plain old-fashioned blackmail. Just as I'm blackmailing you now."

"Then she was in trouble before; this girl, I mean. If it's a bummer, she doesn't have to make the trip. Unless she's into somebody and owes what she can't pay for."

"Who is Nimrod?" Matlock asked the question softly, without emphasis. But the question caused the young man to turn and walk away.

"I don't know that. I don't have that information."

Matlock got out of the chair and stood motionless. "I'll ask you just once more, and if I don't get an answer, I'll walk out the door and you'll be finished.

A very promising life will be altered drastically—if you have a life. . . . Who is Nimrod?"

The boy whipped around and Matlock saw the fear again. The fear he had seen on Lucas Herron's face, in Lucas Herron's eyes.

"So help me Christ, I can't answer that!"

"Can't or won't?"

"Can't. I *don't know!*"

"I think you do. But I said I'd only ask you once. That's it." Matlock started for the apartment door without looking at the student.

"No! . . . Goddamn it, I *don't know!* . . . How *could* I know? You can't!" Pace ran to Matlock's side.

"Can't what?"

"Whatever you said you'd do. . . . Listen to me! I don't know who they are! I don't have . . ."

"They?"

Pace looked puzzled. "Yeah. . . . I guess 'they.' I don't know. I don't have any contact. Others do; I don't. They haven't bothered me."

"But you're aware of them." A statement.

"Aware. . . . Yes, I'm aware. But *who*, honest to God, *no!*"

Matlock turned and faced the student. "We'll compromise. For now. Tell me what you *do* know."

And the frightened young man did. And as the words came forth, the fear infected James Matlock.

Nimrod was an unseen master puppeteer. Faceless, formless, but with frightening, viable authority. It wasn't a *he* or a *they*— it was a *force*, according to Alan Pace. A complex abstraction that had its elusive tentacles in every major university in the Northeast, every municipality that served the academic landscape, all the financial pyramids that funded the complicated structures of New England's higher education. "And points south," if the rumors had foundation.

Narcotics was only one aspect, the craw in the throats of the criminal legions—the immediate reason for the May conference, the Corsican letter.

Beyond drugs and their profits, the Nimrod imprimatur was stamped on scores of college administrations. Pace was convinced that curriculums were being shaped, university personnel hired and fired, degree and scholarship policies, all were expedited on the Nimrod organization's instructions. Matlock's memory flashed back to Carlyle. To Carlyle's assistant dean of admissions—a Nimrod appointee, according to the dead Loring. To Archer Beeson, rapidly rising in the history department; to a coach of varsity soccer; to a dozen other faculty and staff names on Loring's list.

How many more were there? How deep was the infiltration?

Why?

The prostitution rings were subsidiary accommodations. Recruitments were made by the child-whores among themselves; addresses were provided, fees established. Young flesh with ability and attractiveness could find its way to Nimrod and make the pact. And there was "freedom," there was "bread" in the pact with Nimrod.

And "no one was hurt"; it was a victimless crime.

"No crime at all, just freedom, man. No pressures over the head. No screaming zonkers over scholarship points."

Alan Pace saw a great deal of good in the elusive, practical Nimrod. More than good.

"You think it's all so different from the outside—straight? You're wrong, mister. It's mini-America: organized, computerized, and very heavy with the corporate structure. Hell, it's patterned on the American syndrome; it's company *policy*, man! It's GM, ITT, and Ma Bell—only someone was smart enough to organize the groovy groves of academe. And it's growing fast. Don't fight it. Join it."

"Is that what you're going to do?" asked Matlock.

"It's the way, man. It's the faith. For all I know *you're* with it now. Could be, you're a recruiter. You guys are everywhere; I've been expecting you."

"Suppose I'm not?"

"Then you're out of your head. And over it, too."

If one watched the white station wagon and its driver heading back toward the center of New Haven, one would have thought—if he thought at all—that it was a rich car, suitable to a wealthy suburb, the man at the wheel appropriately featured for the vehicle.

Such an observer would not know that the driver was barely cognizant of the traffic, numbed by the revelations he'd learned within the hour; an exhausted man who hadn't slept in forty-eight hours, who had the feeling that he was holding onto a thin rope above an infinite chasm, expecting any instant that his lifeline would be severed, plunging him into the infinite mist.

Matlock tried his best to suspend whatever thought processes he was capable of. The years, the specific months during which he'd run his academic race against self-imposed schedules had taught him that the mind—at least his mind—could not function properly when the forces of exhaustion and overexposure converged.

Above all, he had to function.

He was in uncharted waters. Seas where tiny islands were peopled by grotesque inhabitants. Julian Dunoises, Lucas Herrons; the Bartolozzis, the Aiellos, the Sharpes, the Stocktons, and the Paces. The poisoned and the poisoners.

Nimrod.

Uncharted waters?

No, they weren't uncharted, thought Matlock.

They were well traveled. And the travelers were the cynics of the planet.

He drove to the Sheraton Hotel and took a room.

He sat on the edge of the bed and placed a telephone call to Howard Stockton at Carmount. Stockton was out.

In brusque, officious tones, he told the Carmount switchboard that Stockton was to return his call—he looked at his watch; it was ten of two—in four hours. At six o'clock. He gave the Sheraton number and hung up.

He needed at least four hours' sleep. He wasn't sure when he would sleep again.

He picked up the telephone once more and requested a wake-up call at five forty-five.

As his head sank to the pillow, he brought his arm up to his eyes. Through the cloth of his shirt he felt the stubble of his beard. He'd have to go to a barbershop; he'd left his suitcase in the white station wagon. He'd been too tired, too involved to remember to bring it to his room.

The short, sharp three rings of the telephone signified the Sheraton's adherence to his instructions. It was exactly quarter to six. Fifteen minutes later there was another ring, this one longer, more normal. It was precisely six, and the caller was Howard Stockton.

"I'll make this short, Matlock. You got a contact.

Only he doesn't want to meet *inside* the Sail and Ski. You go to the East Gorge slope—they use it in spring and summer for tourists to look at the scenery—and take the lift up to the top. You be there at eight thirty this evenin'. He'll have a man at the top. That's all I've got to say. It's none of *mah business!*"

Stockton slammed down the telephone and the echo rang in Matlock's ear.

But he'd made it! *He'd made it!* He had made the contact with Nimrod! With the conference.

He walked up the dark trail toward the ski lift. Ten dollars made the attendant at the Sail and Ski parking lot understand his problem: the nice-looking fellow in the station wagon had an assignation. The husband wasn't expected till later—and, what the hell, that's life. The parking lot attendant was very cooperative.

When he reached the East Gorge slope, the rain, which had threatened all day, began to come down. In Connecticut, April showers were somehow always May thunderstorms, and Matlock was annoyed that he hadn't thought to buy a raincoat.

He looked around at the deserted lift, its high double lines silhouetted against the increasing rain, shining like thick strands of ship hemp in a fogged harbor. There was a tiny, almost invisible light in the shack which housed the complicated, hulking machines that made the lines ascend. Matlock approached the door and knocked. A small, wiry-looking man opened the door and peered at him.

"You the fella goin' up?"

"I guess I am."

"What's your name?"

"Matlock."

"Guess you are. Know how to catch a crossbar?"

"I've skied. Arm looped, tail on the slat, feet on the pipe."

"Don't need no help from me. I'll start it, you get it."

"Fine."

"You're gonna get wet."

"I know."

Matlock positioned himself to the right of the entrance pit as the lumbering machinery started up. The lines creaked slowly and then began their halting countermoves, and a crossbar approached. He slid himself onto the lift, pressed his feet against the footrail, and locked the bar in front of his waist. He felt the swinging motion of the lines lifting him off the ground.

He was on his way to the top of the East Gorge, on his way to his contact with Nimrod. As he swung upward, ten feet above the ground, the rain became, instead of annoying, exhilarating. He was coming to the end of his journey, his race. Whoever met him at the top would be utterly confused. He counted on that, he'd planned it that way. If everything the murdered Loring and the very-much-alive Greenberg had told him was true, it couldn't be any other way. The total secrecy of the conference; the delegates, unknown to each other; the oath of "Omerta," the subculture's violent insistence on codes and countercodes to protect its inhabitants—it *was* all true. He'd seen it all in operation. And such complicated logistics—when sharply interrupted—inevitably led to suspicion and fear and ultimately confusion. It was the confusion Matlock counted on.

Lucas Herron had accused him of being influenced by plots and counterplots. Well, he wasn't *influenced* by them—he merely *understood* them. That was different. It was this understanding which had led him one step away from Nimrod.

The rain came harder now, whipped by the wind which was stronger off the ground than on it. Matlock's crossbar swayed and dipped, more so each time he reached a rung up the slope. The tiny light in the machine shack was now barely visible in the darkness and the rain. He judged that he was nearly halfway to the top.

There was a jolt; the machinery stopped. Matlock gripped the waist guard and peered above him through the rain trying to see what obstruction had hit the wheel or the rung. There was none.

He turned awkwardly in the narrow perch and squinted his eyes down the slope toward the shack. There was no light now, not even the slightest illumination. He held his hand up in front of his forehead, keeping the rain away as best he could. He had to be mistaken, the downpour was blurring his vision, perhaps the pole was in his line of sight. He leaned first to the right, then to the left. But still there was no light from the bottom of the hill.

Perhaps the fuses had blown. If so, they would have taken the bulb in the shack with them. Or a short. It was raining, and ski lifts did not ordinarily operate in the rain.

He looked beneath him. The ground was perhaps fifteen feet away. If he suspended himself from the footrail, the drop would only be eight or nine feet. He could handle that. He would walk the rest of the way up the slope. He had to do it quickly, however. It might take as long as twenty minutes to climb to the top, there was no way of telling. He couldn't take the chance of his contact's panicking, deciding to leave before he got to him.

"Stay right where you are! Don't unlatch that harness!"

The voice shot out of the darkness, cutting through the rain and wind. Its harsh command paralyzed Matlock as much from the shock of surprise as from fear. The man stood beneath him, to the right of the lines. He was dressed in a raincoat and some kind of cap. It was impossible to see his face or even determine his size.

"Who are you?! What do you want?!"

"I'm the man you came to meet. I want to see that paper in your pocket. Throw it down."

"I'll show you the paper when I see *your* copy. That's the deal! That's the deal I made."

"You don't understand, Matlock. Just throw the paper down. That's all."

"What the hell are you talking about?!"

The glare of a powerful flashlight blinded him. He reached for the guard rail latch.

"Don't touch that! Keep your hands straight out or you're dead!"

The core of the high-intensity light shifted from his face to his chest, and for several seconds all Matlock saw were a thousand flashing spots inside his eyes. As his sight returned, he could see that the man below him was moving closer to the lines, swinging the flashlight toward the ground for a path. In the glow of the beam, he also saw that the man held a large, ugly automatic in his right hand. The blinding light returned to his face, now shining directly beneath him.

"Don't threaten me, punk!" yelled Matlock, remembering the effect his anger had on Stockton at four that morning. "Put that goddamn gun away and help me down! We haven't much time and I don't like games!"

The effect now was not the same. Instead, the man beneath him began to laugh, and the laugh was sickening. It was, more than anything else, utterly genuine. The man on the ground was enjoying himself.

"You're very funny. You look funny sitting there on your ass in midair. You know what you look like? You look like one of those bobbing monkey targets in a shooting gallery! *You know what I mean?* Now, cut the bullshit and throw down the paper!"

He laughed again, and at the sound everything was suddenly clear to Matlock.

He hadn't made a contact. He hadn't cornered anyone. All his careful planning, all his thought-out actions. All for nothing. He was no nearer Nimrod now than he was before he knew Nimrod existed.

He'd been trapped.

Still, he had to try. It was all that was left him now.

"You're making the mistake of your life!"

"Oh, for Christ's sake, knock it off! Give me the paper! We've been looking for that fucking thing for a week! My orders are to get it *now!*"

"I can't give it to you."

"I'll blow your head off!"

"I said I *can't!* I didn't say I *wouldn't!*"

"Don't shit me. You've got it on you! You wouldn't have come here without it!"

"It's in a packet strapped to the small of my back."

"Get it out!"

"I told you, I can't! I'm sitting on a four-inch slat of wood with a footrail and I'm damn near twenty feet in the air!"

His words were half lost in the whipping rain. The man below was frustrated, impatient.

"*I said get it out!*"

"I'll have to drop down. I can't reach the straps!" Matlock yelled to be heard. "I can't *do* anything! I haven't got a gun!"

The man with the large, ugly automatic moved back several feet from the lines. He pointed both the powerful beam and his weapon at Matlock.

"O.K., come on down! You cough wrong and your head's blown off!"

Matlock undid the latch, feeling like a small boy on top of a ferris wheel wondering what could happen if the wheel stopped permanently and the safety bar fell off.

He held onto the footrail and let the rest of him swing beneath it. He dangled in the air, the rain soaking him, the beam of light blinding him. He had to think now, he had to create an instant strategy. His life was worth far less than the lives at Windsor Shoals to such men as the man on the ground.

"Shine the light down! I can't see!"

"Fuck that! Just drop!"

He dropped.

And the second he hit the earth, he let out a loud, painful scream and reached for his leg.

"Aaaahhh! My ankle, my foot! I broke my goddamn ankle!" He twisted and turned on the wet overgrowth, writhing in pain.

"Shut up! Get me that paper! *Now!*"

"*Jesus Christ!* What do you *want* from me? My ankle's turned *around!* It's *broken!*"

"Tough! Give me the paper!"

Matlock lay prostrate on the ground, his head moving back and forth, his neck straining to stand the pain. He spoke between short gasps.

"Strap's here. Undo the strap." He tore at his shirt displaying part of the canvas belt.

"Undo it yourself. Hurry up!"

But the man came closer. He wasn't sure. And closer. The beam of light was just above Matlock now. Then it moved to his midsection and Matlock could see the large barrel of the ugly black automatic.

It was the second, the instant he'd waited for.

He whipped his right hand up toward the weapon, simultaneously springing his whole body against the legs of the man in the raincoat. He held the automatic's barrel, forcing it with all his strength toward the ground. The gun fired twice, the impact of the explosions nearly shattering Matlock's hand, the sounds partially muted by wet earth and the slashing rain.

The man was beneath him now, twisting on his side, thrashing with his legs and free arm against the heavier Matlock. Matlock flung himself on the pinned arm and sank his teeth into the wrist above the hand holding the weapon. He bit into the flesh until he could feel the blood spurting out, mingled with the cold rain.

The man released the automatic, screaming in anguish. Matlock grabbed for the gun, wrested it free, and smashed it repeatedly into the man's face. The powerful flashlight was in the tall grass, its beam directed at nothing but drenched foliage.

Matlock crouched over the half-conscious, bloody face of his former captor. He was out of breath, and the sickening taste of the man's blood was still in his mouth. He spat a half dozen times trying to cleanse his teeth, his throat.

"O.K.!" He grabbed the man's collar and yanked his head up. "Now you tell me what happened! This was a trap, wasn't it?"

"The paper! I gotta get the paper." The man was hardly audible.

"I was *trapped, wasn't I!* The whole last week was a trap!"

"Yeah. . . . Yeah. The paper."

"That paper's pretty important, isn't it?"

"They'll kill you . . . they'll kill you to get it! You stand no chance, mister. . . . No chance . . ."

"Who's *they?!*"

"I don't know . . . don't know!"

"*Who's Nimrod?*"

"I don't know . . . 'Omerta'! . . . 'Omerta'!"

The man opened his eyes wide, and in the dim spill of the fallen flashlight, Matlock saw that something had happened to his victim. Some thought, some concept overpowered his tortured imagination. It was painful to watch. It was too close to the sight of the panicked Lucas Herron, the terrified Alan Pace.

"Come on, I'll get you down the slope. . . ."

It was as far as he got. From the depths of his lost control, the man with the blood-soaked face lunged forward, making a last desperate attempt to reach the gun in Matlock's right hand. Matlock yanked back; instinctively he fired the weapon. Blood and pieces of flesh flew everywhere. Half the man's neck was blown off.

Matlock stood up slowly. The smoke of the automatic lingered above the dead man, the rain forcing it downward toward the earth.

He reached into the grass for the flashlight, and as he bent over he began to vomit.

Ten minutes later he watched the parking lot below him from the trunk of a huge maple tree fifty yards up the trail. The new leaves partially protected him from the pouring rain, but his clothes were filthy, covered with wet dirt and blood. He saw the white station wagon near the front of the area, next to the stone gate entrance of the Sail and Ski. There wasn't much activity now; no automobiles entered, and those drivers inside would wait until the deluge stopped before venturing out on the roads. The parking lot attendant he'd given the ten dollars to was talking with a uniformed doorman under the carport roof of the restaurant entrance. Matlock wanted to race to the station wagon and drive away as fast as he could, but he knew the sight of his clothes would alarm the two men, make them wonder what had happened on the East Gorge slope. There was nothing to do but wait, wait until someone came out and distracted them, or both went inside.

He hated the waiting. More than hating it, he was frightened by it. There'd been no one he could see or hear near the wheel shack, but that didn't mean no one was there. Nimrod's dead contact probably had a partner somewhere, waiting as Matlock was waiting now. If the dead man was found, they'd stop him, kill him—if not for revenge, for the Corsican paper.

He had no choice now. He'd gone beyond his depth, his abilities. He'd been manipulated by Nimrod as he'd been maneuvered by the men of the Justice Department. He would telephone Jason Greenberg and do whatever Greenberg told him to do.

In a way, he was glad his part of it was over, or soon would be. He still felt the impulse of commitment, but there was nothing more he could do. He had failed.

Down below, the restaurant entrance opened and a waitress signaled the uniformed doorman. He and the attendant walked up the steps to speak with the girl.

Matlock ran down to the gravel and darted in front of the grills of the cars parked on the edge of the lot. Between automobiles he kept looking toward the restaurant door. The waitress had given the doorman a container of coffee. All three were smoking cigarettes, all three were laughing.

He rounded the circle and crouched in front of the station wagon. He crept to the door window and saw to his relief that the keys were in the ignition. He took a deep breath, opened the door as quietly as possible, and leaped inside. Instead of slamming it, he pulled the door shut quickly, silently, so as to extinguish the interior light without calling attention to the sound. The two men and the waitress were still talking, still laughing, oblivious.

He settled himself in the seat, switched on the ignition, threw the gears into reverse, and roared backward in front of the gate. He raced out between the stone posts and started down the long road to the highway.

Back under the roof, on the steps by the front door,

the three employees were momentarily startled. Then, from being startled they became quickly bewildered —and even a little curious. For, from the rear of the parking lot, they could hear the deep-throated roar of a second, more powerful engine. Bright headlights flicked on, distorted by the downpour of rain, and a long black limousine rushed forward.

The wheels screeched as the ominous-looking automobile swerved toward the stone posts. The huge car went to full throttle and raced after the station wagon.

There wasn't much traffic on the highway, but he still felt he'd make better time taking the back roads into Carlyle. He decided to go straight to Kressel's house, despite Sam's proclivity toward hysteria. Together they could both call Greenberg. He had just brutally, horribly killed another human being, and whether it was justified or not, the shock was still with him. He suspected it would be with him for the remainder of his life. He wasn't sure Kressel was the man to see.

But there was no one else. Unless he returned to his apartment and stayed there until a federal agent picked him up. And then again, instead of an agent, there might well be an emissary from Nimrod.

There was a winding S-curve in the road. He remembered that it came before a long stretch through farmland where he could make up time. The highway was straighter, but the back roads were shorter as long as there was no traffic to speak of. As he rounded the final half-circle, he realized that he was gripping the wheel so hard his forearms ached. It was the muscular defenses of his body taking over, controlling his shaking limbs, steadying the car with sheer unfeeling strength.

The flat stretch appeared; the rain had let up. He pushed the accelerator to the floor and felt the station wagon surge forward in overdrive.

He looked twice, then three times, up at his rear-view mirror, wary of patrol cars. He saw headlights behind him coming closer. He looked down at his speedometer. It read eighty-seven miles per hour and still the lights in the mirror gained on him.

The instincts of the hunted came swiftly to the surface; he knew the automobile behind him was no police car. There was no siren penetrating the wet stillness, no flashing light heralding authority.

He pushed his right leg forward, pressing the accelerator beyond the point of achieving anything further from the engine. His speedometer reached ninety-four miles per hour—the wagon was not capable of greater speed.

The headlights were directly behind him now. The unknown pursuer was feet, inches from his rear bumper. Suddenly the headlights veered to the left, and the car came alongside the white station wagon.

It was the same black limousine he had seen after Loring's murder! The same huge automobile that had raced out of the darkened driveway minutes after the massacre at Windsor Shoals! Matlock tried to keep part of his mind on the road ahead, part on the single driver of the car, which was crowding him to the far right of the road. The station wagon vibrated under the impact of the enormous speed; he found it more and more difficult to hold the wheel.

And then he saw the barrel of the pistol pointed at him through the window of the adjacent automobile. He saw the look of desperation in the darting eyes behind the outstretched arm, trying to steady itself for a clean line of fire.

He heard the shots and felt the glass shattering into his face and over the front seat. He slammed his foot into the brake and spun the steering wheel to the right, jumping the shoulder of the road, careening violently into and through a barbed-wire fence and onto a rock-strewn field. The wagon lunged into the grass, perhaps fifty or sixty feet, and then slammed into a cluster of rocks, a property demarcation. The headlights smashed and went out, the grill buckled. He was thrown into the dashboard, only his upheld arms keeping his head from crashing into the windshield.

But he was conscious, and the instincts of the hunted would not leave him.

He heard a car door open and close, and he knew the killer was coming into the field after his quarry. After the Corsican paper. He felt a trickle of blood rolling down his forehead—whether it was the graze of a bullet or a laceration from the flying glass, he couldn't be sure—but he was grateful it was there. He'd need it now, he needed the sight of blood on his forehead. He remained slumped over the wheel, immobile, silent.

And under his jacket he held the ugly automatic he had taken from the dead man in the raincoat on the slope of East Gorge. It was pointed under his left arm at the door.

He could hear the mushed crunch of footsteps on the soft earth outside the station wagon. He could literally feel—as a blind man feels—the face peering through the shattered glass looking at him. He heard the click of the door button as it was pushed in and the creaking of the hinges as the heavy panel was pulled open.

A hand grabbed his shoulder. Matlock fired his weapon.

The roar was deafening; the scream of the wounded man pierced the drenched darkness. Matlock leaped out of the seat and slammed the full weight of his body against the killer, who had grabbed his left arm in pain. Wildly, inaccurately, Matlock pistol-whipped the man about his face and neck until he fell to the ground. The man's gun was nowhere to be seen, his hands were empty. Matlock put his foot on the man's throat and pressed.

"I'll stop when you signal you're going to talk to me, you son of a bitch! Otherwise I *don't* stop!"

The man sputtered, his eyes bulged. He raised his right hand in supplication.

Matlock took his foot away and knelt on the ground over the man. He was heavy set, black-haired, with the blunt features of a brute killer.

"Who sent you after me? How did you know this car?"

The man raised his head slightly as though to answer. Instead, the killer whipped his right hand into his waist, pulled out a knife, and rolled sharply to his left, yanking his gorilla-like knee up into Matlock's groin. The knife slashed into Matlock's shirt, and he knew as he felt the steel point crease his flesh that he'd come as close as he would ever come to being killed.

He crashed the barrel of the heavy automatic into the man's temple. It was enough. The killer's head snapped back; blood matted itself around the hairline. Matlock stood up and placed his foot on the hand with the knife.

Soon the killer's eyes opened.

And during the next five minutes, Matlock did what he never thought he would be capable of doing—he tortured another man. He tortured the killer with the killer's own knife, penetrating the skin around and below the eyes, puncturing the lips with the same steel point that had scraped his own flesh. And when the man screamed, Matlock smashed his mouth with the barrel of the automatic and broke pieces of ivory off the killer's teeth.

It was not long.

"The paper!"

"What else?"

The writhing killer moaned and spat blood, but would not speak. Matlock did; quietly, in total conviction, in complete sincerity.

"You'll answer me or I'll push this blade down through your eyes. I don't care anymore. Believe me."

"The old man!" The guttural words came from deep inside the man's throat. "He said he wrote it down. . . . No one knows. . . . You talked to him. . . ."

"What old . . ." Matlock stopped as a terrifying thought came into his mind. *"Lucas Herron?! Is that who you mean?!"*

"He said he wrote it down. They think you know. Maybe he lied. . . . For Christ's sake, he could have lied. . . ."

The killer fell into unconsciousness.

Matlock stood up slowly, his hands shaking, his whole body shivering. He looked up at the road, at the huge black limousine standing silently in the diminishing rain. It would be his last gamble, his ultimate effort.

But something was stirring in his brain, something

elusive but palpable. He had to trust that feeling, as he had come to trust the instincts of the hunter and the hunted.

The old man!

The answer lay somewhere in Lucas Herron's house.

He parked the limousine a quarter of a mile from Herron's Nest and walked toward the house on the side of the road, prepared to jump into the bordering woods should any cars approach.

None did.

He came upon one house, then another, and in each case he raced past, watching the lighted windows to see if anyone was looking out.

No one was.

He reached the edge of Herron's property and crouched to the ground. Slowly, cautiously, silently he made his way to the driveway. The house was dark; there were no cars, no people, no signs of life. Only death.

He walked up the flagstone path and his eye caught sight of an official-looking document, barely visible in the darkness, tacked onto the front door. He approached it and lit a match. It was a sheriff's seal of closure.

One more crime, thought Matlock.

He went around to the back of the house, and as he stood in front of the patio door, he remembered vividly the sight of Herron racing across his manicured lawn into the forbidding green wall which he parted so deftly and into which he disappeared so completely.

There was another sheriff's seal on the back door. This one was glued to a pane of glass.

Matlock removed the automatic from his belt and as quietly as possible broke the small-paned window to the left of the seal. He opened the door and walked in.

The first thing that struck him was the darkness. Light and dark were relative, as he'd come to understand during the past week. The night had light which the eyes could adjust to; the daylight was often deceptive, filled with shadows and misty blind spots. But inside Herron's house the darkness was complete. He lit a match and understood why.

The windows in the small kitchen were covered with shades. Only they weren't ordinary window shades, they were custom built. The cloth was heavy and attached to the frames with vertical runners, latched at the sills by large aluminum hasps. He approached the window over the sink and lit another match. Not only was the shade thicker than ordinary, but the runners and the stretch lock at the bottom insured that the shade would remain absolutely flat against the whole frame. It was doubtful that any light could go out or come in through the window.

Herron's desire—or need—for privacy had been extraordinary. And if all the windows in all the rooms were sealed, it would make his task easier.

Striking a third match, he walked into Herron's living room. What he saw in the flickering light caused him to stop in his tracks, his breath cut short.

The entire room was a shambles. Books were strewn on the floor, furniture overturned and ripped apart, rugs upended, even sections of the wall smashed. He could have been walking into his own apartment the night of the Beeson dinner. Herron's living room had been thoroughly, desperately searched.

He went back to the kitchen to see if his preoccupation with the window shades and the darkness had played tricks on his eyes. They had. Every drawer was pulled open, every cabinet ransacked. And then he saw on the floor of a broom closet two flashlights. One was a casement, the other a long-stemmed Sportsman. The first wouldn't light, the second did.

He walked rapidly back into the living room and tried to orient himself, checking the windows with the beam of the flashlight. Every window was covered, every shade latched at the sill.

Across the narrow hallway in front of the narrower stairs was an open door. It led to Herron's study, which was, if possible, more of a mess than his living room. Two file cabinets were lying on their sides, the backs torn off; the large leather-topped desk was pulled from the wall, splintered, smashed on every flat surface. Parts of the wall, as the living room, were broken into. Matlock assumed these were sections which had sounded hollow when tapped.

Upstairs, the two small bedrooms and the bath were equally dismantled, equally dissected.

He walked back down the stairs, even the steps had been pried loose from their treads.

Lucas Herron's home had been searched by professionals. What could he find that they hadn't? He wandered back into the living room and sat down on what was left of an armchair. He had the sinking feeling that his last effort would end in failure also. He lit a cigarette and tried to organize his thoughts.

Whoever had searched the house had not found

what they were looking for. Or had they? There was no way to tell, really. Except that the brute killer in the field had screamed that the old man "had written it down." As if the fact was almost as important as the desperately coveted Corsican document. Yet he had added: ". . . maybe he lied, he could have lied." *Lied?* Why would a man in the last extremity of terror add that qualification to something so vital?

The assumption had to be that in the intricate delicacy of a mind foundering on the brink of madness, the worst evil was rejected. Had to be rejected so as to hold onto what was left of sanity.

No. . . . No, they had not found whatever it was they *had to find.* And since they hadn't found it after such exhaustive, extraordinary labors—it didn't *exist.*

But he knew it did.

Herron may have been involved with Nimrod's world, but he was not born of it. His was not a comfortable relationship—it was a tortured one. Somewhere, someplace he had left an indictment. He was too good a man not to. There had been a great decency in Lucas Herron. Somewhere . . . someplace.

But where?

He got out of the chair and paced in the darkness of the room, flicking the flashlight on and off, more as a nervous gesture than for illumination.

He reexamined minutely every word, every expression used by Lucas that early evening four days ago. He was the hunter again, tracking the spoor, testing the wind for the scent. And he was close; goddamn it, he was close! . . . Herron had *known* from the second he'd opened his front door what Matlock was after. That instantaneous, fleeting moment of recognition had been in his eyes. It had been unmistakable to Matlock. He'd even said as much to the old man, and the old man had laughed and accused him of being influenced by plots and counterplots.

But there'd been something else. Before the plots and counterplots. . . . Something *inside*. In this room. Before Herron suggested sitting *outside*. . . . Only he hadn't *suggested*, he'd made a statement, given a command.

And just before he'd given the command to rear-march toward the backyard patio, he'd walked in silently, *walked in silently*, and startled Matlock. He had opened the swinging door, *carrying* two filled glasses, and Matlock *hadn't heard* him. Matlock pushed the button on the flashlight and shot the beam to the base of the kitchen door. There was no rug, nothing to muffle footsteps—it was a hardwood floor. He crossed to the open swing-hinged door, walked through the frame, and shut it. Then he pushed it swiftly open in the same direction Lucas Herron had pushed it carrying the two drinks. The hinges clicked as such hinges do if they are old and the door is pushed quickly—*normally*. He let the door swing shut and then he pressed against it slowly, inch by inch.

It was silent.

Lucas Herron had made the drinks and then *silently* had eased himself back into the living room so he wouldn't be heard. So he could observe Matlock without Matlock's knowing it. And then he'd given his firm command for the two of them to go outside.

Matlock forced his memory to recall *precisely* what Lucas Herron said and did at that *precise* moment.

". . . we'll go out on the patio. It's too nice a day to stay inside. Let's go."

Then, *without waiting for an answer*, even a mildly enthusiastic agreement, Herron had walked *rapidly* back through the kitchen door. No surface politeness, none of the courtly manners one expected from Lucas.

He had given an order, the firm command of an officer and a gentleman.

By Act of Congress.

That was *it!* Matlock swung the beam of light over the writing desk.

The photograph! The photograph of the marine officer holding the map and the Thompson automatic in some tiny section of jungle on an insignificant island in the South Pacific.

"I keep that old photograph to remind myself that time wasn't always so devastating."

At the precise moment Herron walked through the door, Matlock had been looking closely at the photograph! The fact that he was doing so disturbed the old man, disturbed him enough for him to insist that they go outside instantly. In a curt, abrupt manner so unlike him.

Matlock walked rapidly to the desk. The small cellophane-topped photograph was still where it had been—on the lower right wall above the desk. Several larger glass-framed pictures had been smashed; this one was intact. It was small, not at all imposing.

He grabbed the cardboard frame and pulled the photo off the single thumbtack which held it to the wall. He looked at it carefully, turning it over, inspecting the thin edges.

The close, harsh glare of the flashlight revealed scratches at the upper corner of the cardboard. Fingernail scratches? Perhaps. He pointed the light down on the desk top. There were unsharpened pencils, scraps of note paper, and a pair of scissors. He took the scissors and inserted the point of one blade between the thin layers of cardboard until he could rip the photograph out of the frame.

And in that way he found it.

On the back of the small photograph was a diagram drawn with a broad-tipped fountain pen. It was in the shape of a rectangle, the bottom and top lines filled in with dots. On the top were two small lines with arrows, one straight, the other pointing to the right. Above each arrowhead was the numeral 30. Two 30s.

Thirty.

On the sides, bordering the lines, were childishly drawn trees.

On the top, above the numbers, was another simplified sketch. Billowy half-circles connected to one another with a wavy line beneath. A cloud. Underneath, more trees.

It was a map, and what it represented was all too apparent. It was Herron's back yard; the lines on three sides represented Herron's forbidding green wall.

The numerals, the 30s, were measurements—but they were also something else. They were contemporary symbols.

For Lucas Herron, chairman for decades of Romance Languages, had an insatiable love for words and their odd usages. What was more appropriate than the symbol "30" to indicate finality?

As any first year journalism student would confirm, the number 30 at the bottom of any news copy meant the story was finished. It was over.

There was no more to be said.

Matlock held the photograph upside down in his left hand, his right gripping the flashlight. He entered the woods at midsection—slightly to the left—as indicated on the diagram. The figure 30 could be feet, yards, meters, paces—certainly not inches.

He marked off thirty twelve-inch spaces. Thirty feet straight, thirty feet to the right.

Nothing.

Nothing but the drenched, full overgrowth and underbrush which clawed at his feet.

He returned to the green wall's entrance and decided to combine yards and paces, realizing that paces in such a dense, jungle-like environment might vary considerably.

He marked off the spot thirty paces directly ahead and continued until he estimated the point of yardage. Then he returned to the bent branches where he had figured thirty paces to be and began the lateral trek.

Again nothing. An old rotted maple stood near one spot Matlock estimated was thirty steps. There was nothing else unusual. He went back to the bent branches and proceeded to his second mark.

Thirty yards straight out. Ninety feet, give or take a foot or two. Then the slow process of thirty yards through the soaking wet foliage to his next mark. Another ninety feet. Altogether, one hundred and eighty feet. Nearly two-thirds of a football field.

The going was slower now, the foliage thicker, or so it seemed. Matlock wished he had a machete or at least some kind of implement to force the wet branches out of his way. Once he lost count and had to keep in mind the variation as he proceeded—was it twenty-one or twenty-three large steps? Did it matter? Would the difference of three to six feet really matter?

He reached the spot. It was either twenty-eight or thirty. Close enough if there was anything to be seen. He pointed the flashlight to the ground and began slowly moving it back and forth laterally.

Nothing. Only the sight of a thousand glistening weeds and the deep-brown color of soaked earth. He kept swinging the beam of light, inching forward as he did so, straining his eyes, wondering every other second if he had just covered that particular section or not—everything looked so alike.

The chances of failure grew. He could go back and begin again, he thought. Perhaps the 30s connoted some other form of measurement. Meters, perhaps, or multiples of another number buried somewhere in the diagram. The dots? Should he count the dots on the bottom and top of the rectangle? Why were the dots there?

He had covered the six-foot variation and several feet beyond.

Nothing.

His mind returned to the dots, and he withdrew the photograph from his inside pocket. As he positioned himself to stand up straight, to stretch the muscles at the base of his spine—pained by crouching—his foot touched a hard, unyielding surface. At first he thought it was a fallen limb, or perhaps a rock.

And then he knew it was neither.

He couldn't see it—whatever it was, was underneath a clump of overgrown weeds. But he could feel the outline of the object with his foot. It was straight, precisely tooled. It was no part of a forest.

He held the light over the cluster of weeds and saw that they weren't weeds. They were some kind of small-budded flower in partial bloom. A flower which did not need sunlight or space.

A jungle flower. Out of place, purchased, replanted.

He pushed them out of the way and bent down. Underneath was a thick, heavily varnished slab of wood about two feet wide and perhaps a foot and a half long. It had sunk an inch or two into the ground; the surface had been sanded and varnished so often that the layers of protective coating reached a high gloss, reflecting the beam of the flashlight as though it were glass.

Matlock dug his fingers into the earth and lifted up the slab. Beneath it was a weathered metal plaque, bronze perhaps.

For Major Lucas N. Herron, USMCR
In Gratitude from the Officers and Men of
Bravo Company, Fourteenth Raider Battalion,
First Marine Division
Solomon Islands—South Pacific
May 1943

Seeing it set in the ground under the glare of light, Matlock had the feeling he was looking at a grave.

He pushed away the surrounding mud and dug a tiny trench around the metal. On his hands and knees, he slowly, awkwardly lifted the plaque up and carefully placed it to one side.

He had found it.

Buried in earth was a metal container—the type used in library archives for valuable manuscripts. Airtight, weatherproofed, vacuumed, a receptacle for the ages.

A coffin, Matlock thought.

He picked it up and inserted his cold, wet fingers under the lever of the coiled hasp. It took considerable strength to pull it up, but finally it was released.

There was the rush of air one hears upon opening a tin of coffee. The rubber edges parted. Inside Matlock could see an oilcloth packet in the shape of a notebook.

He knew he'd found the indictment.

The notebook was thick, over three hundred pages, and every word was handwritten in ink. It was in the form of a diary, but the lengthy entries varied enormously. There was no consistency regarding dates. Often days followed one another; at other times entries were separated by weeks, even months. The writing also varied. There were stretches of lucid narrative followed by incoherent, disjointed rambling. In the latter sections the hand had shaken, the words were often illegible.

Lucas Herron's diary was a cry of anguish, an outpouring of pain. A confessional of a man beyond hope.

As he sat on the cold wet ground, mesmerized by Herron's words, Matlock understood the motives behind Herron's Nest, the forbidding green wall, the window shades, the total isolation.

Lucas Herron had been a drug addict for a quarter of a century. Without the drugs, his pain was unendurable. And there was absolutely nothing anyone could do for him except confine him to a ward in a Veterans' Hospital for the remainder of his unnatural life.

It was the rejection of this living death that had plunged Lucas Herron into another.

Major Lucas Nathaniel Herron, USMCR, attached to Amphibious Assault Troops, Raider Battalions, Fleet Marine Force, Pacific, had led numerous companies of the Fourteenth Battalion, First Marine Division, in ranger assaults on various islands throughout the Japanese-held Solomons and Carolinas.

And Major Lucas Herron had been carried off the tiny island of Peleliu in the Carolinas on a stretcher, having brought two companies back to the beach through jungle fire. None thought he could survive.

Major Lucas Herron had a Japanese bullet imbedded at the base of his neck, lodged in a section of his nervous system. He was not expected to live. The doctors, first in Brisbane, then San Diego, and finally at Bethesda, considered further operations unfeasible. The patient could not survive them; he would be reduced to a vegetable should even the slightest complication set in. No one wished to be responsible for that.

They put the patient under heavy medication to relieve the discomfort of his wounds. And he lay there in the Maryland hospital for over two years.

The stages of healing—partial recovery—were slow and painful. First, there were the neck braces and the pills; then the braces and the metal frames for walking, and still the pills. At last the crutches, along with the braces and always the pills. Lucas Herron came back to the land of the living—but not without the pills. And in moments of torment—the needle of morphine at night.

There were hundreds, perhaps thousands, like Lucas Herron, but few had his extraordinary qualifications—for those who sought him out. An authentic hero of the Pacific war, a brilliant scholar, a man above reproach.

He was perfect. He could be used perfectly.

On the one hand, he could not live, could not endure, without the relief afforded him by the narcotics —the pills and the increasingly frequent needles. On the other hand, if the degree of his dependence was known medically, he would be returned to a hospital ward.

These alternatives were gradually, subtly made clear to him. Gradually in the sense that his sources of supply needed favors now and then—a contact to be made in Boston, men to be paid in New York. Subtly, in that when Herron questioned the involvement, he was told it was really quite harmless. Harmless but *necessary*.

As the years went by, he became enormously valuable to the men he needed so badly. The contact in Boston, the men to be paid in New York, became more and more frequent, more and more *necessary*. Then Lucas was sent farther and farther afield. Winter vacations, spring midterms, summers: Canada, Mexico, France ... the Mediterranean.

He became a courier.

And always the thought of the hospital ward on his tortured body and brain.

They had manipulated him brilliantly. He was never exposed to the results of his work, never specifically aware of the growing network of destruction he was helping to build. And when finally he learned of it all, it was too late. The network had been built.

Nimrod had his power.

April 22, 1951. At midterm they're sending me back to Mexico. I'll stop at the U. of M.—as usual—and on the way back at Baylor. A touch of irony: the bursar here called me in, saying Carlyle would be pleased to help defray my "research" expenses. I declined, and told him the *disability allowance* was sufficient. Perhaps I should have accepted. . . .

June 13, 1956. To Lisbon for three weeks. A routing map, I'm told, for a small ship. Touching the Azores, through Cuba (a mess!), finally into Panama. Stops—for me—at the Sorbonne, U. of Toledo, U. of Madrid. I'm becoming an academic gadfly! I'm not happy about methods—who could be?—but neither am I responsible for the archaic laws. So many, many can be helped. They need help! I've been in touch with scores on the telephone—they put me in touch—men like myself who couldn't face another day without help. . . . Still, I worry. . . . Still, what can I do? Others would do it, if not me . . .

February 24, 1957. I'm alarmed but calm and reasonable (I hope!) about my concerns. I'm told now that when they send me to make contacts I am the *messenger* from *"Nimrod"!* The name is a code—a meaningless artifice, they say —and will be honored. It's all so foolish—like the intelligence information we'd receive from MacArthur's HQ in So-Pac. *They* had *all* the codes and *none* of the *facts.* . . . The pain is worse, the medics said it would get worse. But . . . "Nimrod's" considerate. . . . As I am. . . .

March 10, 1957. They were angry with me! They withheld my dosage for two days—I thought I would kill myself! I started out in my car for the VA hospital in Hartford, but they stopped me on the highway. They were in a Carlyle *patrol car*—I should have known they had the police here! . . . It was either *compromise* or

the *ward!* . . . They were right! . . . I'm off to
Canada and the job is to bring in a man from
North Africa. . . . I *must* do it! The calls to me
are constant. This evening a man—Army, 27th—
Naha casualty—from East Orange, N.J., said
that he and six others *depended* on me! There
are so many like ourselves! Why? Why, for God's
sake, are we *despised?* We need *help* and all
that's offered to us are the *wards!* . . .

August 19, 1960. I've made my position clear!
They go too far . . . "Nimrod" is not just a code
name for a location, it's also a *man!* The geog-
raphy doesn't change but the man does. They're
not helping men like me any longer—well, maybe they are—but it's more than *us!* They're
reaching out—they're *attracting* people—for a
great deal of money! . . .

August 20, 1960. Now they're threatening me.
They say I'll have no more once my cabinet's
empty. . . . I don't care! I've enough for a week
—with luck—a week and a half. . . . I wish I
liked alcohol more, or that it didn't make me
sick. . . .

August 28, 1960. I shook to my ankles but I
went to the Carlyle Police Station. I wasn't thinking. I asked to speak with the highest man in authority and they said it was after five o'clock—
he had gone home. So I said I had information
about narcotics and within ten minutes the chief
of police showed up. . . . By now I was obvious—
I couldn't control myself—I urinated through my
trousers. The chief of police took me into a small
room and opened his kit and administered a
needle. He was from Nimrod! . . .

October 7, 1965. This Nimrod is displeased

with me. I've always gotten along with the Nimrods—the two I've met, but this one is sterner, more concerned with my accomplishments. I refuse to touch *students*, he accepts that, but he says I am getting silly in my classroom lectures, I'm not bearing down. He doesn't care that I don't *solicit*—he doesn't want me to—but he tells me that I should be—well, be more conservative in my outlook. . . . It's strange. His name is Matthew Orton and he's an insignificant aide to the lieutenant governor in Hartford. But he's Nimrod. And I'll obey. . . .

November 14, 1967. The back is intolerable now—the doctors said it would *disintegrate*—that was *their* word—but not like *this!* I can get through forty minutes of a lecture and then I *must* excuse myself! . . . I ask always—is it worth it? . . . It must be or I wouldn't go on. . . . Or am I simply too great an egoist—or too much a coward—to take my life? . . . Nimrod sees me tonight. In a week it's *Thanksgiving*—I wonder where I will go. . . .

January 27, 1970. It *has* to be the end now. In C. Fry's beautiful words, the "seraphic strawberry, beaming in its bed" must turn and show its nettles. There's nothing more for me and Nimrod has infected too many, too completely. I will take my life—as painlessly as possible—there's been so much pain. . . .

January 28, 1970. I've tried to kill myself! I can't *do* it! I bring the gun, then the knife to the point, but it *will not happen!* Am I *really* so infused, so infected that I cannot accomplish that which is most to be desired? . . . Nimrod will kill me. I know that and he knows it better.

January 29, 1970. Nimrod—he's now *Arthur Latona!* Unbelievable! The same *Arthur Latona*
who built the middle-income housing projects in
Mount Holly!—At any rate, he's given me an unacceptable order. I've *told* him it's *unacceptable*.
I'm far too valuable to be discarded and I've
told him that, *too*. . . . He wants me to carry a
great deal of money to Toros Daglari in Turkey!
. . . Why, oh why, can't my life be *ended?* . . .

April 18, 1971. It's a wondrously strange world.
To survive, to exist and breathe the air, one does
so much one comes to loathe. The total is frightening . . . the excuses and the rationalizations are
worse. . . . Then something happens which sus-
pends—or at least postpones—all necessity of
judgment. . . . The pains shifted from the neck
and spine to the lower sides. I knew it had to be
something else. Something *more.* . . . I went to
Nimrod's doctor—as I must—always. My weight
has dropped, my reflexes are pathetic. He's worried and tomorrow I enter the private hospital in
Southbury. He says for an exploratory. . . . I
know they'll do their best for me. They have
other trips—very important trips, Nimrod says.
I'll be traveling throughout most of the summer,
he tells me. . . . If it wasn't me, it would be
someone else. The pains are terrible.

May 22, 1971. The old, tired soldier is home.
Herron's Nest is my salvation! I'm minus a kidney. No telling yet about the other, the doctor
says. But I know better. I'm dying. . . . Oh, God,
I welcome it! There'll be no more trips, no more
threats. Nimrod can do no more. . . . They'll
keep me alive, too. As long as they can. *They
have to now!* . . . I hinted to the doctor that I've

kept a record over the years. He just stared at me speechless. I've never seen a man so frightened. . . .

May 23, 1971. Latona—Nimrod—dropped by this morning. Before he could discuss anything, I told him I knew I was dying. That nothing mattered to me now—the decision to end my life was made, not by me. I even told him that I was prepared—relieved; that I had tried to end it myself but couldn't. He asked about *"what you told the doctor."* He wasn't able to say the *words!* His *fear* blanketed the living room like a heavy mist. . . . I answered calmly, with great authority, I think. I told him that whatever records there were would be given to him—*if my last days or months were made easier for me. He* was furious but he knew there wasn't anything he could do. What can a person do with an old man in pain who knows he's going to die? What arguments are left?

August 14, 1971. Nimrod is dead! Latona died of a coronary! Before *me,* and there's irony in that! . . . Still the business continues without change. Still I'm brought my supplies every week and every week the frightened messengers ask the questions—where are they? Where are the records?—they come close to threatening me but I remind them that Nimrod had the word of a dying old man. Why would I change that? . . . They retreat into their fear. . . . A new Nimrod will be chosen soon. . . . I've said I didn't want to know—and I don't!

September 20, 1971. A new year begins for Carlyle. My last year, I know that—what responsibilities I can assume, that is. . . . Nimrod's death has given me courage. Or is it the knowledge of my own? God knows I can't undo much but I can try! . . . I'm reaching out, I'm finding a few who've been hurt badly, and if nothing else I offer help. It may only be words, or advice, but just the knowledge that *I've been there* seems to be comforting. It's always such a shock to those I speak with! Imagine! The "grand old bird"! The pains and the numbness are nearly intolerable. I may not be able to wait. . . .

December 23, 1971. Two days before my last Christmas. I've said to so many who've asked me to their homes that I was going into New York. Of course, it's not so. I'll spend the days here at the Nest. . . . A disturbing note. The messengers tell me that the new Nimrod is the sternest, strongest one of all. They say he's ruthless. He orders executions as easily as his predecessors issued simple requests. Or are they telling me these things to frighten me? That can't frighten me!

February 18, 1972. The doctor told me that he'd prescribe heavier "medication" but warned me not to overdose. He, too, spoke of the new Nimrod. Even he's worried—he implied that the man was mad. I told him I didn't want to know anything. I was out of it.

February 26, 1972. I can't believe it! Nimrod *is* a *monster!* He's *got* to be *insane!* He's demanded that all those who've been working here over three years be cut off—sent out of the country—and if they refuse—be killed! The doctor's leaving next week. Wife, family, practice. . . . Latona's widow was murdered in an "automobile accident"! One of the messengers—Pollizzi —was shot to death in New Haven. Another— Capalbo—OD'd and the rumor is that the dose was administered!

April 5, 1972. From Nimrod to me—deliver to the messengers any and all records or he'll shut off my supplies. My house will be watched around the clock. I'll be followed wherever I go. I'll not be allowed to get any medical attention whatsoever. The combined effects of the cancer and the withdrawal will be beyond anything I can imagine. What Nimrod doesn't know is that before he left the doctor gave me enough for several months. He frankly didn't believe I'd last that long. . . . For the first time in this terrible, horrible life, I'm dealing from a position of strength. My life is firmer than ever because of death.

April 10, 1972. Nimrod is near the point of hysterics with me. He's threatened to expose me— which is meaningless. I've let him know that through the messengers. He's said that he'll destroy the whole Carlyle campus, but if he does that he'll destroy himself as well. The rumor is that he's calling together a conference. An important meeting of powerful men. . . . My house is now watched—as Nimrod said it would be— around the clock. By the Carlyle police, of course. Nimrod's private army!

April 22, 1972. Nimrod has won! It's horrifying, but he's won! He sent me two newspaper clippings. In each a student was killed by an overdose. The first a girl in Cambridge, the second a boy from Trinity. He says that he'll keep adding

to the list for every week I withhold the records.
. . . Hostages are executed!—He's got to be
stopped! But how? What can I *do?* . . . I've got
a plan but I don't know if I can do it—I'm going
to try to *manufacture* records. Leave them intact. It will be difficult—my hands shake so
sometimes! Can I possibly get through it?—
I have to. I said I'd deliver a *few* at a time. For
my *own* protection. I wonder if he'll agree to
that?

April 24, 1972. Nimrod's unbelievably evil, but
he's a realist. He knows he can do nothing else!
We both are racing against the time of my death.
Stalemate! I'm alternating between a typewriter
and different fountain pens and various types of
paper. The killings are suspended but I'm told
they will resume if I miss *one* delivery! Nimrod's
hostages are in my hands! Their executions can
be prevented only by me!

April 27, 1972. Something strange is happening! The Beeson boy phoned our contact at Admissions. Jim Matlock was there and Beeson suspects him. He asked questions, made an ass of himself with Beeson's wife. . . . Matlock isn't on any
list! He's no part of Nimrod—on either side. He's
never purchased a thing, never sold. . . . The Carlyle patrol cars are always outside now. Nimrod's
army is alerted. What is it?

April 27, 1972—P.M. The messengers came—
two of them—and what they led me to believe is
so incredible I cannot write it here. . . . I've never
asked the identity of Nimrod, I never wanted to
know. But panic's rampant now, something is
happening beyond even Nimrod's control. And

the messengers told me who Nimrod is. . . . They *lie! I cannot, will not believe it!* If it is true we are all in hell!

Matlock stared at the last entry helplessly. The hand-writing was hardly readable; most of the words were connected with one another as if the writer could not stop the pencil from racing ahead.

April 28. Matlock was here. He knows! Others know! He says the government men are involved now. . . . It's over! But what they can't under-stand is what will happen—a bloodbath, killings —executions! Nimrod can do *no less!* There will be so much *pain.* There will be mass killing and it will be provoked by an insignificant teacher of the Elizabethans. . . . A messenger called. Nim-rod *himself* is coming out. It is a confrontation. Now I'll know the truth—who he really is. . . . If he's who I've been led to believe—somehow I'll get this record out—somehow. It's all that's left. It's my turn to threaten. . . . It's over now. The pain will soon be over, too. . . . There's been so much pain . . . I'll make one final entry when I'm sure. . . .

Matlock closed the notebook. What had the girl named Jeannie said? *They* have the *courts,* the *police,* the *doctors.* And Alan Pace. He'd added the major university administrations—all over the Northeast. Whole academic policies; employments, deployments, curriculums—sources of enormous financing. *They* have it *all.*

But Matlock had the indictment.

It was enough. Enough to stop Nimrod—whoever he was. Enough to stop the bloodbath, the executions. Now he *had* to reach Jason Greenberg.

Alone.

Carrying the oilcloth packet, he began walking toward the town of Carlyle, traveling the back roads on which there was rarely any night traffic. He knew it would be too dangerous to drive. The man in the field had probably recovered sufficiently to reach someone —reach Nimrod. An alarm would be sent out for him. The unseen armies would be after him now. His only chance was to reach Greenberg. Jason Greenberg would tell him what to do.

There was blood on his shirt, mud caked on his trousers and jacket. His appearance brought to mind the outcasts of Bill's Bar & Grill by the railroad freight yards. It was nearly two thirty in the morning, but such places stayed open most of the night. The blue laws were only conveniences for them, not edicts. He reached College Parkway and descended the hill to the yards.

He brushed his damp clothes as best he could and covered the bloodstained shirt with his jacket. He walked into the filthy bar; the layers of cheap smoke were suspended above the disheveled customers. A jukebox was playing some Slovak music, men were yelling, a stand-up shuffleboard was being abused. Matlock knew he melted into the atmosphere. He would find a few precious moments of relief.

He sat down at a back booth.

"What the hell happened to *you?*"

It was the bartender, the same suspicious bartender whom he'd finally befriended several days ago. Years . . . ages ago.

"Caught in the rainstorm. Fell a couple of times. Lousy whisky. . . . Have you got anything to eat?"

"Cheese sandwiches. The meat I wouldn't give you. Bread's not too fresh either."

"I don't care. Bring me a couple of sandwiches. And a glass of beer. Would you do that?"

"Sure. Sure, mister. . . . You sure you want to eat here? I mean, I can tell, this ain't your kind of place, you know what I mean?"

There it was again. The incessant, irrelevant question; the dangling interrogative. *You know what I mean . . . ?* Not a question at all. Even in his few moments of relief he had to hear it once more.

"I know what you mean . . . but I'm sure."

"It's your stomach." The bartender trudged back to his station.

Matlock found Greenberg's number and went to the foul-smelling pay phone on the wall. He inserted a coin and dialed.

"I'm sorry, sir," the operator said, "the telephone is disconnected. Do you have another number where the party can be reached?"

"Try it again! I'm sure you're wrong."

She did and she wasn't. The supervisor in Wheeling, West Virginia, finally informed the operator in Carlyle, Connecticut, that any calls to a Mr. Greenberg were to be routed to Washington, D.C. It was assumed that whoever was calling would know where in Washington.

"But Mr. Greenberg isn't expected at the Washing-

ton number until early A.M.," she said. "Please inform
the party on the line."

He tried to think. Could he trust calling Washington, the Department of Justice, Narcotics Division?
Under the circumstances, might not Washington—for
the sake of speed—alert someone in the Hartford vicinity to get to him? And Greenberg had made it clear
—he didn't trust the Hartford office, the Hartford
agents.

He understood Greenberg's concern far better now.
He had only to think of the Carlyle police—Nimrod's
private army.

No, he wouldn't call Washington. He'd call Sealfont. His last hope was the university president. He
dialed Sealfont's number.

"James! Good Lord, James! Are you all right?!
Where in heaven's name have you *been?!*"

"To places I never knew were there. Never knew
existed."

"But you're all right? That's all that matters! Are
you all right?!"

"Yes, sir. And I've got everything. I've got it all.
Herron wrote everything down. It's a record of twenty-three years."

"Then he *was* part of it?"

"Very much so."

"Poor, *sick* man. . . . I don't understand. However,
that's not important now. That's for the authorities.
Where are you? I'll send a car. . . . No, I'll come myself. We've all been so worried. I've been in constant
touch with the men at the Justice Department."

"Stay where you are," Matlock said quickly. "I'll get
to you myself—everyone knows your car. It'll be
less dangerous this way. I know they're looking for

me. I'll have a man here call me a taxi. I just wanted to make sure you were home."

"Whatever you say. I must tell you I'm relieved. I'll call Kressel. Whatever you have to say, he should know about it. That's the way it's to be."

"I agree, sir. See you shortly."

He went back to the booth and began to eat the unappetizing sandwiches. He had swallowed half the beer when from inside his damp jacket, the short, hysterical beeps of Blackstone's Tel-electronic seared into his ears. He pulled out the machine and pressed the button. Without thinking of anything but the number 555-6868 he jumped up from the seat and walked rapidly back to the telephone. His hand trembling, he awkwardly manipulated the coin and dialed.

The recorded words were like the lash of a whip across his face.

"Charger Three-zero is canceled."

Then there was silence. As Blackstone had promised, there was nothing else but the single sentence— stated but once. There was no one to speak to, no appeal. Nothing.

But there had to be! He would not, *could not*, be cut off like this! If Blackstone was canceling him, he had a right to know *why!* He had a right to know that Pat was *safe!*

It took several minutes and a number of threats before he reached Blackstone himself.

"I don't have to talk to you!" The sleepy voice was belligerent. "I made that clear! . . . But I don't mind because if I can put a trace on this call I'll tell them where to find you the second you hang up!"

"Don't threaten me! You've got too much of my

money to threaten me. . . . Why am I canceled? I've got a right to know that."

"Because you stink! You stink like garbage!"

"That's not good enough! That doesn't *mean* anything!"

"I'll give you the rundown then. A warrant is out for you. Signed by the court and . . ."

"For *what*, goddamn it? Protective custody?! *Preventive detention?!*"

"For *murder*, Matlock! For conspiracy to distribute *narcotics!* For aiding and abetting known narcotics *distributors!* . . . You sold *out!* Like I said, you *smell!* And I hate the business you're in!"

Matlock was stunned. Murder? Conspiracy! What was Blackstone talking about?

"I don't know what you've been told, but it's not true. None of it's *true!* I risked my life, my *life*, do you *hear* me! To bring what I've got . . ."

"You're a good talker," interrupted Blackstone, "but you're careless! You're also a ghoulish bastard! There's a guy in a field outside of Carlyle with his throat slit. It didn't take the government boys ten minutes to trace that Ford wagon to its owner!"

"I didn't *kill* that man! I swear to Christ I *didn't kill him!*"

"No, of course not! And you didn't even *see* the fellow whose head you shot off at East Gorge, did you? Except that there's a parking lot attendant and a couple of others who've got you on the scene! . . . I forgot. You're also stupid. You left the parking ticket under your windshield wiper!"

"Now, wait a minute! *Wait a minute!* This is all *crazy!* The man at East Gorge asked to meet me there! He tried to *murder me!*"

"Tell that to your lawyer. We got the whole thing

—straight—from the Justice boys! I demanded that. I've got a damned good reputation. . . . I'll say this. When you sell out, you sell *high!* Over sixty thousand dollars in a *checking* account. Like I said, you *smell,* Matlock!"

He was so shocked he could not raise his voice. When he spoke, he was out of breath, hardly audible. "Listen to me. You've *got* to listen to me. Everything you say . . . there are explanations. Except the man in the field. I don't understand that. But I don't care if you believe me or not. It doesn't matter. I'm holding in my hand all the vindication I'll ever need. . . . What *does* matter is that you watch *that girl!* Don't cancel me out! *Watch her!*"

"Apparently you don't understand English very well. You *are* canceled! Charger Three-zero is *canceled!*"

"What about the girl?"

"We're not irresponsible," said Blackstone bitterly. "She's perfectly safe. She's under the protection of the Carlyle police."

There was a general commotion at the bar. The bartender was closing up and his customers resented it. Obscenities were shouted back and forth over the beer-soaked, filthy mahogany, while cooler or more drunken heads slowly weaved their way toward the front door.

Paralyzed, Matlock stood by the foul-smelling telephone. The roaring at the bar reached a crescendo but he heard nothing; the figures in front of his eyes were only blurs. He felt sick to his stomach, and so he held the front of his trousers, the oilcloth packet with Lucas Herron's notebook between his hands and his belt. He thought he was going to be sick as he had been sick beside the corpse on the East Gorge slope.

But—there was no time. Pat was held by Nimrod's private army. He had to act *now*. And when he acted, the spring would be sprung. There would be no re-winding.

The horrible truth was that he didn't know where to begin.

"What's the matter, mister? The sandwiches?"

"What?"

"Ya look like you're gonna throw up."

"Oh? . . . No." Matlock saw for the first time that al-most everyone had left the place.

The notebook! The notebook would be the ransom! There would be no tortured decision—not for the plastic men! Not for the *manipulators!* Nimrod could have the notebook! The indictment!

But then what? Would Nimrod let her live? Let him live? . . . What had Lucas Herron written: "The new Nimrod is a monster . . . ruthless. He orders exe-cutions. . . ."

Nimrod had murdered with far less motive than someone's knowledge of Lucas Herron's diaries.

"Look, mister. I'm sorry, but I gotta close up."

"Will you call a taxi for me, please?"

"A taxi? It's after three o'clock. Even if there was one, he wouldn't come down *here* at three o'clock in the morning."

"Have you got a car?"

"Now wait a minute, mister. I gotta clean up and ring out. I had some action tonight. The register'll take me twenty minutes."

Matlock withdrew his bills. The smallest denomina-tion was a hundred. "I've got to have a car—right away. How much do you want? I'll bring it back in an hour—maybe less."

The bartender looked at Matlock's money. It wasn't a normal sight. "It's a pretty old heap. You might have trouble driving it."

"I can drive *anything!* Here! Here's a hundred! If I wreck it you can have the whole roll. Here! Take it, for Christ's sake!"

"Sure. Sure, mister." The bartender reached under his apron and took out his car keys. "The square one's the ignition. It's parked in the rear. Sixty-two Chevy. Go out the back door."

"Thanks." Matlock started for the door indicated by the bartender.

"Hey, mister!"

"What?"

"What's your name again? . . . Something 'rock'? I forgot. I mean, for Christ's sake, I give you the car, I don't even know your name!"

Matlock thought for a second. "Rod. Nimrod. The name's Nimrod."

"That's no name, mister." The burly man started toward Matlock. "That's a spin fly for catchin' trout. Now, what's your name? You got my car, I gotta know your name."

Matlock still held the money in his hand. He peeled off three additional hundreds and threw them on the floor. It seemed right. He had given Kramer four hundred dollars for his station wagon. There should be symmetry somewhere. Or, at least, meaningless logic.

"That's four hundred dollars. You couldn't get four hundred dollars for a '62 Chevy. I'll bring it back!" He ran for the door. The last words he heard were those of the grateful but confused manager of Bill's Bar & Grill.

"Nimrod. Fuckin' joker!"

The car was a heap, as its owner had said. But it moved, and that was all that mattered. Sealfont would help him analyze the facts, the alternatives. Two opinions were better than one; he was afraid of assuming the total responsibility—he wasn't capable of it. And Sealfont would have people in high places he could contact. Sam Kressel, the liaison, would listen and object and be terrified for his domain. No matter; he'd be dismissed. Pat's safety was uppermost. Sealfont would see that.

Perhaps it was time to threaten—as Herron ultimately had threatened. Nimrod had Pat; he had Herron's indictment. The life of one human being for the protection of hundreds, perhaps thousands. Even Nimrod had to see their bargaining position. It was irrefutable, the odds were on their side.

He realized as he neared the railroad depot that this kind of thinking, by itself, made him a manipulator, too. Pat had been reduced to *quantity X*, Herron's diaries, *quantity Y*. The equation would then be postulated and the mathematical observers would make their decisions based on the data presented. It was the ice-cold logic of survival; emotional factors were disregarded, consciously despised.

Frightening!

He turned right at the station and started to drive up College Parkway. Sealfont's mansion stood at the end. He went as fast as the '62 Chevy would go, which wasn't much above thirty miles an hour on the hill. The streets were deserted, washed clean by the storm. The store fronts, the houses, and finally the campus were dark and silent.

He remembered that Kressel's house was just a half block off College Parkway on High Street. The detour would take him no more than thirty seconds. It was worth it, he thought. If Kressel hadn't left for Seal-font's, he would pick him up and they could talk on the way over. Matlock *had* to talk, *had* to begin. He couldn't stand the isolation any longer.

He swung the car to the left at the corner of High Street. Kressel's house was a large gray colonial set back from the street by a wide front lawn bordered by rhododendrons. There were lights on downstairs. With luck, Kressel was still home. There were two cars, one in the driveway; Matlock slowed down.

His eyes were drawn to a dull reflection at the rear of the driveway. Kressel's kitchen light was on; the spill from the window illuminated the hood of a third car, and the Kressels were a two-car family.

He looked again at the car in front of the house. It was a Carlyle patrol car. The Carlyle police were in Kressel's house!

Nimrod's private army was with *Kressel!*

Or was Nimrod's private army with *Nimrod?*

He swerved to the left, narrowly missing the patrol car, and sped down the street to the next corner. He turned right and pressed the accelerator to the floor. He was confused, frightened, bewildered. If Sealfont had called Kressel—which he had obviously done—and Kressel worked with Nimrod, or *was* Nimrod, there'd be other patrol cars, other soldiers of the private army waiting for him.

His mind went back to the Carlyle Police Station —a century ago, capsuled in little over a week—the night of Loring's murder. Kressel had disturbed him then. And even before that—with Loring and Green-berg—Kressel's hostility to the federal agents had been outside the bounds of reason.

Oh, Christ! It was so clear now! His instincts had been right. The instincts which had served him as the *hunted* as well as the *hunter* had been true! He'd been watched *too* thoroughly, his every action anticipated. Kressel, the *liaison*, was, in fact, Kressel the tracker, the seeker, the supreme killer.

Nothing was ever as it appeared to be—only what one sensed behind the appearance. Trust the senses.

Somehow he had to get to Sealfont. Warn Sealfont that the Judas was Kressel. Now they *both* had to protect themselves, establish some base from which they could strike back.

Otherwise the girl he loved was lost.

There couldn't be a second wasted. Sealfont had certainly told Kressel that he, Matlock, had Lucas Herron's diaries, and that was all Kressel would need to know. All Nimrod needed to know.

Nimrod had to get possession of both the Corsican paper *and* the diaries; now he knew where they were. His private army would be told that this was its moment of triumph or disaster. They would be waiting for him at Sealfont's; Sealfont's mansion was the trap they expected him to enter.

Matlock swung west at the next corner. In his trouser pocket were his keys, and among them was the key to Pat's apartment. To the best of his knowledge, no one knew he had such a key, certainly no one would expect him to go there. He had to chance it; he couldn't risk going to a public telephone, risk being seen under a street lamp. The patrol cars would be searching everywhere.

He heard the roar of an engine behind him and felt the sharp pain in his stomach. A car was following him—closing in on him. And the '62 Chevrolet was no match for it.

His right leg throbbed from the pressure he exerted on the pedal. His hands gripped the steering wheel as he turned wildly into a side street, the muscles in his arms tensed and aching. Another turn. He spun the wheel to the left, careening off the edge of the curb back into the middle of the road. The car behind him maintained a steady pace, never more than ten feet away, the headlights blinding in the rear-view mirror.

His pursuer was *not* going to close the gap between them! Not then. Not at that moment. He could have done so a hundred, two hundred yards ago. He was waiting. Waiting for something. But what?

There was so *much* he couldn't understand! So much he'd miscalculated, misread. He'd been out-maneuvered at every important juncture. He was what they said—an amateur! He'd been beyond his depth from the beginning. And now, at the last, his final assault was ending in ambush. They would kill him, take the Corsican paper, the diaries of indictment. They would kill the girl he loved, the innocent child whose life he'd thrown away so brutally. Sealfont would be finished—he knew too much now! God knew how many others would be destroyed.

So be it.

If it had to be this way, if hope really had been taken from him, he'd end it all with a gesture, at least. He reached into his belt for the automatic.

The streets they now traveled—the pursuer and the pursued—ran through the outskirts of the campus, consisting mainly of the science buildings and a number of large parking lots. There were no houses to speak of.

He swerved the Chevrolet as far to the right as possible, thrusting his right arm across his chest, the barrel of the pistol outside the car window, pointed at the pursuing automobile.

He fired twice. The car behind him accelerated; he

felt the repeated jarring of contact, the metal against metal as the car behind hammered into the Chevrolet's left rear chassis. He pulled again at the trigger of the automatic. Instead of a loud report, he heard and felt only the single click of the firing pin against an unloaded chamber.

Even his last gesture was futile.

His pursuer crashed into him once more. He lost control; the wheel spun, tearing his arm, and the Chevrolet reeled off the road. Frantic, he reached for the door handle, desperately trying to steady the car, prepared to jump if need be.

He stopped all thought; all instincts of survival were arrested. Within those split seconds, time ceased. For the car behind him had drawn parallel and he saw the face of his pursuer.

There were bandages and gauze around the eyes, beneath the glasses, but they could not hide the face of the black revolutionary. Julian Dunois.

It was the last thing he remembered before the Chevrolet swerved to the right and skidded violently off the road's incline.

Blackness.

Pain roused him. It seemed to be all through his left side. He rolled his head, feeling the pillow beneath him.

The room was dimly lit; what light there was came from a table lamp on the other side. He shifted his head and tried to raise himself on his right shoulder. He pushed his elbow into the mattress, his immobile left arm following the turn of his body like a dead weight.

He stopped abruptly.

Across the room, directly in line with the foot of the bed, sat a man in a chair. At first Matlock couldn't distinguish the features. The light was poor and his eyes were blurred with pain and exhaustion.

Then the man came into focus. He was black and his dark eyes stared at Matlock beneath the perfectly cut semicircle of an Afro haircut. It was Adam Williams, Carlyle University's firebrand of the Black Left.

When Williams spoke, he spoke softly and, unless Matlock misunderstood—once again—there was compassion in the black's voice.

"I'll tell Brother Julian you're awake. He'll come in to see you." Williams got out of the chair and went to the door. "You've banged up your left shoulder. Don't try to get out of bed. There are no windows in here. The hallway is guarded. Relax. You need rest."

"I don't have *time* to rest, you *goddamn fool!*" Matlock tried to raise himself further but the pain was too great. He hadn't adjusted to it.

"You don't have a choice." Williams opened the door and walked rapidly out, closing it firmly behind him.

Matlock fell back on the pillow. . . . Brother Julian. . . . He remembered now. The sight of Julian Dunois's bandaged face watching him through the speeding car window, seemingly inches away from him. And his ears had picked up Dunois's words, his commands to his driver. They had been shouted in his Caribbean dialect.

"Hit him, mon! Hit him again! Drive him *off*, mon!"

And then everything had become dark and the darkness had been filled with violent noise, crashing metal, and he had felt his body twisting, turning, spiraling into the black void.

Oh, God! How long ago was it? He tried to lift up his left hand to look at his watch, but the arm barely moved; the pain was sharp and lingering. He reached over with his right hand to pull the stretch band off his wrist, but it wasn't there. His watch was gone.

He struggled to get up and finally managed to perch on the edge of the bed, his legs touching the floor. He pressed his feet against the wood, thankful that he could sit up. . . . He had to put the pieces together, to reconstruct what had happened, where he was going.

He'd been on his way to Pat's. To find a secluded telephone on which to reach Adrian Sealfont. To warn him that Kressel was the enemy, Kressel was Nimrod. And he'd made up his mind that Herron's diaries would be Pat's ransom. Then the chase had begun, only it wasn't a chase. The car behind him, commanded by Julian Dunois, had played a furious game of terror. It had toyed with him as a lethal mountain cat might play with a wounded goat. Finally it had attacked—steel against steel—and driven him to darkness.

Matlock knew he had to escape. But *from where* and *to whom?*

The door of the windowless room opened. Dunois entered, followed by Williams.

"Good morning," said the attorney. "I see you've managed to sit up. That's good. It augurs well for your very abused body."

"What time is it? Where am I?"

"It's nearly four thirty. You are in a room at Lumumba Hall. You see? I withhold nothing from you. . . . Now, you must reciprocate. You must withhold nothing from me."

"Listen to me!" Matlock kept his voice steady. "I have no fight with you, with *any* of you! I've got . . ."

"Oh, I disagree," Dunois smiled. "Look at my *face*. It's only through enormous good fortune that I wasn't blinded by you. You tried to crush the lenses of my glasses into my eyes. Can you imagine how my work would suffer if I were blind?"

"Goddamn it! You filled me with acid!"

"And you provoked it! You were actively engaged in pursuits inimicable to our brothers! Pursuits you had no *right* to engage in . . . But this is concentric debate. It will get us nowhere. . . . We *do* appreciate what you've brought us. Beyond our most optimistic ambitions."

"You've got the notebook. . . ."

"*And* the Corsican document. The Italian invitation

we knew existed. The notebook was only a rumor. A rumor which was fast being ascribed to fiction until tonight—this morning. You should feel proud. You've accomplished what scores of your more experienced betters failed to accomplish. You found the treasure. The *real* treasure."

"I've got to have it back!"

"Fat chance!" said Williams, leaning against the wall, watching.

"If I don't get it back, a girl will *die!* Do whatever you goddamn well please with me, but let me *use* it to get her back. Christ! Please, *please!*"

"You feel deeply, don't you? I see tears in your eyes. . . ."

"Oh, *Jesus!* You're an *educated man!* You can't *do* this! . . . *Listen!* Take whatever information you want out of it! Then give it to me and let me go! . . . I swear to you I'll come back. Give her a chance. Just give her a *chance!*"

Dunois walked slowly to the chair by the wall, the chair in which Adam Williams sat when Matlock awoke. He pulled it forward, closer to the bed, and sat down, crossing his knees gracefully. "You feel helpless, don't you? Perhaps . . . even without hope."

"I've been through a great deal!"

"I'm sure you have. And you appeal to my reason . . . as an *educated man.* You realize that it is within my scope to help you and therefore I am superior to you. You would not make such an appeal if it were not so."

"Oh, Christ! Cut that out!"

"Now you know what it's like. You are helpless. Without hope. You wonder if your appeal will be lost on a deaf ear. . . . Do you really, for one second, think that I care for the life of Miss Ballantyne? Do you honestly believe she has any priority for me? Any *more* than the lives of *our* children, *our* loved ones mean anything to you!"

Matlock knew he had to answer Dunois. The black would offer nothing if he evaded him. It was another game—and he had to play, if only briefly.

"I don't deserve this and you know it. I loathe the people who won't do anything for them. You know me—you've made that clear. So you must know that."

"Ahh, but I *don't* know it! You're the one who made the choice, the decision to work for the superior man! The *Washington* man! For decades, two *centuries, my* people have appealed to the *superior Washington man!* 'Help us,' they cry. 'Don't leave us without hope!' they scream. But nobody listens. Now, you expect me to listen to you?"

"Yes, I *do!* Because I'm not your enemy. I may not be everything you want me to be, but I'm not your enemy. If you turn me—and men like me—into objects of hatred, you're *finished.* You're outnumbered, don't forget that, Dunois. We won't storm the barricades every time you yell 'foul,' but we hear you. We're willing to help; we want to help."

Dunois looked coldly at Matlock. "Prove it."

Matlock returned the black's stare. "Use me as your bait, your hostage. Kill me if you have to. But get the girl out."

"We can do that—the hostaging, the killing—without your consent. Brave but hardly proof."

Matlock refused to allow Dunois to disengage the stare between them. He spoke softly. "I'll give you a statement. Written, verbal—on tape; freely, without force or coercion. I'll spell it all out. How I was used, what I did. Everything. You'll have your Washington men as well as Nimrod."

Dunois folded his arms and matched Matlock's quiet voice. "You realize you would put an end to your professional life; this life you love so much. No university administration worthy of its name would consider you for a position. You'd never be trusted again. By any factions. You'd become a pariah."

"You asked for proof. It's all I can offer you."

Dunois sat immobile in the chair. Williams had straightened up from his slouching position against the wall. No one spoke for several moments. Finally Dunois smiled gently. His eyes, surrounded by the gauze, were compassionate.

"You're a good man. Inept, perhaps, but persevering. You shall have the help you need. We won't leave you without hope. Do you agree, Adam?"

"Agreed."

Dunois got out of the chair and approached Matlock.

"You've heard the old cliché, that politics make strange bedfellows. Conversely, practical objectives often make for strange political alliances. History bears this out. . . . We want this Nimrod as much as you do. As well as the Mafiosi he tries to make peace with. It is they and their kind who prey upon the children. An example must be made. An example which will instill, terror in other Nimrods, other Mafiosi. . . . You shall have help, but this is the condition we demand."

"What do you mean?"

"The disposition of Nimrod and the others will be left to us. We don't trust your judges and your juries. Your courts are corrupt, your legalistics no more than financial manipulations. . . . The barrio addict is thrown into jail. The rich gangsters appeal. . . . No, the disposition must be left to us."

"I don't care about that. You can do whatever you like."

"Your not caring is insufficient. We demand more than that. We must have our guarantee."

"How can I give a guarantee?"

"By your silence. By not acknowledging our presence. We will take the Corsican paper and somehow we will find the conference and be admitted. We will extract what we want from the diaries—that's being done now, incidentally. . . . But your *silence* is the paramount issue. We will help you now—on a best-efforts basis, of course—but you must never mention our involvement. Irrespective of what may happen, you must not, directly or indirectly, allude to our participation. Should you do so, we will take your life and the life of the girl. Is this understood?"

"It is."

"Then we are in agreement?"

"We are."

"Thank you," said Dunois, smiling.

As Julian Dunois outlined their alternatives and began to formulate strategy, it became clearer to Matlock why the blacks had sought him out with such concentration—and why Dunois was willing to offer help. He, Matlock, had the basic information they needed. Who were his contacts? Both inside and without the university? Who and where were the government men? How were communications expedited?

In other words—whom should Julian Dunois *avoid* in his march to Nimrod?

"I must say, you were extraordinarily unprepared for contingencies," Dunois said. "Very slipshod."

"That occurred to me, too. But I think I was only partially to blame."

"I dare say you were!" Dunois laughed, joined by Williams. The three men remained in the windowless room. A card table had been brought in along with several yellow pads. Dunois had begun writing down every bit of information Matlock supplied. He double-checked the spelling of names, the accuracy of addresses—a professional at work; Matlock once again experienced the feeling of inadequacy he had felt when talking with Greenberg.

Dunois stapled a number of pages together and

started on a fresh pad. "What are you doing?" asked Matlock.

"These will be duplicated by a copier downstairs. The information will be sent to my office in New York. . . . As will a photostat of every page in Professor Herron's notebook."

"You don't fool around, do you?"

"In a word—no."

"It's all I've got to give you. Now, what do we do? What do *I* do? I'm frightened, I don't have to tell you that. I can't even let myself think what might happen to her."

"*Nothing* will happen. Believe me when I tell you that. At the moment, your Miss Ballantyne is as safe as if she were in her mother's arms. Or yours. She's the bait, not you. The bait will be kept fresh and unspoiled. For you have what they want. They can't survive without it."

"Then let's make the offer. The sooner the better."

"Don't worry. It will be made. But we must decide carefully—aware of the nuances—how we do it. So far, we have two alternatives, we agreed upon that. The first is Kressel, himself. The direct confrontation. The second, to use the police department, to let your message to Nimrod be delivered through it."

"Why do that? Use the police?"

"I'm only listing alternatives. . . . Why the police? I'm not sure. Except that the Herron diaries state clearly that Nimrod was replaced in the past. This current Nimrod is the third since the position's inception, is that not correct?"

"Yes. The first was a man named Orton in the lieutenant governor's office. The second, Angelo Latona, a builder. The third, obviously, Kressel. What's your point?"

"I'm speculating. Whoever assumes the position of Nimrod has authoritarian powers. Therefore, it is the position, not the man. The man can make whatever he can of the office."

"But the office," interrupted Williams, "is given and taken away. Nimrod isn't the last voice."

"Exactly. Therefore, it might be to Matlock's advantage to let the word leak out very specifically that it is *he* who possesses the weapon. That Kressel—Nimrod—must exercise great caution. For everyone's sake."

"Wouldn't that mean that more people would be after me?"

"Possibly. Conversely, it could mean that there'd be a legion of anxious criminals protecting you. Until the threat you impose is eliminated. No one will act rashly until that threat is taken away. No one will want Nimrod to act rashly."

Matlock lit a cigarette, listening intently. "What you're trying to do then is to partially separate Nimrod from his own organization."

Dunois snapped the fingers of both hands, the sound of castanets, applause. He smiled as he spoke.

"You're a quick student. It's the first lesson of insurgency. One of the prime objectives of infiltration. Divide. Divide!"

The door opened; an excited black entered. Without saying a word, he handed Dunois a note. Dunois read it and closed his eyes for several moments. It was his way of showing dismay. He thanked the black messenger calmly and dismissed him politely. He looked at Matlock but handed the note to Williams.

"Our stratagems may have historic precedence, but I'm afraid for us they're empty words. Kressel and his wife are dead. Dr. Sealfont has been taken forcibly from his house under guard. He was driven away in a Carlyle patrol car."

"What? Kressel! I don't believe it! It's not true!"

"I'm afraid it is. Our men report that the two bodies were carried out not more than fifteen minutes ago. The word is murder and suicide. Naturally. It would fit perfectly."

"Oh, Christ! Oh, Jesus Christ! It's my fault! I made them do it! I *forced* them! Sealfont! Where did they take him?"

"We don't know. The brothers on watch didn't dare follow the patrol car."

He had no words. The paralysis, the fear, was there again. He reeled blindly into the bed and sank down on it, sitting, staring at nothing. The sense of futility, of inadequacy, of defeat was now overwhelming. He had caused so much pain, so much death.

"It's a severe complication," said Dunois, his elbows on the card table. "Nimrod has removed your only contacts. In so doing, he's answered a vital question, prevented us from making an enormous error—I refer to Kressel, of course. Nevertheless, to look at it from another direction, Nimrod has reduced our alternatives. You have no choice now. You must deal through his private army, the Carlyle police."

Matlock looked numbly across at Julian Dunois. "Is that all you can *do?* Sit there and coolly decide a next move? . . . Kressel's *dead.* His *wife* is *dead.* Adrian Sealfont's probably killed by now. These were my *friends!*"

"And you have my sympathies, but let me be honest: I don't regret the loss of the three individuals. Frankly, Adrian Sealfont is the only *real* casualty—we might have worked with him, he was brilliant—but this loss does not break my heart. We lose thousands in the barrios every month. I weep for them more readily. . . . However, to the issue at hand. You really don't have a choice. You must make your contact through the police."

"But that's where you're wrong." Matlock felt suddenly stronger. "I *do* have a choice. . . . Greenberg left West Virginia early this morning. He'll be in Washington by now. I have a number in New York that can put me in touch with him. I'm getting hold of Greenberg." He'd done enough, caused enough anguish. He couldn't take the chance with Pat's life. Not any longer. He wasn't capable.

Dunois leaned back in his chair, removing his arms from the card table. He stared at Matlock. "I said a little while ago that you were an apt student. I amend that observation. You are quick but obviously superficial. . . . You will *not* reach Greenberg. He was not part of our agreement and you *will not* violate that agreement. You will carry through on the basis we agree upon or you will be subject to the penalties I outlined."

"Goddamn it, don't threaten me! I'm sick of threats!" Matlock stood up. Dunois reached under his jacket and took out a gun. Matlock saw that it was the black automatic he had taken from the dead man on the East Gorge slope. Dunois, too, rose to his feet.

"The medical report will no doubt estimate your death to be at dawn."

"For God's sake! The girl is being held by killers!"

"So are you," Dunois said quietly. "Can't you *see* that? Our motives are different, but make no mistake about it. We are *killers*. We *have* to be."

"You wouldn't go that far!"

"Oh, but we would. We have. And much, much further. We would drop your insignificant corpse in front of the police station with a note pinned to your bloodstained shirt. We would *demand* the death of the girl prior to any negotiations. They would readily agree, for neither of us can take the chance of her living. Once she, too, is dead, the giants are left to do battle by themselves."

"You're a monster."

"I am what I have to be."

No one spoke for several moments. Matlock shut his eyes, his voice a whisper. "What do I do?"

"That's much better." Dunois sat down, looking up at the nervous Adam Williams. Briefly, Matlock felt a kinship with the campus radical. He, too, was frightened, unsure. As Matlock, he was ill-equipped to deal with the world of Julian Dunois or Nimrod. The Haitian seemed to read Matlock's thoughts.

"You must have confidence in yourself. Remember, you've accomplished far more than anyone else. With far less resources. And you have extraordinary courage."

"I don't feel very courageous."

"A brave man rarely does. Isn't that remarkable? Come, sit down." Matlock obeyed. "You know, you and I are not so different. In another time, we might even be allies. Except, as many of my brothers have noted, I look for saints."

"There aren't any," Matlock said.

"Perhaps not. And then again, perhaps . . . we'll debate it some other time. Right now, we must plan. Nimrod will be expecting you. We can't disappoint him. Yet we must be sure to guard ourselves on all flanks." He pulled closer to the table, a half-smile on his lips, his eyes shining.

The black revolutionary's strategy, if nothing else, was a complex series of moves designed to protect Matlock and the girl. Matlock grudgingly had to acknowledge it.

"I have a double motive," Dunois explained. "The second is, frankly, more important to me. Nimrod will not appear himself unless he has no other choice, and I want Nimrod. I will not settle for a substitute, a camouflage."

The essence of the plan was Herron's notebook itself, the last entries in the diary.

The identity of Nimrod.

"Herron states explicitly that he *would* not write the name intimated by the messengers. Not that he couldn't. His feeling obviously was that he could not implicate that man if the information was incorrect. Guilt by innuendo would be abhorrent to him. Like yourself, Matlock; you refused to offer up Herron on the basis of an hysterical phone call. He knew that he might die at any given moment; his body had taken about as much abuse as it could endure. . . . He had to be positive." Dunois, by now, was drawing meaningless geometric shapes on a blank page of yellow paper.

"And then he was murdered," said Matlock. "Made to look like suicide."

"Yes. If nothing else, the diaries confirm that. Once Herron had proved to himself who Nimrod was, he would have moved heaven and earth to include it in the notebook. Our enemy cannot know that he did not. That is our Damocletian sword."

Matlock's first line of protection was to let the chief

of the Carlyle police understand that he, Matlock, knew the identity of Nimrod. He would reach an accommodation solely with Nimrod. This accommodation was the lesser of two evils. He was a hunted man. There was a warrant out for his arrest of which the Carlyle police surely were aware. He might conceivably be exonerated from the lesser indictments, but he would not escape the charge of murder. Possibly, two murders. For he had killed, the evidence was overwhelming, and he had no tangible alibis. He did not know the men he had killed. There were no witnesses to corroborate self-defense; the manner of each killing was grotesque to the point of removing the killer from society. The best he could hope for was a number of years in prison.

And then he would spell out his terms for an accommodation with Nimrod. Lucas Herron's diaries for his life—and the life of the girl. Certainly the diaries were worth a sum of money sufficient for both of them to start again somewhere.

Nimrod could do this. Nimrod *had* to do it.

"The key to this . . . let's call it phase one . . . is the amount of conviction you display." Dunois spoke carefully. "Remember, you are in panic. You have taken lives, killed other human beings. You are not a violent man but you've been forced, coerced into frightening crimes."

"It's the truth. More than you know."

"Good. Convey that feeling. All a panicked man wants is to get away from the scene of his panic. Nimrod must believe this. It guarantees your immediate safety."

A second telephone call would then be made by Matlock—to confirm Nimrod's acceptance of a meeting. The location, at this point, could be chosen by

Nimrod. Matlock would call again to learn where.
But the meeting must take place before ten o'clock in
the morning."

"By now, you, the fugitive, seeing freedom in sight,
suddenly possess doubts," said Dunois. "In your gathering hysteria, you need a guarantee factor."

"Which is?"

"A third party; a mythical third party. . . ."

Matlock was to inform the contact at the Carlyle
Police Headquarters that he had written up a complete statement about the Nimrod operation. Herron's
diaries, identities, everything. This statement had been
sealed in an envelope and given to a friend. It would
be mailed to the Justice Department at ten in the
morning unless Matlock instructed otherwise.

"Here, phase two depends again on conviction, but
of another sort. Watch a caged animal whose captors
suddenly open the gate. He's wary, suspicious; he
approaches his escape with caution. So, too, must our
fugitive. It will be expected. You have been most resourceful during the past week. By logic you should
have been dead by now, but you survived. You must
continue that cunning."

"I understand."

The last phase was created by Julian Dunois to
guarantee—as much as was possible in a "best-efforts
situation"—the reclaiming of the girl and the safety of
Matlock. It would be engineered by a third and final
telephone call to Nimrod's contact. The object of the
call was to ascertain the specific location of the meeting and the precise time.

When informed of both, Matlock was to accept
without hesitation.

At first.

Then moments later—seemingly with no other rea-

son than the last extremity of panic and suspicion—
he was to reject Nimrod's choice.

Not the time—the location.

He was to hesitate, to stutter, to behave as close to
irrationality as he could muster. And then, suddenly,
he was to blurt out a second location of his *own*
choice. As if it had just come to mind with no
thoughts of it before that moment. He was then to
restate the existence of the nonexistent statement
which a mythical friend would mail to Washington at
ten in the morning. He was then to hang up without
listening further.

"The most important factor in phase three is the
recognizable consistency of your panic. Nimrod must
see that your reactions are now primitive. The act itself is about to happen. You lash out, recoil, set up
barriers to avoid his net, should that net exist. In your
hysteria, you are as dangerous to him as a wounded
cobra is deadly to the tiger. For rationality doesn't
exist, only survival. He now must meet you himself,
he now must bring the girl. He will, of course, arrive
with his palace guard. His intentions won't change.
He'll take the diaries, perhaps discuss elaborate plans
for your accommodation, and when he learns that
there is no written statement, no friend about to mail
it, he'll expect to kill you both. . . . However, none of
his intentions will be carried out. For we'll be waiting
for him."

"How? How will you be waiting for him?"

"With my own palace guard. . . . We shall now, you
and I, decide on that hysterically arrived at second
location. It should be in an area you know well, perhaps frequent often. Not too far away, for it is presumed you have no automobile. Secluded, because
you are hunted by the law. Yet accessible, for you

must travel fast, most likely on back roads."

"You're describing Herron's Nest. Herron's house."

"I may be, but we can't use it. It's psychologically inconsistent. It would be a break in our fugitive's pattern of behavior. Herron's Nest is the root of his fear. He wouldn't go back there. . . . Someplace else."

Williams started to speak. He was still unsure, still wary of joining Dunois's world. "I think, perhaps . . ."

"What, Brother Williams? What do you think?"

"Professor Matlock often dines at a restaurant called the Cheshire Cat."

Matlock snapped his head up at the black radical. "You too? You've had me followed."

"Quite often. We don't enter such places. We'd be conspicuous."

"Go on, brother," broke in Dunois.

"The Cheshire Cat is about four miles outside Carlyle. It's set back from the highway, which is the normal way to get there, about half a mile, but it also can be reached by taking several back roads. Behind and to the sides of the restaurant are patios and gardens used in the summer for dining. Beyond these are woods."

"Anyone on the premises?"

"A single night watchman, I believe. It doesn't open until one. I don't imagine cleanup crews or kitchen help get there before nine thirty or ten."

"Excellent." Dunois looked at his wristwatch. "It's now ten past five. Say we allow fifteen minutes between phases one, two, and three and an additional twenty minutes for traveling between stations, that would make it approximately six fifteen. Say six thirty for contingencies. We'll set the rendezvous for seven. Behind the Cheshire Cat. Get the notebook, brother. I'll alert the men."

Williams rose from his chair and walked to the door. He turned and addressed Dunois. "You won't change your mind? You won't let me come with the rest of you?"

Dunois didn't bother to look up. He answered curtly. "Don't annoy me. I've a great deal to think about."

Williams left the room quickly.

Matlock watched Dunois. He was still sketching his meaningless figures on the yellow pad, only now he bore down on the pencil, causing deep ridges on the paper. Matlock saw the diagram emerging. It was a series of jagged lines, all converging.

They were bolts of lightning.

"Listen to me," he said. "It's not too late. Call in the authorities. Please, for Christ's sake, you can't risk the lives of these kids."

From behind his glasses, surrounded by the gauze bandages, Dunois's eyes bore into Matlock. He spoke with contempt. "Do you for one minute think I would allow these children to tread in waters I don't even know *I* can survive? We're not your Joint Chiefs of Staff, Matlock. We have greater respect, greater love for our young."

Matlock recalled Adam Williams' protestations at the door. "That's what Williams meant then? About coming with you."

"Come with me."

Dunois led Matlock out of the small, windowless room and down the corridor to a staircase. There were a few students milling about, but only a few. The rest of Lumumba Hall was asleep. They proceeded down two flights to a door Matlock remembered as leading to the cellars, to the old, high-ceilinged chapter room in which he'd witnessed the frightening performance of the African tribal rite. They descended the stairs and, as Matlock suspected, went to the rear of the cellars, to the thick oak door of the chapter room. Dunois had not spoken a word since he'd bade Matlock follow him.

Inside the chapter room were eight blacks, each well over six feet tall. They were dressed alike: dark, tight-fitting khakis with open shirts and black, soft leather ankle boots with thick rubber soles. Several were sitting, playing cards; others were reading, some talking quietly among themselves. Matlock noticed that a few had their shirt sleeves rolled up. The arms displayed were tautly muscular, veins close to the skin. They all nodded informally to Dunois and his guest. Two or three smiled intelligently at Matlock, as if to put him at ease. Dunois spoke softly.

"The palace guard."

"My God!"

"The elite corps. Each man is trained over a period of three years. There is not a weapon he cannot fire or fix, a vehicle he cannot repair . . . or a philosophy he cannot debate. Each is familiar with the most brutal forms of combat, traditional as well as guerrilla. Each is committed until death."

"The terror brigade, is that it? It's not new, you know."

"Not with that description, no, it wouldn't be. Don't forget, I grew up with such dogs at my heels. Duvalier's Ton Ton Macoute were a pack of hyenas; I witnessed their work. These men are no such animals."

"I wasn't thinking of Duvalier."

"On the other hand, I acknowledge the debt to Papa Doc. The Ton Ton's concept was exciting to me. Only I realized it had to be restructured. Such units are springing up all over the country."

"They sprung up once before," Matlock said. "They

were called 'elite' then, too. They were also called 'units'—SS units."

Dunois looked at Matlock and Matlock saw the hurt in his eyes. "To reach for such parallels is painful. Nor is it justified. We do what we have to do. What is right for us to do."

"Ein Volk, Ein Reich, Ein Fuehrer," said Matlock softly.

34

Everything happened so fast. Two of Dunois's elite guard were assigned to him, the rest left for the rendezvous with Nimrod, to prepare themselves to meet another elite guard—the selected few of Nimrod's private army who undoubtedly would accompany him. Matlock was ushered across the campus by the two huge blacks after the word came back from scouts that the path was clear. He was taken to a telephone booth in the basement of a freshman dormitory, where he made his first call.

He found that his fear, his profound fear, aided the impression Dunois wanted to convey. It wasn't difficult for him to pour out his panicked emotions, pleading for sanctuary, for, in truth, he *felt* panicked. As he spoke hysterically into the phone, he wasn't sure which was the reality and which the fantasy. He wanted to be free. He wanted Pat to live and be free with him. If Nimrod could bring it all about, why not deal with Nimrod in good faith?

It was a nightmare for him. He was afraid for a moment that he might yell out the truth and throw himself on the mercy of Nimrod.

The sight of Dunois's own Ton Ton Macoute kept bringing him back to his failing senses, and he ended the first telephone call without breaking. The Carlyle police "superintendent" would forward the information, receive an answer, and await Matlock's next call.

The blacks received word from their scouts that the second public telephone wasn't clear. It was on a street corner, and a patrol car had been spotted in the area. Dunois knew that even public phones could be traced, although it took longer, and so he had alternate sites for each of the calls, the last one to be made on the highway. Matlock was rushed to the first alternate telephone booth. It was on the back steps of the Student Union.

The second call went more easily, although whether that was an advantage was not clear. Matlock was emphatic in his reference to the mythical statement that was to be mailed at ten in the morning. His strength had its effect, and he was grateful for it. The "superintendent" was frightened now, and he didn't bother to conceal it. Was Nimrod's private army beginning to have its doubts? The troops were, perhaps, picturing their own stomachs blown out by the enemy's shells. Therefore, the generals had to be more alert, more aware of the danger.

He was raced to a waiting automobile. It was an old Buick, tarnished, dented, inconspicuous. The exterior, however, belied the inside. The interior was as precisely tooled as a tank. Under the dashboard was a powerful radio; the windows were at least a half-inch thick, paned, Matlock realized, with bulletproof glass. Clipped to the sides were high-powered, short-barreled rifles, and dotted about the body were rubber-flapped holes into which these barrels were to be inserted. The sound of the engine impressed Matlock instantly. It was as powerful a motor as he'd ever heard.

They followed an automobile in front of them at

moderate speed; Matlock realized that another car had taken up the rear position. Dunois had meant it when he said they were to cover themselves on all flanks. Dunois was, indeed, a professional.

And it disturbed James Matlock when he thought about the profession.

It was black. It was also *Ein Volk, Ein Reich, Ein Fuehrer.*

As was Nimrod and all he stood for.

The words came back to him.

". . . *I'm getting out of this goddamn country, mister. . . .*"

Had it come to that?

And: ". . . *You think it's all so different? . . . It's mini-America! . . . It's company policy, man!*"

The land was sick. Where was the cure?

"Here we are. Phase three." The black revolutionary in command tapped him lightly on the arm, smiling reassuringly as he did so. Matlock got out of the car. They were on the highway south of Carlyle. The car in front had pulled up perhaps a hundred yards ahead of them and parked off the road, its lights extinguished. The automobile behind had done the same.

In front of him stood two aluminum-framed telephone booths, placed on a concrete platform. The second black walked to the right booth, pushed the door open—which turned on the dull overhead light—and quickly slid back the pane of glass under the light, exposing the bulb. This he rapidly unscrewed so that the booth returned to darkness. It struck Matlock—impressed him, really—that the Negro giant had eliminated the light this way. It would have been easier, quicker, simply to have smashed the glass.

The objective of the third and final call, as Dunois

had instructed, was to reject Nimrod's meeting place. Reject it in a manner that left Nimrod no alternative but to accept Matlock's panicked substitute: the Cheshire Cat.

The voice over the telephone from the Carlyle police was wary, precise.

"Our mutual friend understands your concerns, Matlock. He'd feel the same way you do. He'll meet you with the girl at the south entrance of the athletic field, to the left of the rear bleachers. It's a small stadium, not far from the gym and the dormitories. Night watchmen are on; no harm could come to you. . . ."

"All right. All right, that's O.K." Matlock did his best to sound quietly frantic, laying the groundwork for his ultimate refusal. "There are people around; if any of you tried anything, I could scream my head off. And I *will!*"

"Of course. But you won't have to. Nobody wants anyone hurt. It's a simple transaction; that's what our friend told me to tell you. He admires you. . . ."

"How can I be sure he'll bring Pat? I have to be sure!"

"The *transaction*, Matlock." The voice was oily, there was a hint of desperation. Dunois's "cobra" was unpredictable. "That's what it's all about. Our friend wants what you found, remember?"

"I remember. . . ." Matlock's mind raced. He realized he had to maintain his hysteria, his unpredictability. But he had to switch the location. Change it without being suspect. If Nimrod became suspicious, Dunois had sentenced Pat to death. "And you tell our *friend* to remember that there's a statement in an envelope addressed to men in Washington!"

"He knows that, for Christ's sake, I mean . . . he's

concerned, you know what I mean? Now, we'll see you at the field, O.K.? In an hour, O.K.?"

This was the moment. There might not come another.

"No! Wait a minute. . . . I'm not going on that campus! The Washington people, they've got the whole place watched! They're all around! They'll put me away!"

"No, they won't. . . ."

"How the hell do you know?"

"There's nobody. So help me, it's *O.K.* Calm down, please."

"That's easy for you, not me! No, I'll tell you where. . . ."

He spoke rapidly, disjointedly, as if thinking desperately while talking. First he mentioned Herron's house, and before the voice could either agree or disagree, he rejected it himself. He then pinpointed the freight yards, and immediately found irrational reasons why he could not go there.

"Now, don't get so excited," said the voice. "It's a simple transaction. . . ."

"That restaurant! Outside of town. The Cheshire Cat! Behind the restaurant, there's a garden. . . ."

The voice was confused trying to keep up with him, and Matlock knew he was carrying off the ploy. He made last references to the diaries and the incriminating affidavit and slammed the telephone receiver into its cradle.

He stood in the booth, exhausted. Perspiration was dripping down his face, yet the early morning air was cool.

"That was handled very nicely," said the black man in command. "Your adversary chose a place within the college, I gather. An intelligent move on his part. Very nicely done, sir."

Matlock looked at the uniformed Negro, grateful for his praise and not a little astonished at his own resourcefulness. "I don't know if I could do it again."

"Of course you could," answered the black, leading Matlock toward the car. "Extreme stress activates a memory bank, not unlike a computer. Probing, rejecting, accepting—all instantaneously. Until panic, of course. There are interesting studies being made regarding the varying thresholds."

"Really?" said Matlock as they reached the car door. The Negro motioned him inside. The car lurched forward and they sped off down the highway flanked by the two other automobiles.

"We'll take a diagonal route to the restaurant using the roads set back in the farm country," said the black behind the wheel. "We'll approach it from the southwest and let you off about a hundred yards from a path used by employees to reach the rear of the building. We'll point it out to you. Walk directly to the section of the gardens where there's a large white arbor and a circle of flagstones surrounding a goldfish pond. Do you know it?"

"Yes, I do. I'm wondering how *you* do, though."

The driver smiled. "I'm not clairvoyant. While you were in the telephone booth, I was in touch with our men by radio. Everything's ready now. We're prepared. Remember, the white arbor and the goldfish pond. . . . And here. Here's the notebook and the envelope." The driver reached down to a flap pocket on the side of his door and pulled out the oilcloth package. The envelope was attached to it by a thick elastic band.

"We'll be there in less than ten minutes," said the man in command, shifting his weight to get comfortable. Matlock looked at him. Strapped to his leg—sewn into the tight-fitting khaki, actually—was a leather scabbard. He hadn't noticed it before and knew why. The bone-handled knife it contained had only recently been inserted. The scabbard housed a blade at least ten inches long.

Dunois's elite corps was now, indeed, prepared.

He stood at the side of the tall white arbor. The sun had risen over the eastern curve, the woods behind him still heavy with mist, dully reflecting the light of the early morning. In front of him the newly filled trees formed corridors for the old brick paths that converged into this restful flagstone haven. There were a number of marble benches placed around the circle, all glistening with morning moisture. From the center of the large patio, the bubbling sounds of the man-made goldfish pond continued incessantly with no break in the sound pattern. Birds could be heard activating their myriad signals, greeting the sun, starting the day's foraging.

Matlock's memory wandered back to Herron's Nest, to the forbidding green wall which isolated the old man from the outside world. There were similarities, he thought. Perhaps it was fitting that it should all end in such a place.

He lit a cigarette, extinguishing it after two intakes of smoke. He clutched the notebook, holding it in front of his chest as though it were some impenetrable shield, his head snapping in the direction of every sound, a portion of his life suspended with each movement.

He wondered where Dunois's men were. Where had

the elite guard hidden itself? Were they watching him, laughing quietly among themselves at his nervous gestures—his so obvious fear? Or were they spread out, guerrilla fashion? Crouched next to the earth or in the low limbs of the trees, ready to spring, prepared to kill?

And who would they kill? In what numbers and how armed would be Nimrod's forces? Would Nimrod come? Would Nimrod bring the girl he loved safely back to him? And if Nimrod did, if he finally saw Pat again, would the two of them be caught in the massacre which surely had to follow?

Who *was* Nimrod?

His breathing stopped. The muscles in his arms and legs contorted spastically, stiffened with fear. He closed his eyes tightly—to listen or to pray, he'd never really know, except that his beliefs excluded the existence of God. And so he listened with his eyes shut tight until he was sure.

First one, then two automobiles had turned off the highway and had entered the side road leading to the entrance of the Cheshire Cat. Both vehicles were traveling at enormous speeds, their tires screeching as they rounded the front circle leading into the restaurant parking area.

And then everything was still again. Even the birds were silent; no sound came from anywhere.

Matlock stepped back under the arbor, pressing himself against its lattice frame. He strained to hear—anything.

Silence. Yet not silence! Yet, again, a sound so blended with stillness as to be dismissed as a rustling leaf is dismissed.

It was a scraping. A hesitant, halting scraping from one of the paths in front of him, one of the paths hidden amongst the trees, one of the old brick lanes leading to the flagstone retreat.

At first it was barely audible. Dismissible. Then it became slightly clearer, less hesitant, less unsure.

Then he heard the quiet, tortured moan. It pierced into his brain.

"Jamie . . . Jamie? Please, Jamie. . . ."

The single plea, his name, broke off into a sob. He felt a rage he had never felt before in his life. He threw down the oilcloth packet, his eyes blinded by tears and fury. He lunged out of the protective frame of the white arbor and yelled, roared so that his voice startled the birds, who screeched out of the trees, out of their silent sanctuary.

"Pat! Pat! Where are you? Pat, my God, where? *Where!*"

The sobbing—half relief, half pain—became louder.

"Here. . . . Here, Jamie! Can't see."

He traced the sound and raced up the middle brick path. Halfway to the building, against the trunk of a tree, sunk to the ground, he saw her. She was on her knees, her bandaged head against the earth. She had fallen. Rivulets of blood were on the back of her neck; the sutures in her head had broken.

He rushed to her and gently lifted up her head.

Under the bandages on her forehead were layers of three-inch adhesive tape, pushed brutally against the lids of her eyes, stretched tight to her temples—as secure and unmovable as a steel plate covering her face. To try and remove them would be a torture devised in hell.

He held her close and kept repeating her name over and over again.

"Everything will be all right now. . . . Everything will be all right. . . ."

He lifted her gently off the ground, pressing her face against his own. He kept repeating those words of comfort which came to him in the midst of his rage.

Suddenly, without warning, without any warning at all, the blinded girl screamed, stretching her bruised body, her lacerated head.

"Let them have it, for God's sake! Whatever it is, *give it to them!*"

He stumbled down the brick path back to the flagstone circle.

"I will, I will, my darling. . . ."

"Please, Jamie! Don't let them touch me again! *Ever again!*"

"No, my darling. Not ever, not ever. . . ."

He slowly lowered the girl onto the ground, onto the soft earth beyond the flagstones.

"Take the tape off! Please take the tape off."

"I can't now, darling. It would hurt too much. In a little . . ."

"I don't *care!* I can't stand it any longer!"

What could he do? What was he supposed to *do?* Oh, God! Oh, God, you son-of-a-bitching God! *Tell me! Tell me!*

He looked over at the arbor. The oilcloth packet lay on the ground where he had thrown it.

He had no choice now. He did not care now.

"Nimrod! . . . *Nimrod! Come to me now, Nimrod! Bring your goddamn army! Come on and get it, Nimrod! I've got it here!*"

Through the following silence, he heard the footsteps.

Precise, surefooted, emphatic.

On the middle path, Nimrod came into view.

Adrian Sealfont stood on the edge of the flagstone circle.

"I'm sorry, James."

Matlock lowered the girl's head to the ground. His mind was incapable of functioning. His shock was so total that no words came, he couldn't assimilate the terrible, unbelievable fact in front of him. He rose slowly to his feet.

"Give it to me, James. You have your agreement. We'll take care of you."

"No. . . . No. No, I don't, I *won't believe* you! This isn't so. This isn't the way it can be. . . ."

"I'm afraid it is." Sealfont snapped the fingers of his right hand. It was a signal.

"No. . . . No! No! No!" Matlock found that he was screaming. The girl, too, cried out. He turned to Sealfont. "They said you were taken away! I thought you were dead! I blamed myself for your death!"

"I wasn't taken, I was escorted. Give me the diaries." Sealfont, annoyed, snapped his fingers again. "And the Corsican paper. I trust you have both with you."

There was the slightest sound of a muffled cough, a rasp, an interrupted exclamation. Sealfont looked quickly behind him and spoke sharply to his unseen forces.

"Get out here!"

"Why?"

"Because we *had* to. *I* had to. There was no alternative."

"No alternative?" Matlock couldn't believe he had heard the words. "No alternative to *what?*"

"Collapse! We were financially exhausted! Our last reserves were committed; there was no one left to appeal to. The moral corruption was complete: the pleas of higher education became an unprofitable, national bore. There was no other answer but to assert our own leadership . . . over the corruptors. We did so, and we survived!"

In the agonizing bewilderment of the moment, the pieces of the puzzle fell into place for Matlock. The unknown tumblers of the unfamiliar vault locked into gear and the heavy steel door was opened. . . . Carlyle's extraordinary endowment. . . . But it was more than Carlyle; Sealfont had just said it. The *pleas* had become a *bore!* It was subtle, but it was there!

Everywhere!

The raising of funds throughout all the campuses continued but there were no cries of panic these days; no threats of financial collapse that had been the themes of a hundred past campaigns in scores of colleges and universities.

The general assumption to be made—if one bothered to make it—was that the crises had been averted. Normality had returned.

But it *hadn't*. The norm had become a monster.

"Oh, my God," said Matlock softly, in terrified consternation.

"He was no help, I can assure you," replied Sealfont. "Our accomplishments are extremely human. Look at us now. *Independent!* Our strength growing systematically. Within five years every major university in the Northeast will be part of a self-sustaining federation!"

"You're diseased. . . . You're a *cancer!*"

"We *survive!* The choice was never really that difficult. No one was going to stop the way things were. Least of all ourselves. . . . We simply made the decision ten years ago to alter the principal players."

"But *you* of all people . . ."

"Yes. I was a good choice, wasn't I?" Sealfont turned once again in the direction of the restaurant, toward the sleeping hill with the old brick paths. He shouted. "I told you to come out here! There's nothing to worry about. Our friend doesn't care who you are. He'll soon be on his way. . . . Won't you, James?"

"You're *insane*. You're . . ."

"Not for a *minute!* There's no one saner. Or more practical. . . . History repeats, you should know that. The fabric is torn, society divided into viciously opposing camps. Don't be fooled by the dormancy; scratch the surface—it bleeds profusely."

"You're *making* it bleed!" Matlock screamed. There was nothing left; the spring had sprung.

"On the contrary! You pompous, self-righteous *ass!*" Sealfont's eyes stared at him in cold fury, his voice scathing. "Who gave you the right to make pronouncements? Where were you when men like myself—in *every institution*—faced the very real prospects of closing our doors! You were safe; we *sheltered* you. . . . And our appeals went unanswered. There wasn't room for our needs . . ."

"You didn't try! Not hard enough . . ."

"Liar! *Fool!*" Sealfont roared now. He was a man possessed, thought Matlock. Or a man tormented. "What was *left?* Endowments? Dwindling! There are other, more *viable tax incentives!* . . . Foundations? Small-minded tyrants—smaller allocations! . . . The Government? *Blind! Obscene!* Its priorities are bought! Or returned in kind at the ballot box! We had no funds; we bought no votes! For us, the system had collapsed! It was finished! . . . And no one knew it better than I did. For years . . . begging, pleading; palms outstretched to the ignorant men and their pompous *committees*. . . . It was hopeless; we were killing ourselves. Still no one listened. And always . . . *always*—behind the excuses and the delays—there was the snickering, the veiled reference to our common God-given frailty. After all . . . we were *teachers*. Not *doers*. . . ."

Sealfont's voice was suddenly low. And hard. And utterly convincing as he finished. "Well, young man, we're *doers now*. The system's damned and rightly so. The leaders never learn. Look to the children. They saw. They understood. . . . And we've enrolled them. Our alliance is no coincidence."

Matlock could do no more than stare at Sealfont. Sealfont had said it: *Look to the children. . . . Look, and behold. Look and beware.* The leaders never learn. . . . Oh, God! Was it so? Was it really the way things were? The Nimrods and the Dunoises. The "federations," the "elite guards." Was it happening all over again?

"Now James. Where is the letter you spoke of? Who has it?"

"Letter? What?"

"The letter that is to be mailed this morning. We'll stop it now, won't we?"

"I don't understand." Matlock was trying, trying *desperately* to make contact with his senses.

"Who has the letter!"

"The letter?" Matlock knew as he spoke that he was saying the wrong words, but he couldn't help himself. He couldn't stop to think, for he was incapable of thought.

"The letter! . . . There *is* no *letter, is there?!* There's . . . no 'incriminating statement' typed and ready to be mailed at ten o'clock in the morning! You were lying!"

"I was lying. . . . Lying." His reserves had been used up. There was nothing now but what was so.

Sealfont laughed softly. It wasn't the laugh Matlock was used to hearing from him. There was a cruelty he'd not heard before.

"Weren't you clever? But you're ultimately weak. I knew that from the beginning. You were the government's perfect choice, for you have no really firm commitments. They called it mobility. I knew it to be unconcerned flexibility. You talk but that's all you do. It's meaningless. . . . You're very representative, you know." Sealfont spoke over his shoulder toward the paths. "All right, *all* of you! Dr. Matlock won't be in a position to reveal any names, any identities. Come out of your hutches, you rabbits!"

"Augh . . ."

The guttural cry was short, punctuating the stillness. Sealfont whipped around.

Then there was another gasp, this the unmistakable sound of a human windpipe expunging its last draft of air.

And another, this coupled with the beginnings of a scream.

"Who is it? Who's up there?" Sealfont rushed to the path from which the last cry came.

He was stopped by the sound of a terrifying shout —cut short—from another part of the sanctuary. He raced back; the beginnings of panic were jarring his control.

"Who's up there?! Where are all of you? *Come down here!*"

The silence returned. Sealfont stared at Matlock.

"What have you done? What have you done, you

unimportant little man? Whom have you brought with you? *Who is up there? Answer me!"*

Even if he'd been capable, there was no need for Matlock to reply. From a path at the far end of the garden, Julian Dunois walked into view.

"Good morning, Nimrod."

Sealfont's eyes bulged. "Who *are* you? Where are my men?!"

"The name is Jacques Devereaux, Heysoú Daumier, Julian Dunois—take your choice. You were no match for us. You had a complement of ten, I had eight. No match. Your men are dead and how their bodies are disposed of is no concern of yours."

"Who *are* you?"

"Your enemy."

Sealfont ripped open his coat with his left hand, plunging his right inside. Dunois shouted a warning. Matlock found himself lurching forward toward the man he'd revered for a decade. Lunging at him with only one thought, one final objective, if it had to be the end of his own life.

To kill.

The face was next to his. The Lincoln-like face now contorted with fear and panic. He brought his right hand down on it like the claw of a terrified animal. He ripped into the flesh and felt the blood spew out of the distorted mouth.

He heard the shattering explosion and felt a sharp, electric pain in his left shoulder. But still he couldn't stop.

"Get off, Matlock! For God's sake, get off!"

He was being pulled away. Pulled away by huge black muscular arms. He was thrown to the ground, the heavy arms holding him down. And through it all he heard the cries, the terrible cries of pain and his name being repeated over and over again.

"Jamie . . . Jamie . . . Jamie . . ."

He lurched upward, using every ounce of strength his violence could summon. The muscular black arms were taken by surprise; he brought his legs up in crushing blows against the ribs and spines above him.

For a few brief seconds, he was free.

He threw himself forward on the hard surface, pounding his arms and knees against the stone. Whatever had happened to him, whatever was meant by the stinging pain, now spreading throughout the whole left side of his body, he had to reach the girl on the ground. The girl who had been through such terror for him.

"Pat!"

The pain was more than he could bear. He fell once more, but he had reached her hand. They held each other's hands, each trying desperately to give comfort to the other, fully aware that both might die at that moment.

Suddenly Matlock's hand went limp.

All was darkness for him.

He opened his eyes and saw the large black kneeling in front of him. He had been propped up into a sitting position at the side of a marble bench. His shirt had been removed; his left shoulder throbbed.

"The pain, I'm sure, is far more serious than the wound," said the black. "The upper left section of your body was badly bruised in the automobile, and the bullet penetrated below your left shoulder cartilage. Compounded that way, the pain would be severe."

"We gave you a local anesthetic. It should help." The speaker was Julian Dunois, standing to his right.

"Miss Ballantyne has been taken to a doctor. He'll remove the tapes. He's black and sympathetic, but not so much so to treat a man with a bullet wound. We've radioed our own doctor in Torrington. He should be here in twenty minutes."

"Why didn't you wait for him to help Pat?"

"Frankly, we have to talk. Briefly, but in confidence. Secondly, for her own sake, those tapes had to be removed as quickly as possible."

"Where's Sealfont?"

"He's disappeared. That's all you know, all you'll ever know. It's important that you understand that. Because, you see, if we must, we will carry out our threat against you and Miss Ballantyne. We don't wish to do that. . . . You and I, we are not enemies."

"You're wrong. We are."

"Ultimately, perhaps. That would seem inevitable. Right now, however, we've served each other in a moment of great need. We acknowledge it. We trust you do also."

"I do."

"Perhaps we've even learned from each other."

Matlock looked into the eyes of the black revolutionary. "I understand things better. I don't know what you could have learned from me."

The revolutionary laughed gently. "That an individual, by his actions—his courage, if you like—rises above the stigma of labels."

"I don't understand you."

"Ponder it. It'll come to you."

"What happens now? To Pat? To me? I'll be arrested the minute I'm seen."

"I doubt that sincerely. Within the hour, Greenberg will be reading a document prepared by my organization. By me, to be precise. I suspect the contents will become part of a file buried in the archives. It's most embarrassing. Morally, legally, and certainly politically. Too many profound errors were made. . . . We'll act this morning as your intermediary. Perhaps it would be a good time for you to use some of your well-advertised money and go with Miss Ballantyne on a long, recuperative journey. . . . I believe that will be agreed upon with alacrity. I'm sure it will."

"And Sealfont? What happens to him. Are you going to kill him?"

"Does Nimrod deserve to die? Don't bother to answer; we'll not discuss the subject. Suffice it to say he'll remain alive until certain questions are answered."

"Have you any idea what's going to happen when he's found to be missing?"

"There will be explosions, ugly rumors. About a great many things. When icons are shattered, the believers panic. So be it. Carlyle will have to live with it. . . . Rest, now. The doctor will be here soon." Dunois turned his attention to a uniformed Negro who had come up to him and spoken softly. The kneeling black who had bandaged his wound stood up. Matlock watched the tall, slender figure of Julian Dunois, quietly, confidently issuing his instructions, and felt the pain of gratitude. It was made worse because Dunois suddenly took on another image.

It was the figure of death.

"Dunois?"

"Yes?"

"Be careful."

EPILOGUE

The blue-green waters of the Caribbean mirrored the hot afternoon sun in countless thousands of swelling, blinding reflections. The sand was warm to the touch, soft under the feet. This isolated stretch of the island was at peace with itself and with a world beyond that it did not really acknowledge.

Matlock walked down to the edge of the water and let the miniature waves wash over his ankles. Like the sand on the beach, the water was warm.

He carried a newspaper sent to him by Greenberg. Part of a newspaper, actually.

KILLINGS IN CARLYLE, CONN.

23 SLAIN, BLACKS AND WHITES, TOWN STUNNED, FOLLOWS DISAPPEARANCE OF UNIVERSITY PRESIDENT

CARLYLE, MAY 10—On the outskirts of this small university town, in a section housing large, old estates, a- bizarre mass killing took place yesterday. Twenty-three men were slain; the federal authorities have speculated the killings were the result of an ambush that claimed many lives of both the attackers and the attacked. . . .

There followed a cold recitation of identities, short summaries of police file associations.

Julian Dunois was among them.

The specter of death had not been false; Dunois hadn't escaped. The violence he engendered had to be the violence that would take his life.

The remainder of the article contained complicated speculations on the meaning and the motives of the massacre's strange cast of characters. And the possible connection to the disappearance of Adrian Sealfont.

Speculations only. No mention of Nimrod, nothing of himself; no word of any long-standing federal investigation. Not the truth; nothing of the truth.

Matlock heard his cottage door open, and he turned around. Pat was standing on the small veranda fifty yards away over the dune. She waved and started down the steps toward him.

She was dressed in shorts and a light silk blouse; she was barefoot and smiling. The bandages had been removed from her legs and arms, and the Caribbean sun had tanned her skin to a lovely bronze. She had devised a wide orange headband to cover the wounds above her forehead.

She would not marry him. She said there would be no marriage out of pity, out of debt—real or imagined. But Matlock knew there would be a marriage. Or there would be no marriages for either of them. Julian Dunois had made it so.

"Did you bring cigarettes?" he asked.

"No. No cigarettes," she replied. "I brought matches."

"That's cryptic."

"I used that word—cryptic—with Jason. Do you remember?"

"I do. You were mad as hell."

"You were spaced out . . . In hell. Let's walk down to the jetty."

"Why did you bring matches?" He took her hand, putting the newspaper under his arm.

"A funeral pyre. Archeologists place great significance in funeral pyres."

"What?"

"You've been carrying around that damned paper all day. I want to burn it." She smiled at him, gently.

"Burning it won't change what's in it."

Pat ignored his observation. "Why do you think Jason sent it to you? I thought the whole idea was several weeks of nothing. No newspapers, no radios, no contact with anything but warm water and white sand. He made the rules and he broke them."

"He *recommended* the rules and knew they were difficult to live by."

"He should have let someone else break them. He's not as good a friend as I thought he was."

"Maybe he's a better one."

"That's sophistry." She squeezed his hand. A single, overextended wave lapped across their bare feet. A silent gull swooped down from the sky into the water offshore; its wings flapped against the surface, its neck shook violently. The bird ascended screeching, no quarry in its beak.

"Greenberg knows I've got a very unpleasant decision to make."

"You've made it. He knows that, too."

Matlock looked at her. Of course Greenberg knew; she knew, too, he thought. "There'll be a lot more pain; perhaps more than justified."

"That's what they'll tell you. They'll tell you to let them do it their way. Quietly, efficiently, with as little embarrassment as possible. For everyone."

"Maybe it's best; maybe they're right."

"You don't believe that for a second."

"No, I don't."

They walked in silence for a while. The jetty was in front of them, its rocks placed decades, perhaps centuries ago, to restrain a long-forgotten current. It was a natural fixture now.

As Nimrod had become a natural fixture, a logical extension of the anticipated; undesirable but nevertheless expected. To be fought in deep cover.

Mini-America . . . just below the surface.

Company policy, man.

Everywhere.

The hunters, builders. The killers and their quarry were making alliances.

Look to the children. They understand . . . We've enrolled them.

The leaders never learn.

A microcosm of the inevitable? Made unavoidable because the needs were real? Had been real for years?

And still the leaders would not learn.

"Jason said once that truth is neither good nor bad. Simply truth. That's why he sent me this." Matlock sat down on a large flat rock; Pat stood beside him. The tide v·as coming in and the sprays of the small waves splashed upward. Pat reached over and took the two pages of the newspaper.

"This is the truth then." A statement.

"Their truth. Their judgment. Assign obvious labels and continue the game. The good guys and the bad guys and the posse will reach the pass on time. Just in time. This time."

"What's your truth?"

"Go back and tell the story. All of it."

"They'll disagree. They'll give you reasons why you shouldn't. Hundreds of them."

"They won't convince me."

"Then they'll be against you. They've threatened; they won't accept interference. That's what Jason wants you to know."

"That's what he wants me to think about."

Pat held the pages of the newspaper in front of her and struck a wooden island match on the dry surface of a rock.

The paper burned haltingly, retarded by the Caribbean spray.

But it burned.

"That's not a very impressive funeral pyre," said Matlock.

"It'll do until we get back."